AN
SEVENTEENTH-CENTURY FICTION

PAUL SALZMAN is currently a Senior Lecturer in the English Department at La Trobe University, Melbourne, Australia. He is the author of *English Prose Fiction 1558–1700: A Critical History* (Oxford: Clarendon Press); *The New Diversity: Australian Fiction 1970–1988* (written with Ken Gelder, Melbourne: McPhee Gribble Publishers); and editor of *An Anthology of Elizabethan Prose Fiction* (The World's Classics).

THE WORLD'S CLASSICS

An Anthology of Seventeenth-Century Fiction

Edited with an Introduction by
PAUL SALZMAN

Oxford   New York
OXFORD UNIVERSITY PRESS

Oxford University Press, Walton Street, Oxford OX2 6DP

Oxford New York Toronto
Delhi Bombay Calcutta Madras Karachi
Kuala Lumpur Singapore Hong Kong Tokyo
Nairobi Dar es Salaam Cape Town
Melbourne Auckland Madrid

and associated companies in
Berlin Ibadan

Oxford is a trade mark of Oxford University Press

British Library Cataloguing in Publication Data
Data available

Library of Congress Cataloging in Publication Data
An Anthology of seventeenth-century fiction / edited with an introduction
by Paul Salzman.
p. cm. — (The World's classics)
Includes bibliographical references and index.
1. English fiction — Early modern, 1500-1700. I. Salzman, Paul.
II. Title: Anthology of 17th-century fiction. III. Series.
PR1295.A58 1991 823'.408 dc20 90 44123

ISBN 0 19 282619 0

3 5 7 9 10 8 6 4 2

Printed in Great Britain by
BPC Paperbacks Ltd
Aylesbury, Bucks

ACKNOWLEDGEMENTS

THIS anthology is the third book arising from an interest in sixteenth- and seventeenth-century prose fiction that began fifteen years ago. I am particularly grateful to Oxford University Press, which has published all three volumes, and to its skilled editors, Kim Scott Walwyn and Judith Luna.

The La Trobe University School of Humanities provided research funding which enabled me to employ Michael Connor, who offered invaluable assistance in assembling the texts and bibliography. I would also like to thank Iain Topliss, and especially Gregory Kratzmann, for help with some troublesome notes. James L. Forrest and Roger Sharrock generously granted permission to base the extract from *Mr Badman* on their Oxford edition. Susan Bye criticized the introduction, helped with the proof-reading, and kept me sane, as usual.

CONTENTS

CONTENTS

INTRODUCTION

FOR too long, the prose fiction of the seventeenth century has been seen as a series of more or less successful rehearsals for the eighteenth-century novel. While Elizabethan fiction was often treated in a similar fashion, it has always been more visible and more subject to analysis from scholars interested in it within the context of its own period.[1] Seventeenth-century fiction had no acknowledged masterpiece to match Sir Philip Sidney's *Arcadia*, one of the key monuments of Elizabethan culture. John Bunyan's *Pilgrim's Progress* comes closest to adopting this role, but it was detached from its context within the fiction that surrounded it and placed instead within a religious, moral, or spiritual tradition.

Scholars have tended to see the fiction of the seventeenth century through the constricting norm of the 'realist novel' as it was developed in the eighteenth and nineteenth centuries. This is evident in the very titles of their studies; for example, Charlotte Morgan's *The Rise of the Novel of Manners* (1911), or E. A. Baker's *History of the English Novel*, iii (1929). This culminated in Ian Watt's much more sophisticated, and still influential study, *The Rise of the Novel* (1957). In establishing the nature of the 'new' literary form of the eighteenth-century novel, Watt saw it as a movement away from the romance conventions that he characterized as dominating the fiction of the preceding century.

In recent years, a series of important theoretical debates have been conducted over the transition from earlier forms of narrative to the eighteenth-century novel. While different in theoretical orientation, they have all followed Watt in viewing the fiction of the seventeenth century through what might be called a teleological perspective, reading the works of earlier periods as if they were moving towards a finally developed novel form. This is evident in Lennard Davis's search, theoretically influenced by

---

[1] For a discussion of the relationship between 16th- and 17th-century fiction, see Paul Salzman, *English Prose Fiction 1558–1700: A Critical History* (Oxford, 1985).

the work of Michel Foucault, for the origins of the novel in
changes in the status of reportage in the seventeenth-century;
these changes affected what Davis calls the 'news/novels'
discourse during this period.[2] Michael McKeon has offered an
even more complex account of generic change leading up to the
establishment of the novel, in his case influenced by Mikhail
Bakhtin's theory of the nature of the novel.[3] McKeon once again
sees the seventeenth century as a period of transition, when
radical changes in notions of truth and notions of virtue laid the
groundwork for the eighteenth-century novel form. Far and away
the most extensive treatment of the subject, McKeon's study
looks at seventeenth-century fiction only in so far as it provides a
context for changing conceptions of the novel as against the
romance form. Similarly, J. Paul Hunter looks carefully at
changing audiences for fiction as well as changing narrative
conventions, especially in journalism.[4]

All these studies are valuable contributions to our understanding of the creation of the novel form, as well as addressing
general questions of literary change. But they have had the effect
of rendering seventeenth-century prose fiction less visible than
ever. This situation is beginning to change, especially under the
influence of major editorial and critical work on John Bunyan,
and a strong interest in the position of women writers during this
period, particularly those who contributed to the development of
fiction in various forms.[5] Greater attention to specific examples
of seventeenth-century fiction should widen general awareness
of just how complex and varied it was. This anthology is an

---

[2] Lennard J. Davis, *Factual Fictions: The Origins of the English Novel* (New York,
1983).

[3] Michael McKeon, *The Origins of the English Novel 1600–1740* (Baltimore,
1987); McKeon's response to Davis's book is also important: 'The Origins of the
English Novel', *Modern Philology*, 82 (1984), 76–86.

[4] J. Paul Hunter, *Before Novels* (New York, 1989), unavailable to me at the time
of going to press); 'Novels and "the Novel": The Poetics of Embarrassment',
Modern Philology, 85 (1988), 480–98; ' "News and New Things": Contemporaneity
and the Early English Novel', *Critical Enquiry*, 14 (1988), 493–515. A study which
does look back at one aspect of seventeenth-century fiction in detail is Henry
Knight Miller, *Henry Fielding's Tom Jones and the Romance Tradition* (Victoria,
1976).

[5] See the entries in the Select Bibliography for examples.

attempt to introduce a representative sampling to a wider audience.

Between 1600 and 1700 about 450 works of prose fiction (including translations) were published in England—the exact number varies depending on how one defines the category of prose fiction.[6] The main problem in understanding the nature of this material is, to begin with, very much a matter of categorization. As, in their very different ways, both Davis and McKeon have shown, writers during this period did not use the modern genre of the novel as a category, nor would they have subsumed so many disparate works under the heading 'prose fiction'. Too much generic categorizing and subcategorizing produces a sense of early fiction as an atomistic genealogy of super-refined divisions. On the other hand, it is evident even from the selection in this volume that authors did see themselves as part of an ongoing process of narrative experimentation. Thus Congreve, at the end of the century, offers a definition of the novel as opposed to the romance; Aphra Behn offers a very stylized story as the 'whole truth'; Margaret Cavendish examines the nature of romance as pure fancy in opposition to fictional 'truth'; Bunyan pits his moral historicizing against the immoral criminal biography, which is exemplified by *Don Tomazo* and its dubious claims to be a 'moral history'; Percy Herbert sees the romance form as absolutely necessary to encompass the astonishing events of the Civil War, while Mary Wroth bends the romance form to encompass women's responses to this patriarchal mode.

What we see here is something like a continuing dialogue over the means and ends of prose fiction, which might well justify its use as a loose but convenient category for considering a variety of seventeenth-century works. These works have some links to earlier traditions of prose fiction, particularly to the long and complex history of the romance form. When read chronologically, as they are presented here, it is possible to see changes occurring, most obviously at the level of prose style, but also in relation to plot and characterization. The seventeenth century saw a continuation of a general increase in literacy, which seems

[6] See Salzman, *English Prose Fiction*, ch. 9; the standard bibliography is Charles C. Mish, *English Prose Fiction 1600 to 1700: A Chronological Checklist* (Charlottesville, 1967).

to be reflected in the very diverse range of fiction written for a variety of readers.[7] I have tried to provide, through my selection, some sense of the range of this fiction. Unfortunately, this has necessitated the use of extracts in three cases, rather than entire works. *Urania* and *The Princess Cloria* are so massive that a selection from each might well seem more than enough. Although the whole work is now available in an authoritative text, [8] some experience of *Mr Badman* seems to me to be essential in any attempt at an overview of the fiction of the period.

While many readers may use this anthology for the sake of a single work, it is intended to be read as a whole. Taken together, these works offer a lively excursion through the diversity of seventeenth-century prose narrative. In different ways, they indicate a complex meditation on the relationship between fictional narrative and a variety of social issues that occurred during the seventeenth century. Wroth, Cavendish and Behn use the romance, Utopia/imaginary voyage, and Restoration novella forms respectively, to explore the constraints of female roles, and the possibility of circumventing those constraints. What could be called the politicization of fiction during this period is evident, not just in the elaborate political allegory of *The Princess Cloria*, but even in *Don Tomazo*, partly written to create sympathy for Thomas Dangerfield's dubious role in the Popish Plot. When read on their own terms, these narratives should repay the closest scrutiny, and challenge the assumption that the seventeenth century was a low point for prose fiction.

URANIA

MARY WROTH is just beginning to take her place as an important figure in the recent remapping of Renaissance literature. She was the daughter of Sir Philip Sidney's brother Robert, and accordingly was part of a family renowned for its literary

---

[7] See David Cressy, *Literacy and the Social Order* (Cambridge, 1980); Salzman, *English Prose Fiction*, 110–11, 265–70; and for a fascinating study of a genre not really represented here, see Margaret Spufford, *Small Books and Pleasant Histories: Popular Fiction and its Readership in Seventeenth-Century England* (London, 1981).

[8] John Bunyan, *Mr Badman*, ed. James F. Forrest and Roger Sharrock (Oxford, 1988).

production and patronage.[9] Apart from Wroth's famous uncle, her father and her aunt, Mary, Countess of Pembroke, both wrote and translated poetry. She married Robert Wroth in 1603. During this period she had a prominent place in the court of King James, and her role as a poet, as well as patron, was acknowledged frequently by Ben Jonson, who stated in a sonnet to her that 'Since I exscribe your sonnets [I] am become | A better lover and much better poet'.[10]

Wroth's poetry was, like that of most noble authors in the Renaissance, written for private circulation only.[11] But after the death of her husband in 1614, closely followed by the birth of a son, she was left in severe financial difficulties, which were compounded by the reversion of much of her estate after the death of her son in 1616. It has also been suggested that she lost favour at court because of her affair with her cousin, William Herbert, Earl of Pembroke, and the two illegitimate children she bore.[12]

It seems probable that Wroth began to write *Urania* around 1618. Its publication in 1621 might partly have been an attempt to alleviate her financial crisis.[13] However, the landmark appearance of probably the first published work of prose fiction in English by a woman was a disaster for Wroth. One of the numerous inset-stories in *Urania* was a thinly disguised account of the scandal surrounding the marriage of Lord Edward Denny's daughter Honora to James Hay, and Hay's subsequent marriage to Lucy Percy after Honora's death.[14] Denny was

[9] Biographical information is principally derived from Josephine A. Roberts's introduction to her excellent edition. *The Poems of Lady Mary Wroth* (Baton Rouge, La, 1983).

[10] 'A Sonnet to the Noble lady, the Lady Mary Wroth', in *The Complete Poems*, ed. George Parfitt (Harmondsworth, 1975), 165.

[11] Recently two MSS of Wroth's pastoral play *Love's Victory* have been discovered; see Carolyn Ruth Swift, 'Feminine Self-Definition in Lady Mary Wroth's *Love's Victorie*', *English Literary Renaissance*, 19 (1989), 171–88.

[12] See Roberts, *Poems of Lady Mary Wroth*, 24–6.

[13] Roberts rightly notes (35) that Wroth could not have expected to make a great deal of money from *Urania*, but this still seems a reasonable explanation for what must have seemed a risky venture.

[14] See John J. O'Connor, 'James Hay and *The Countess of Montgomery's Urania*', *Notes and Queries*, 200 (1955), 150–2; Paul Salzman, 'Contemporary References in Mary Wroth's *Urania*', *Review of English Studies*, 29 (1978), 178–81.

outraged by his family's presence in *Urania* . He wrote furious letters to Wroth, containing some vitriolic poetry, including the ominous warning to future female authors: 'leave idle books alone | For wise and worthier women have writ none.'[15] Wroth replied in kind, but Denny succeeded in having *Urania* withdrawn from sale. A continuation of the romance, which Wroth wrote, was never published.[16]

As is apparent from Book I of *Urania*, published here for the first time since its original appearance, Wroth produced a massive romance.[17] Its title-page echoes her uncle's famous romance, *The Countess of Pembroke's Arcadia*, still enormously popular when *Urania* was published in 1621. But Wroth produced a very different kind of romance to Sidney's. Wroth greatly sharpens the gentle questioning of the heroic ideal that is evident at times in Sidney's *Arcadia*. Jealousy and inconstancy are rife in *Urania*, and as much attention is paid to the female characters as is paid to the 'heroes'.

A critical debate seems to be emerging over Wroth's depiction of women, initially seen more as victims, but recently Naomi Miller has stressed that 'While translating from social into literary terms the precariousness of the female position in Jacobean society, Wroth nevertheless affirms the resilience rather than victimization of the female character.'[18] It is perhaps more useful to note a balance of these two positions played out in *Urania*. There is female friendship, independence, and support; but also female deceit, and considerable victimization at the hands of inconstant men. In the unpublished continuation of the

---

[15] A full account is in Josephine A. Roberts, 'An Unpublished Literary Quarrel Concerning the Suppression of Mary Wroth's *Urania*', *Notes and Queries*, 222 (1977), 532–5, who also prints the poems in her edition of Wroth, 32–5.

[16] The MS, itself unfinished, is in the Newberry Library.

[17] Readers can evidently look forward to a complete text of *Urania* being prepared by Wroth's editor, Josephine A. Roberts.

[18] See Salzman, *English Prose Fiction*, 141–4; Carolyn Ruth Swift, 'Feminine Identity in Lady Mary Wroth's Romance *Urania*', *English Literary Renaissance*, 14 (1984), 328–46; Gary F. Waller, 'Struggling into Discourse: The Emergence of Renaissance Women's Writing', in *Silent But for the Word*, ed. Margaret Patterson Hannay (Kent, Ohio, 1985), 248; Elaine V. Beilin, *Redeeming Eve: Women Writers of the English Renaissance* (Princeton, NJ, 1987), ch. 8; Naomi J. Miller, ' "Not much to be marked": Narrative of the Woman's Part in Lady Mary Wroth's *Urania*', *Studies in English Literature*, 29 (1989), 123.

romance, the men and women we meet in Book I are married, have children, grow old, and die—an indication that Wroth's reworking of traditional romance motifs grew even more radical as she went on.

Even in Book I, Wroth initiates an examination of the problems of identity, of assuming the right role, of penetrating disguises, both literally and metaphorically. This issue is relevant to both male and female identity in *Urania*. Whether there are many more true scandals like Edward Denny's in *Urania* remains uncertain (two more have been identified, one of them being an account of the notorious Overbury affair),[19] but the familial, social, and sexual interrelationships in *Urania* certainly reflect the tense world of Jacobean court politics. Wroth's decision to recall the medieval romance's proliferation of interconnecting subsidiary stories may prove something of a barrier to a modern reader, but it enables her to examine an enormous range of personal and political situations through an impressively differentiated range of characters. In the first book of the romance, much of this range is represented, from the political intrigues at various courts to the superb domestic portrait of the marriage of Parselius and Dalinea.

THE PRINCESS CLORIA

ANOTHER important way in which the romance form took on a new response to social issues in the seventeenth century was through its direct engagement with history and politics. While Sidney's *Arcadia* considers a wide variety of issues connected with the uses and abuses of political power, the discussion remains general and theoretical. In 1621 John Barclay published a romance in Latin called *Argenis*, which dealt directly with French political history, disguising real events and characters under romance names. *Argenis* was immensely popular, admired by no less a person than James I, who commissioned Ben Jonson to translate it into English (it perished in the fire which destroyed Jonson's library in 1623). It was eventually translated twice, by

[19] See Roberts, *Poems of Lady Mary Wroth*, 35.

Kingesmill Long (1625) and by Sir Robert Le Grys (1628).[20]
Argenis pointed towards the romance's direct engagement with
contemporary political controversy.

Annabel Patterson has described how the court of Charles I
increasingly used the romance form as an ideologically charged
means of self-representation.[21] This is even evident in Charles's
presentation of himself during his trial and execution. It is in this
context that a number of writers with royalist sympathies used the
romance form during the Interregnum as some protection for the
disguised, or allegorical, presentation of the events of the Civil
War and its aftermath. Five of these romances have survived,
though it seems likely that more were written. *The Princess Cloria*
is the most elaborate and impressive, presenting, in its final form,
a detailed and sophisticated account of all the events of the Civil
War, reaching right back to the reign of Elizabeth I for
explanations of how the war began, ranging across the political
situation of Europe as a whole, and concluding with the
Restoration.

The first part of *The Princess Cloria* was published in 1653
under the title *Cloria and Narcissus*. The entry in the Stationers'
Register for the publication of the second part, which appeared
in 1654, reveals the identity of the anonymous author, who was
Sir Percy Herbert of Powis. Even when the full text of the
romance was published in 1661, after the Restoration, and again
in 1665, Herbert remained anonymous. This may have been
because the romance, though reflecting Herbert's strong royalist
sympathies, also reflects, to some extent, his family's Catholicism, and it also contains some criticism of the policies that led to
the Civil War. Herbert's only other published work that I can
trace was a philosophical meditation entitled *Certain Conceptions,
or, Considerations of Sir Percy Herbert . . . Directed to his Son* (1650).

The fairly brief extract from *The Princess Cloria* that I have
included here—the opening of the romance, and two short
passages depicting Euarchus (Charles I) dealing with his captivity

---

[20] Information on the context of *The Princess Cloria* and political romance in
general may be found in Paul Salzman, '*The Princess Cloria* and the Political
Romance in the 1650s', *Southern Review* (Adelaide), 14 (1981), 236–46; Annabel
Patterson, *Censorship and Interpretation* (Madison, Wis., 1984), ch. 4; and
Salzman, *English Prose Fiction*, ch. 11.

[21] Patterson, *Censorship and Interpretation*, 166–76.

and trial—illustrates the skill with which Herbert blends
romance motifs and political, as well as historical, analysis. The
preface, printed here in full, is an extremely important contribution to the growing analysis, during the seventeenth century, of
the relationship between fictional genres and ideological ends.
Herbert begins the romance with an overview of the chaos
caused by the Thirty Years War in Europe. As a whole, *The
Princess Cloria* is an important exploration of the discrepancy
between morality and political expediency.

THE BLAZING WORLD

WHILE Mary Wroth may have aroused the ire of some of her
readers, the second woman in this anthology generally aroused
ridicule. Margaret Cavendish, Duchess of Newcastle, published
her first book in 1653. She went on to produce plays, letters,
short stories, poems, a biography of her husband, and a number
of scientific and philosophical treatises. She was undoubtedly a
highly individual, not to say eccentric, figure, who was capable of
ignoring varying degrees of prejudice about female roles that
surrounded her.[22] Cavendish received little praise during her
lifetime, apart from the support of her admiring husband and
those seeking her patronage. It is often difficult to determine
whether her 'madness' might not have consisted mostly of her
daring to enter the masculine worlds of letters, science, and
philosophy, coupled with her determination to maintain her own
individuality, whether in matters of dress, or opinion.

Even recent assessments have often seen Cavendish in this
perjorative way. Sandra Gilbert and Susan Gubar, in their
influential study of women writers, *The Madwoman in the Attic*, focus
in a rather negative fashion on Cavendish as a victim of her society's
limited view of women: 'finally the contradictions between her
attitude towards her gender and her sense of her own vocation
seem really to have made her in some sense "mad." '[23] While

---

[22] The best brief biography is the first chapter in Sara Heller Mendelson, *The
Mental World of Stuart Women* (Brighton, 1987); but see also Douglas Grant,
Margaret the First (London, 1957).
[23] Sandra Gilbert and Susan Gubar, *The Madwoman in the Attic* (New Haven,
Conn., and London, 1979), 63.

attempting to rescue her from these charges of madness, Sylvia Bowerbank has dismissed the bulk of Cavendish's works for their disorder, offering a particularly harsh view of *The Blazing World* as 'tedious chaos'.[24]

This anthology will give readers the opportunity to judge for themselves whether *The Blazing World* is readable. It was first published, as its preface indicates, as an addendum to one of Cavendish's scientific works, *Observations Upon Experimental Philosophy*, which was partly intended to be a critique of Robert Hooke's *Micrographia* (1665). Cavendish's views on science and philosophy are prominent in *The Blazing World*, as the Empress creates her own equivalent of the Royal Society, an institution that Cavendish was permitted to visit once but never, of course, to join. Before jumping to any conclusions about the absurdity of Cavendish's views, it is important to realize that they are no odder, to a modern reader, than the views of many respected seventeenth-century pioneers of the new science.

Both in the preface and in the narrative itself, Cavendish offers an important defence of the role of the imagination, or fancy. *The Blazing World* constructs what could surely be seen as a Utopia, which allows a woman to overturn the constraints imposed on her by a rigidly patriarchal society. Cavendish makes it quite clear, poignantly clear, that this *is* mere fancy, just as her self-conscious inclusion of herself within the narrative is often the vehicle for gentle self-mockery.

In a provocative account of Cavendish in the context of seventeenth-century women who embraced Tory ideology, Catherine Gallagher examines the absolutism present throughout her work, and prominent in the image of the Empress of the Blazing World. Gallagher reminds us that during this period 'women were excluded from all state offices except that of monarch'.[25] In the real world, Cavendish was excluded from centres of power, especially the intellectual power that so fascinated her. Cavendish's very isolation produces a fantasy of an absolute female ruler, but with the critical provision that all

---

[24] Sylvia Bowerbank, 'The Spider's Delight: Margaret Cavendish and the "Female" Imagination', *English Literary Renaissance*, 14 (1984), 402.

[25] Catherine Gallagher, 'Embracing the Absolute: The Politics of the Female Subject in Seventeenth-Century England', *Genders*, 1 (1988), 27.

this is solipsistic: a world created within the author's mind, just as the reader might create a similar world. This is acknowledged by the fact that Cavendish's own appearance in *The Blazing World* is as the Empress's friend, and when she wants a world of her own, she is only able to create it in her imagination, even within the narrative itself.

On the other hand, it is also possible to see the 'Platonic' friendship between Cavendish's persona and the Empress as an idealized female companionship unattainable in Cavendish's society. Another notable aspect of the Blazing World is its provisional nature, not just at the level of its attenuated existence as a world, but even at the level of the Empress's shifting political reforms. *The Blazing World* is not intended to be a *rational* Utopia, because that would contradict the philosophy that the author espouses. It deserves to be seen as a pioneering female, and perhaps even feminist, Utopia.

DON TOMAZO

PICARESQUE narrative has been the favourite hunting ground for historians of the novel looking for the antecedents of a writer like Daniel Defoe. In England, picaresque and criminal narrative has a long history of its own, extending back to sixteenth-century cony-catching pamphlets; these were stories of tricksters, con men (from cony-, or rabbit-, catchers), who preyed on naïve targets, usually country visitors to London.[26] Although these narratives pretended to be moral warnings for unsuspecting victims, they were extremely ambiguous, tending to revel in the skills of the trickster as much as condemning the trick.

In the seventeenth century these narratives continued to be popular, and were joined by the sophisticated Spanish picaresque novels *Lazarillo de Tormes* (1554) and Mateo Aleman's *Guzman de Alfarache* (1599). Both went through a number of reprintings in English translation, particularly James Mabbe's translation of *Guzman* as *The Rogue*, which was first published in 1622. By the time *Don Tomazo* was published in 1680, a diverse tradition of

---

[26] A useful and readable collection is available: *Cony-Catchers and Bawdy Baskets*, ed. Gamini Salgado (Harmondsworth, 1972).

criminal–picaresque narrative was in existence. *Don Tomazo* itself is part of a further development in this tradition: what has become known as the criminal biography.[27] Writers offered the eager reading public what purported to be the true biography or autobiography of a notorious criminal. Perhaps the most successful of these, at least from a marketing point of view, were a variety of accounts of Mary Carleton, a particularly skilled impostor, whose activities included masquerading as a German princess.[28]

Thomas Dangerfield, the subject and purported author of *Don Tomazo*, was an even more notorious figure. Spiro Peterson has explained how *Don Tomazo* forms part of Dangerfield's complex and scurrilous involvement in the Popish Plot and its aftermath.[29] *Don Tomazo* was published when Dangerfield was being presented as an informer by one Mrs Cellier, who appears at the end of the narrative (p. 445). While Dangerfield was meant to expose a Catholic conspiracy, his unreliable performances in court led to the betrayal of Cellier. On all occasions he was proven to be completely untrustworthy as a witness.

Don Tomazo seems intended at one level to provide an introduction to Dangerfield as an engaging rogue, in order to further his political ends. The narrative, by slipping into the first person at times, hints to the reader that perhaps Dangerfield himself is the author (and it is usually presented, as it is here for the sake of convenience, as being by Dangerfield). The truth will never be determined, and the effectiveness and vigour of the narrative does not depend upon its authorship. The hints at its 'truthfulness' about Dangerfield only add a certain frisson—or, at least, so they must have done for its first readers.

The narrative technique of *Don Tomazo* is most impressive: a skilful blend of irony, broad comedy, and the typical cony-catching mixture of didactic comment and amoral exuberance. The narrative voice is extremely self-conscious, and also highly

---

[27] See the excellent anthology, Spiro Peterson (ed.), *The Counterfeit Lady Unveiled* (New York, 1961); Robert R. Singleton, 'English Criminal Biography 1651–1722', *Harvard Library Bulletin*, 18 (1970).

[28] See Ernest Bernbaum, *The Mary Carleton Narratives 1663–1673* (Cambridge, Mass., 1914); C. F. Main, 'The German Princess, or, Mary Carleton in Fact and Fiction', *Harvard Library Bulletin*, 10 (1956), 165–85.

[29] Peterson (ed.), *The Counterfeit Lady Unveiled*, 180–2.

educated, both in the picaresque tradition itself, and in a wider context, as the occasional classical references indicate. There is generally considerable ironic distance between the narrative voice and Tomazo's activities, though the irony is as much at the expense of Tomazo's victims as it is directed at the activities of 'gusmanry' (roguery). The early account of Tomazo's childhood is particularly effective, and overall the narrative is an engaging performance.

MR BADMAN

SOME of the moral issues skirted around by *Don Tomazo* are at the centre of John Bunyan's *The Life and Death of Mr Badman*. In this work Bunyan offers a counterbalance to *The Pilgrim's Progress*: an account of an individual's moral failure and decline, as opposed to Christian's journey to heaven. James Forrest and Roger Sharrock, the editors of *Mr Badman* for the complete Oxford *Bunyan*, point to a variety of literary forms which lie behind the narrative: the dialogue, collections of judgement stories, the exemplum, the posthumous, as well as the picaresque and rogue tradition.[30]

Bunyan stages a conversation between Wiseman and the rather naïve Attentive, in order to warn of the dangers of an ungodly life. He focuses on the same kind of rogue figure found in the criminal fiction discussed above, but was conscious of the moral ambiguity present in the English rogue tradition. *Mr Badman* is carefully structured to forestall the potential allure of the rogue figure, so that we will not offer the kind of sympathy to Badman that we might offer to Don Tomazo.

Even though Bunyan keeps a firm grip on his didactic purpose, he uses all the devices of the rogue tradition to evoke the world of Badman as vividly as possible. In the extracts presented here, we see Badman's duplicitous courtship (including what modern readers may see as a particularly harsh view of his wife's gullible acquiescence); some wonderful examples of God's judgement; and Badman's temporary and hypocritical repentance. All three sections illustrate *Mr Badman*'s major theme: the need for

[30] *The Life and Death of Mr Badman*, ed. James F. Forrest and Roger Sharrock (Oxford, 1988), pp. xv–xxx.

intense spiritual vigilance. Forrest and Sharrock stress the
effectiveness of Bunyan's decision to avoid exposing Badman to
any of the spectacular visitations of God's justice outlined in the
inset-stories: 'the work leaves an overwhelming impression of the
ugliness and sheer uncomfortableness of his way of life just
because he is left to his sins without the folk-tale intervention of
demons.'[31]

The marginal glosses stress the didactic intention behind *Mr
Badman*, and initially both they and the dialogue form may seem
alien to the modern reader. However, Bunyan is able to offer all
the pleasure of striking verisimilitude of character and situation,
while never losing sight of his principal moral purpose. Especially
when read alongside a work like *Don Tomazo*, *Mr Badman* can be
seen as a remarkable spiritual contribution to an otherwise
dramatically secular genre.

INCOGNITA

IN the preface to *Incognita*, William Congreve offers a much-
quoted account of the differences between the romance and the
novel. By 'novel', Congreve had in mind the French *nouvelle*
form, which had become extremely popular in England during
the 1680s, both through large numbers of translations from the
French, and through some English imitations.[32] As Congreve
explains, the 'novel' is 'of a more familiar nature' than the
romance. *Incognita* is not intended to provide what modern
readers might look for in a novel, for the notion of verisimilitude
outlined by Congreve is still subject to conventions of characterization that now seem more suited to what we call, far too
generally, 'romance'.

The sophistication of Congreve's preface, not to mention
Incognita itself, is remarkable given that Congreve was probably
as young as eighteen when he wrote it. [33] The young lovers,

[31] *The Life and Death of Mr Badman*, p. xxvi.

[32] For the development of fiction after the Restoration see Salzman, *English
Prose Fiction*, ch. 17, and Benjamin Boyce, 'The Effect of the Restoration on Prose
Fiction', *Tennessee Studies in Literature*, 6 (1961), 77–82.

[33] See John C. Hodges, *William Congreve: Letters and Documents* (London,
1964).

Aurelian, Hippolito, Juliana, and Leonora, are inspected by a narrative voice that sounds as if it stems from someone three times the author's age. The narrator's irony has been the subject of a range of critical opinions. Some writers have stressed the serious side of *Incognita*, seeing it as a portrait of youthful love, and even as an account of the nature of providence.[34] Others have offered it to modern readers as a totally self-conscious and ironical narrative.[35] For Michael McKeon, *Incognita* represents a stage in the complex changes that moved narrative from the romance to the novel. He notes the ironic distance between the young lovers' characterizations of themselves and their situation, and the narrator's knowing and detached assessment: 'Congreve's personages are figures out of an idealizing romance, satirized most of all for an indefatigable credulousness that conomically evokes also the gullibility of the average romance reader.'[36]

Readers will have to decide this controversy for themselves. As is so often the case with polarized critical viewpoints, the answer seems to lie somewhere in between, with *Incognita* representing a balance between ironic detachment and the satisfaction of romantic (if not romance) expectations. In the preface, Congreve is concerned to draw the reader's attention to the skill of the plot, an imitation of 'dramatic writing'; that is, it makes use of the dramatic unities. In later stage comedies, most famously in *The Way of the World* (1699), Congreve was able to combine the plot and witty irony of *Incognita* with a more complex characterization. In his 'novel', he is more concerned to display the poised style of his narrator, and ring the changes in a dramatically structured plot.

Throughout *Incognita*, the sense of display is paramount. The characters themselves, beneath their various disguises, are always conscious of the games they are playing, and the reactions of their audiences, thus establishing a continuity with the ironic

[34] See I. M. Westcott, 'The Role of the Narrator in Congreve's *Incognita*', *Trivium*, 11 (1976), 40–8; Aubrey Williams, 'Congreve's *Incognita* and the Contrivances of Providence', in M. Mack, (ed.), *Imagined Worlds* (London, 1968), 3–18, and also in his *An Approach to Congreve* (New Haven, Conn., 1979), ch. 5.

[35] e.g. Helga Drougge, *The Significance of Congreve's 'Incognita'* (Uppsala, 1976).

[36] McKeon, *Origins of the English Novel*, 62.

stance of the narrator. The whole performance of *Incognita* as narrative is self-conscious, and it could be said that, of all the writers represented here, the precocious Congreve is most in control of his medium.

THE UNFORTUNATE HAPPY LADY

SINCE Virginia Woolf singled out Aphra Behn as the precursor of later professional women writers in *A Room of One's Own* (1929), Behn's life, rather than her works, has been the subject of some fascination. Even though her play *The Rover* has been successfully revived for the stage, and her fiction is now more readily available, there are more biographical studies than critical studies in print.[37] Behn certainly led a fascinating life, and her biographers face many interesting unanswered questions. But to some extent at least, the effect of this interest has been to divert attention away from her literary works. Recognition of what one scholar has called 'the remarkable quality and quantity of her literary achievements' will, without doubt, increase as the works themselves become more readily available to readers.[38]

Behn turned to prose fiction very late in her writing career, after her long and successful production of plays—twenty-two in all, including adaptations—was hampered by changes in the theatre companies which dried up the demand. Behn was ailing when she began writing fiction, and only four of the twelve works she wrote were published in her lifetime (she died in 1689). At the time of her death she had an uncertain reputation as a female author: she had been both satirized, but also strongly supported by such notable figures as Dryden. Increasingly Behn championed freedom for women to take their places alongside men; a

---

[37] Three recent biographies are: Maureen Duffy, *The Passionate Shepherdess* (London, 1977); Angeline Goreau, *Reconstructing Aphra* (New York, 1980); and Mendelson, *The Mental World of Stuart Women*, ch. 3. Mendelson's is by far the most sophisticated and reliable account.

[38] Robert Adams Day, 'Aphra Behn and the Works of the Intellect', in Mary Anne Schofield and Cecilia Macheski (eds.), *Fetter'd or Free? British Women Novelists 1670–1815* (Athens, Ohio, 1986), 372; Maureen Duffy has produced a selection of Behn's fiction, *Oroonoko and other Stories* (London, 1986), and an edition of *Love Letters Between a Nobleman and his Sister* (London, 1987).

typical expression is in the epilogue to her play *Sir Patient Fancy* (1678):

> I here and there o'erheard a coxcomb cry
> Ah, rot it—'tis a woman's comedy . . .
> Why in this age has heaven allowed you more
> And women less of wit than heretofore?
> We once were famed in story, and could write
> Equal to men; could govern, nay, could fight . . . [39]

Though published posthumously in 1698, *The Unfortunate Happy Lady* was probably written in 1684, some years before Congreve wrote *Incognita*. It shares something of Congreve's narrative voice, a common technique in the Restoration tale, as noted above. Janet Todd has aptly described the narrative voice that Behn developed for her prose fiction:

When less obtrusive, the narrator is still a presence, older, experienced, commonsensical and knowledgeable in the ways of the world but not all knowing of events, breezy but not insensitive. She is not authoritative—hers is only a 'female pen'—and she reconstructs, she declares, from her own experiences or from the tales of others, often presenting without comment but often placing with her wiser opinion, insisting on her authenticity, but sailing close at times to self-parody in her claims.[40]

This narrative voice is evident in *The Unfortunate Happy Lady* . In contrast to *Incognita*'s foreign setting and stylized plot and characters, *The Unfortunate Happy Lady* is more like a Restoration comedy in its use of London settings, realistic dialogue and an unexpected plot. The increasingly independent and resourceful Philadelphia is one of Behn's most interesting female characters, in so far as she remains an attractive portrait of a moral, but pragmatic woman. She might be seen as a development of the female characters explored initially by Mary Wroth; like them, Philadelphia resists being written into a patriarchal story.

However, there are some complications involved in this aspect of Behn's narrative. The ironically named Philadelphia forgives her brother, after his fortunes have been reversed, for placing her

---

[39] Quoted in Mendelson, *The Mental World of Stuart Women*, 144.
[40] Janet Todd, *The Sign of Angellica: Women, Writing, And Fiction 1660–1800* (London, 1989), 77.

in a brothel; but rewarding him with the hand of her step-
daughter seems to be close to another example of the treatment
of women as objects of exchange, even when a woman is doing
the exchanging. The action does not seem entirely necessary for
the narrative's conventional happy ending; however, it is clearly
important for Behn that Philadelphia should, at the conclusion of
her story, be in complete control. *The Unfortunate Happy Lady*,
like all the fiction in this volume, indicates the constant
experimentation that enlivened seventeenth-century narrative.

NOTE ON THE TEXTS

I HAVE followed the same principle of relatively conservative modernization in this volume as I did with *An Anthology of Elizabethan Prose Fiction* (Oxford, 1987). All spelling has been modernized; direct speech has been marked by inverted commas; punctuation has generally been altered to clarify the sense; and paragraphing has been changed to fit modern conventions. With the possible exception of *Urania*, these seventeenth-century narratives do not present the same difficulties for the modern reader as Elizabethan works. However, all unusual words have been glossed in the Explanatory Notes.

This is not a scholarly edition with full critical apparatus. However, as the details set out below indicate, each text has been edited afresh from the original printed source, the one exception being the extract from *Mr Badman*, taken from the Oxford text. The copy-texts have been collated with significant later texts, and I have, in the Notes, indicated particularly important or interesting emendations and variant readings. Obvious errors have been corrected without comment.

Urania: The copy-text is a Folger Library copy of the 1621 edition (the only one published). The poems have been checked against the texts in Josephine A. Roberts (ed.), *The Poems of Lady Mary Wroth* (Baton Rouge, La., 1983).

The Princess Cloria: The copy-text is a Henry E. Huntington Library copy of the first edition (1661). This has been checked against the second edition (1665) and the first appearance of Book I as *Cloria and Narcissus* (1653).

The Blazing World: The copy-text is a Harvard Library copy of the first edition (1666). This has been checked against the second edition (1667).

Don Tomazo: The copy-text is a Henry E. Huntington Library copy of the first edition (1680). This has been checked against the edition in Spiro Peterson (ed.), *The Counterfeit Lady Unveiled and Other Criminal Fiction of Seventeenth Century England* (New York, 1961).

Mr Badman: The text has been modernized from the authoritative Oxford edition: James F. Forrest and Roger Sharrock (eds.), *The Life and Death of Mr Badman* (Oxford, 1988).

Incognita: The copy-text is a Bodleian Library copy of the first edition (1692). This has been checked against the second edition (1700), and also against A. Norman Jeffares (ed.), *Incognita and The Way of the World* (London, 1966).

The Unfortunate Happy Lady: The copy-text is a University of Illinois Library copy of the first edition (1698). This has been checked against the probable second edition: *Histories, Novels and Translations* (1700). The edition of Behn's works edited by Montague Summers (London, 1915), while convenient, is unreliable.

SELECT BIBLIOGRAPHY

BIBLIOGRAPHIES

Charles C. Mish, *English Prose Fiction 1600–1700: A Chronological Checklist* (Charlottesville, NC, 1967), is the standard bibliography, while Paul Salzman, *English Prose Fiction 1558–1700: A Critical History* (Oxford, 1985), has an appended bibliography arranged in generic categories. See also James L. Harner, *English Renaissance Prose Fiction 1500–1660: An Annotated Bibliography of Criticism* (Boston, 1978, 1985), with regular supplements; and Jerry C. Beasley, *English Fiction 1660–1800: A Guide to Information and Sources* (Detroit, 1978).

ANTHOLOGIES

Charles C. Mish, *Short Fiction of the Seventeenth Century* (New York, 1963) and *Restoration Prose Fiction 1666–1700* (Lincoln, Neb., 1970); Spiro Peterson *The Counterfeit Lady Unveiled and Other Criminal Fiction of Seventeenth Century England* (New York, 1961); Philip Henderson, *Shorter Novels: Seventeenth Century* (London, 1930, repr. 1967).

GENERAL STUDIES

Still of some interest are four older studies of the period: J. J. Jusserand, *The English Novel in the Time of Shakespeare* (1890, repr. London, 1967); Charlotte Morgan, *The Rise of the Novel of Manners* (London, 1911); E. A. Baker, *The History of the English Novel*, iii (1929, repr. New York, 1957); and A. J. Tieje, *The Theory of Characterization in Prose Fiction Prior to 1740* (Minneapolis, 1916). The fiction as a whole is surveyed most comprehensively in Paul Salzman, *English Prose Fiction 1558–1700* (Oxford, 1985); see also Charles C. Mish, 'English Short Fiction in the Seventeenth Century', *Studies in Short Fiction*, 6 (1968–9), 233–330.

As noted in the Introduction, the work of three important theorists on the origins of the novel form is of interest: Lennard J. Davis, *Factual Fictions* (New York, 1983); Michael McKeon, *The Origins of the English Novel 1600–1740* (Baltimore, 1987), and 'The Origins of the English Novel', *Modern Philology*, 82 (1984), 76–86; J. Paul Hunter, *Before Novels* (New York, 1989, unavailable to me at the time of going to press),

'Novels and "the Novel": The Poetics of Embarrassment', *Modern Philology*, 85 (1988), 480–98, and ' "News and New Things": Contemporaneity and the Early English Novel', *Critical Enquiry*, 14 (1988), 493–515.

On the readership for popular fiction see Margaret Spufford, *Small Books and Pleasant Histories* (London, 1981). On two important genres in translation see Dale B. J. Randall, *The Golden Tapestry: A Critical Survey of Non Chivalric Spanish Fiction in English Translation 1543–1657* (Durham NC, 1963), and T. P. Haviland, *The Roman de Longue Haleine on English Soil* (Philadelphia, 1931). On the picaresque see Walter L. Reed, *An Exemplary History of the Novel: The Quixotic Versus the Picaresque* (Chicago, 1981); Richard Bjornson, *The Picaresque Hero in European Fiction* (Madison Wis., 1977). Percy G. Adams, *Travel Literature and the Evolution of the Novel* (Lexington, Ky., 1983) is extremely thorough; see also his earlier *Travelers and Travel Liars 1660–1800* (Berkeley, Calif., 1962). There is some general treatment of romance genres in the period in Henry Knight Miller, *Henry Fielding's Tom Jones and the Romance Tradition* (Victoria, BC 1976). The best general accounts of women writers of fiction in the period are contained in B. G. MacCarthy, *Women Writers: Their Contribution to the English Novel* (Cork, 1944); Dale Spender, *Mothers of the Novel* (London, 1986), not always wholly reliable; Jane Spencer, *The Rise of the Woman Novelist From Aphra Behn to Jane Austen* (Oxford, 1986); Janet Todd, *The Sign of Angellica: Women, Writing and Fiction, 1660–1800* (London, 1989). More specialized articles include Benjamin Boyce, 'The Effect of the Restoration on Prose Fiction', *Tennessee Studies in Literature*, 6 (1961), 77–82; Kristiaan P. Aercke, 'Theatrical Background in English Novels of the Seventeenth Century', *Journal of Narrative Technique*, 18 (1988), 120–36.

URANIA

On the *roman-à-clef* element, see John J. O'Connor, 'James Hay and *The Countess of Montgomery's Urania*', *Notes and Queries*, 200 (1955), 150–2; Josephine A. Roberts, 'An Unpublished Literary Quarrel Concerning the Suppression of Mary Wroth's *Urania*', *Notes and Queries*, 222 (1977), 532–5; Paul Salzman, 'Contemporary References in Mary Wroth's *Urania*', *Review of English Studies*, 24 (1978), 178–81. The most reliable biographical account is contained in the introduction to Josephine A. Roberts (ed.), *The Poems of Lady Mary Wroth* (Baton Rouge, La, 1983), which has excellent notes on the poems taken from *Urania* and a useful genealogical chart of the main characters. There is a brief account of *Urania* in B. G. MacCarthy, *Women Writers: Their Contribution to the*

English Novel (Cork, 1944). Recent detailed studies include: Paul Salzman, *English Prose Fiction 1558–1700: A Critical History* (Oxford, 1985), ch. 10; Carolyn Ruth Swift, 'Feminine Identity in Lady Mary Wroth's Romance *Urania*', *English Literary Renaissance*, 14 (1984), 328–46; Margaret Patterson Hannay, 'Mary Sidney, Lady Wroth', in Katherine M. Wilson (ed.), *Women Writers of the Renaissance and Reformation* (Athens, G., 1987), 548–65; Elaine V. Beilin, *Redeeming Eve: Women Writers of the English Renaissance* (Princeton, NJ, 1987), ch. 8; Naomi J. Miller, ' "Not much to be marked": Narrative of the Woman's Part in Lady Mary Wroth's *Urania*', *Studies in English Literature*, 29 (1989), 121–37.

THE PRINCESS CLORIA

See Paul Salzman, '*The Princess Cloria* and the Political Romance in the 1650s', *Southern Review* (Adelaide), 14 (1981), 236–46, and *English Prose Fiction 1558–1700* (Oxford, 1985), ch. 11. An important discussion of the whole genre is contained in Annabel Patterson, *Censorship and Interpretation* (Madison, Wis., 1984), ch. 4.

THE BLAZING WORLD

The standard biography of Cavendish is Douglas Grant, *Margaret the First* (London, 1957), but there is a much more sophisticated account in Sara Heller Mendelson, *The Mental World of Stuart Women* (Brighton, 1987), ch. 1. Some discussion of *The Blazing World* in Henry Ten Eyck Perry, *The First Duchess of Newcastle and her Husband as Figures in Literary History* (1918, repr. New York, 1968); more detailed accounts include: Paul Salzman, *English Prose Fiction 1558–1700* (Oxford, 1985) ch. 16; Sylvia Bowerbank, 'The Spider's Delight: Margaret Cavendish and the "Female" Imagination', *English Literary Renaissance*, 14 (1984), 392–408; Janet Todd, *The Sign of Angellica* (London, 1989), ch. 3. Studies with an emphasis on Cavendish's ideas include Sophia B. Blaydes, 'Nature is a Woman: The Duchess of Newcastle and Seventeenth Century Philosophy', in D. C. Mell et al. (eds.), *Man*, [sic] *God and Nature in the Enlightenment* (East Lansing, Mich., 1988), 51–64; Catherine Gallagher, 'Embracing the Absolute: The Politics of the Female Subject in Seventeenth-Century England', *Genders*, 1 (1988), 24–9; Lisa T. Sarahsohn, 'A Science Turned Upside Down: Feminism and the Natural Philosophy of Margaret Cavendish', *Huntington Library Quarterly*, 47 (1984), 289–307.

DON TOMAZO

The world of real rogues and the real Dangerfield is examined in Maurice Petherick, *Restoration Rogues* (London, 1951). There is a brief discussion of *Don Tomazo* as criminal biography in Paul Salzman, *English Prose Fiction 1558–1700*, (Oxford, 1985), ch. 13; and a good introduction to the presentation of the text in Spiro Peterson (ed.), *The Counterfeit Lady Unveiled* (New York, 1961). See also Philip Bordinat, 'Thomas Dangerfield: A Talent Gone Wrong', *Bulletin of the West Virginia Association of College English Teachers*, 8 (1983), 23–31.

MR BADMAN

The standard edition, with a full introduction, is James F. Forrest and Roger Sharrock (eds.), *The Life and Death of Mr Badman* (Oxford, 1988). For critical accounts see Maurice Hussey, 'John Bunyan and the Books of God's Judgements', *English*, 7 (1948–9); Charles W. Baird, *John Bunyan: A Study in Narrative Technique* (New York, 1977); Lynn Veach Sadler, *John Bunyan* (Boston, 1979); Beatrice E. Batson, *John Bunyan: Allegory and Imagination* (London, 1984); Paul Salzman, *English Prose Fiction 1558–1700* (Oxford, 1985), ch. 14; Roger Sharrock, '*The Life and Death of Mr Badman*: Facts and Problems', *Modern Language Review*, 82 (1987), 15–29. Also of considerable interest is Christopher Hill, *A Turbulent, Seditious and Factious People: John Bunyan and His Church* (Oxford, 1988).

INCOGNITA

The main critical accounts are: E. S. de Beer, 'Congreve's *Incognita*: The Source of Its Setting', *Review of English Studies*, 8 (1932), 74–6; Aubrey Williams, 'Congreve's *Incognita* and the Contrivances of Providence', in Maynard Mack (ed.), *Imagined Worlds* (London, 1968), 3–18, and in his *An Approach to Congreve* (New Haven, Conn. 1979); I. M. Westcott, 'The Role of the Narrator in Congreve's *Incognita*', *Trivium*, 11 (1976), 40–8; Irene Simon, 'Early Theories of Prose Fiction: Congreve and Fielding', in Maynard Mack (ed.), *Imagined Worlds* (London, 1968); Helga Drougge, *The Significance of Congreve's 'Incognita'* (Uppsala, 1976); Paul Salzman, *English Prose Fiction 1558–1700* (Oxford, 1985), ch. 17; Brian Corman, 'Congreve, Fielding, and the Rise of Some Novels', in Shirley Strum Kenny (ed.), *British Theater and Other Arts 1660–1800* (Washington, DC, 1983), 257–70; and some interesting analysis in Michael McKeon, *The Origins of the English Novel 1600–1740* (Baltimore, 1987).

THE UNFORTUNATE HAPPY LADY

There are three biographical studies of Aphra Behn: Maureen Duffy, *The Passionate Shepherdess* (London, 1977); Angeline Goreau, *Reconstructing Aphra* (Oxford, 1980); and Sara Heller Mendelson, *The Mental World of Stuart Women* (Brighton, 1987), ch. 3. Mendelson's is by far the most reliable and useful account. See also Robert Adams Day, 'Aphra Behn's First Biography', *Studies in Bibliography*, 22 (1969), 227–40. A useful bibliography is available: Mary Ann O'Donnell, *Aphra Behn: An Annotated Bibliography* (New York, 1986). *The Unfortunate Happy Lady* has received only passing mention in most studies of Behn's fiction; of interest are: Frederick M. Link, *Aphra Behn* (New York, 1968); George Woodcock, *The Incomparable Aphra* (London, 1948); Rowland Hill, 'Aphra Behn's Use of Setting', *Modern Language Quarterly*, 7 (1946); Gary Kelly, ' "Intrigue" and "Gallantry": The Seventeenth-Century French Nouvelle and "Novels" of Aphra Behn', *Revue de littérature comparée*, 218 (1981), 184–94; Paul Salzman, *English Prose Fiction*, 1558–1700 (Oxford, 1985), ch. 17; Jane Spencer, *The Rise of the Woman Novelist* (Oxford, 1986), ch. 2; Janet Todd, *The Sign of Angellica* (London, 1989), ch. 4.

MARY WROTH

Urania

(1621)

The Countess of Montgomery's Urania. Written by the Right Honourable the Lady Mary Wroath, daughter to the Right Noble Robert Earl of Leicester, and niece to the ever-famous and renowned Sir Philip Sidney, Knight, and to that most exalt[ed] Lady Mary, Countess of Pembroke, late deceased.

The First Book

WHEN the Spring* began to appear like the welcoming messenger of Summer, one sweet (and in that more sweet) morning, after Aurora had called all careful eyes to attend the day, forth came the fair shepherdess Urania (fair indeed, yet that far too mean a title for her who, for beauty, deserved the highest style could be given by best-knowing judgements. Into the mead she came where usually she drave her flocks to feed, whose leaping and wantonness showed they were proud of such a guide. But she, whose sad thoughts led her to another manner of spending her time, made her soon leave them, and follow her late begun custom which was, while they delighted themselves, to sit under some shade bewailing her misfortune; while they fed, to feed upon her own sorrow and tears—which at this time she began again to summon, sitting down under the shade of a well-spread beech, the ground then blessed and the tree with full and fine-leaved branches growing proud to bear and shadow such perfections. But she regarding nothing in comparison of her woe, thus proceeded in her grief.

'Alas Urania,' said she, 'the true servant of misfortune! Of any misery that can befall woman, is not this the most and greatest which thou art fallen into? Can there be any near the unhappiness of being ignorant, and that in the highest kind, not being certain of mine own estate or birth? Why was I not still continued in the belief I was, as I appear, a shepherdess, and daughter to a shepherd? My ambition then went no higher than this estate, now flies it to a knowledge. Then was I contented, now perplexed. Oh ignorance, can thy dullness yet procure so sharp a pain, and that such a thought as makes me now aspire unto knowledge? How did I joy in this poor life, being quiet, blessed in the love of those I took for parents. But now by them I know the contrary, and by that knowledge, not to know myself. Miserable Urania, worse art thou now than these thy lambs, for they know their dams, while thou dost live unknown of any.'

By this were others come into that mead with their flocks; but she, esteeming her sorrowing thoughts her best and choicest company, left that place, taking a little path which brought her to the further side of the plain to the foot of the rocks, speaking as she went these lines, her eyes fixed upon the ground, her very soul turned into mourning.

> Unseen, unknown, I here alone complain
>   To rocks, to hills, to meadows and to springs,
> Which can no help return to ease my pain
>   But back my sorrows the sad echo brings.
> Thus still increasing are my woes to me,
>   Doubly resounded by that moanful voice,
> Which seems to second me in misery,
>   And answer gives like friend of mine own choice.
> Thus only she doth my companion prove,
>   The others silently do offer ease,
> But those that grieve, a grieving note do love;
>   Pleasures to dying eyes bring but disease:*
>   And such am I, who daily ending live,
> Wailing a state which can no comfort give.

In this passion she went on till she came to the foot of a great rock. She, thinking of nothing less than ease, sought how she might ascend it, hoping there to pass away her time more peaceably with loneliness—though not to find least respite from her sorrow, which so dearly she did value as by no means she would impart it to any. The way was hard, though by some windings making the ascent pleasing. Having attained the top, she saw under some hollow trees the entry into the rock. She, fearing nothing but the continuance of her ignorance, went in, where she found a pretty room, as if that stony place had yet in pity given leave for such perfections to come into the heart as chiefest and most beloved place, because most loving. The place was not unlike the ancient (or the descriptions of ancient) hermitages, instead of hangings, covered and lined with ivy, disdaining ought else should come there, that being in such perfection. This richness in nature's plenty made her stay to behold it, and almost grudge the pleasant fullness of content that place might have, if sensible, while she must know to taste of torments.

As she was thus, in passion mixed with pain, throwing her eyes as wildly as timorous lovers do for fear of discovery, she perceived a little light, and such a one as a chink doth oft discover to our sights. She, curious to see what this was, with her delicate hands put the natural ornament aside, discerning a little door which she putting from her, passed through it into another room, like the first in all proportion, but in the midst there was a square stone, like to a pretty table, and on it a wax candle burning, and by that a paper which had suffered itself patiently to receive the discovering of so much of it as presented this sonnet (as it seemed, newly written) to her sight.

> Here all alone in silence might I mourn,
> But how can silence be where sorrows flow?
> Sighs with complaints have poorer pains outworn,
> But broken hearts can only true grief show.
>
> Drops of my dearest blood shall let Love know
> Such tears for her I shed, yet still do burn,
> As no spring can quench least part of my woe,
> Till this live earth again to earth doth turn.
>
> Hateful all thought of comfort is to me,
> Despised day, let me still night possess,
> Let me all torments feel in their excess,
> And but this light allow my state to see
>
> Which still doth waste, and wasting as this light
> Are my sad days unto eternal night.

'Alas Urania,' sighed she, 'how well do these words, this place, and all agree with thy fortune! Sure, poor soul, thou wert here appointed to spend thy days, and these rooms ordained to keep thy tortures in, none being assuredly so matchlessly unfortunate.'

Turning from the table, she discerned in the room a bed of boughs, and on it a man lying, deprived of outward sense, as she thought, and of life, as she at first did fear, which strake her into a great amazement. Yet having a brave spirit, though shadowed under a mean habit, she stepped unto him, whom she found not

dead, but laid upon his back, his head a little to herwards, his
arms folded on his breast, hair long, and beard disordered,
manifesting all care but care itself had left him. Curiousness thus
far afforded him as to be perfectly discerned the most exact piece
of misery. Apparel he had suitable to the habitation, which was a
long grey robe.

This grieveful spectacle did much amaze the sweet and
tender-hearted shepherdess, especially when she perceived (as
she might by the help of the candle) the tears which distilled from
his eyes, who, seeming the image of death, yet had this sign of
worldly sorrow, the drops falling in that abundance as if there
were a kind strife among them to rid their master first of that
burdenous carriage, or else meaning to make a flood and so
drown their woeful patient in his own sorrow; who yet lay still,
but then fetching a deep groan from the profoundest part of his
soul, he said:

'Miserable Perissus, canst thou thus live, knowing she that
gave thee life is gone? Gone, O me, and with her all my joy
departed! Wilt thou, unblessed creature, lie here complaining for
her death and know she died for thee? Let truth and shame make
thee do something worthy of such a love, ending thy days like thy
self, and one fit to be her servant. But that I must nòt do. Then
thus remain and foster storms, still to torment thy wretched soul
withal, since all are little, and too too little, for such a loss. O
dear Limena, loving Limena, worthy Limena, and more rare,
constant Limena! Perfections delicately feigned to be in women
were verified in thee. Was such worthiness, framed only to be
wondered at by the best, but given as a prey to base and unworthy
jealousy? When were all worthy parts joined in one, but in thee,
my best Limena? Yet all these grown subject to a creature
ignorant of all but ill, like unto a fool who, in a dark cave that hath
but one way to get out, having a candle but not the understanding
what good it doth him, puts it out. This ignorant wretch, not
being able to comprehend thy virtues, did so by thee in thy
murder, putting out the world's light, and men's admiration.
Limena, Limena; O my Limena!'

With that, he fell from complaining into such a passion as
weeping and crying were never in so woeful a perfection as now
in him, which brought as deserved a compassion from the

excellent shepherdess, who already had her heart so tempered with grief as that it was apt to take any impression that it would come to feel withal. Yet taking a brave courage to her, she stepped unto him. Kneeling down by his side and gently pulling him by the arm, she thus spake:

'Sir,' said she, 'having heard some part of your sorrows, they have not only made me truly pity you, but wonder at you, since, if you have lost so great a treasure, you should not lie thus, leaving her and your love unrevenged, suffering her murderers to live while you lie here complaining. And if such perfections be dead in her, why make you not the phoenix of your deeds live again, as to new life raised out of the revenge you should take on them? Then were her end satisfied and you deservedly accounted worthy of her favour, if she were so worthy as you say.'

'If she were! O God,' cried out Perissus, 'what devilish spirit art thou that thus dost come to torture me? But now I see you are a woman, and therefore not much to be marked, and less resisted. But if you know charity, I pray you now practise it and leave me, who am afflicted sufficiently without your company; or if you will stay, discourse not to me.'

'Neither of these will I do,' said she. 'If you be then,' said he, 'some fury of purpose sent to vex me, use your force to the uttermost in martyring me, for never was there a fitter subject than the heart of poor Perissus is.' 'I am no fury,' replied the divine Urania, 'nor hither come to trouble you, but by accident lighted on this place, my cruel hap being such as only the like can give me content. While the solitariness of this like cave might give me quiet, though not ease; seeking for such a one I happened hither, and this is the true cause of my being here, though now I would use it to a better end if I might. Wherefore, favour me with the knowledge of your grief, which heard, it may be I shall give you some counsel and comfort in your sorrow.'

'Cursed may I be,' cried he, 'if ever I take comfort, having such cause of mourning. But because you are, or seem to be, afflicted, I will not refuse to satisfy your demand, but tell you the saddest story that ever was rehearsed by dying man to living woman, and such a one as I fear will fasten too much sadness in you. Yet should I deny it, I were to blame, being so well known to these senseless places as, were they sensible of sorrow, they would

condole, or else amazed at such cruelty, stand dumb (as they do)
to find that man should be so inhuman.

'Then fair shepherdess, hear myself say my name is Perissus.
Nephew I am to the King of Sicily, a place fruitful and plentiful
of all things, only niggardly of good nature to a great man in that
country, whom I am sure you have heard me blame in my
complaints. Heir I am as yet to this King, mine uncle, and truly
may I say so, for a more unfortunate prince never lived, so as I
inherit his crosses, howsoever I shall his estate.

'There was in this country (as the only blessing it enjoyed) a
lady, or rather a goddess for incomparable beauty and matchless
virtues, called Limena, daughter to a duke but princess of all
hearts. This star coming to court to honour it with such light, it
was in that my blessed destiny to see her and be made her servant
—or, better to say, a slave to her perfections. Thus long was I
happy, but now begins the tragedy. For, wars falling out between
the people and the gentlemen, the King was by the people
(imagining he took the other part) brought unto some danger and
so great an one as rudeness joined with ill-nature could bring
him into, being at last besieged in a stronghold of his, all of us his
servants and gentle subjects striving for his good and safety, in
this time nothing appearing but danger, and but wise force to
preserve men's lives and estates unto them, everyone taking the
best means to attain unto their good desires.

'The Duke, father to the best and truest beauty, would yet
bestow that upon a great lord in the country, truly for powerful
command and means a fit match for any but the wonder of
women, since none could without much flattery to himself think
he might aspire to the blessing of being accounted worthy to be
her servant, much less her husband. She, seeing it was her
father's will, esteeming obedience beyond all passions how
worthily soever suffered, most dutifully though unwillingly said
she would obey, her tongue faintly delivering what her heart so
much detested, loathing almost itself for consenting in show to
that which was most contrary to itself. Yet thus it was concluded,
and with as much speed as any man would make to an eternal
happiness.

'While of this, and so my misfortune, I remained ignorant, till
one day the wars being a little ceased—though not ended, the

siege still continuing—I stole from mine uncle to see my heart, which she kept safe with her. But when I came thither, I found, or feared I found, no room for it. She who had it being in the power of mine enemy (for so I accounted him, when he enjoyed my loss), my hopes being frustrate, my joys lost and spoiled, I grew from my self, my senses failed me, a trembling possessed my whole body, so as this distemper was marked and pitied of all. But what did comfort me was that she did seem to pity me. Then did I bless my torments that had procured me such a favour. There were none but carefully sought my health, especially her husband, whose diligence was as tedious as his wife's was my only joy. Grieved I was to stay and see my misery, yet sad I was to go from seeing her, who gave me (though a barred) delight in beholding her. But knowing passion the greater lord over my strength, I took my leave, pretending business, having only taken the opportunity that way afforded me to visit them, passing so near by them. They all seemed sorry for my going, and Limena indeed was so.

'Then by unused paths I got back to the King, often as I rode looking to that place where I left my soul prisoner. When I had been awhile at home remembering, or rather never letting the beauty of Limena be absent from me, I say remembering her and my everlasting wretched state in missing her, calling my mischief by his gain to account, I found so much cause to lament as in short time I was but mournful sorrow. My friends grieved, and generally all did show displeasure for me. Only myself found nothing but cause to proceed in this despair, love having truly changed me to that most low and still unlucky fate. Business of state I neglected, going about as in a dream led by the cruellest of hellish spirits, Despair, till I was awaked by a command to go and lead some troops, which were gathered by the King's friends, together coming to raise the siege, yet desiring me to be their head.

'I went, and thus far willingly, having so much hope left me as to think I might by this means conclude my afflictions with my end. Yet first I resolved to write unto her, that she might know she had so unblessed a creature to her servant. When I had written my letter with shaking hands, and yet a more shaking heart, I gave it to a page of mine who was newly come unto me, and never had been seen in her father's house, giving him besides directions how to carry himself, which he discreetly did observe and found as fit an opportunity as could be wished. For her husband being gone to an ancient house of his, she walked alone into a little grove below the place of her abiding. He perceiving her knew straight it was she, wherefore he followed her, having before hid himself in the uppermost part of the thicket, expecting occasion whereby to perform his master's command. He then, seeing it offered, would not neglect it, though somewhat timorously, esteeming her for her excellencies rather some goddess of those woods than an earthly creature. But remembering the infinite (yet not sufficient) praises I had given her, concluded it could be none other than Limena, so as coming to her, he on his knees delivered the letter, saying these words: The woeful Perissus his lord and master presented that with his service to her.

'This, though but little, was more than I could have said if in his place, for Lord how was I afflicted with millions of doubts how it might be delivered; then, whether she would accept of it; and most, what she would conceive of my boldness—quaking when I gave it him, knowing how wretched a creature I must be if it offended her, yet wishing I might have had the paper's place once more to have been touched by her, though if it brought dislike, for that to have suffered martyrdom.

'But she, for my happiness, took it, and with a pretty blush read it, which since I perceived did spring from love, yet blushed to see itself so lively in her cheeks. When she had read it, "Good youth," said she, "commend me to your lord, but for his letter, say it needs no answer till he come himself and fetch one."

'With this he returned, and so with much comfort to me, hope being glad to build on any small ground, how much more then on so likely a possibility. I then Hope's servant, as before only slave to despair, made all haste I could to see her, having good and welcome means afforded me, being able with convenience to take her father's house in my way to the new-raised army. Thither I came which, though in a wild forest, yet it was pretended I left the great roads for my better safety. Thus was a colour set upon my love, which but for her service and so the safelier to serve her, would suffer any gloss but truth in affection.

'Being there arrived, I was extremely welcomed of all. Her father, a grave and wise man, discoursed with me of business of state; after him, and for all supper time, her husband discoursed of hunting, an exercise fit for such a creature. Neither of these brought my mistress from a grave and almost sad countenance, which made me somewhat fear, knowing her understanding and experience, able and sufficient to judge or advise in any matter we could discourse of. But modesty in her caused it, only loving knowledge, to be able to discern men's understandings by their arguments, but no way to show it by her own speech. This (and withal fear of discovering some passions which she, though excelling in wit and judgement, yet could not govern—at least guiltiness forced her to think so) was the reason she held her gravity. Yet after she grew more merry, and I, finding a fit time by her husband's going out of the chamber with some company that was there, humbly desired an answer of my letter. She blushing, and as if ashamed so much innocent virtue should be discovered with my lover-like importunity in her, though strong in constancy, yet woman's affection gained so much by looks and sweet, though fearing, words as I was resolved and assured of her love—which made me, proud of such a treasure, begin to dispose part of it to my benefit, for looking about and seeing everyone's eyes carried their own ways, I kissed her.

'She, not offended, yet said "Let not my freedom make you dispose otherwise than virtuously with me." I vowed more than that liberty I would not ask, which I know, if I had offered, her virtue would have refused. Nor truly would my dear and worthy affection permit me to demand, and this held our loves more firm, when tied by virtue.

'But not to hold you long with this (which yet to me is some ease for the present, although the bitterer the conclusion is that follows). We had as many such meetings as true or feigned means could compass us, till our misery was such as this wild man her husband, whether out of true consideration of his great unworthiness, or proceeding from his froward disposition, I know not, grew jealous—an humour following base minds as readily as thunder doth the lightning. Then had he rashness to accompany the other, which framed a determination, which was soon altered from that name by performance, that she should stay no longer with her father but go with him to his own house. This I had notice of, but all that we could do could not hinder the accomplishing his will and save her honour, which to me more dear than mine own life was esteemed.

'But the night before her going, I came thither, where I found the accustomed entertainment, he using me with all show of respect which in that kind I embraced, our hearts being as far from meaning truth in giving or accepting as truth is from bare compliment, but greatness in me made him use it and care in me of my better self to receive it, my heart swelling with hate and scorn even almost to breaking when I did see him.

'That night I saw her, and but spake to her, so curiously her husband watched us—yet could he not keep our eyes, but by them we did deliver our souls, he only able to keep her dainty body in his wicked prison. The next day they went, and so went all worth with this odd man to have her delicacy kept like a diamond in a rotten box. Yet she, considering it to be to no purpose to contend where she was miserably bound to obey, observed him as well as she could bring her spirit to consent to; yet did he begin for her welcome to grow cursed to her. With her servants he first began, finding or, better to say, framing occasions to be rid of them all, placing of his own about her, which she suffered, only contenting herself with the memory of our loves. Yet, wanting the true content which was in our conversation, she grew sad, and keeping much within, grew pale, her rosy cheeks and lips changing to wanness. But this was all the change, her noble heart free from such a sin.

'This was but part of her affliction, still vexing her sweet disposition with speaking slightly of me, and then telling her of her love to me, which brought her into that pass as at last I was not named but she would blush. Then would he revile her and vilely use her; but she patiently and silently bare all, not suffering me to have notice of it, lest it might—as it should have done—move me to revenge her wrong for my sake endured. Thus it rested, she restlessly bearing all the ills that froward nature mixed with peevish and spiteful jealousy could afflict upon the purest mind, using no other means but gentle and mild persuasions, which wrought no more in him but that still his madness increased.

'Now was his house not far from the way which I must pass between the camp and the great city of Siracusa, being one of the chief of that kingdom, and which at that time had yielded itself again unto the King. I, hearing Philargus (for so was this unworthy man called) was at his house with his truly virtuous wife, whom my soul longed to see, I resolved to lodge there that night, not (alas) mistrusting the misfortune, but coveting to see her whom more than my heart I loved, or loved my heart the better for being hers.

'So I went thither, where I was by him exceedingly well welcomed in outward show, though his meaning was contrary, which I should have found had his devilish plots been ready, jealousy having now blinded him to all good nature or judgement. She, poor lady (poor only in this fortune) sad and grieved, all her smiles turned into sighs and thinkings, which made me fear and wonder, wondering at the change of her beauty, which yet in paleness showed excellency, and fear I did lest my absence had offended her. But I was deceived, while I least thought of the true cause, or could imagine such villainy plotted against so rare perfections.

'Desirous to know the cause, I remained almost impatient, not venturing to speak to her before her husband, for hurting her [sic]. But he going out of the room after we had supped, either to cover the flames which were ready to break out in huge fires of his mistrust, or to have the company fitter for him, affecting still to be chief, his absence howsoever gave me opportunity to demand the reason of her strangeness. She sighed to hear me call it so, and with tears told me the reason, concluding: "And thus do you see my Lord," said she, "the torments I suffer for your love, yet do you more torture me with doubting me, who have no happiness left me but the knowledge of my faith to you, all afflictions being welcome to me which for your sake I suffer."

'Between rage and pain I remained amazed, till she, taking me by the hand, brought me more woefully to myself with these words: "And yet am I brought to a greater mischief"—with that fixing her weeping eyes upon mine, which affectionately answered hers with looks and tears. "I must, my Lord," said she, "entreat you to refrain this place, since none can tell what danger may proceed from mad and unbridled jealousy." "Refrain your

sight! Command me then to die," said I. "Have I deserved to be
thus punished? Shall his brutishness undo my blessings? Yet this
place I will [*sic*], since you will have it so, hoping you will find
some means to let me know Philargus' house is not in all places."

' "That I will do, or die," said she. "Miserable wretch," cried I,
"art thou born to such fortune as to have this lady love thee, and
her unmatched goodness to suffer for one so worthless as
thyself?" "No, no, my Lord," said she, "in this you wrong me and
that judgement which heretofore you said was in me, since if you
were unworthy, then my choice was unperfect. But you are
worthy, and I worthily chose you. I loved you, and constantly
loved you, and in this do I best allow of my own judgement." "I
hope that love is not clean gone," cried I, my speech by love
directed to say thus, "nor will you forget me, though from our
most desired meetings we must be barred." "My love, my Lord,"
said she, "had and hath too sure a ground to know remove. I too
truly loved and do love you, ever to forget it or to let it have least
shadow of lessening, though veiled in absence, but rather—if
increase can be where all is already possessed—it shall increase,
love living best where desert and sufferance join together. And
for witness of it take this," said she, bestowing her picture upon
me—which is all the Limenas I shall now enjoy, or ever did,
more than her loved and best beloved sight.

'The case was blue, commanding me withal to love that colour,
both because it was hers, and because itself betokened truth. By
this time her husband was come, who told us 'twas time to go
rest. We obeyed, and this was the last time that ever I saw my
dear and most worthily accounted dear Limena, for the next
morning I was by day to be at the city, and so from thence to
return to the camp.

'Thus took I my leave and my last leave of virtuous Limena,
whose sad face, but sadder soul, foretold our following harm and
succeeding ruin. For within few days after my return to the camp,
there came a messenger early in the morning, and (O, too early
for my fortune) whom I straight knew to be Limena's faithful
servant. At first it brought joy to me, seeing a letter in his hand,
but soon was that turned to as much mourning, cursing my hands
that took it and eyes that read so lamentable a letter, the contents
—nay that itself—being this, and the very same my mistress sent
and, woe is me, the last she ere can send.'

Urania read it, while he with tears and groans gave the true period to it. The letter said thus:

'My only Lord, think not this or the manner strange I now send, knowing already some part of the undeserved course taken with me. Only pity her who, for your sake, suffers patiently. Accept these my last lines, and with them the sincerest love that ever woman gave to man. I have not time to speak what I would, therefore let this satisfy you, that the many threatenings I have heard are come in some kind to end, for I must presently die, and for you—which death is most welcome, since for you I must have it, and more pleasing than life without you. Grant me then these last requests, which even by your love I conjure you not to deny me: that you love my poor memory and as you will love that, or ever loved me, revenge not my death on my murderer who, how unworthy soever he was, or is, yet he is my husband. This is all, and this grant, as I will faithfully die.

Yours.'

'Alas, fair shepherdess,' said he, 'is this a letter without much sorrow to be read, and is not this a creature of all others to be beloved? Never let him breathe that will not heartily and most heartily lament such a misfortune.' ' 'Tis true,' said Urania, 'reason and worth being companions. But yet I hear not the certainty or manner of her death; then will I not fail to lament with you.' 'Alas,' said he, 'hear it of me, only fit to tell that story. After my departure from his house to the city, and so to the camp, the jealous wretch, finding my lady retired into a cabinet she had, where she used to pass away some part of her unpleasant life, coming in, he shut the door, drawing his sword and looking with as much fury as jealous spite could with rage demonstrate. His breath short, his sword he held in his hand, his eyes sparkling as thick and fast as an unperfectly kindled fire with much blowing gives to the blower; his tongue stammeringly with rage bringing forth these words: "Thou hast wronged me, vile creature, I say thou has wronged me."

'She, who was compounded of virtue, and her spirit, seeing his wild and distracted countenance, guessed the worst, wherefore mildly she gave this answer. "Philargus," said she, "I know in

mine own heart I have not wronged you, and God knows I have
not wronged myself." "These speeches," said he, "are but the
followers of your continued ill and false living. But think no
longer to deceive me, nor cozen yourself with the hope of being
able, for in both you shall find as much want as I do of your faith
to me. But if you will speak, confess the truth, O me, the truth:
that you have shamed yourself in my dishonour. Say you have
wronged me, giving your honour and mine to the loose and
wanton pleasure of Perissus. Was I not great enough, amiable,
delicate enough, but for lasciviousness you must seek and woo
him? Yet Limena, I did thus deserve you, that once better than
myself I loved you, which affection lives in the extremity still, but
hath changed the nature, being now as full of hate as then
abounding in love, which shall instantly be manifested if you
consent not to my will, which is that without dissembling
speeches or flattering fineness you confess your shameful love
to the robber of my bliss. You may deny it, for how easy is it to be
faulty in words, when in the truth of truth you are so faulty. But
take heed! Unfeignedly answer, or here I vow to sacrifice your
blood to your wanton love."

' "My Lord," said she, "threatenings are but means to
strengthen free and pure hearts against the threateners, and this
hath your words wrought in me, in whom it were a foolish
baseness for fear of your sword or breath to confess what you
demand. If it were true, far more did I deserve eternal
punishment if I would belie him and myself for dread of a bare
threatening, since sure that sword, were it not for danger to itself,
would if any nobleness were in it or its master, choose rather to
dye itself in the blood of a man than be seen in the wranglings
between us. Yet do I not deny my love to Perissus in all noble and
worthy affection, being I think nursed with me, for so long have I
borne this respective love to him as I know no part of my memory
can tell me the beginning. Thus partly you have your willing
assurance, that that unseparable love I bear him was before I
knew you, or perfectly myself, and shall be while I am—yet
always thus in a virtuous and religious fashion."

' "Oh God," cried out Philargus, "what do I hear? Or what can
you style virtuous and religious, since it is to one besides your
husband? Hath shame possessed you and excellent modesty

abandoned you? You have in part satisfied me indeed, but thus to see that I have just occasion to seek satisfaction for this injury. Wherefore, resolve instantly to die, or obey me. Write a letter straight before mine eyes unto him; conjure him with those sweet charms, which have undone mine honour and content, to come unto you. Let me truly know his answer and be secret, or I vow thou shalt not many minutes outlive the refusal."

'She, sweetest soul, brought into this danger (like one being between a flaming fire and a swallowing gulf, must venture into one, or standing still, perish by one) stood awhile not amazed, for her spirit scorned so low a passion, but judicially considering with herself what might be good in so much ill, she with modest constancy and constant determination made this answer:

'"This wretched and unfortunate body is, I confess, in your hands, to dispose of to death if you will, but yet it is not unblessed with such a mind as will suffer it to end with any such stain as so wicked a plot and miserable consent might purchase. Nor will I blot my father's house with treason. Treason? Nay, the worst of treasons, to be a traitor to my friend. Wherefore, my Lord, pardon me, for I will with more willingness die than execute your mind, and more happily shall I end, saving him innocent from ill, delivering my soul pure and I unspotted of the crime you tax me of, or a thought of such dishonour to myself. I might have said to *you*, but that this cruel course makes me thus part my honour from you; yet can you not part infamy and reproach from you, nor me."

'Said he: "Prepare then quickly, this shall be your last." "My Lord," said she, "behold before your eyes the most distressed of women, who if you will thus murder is here ready." Then, untying a dainty, embroidered waistcoat, "See here," said she, "the breast"—and a most heavenly breast it was!—"which you so dearly loved, or made me think so, calling it purest warm snow. Yet never was the colour purer than my love to you, but now 'tis ready to receive that stroke shall bring my heart blood, cherished by you once, to dye it, in revenge of this my wrong revenge. Nay, such revenge will my death have, as though by you I die, I pity your ensuing overthrow."

'Whether these words or that sight (which not to be seen without adoring) wrought most, I know not, but both together so

well prevaile[d] as he stood in a strange kind of fashion, which
she, who now was to act her part for life or death, took advantage
of. "And this your cruelty will more appear when it is known you
gave no time for consideration or repentance," said she. "You
deserve no such favour from me," said he, "but rather that I
should without giving ear to that bewitching tongue have
revenged my harm. But since I have committed this first, like
faulty men I must fall into another. Charity, but no desert of
yours, procures this favour for you. Two days I give you, at the
end of which be sure to content me with your answer, or content
your self with present death."

'The joy she at this conceived was as if assured life had been
given her, wherefore humbly thanking him, she promised to
satisfy him so fully at that time as he should (she hoped) be
pleased with it. Away he went, leaving her to her busy thoughts,
yet somewhat comforted since so she might acquaint me with her
afflictions, for which cause grieving that I should be ignorant of
the true means to her end, she so prettily gained that little time
for the rarest lamp of excellent life to endure.

'Then called she a faithful servant of hers, and the same who
brought me the doleful letter. First she conjured him by the faith
he bare her to obey what she commanded and to be secret. Then
related she this soul-rendering story to him, which she enjoined
him truly to discover to me, by his help getting pen and paper,
and having written that dolorous—yet sweet, because loving—
letter, sent him to me that day she was to give her answer, which
she assured him should be a direct refusal, esteeming death more
pleasing and noble than to betray me, who (for my now grief
mixed with that blessing) she enriched with her incomparable
affection, giving him charge to deliver it to mine own hands and
besides to stay with me, assuring him I would most kindly entreat
him for her sake, which she might truly warrant him, being
commandress of my soul.

'He found me in my tent ready to go forth. With a wan and sad
countenance, he gave that and my death together, then telling the
lamentable story I now delivered you. With floods of tears and
storms of sighs he concluded: "And by this is the rarest piece of
womankind destroyed."

'Had I grown into an ordinary passion like his, of weeping,
sobbing or crying, it had not been fit for the excessive loss I was

fallen into, wherefore like a true castaway of fortune, I was at that
instant metamorphosed into misery itself, no other thing being
able to equal me, no more than any, except the own fellow to a
cockleshell can fit the other.* This change yet in me, which to
myself was so sudden as I felt it not, was so marked by my
friends, and by all admired, as those who feared the least doubted
my end—which would it then had happened, since if so, the
earth no longer had born such a wretch, this sad place been
molested with a guest perpetually filling it, and these places near
with my unceasing complaints. Despair having left me no more
ground for hope but this: that ere long I shall ease them all, death
proving merciful unto me in delivering this grief-full body to the
rest of a desired grave.'

'My Lord Perissus,' said Urania, 'how idle and unprofitable
indeed are these courses, since if she be dead, what good can
they bring to her? And, not being certain of her death, how unfit
are they for so brave a prince who will, as it were, by will without
reason willfully lose himself. Will not any, till the contrary be
known, as properly hope as vainly despair? And can it be
imagined her husband, who passion of love did in his fury so
much temper, should have so cruel a hand, guided by so savage a
heart, or seen by so pitiless eyes, as to be able to murder so sweet
a beauty? No, my Lord, I cannot believe but she is living, and that
you shall find it so, if unreasonable stubborn resolution bar you
not, and so hinder you from the eternal happiness you might
enjoy.'

'Only, rare shepherdess,' said the love-killed Perissus, 'how
comfortable might these speeches be to one who were able to
receive them, or had a heart could let in one sign of joy. But to
me they are rather bitter, since they but cherish me the longer to
live in despairful misery. No, she is dead, and with her is all
virtue and beauteous constancy gone. She is dead, for how can
goodness or pity be expected from him who knew nothing more
than desire of ill and cruelty? Thou art dead, and with thee all my
joys departed; all faith, love and worth are dead, to enjoy some
part of which, in short time I will be with thee, that though in life
we were kept asunder, in death we may be joined together, till
which happy hour I will thus still lament thy loss.'

'If you be resolved,' said the dainty Urania, 'folly it were to
offer to persuade you from so resolute a determination. Yet being

so brave a prince, stored with all virtuous parts, discretion and judgement, methinks, should not suffer you to bury them in the poor grave of love's passion, the poorest of all other. These invite me, as from yourself, to speak to yourself. Leave these tears and woman-like complaints, no way befitting the valiant Perissus, but like a brave prince, if you know she be dead, revenge her death on her murderers, and after, if you will celebrate her funerals with your own life-giving, that will be a famous act. So may you gain perpetual glory and repay the honour to her dead, which could not be but touched by her untimely end.'

'Her honour touched, and touched for me? Oh, immortal God,' cried he, 'thou wilt not, I hope, let a slave live should touch on such a thought, nor me to live after it were borne, if not to sacrifice my blood to wash away the stain. But I pray you, since you undertake thus to advise me, how can I do this, and yet obey my Limena's command in not revenging her death?' 'Why that,' replied the discreet Urania, 'proceeded wholly from the love she bare you, which rather is another motive to stir you if you consider it, since the danger she apprehended you would run into, to right so delicate yet unhappily injured a lady, and for you injured, forced her to use her authority for your safety. But let not that prevail, nor hinder a deadly revenge for so detestable a fact. Thus shall you approve yourself a brave and worthy lover, deserving her who best deserved; but let it never be said Perissus ended unrevenged of Philargus, and concluded his days like a fly in a corner.'

These words wrought so far in the noble heart of Perissus as, rising from his leafy cabin, then thus said he. 'Is Perissus the second time conquered? I must obey that reason which abounds in you and to you shall the glory of this attempt belong. Now will I again put on those habits which of late I abandoned, you having gained the victory over my vow. But I beseech you, tell me who my counsellor is, for too much judgement I find in you to be directly, as you seem, a mere shepherdess, nor is that beauty suitable to that apparel.'

'My name,' said she, 'is Urania,* my bringing up hath been under an old man and his wife who, till lately, I took for my father and mother, but they telling me the contrary, and the manner of their finding me, makes me find I am lost, and so in truth is much of my content, not being able to know any more of myself. I delighted before to tend a little flock the old pair put into my hands; now am I troubled how to rule my own thoughts.' 'This do I well credit,' said Perissus, 'for more like a princess than a shepherdess do you appear, and so much do I reverence your wisdom as next unto Limena I will still most honour you. And therefore, fair Urania (for so I hope you will give me leave to call you), I vow before heaven and you that I will never leave off my arms until I have found Philargus and on him revenged my lady's death, and then to her love and memory offer up my afflicted life —but first shall you have notice of the success which, if good, shall be attributed to you, if ill, but to the continuance of my ill destiny. But if your fortune call you hence before you shall be found by them I will employ (since the world hath not a place can keep the beauty of Urania hidden—if seen, then will it not be adored?), they shall not leave till they have found you. Nor will you scorn that name from me, who shall now leave you the incomparable Urania.'

With these words they went out of the cave, he straight going to a large holly tree (the place rich with trees of that kind), on which, at his coming to that melancholy abiding, he had hung his armour, meaning that should there remain in memory of him, and as a monument after his death, to the end that whosoever did find his body might by that see he was no mean man, though subject to fortune. Them he took down and armed himself, but while he was arming, Urania entreated him to do one thing more for her, which was to tell her how he came to that place.

'And that was ill forgot, most fair Urania,' said he. 'Then know that as soon as I had received that letter so full of sorrow, and heard all that miserable relation, I was forced, notwithstanding the vow I had to myself made of this solitary course you have relieved me from, to go against the enemy who, with new forces and under a new leader, were come within sight of our army. I, thinking all mischiefs did then conspire together against me, with an enraged fury went towards them, hoping (and that only hope was left me) in that encounter to end my life and care together in the battle—yet not slightly to part with it, in my soul wishing everyone I had to deal withal had been Philargus.

'This wish after made me do things beyond myself, forcing not

only our company and party to admire me, but also the contrary
to be discouraged, so as we got the day, and not only that but an
end of the wars, for the chief traitors being either killed or taken,
the rest that outlived the bloody slaughter yielded themselves to
mercy, whom in my uncle's name I pardoned on condition that
instantly they disbanded and everyone retire to his own home.

'This done, and my uncle quietly settled in his seat, in the
midst of those triumphs which were for this happy victory I stole
away, leaving a letter with my new servant directed to the King
wherein I humbly asked pardon for my private departure and
with all the entreaties that I could frame, persuaded him to
entertain that servant of mine and to accept of him as
recommended by me and accordingly to esteem of him. Then
took I my way first to her father's, to know the manner and
certainty—where I found unspeakable mourning and sadness,
her mother ready to die with her, as if she had brought her forth
to be still as her life, that though two, yet like those eyes that one
being struck in a certain part of it, the other unhurt doth lose
likewise the sight. So she, having lost her, lost likewise all
comfort with her. The servants mourned and made pitiful
lamentations. I was sorry for them, yet gratefully took their
mourning, for methought it was for me, none being able to grieve
sufficiently but myself for her loss. When her mother saw me,
who ever she well-loved, she cried out these words:

' "O my Lord, see here the miserable woman deprived of all
joy, having lost my Limena, your respected friend. Full well do I
now remember your words, when with gentle and mild persuasions you would have had us stay her going from this place unto
his house. Would we had then feared or believed; then had she
been safe, whereas now she is murdered."

' "Murdered!" cried I. "O speak again—but withal, how?"
"Her husband," said she, "led her forth, where in a wood thick
enough to shade all light of pity from him, he killed her and then
burnt her, her clothes found in the wood besmeared with blood
and hard by them the remnant of a great fire. They, with such
store of tears as had been able to wash them clean and quench
the fire, were brought to the house by those who went to seek
her, seeing her long stay—not mistrusting harm, but that
they had forgotten themselves. The rest, seeing this doleful

spectacle, rent their hair and gave all testimony of true sorrow. Then came these news to us; how welcome judge you, who I see feel sorrow with us. Her father and brothers armed themselves and are gone in search of him, who was seen with all speed to pass towards the sea. Thus hear you the daughter's misfortune, which must be followed by the mother's death; and God send that as soon as I wish my lord and sons may meet with that ungrateful wretch to revenge my miserable child's loss."

'This being done, she swooned in my arms, myself, being still in my transformed estate, helped her as much as I could. Then, delivering her to her servants, I took my leave, buying this armour to go unknown till I could find a place sad enough to pass away my mournful hours in. Many countries I went through and left, for all were too pleasant for my sorrow, till at last I lighted on this happy one, since in it I have received as much comfort by your kind and wise counsel as is possible for my perplexed heart to entertain.'

By this time he was fully armed, which made the sweet Urania admire him, and if more pity had lodged in her than before she had afforded him, his goodly personage and doleful looks so ill agreeing had purchased, for she did pity him so much as this had almost brought the end of some kind of pity, or pity in some kind love, but she was ordained for another, so as this proved but a fine beginning to make her heart tender against the other's coming.

Now was he ready to depart, wherefore they came down from the rock, when being at the bottom they met a young shepherd whose heart Urania had (although against her will) conquered. This lad she entreated to conduct Perissus to the next town, which he most willingly consented to, thinking himself that day most happy when she vouchsafed to command him; withal she enjoined him not to leave him till he saw him shipped, which he performed, coming again to her to receive thanks more welcome to him than if a fine new flock had been bestowed on him.

Perissus gone, Urania for that night drove her flock homeward, giving a kind look unto the rock as she returned, promising often to visit it for brave Perissus' sake and to make it her retiring place, there to pass some of her melancholy hours in. The next morning, as soon as light did appear or she could see light (which sooner she might do than any, her eyes making day before day itself was seen), with her flock she betook herself to the meadow, where she thought to have met some of her companions. But being early, her thoughts having kept more careful watch over her eyes, thought itself grown peremptory with such authority, she found none come, wherefore leaving the flock to the charge of a young lad of hers, took her way towards the rock, her mind faster going than her feet, busied still, like one holding the compass, when he makes a circle, turns it round in his own centre, so did she, her thoughts encircled in the ignorance of her being.

From this she was a little moved by the coming of a pretty lamb towards her who, with pitiful cries and bleatings, demanded her help—or she with tender gentleness imagined so. Wherefore she took it up and, looking round about if she could see the dam, perceiving none, wandered a little amongst bushes and rude places till she grew something weary, when sitting down she thus began to speak.

'Poor lamb,' said she, 'what moan thou makest for loss of thy dear dam. What torments do I then suffer, which never knew my mother? Thy miss is great, yet thou, a beast, mayest be brought up and soon contented, having food, but what food can be given me, who feeds on nothing but despair? Can that sustain me? No, want of knowledge starves me, while other things are plentiful. Poor innocent thing, how doth thy wailing suit with mine. Alas, I pity thee, myself in some kind wanting such a pity.'

Then she did hear a noise in the bushes. Looking what it should be, she saw a fierce she-wolf come furiously towards her. She, who (though a spirit matchless lived in her) perceiving her, wished the beast further, yet taking her wonted strength of heart and virtuous thoughts together, she thus said: 'O Heaven defend me, miserable creature, if thou please. If not, grant me this blessing: that as I shall here end, not knowing any parents to sorrow for me, so those parents, if living, may never know my loss, lest they do grieve for me.'

As she thus religiously gave her thoughts and her last, as she thought, to the Highest, the beast running towards her of a sudden stood still—one might imagine seeing such a heavenly creature did amaze her, and threaten for meddling with her. But such conceits were vain, since beasts will keep their own natures.*

The true reason being, as soon appeared, the hasty running of two youths who, with sharp spears, soon gave conclusion to the supposed danger, killing the wolf as she stood hearkening to the noise they made. But they, not seeing Urania, who on her knees was praising God, said one to another 'Alas, have we hasted to kill this beast, which now is not for our turn, little help can this give to our sick father.'

Urania then looked up, hearing human voices, which she so little expected as only death was that she looked for; but then perceived the two young men, whose age might be judged to be some seventeen years. Faces of that sweetness as Venus' love could but compare with them, their hair which never had been cut hung long, yet longer much it must have been had not the dainty natural curling somewhat shortened it, which as the wind moved the curls so prettily played as the sunbeams in the water. Their apparel goats' skins cut into no fashion, but made fast about them in that sort as one might see by their sight they were wild, yet that wildness was governed by modesty; their skin most bare, as arms and legs and one shoulder, with part of their thighs. But so white was their skin as seemed the sun, in love with it, would not hurt, nor the bushes so much as scratch. On their feet they had a kind of shoes which came up to the ankle.

Thus they were before the prime of shepherdesses, who coming to them and saluting them, they stepped back in wonder to see that beauty which yet in the masculine they came near to. Then, laying admiration so far apart as to keep themselves safe from rudeness in some kind, one of them began.

'Divine creature, pardon this our boldness, which hath brought us thus rudely to your presence. If we have offended, let our humility in sorrow excuse us, or if this beast we have killed was favoured by you, take us, who are rude men, to serve you in that stead. In the meantime, accept our petition to be forgiven our fault.'

Urania, who had before in their outsides seen enough to be wondered at, hearing their speech bred more admiration. She answered them: 'Your beauties, mixed with so much mildness and sweetness, might plead for you if you had offended, which I saw not—but in having given too much respect to me, the most miserable of women. Nor any rudeness see I, but in that beast which you have so manfully destroyed. If your habits show wildness, your speech takes away that error, nor have you committed any fault if not in saving me to live to greater miseries.'

The young men then blushing, humbly thanking her, were taking their leaves when she courteously desired them that since they had rescued her, she might know the men that saved her, and the adventure brought them thither. They answered with all their hearts they would satisfy her demand, but for that time desired to be excused, since they were sent by their old, weak father to get some food for him which when they had done they would return to her. She, hearing this, 'Alas,' said she, 'shall you, who have kept me out of the throat of a ravening wolf, want what I may help you to? Go to your father. I will accompany you; this lamb shall feed him, at this time sent of purpose, without doubt, to cherish so good and blessed a man as is father to two such sons. And then may I know your story and his together.'

They, happy to see so fit a dish for his age, on their knees would have thanked her, but she hindered them, and so together they went towards the place where he remained, which was in a cave under a great rock near to the sea. When they arrived at the place, the elder of the two went in, telling the old man of the fair shepherdess's coming and her kindness to him. Wherefore he sent out a young maid, who was clothed in plain but neat apparel, of such beauty as who had seen her alone would have thought her incomparable, but Urania excelled her; meeting of her, knowing by the youth she was his sister, most sweetly saluted her, taking her by the hand, went in, where they found an old man so feeble as he had but his tongue left to serve himself or them withal— and well did it serve him for the good of the young men, thus beginning to Urania:

'Admired shepherdess, and most worthy to be so, since the inward beauty of your mind so much excels the peerless excellency of your outward perfections, as virtue excels beauty, see here a poor sign of greatness overwhelmed with misfortune, and be as you are, all excelling, a happy means to aid an else destroyed hope of rising. Sit down here and grudge not me that honour, for before the story be ended you will see more reason to pity than scorn, and you my sons and daughter, come near, for now shall you know that which I have till this present kept from you for fear I should not else have held you in this poor but quiet living.'

They being ready to sit and hear the story, a man's voice made them stay, and Urania entreated, as in less danger if seen than the other, to go forth. She perceived a gentleman of that delicacy for a man as she was struck with wonder, his sweetness and fairness such as the rarest painters must confess themselves unable to counterfeit such perfections, and so exquisite proportion. He had a mantle richly embroidered with pearl and gold, the colour of that and his other apparel being watchet* suitably embroidered; his hair fair and shining, so young he was as he had but the sign of a beard. Arms he had none, save a sword to defend himself, or offend his enemies.

He came softly and sadly on towards the rock, but his eyes to the seaward. She beholding him said 'Oh sweet island, how mayest thou indeed boast thyself for being the harbour of all excellent persons.' He, whose mind was distant from him, held his eyes and thoughts as at first fixed, beseeching the sea, if she had Amphilanthus in her power, she would be pitiful unto him. After he had concluded these words, he (whose soul was absent from him) looked towards the island, when his eyes were soon called to admire and admiringly behold the rare shepherdess, who in the same kind of wonder looked on him. He, ravished with the sight, scarce able to think her an earthly creature, stood gazing on her. She, who—poor soul—had with the sight of Perissus given leave for love to make a breach into her heart, the more easily after to come in and conquer, was in so great a passion as they seemed like two masterpieces framed to demonstrate the best and choicest skill of art.

At last, as men have the stronger and bolder spirits, he went unto her, not removing his eyes in the least from hers, and with a brave but civil manner thus spake unto her. 'If you be, as you seem, an incomparable shepherdess, let me be so much favoured of you as to be permitted to ask some questions. But if you be a heavenly person, as your rareness makes me imagine, let me know, that by the humble acknowledging my fault I may gain pardon.'

'Alas sir,' said Urania, 'so far am I from a heavenly creature as

I esteem myself the most miserable on earth, wherefore if any service I can do may pleasure you, I beseech you, command me, so may I receive some happiness which I shall obtain in obeying you.' 'What I will demand,' said he, 'shall be such things as you may easily grant, and by that make me your servant. I desire to know what this place is, but most what you are, for never can I believe you are as you seem, unless for the greater wonder all excellency should be masked under this shepherdess' attire.'

'For the perfections in me, as you call them,' said Urania, 'were they not made perfect by so excellent a speaker, would be of no more value than the estimation I make of my poor beauty. Touching your demands, I will as well as I can satisfy you in them. This island is called Pantaleria, governed by an ancient worthy lord called Pantalerius, who having received some discontent in his own country, with his family and some others that loved and served him, came hither, finding this place unpossessed, and so named it after his own name, having ever since in great quiet and pleasure remained here, himself and all the rest taking the manner and life of shepherds upon them, so as now this place is of all these parts most famous for those kind of people. For myself, I can say nothing but that my name is Urania, an old man and his wife having bred me up as their own till within these few days they told me that which now more afflicts me than the poverty of my estate did before trouble me, making me so ignorant of myself as I know no parents. For they told me that I was by them found hard by the seaside, not far from these rocks, laid in a cradle with very rich clothes about me, a purse of gold in the cradle and a little writing in it which warned them that should take me up to look carefully to me, to call me Urania, and when I came to sixteen years of age to tell this to me, but by no means before. This they have truly performed, and have delivered me the mantle and purse, that by them, if good fortune serve, I may come to knowledge; enjoining me besides not to keep this my story secret from any, since this sweet place, enticing many into it, may chance to bring someone to release me from this torment of ignorance.'

'It could not be otherwise,' said he, 'since such sweetness and peerless loveliness are matched together.' 'But now,' said Urania, 'let me know, I beseech you, who I have discovered myself unto.'

'Let us sit down,' said he, 'under these rocks, and you shall know both who I am, and the cause of my coming hither.' 'Nay,' answered Urania, 'if it please you, let us rather go into a cave hard by where I have left an old, weak man, ready to tell me his story—having with him two of the finest youths and a maid of the rarest beauty that eye can behold—and desirous he is to speak, for long he cannot endure.'

So together they came into the cave, the grave man reverently with bowing down his head saluting him thus: 'Brave Sir—for majesty do I perceive in your countenance, which makes me give you this title—welcome to my poor abiding, and most welcome since now, I trust, I shall dispose of my sons according to my long wish and desire. Sit, I beseech you, down, and tell me who you are, that then I may discourse to you the lamentable fortune I and these my children are fallen into.'

The stranger sat down between the old man and the excellent shepherdess, beginning his tale thus. 'My name,' said he, 'is Parselius, Prince of Morea, being eldest son unto the King thereof. Which country I left with a dear friend of mine who, besides the untying band of friendship we live linked in, is my kinsman and heir to the kingdom of Naples, called Amphilanthus, resolving not to return till we had heard news of a lost sister of his who in the first week after her birth was stolen away. Since which time, an old man, whether by divination or knowledge, assured the King her father she is living. Wherefore, the most brave of princes Amphilanthus resolved to seek her. Myself, loving him as well or better than myself, would not be denied to accompany him, for having been ever bred in nearness of affections, as well as in conversation, together, it could not be but we must, like the soul and body, live and move.

'So we betook ourselves to the sea, leaving Morea, passing many adventures in diverse countries, still seeking the least frequented and privatest places, keeping to the West, for that way we were directed by the wise man. At last we arrived in Sicily, which country we found in great trouble, wars being broke out again after the departure of Perissus, nephew to the King, who had settled the state in good peace and quiet. But their hearts either not fully reconciled, or only reconciled to him after his departure, which as we heard was strange and sudden being never since heard of, they rebelled again. But we soon appeased the business, settling the King in his seat with quiet and safety. Then did Amphilanthus and I, though against my heart, part our bodies (but never shall our minds be parted), he in one ship, taking I know not justly what course, but I trust the happiest; myself, guided by fortune, not appointing any one place to bend to, was brought hither, promising at our parting to meet in his father's court in Italy within twelve months after. But shorter I hope now my journey will be, since I verily believe you, most fair shepherdess, are the lost princess, and rather do I think so because you much resemble Leonius, the younger brother to Amphilanthus, whose beauty in man cannot be equalled, though surpassed by you.'

When he had concluded, the old man, with tears, thus said: 'O almighty God, how great are thy blessings to me, that before I die thou dost thus bring the most desired happiness I could wish for, in sending hither that prince who only can restore our good unto us. Most mighty and worthily honoured prince, see here before your royal presence the unfortunate King of Albania, who in the wars between Achaea and Macedon, taking part with Achaea, was beaten out of my country and forced to wander, seeking safety far from the place where my safety ought most to have been. I came to your father's court, it is true, poor and unlike a prince, which sight took away so much as pity, courtiers rather out of their bravery condemning than compassionating extremity. Besides, your mother being sister to the Macedonian King then living, would not permit me any favour, my kingdom in the meanwhile spoiled and parted among such as could prevail by strength and policy to get shares. When I found myself in this misery, with my wife and some few friends we went away, leaving Morea and all hope of gaining any good in Greece.

'Following what course our stars would guide us to we came hither, where it pleased God to bless us with these two boys and this daughter, after whose being seven years old she died.* Yet for all it is and was a joy to me to see of my own for my posterity, finding that likelihood of princely virtues as (I hope) shall be one day manifested, it hath grieved me to think how I should leave them. But now my hopes are revived, since I trust that danger is past, your noble and magnanimous virtues being such as to take pity of any, how much more then will your honour be to assist distressed princes? And now may you well do it, since a servant of mine, who I have often sent thither to see how things pass, doth assure me your uncle is dead, and a mighty lord being next heir-male, which by the laws of the country was otherwise, hath got the crown, having enclosed your fair young cousin, right heir to the kingdom of Macedon, being only daughter to the late King, in a strong tower till she be of age, and then to marry her, or if she refuse to keep her there still, and this is the best she can expect. Wherefore, Sir, thus you are bound to rescue her; then I beseech you take these two young men into your protection, who till now knew no other than that they were mean boys, I not daring to let them know their birth, lest those great spirits which live in them should have led them into some dangerous course. But still I have kept them under, making them know hardness and misery, the better still to endure it, if so cross their fortunes be, or if they come to enjoy their right they may know the better to command, having so well learned to obey and serve. And most delicate shepherdess, do you I pray accept of this young maid for your friend and companion, since if you be the King of Naples' daughter, or any other prince's, you need not scorn the company of the Albanian King's daughter.'

Parselius, taking the old King in his arms, 'And is it my good fortune, most famous King of Albania,' said he, 'to have it in my power to serve so excellent a prince? Doubt not then but I will with all faithful love and diligence, as soon as I have concluded this search with meeting my dearest friend in Italy, go into Morea and from thence carry such forces as shall, with my other friends I will join with me, restore you to your right, and pull down that Macedonian usurper, were it but for wronging you. But since I have so fair an occasion to revenge such injuries offered so virtuous a prince as yourself, in keeping a kingdom and usurping another from his rightful Queen, I am doubly bound. Your sons I accept to be my companions, and as brothers to me will I be careful of them.'

The like did Urania promise for the young lady. Then the old King, before overcharged with sorrow was now so ravished with joy as not being able to sustain, bursting into floods of kind tears, and his soul turned into a passion of joy unsupportable—being only able to kiss the prince Parselius and Urania, embracing, blessing and kissing his children, giving them charge faithfully and lovingly to observe and love that brave prince and sweet shepherdess—like a child for quiet ending gave up the ghost in their arms he best did love.

Great sorrow was made among them for his death, but then growing almost night, Urania for that time went home, leaving the three to attend the King's body till the next morning, directing Parselius to the sad abiding of the perplexed Perissus, promising to come to the cave by sun rising to dispose of all things.

Urania being come home, little meat contented her, making haste to her lodging, that there she might discourse with herself of all her afflictions privately and freely. Throwing herself on her bed she thus began: 'Alas Urania, how doth misery love thee, that thus makes thee continually her companion! What is this new pain thou feelest? What passion is this thy heart doth entertain? I have heard my imagined father, and many more, talk of a thing called love, and describe it to be a delightful pain, a sought and cherished torment, yet I hope this is not that, for slave am I enough already to sorrow, no need have I then to be oppressed with passion. Passion, oh passion yet thou rulest me! Ignorant creature, to love a stranger and a prince. What hope hast thou that, because thou art not known, thou shouldst be known to love in the best place? I had rather yet offend so than in a mean choice, since if I be daughter of Italy, I chose but in mine own rank, if meaner, ambition is more noble than baseness. Well then, if I do love, my only fault is in too soon loving, but neither in love nor choice. Love, plead for me, since if I offend it is by thy power, and my faults must, as made, be salved by thee. I confess I am won and lost if thou, brave prince, pity not and save me. Sweet chastity, how did I love, and honour thee; nay, almost vow myself unto thee. But I have failed. Love is the more powerful god, and I was born his subject.'

With that she rose up and went to the window to see if it were day, never knowing before what it was to wish for anything (except the knowledge of herself), now longs for day, watches the hours, deems every minute a year and every hour an age till she again enjoyed Parselius' sight, who all that night took as little rest, hope, love and fear so vexing him and tyrannizing over him as sleep durst not close nor seize his eyes to any the least slumber, all his content being in thinking on Urania, wishing from his soul she were the lost princess, that then they might happily enjoy which wish by love was chid, since love was able in him to make her great enough and those wishes were but to add to that which ought to be so perfect as itself should of itself be sufficient to make happiness, which is the greatest greatness. Then did he resolve, whatsoever she was, to make her his wife. His father, country, friend and all must love Urania. Thus all must yield to her, or lose him already yielded.

He, whose youth and manlike conversation scorned the poor name and power of love, is now become his bondman; cries out on nothing but Urania; thinks of nothing, hopes for nothing but the gain of her perfections to his love—accusing this night for spitefully being longer than any other that ever he knew, affection and desire making it appear tedious unto him. And why? Because it kept Urania from him.

'O,' would he say, 'how happy wert thou, Parselius, to land on this shore, where thou hast gained the goddess of the earth to be thy mistress, Urania to be thy love.' But then would a lover's fear take him, making him tremblingly sigh and say, 'But if she should not love again, wretch of all men, what would become of thee?' Courage then joining with hope would bring him from that sad despair, giving him this comfort. 'Yet sure,' said he, 'her heart was not framed of so excellent temper, her face of such beauty, and herself wholly made in perfectness, to have cruelty lodged in her. No, she was made for love; then she must love, and if so, pity will claim some part; and if any, or to any, who more deserves it than myself who most affecteth her?'

With that he went to the mouth of the rock, from whence he might discover all the plains, carefully and lovingly beholding them. 'You blessed plains,' said he, 'which daily have that treasure which, the rest of the world wanting, confesseth sense of poverty; dull earth, ignorant of your riches, neither knowing nor caring how to glory sufficiently for bearing and continually touching such perfections, why dost not thou with all excellencies strive to delight her, sending forth soft and tender grass mixed with sweetest flowers when she will grace thee, suffering thee to kiss her feet as she doth tread on thee? But when she lies on thee, dost thou not then make thyself delicate and change thy hardness to daintiness and softness, happy, most happy in her sweet weight? And yet when she doth leave thee, do not the flowers fade and grass die for her departure?'

Then he perceived her coming afar off down the plains, her flock some feeding, but most leaping and wantonly playing before her. 'And well may you do this, most lucky flock,' said he, 'having such a commandress and so fair a guardian. Well doth joy become you, showing you sensibly do know the blessing you enjoy. But what will you do when she shall leave you? Leave this pleasure, pine, starve, and die with so great misery! Alas, I pity you, for such a change will be. And what wilt thou, sweet island, do? Let in the sea, be drowned, and lose thy pleasant solitariness!'

Having thus said, he left the desolate rock and went to meet her, who with equal love and kindness met him. Such indeed was their affection as can be expressed by nothing but itself, which was most excellent. When the first passion was past, which joy governed for sight, love taking the place of speech, 'Ah Urania,' said he, 'how did the sun show himself in his brightest and most glorious habits to entertain thee in these meads, coveting to win thy favour by his richness, triumphing in his hope of gain. What moved thy sight then in my soul? Think you not it grew to ravishing of my senses?'

'The sun,' said she, 'shined (methought) most on you, being as if so fond as he did give himself to be your servant, circling you about as if he meant that you should be the body and himself serve for your beams.' With that he took her hand and, with an affectionate soul, kissed it. Then went they together to the cave where the two young savage princes and their sister attended them. Then did they privately bury the old King, promising (if business went well, that they by Parselius' favour might recover their right) to fetch his worthy body and lay it with the other famous kings of Albania.

This being agreed upon, they went out of the cave, Steriamus and Selarinx (for so the young princes were called) went first in their savage habits, which they resolved to wear till they came where they might fit themselves with apparel and arms befitting their estates, Parselius then promising to knight them. Next after them went the Morean prince leading Urania, and she holding Selarina by the hand.

Being come into the plain, Parselius again speaking to Urania, urged the likelihood of her being the lost princess, besides assuring her howsoever of no lower estate if she would go with him. She made him this answer: 'A prince,' said she, 'can demand or promise but princely things. I believe you to be so because you say so, and that face, methinks, should not dissemble. Out of this I credit you, and so consent to go with you; then nobly and virtuously, as I trust you, dispose of me.'

He, casting up his eyes to heaven, 'Let me, nor my attempts prosper,' said he 'when I break faith and virtuous respect to you! Now let us to the ship.' 'Nay I beseech you, first,' said she, 'permit me to take my leave of my good friends and formerly supposed parents, lest my absence bring their death, if ignorant of my fortune. Besides, we will carry the mantle and purse with us.'

He soon agreed unto it, and so together they went to the house, the late abiding of the matchless shepherdess, where they found the good old folks sitting together before the door expecting the return of Urania. But when they saw her come so accompanied, they wondered at it; and though poor, yet were they civil, wherefore they went towards them and, hearing by the fair shepherdess who the princes were, kneeled down and would have kissed the hand of Parselius. But he, who respected them for their care of Urania, would not permit them to do so much reverence, lifting them up and embracing them, told them the same story of his travel and cause thereof, as he had done to Urania, and then concluded that the likelihood of her being that sought for princess was the reason why they agreed to go together, he promising to conduct her safely into Italy, and if she proved the princess, to deliver her to her father, which verily he believed he should do—and seldom do men's imaginations in that kind fail, especially having so good grounds to lay their hopes upon.

The old folks, sorry to part with Urania, yet knowing she was not ordained to tarry with them, would not seem to contradict their wills. Wherefore, fetching the mantle and purse with the little writing, delivered them to Urania, whose good disposition was such as she could not refrain from tears when she parted with them, they wishing their age would have permitted them to have attended her, but being feeble, it was not for them to travel, especially to go so uncertain a journey. But in their place they desired their daughter might serve her, which she willingly consented to.

Thus, everything concluded, they took their leaves and way to the ship, which they found where Parselius had left her, but not as he had parted from her, for much more company was in her and a strange encounter: he found his servants prisoners, his arms possessed, and all his goods in the hands of a pirate. Yet had he governed it so as this misadventure was not discovered till they were aboard. Parselius alone, in regard of his company and some women, would nevertheless have ventured his life to have kept Urania free, such was his love, by none to be surpassed. His compassion likewise was great on the other princess. In himself, feeling the just cause, as he thought, they had to mistrust him, and his promises to be valueless, this accident being the first of their hoped-for joys.

But she, whose truth in belief would not permit her to have the least part of suspicion to enter, much less lodge in her breast against him, hindered that brave but doubtful attempt, using these speeches to him. 'Be satisfied my dearest friend,' said she, 'and hazard not yourself in this kind, seeking to alter what is ordained by fate, and therefore not to be changed, but rather give us example as confidently and mildly to suffer this adversity, as happily we might have enjoyed the other we expected.'

He only with a languishing but (to her) loving look, answered her, when the pirate, contrary to their expectation, came, and kneeling down before Urania, used these words. 'Let not, fairest princess, this accident trouble you, since your imprisonment shall be no other than the command of me and mine. Neither, most noble Sir, be you or these others offended, for sooner will I do violence on myself than any way wrong those that come with this lady. Be patient, and you shall soon see the cause of my taking this noble prey.'

This said, he rose and, placing them all on fine seats in the cabin, where lately the prince had sat free from both the bands of love and imprisonment, himself sitting before them began his discourse in this manner (while the ship under sail was guided the way which he directed the pilot). 'My name,' said he, 'is Sandringall, born and bred in the land of Rumania, being servant to the King thereof. This King lived long, as one may say, the favourite of fortune, being blessed in his government with peace and love of his people, but principally happy in two children, a son, and a daughter younger by some years than her brother, he being called Antissius and she Antissia—promising in their youths all comfort to succeed in their age. But destiny herein commanded, disposing quite other ways, and thus it was. The King, my master, having in his youth been a brave and valiant prince, giving himself unto the seeking and finishing adventures, a strict league of friendship grew between him and the King of Achaea, for whose sake he left his country with a great army, assisting him against his Macedonian enemy. After returning with honour and content, the Achaean King, grateful for such a courtesy, being grown in years, sent ambassadors to demand his daughter in marriage for his son, and withal to have the princess sent unto him to be brought up together to the end that conversation (a ready friend to love) might nurse their affections so well as she might as contentedly be his daughter, as it was affectionately desired of him

'His son, as towardly a prince as those parts had, called Leandrus, with whom few Christian princes will compare, except the two cousins Parselius and Amphilanthus. But to my discourse. My master soon consented to the Achaean King's demand, which although for the farness of the country he might have refused, yet the nearness of their loves was such as he could not deny him or his request, resolving instantly to send the one half of his happiness to his old friend, and for this end he sent for me. But herewithal begins my misery, caused by my treachery, which heartily I repent and am ashamed of.

'I being arrived at his court, out of an ancient confidence which he had of my loyalty to him, committed this charge unto me: to see his Antissia carefully conducted and delivered to the King of Achaea, giving me directions and council how to carry myself, besides sole authority and power in this ambassage. Thus we departed, my wife attending on her person. Accompanied we were with most of the nobility, their loves being such as they parted not till they saw the young princess shipped. Covetousness (a dangerous sin in this time) bred in my wife, seeing the infinite riches the father had sent with his child. Her persuasions besides (or rather, joined to the devilish sense of gain) made me consent to detestable wickedness. Led by this wicked subtlety, we resolved not to take our way to Achaea, but to put into some island, there to sell the jewels and leave the princess in a religious house, not to be known while her dear parents should esteem her lost, we using the gain to our own profits.

'More cunningly to carry this, we sent a servant of ours before into the ship with such provision as our plot required. Towards night, the sweet young lady embarked, with belief to go into Achaea, we purposing nothing less, for in the dead time of the night we set the ship on fire, having before, when most slept, conveyed the treasure into the longboat. Then, with as much amazement as any (nothing like the bellows of that fuel) I took the princess in mine arms, leaping into the boat, calling to my wife to follow me, withal cutting the cord lest others should leap in. She leaped, but short, her sin so heavy drowning her, and my trusty servant with all the knights, in number twenty, and the ladies sent to attend Antissia, were drowned or burned, or both.

'Then played I the waterman, making towards the next shore we could discover. Day breaking gave us sight of one, yet only for flattering hope to play withal, not to be enjoyed, for instantly were we set on by rovers, who kept about these coasts. The princess they took from me, and all the treasure, leaving me in the boat, and towing it by the ship in the midst of the sea, left me with bread and water for two days, but without oar, sail or hope. Yet such and so favourable was my destiny as within that time a pirate, scouring the seas, took me up, who not long after was set upon by another. But then did the first arm me to serve him, which in gratitude I did, and so well defended him as we had the victory by the death of the other, slain with my hand. For requital hereof, he bestowed the new-won bark upon me, and men to serve me. Glad was I of this, having means to search for the princess, which I vowed with true and humble repentance to perform, never giving over till I had found the lost Antissia, or ended my life in the service. And this is the reason I took you, for having landed here and by chance seen you, I straight remembered your face, wherefore I determined by some way or other to compass the means to get you before my parting hence, and had not this happy occasion befallen me, some other had not failed to achieve my purpose. Then tell me where have you been these ten years, for so long it is since you were lost, and withal, I beseech you, let my submission and repentance gain my pardon.'

'Truly,' said Urania, 'you have told so ill a tale as, if I were the lost princess, I should scarce forget so great an injury. But satisfy yourself with this, and the hope of finding her, while you have in your power one who, alas, is lost too.'

The pirate at this grew much troubled and perplexed for so unadvisedly having discovered his former ill. Thus they remained, the pirate vexed, Urania grieved, Parselius in soul tormented, the others moved as much as respect in them to the other two could move in noble minds, least, or not at all, thinking of themselves in comparison of them; all sitting with arms crossed and eyes cast down upon the earth except the pirate, whose mind was busied with higher thoughts, none knowing to what end they would have ascended had not a voice awaked them, which came from a sailor who bade them prepare.

This called not the rest from their sorrow, nor moved Urania so much as to hear it, who sat not tearless, though speechless, while her sighs accompanied the wind in loud blowing. Sandringall, looking forth, saw the cause of the cry proceeded from the sight of the great pirate of Syracusa, whose force was thereabouts too well known. Then did he take his arms, delivering Parselius his own into his hands, entreating his aid. Parselius lifted up his eyes, and as he raised them he placed them on Urania, as the sphere where they alone should move, using these words: 'Now have we some hope, since once more I possess my arms', those (in show) savage youths helping him.

By this time was the other ship come to them, when there began a cruel fight between them. Being grappled, Parselius encountered the chief pirate; Sandringall, a black knight, who was so strong and valiant as Sandringall gained much honour so long to hold out with him. Parselius killed his enemy when at that instant the black knight strake the head of Sandringall from his shoulders, which Parselius seeing, 'Farewell Sandringall,' said

he, 'now are Antissia and Leandrus well revenged for thy
treason.'

With that, the black knight commanded his part to be quiet,
himself throwing down his sword and pulling off his helmet, ran
and embraced Parselius, who knowing him to be Leandrus,
with as much affection held him in his arms. Thus was
the business ended, all growing friends by their example. Then
were all the prisoners brought forth of both the ships, amongst
whom he knew one to be the squire of his dear friend and cousin
Amphilanthus, and two gentlemen who had mortal hatred, as it
did appear, one unto the other, for no sooner came they together
but they would have buffeted each other, wanting weapons to do
more. The one of them Leandrus took into his custody, while the
other began his story thus.

'My lords,' said he, 'first let me beseech pardon for this
rudeness; next, claim justice on this villain, who hath not only
wronged me, but in his unmannerly discourse injured the bravest
Christian princes. And that you may know the truth, give me
liberty to speak this to you. My name is Allimarlus, born in
Rumania, and page I was unto the King thereof. But being come
to man's estate, and so much knowledge as to see and
commiserate my master's misery, which had the flood from two
springs.* The first was the loss of his daughter Antissia, being
sent under the conduct of his faithful (as he esteemed) servant
Sandringall, who so well he trusted as he would have ventured
his life in his hands—which appeared in putting the fair Antissia
in his power, who as himself he loved, to be delivered to the King
of Achaea, desiring a match between her and the King's son,
called the hopeful Leandrus, but in the way the ship was spoiled
by an unlucky fire, and she (as it was conjectured) lost, which
since proved otherwise, not being swallowed by the unmerciful
sea, but betrayed by her guardian and stolen again from him by
rovers, since which time little news hath been heard of her,
saving hope of her living. The other and greater affliction was,
and is, a wicked woman he hath made his wife, after the death of
his virtuous Queen, who died as soon as she had seen her
worthily beloved son Antissius blessed with a son, whom they
called after his own name, who having endured a long and
painful search for his sister, at his return took a sweet and

excellent lady called Lucenia to wife, who though she were not the fairest, yet truly was she beautiful, and as fair as any in goodness, which is the choicest beauty.

'But this second marriage made them first know misery, the King old and passionately doting on her; she young, politic and wicked, being the widow of a nobleman in the country whose beastliness and cruelty cost the prince his life and bred the ruin of the state, as I have, since my departure from thence, understood by a knight of that country. But to my discourse. The King one day, after he had banished his son Antissius the court, and by her damnable counsel put such jealousy into his head as he now feared and hated him that once was three parts of his joy—this, and the loss of his other comfort Antissia, did so perplex him as one day, being at dinner, he began with tears to speak of Antissius, blaming his unnaturalness to him in his age, who had so tenderly and lovingly cherished his youth. But little of that she would suffer him to discourse of, lest his deserved pity might have hindered her ends, and so her plots have failed or been discovered. Then spake he of his young friend and once hoped for son Leandrus, who in search of Antissia was said to be slain by reason that his squire returned to the court (after long seeking his lord, who by misadventure he had lost), bringing his armour shrewdly cut and battered, which he had found in a meadow, but no news of his master—only this probability of his loss a country fellow gave him, telling him that gallant men in gay armours had not far off performed a gallant fight, wherein some were killed, and one knight's body carried thence by a lady who followed the knight, having but one more with her. Whither they went or more of the matter he could not tell.

'With this and the armour, he returned to the old King, who, the kindest of fathers, did accordingly suffer for this too likely disaster. From that he fell to the last and first of his misfortune, speaking of Antissia and bewailing her loss, concluding "How miserable am I of all men, that do live to lament for these many afflictions. One child dead by his living undutifulness, the other lost by treachery in a man I most trusted, and to be besides the occasion to bereave my dearest friend of his only comfort, which as one of my equal sorrows I esteem."

'I, seeing his vexation, and just cause of mourning, offered my

best service in seeking the princess, who not being dead, I might
hope to find and bring some content unto his age. He, hearing
me say this, fell upon my neck, kissing my forehead, and yet
weeping so as they resembled the watery and parting kisses the
sweet rivers give the sweeter banks, when with ebbing they must
leave them. So did his tears, so did his kisses on my face, both
meet and part. At last, his joy-mixed sorrow let him speak these
words: "And wilt thou, O Allimarlus, do this for me? Shall I yet
find so true a friend?" "A servant, and a faithful one," said I,
"who will not live if not to serve you, and so my faith to live in
me."

'Then he took me up in his arms and, calling for a sword of
his, which he had worn in most of his adventures, gave that with
the honour of knighthood to me. Then, kissing his hands and the
Queen's, I took my leave. He, though glad to find my loyalty, and
hoping to hear some news of his daughter, yet was sorry to part
with me: so few were left that he could trust, his kind wife having
taken care that her minions and favourites should most attend his
person.

'Long time was I not landed in Greece, in that part called
Morea, before I met an old man who told me something of the
princess, but nothing of her certain abode. Yet I rejoiced to hear
of her, not doubting but to bring her to delight her grieved father,
who never indeed tasted of true happiness since her loss, that
being the thread to his succeeding miseries. That old man
likewise told me I was in my way of finding her if I held on to
Laconia. I earnestly desired his company, which he afforded me,
and so we went together, resolving still to enquire and to leave no
likely place unsought in all Greece till we had found her.

'A pretty space we thus continued, the old man passing away
the time with good discourse, which made the way seem shorter,
telling me many adventures which had befallen him in his youth,
having led the life that most brave spirits use. But one I best
remember, being his own story, the place wherein we then were
producing it, it was this—and in truth worthy of note. "Whatsoever
I now, fair knight," said he, "appear to be, know I am in birth
quite contrary. Poor and alone now; once a duke, and one of the
mightiest, richest, ancientest and sometimes happiest of these
parts, this country wherein you are being mine, only subject in

homage to the famous King of Morea. My education had been most in the court; my time, some spent there, some time abroad. But weary at last of either, as a hound will be who never so well loving hunting, will at last take rest, so did I lie down at mine own home, determining to end my days in quiet plenteousness, taking my own delight, to add unto which I brought with me a virtuous lady, and such a one as might for goodness equal any of her rank and truly not unbeautiful. Yet so much was I besotted on a young man, whom I had unfortunately chosen for my companion, as at last all delights and pastimes were to me tedious and loathsome if not liking or begun by him. Nay, my wife's company in respect of his was unpleasing to me.

'"Long time this continued, which continuance made me issueless, wherefore I made him my heir, giving him all the present honour I could in my own power, or by the favour of the King (who ever graced me much) procure him. But he, the son of wickedness, though adopted to me, esteeming possession far better than reversion, gave place so much to covetousness as murder crept into credit to attain the profit, wherefore he practised to make me away. My friends and kindred had before left me, expecting nothing but my ruin, seeing me so bewitched with my undoing. The plot was laid, and I thus betrayed where most I trusted.

'"The time being come for the execution, the hired man (being mine more for justness than his for rewards) came unto me, and upon promise of secrecy, discovered the truth unto me, making me besides promise to be persuaded by him, which was for some time to retire myself till a party were made in the country strong enough to pull down his pride, who had gained such power as he was grown more powerful than myself. Then might I be myself, and rule in safety.

'"I consented to the concealing, but never could be won to think of harming him whose ingratitude I believed sufficiently would one day burden him. But how often did I entreat and beseech him to perform his part, and satisfy his master in killing me, whose falseness and wickedness more grieved me than ten deaths (could I have suffered so many). Yet his honest care overruled me, and I submitted to his counsel.

'"Then took he my clothes, apparelling me fit for the change of my fortune. He, poor man, returning to my castle (for so till then it was), credibly reporting that I, going to swim—as often I did in this sweet river which runs along this valley—I was drowned, we being then in that place, and indeed the sweetest in the world. This in some kind was true," said he, "for drowned I was in sorrow and tears, which could they have made a stream for bigness answerable to their swift falling, had questionless made his framed report true.

' "This being told, the Duke, as then by my imagined death imaginarily he was, did make show of insupportable grief, being so possessed as he seemed disposed of senses, furiously and suddenly stabbing the good man who for my life lost his own. This was counted a passionate act, love transporting him so much beyond himself as he was not able to resist his own fury, while his devilish cunning did both set a gloss upon his brutishness and keep his treason unrevealed, the poor soul falling dead at his feet while he said, 'Take this for thy detested news-bringing.' Then did he make a solemn funeral for my dead mind, though living body. He apparelled himself and his court in mourning, which gave much content to the people who loved me, while indeed their black was but the true picture of his inward foulness.

' "My wife did presently retire to a house herself had built. But when he had (as he thought) sufficiently played with the people, he began to exercise his authority, beginning with my wife, picking a quarrel to bereave her of her estate, which he in short time did, turning her to seek her fortune. Patiently she took it. Having yet some jewels left her, she bought a little house in a thick and desert wood, where she was not long before I came unto her, discovering myself to both our equal passions of joy and sorrow. Privately we there continued many years, God in our poverty giving us an unexpected blessing, which was a daughter, who grew up and served us for a servant our means would not allow us, though our estates required it.

' "Seventeen years we thus concealed lived, but then, as joys so tortures will have end: the Duke in all pleasure and plenty, I in misery and poverty. One day the young prince accompanied with his most noble companion Amphilanthus (who for the honour of Greece was bred with him) and many other brave young nobles who attended them, went forth to see a flight at the brook, when after a flight or two the prince's hawk went out at a check, which made them all follow her and so long as, at the last (for rescue of my afflictions), they were brought to my poor abiding, which by reason of the farness from the court, and foulness of the weather (a sudden storm then falling) they accepted for their lodging, which although so mean as could be, yet they pleased to like it, rather looking into my heart for welcome (where they found it) than into the meanness of the place.

' "After they had refreshed themselves and discoursed freely with me, it pleased my prince to say that my estate and life agreed not with my conversation, wherefore he would not be denied, but needs must know the truth, which out of obedience more than desire, with heart-tearing grief I discoursed to him. He gave few words for answer, but commanded me the next day with my wife and daughter to attend him to the court, which fain I would have refused, foreseeing that which soon after followed: the destruction of my once most loved friend, who, though he had changed gratefulness to the contrary, and love to hate, yet my affection could not so much alter itself as to hate where once so earnestly I affected, or seek revenge on him whose good I ever wished.

' "But we obeyed. Then the sweet young prince presented me to his father, who instantly called me to mind, remembering many adventures which in our youths we had passed together; pitying my fortune as much as he had in younger days affected me. Yet glad in some kind to recompense my faithful service to him, instantly sent for the usurper, who by reason of a journey the King made to see his realm and show it to his son before his departure, who was to go thence with his excellent cousin in a search by them undertaken, was come near to the place of the tyrant's abode. He refused to come, but soon by force he was brought before the King, who with mild fashion and royal majesty examined the business—which he confessed, but rather with a proud scorn than repentant heart. Wherefore the King, with just judgement, degraded him, committing him to a strong tower whereinto he was walled up, meat given him in at the window and there to end his days, which were not long: pride swelling him so with scorn of his fall as he burst and died.

' "The dukedom after this sentence was restored to me; but

truly I was not able to recover my former loss, wherefore humbly
thanking the King and his son, besought them to give me leave to
bestow it on my daughter, which was granted me—my wife,
thinking she had seen enough when I was myself again, departing
this life with joy and content. Besides, I made one suit more,
which was that since the prince had with so much favour begun
to honour me, it would please him to proceed so far as to bestow
one of his young lords in marriage on my daughter. The King
and prince both took this motion most kindly, wherefore
choosing a hopeful young lord, and him the prince most loved,
gave him to her.

' "The marriage was with much honour celebrated in the
court, at which for their unspeakable honour Parselius (for so the
prince is called) and Amphilanthus, prince of Naples, were made
knights, and bravely for the beginning of their succeeding glory
began those sports of field, as since have made them famous over
the world. This ended, I went away, kissing the King's and
prince's hands, undertaking a pilgrimage, which performed, I
returned to this place where like a hermit still I live, and will
continue while life is in me. This valley, those steepy,* woody
hills and the cave I rest in shall be all the courts or palaces that
these old eyes shall ever now behold."

'As thus we travelled on, determining to conclude that day's
journey with the end of his story, and resting in his cell that night,
we were called from that resolution by a noise within the wood of
horse and clashing of armour, which drew me to see what the
matter was. Arriving at the place, we found two gentlemen
cruelly fighting and by them many more slain. But that which
most amazed us was that, hard by them on the ground, was one
of the mirrors for beauty to see herself lively in, so fair indeed is
she, and such a fairness hath she, as mine eyes never saw her
equal, if not that rare shepherdess by you or the incomparable
Lady Pamphilia, sister to the noble prince Parselius, who I need
but name, the world being sufficiently filled with his fame.

'This lady lay along, her head upon her hand; her tears ran in
as great abundance as if they meant to preserve themselves in
making some pretty brook of truest tears. Her breath she took
rather in sighs and sobs than quiet breathing, yet did not this
alter the colour or feature of her heavenly beauty, but resembling

the excellent workmanship of some delicately proportioned fountain which lets the drops fall without hurting itself, or like a shower in April while the sun yet continues clear and bright—and so did she seem to our eyes.

'As we were admiring her, there came a knight in black armour, his shield suitable to it without any device, who not seeing the lady, stepped to the two combatants, willing them to hold their hands till he did understand the cause of their enmity. They, refusing it, turned both on him, one striking him forcibly on the shoulder. He, seeing their rudeness, and feeling himself smart, forgot parting and made himself a party, sticking one of them such a blow as made him fall dead at his feet, whereupon the other yielded, delivering his sword and turning to the lady, who now the knight saw with admiration for her fairness and sorrow. Unbinding her and sitting down by her, finding I was likewise a stranger, called me and the good hermit to hear the discourse, which the vanquished man delivered in this manner.

' "Two of those which here you see lie slain were half brothers, sons to one mother, the one of them my master. Who, on a day after a long chase of a stag, happened into a merchant's house not far hence, where this lady did then remain. They were civilly and courteously entertained, for being gentlemen well born, and in their fashion pleasing, they were respected and beloved of most, never having attempted, or to man's knowledge embraced or let in a thought contrary to virtue, till their coming thither, where they resolved a course worse than man could of man imagine, if not proved by experience. For there they saw that lady, desired her, and plotted to obtain her, purposing with all ill means to enjoy her, nothing being able to give other end to their wicked minds but this, whereto their beastliness and true justice hath brought them, having made this place their bed of death as it was meant for their lascivious desires.

' "Great they did imagine her of birth, by the honour done unto her. This was another spur to their devilish longing. Yet to be certain, with a good fashion dissembling their inward intent (as well they could, for they were courtiers) entreated the merchant to tell who this lady was, that they might accordingly honour and respect her. He told them her name was Antissia, and that she was daughter to the great King of Rumania,

betrayed by her guardian, taken from him again by rovers and sold
by them on this coast, at the town called S. Anzolo, 'Where I, a
merchant,' said he, 'bought her, they not knowing who they sold
nor I what I had bought, till some days after she herself (entreating
me no more to suffer her to be made merchandise, but to carry
her to her father, who would reward me sufficiently for my pains)
told me the unexpected secret.' The brothers, hearing this,
inflamed more than before, beauty first enticing them, then
ambition wrought to compass a king's daughter to their pleasure,
much commending themselves for placing their loves so worthily,
yet still forgetting how unworthy and dishonourable their love
was. Desire makes them now politic, casting all ways how they
might betray her. Consulting together, they at last concluded to
get the princess into the garden walk, having before appointed
these slain men to attend at a door which opened into the field,
which they opening, persuaded her to go out a little into so sweet
an air.

'"She, fearing nothing, went with them, when no sooner she
was forth but she found she was betrayed. Crying for help would
not avail her, yet the pitifulness of it brought forth most of the
house, who perceiving what was intended and near acted, no fury
could be compared to theirs (and fury indeed it was) for they,
but five and unarmed, attempted to rescue her from us, being all
these, and two of them so amorous as they in that raging passion
(love being at the best a mild frenzy) would have been able—or
thought themselves so—to have withstood them and many more,
especially their mistress being in presence. This noise also
brought forth the good woman, wife to the honest merchant,
where began so pitiful a moanful complaining between her and
this princess as truly moved compassion in all my heart, I am
sure, weeping for them. Yet the mad lovers had sense of nothing
but their worst desires."

'With these words, the princess fell into a new sorrow, which
the knight perceiving (whose heart was never but pitiful to fair
ladies) persuaded the sad Antissia so well as he proceeded.
"Then being possessed of the lady, my master led the way,
bringing his brother and us to this banquet, this place being set
down for her dishonour, but destined for their graves.

'"Then grew a strife for the first enjoying of her; so far it proceeded as from words they fell to blows, and so in short time to this conclusion, for they fighting, we, following our masters' example, followed them in death likewise, all but myself, and I now at your mercy."

'He had but concluded his story when I, pulling off my helmet, kneeling down to the princess, told her who I was and likewise my search for her, which she (with as much joy as on a sudden could enter into so sad a mind) received with gracious thankfulness. Now had the black knight in like manner discovered his face, which so excellent in loveliness—I cannot say fairness—as the whitest beauty must yield to such a sweetness, and yet doth his mind as far excel his person as his person doth all others that I have seen, and so will I allow—for this was Amphilanthus, who with mild, yet a princely manner told the princess that she might leave her sorrow, being fallen into his hands, where she should have all honour and respect, and within short time by himself be delivered to her father. But first he was to perform his promise to his dearest friend and cousin Parselius in meeting him in Italy, the time prefixed being almost expired, and his search utterly fruitless.'

'But I pray sir,' said Parselius, 'how came that brave prince again into Morea?' 'By a violent storm,' said he, 'wherein he suffered shipwreck. This done, Amphilanthus, Antissia, the hermit and myself took our ways to the merchant's house, whom we found returned, but ready again to have left his house, filled with discontent and passion for the unhappy accident, his wife in that desperate grief as hardly could she have endured with life had not the blessed return of Antissia given comfort, like life unto her sorrows. The servant to the slain knight guided us within sight of the house, but then with pardon and liberty of going his own way, he departed.

'That night we rested there, the next morning parted our selves. Amphilanthus, Antissia, the merchant and his wife took their journey together towards the court, there to leave her till he had found Parselius, and so end his vow; the old hermit returned to his private devotions; myself took my way to the next port, to ship myself for Rumania. In the same ship was also this man who, hearing me discourse of my adventures with the master of the ship, gave ill language of Amphilanthus, then of Parselius, saying they were cozeners and not princes, but some odd fellows taking good names upon them, since it was very unlikely so great persons should be so long suffered abroad and travel in such sort alone and more like runaways than princes.

'These* much moved me, but to put me quite out of patience he went on, giving viler and more cursed speeches of my own lord. This made me strike him, and so we fell together so close as one or both had died for it had not the company parted us, and after we had again gone to it, but that this ship came and took us and so made us prisoners to save our lives. But now Sirs, if you do not justice you wrong yourselves in not revenging so great an injury done to the bravest princes.'

Parselius replied: 'We were not worthy to live if we did not right so worthy a gentleman as yourself, and revenge the wrong done to so great princes, whose greatness yet cannot keep ill tongues in awe sufficiently, but that in absence they are often wronged, and therefore friends must revenge that which they, ignorant of otherwise, may suffer. But herein we may be thought partial, for this knight you see is Leandrus, myself Parselius, one of the cozening princes (as it pleased his honesty to call me). I would advise, therefore, that this rare shepherdess should appoint him his punishment.'

The young knight kneeled down to have kissed the hands of the two princes. They, taking him up, gave him thanks for his discourse, commending him much for his loyalty and valour. Urania, who was as heartily angry as the knight, seeing her Parselius thus wronged, could find no less punishment for him than death. But then the prince did with sweet persuasions mitigate her fury, but brought it no lower than to public whipping, submission and recantation, lastly, humbly on his knees to ask pardon of the Rumanian knight.

All now satisfied but Urania (who could not easily forgive an injury done to her other self) sent him ashore to the next land they saw. Then did the knight again speak: 'My lord Parselius, with your leave, I beseech you permit me to take so much boldness as to beseech my lord Leandrus to do me so much honour as to tell me the adventure which caused the report and suspicion of his death.' They both agreeing, Leandrus thus began.

'After I had left you, most noble Parselius, I went to my own country to visit my father, where still I heard the noise of Antissia's loss, the likelihood of her beauty, the grief of parents and the wrong done to myself. These did not only invite but command me to be diligent in making all these pieces join again in the first body of content, which I persuaded myself able to do by seeking and finding of her. The one I resolved, the other I nothing doubted. Then, with my father's consent, I left Achaea, taking my way among the Greek islands, and passing the archipelago. I left no island that had a league of land unsought or unseen. Then shipped I myself and passed into your Morea.

'So, after I had seen all those places, I went again to sea, resolving afterwards to take towards Italy, whither for farness it might be the traitors had carried her, my companion then leaving me to go to his heart, which he had left in Sicilia. But being in the island of Cephalonia, there was a solemn and magnificent feast held, which was by reason of a marriage between the lord's daughter of that island and the lord of Zante's son, a fine and sprightful youth, jousts, tilts and all other such warlike exercises being proclaimed.

'Hearing this, I would needs show myself one as forward as any stranger to honour the feast. The first day (which was the wedding day) arms were laid aside, and only dancing and feasting exercised, after supper everyone preparing for the dancing again. With the sound of trumpets, there entered one in habit and fashion like a commander of horse, who delivered some few lines to the new-married pair, dedicated as to their honour and joy, which they received most thankfully, promising freedom and welcome to the whole company. Then entered in twenty gentlemen presenting soldiers, and so danced in their kind, making a brave and commendable demonstration of courtship in the bravest profession, honour abounding most where nobleness in valour and bounty in civility agree together. After, they went to a rich banquet. The brave masquers, discovering themselves, were found to be gentlemen of both islands, equally divided in number as their affections ought to be to either, and therefore had put themselves into the evenest and perfectest number of ten and ten.

'But to leave sport and come to earnest, the manner of that

place was that from the banquet the bride must be stolen away (to bed, the meaning is), but she took to the fields. Most did miss her, for there wanted no respective care of her, but all were satisfied with the fashion, correcting such as spake suspiciously, and expecting to be called to see her in bed, waited the calling. But the time being long, some hastier than the rest went to the chamber, where they found she had not been. This was instantly blown abroad. All betook themselves to arms who could bear any, the ladies to their tears, everyone amazed, and chiefly the bridegroom perplexed; the old fathers vexed; the mothers tore their grey locks. Such disorder in general as cannot be expressed but by the picture of the same accident. Some mistrusted the masquers, but soon they cleared themselves, putting on arms and being as earnest as any in the search.

'I, a stranger, and loving business, would needs have accompanied them, which the favour of a nobleman with whom I had got some little acquaintance did well aid me in, whose fortunes were in finding them more happy than any others, overtaking them when they thought themselves most secure, being together laid within a delicate vineyard, a place able to hide them and please them with as much content as Paris felt when he had deceived the Greek King of his beautiful Helen, laughing at the fine deceit and pitying in a scornful fashion those who with direct pain and meaning* followed them, commending their subtleties and fine craftiness in having so deceived them. Kissing and embracing, they joyfully remained in their stolen comforts till we rudely breaking in upon them made them as fearfully rush up as a tapist* buck will do when he finds his enemies so near. Yet did not our coming any whit amaze them, but that they were well able to make use of the best sense at that time required for their good, which was speech, uttering it in this manner.

' "My lords," said they, "if ever you have known love, that will (we hope) now withhold you from crossing lovers. We confess, to the law we are offenders, yet not to the law of love. Wherefore, as you have loved, or do, or may, pity us and be not the means that we too soon sacrifice our bloods on the cruel altar of revenge while we remain the faithful vassals of Venus. Let not your hands be soiled in the blood of lovers. What can wash away so foul a stain? You may bring us, it is true, unto our just deserved ends,

but then take heed of a repentant, gnawing spirit, which will
molest you when you shall be urged to remember that you caused
so much faithful and constant love to be offered to the triumph of
your conquest over a lover unarmed, wanting all means of
resistance but pure affections to defend himself withal, and a
woman only strong in truth of love."

'For my part, she won me; my companion was by him gained,
so as, promising assistance in place of arms, and help instead of
force, we sat down together, he beginning his discourse in this
manner.

' "To make long speeches, striving to be held an orator, or with
much delicacy to paint this story, the time affords not the one,
our truth and love requires not the other. Wherefore, as plainly
as truth itself demands, I will tell you the beginning, success and
continuance of our fortunate (though crossed) affections. I loved
this lady before she had seen this young lord. She likewise had
only seen my love, and only tied herself to that, before he saw
her. Love made me her slave, while she suffered as by the like
authority. I sued, she granted; I loved, she requited, happiness
above all blessings to be embraced. Our eyes kept just measure of
looks, being sometimes so enchained in delightful links of each
other's joy-tying chain (for so we made up the number of our
beholdings) as hard it was to be so unkindly found as to separate
so dear a pleasure.

' "Our hearts held even proportion with our thoughts and eyes,
which were created, nursed and guided by those, or rather one
heart's power. But parents having (were it not for Christianity I
should say) a cruel and tyrannical power over their children,
brought this, to us, disastrous fortune. For, discovering our loves,
set such spies over us (scorning that I, being the younger brother
to an Earl, should have such happiness as to enjoy my princess),
as we could never come to enjoy more than bare looks, which yet
spake our true meanings, as after it was discovered.

' "This course enraged us, vowing to have our desires upon
any terms whatsoever, always considered with true nobleness and
virtue. Thus resolved, we continued till her father, concluding
this match, shut her up in a tower wherein he then kept (in her)
his choicest treasure, till this day of her marriage, which
opportunity we took, purposing . . ."

'More he would have said, as it seemed, truly to manifest the virtuous determination they had in their accomplishment of their desires, when he was hindered by the rushing in of others with their horses. Rising, we discerned the deceived youth with some others in his company, fate, like his love, having guided him to that place. In charity we could not leave our first professed friends, nor could I part myself from such and so true love; wherefore, resolutely taking my companion's part, defended the lovers, pity then taking the place of justice in our swords. The husband being unfortunately slain by my companion, truly I was sorry for him, and glad it was not I had done it.

'But soon followed a greater and more lamentable misfortune. For one of the young lord's servants, seeing his master slain, pressed in, unregarded or doubted, upon the unarmed lover, who was this while comforting his mistress and, not expecting danger, was on the sudden thrust into the back as he was holding his only comfort in his arms. He soon (alas, and so forever) left his dear embracement, turning on him who hurt him, repaying the wrong with giving him his death, but then soon followed his own, the wound being mortal which he had received, yet not so suddenly but that he saw the destruction of his enemies. We being as fierce as rage and revenge could make us, then he remaining alone (besides myself) alive, and yet dying, giving me infinite thanks for my love and willing rescue lent him, with many doleful and (in affection) lamentable groans and complaints, he took his leave of his only and best beloved, then of me, to whom he committed the care of her and his body. Then, kissing her, departed.

'But what shall I say of her? Imagine, great prince and all this brave company, what she did. You will say: she wept, tore her hair, rent her clothes, cried, sobbed, groaned. No! She did not thus; she only embraced him, kissed him, and with as deadly a paleness as death could with most cunning counterfeit, and not execute, she entreated me to conduct her to the next religious house where she would remain till she might follow him. I admired her patience, but since more wondered at her worth. O women, how excellent are you when you take the right way! Else, I must confess, you are the children of men and, like them, fault-full.

'The body we took with the help of a litter which passed by,

having before conveyed a hurt knight to the same monastery next
to that place, and in that we conveyed it thither, where we buried
him and almost drowned him in our tears. Thinking then to have
removed, she fell ill; not sick in body but dead in heart, which
appeared, for within two days she died, leaving this world to meet
and once more joy in him, who more than a world, or ten
thousand worlds, she loved and still desired, which made her
choose death, being her then greater joy—burying them together
a little without the house, the order of that place not permitting
them to be laid within it.

'After this sad but honest performance of my word, I went on
in my journey, meeting within few days after a page belonging to
my dead friend, who with his master's armour followed him, love
and obedience bringing it into his mind. The armour was good,
being that which I now wear, my own hacked and cut in many
places. With much sorrow the youth received the woeful tidings
of his master. Then obtained I so much as to have those arms,
which with violent sorrow he consented to, helping me to arm
myself in them, though so as, had I been any but his dead lord's
friend, he sooner and more willingly would have wound into his
funeral shirt. He took my armour and laid it together under a tree
which grew in the midst of a fair and pleasant plain. Then,
although against my will, he kissed my hands and with as much
true-felt sorrow as could lodge in so young years, took his leave
of me, only beseeching me, when I remembered my unfortunate
friend, I would also with some pity think on his misery.

'This was my adventure. And then passed I by sea till on a rock
I suffered shipwreck, being taken up by this famous pirate whom
you so valiantly have slain, being I assure you none of your least
victories, he having had as much strength and skill as in any one
man need remain. But knowing me, and some power I have with
the King of Sicily, my dear and worthy friend Perissus his uncle,
whose excellent company I gained in Achaea, he then being
there, and with whom I travelled many months, almost years, till I
began this search, this man, on condition I would mediate for
him to the King or his nephew, let me go at liberty and armed in
his ship till such time as we fortuned to land—always concluded
that while I was with him I should defend him with my best
means. This made me resist you till heaven told me my error,

which I repent and heartily ask pardon for. And this sure was the reason that my page imagined my death, if he found (as by all likelihood he did) my arms.'

Then did Parselius again embrace Leandrus. Turning to the squire of Amphilanthus, he demanded what he knew of his master. 'Truly,' replied he, 'nothing but the joy I conceive to hear by this gentle knight that he is living. I parted from him in a great storm, having been in Germany, sent thither with an army from the Pope to assist the Emperor against the Duke of Saxony, who was slain by his hand, and for this act was by the Emperor and the other princes made King of the Romans, having protected the empire against such an enemy—since till now never having heard news of him. But he meant to seek still for you, and therefore left Germany and in the Mediterranean sea my self, ship and all my lord's treasure was taken by this pirate, whom your valour hath destroyed.'

Thus with prosperous wind and infinite joy for Amphilanthus his new title and honour, they sailed towards Italy, hoping to land not far from the town where the King of Naples at that time kept his court, which was at that great city. But being within the sight of the shore, because it then was evening they resolved not to land till the next morning and so take the day before them. This thought the best (like men's counsels) proved the worst; for in the night rose a terrible and fearful storm, being so violent as it took not away rest only, but knowledge from the pilot, being only able within some hours to assure them that they were far distant from Italy.

The tempest continued in as great (if no greater) fury, nor any more comfort had they save that now they enjoyed light and yet could that light scarce be counted day, being but as daybreak before the sun rising, so as it was but as to distinguish the time of day from night, or as if it were to hold a candle to them the more to see their danger, so thick, cloudy and uncomfortable as they could discern nothing but what was nearest them, which was peril.

Cunning now prevailed not, for the most skilful confessed that now he was artless, heavenly powers working above the knowledge of earthly creatures. Which way they were by force carried was utterly unknown to them. Sails, tackling were gone;

the mast, either by force or hope of safety cast overboard; thunder, lightning, wind, rain, they wanted not, none being able to express the desperateness of this storm but by saying it was the picture of the last day for violence, but like the world for strangeness and uncertainty.

Thus they continued in the day, having only the shadow of a day and in the night fearful flames, which yet they thanked, because by them they could discern themselves. When heaven did think this storm had lasted long enough cross to those, though crossed, yet still most loving lovers, it commanded the seas to be at quiet, which being performed, the pilot again began to use his skill, which first had means to let him know that so far they were from the place resolved on as, instead of the coast of Italy, they were within sight of the island of Cyprus.

This not only amazed them, but much troubled them, considering the barbarousness of the people who there inhabited, and their extremity such as, of necessity, they must land to replenish their wants, caused by the rigour of the tempest. Yet were they come to such a part of the country as there was no harbour or port to ride or land at, wherefore they were forced to coast the country, night again like an evil spirit possessing them, almost all tired and weary with the length and violence of the storm.

Some were laid down to see if rest would possess them; others fallen asleep; none enduring it like the excellent Urania, which brought comfort (though in sorrow) to the loving and noble Parselius, never showing fear or trouble, encouraging all. And yet she did fear, but seeing his, she dissembled hers, in care of not further harming him. She, I say, when all were gone to rest, stood as sentinel but by her own appointment, love commanding her soul to take no advantage of restful hours, which she obediently did, sleep never but by love's liberty possessing her eyes. Which freedom her passion had not yet allowed her, but molesting her patient sweetness, caused her to walk up and down in the amaze of her trouble.

The moon (though coldly) smiling on her and her love, she perceived a great fire, whereupon she called the company, demanding what their opinions were of it. They could not give her a direct answer till, being come somewhat nearer, they

perceived it was a ship was fallen afire in the midst of the sea, and
right against it a very good harbour. Pity and noble compassion
straight moved in them, so as they haled to the burning bark to
know if there were any by ill fortune in her and, if so, to succour
them. But hearing no answer, they concluded she was empty,
wherefore passing on they landed in the island. Which no sooner
was done but their former wonder was increased by the sudden
falling afire of their own ship, which had but delivered herself of
them, and then as a martyr suffered for the pain they had in her
endured.

But this past, admiration brought new sorrow to them,
considering they were in a strange country among barbarous
people, deprived of all hope to get thence any more, but there to
continue at the mercy of unchristened creatures. Parselius
wished, but still found himself further from succour of any but
his fruitless wishes, all his tormenting grief being for Urania.
Urania did as he did, justly requiting his pain, for all hers was for
him. All lamented and pitied Urania, and the dainty Selarina,
who mildly yet with a more womanlike manner suffered these
afflictions, loving and pitying Urania, being an obligation they
were all in their hearts, as they found, bound unto. Leandrus
sorrowed for her, and bewailed the two young princes, whose
father had lost his kingdom for his love to his father, which
stirred in him a commiserate passion.

Thus all for others grieved, pity extended so as all were careful
but of themselves most careless, yet their mutual care made them
all cared for. Parselius with a brave courage at last advised them
to go on, yet left it to their own minds, fearing to persuade lest
harm might after follow. Grieve, fear and persuade they did, and
all distractedly, so much they feared, and most was for Urania—
so much can worth, sweetness and beauty work in noble minds.
His advice was to go on, and this was allowed, for what could he
propound that Urania liked not of? And if she consented, what
spirit could deny? Thus on they went (but as in a labyrinth
without a thread) till they came within sight of a rare and
admirable palace.*

It was situated on a hill, but that hill formed, as if the world
would needs raise one place of purpose to build love's throne
upon, all the country besides humbly plain, to show the

subjection to that powerful dwelling. The hill whereon this palace stood was just as big as to hold the house, three sides of the hill made into delicate gardens and orchards; the further side was a fine and stately wood. This sumptuous house was square, set all upon pillars of black marble, the ground paved with the same, every one of those pillars presenting the lively image (as perfectly as carving could demonstrate) of brave and mighty men and sweet and delicate ladies, such as had been conquered by love's power—but placed there as still to maintain and uphold the honour and house of love.

Coming towards it, they imagined it some magical work, for so daintily it appeared in curiosity as it seemed as if it hung in the air, the trees, fountains and all sweet delicacies being discerned through it. The upper story had the gods most fairly and richly appearing in their thrones, their proportions such as their powers and qualities are described. As Mars in arms, weapons of war about him, trophies of his victories and many demonstrations of his war-like Godhead; Apollo with music; Mercury; Saturn and the rest in their kind.

At the foot of this hill ran a pleasant and sweetly passing river, over which was a bridge on which were three towers. Upon the first was the image of Cupid, curiously carved with his bow bent and quiver at his back, but with his right hand pointing to the next tower, on which was a statue of white marble representing Venus, but so richly adorned as it might, for rareness and exquisiteness, have been taken for the goddess herself and have caused as strange an affection as the image did to her maker when he fell in love with his own work. She was crowned with myrtle and pansies, in her left hand holding a flaming heart, her right directing to the third tower, before which, in all dainty riches and rich delicacy, was the figure of Constancy, holding in her hand the keys of the palace—which showed that place was not to be open to all, but to few possessed with that virtue.

They all beheld this place with great wonder, Parselius resolving it was some enchantment, wherefore was the nicer how they proceeded in the entering of it. While they were thus in question, there came an aged man with so good a countenance and grave aspect as it struck reverence into them, to be showed to him by them. He saluted them thus: 'Fair company, your beholding this place with so much curiosity, and besides your habits, makes me know you are strangers, therefore fit to let you understand the truth of this brave building, which is dedicated to love. Venus (whose priest I am), thinking herself in these latter times not so much, or much less honoured than in ages past, hath built this, calling it the Throne of Love. Here is she daily served by myself and others of my profession, and here is the trial of false or faithful lovers.

'Those that are false, may enter this tower, which is Cupid's tower, or the Tower of Desire. But therein once enclosed, they endure torments fit for such a fault. Into the second any lover may enter, which is the Tower of Love, but there they suffer unexpressible tortures in several kinds as their affections are most incident to, as jealousy, despair, fear, hope, longings and such like. The third, which is guarded by Constancy, can be entered by none till the valiantest knight with the loyalest lady come together and open that gate, when all these charms shall have conclusion. Till then, all that venture into these towers remain prisoners. This is the truth. Now, if your hearts will serve you, adventure it.'

They thanked the old man for his relation, but told him they had some vows to perform first, which ended, they would adventure for imprisonment in so rare a prison. The old priest left them and they, weary, laid them down near the Tower of Desire, refreshing themselves with some little meat which Urania's maid had in her scrip. But wanting drink, they all went to the river, whereof they had but drunk, when in them several passions did instantly abound.

Parselius forgot all but his promise to the dead King of Albania, for the settling his sons in that kingdom. Leandrus, afflicted with the loss of Antissia, must straight unto Morea to find her and take her from Amphilanthus. Steriamus and Selarinus would not be refused the honour of knighthood, Mars having so possessed them with his warlike disposition as worlds to their imaginations were too little to conquer, therefore Albania was already won. Urania, whose heart before was only fed by the sweet looks and pleasing conversation of Parselius, loves him now so much as she imagines she must try the adventure, to let him see her loyalty is such as for, his love and by it, she would end the enchantment. Selarina thought she saw within the gardens a young prince with a crown upon his head who beckoned to her, wherefore she would go at such a call. Urania's maid beheld, as she believed, Allimarlus in the second tower, kissing and embracing a blackamoor, which so far enraged her, being passionately in love with him, as she must go to revenge herself of that injury.

These distractions carried them all as their passions guided them. Parselius, having knighted the two princes, took their way to the next port, Urania now not seen or thought on, Leandrus, hasting another way to find means for his journey, Selarina to the tower, and knocked with that fervent desire to accomplish her end as the gate opened. All the three rushed in, striving who should be first. But Selarina was then soon made to know she should not contend with Urania, wherefore she was locked into the first tower, burning with desire to come to that sweet prince which still she sees before her; he calling, she with uncessant desire striving to go to him.

Urania went on when, entering the second tower, guarded by Venus, she was therein enclosed, whenas thus much sense came to her as to know she had left Parselius, which strake her into a mourning passion, confessing that an unpardonable fault, and what he in justice could not excuse. Then despair possessed her so as there she remained, loving in despair and, despairing, mourned. The shepherdess her servant, continuing her first passion, got into that tower too, where she still saw her affliction, striving with as much spiteful jealousy as that fury could vex her withal to come at the moor to pull her from her knight. Thus were the women for their punishment left prisoners in the throne of Love, which throne and punishments are daily built in all human hearts.

But how did the honest Allimarlus carry himself in all these changes? Alas, with much grief and sorrow for this misfortune, he, not having drank, being the only sensible man left; wherefore, fearing more the harm of Parselius and his companions than the ladies, who were without question safe, though far from being free, he followed them, lest harm might from those furious humours grow.

They made such haste as no rest could invite their stay till they were tired with their own minds' travail, and then, all three lying down in one another's arms, they yielded unto sleep. In which new torments vexed them, for then did they come a little to themselves (or a little more from themselves in another kind), and as men long held in a trance, awaked. Parselius, weeping for Urania's unkindness, who had (as he dreamed) forsaken him, and left him sleeping while she went with another. The two princes bewailing the death of their sister, who they imagined taken violently from them and sacrificed to Venus.

Thus they again fall into strange and new distractions, which grieved the young knight's very soul to see; but having no hope of seeing them restored while they continued in that island, soothing them up in their own opinions, knowing it dangerous and idle to cross madmen, with gentle persuasions gained Parselius to go with him, when he promised to bring him where Urania with her new friend did abide, and then he might recover her and kill his enemy. The others he likewise gained, promising they should have the means to kill their adversaries likewise.

Thus he got them thence, travelling in this sort until they came to the seaside, where they found a small bark, and in her two persons, an old man and a little boy, being fishers, and having taken some, had then newly put ashore to dress and so to satisfy their hungers with their game. The Rumanian knight saluted the old man, entreating that that company might go into his boat, and time it was to prevent the coming harm, for then were they ready to run into the sea. But by force they got them into the bark, where no sooner they were, having freed themselves from the land (which was the nature of those charms) but their good spirits again possessed them.

Then did Parselius bewail Urania, cry out of his miserable fortune in having lost her, beseech everyone to pity with him so great a mischief. The knight wept to see these changes, but then mildly told him all that had happened. Grieved Parselius did remain, but considering heavenly powers had caused this, he the more quietly endured it, yet not without a bleeding heart and often showering eyes. 'O Urania,' would he cry, 'how justly mayest thou hate me for leaving thee! Damned country, can it be that thou wert ordained for love to have a throne in and yet to be the hell of lovers?' Much more he cried and sorrowed out, while the old man had gained the knowledge of this adventure from Allimarlus, who was by him known, so as beseeching Parselius to lay by his mourning or at least to 'Give ear to this story,' said he, 'which will increase compassion and passion in you.' With that the grave old man began thus:

'Lamentation, brave princes, is that which I must treat of, but first I must tell you, as one of the parts of this story, I am called Selencius. Brother I am to the King of Rumania, lord to this young knight; and thus from me (the most unfortunate of princes) hear the woefullest and most disastrous history that ever princely ears gave attention to. I was brother and sometime heir to this unhappy King, being thought lost but after found in such an adventure of enchantment as this seems to be. Returned, married, and was blessed with two children, of whom I am sure this gentleman hath already discoursed unto you, wherefore that part I will leave, and come to the last.

'My nephew Antissius being come from the fruitless search of his sister Antissia, my brother would needs marry him to a lady in the country which he (although never having been in love) might have questioned. Yet he ever loved to obey his father, and so they were married. O Antissius, worthy Antissius!' With that, the tears ran down his long white beard, resembling drops in snow, stopping his breath that scarce the last word could be heard. In this time did all the princes join, concluding it with sobs and groans, everyone having equal feeling of sorrow, though for several things. At last he cried out these words:

'Pardon, great prince, this sad interruption in my story, which I am forced to do, heart-rending sorrow making me ever do so, when I think of (much more name) my dearest nephew and his unfortunate loss, being such a wound to that country as none can imagine but ourselves, who daily feel the misery. He, being married by his father's command, who longed to see some fruit from so worthy a stock, his obedience having mastered his affection, which rather was to follow arms than fall into the arms of love, he worthily loved his wife and lovingly lived with her, within that year being blessed with a son whom, after his father, they called Antissius.

'With this joyed-at birth began the ruin of all—yet not because of his birth, for in him we have yet our last hope, but by reason that the grandmother lived but to kiss her babe, after whose death the King again married; and her, whose wickedness I am sure hath come unto your ears. This malicious creature, after she had caused Antissius to be banished, and most honest men to lose their lives or places, she yet not satisfied with such sins as never the earth suffered in one body the weight of more—treason, adultery, witchcraft and murder were plentifully in her—yet while he lived she was not contented, wherefore to bring this to pass was now her only study.

'In this time some one or two honest hearts were left, who gave the King warning of her, venturing their heads to save his body from harm, her immoderate desires so much known as they cried out against her. She, being a Queen, salved not nor covered her sin, which in her greatness appeared the greater fault, a spot being more marked in a diamond than in an ordinary piece of glass. Long time it was ere his honest and unspotted love would believe it or hearken to it, while she delighted herself in her own shame and his dishonour

'At last, though extreme loath, he seemed to see it; slaking his violent love to her and oft refraining her bed made her discern it, though delighting herself so much with others had somewhat blinded her from seeing what, but for policy, she cared little for. But then did she never leave the poor man, with her flatterings and dissembling falsehoods, till she had gained the cause and ground of his most just offence and deserved mistrust and unusual strangeness, which at last (undone by her bewitching fawnings) she gained.

'Then had she enough, vowing to be revenged on all, and under this colour to execute her malice and purge her spleen upon the famous prince his son, which by her cruel practices she at last unfortunately brought to pass. For first, by means as she pretended that she was slandered, she got her good, honest husband to banish any who had in the least spoken of her lightness, putting into that number those whom she hated, having suffered (as she alleged) as much by their slanderous reports as almost, if it had been a truth, she had merited, wishing she had still continued widow rather than to come to this height of honour, and having it to fall so low as into the shame of dishonour; beseeching him thoroughly to revenge her, or to permit her to retire to the most lonely and private life, rather than there openly to sink under shame and infamy; or if she could be found faulty, then to cut off her head, far unfit to live wife to so virtuous and good a King.

'To satisfy her, whose dissemblings were of force to bring new heat into his aged heart which, like old wood, will presently kindle, he struck off the heads of those loyal servants who had honestly (though undiscreetly) told him of her sin, men not loving that discourse of any. This done, he came to receive thanks. But she telling him this was nothing, and unless he would do more to right her, so shamefully wronged, she would go away and execute some mischief on herself, her spirit and conscience not being able to sustain themselves enduring such abuse, and then (if ever he loved her) he would be sorry he had wronged so true and faithfully loving a wife, while he did credit pickthanking counsellors.

'He, seeing this passion in his dear wife, vowed revengeful justice on all she could accuse. Upon this vow, and some other assurance which was given by execution, her holy majesty seemed somewhat satisfied, and then contented (as it were) to live, having new life given in her justice and faith-trying honour. She came abroad, but oft-times blushing. Modesty was the colour put upon it, when indeed it was affection to a young lord in the court, who after she found she could not win with all enticements and love-shows, she accused him for seeking her, and so with many more lost his head.

'Now was Antissius and his virtuous wife confined to a castle some twenty miles from the court, he being accused of popularity and aspiring to the crown. This was the power of that insatiable monster, as she could and would banish from him his best and only true comforts. My nephew's misfortune increasing, and his hate to live growing every day stronger in him, he gained for all this the Queen's leave to go and live with me—she willing to it, hoping his former ill usage would provoke him to that he might die for, else she would find a means to compass it.

'But few plots needed, this being the beginning, and his soon following overthrow; for the people finding her government absolute, and that being bent to the ruin of the land, followed the virtuous prince in great numbers and at all times, which he, as much as in him lay, did put off and avoid, yet not so but that the Queen wrought cunningly enough upon it to mix jealousy with the father's love to his son, she never ceasing to wish the subjects' love as great and firm to his Majesty as she and all others saw their hearts were placed upon his worthy son—which though he for his affection to him did not yet make use of, "Yet it is a fine thing," said she, "to be a King, and a terrible matter to be tempted, were you not safely blessed with so honest a son. And therefore you must trust more to the loyalty of Antissius . . . " than the faith of his people who, he might perceive, regarded nothing less than their due respect to him.

'Sparingly she spake well of him, but freely to make suspicion. Thus now was he fallen into the path which led to the court of her malice. For, buzzing these things in his old and fearful ears, she at last brought to this fullness of ill. One day, as she had appointed (being privately with the King in a gallery), two of the council came in, in haste yet a dissembling fear in their faces, counterfeiting need, but doubt and unwillingness to discover what moved in them this sudden approach. The King urged them, when with tears they told him that they had gained knowledge of a dangerous conspiracy which was plotted and to be instantly executed upon the persons of his Majesty and his most royal Queen by Antissius and myself, the treason being this: to depose him, kill the Queen, banish the council, make himself monarch of Rumania, dispose the offices already disposed of among his favourites, and the whole realm as he best liked to his followers and associates, and in this kind make a conquest of it.

' "Then alas sir," said they, "what will become of poor Rumania when your virtue and wisdom shall be put by? Their government and his green capacity and those wild-headed counsellors shall rule over us, who were fitter at school to learn obedience and loyalty than to sway a sceptre—besides the wrong and sin taking the lawful prince from among his people."

'This related and seconded by the Queen, who still in a double manner cleared and condemned poor Antissius, whose just and virtuous heart never thought of such a treason, nor of her (if not with sorrow for her wickedness). It wrought so far in the jealous breast of the old man, as he manifested his crediting it and with all the fear he conceived of it, expressing as much hate to his son as such a wicked practice might justly challenge. Then hastily (as fear is always sudden), he demanded advice with the best and readiest way to avoid the danger.

'They yet having gone but half way of their devilish progress replied that, since it pleased him to have such confidence in them as to ask their advice in so great a business, they would as honestly discharge themselves, and this they held the safest and the best course, which was that the prince (who they must still love and reverence, and whose fault cut their hearts to think of) should be sent for, but in such manner as he should have no cause to distrust, lest then he went about to gain by force what they before had been informed he hoped to compass by a private conspiracy. This advice, and the plot itself, he imparted to some more of the council, who already were sufficiently instructed in their parts, and so accordingly agreed, consenting, nay commending the grave, careful and honest advice of the other two.

'Then was a messenger straight dispatched to the prince (who like a brave but innocent hart came into the toil),* with orders to come himself, his wife and son unto the King, whose age and weakness being great, and his affection only left strong in him towards him and his, would have them nearer to him, and for that he would recompense him for the injuries in former times done to him.

'I was not at home, for had I been, the journey surely had been hindered; while Antissius, doubting no treason, his noble heart being free from thinking any, in haste (hoping that way to express the joy he felt by these unexpected glad tidings) posted to the court, leaving word that I (who was to return in a very short time after) should with all convenient speed accompany his wife and son to the King.

'Few days he had rid before he was encountered with a troop of horse under the command of an ancient friend of his, and a friend indeed he was in this action, being betrayed as well as he, sent under colour of love to the prince, who since he had (or at least it being thought he had) so much disliked his father as he had forbid him his once-held dearest sight, and that the people had taken notice of it in a dangerous kind, to prevent any bold or hazardous attempt might happen by a rude multitude, the Queen had sent this troop to guard him, and that she, knowing love this gentleman bare Antissius, had made choice of him to conduct his person thither.

'Antissius was somewhat troubled with this accident, wondering why she should be on the sudden so kind, knowing that there was none whose ruin she and her godly crew more shot at. Yet could not he (who saw only with the eyes of virtue) pierce into this plot. Mildly and graciously he saluted the captain and his men, yet telling them his innocency had been guard enough for his person.

'They went on, but when they were within sight of the great city of Constantinople, the court then being there, they perceived a far greater number of soldiers, with which sight he saw his end, and soon heard the sentence of his death. For then did they set upon him, crying "Down with that traitor, that disobedient child; the incurable grief of his loving father, the dishonour of our country and the canker of the state's quiet!" With these cries they rushed violently upon the prince.

'The first troop, seeing this treason, did their best to defend Antissius, but their lives could not buy his safety, in vain striving to alter destiny, the period of his days being come with a blow given him by a traitorous villain which strake his head in two. Grief of this accident turned to fury, his party fighting as if Antissius had been in everyone, and so to be defended. But that was past, their loves only living to him. Yet died it too, for none were left of the whole troop but the captain and some ten more. The Queen's men having gained almost what they sought, fully to give her satisfaction in his death, yet wanted part, since they could not get his body be made a present to her cruelty. For the captain, perceiving their drift, hindered them of it, taking him up when he saw the unlucky blow given, and in the heat of the fight fled away with it, knowing this a better piece of service than to have lost his life in revenge at that time, since to better purpose he might save it in serving his son to have a just and fit requital for such a wickedness, on those shameful murderers.

'They came with this body of the most beloved prince, while he lived, and the most pitied and honoured after death, to my house. Just as I returned did I encounter this sad and disastrous adventure. Instead of a brave, courageous and (with it) pleasing presence, I met his bloodless, pale and martyred body. There I saw the hope of our country and comfort of mine age changed again into our first being. So much it afflicted me as I stood amazed with grief, speechless and senseless of sense, but sorrow; till, sorrow being pleased to make me have more feeling of her power, gave me leave to let these words come from me.

'"O Antissius, hath life been lent me to see this day! Miserable man, miserable country, wretched age, wherein such cruelty doth reign. O Antissius!" But then, by their honest, good persuasions telling me the necessity and ensuing dangers, if not prevented, that the rest living might fall into, I strove to endure this calamity with as much patience as so miserable a man could let sink into him, and indeed for this young youth's sake, who is the young Antissius, heir to these miseries and the overthrown estate of Rumania.

'But then followed a second cause of grief. For his virtuous wife came to us who, hearing such loud cries and distracted noises, left her chamber, following the cries till they brought her to that most lamentable spectacle. When she saw the cause of their wailing, she put them aside, going to the body and kneeling down by it, used these words: "My dear, was it for this that unnatural father and monster of women sent for thee? That no sooner thou shouldst see thy father's house but with it thou must see thy house of death? Alas, wert thou too good, too hopeful, too full of all virtues to live among us, who can now but assist thee with our tears. But long shall not this worldly sorrow triumph over me in thy loss, for I must and will be with thee." With that, kissing the pale lips of her dearest love, and as it were breathing her (though not last, but foretelling) last breath into him, she rose and, rising, a little seemed to smile joy within her (for assured going to him) having caused that countenance, which by some was disliked, not being, to their weak apprehensions, sad enough for such a cause of woe.

'As soon as she had left the body, she came to me, earnestly entreating me that I would suffer none to trouble her, she having some private devotions to perform, which being ended, I should be welcome to her. For my part, I so little mistrusted her intent, or imagined a woman had so strong a spirit as to die when she would, granted what she asked, being confident her goodness would keep her from doing any violence on herself. Having left

me, she went to the room where her young son lay, and then fast
sleeping, whenas weeping over him (as the maids since told me)
"Well mayest thou sleep, dear heart," said she, "for long, I fear,
thy quiet will not last, thy being son to so worthy a father and
unfortunate a mother must cast some storms on thee, it being
fault enough in thee to have such parents. At least thy wicked
grandmother will think so who, hating truth, will make thee
suffer for thy father's sake. Sleep then quietly, my sweet and lost
Antissius, nor now look up to see thy woeful mother, or to take
her last farewell, but thus receive her blessing which, as the
blessing of her own soul, she wishes may come and stay upon
thee, God sending thee a more happy life than thy valiant father
had. Let his gifts of virtue, courage and magnanimity live in thee,
and his misfortunes take their grave in me. Alas Antissius, my
only sweet babe, I must leave thee."

'Then again kissing him, she said "This is the difference in
affection twixt a husband and a child, otherwise no fear of
misfortune should carry me from thee, but, my sweetest, I must
go, leaving Antissius, to fly to Antissius. And good maids," said
she, "have a kind and just care of this young prince, he may live
to requite your pains and revenge the wrongs done to his
distressed parents." They vowed all faith and dutiful service to
him. Then again, as loath it must be the last, she kissed him and
so went to her chamber; yet at the door turning back
affectionately and with watery eyes cast her last and kindest
farewell look on him.

'When she came into her chamber, she locked the door, not
suffering any to stay or come to her, where she continued till (I
thinking her stay long, besides having business with her
concerning the dead prince) I went to her lodgings, where long I
knocked, and indeed so long as it vexed me. But after, fear
possessed me, when I considered what the danger might be, and
her freedom and liberty such as none had ever received that
dishonour of being barred her presence.

'Wherefore I sent for some of my servants, who by my
command broke open the door. Entering the room, we found her
laid upon her bed newly dead, yet her own accustomed
sweetness in her, lying as straight and unmoved as if death had
only then shown he could in pangs be mild, yet receive his gain,

so as well it may be said he deprived her of her life yet left her own beauty and grace to triumph over his fury. By the bedside stood a table covered with a carpet of crimson velvet, and on the board a letter, which I took up and, seeing it directed to me, I read it, and here (brave princes) you may see the very same my dearest niece left to me, which never will I part with till time give end unto my days, or life to accomplish her desires.'

The letter was this:

'Since it hath pleased God for the overthrow of this land, and grief of all good hearts (among which you and I hold the nearest places in sorrow) to cut this thread of admiration in sunder and leave the heavy burden of lamentation upon us, taking away our joy, our comfort, our only hope, Antissius, I feel myself altogether unable to sustain so great and killing a loss. Then let me crave this of you (which the assurance of your love to your dead nephew and dying niece emboldeneth me to ask): that you will grant these three things, and see them accomplished. Let the love you bare to your dead nephew continue and live in the same strength to your living nephew. Let nothing hinder you from seeking a deadly revenge on his murderers. Lastly, let me be here privately buried with him. Let these requests be welcome to you, my dearest uncle, and not deny the dying Lucenia.'

'No stranger, I think, would have denied so just requests proceeding from a lady of her worth, and being dying, what then wrought in me, who wanted not love or resolution of revenge? One of her desires I instantly performed, for I buried her with her husband, and then upon the tomb myself, the captain and the servants to the lost Antissius took a solemn oath to have revenge—but by the bravest princes, whose worths must needs abhor so detestable practices; other means, though they deserved the worst and basest, honest and noble hearts did detest them.

'This done, we parted every one a several way and to a several King, to make our misery more manifest, out of justice demanding their aid to pull down wickedness and again settle worth in Rumania; myself remaining one whole year after near the Hellespont, disguised and almost begging my living, with this my last hope. Still they sought us while we were among them, but then perceiving the continual hazard, and ableness in this latter Antissius to travel, we left Greece, myself alone going with him.

But how this was discovered, or that this young man must inherit his father's misfortunes, we hardly did escape taking. Upon the missing of us, ambassadors were sent in all haste to all the near princes, to whom with much falsehood their false fault was covered with as foul a veil, working so far as belief, or fear of war, made show of, so much as prevented the succour we had hoped for.

'Finding this, we took this boat, coasting (not daring to stay anywhere) till we could be secure. Many places we have seen, but found none to rescue misfortune, not caring whither we went so we were freed from her malicious power. Hither fate hath brought us, and here we have found and served some noblemen and good princes, who have promised their help. So as if you, brave prince Parselius, and these with you will likewise assist us, I fear not, but assure myself of our hoped for comfort. Thus, if pity dwell in you, you will pity us, and this, Allimarlus, is your lord and prince.'

Parselius then embraced him, so did Steriamus and Selarinus; all promising (their former vows and business ended) they would attend and rescue them. In the meantime, they would advise them to leave that shore for fear of danger, considering the charms which yet to any but such as adventured the towers or unfortunately drank of the river were nothing, yet that, scarce known, made cause of doubt.

So they resolved, and betook themselves to the sea, when they saw floating upon the water a man past sense or power to help himself, being now subject to the sea and the disposition she might be in to destroy him or succour him. Parselius in charity willed them to go towards him, the tide bringing him apace (as in love of him) that way. Being near, he perceived the man to be his dear friend Leandrus, who (in the same fury they had before fallen into, but wanting such helps as they had) ran into the sea, missing a boat to convey him but not fury to cast away himself, crying out he would have Antissia in spite of the valiantest black knight. But quickly was he cooled with loss of strength to save himself from loss; senses were come to him, but alas too soon to lose them again, and life with them, if this happy adventure had not come unto him. For then cried out Parselius, 'O take up that worthy body; save that noble person from such loss.'

With this, they made to him, taking him up and, after much

care, getting life again to put itself into the cage of the body. When, knowing his friends, but forgetting all things else, they embraced as souls would (if not by a greater joy hindered) rejoice in the other world for encountering their best friends. On they rowed, sometimes Parselius and the other princes aiding the old man, taking their turns till they discovered a Morean ship, to which they haled. She coming, and her rulers knowing their prince, with all joy and duty received him and his company into her.

Then securely they sailed towards Greece, where being landed in Morea, they determined that since instant aid could not be given them, they should there in a strong castle remain, not prisoners but commanders of that place, being an impregnable fort, and in such a place as none could land without their favour. So might they use the opportunity of place and time.

The Rumanian knight, after this place was by the prince delivered to Seleucius and his nephew Antissius, in the same ship had thither brought them, took again to the sea, intending to go into Rumania, and so hired them for Constantinople. But soon were they altered, for meeting another ship which desired to know something (the cause of that ship's journey being for discovery) he found in her the ancient servant and the same faithful captain who had so loyally served the first Antissius. Finding him (and by him, that the prince was to be found), he with him returned to the castle, where being received, and ready to make his discourse, I will leave him and go again to Parselius, who took the directest way to the court, which was then kept in Arcadia, being a time the King had in pleasure made a journey that way to delight himself in that most delightful country.

Being there arrived, no joy could be compared to the King's and Queen's, seeing their dearest son returned. But little joy felt he, Urania being lost, which only to Pamphilia he discovered, who out of a dear and sisterly affection the like bewailed absence.* Sports and pleasures were every day offered, while he still knew of none, being in them as in another world—only wherein his own person was required, there his valour failed not, though his soul which governed that was otherwhere.

Some days this lasted, but Parselius, whose love still urged him, could have no rest, colouring his pain with the loss of his friend and cousin, which indeed was the cause, but in the feminine gender. The King was the less displeased because it was on so worthy a subject, yet he was sorry, being the lovingest of fathers, that his dearest son should be displeased, and most troubled when he saw he would not stay, but again go seek his friend. Yet before his depart, he gained the promise of his father to raise men to assist Steriamus in his journey to conquer his right, which was granted both for that just cause and likewise because the fair young princess Meriana, Queen of Macedon, by right should be unto her right restored.

Thus departed Parselius, leaving Steriamus and his brother to attend their business and see the men raised, himself promising, within fit time to take their journey, to return. Leandrus, likewise accompanying Parselius to the court, gave his word to use his best power in gaining forces from his father to assist in this deserved occasion, they having suffered for their parents' loves. To which end he went into Achaea, giving his hand to Parselius to be with him in Morea within six months, which was the time appointed for their marching forwards towards Macedon or Albania as at their next meeting they would agree on.

Thus they parted: Parselius as his destiny would guide him, Leandrus to Achaea, and the other princes remaining in Arcadia with the King, very much esteemed of. But soon after the court removed nearer to the sea, while Amphilanthus, who hath been too long forgot, not being time enough remembered, being the most matchless prince, with the fair Antissia, being in the merchant's house, as the Rumanian knight told Parselius, finding fit time and longing to meet his friend, with the princess and the honest pair took their way towards the court where the King lived.

By the way, it was Antissia's fortune to mark (with so yielding a heart) the loveliness, sweetness, bravery and strength of the famous Amphilanthus, which in many adventures he made testimony of in her sight, before their gaining the court, as this (alas) made her acknowledge she had seen but him who might be thought a prince, she had heard of none but him, all others' virtues being single in them, but knit in one in him. This made her like, that made her love, and so she did (poor lady) to her lost liberty. He, the more he saw her respect to him, answered it with his to her. Kindness then betrayed them, she showing it, he (as a kind hearted prince to ladies) receiving it.

By this time they were content to think they loved, and so to know those pains. He was not unexperienced, therefore soon saw remedy must be given, and cruelty he imagined it would be in him, who discerned he might by his art help her, if he refused that good to one so fair and so kindly loving. This made him in charity watch his opportunity, or at least not to lose any, being most with her, and contentedly, because lovingly passing the time, entertaining themselves with fine discourse many hours together. The good people, weary with travelling or seeking other necessaries for them, necessarily leaving them then, not without much complaining of their absence.

At last they came unto the court, being two months after the departure of Parselius, and the next week after the secret departure of Steriamus, which was such as hereafter you shall hear. His arrival was as pleasing to the people and prince as fair weather is after a storm, or plenty following a great dearth, so generally and particularly was he beloved; his enemies (for no great man, nor good man lives without) being forced in truth to confess he deserved much admiration. He came pleasantly thither and for some days continued so. But after, whether miss of his friend Parselius, or some other private cause to himself moved him, is not known, but sad he grew and, shunning all other company, would retire himself with Antissia into Pamphilia's chamber, where he would, when he spoke, direct his speech to her, still blaming her brothers for so strangely leaving their country. He could not offer speech to her which she received not with much respect, yet was she generally the most silent and discreetly retired of any princess.

But one day, as they were alone together, some discourse falling out of the beauty of ladies, Amphilanthus gave so much commendations of Antissia as she, between dislike and a modest affection, answered he had spoke sufficiently in her praise. 'For truly my lord,' said she, 'methinks there is not that beauty in her as you speak of, but that I have seen as fair and delicate as she. Yet in truth she's very white; but that extreme whiteness I like not so well as where that (though not in that fullness) is mixed with sweet loveliness. Yet I cannot blame you to think her peerless, who views her but with the eyes of affection.'

Amphilanthus gave this reply: that he till then had never seen so much womanish disposition in her as to have so much pretty envy in her, yet in his opinion (except herself) he had not seen any fairer. Antissia with that came to them, which brought them into other discourses, till they were forced to part. They gone, Pamphilia alone began to breathe out her passions, which to none she would discover, resolving rather so to perish than that any third should know she could be subject to affection.

'Alas,' would she say, weeping, to herself, 'what have I deserved to be thus tyrannically tortured by love, and in his most violent course, to whom I have ever been a most true servant? Had I wronged his name, scorned his power or his might, then I had been justly censured to punishment; but ill kings, the more they see obedience, tread the more upon their subjects—so doth this all-conquering king. O love, look but on me, my heart is thy prey, my self thy slave. Then take some pity on me.'

Being heavy, she went into her bed, but not with hope of rest, but to get more liberty to express her woe. At last, her servants gone, and all things quiet but her ceaseless mourning soul, she softly rose out of her bed, going to her window and, looking out, beheld the moon who was then fair and bright in herself, being almost at the full, but rounded about with black and broken clouds. 'Ah Diana,' said she, 'how do my fortunes resemble thee! My love and heart as clear and bright in faith as thou art in thy face, and the fullness of my sorrows in the same substance. And as thy wane must be, so is my wane of hopes in my love, affections in him being as cold to me as thou art in comparison of the sun's heat; broken joys, black despairs, encircling me as those dissevered clouds do strive to shadow by strait compassing thy best light.'

When she had (as long as her impatient desires would permit her) beheld the chaste goddess, she went to her bed again, taking a little cabinet with her wherein she had many papers and, setting a light by her, began to read them. But few of them pleasing her, she took pen and paper and, being excellent in writing, writ these verses following.

> Heart drops distilling like a new cut vine
> Weep for the pains that do my soul oppress,
>   Eyes do no less
> For if you weep not, be not mine,

Silly woes that cannot twine
    An equal grief in such excess.

You first in sorrow did begin the act,
You saw and were the instruments of woe.
    To let me know
That parting would procure the fact
Wherewith young hopes in bud are wracked
    Yet dearer eyes the rock must show.

Which never weep, but killingly disclose
Plagues, famine, murder in the fullest store,
    But threaten more.
This knowledge cloys my breast with woes
T'avoid offence my heart still chose
    Yet failed, and pity doth implore.

When reading them over again, 'Fie passion,' said she, 'how foolish canst thou make us! And when with much pain and business thou hast gained us, how dost thou then dispose us unto folly, making our choicest wits testimonies to our faces of our weaknesses and, as at this time dost, bring my own hands to witness against me, unblushingly showing my idleness to me.'

Then took she the new-writ lines and as soon almost as she had given them life, she likewise gave them burial. 'And yet,' said she, 'love must do thus, and sure we love his force the better for these fancies.' Then, putting out the light, lest that should; too soon waste, beholding her passions, which in hotter flames continued (then the united one of the candle could aspire to comparison with the smallest of millions of them) turning her in her bed with a deep love-sigh, she cried 'O love, thou dost master me!'

Thus did the love-wounded princess pass that night, or the greater part of it. Convenient time for sports in the morning being come, the King sent for her to attend him and the Queen, to see a match which was made at the jousts, only partly to please the King, but mostly to welcome Amphilanthus. Pamphilia and Antissia were placed together, Antissia dearly loving her for her cousin's sake, whom so well she loved as she gloried to have all ears and eyes partake the knowledge of it. Pamphilia did embrace her company, being excelling* in sweet conversation, as far as pleasant and harmless mirth could extend, and fit was such a companion for the melancholy which abounded in the princess.

Being at the window, and all having once run over, Amphilanthus gained the first honour, whereat Antissia, being joyful, 'Well may it be bestowed on him,' said she, 'for sure none can in all brave exercises come near your matchless cousin for delicate fineness and peerless power.' ''Tis true,' said Pamphilia, 'yet if you saw my brother Parselius you would (and indeed must) confess he comes the nearest to him and nearly matches him.' 'I know not him,' said Antissia, 'but if he do but second this, you may boldly say no princess living can compare with you for a cousin and a brother.'

By this the match was ended, and the knights coming to the King, he gave them thanks, embracing his best-beloved nephew. Then went each one to his mistress to receive their opinions in the defence of their favours, Antissia telling Amphilanthus that in her mind he alone deserved the honour of that day. He replied, her wishes and favour did purchase him that honour, more power living in them than in his arm or skill. Then did all return, the knights conducting every one his lady. Pamphilia went alone, for she, not enjoying her love, loved to be alone, as she was alone in perfect and unfortunate loving, thinking so slight a thing as a knight's leading her might be a touch in her thoughts to her spotless affection. Nor would she ever honour anyone with wearing a favour in those sports, having vowed that only one should enjoy all love and faith from her, and in her constancy (this not being known, her passions so wisely governed as she was not mistrusted to love so violently) made her of many to be esteemed proud, while it was that flame which made her burn in the humblest subjection of love's meanest subjects—yet was her choice, like her self, the best. No day passed without some exercises on horseback, wherein Amphilanthus did still add fame unto himself, by that to make Antissia the more his prisoner. But now is the time for his depart in the search of his friend arrived. If it grieved the court to part with him, it surely heartily perplexed her whose life depended on his sight; so it tormented her, as with the flowing of tears her face was martyred so much, as she was not fit to come in company, having turned her delightfulness to sorrows, feigning herself ill and so keeping her chamber, being seen of none but of Pamphilia, to whom she had freely discoursed both her affection and success in her love, who like a worthy friend accompanied her in this sorrow.

The night before he was to go, he came into her chamber to bid her farewell, and to entreat her to remain there till his return, the King having given him his promise that all honour and respect should be used to her. The princess Pamphilia, he durst say, would do the like, and for his own part, care and diligence should not want in him to make his speedy return. The poor lady could but with a speechless mourning behold him, holding his hand fast in hers. At last sorrow brought forth these words for her: 'My lord, God knows how I lament for your going; how much more must your absence afflict me? As you see the one, and may judge of the other, have pity in hastening hither to her who, till then, daily will find a death-like life.'

So he took his leave of her, promising to perform her commands. Then, turning to Pamphilia (who had all this while beheld this so sad but loving parting), 'Madam,' said he, 'is there anything left to make me so happy as that it may be in my fortunes to serve you, and so to be blessed with your employments.' 'My lord,' said she, 'it is sufficient to be commanded by one, and so beautiful a lady. For my part, I will entreat your speedy return, and that you bring my brother with you.'

With this, he left the ladies, one to lament, the other forced to comfort. His journey he took directly toward the sea, meaning at the first convenient port to take shipping and so to pass into Italy, whither, it might be, his friend was gone according to their first agreement. But coming into a place not the richest, but well distant from the worst of countries, in a part within some leagues from the sea, the least inhabited of any of those quarters, being somewhat hilly and desert-like, he went among some of those hills to rest himself, choosing one, the side of it being a fine wood, the foot of it beautified with a pleasant and swift river, before it a pretty plain which went not far before another hill proudly overlooked her lowliness. His horse he gave to his squire, himself walking down into the wood and being taken with the pleasures of that place, he laid himself among them on the ground, speaking these words:

'What destiny is this, unhappy man, that no time will be permitted me to endure happy in? How is the world deceived in thinking happiness consists alone in being beloved, whenas if it proceeds from other than their own chosen love it is a punishment like as the being crammed when one is full. Love then, I beseech thee, make me less happy in not being loved, or truly blessed with enjoying her heart who hath made mine her captive. But, oh me, I do fear that she doth love. Wretch that I am, what then must needs befall me? Death, aye cruellest death, when by a love procured.'

More he was saying, and surely had discovered his passions in a greater and more exact manner, but that he was called to attention by a delicate (yet doleful) voice, a lute finely played upon giving music to his song, which was this:

> Adieu sweet sun
> Thy night is near
> Which must appear
> Like mine, whose light but new begun
> Wears as if spun
> By chance, not right,
> Led by a light
> False and pleasing, ever won.

> Come once in view
> Sweet heat and light
> My heavy spirit
> Dulled in thy setting, made anew
> If you renew
> Daisies do grow
> And spring below
> Blessed with thy warmth, so once I grew.

> Wilt thou return,
> Dear bless mine eyes
> Where love's zeal lies
> Let thy dear object mildly burn
> Nor fly, but turn
> 'Tis season now
> Each happy bough
> Both buds and blooms, why should I mourn?

No sooner had he ended his song, but the same voice (though in a more plaining manner) brought forth these words. 'O life, O death, why am I cloyed with one and slave for the other, much more of me desired? False joys, leave; forced pleasure, fly me! Music, why abide you, since joy, pleasure and true music (which is love) abandons me, shuns me? Alas, true piece of misery, I who am despised, hated, scorned and lost. Are these my gains, ungrateful love? Take here thy conquest, and glory in thy purchase while I live loathing myself and all but her by whom I remain a wretched, forlorn slave. Yet some comfort I have to sustain me: that I suffer for the rarest and most excellent of women, and so long Cupid use thy force and tyrannize upon my slaughtered heart.'

These words were to the brave Italian so just the image of his own thoughts as they were as if his, or like two lutes tuned alike and placed, the one struck, the other likewise sounds. So did these speeches agree to his encumbered thoughts. Willing he was to comfort him, but loath to disquiet him, knowing in this cstate loneliness and disburdening of some part of the like grief doth ease one. Wherefore he remained in a doubt what to do, whenas the young man (for so he perceived from such a one the voice did come) not caring which way he did take, or seeing any direct path but that his fantasies led him in, came hard by the place where Amphilanthus lay, who viewing his youth and delicate beauty, admired and pitied him.

He passed on towards the river, his eyes, as it were, imitating the swift running of that stream. His lute he held in his hand, till again having some more verses framed in his mind (perfect lovers never wanting invention) he again played and sung. Having done, 'O love,' said he, 'once ease me, or let death seize me, giving conclusion to my dolorous days. What do I gain by being a prince? What avails it me to hope for a kingdom's government when she who is my kingdom to me, and my princess, doth reject me? Woe is me that ever I knew Morea. Woe is me that ever I beheld Pamphilia. O Pamphilia, would I were but so much honoured as thou wouldst but think me worthy to kiss thy hands. That would revive me, and for that favour would I think myself sufficiently requited for all my torments-bearing.'

Amphilanthus, hearing his cousin named, and the young man discover himself to be a prince, wondering in his travels he had never seen him, desirous to be resolved of his estate and name, with all the true cause of his desperate grief, went towards him courteously, and with respect due to him, saluted him thus. 'Sir, let not, I pray you, my boldness in this interrupting your more pleasing thoughts be displeasing to you, since it is my fortune (not desire to trouble you) which brought me hither, wherefore I hope I shall obtain pardon of you.'

The young prince soberly, and a little blushing, answered. 'No fault can I find with your being here, or anything except my own fortune, which thinks itself never cursed enough to me. But since, as I assure myself, you have heard my passions, till now never known to man, let me know by whom I am discovered.' 'Upon promise to have the like courtesy from you,' replied the valiant King, 'I will not hide myself from you.' He consenting, the stranger prince began. 'Then Sir, know I am called Steriamus, prince and rightful King of Albania, brought unto this country by the virtuous and noble prince Parselius, who hath undertaken to assist me in recovering the kingdom lost in my father's days. But what talk I of a kingdom, having lost the power of my content and happiness. Now Sir, perform your word.'

'I am,' said the other, 'Amphilanthus, King of the Romans.' Steriamus, knowing him to be that famous prince in whose search his friend was gone, fast held him in his arms, crying, 'Yet am I happy to see the most renowned prince breathing before I die! For now may I, ending, say I have seen the worth of the world and feel her greatest cruelty.' Amphilanthus blushed to hear his virtue so extolled, but lovingly embracing in like manner, the Albanian prince was again solicited by him to tell him all his story, which in this manner (sitting down by the river side) he did discourse.

'My self and my brother being brought by that worthy prince to his father's court were there left, he first having received promise and command being given for men's raising to restore me (miserable me) to my kingdom, as I before told you. He took his leave, being gone in the search of you, but promised return within six months into Morea, being now gone into Italy, hoping to meet you there. I remaining, grieved to part with him, but more afflicted with an incurable wound which in that court I received. But before I go any further, I pray tell me whether you have lately seen the princess Pamphilia, for surely then shall I find one pain troubles us, and one cure only for us.'

'I saw her very lately,' replied Amphilanthus, 'being but almost now come from her father's court. But for all that, you may safely go on with your discourse.' 'Then,' said he, 'it was my happiness to see her, but my misery to fall in love with her (cruel she) who if she prove not merciful to me I must for her thus ever suffer. Besides, it hinders my going on in the regaining of Albania, for what is a kingdom to me, being subject to a greater power of the mind? What can that realm prove to me if Pamphilia martyr me? What is a court to one cast down to the lowest of love's slaveries? No Selarinus, thou art worthy and free and therefore fit to rule, and God send thee that and all other good fortunes, and this among the rest: that thou never come to the knowledge of thy miserable brother's end, whose misery did thus begin.

'One day, as the King and Queen were walking in the garden attended on by all the princes, ladies and knights of the court, everyone discoursing as best pleased them, Pamphilia walked alone, none daring to present himself to her, such was the respect all bore unto her and fear of displeasing her. I saw her and, with that sight, lost my self. Love then emboldened me so as, armed with his fire, I went to her and took the boldness to walk by her, and offering discourse (I confess unworthy of her hearing) she entertained me modestly and gravely. Love, for me finding this hope, forced me to use the time and to speak something of itself to her, which she perceiving (yet out of pity not willing too cursedly to deal with me) showed me in her countenance dislike of my speeches. And yet not to put me too much besides myself, called others to her, to add (as she feigned) to her company.

'With a bleeding heart I suffered this disgrace, which yet was by her so handled as none but my own soul could witness it to any. Thus that day passed, sorrow increasing in me and little mirth growing in her. Oft times would she be ready to sigh, but loving that breath which she drew for so loved a cause, she did strive to fetch it back again, or else it was to cover her long breathing. Many days this continued, till one night, standing in a round window in a great gallery, a lady who did much use to accompany the princess (though she be of the Queen's chamber) standing by her, "Madam, said she, "did you ever see so silent a prince as this? Surely if he were to win his kingdom by words, as it must be done by swords, the country might remain a long time without the lawful King."

'Pamphilia looked (O me, a deadly wound that sweetest look did prove) pleasingly upon me, saying "My lord, you see this lady finely begs discourse from you." "Alas, divine princess," said I, "what discourse can proceed from a dead man?" "I never heard till now," said she, "that dead men walked and spake." "Yes madam," cried I, "as you have seen trees continue green in their branches, though the heart be quite dead and consumed away, hollowness only remaining. And so is nothing left in me but empty hope and flourishing despair." "Is there no cure?" said she. "Yes, that there is," said I. "Show it," said she.

'I looking about, and seeing the other lady parted from me, besides hard by a fair glass (many hanging as ornaments in that gallery), I took it up, turning it to her, mine eyes only speaking for me. She (with seeing her face, saw my cause of torment) said as little as I, only taking the glass, turned the other side, which was dull like my gains, and with as much scorn and contempt as could appear in so much beauty (like as if the sun would in spite show himself in a storm) she turned from me.

'I stood still, for indeed I could not move till, for my last comfort, sense came to me to show me I was in no fit place so to betray my passions. Wherefore, getting so much strength (although no more than as men after a long sickness gain when they go with feeble joints the length of a room, so much had I) and that little with much ado brought me to my chamber, where I opened my breast to all sorrow, and let mine eyes make full sea of tears.

'Thus I remained till this resolution took me: to wander I cared not whither, so it were far from knowledge of any and to leave that most cruel beauty to her own content, which yet I fear she hath not, though I truly wish she had. I called my brother to me, telling him he must be secret to me, as he did hope for love from me, which he vowed, not mistrusting what I meant till 'twas too late to go back. With sobs and tears he besought me to alter, but I told him there was no remedy, nor must he break his oath. Then, against his heart, he said he must obey. My charge was this: never to reveal my manner of going, nor ever to seek after me or suffer any that he could hinder.

'Then went I to Pamphilia's chamber, where I humbly desired to speak with her. She gave me leave, but when I was ready to say something, she prevented me. "If you have," said she, "any business, I shall be ready to do you any service in it. But if it be concerning your glass discovery, know this: you shall do best to be silent, for a greater offence you cannot do me." "Alas madam," said I, "have you no pity for me?" "I have pity for any," said she, "leave this folly and I shall wish you well."

'That was so cold a favour for my desires, and my dutiful affection, such to her as not to give her the least cause of dislike, besought her she would honour me but so much as I might kiss her hands before my departure, which was forced by an adventure calling me away. She nobly granted that and said she wished me good fortune. I told her my fortune could only be made by her. "Then can it prove little," said she.

'With trembling and death-like paleness I left her lodgings, having yet the favour which my lips received in touching her fairest hand, which kiss shall never part from me till these my lips do kiss with death. Then wandered I away till I came hither, never finding any place to please me nor, alas, doth this, or can anything but her pity please. Only this is less distasteful than those where greater noises be. Here I am quiet, but for my own quiet, but for my grief, which never gives me rest. In a little cave in the ground is my lodging; one squire attending me, who from a town not far hence fetcheth me provision. This lute (a quality I learned in the court since my coming thither), misfortune and my mistress's disdain, my discourse and companions. And thus lives, and daily dies, the rejected Steriamus.'

Having finished his tale, his eyes flowed again with tears, as if it were their office to give the full stop of his discourse. Amphilanthus embracing him, 'Steriamus,' said he, 'leave these lamentations, for a fury in one who, how worthy soever, yet, being a woman, may change. How many have been condemned for cruelty that after have proved kind enough? Yet speak I not this of Pamphilia, who hath still kept a constant resolution to herself. But sure some strange occasion makes her (so full of judgement and sweetness) carry so strict a course in your affections. Yet let not that make you forget yourself. The poor Albania (poor in missing you) calls upon you; the rest of the world hath need of such princes. Then let not passion overthrow a brave spirit. Absence can bring no hope, presence and desert may, if anything. Or say she never love you: there are other fair ladies who will be liker themselves, pitiful and loving.'

'Never shall other love possess my heart,' cried he, 'and that,
O heavens, still witness for me and behold this vow: that when I
change, it shall be unto death.' Then, shutting his hands one fast
within the other, he groaning said, 'Nor ever let these hands part,
if I part from this my love.' 'Time,' said he, 'will give you (I trust)
unexpected cause of comfort. In the meantime, let us talk of
something else.'

Then Steriamus invited Amphilanthus to the cave, dearly
loving him for his brave advice, but most for his cousin's sake.
There they sat together, lay together, and passed some days
together till the Albanian was overcome with the Italian's (never-
failing) persuading speeches, so as they took their course towards
the sea, falling into that way which brought them directly to the
castle where young Antissius and his uncle were by Parselius left.

There they found them and met the honest captain, who was
brought thither by the Rumanian knight who, after the whole
discourse was told to Amphilanthus, as before it had been to
Parselius, the old prince and young knight, continued the story
thus.

'After that devil of women, the King's wife, had wrought the
ruin of Rumania, proclamations out for the bringing of either or
both of you, for which large sums of money were offered—but if
you could be delivered in alive, those sums and great honours
with brave possessions—you, my lord, made a traitor and you,
Sir, having your head at sale. Then obtained she that her son was
made heir apparent to the crown, and that if the King happened
to die while the new prince was under years, that then she would
govern as protectress until he came of age.

'This sure, she grew weary of the old man, whose age and
dotage (she having employed them to her use, was now cloyed
with them) troubled her. To be rid of him was then her study. At
last, finding an easy way (as she thought), she called one of her
servants to her (being one who ambitiously sought to win the
honour of being her favourite); leading him into a private cabinet,
where she plotted all her wickedness, there she began with false
and forged flatterings to entice him to her purpose. Dissimulation and protestations of her affections she wanted not to draw
him into the yoke of her witchcraft.

' "And what," said she, "though the world do tax me for loving

many? Do not you accuse me, my only dear, for sooner will I die
than wrong your love. If my fashion, which is free and familiar,
make you doubt me, consider why it is, since it were neither
wisdom nor safety for us to use you only kindly in all sights. The
graces others have is but to blind their eyes, which else would be
clearsighted to our ill, and this even by the love you bear me I
conjure you to believe, and this should you well find were I at
liberty and free." "What freedom would you ask?" "To be
myself," said she, "and so to take a husband I could love as I love
you, and so would make you were the old man dead."

' "Is that the bar," cried he, "dear lady? He is dead, or even as
good; for two days is his longest term of life." "That done, enjoy
me, who am only thine, and verily the thing is easy, safe—and
doubtless, do it then, and by it purchase me."

'He, long time bewitched with her craft, allured by her beauty,
and continued in error by her falsehoods, believed she spoke
unfeigned from her heart, letting himself covet that which with
murder (and treacherous murder) they must gain from the true
owner. But he looked no further than his love, to compass which
no means seemed ill, so partial was he to his vile desires. Thus
was his word engaged, and the King's life limited. Which end of
time being come, they enticed the grave man into a park, where
they murdered him, bringing home the old body besmeared in
his own blood, covered with their mantles, as the fault was with
their feigned tales, which were that in the wood certain men,
hired as it was likely by you, set upon him, killed him and
wounded them (showing some slight wounds which they had, for
the greater show of truth, given themselves).

'The Queen, being brought to this sad sight, took on strangely,
rending her clothes, crying and even howling so as most did pity
her, and few or none accuse her guilty of the crime, so cunning
was she in her deep deceits. Then was the council called, who
came in, in show sad, but in hearts joyful, wicked men loving
nothing more than change. They brought also the young King to
his mother, the people being assembled, and the false report of
the King's death delivered, wherewith they were satisfied, pitying
the wounded body, yet crediting the murderers.

'Thus was the poor doting King rewarded for his fondness. A
funeral was made with all ceremonious cost and pomp, the young

unlawful King being that day crowned as soon as the body was interred. This was yet but one part of the play; the other as soon followed. She, thinking herself no way secure (so many knowing of her sin) to avoid punishment on earth, would run yet faster to meet more punishments' cause, in the other world, by heaping murders upon murders. For, inviting all those except her minion to a private banquet, she poisoned them, reserving the favourite for some other virtuous purpose; who, being in the pride of his desires, expecting when he should be made her husband, often urged it. But she put it off with pretence of fear, lest that the too sudden marriage might give occasion to the world to doubt what was most true and what their guiltiness made them mistrust.

'Thus it passed awhile like a calm tide after a tempest; her son and she being in fell possession of all, the neighbour kings sent to condole the death of the King and to congratulate the other, whether out of love, or desire of peace (a sweet thing to spriteless* princes). Among the rest came one who accompanied the ambassador of Morea, a gentleman of excellent parts, winning the love of all that conversed with him, having a modest government over a strong and dainty wit. But as he was in this happy, he was crossed with the violent love of the chasteless Queen who affected him after her wonted fashion, but so fondly and intemperately as she caused most to look with gazing eyes on her.

'He was not of the highest stature, though far from being low; his hair fair and that beard he had something inclined to yellow. She saw this gentleman (who since I learned was son to the Duke of Mantinea, and captain of a troop of horse, which was part of the King's guard, and the noblest part because that company must ever be choice men and all gentlemen). She wooed him; plainly said she loved him. Yet could not this prevail, worth* in him withstanding all her baits, which being meant as refusals, proved enticements to bring her on, like a spaniel that fawns on the man's cruelty.

'Her passions then grown immoderate and ungovernable, years increasing in her and strength of judgement failing her more than in her youth, gave such open testimony of her love as her latter servant (but companion in mischief) perceived it, his confidence having been such as that blinded him long time,

giving liberty and assurance in that to her and her ends, which
were but either politic or lascivious. But he, as having new sight
given him to see her shame and his own together, hate taking the
place of love, his desires flew to the ruin of her, as before to the
continuance of their days in their own pleasures never enough
enjoyed. He plotted to undo her, and watched the opportunity,
which he obtained by his diligent prying—that bringing him to
discover her going into her cabinet with this stranger, pretending
there to show him some jewels.

'They were no sooner within the room (she having but put the
door a little to, not close), but her enraged enemy came and,
finding means of discerning what was to be seen, lost it not but
stood still looking in. She (whose thoughts carried her to higher
points than care) took no heed of that which most concerned her,
for there he saw her with all passionate ardency seek and sue for
the stranger's love, yet he, unmoveable, was no further wrought
than if he had seen a delicate play-boy act a loving woman's part
and, knowing him a boy, liked only his action. Then with much
ado he brought forth these words.

' "Alas madam, why seek you at my hands your dishonour and
my shame? How dare you venture your honour in the power of a
stranger, who likely would use it to his glory and your reproach.
Besides, you know I love one whose worth and truth must not be
hurt or blotted in my fault, my life not worthy to satisfy the crime
should her unspotted loyalty suffer for my sin." "Yet satisfy my
desire," said she, "and then love whom you will." "Love whom
you will!" cried out the furious forsaken, rushing into the room as
much unexpected and unwelcome as thunder in winter, which is
counted prodigious.

'The Queen stood amazed while he used these speeches: "Fie,
faithless woman, verifier of that fault whereof I hoped women
had been slandered, and not subject unto. Have I obeyed you in
your wicked and abominable treasons thus to be rewarded?" She,
finding he had not only found her, but also had discovered her
falsehood, withal considering his rage, she fell at his feet asking
pardon. "Pardon yourself," said he, "if you can, and me, who
want it as drought doth water. Be your protestations, vows and
daily given oaths come to this?"

'With that, most furiously he ran towards her. But the Morean in humanity saved her from hurt by him, but to hinder that he was forced to struggle with him, who was a strong man and then had double power. This noise called in some that waited without. Others ran to tell the King, either to show forwardness in service, or indeed business, not caring what they carry so it be news, wanting the chiefest part, which is judgement to know where, when and what to tell. But in brief, the King came and, finding this unfortunate disorder, not being able to win from them by fair means the truth, to avoid all ill, committed them to prison, from whence (for the speedier and so more secure proceeding) the next morning they were brought to public arraignment. But the King was not present, fearing those things (which after broke forth) would then be blown forth.

'And indeed it was so, for the accused being demanded what he could say in his own defence, said nothing but wherein he must accuse himself. Being urged to that, he confessed all, finishing his speech thus. "For her sake, by her consent, knowledge and command, I slew the King, she having given me her faith (which as a faith I esteemed, but alas it was a shadow put in false light) that she would marry me. This, added to a natural ambition I had to greatness, not judicially weighing how heavy in justice this weight of honour should be so devilishly sought for or attained."

'For this he was condemned to die; the manner: by four wild horses. But before his execution she was examined, with whom few words were used before she confessed herself guilty. She was likewise condemned (for being a subject, she was under the law), and so had her head struck off. The stranger was delivered free again.

'Many pitied her, to whom she had done good (for none can be found so ill that some will not commiserate) yet the most (like the base world) left her, having held with her while her power shined, but now set with her light, running to the rising strength, not to the declined. Few said she was wrongfully put to death, either for love to her or to make business, for no sooner was she dead but one of her ancienter favourites rose in rebellion, the people apt to take any occasion to stir new afflictions. But a great party he hath gotten, and so much gained as the King is now shut up in the great city of Constantinople, the rebel (as the unlawful

King doth call him) besieging him, and vowing never to lay down
arms till he hath gotten him in his power. And now do they all cry
out for Antissius, honouring the very name as a god, wishing for you
Sir, and vowing, if they can recover you, to make you their King.

'Thus have I left them, the General (for so he is called) having
enjoined me to find you out. They are infinite strong, and want
but you and some brave men to govern them. Go now, I beseech
you; never had Rumania more need, nor shall you ever find a
fitter time.'

The princes sat a while in consultation. At last they resolved
presently to take the journey in hand, not holding it good to lose
so fit an opportunity. The squire of Amphilanthus was sent to
find Parselius in Italy, and to acquaint him with their affairs,
withal to entreat his company. This concluded on, all went to
rest, Steriamus desiring, that because his name was not yet
known by desert, it might be still kept secret, and most he desired
it by reason of his vow. They agreed to it, and he was only called
The True Despised, which was all the device in his shield.
Amphilanthus did desire to be held unknown too, but his reason
was that it was not so safe for so famous a man to be commonly
known in so great and imminent dangers; besides, the renown of
him might make many refuse the combat with him, who else he
might for sport or profit encounter. He had Love painted in his
shield, and was called The Knight of Love.

Towards Rumania with prosperous winds they sailed, choosing the way by sea as the shortest and less troublesome. In a fit
and short time they arrived in Rumania, landing a little from the
town for fear of unknown dangers, and so they passed to the
army, where Antissius and his uncle being known, unspeakable
joy was made, the General yielding all into his hands and taking
his authority from him. Upon this, the usurper sent for a truce,
but that was denied. Then he desired (rather than to continue
immured in that kind, besides ready to be famished) that they
would bring three knights into the field, the which number he
would also bring, himself being one, and those six to end the
business, which side overcoming, the other should depart with
peace and never make more war one against another.

This was accepted, Amphilanthus and Steriamus being two,
the third they had not yet appointed, nor would till the day of

combat, still expecting some famous knight, or Parselius himself, might come to fill the number. If none, then the young knight their first acquaintance should be the man. The day come whenas the lists were made without the town, the judges appointed, old Seleucius, uncle to Antissius, and the honest captain Lisandrinus were the judges for their side; on the other were the admiral and marshal of Rumania. The gates were all set open and free liberty given everyone to pass where he listed, only enjoined to go unarmed.

The first that entered into the field was the King, on each hand of him his two companions in fight; before him, six men bare-headed, one carrying his helmet, three other his spears, the two last his sword and shield; his armour was green flowered with gold, the furniture to his horse of the same colour, cut into garlands of laurel and embroidered with gold, but so artificially joined together as they seemed, when the horse stirred, to rise as ready to crown each part of his conquest. In his shield he had a crown of bays held up by a sword. Word he had none, so as it seemed he stayed for that till his hoped for victory had provided one for him. The other knights were both alike in watchet and gold, their devices a blue cloud out of which sparkled fire.

But then came the honour of his sex, never enough admired and beloved Amphilanthus. His armour was white, filleted with rubies, his furniture to his horse crimson embroidered with pearl, his shield with the same device, from which he took his name. Steriamus, according to his fortune, was in tawny wrought all over with black.

As they were entering, a brave gentleman in murry* armour filled with diamonds, his furniture richly wrought with silver and gold, came to Amphilanthus, using these words: 'My lord, your worth cannot be hid, though you have obscured your name. They both (but the former most) ties* me to be your servant, and as the first favour I shall receive, beg the honour of being third in this brave exploit; not that I am so ignorant as to think myself worthy of being your companion, but wholly out of ambition to serve you.'

Amphilanthus, looking upon him, seeing the richness of his arms and the bravery of his personage, being as comely and strong set as ever he had seen any, made him this answer. 'Sir, the honour is mine to gain so brave a companion and friend, wherein I rejoice, and in place of your love to me, give you mine, which is and shall be firm unto you, and with all my heart embrace your offer to be the third, not now doubting of the victory, having so happy a beginning.'

Then they embraced, and taking him on the left hand of him and Steriamus on the right, they went on to the judges, and all six meeting together, speaking some few words one to another, they parted to meet, never more to part on some sides. Amphilanthus encountered one of the watchet knights; Steriamus the King; and the forest knight (so being called because of his device, which was a great and pleasant forest, most pleasantly set forth, as the cunning of the rarest painter could devise) met the other watchet knight.

The first knight lost his stirrup, else there was no advantage on any side and thus they continued the three courses. Then lighting and drawing their swords, there grew the cruellest and yet delightfullest combat (if in cruelty there can be delight) that martial men ever performed, or had been seen by judging eyes, for never was courage, magnanimity, valour, skill and nimbleness joined better together, so as indeed a kingdom was too low a prize for such a combat.

Long it continued, till the Knight of Love, disdaining one man should hold out so long with him, gave him such a wound in the head as therewith he fell down dead at his feet. At the same instant the King gave Steriamus a great hurt in the body, but he was quickly paid with a wound in the belly which gave him his discharge and freed him from any more trouble of ruling or obeying. The Knight of the Forest, seeing his companions' good fortune, knew it his part to accompany them so as with a surely given stroke, the head of the other and last knight fell to kiss his feet.

Steriamus was carried presently into the town, where by the help of a good surgeon he was soon recovered. The judges all in face glad (howsoever some of their hearts were affected) came to them, who with the rest presently proclaimed Antissius King, who was by the people received with much joy at the coronation, which was within short time. Antissius created the General Duke of Neapolis, and Lysandrinus, Duke of Selybria.

All things being in quiet, the Knight of Love would needs
return into Morea, to see things fitting for Steriamus and to
accompany him in his conquest. With him went the Knight of the
Forest, between whom grew so strict a bond of friendship as was
never to be broken, they two lying together in one room,
Steriamus in another, by reason of his hurt. Amphilanthus in the
night often turned and, turning, still did end with sighs. The
Forest Knight perceived it, yet let him alone till the morning,
when being ready to rise, 'My only friend,' said he, 'your last
night's ill rest made mine unpleasing to me, and most because
mine ignorance hinders me from being able to serve you. I
cannot be yet so bold to demand the cause, since what proof have
you of me that I should think you might esteem me worthy of
such a favour? Yet this you may be confident of: that death shall
seize me before I refuse to venture life to obtain your desires and
lose it rather than reveal any secret you shall impart to me.'

Amphilanthus answered that he saw unexpected good happen
to him in all things (especially in this blessed friendship) but in
that which he most sought for. 'Nor would I conceal the cause of
this my pain from you, were it once discovered to her from whom
I suffer it, but till then I must conceal it, and you, I hope, on this
occasion will excuse me. And for proof of your accepting this for
that which it is, being truth, tell me your love, and fortune in it,
which shall bind me to confidence and engage me to the relation
of mine.'

'My lord', said he, 'to satisfy you (which is the all of my
wishes) understand that my poor self (only rich in the honour of
being your friend), hunting one day in a great forest, my father,
the King of Bohemia, and many other princes of Germany being
assembled, it was my fortune, following the sport more eagerly
than the rest, to go so far from my company as I was left in the
woods all night. There I took my lodging, resting free from
passion, if not rage, for wanting judgement so to be lost.

'In this night, and midst of it (for I waked with the dream and
found it was not day) methought I saw a creature for shape a
woman, but for excellency such as all the rareness in that sex,
curiously and skilfully mixed, could but frame such an one, and
yet but such a one in show like a picture well drawn, but the
subject more perfect, apparelled in green, her hair hanging

careless, nothing holding it but a delicate garland which she wore
upon her head made of pansies and woodbines. Her face bare,
boldly telling me not I only, but all hearts must burn in that
pureness. Eyes like the perfectest mixtures of heavenly powers,
not to be resisted but submitted to. Lips fully commanding the
plenty of duty when they seemed to demand obedience. Her neck
the curiousest pillar of white marble; breast of snow or smooth
waves of milk, swelling or falling as the sweet gale of her most
sweet breath did rise or slack. All other parts so exquisite as
none, save only she, can be so excelling.

'This I found in her, who methought came to me using these
words. "Arise, leave Bohemia, and rescue me from the hands of
rebels." I cried out "Stay, O stay, and tell me how and where."
"In Hungaria," said she. With that I waked, having her image so
perfect in my breast as nothing can remove it from me. A pretty
while I lay still, wishing to sleep again, so once more to have
beheld her. But she was too rich a jewel slightly to appear to such
worthless eyes. Contented with that I had seen, I lay feeding on
that and my resolution, which was to seek her.

'When day began to appear, what joy was it to me? But for my
greater comfort I found hard by me this armour laid with this
shield and sword. I stayed not, but put it on, thinking with myself
how to attain to the honour of knighthood, my father having refused
it to me because my elder brother, being weak and sickly, had not
demanded it, resolving I should attend his increase of strength,
my father's whole content being in that son.

'Considering this, I knew it no way to go to him. Wherefore,
armed (my squire carrying my sword) I passed unto the
Emperor's court, who without delay gave me what I demanded,
honouring me with the gift of an excellent horse, and furnishing
me with all conveniences. Then took I my way for Hungary, which
kingdom I had no sooner entered but I met the news of a great
rebellion made by the uncle King's bastard son, called Rodolin-
dus, against the daughter and heir of the second brother, called
Melasinda, who was crowned Queen after the decease of her
uncle and father. But he, envying her greatness, and ambitiously
seeking honour himself, claimed a contract between the King
and his mother with all vows and protestations of marriage.

'Witnesses he produced. True or false, they made a terrible

stir, and brought the fairest Melasinda into great danger. Troops I continually met, some with the Queen, some against her. With much difficulty I passed till I came to an ancient lord's castle within two leagues of the city of Buda, where she was enclosed. This nobleman held with his sovereign, and after much discourse of those affairs he led me into a gallery, where he showed me the picture of that distressed princess, truly I will not say so well drawn as that which remains figured in my heart, but so well as none but her counterfeit could appear so beautiful, and such as I knew it to be the same which in that blessed night in the forest showed herself to me.

'This made me conclude the adventure was reserved for me; wherefore carefully examining all things that had passed, and curiously and affectionately weighing the business and means to achieve the finishing, not leaving anything unasked that might avail, concluding to adventure what e'er came of it.

'The good lord advised me (perceiving my purpose) to be ruled by him, which I consented to, when I found he meant honestly for his princess's good and circumspectly for my safety, by no means suffering me to enter the town as myself (by reason of a great hate had been between our parents), but as an adventurous knight who, hearing of her troubles, offered my service to her.

'She, most fair, most lovely she, accepted me into her service, where I performed what was put into my trust, in two days killing two of the mightiest and strongest knights of all his party. In the end, the council of both sides and the people, weary of war, advised and agreed upon a peace, on those conditions: that he should lay down all claim to the crown, yielding it wholly to her, but in requital she should take him for her husband. This was bitter to her, but this she must do, or be left alone, peopleless and kingdomless.

'I was but one, and unable to set the crown and keep it on her head against the whole state, wherefore loving her so much as not daring to think of any harm to her in giving ill advice (nor could my soul allow her less than the kingdom) with the rest I persuaded for him, till she told me she was sorry she no better deserved my love but that I would think another fitter for it, or she unworthy of mine.

'I swore (and truly) the world had not that treasure I more covetously sought than her enjoying. She urged the unkindness between our parents made me doubt. I firmly vowed her love made me secure and happy, but what I did or said in this was only for her good and safety.

'With much ado and long persuasions, I won her love to me, her yielding for the other, so the match was concluded and peace on all sides, I leading her the day of marriage to her wedding chamber, where I left her to her husband. The next morning she came down into a little garden whereinto no window looked but that in her cabinet, nor key could open but her own. Into this place I was conveyed by her woman a little before where, meeting her, we passed some hours together.

'Thus was I the blessed man, enjoying the world of riches in her love, and he contented after, having what he sought. Thus I lived awhile, till I found him altered, and the face of the court a little changed towards me (for former causes they pretended, forgetting me and what was done by me for them) which made me, fearing her harm, leave the country for awhile, which little time to me already seems ages, being yet but months and few in number, though in love innumerable.

'She was sad and grieved for my going; I played the woman too, and wept at our departing. But soon I hope again that we shall meet; howsoever I will see her, though in private, and venture life for it. After that I left Hungary, I came through many countries till I came into Italy, and so hoping to meet you there, but hearing of your being in Morea, I went cross the sea into that country and so had missed you, but that I fortunately met your squire who, seeking Parselius, enquired of me for him, and I for you of him. We resolved each other, I telling him where I had left him, which was in Elis, after a delicate and strange adventure finishing, and being directed by him how to know you, I was the better instructed to present my service to you, which the fame of your worth had long since dedicated to you.'

'Leave compliments, dear friend,' said Amphilanthus, 'it is not now time to use them, our loves having sealed them up in truth. Give such delicate phrases to your next mistress.' 'My next! Why, think you I will change?' 'If you be wise,' said Amphilanthus, 'and would my fate would change, then were I happy; one such minute, whereof it seems you have had seasons, would be more welcome to me than the crown of Naples, yet would I have her chaste still and then I hope I should with truth and service win her.'

'Is she yet to be won?' said the Bohemian. 'Yes,' said the Italian, 'by me she is, and what tormenteth me is I fear she loves my friend.' 'He is no friend that will not yield to you,' said he. 'I should not love him,' said Amphilanthus, 'if his love to me should exceed that to so incomparable a creature.' 'How know you she doth love?' said the prince. 'I only fear,' said he, 'and dare not hope it is myself; but surely she doth love.' 'Hope and believe,' said he, 'and that will make you bold to show yours to her, and then who can refuse you?' 'Would this were true and then had I the only victory I seek.' 'Adventure, brave prince,' said the Bohemian, 'never yet failed your conquest on men, and women are the weaker and gentler. Besides, you are (the world says happy in those wars) so fortunate and so loving as you cannot fail, nor she resist.'

'I am no coward, though mistrust my strength in her sight; her looks,' said Amphilanthus, 'are to me (if frowning) more terrible than death, yet come what will I must adventure. If I obtain, I will be as free with you as you have been with me, else keep my disgrace, my fortune and affliction from discovery made by my tongue.' 'Will not your face declare it, think you? Therefore to avoid such inconvenience, woo bravely and resolutely and then win joyfully and blessedly.'

Morning being somewhat spent, they rose and so took on their way, Steriamus having yielded to Amphilanthus' earnest persuasion to go with him into the pleasant Morea. Parselius, after he had left his father's court and friends together, with his sad thoughts he betook himself to Elis, and so to ship for Italy to fetch his friend to assist the two princes, and after to go and redeem his heart out of the enchantment.

As he passed along in the country of Elis, one day being so busied as his thoughts had changed him into themselves, his horse carrying him which way he best liked, he was called upon by a rude voice which willed him to know himself better than so proudly to carry himself before a princess. Looking up to see what and who this was, he perceived close by him a troop of ladies all on horseback, and many gentlemen and knights attending them, but one who had adventured to instruct him a little more than the rest, to whom he thus spake. 'Truly sir,' said he, 'this fault was caused by melancholy, not by rudeness, for I have been too well brought up to be uncivil to ladies.' 'It appears so indeed,' said he, 'that thus you stand prating to me and do no reverence to her who best deserves it.'

The prince, angry at his boldness, but unwilling to wrangle with him, only turned to the ladies and made a reverence to them, offering to pass by them. But the first knight seeing that, 'Stay Sir,' said he, 'you have not done all. 'Tis not a courtesy shall serve, for we must see if your valour be equal to your manners.' 'They have commonly gone together,' said Parselius, 'but where are your arms?' 'Hard by,' said the other, 'and that you will too soon find.' 'I'm sure,' said he, 'I have found words enough which may make me hope to scape the better from your blows.'

He went and armed himself. The like did all the rest, while the prince stood beholding the lady, who was of great beauty and bravery, apparelled in a hunting gown of green cut with red, the upper and lower part of her garment embroidered with gold and red, a feather of red and green in her head, the furniture to her horse of the same colour and richness, to whom Parselius thus spake: 'Madam, if I had offended you, the least of your corrections had made me submit, without the fury of your knights who, methinks, were very confident of the due respect you may challenge else, unarmed, they would not have been so forward to the combat.'

'Sir,' said she, 'you are deceived in this, for such is their valour as none yet ever equalled them, especially him that first spake; nor have they reason to trust any further on me than their own swords will warrant them in, but indeed the cause of all this is a vow which I have made, which is this. Myself being daughter to the prince of Elis, which country is in homage subject to the King of Morea, it was my ill fortune to fall in love with the scornful and proud prince of that country, called Parselius, who did not content himself with disdaining me, but boasted of my subjection, and to myself when I with humility besought his favour, he told me he was no subject to love. This hath made me vow revenge, to which end I keep these knights about me, and never meet any stranger that they encounter not, nor shall till we meet him, and if good fortune fall that we win him by combat, I will then win him by love or obtain my will by force.'

By this the knights were come who, setting on the brave prince one after another, he overthrew them all, and left them, most not able to go thence, some stark dead, the best, legs or arms broken. This done, the lady again spake. 'Sir, since fortune and your power hath left me guardless, I hope you will conduct me to the town; besides, let me know who you are.' 'Madam' said he, 'as I take it, by the course of arms you are mine, for if you were to win me by their conquest, by the same reason you must be lost if they be vanquished.'

' 'Tis true sir,' said she, 'and such indeed were the conditions. Yet I had hoped you would never have called that in question.' 'Nor truly madam,' said he, 'do I it with any meaning to keep you, though my victory gives you to me, but to show I am civil and not unmannerly, I will deliver you here to your ladies and pages; that I am not proud or scornful, I kiss your hands; but to let you see I disdain an unworthy love, or a forced one, Parselius bids you thus farewell, and will yet pray that your senses may tell you a lower choice and an humbler mind will prove more fit and happy for you, and such I wish you, since for me you have been distempered.'

Thus he departed, leaving her amazed and afflicted with hate, disdain, scorn and all other she accused him of, till shame overcame and forced her to return to a good old man, her father, whose mild and good example brought her to follow the counsel of Parselius, who held on his journey. Taking ship for Italy, he landed in the kingdom of Naples, those very parts making him remember that which too well still continued in his mind, which was the sweet and delicate island wherein he found the sweetest and delicatest of shepherdesses, the thought of whom brought forth these words, his heart bleeding as fast as before his eyes had shed sad drops.

'O sweet island,' cried he, 'and yet desolate Pantalerea, how do our afflictions suit as one, and so our destinies. Urania hath left thee and thou mournest; Urania hath left me, and I pine. Dearest Urania, dear unto me still, why wouldst thou for novelties leave thy faithful Parselius? Why wouldst thou not be as well then advised as till that time be governed by my counsel? Yet fool, most blame thyself, for why didst thou permit her dainty lips to touch that charmed brook? Nay, still add unto thy folly: why wouldst thou drink so hastily thyself, and so have no means left to help or save? Accursed spring, from whence did run the ruin of my bliss. Bewitching stream, to charm me to the loss of my soul's joys. Spitefulest of the gods or goddesses, was it for revenge because we would not try your charmed house that yet their cruel trial should be made upon us? Unlucky tempest, constraining us to land on that much more unlucky shore.'

Leaving his ship, he went aland, commanding his servants to go to the court, and if they came before him thither, there to attend till his coming—but secretly himself going along the seaside, his mind as unrestingly running on Urania as a hurt bird that never leaves flying till he falls down. No more did he rest, till death-like sleep did force him to obey. Yet were his dreams oft of her, his mind then working and presenting her unto his imagination; as in day his thoughts did to his heart, so did the eyes of his loving soul ever behold her, accusing himself for his folly, fearing the power of the charms whose wicked might might alter her, assuring himself she must be deceived by them if ever she did change.

In this violent fever of sorrow he went on till he discerned a man come from under the rocks that proudly showed their craggy faces, wrinkling in the smiles of their joy for being above the sea which strove by flowing to cover them, but for all that ambition was forced to ebb in penance for that high desire. He came armed at all points, leading in his hand as beautiful a lady as nature could frame and sorrow suffer to appear so, being such an one as both had used their best art to frame and suffer to show excellent. Had she been free, how much more rare must she then of necessity appear, who in misery showed so delicate?

The Morean prince stayed to behold and, beholding, did admire the exquisiteness of that sad beauty, but more than that did the cruelty of the armed man seem wonderful for, leading her to a pillar which stood on the sand (a fit place that the sea might still wash away the memory of such inhumanity), he tied her to it by the hair, which was of great length and sun-like brightness. Then pulled he off a mantle which she wore, leaving her from the girdle upwards all naked, her soft, dainty white hands he fastened behind her with a cord about both wrists, in manner of a cross, as testimony of her cruellest martyrdom.

When she was thus miserably bound to his unmerciful liking, with whips he was about to torment her. But Parselius with this sight was quickly put out of his admiration, hasting to revenge her wrong, setting spurs to his horse he ran as swift as lightning (and as dangerous this happened to the knight) towards them, yet sending his voice with more speed before him, crying 'Vile traitor, hold thy hands and turn thy spite on me, more fit to encounter stripes', hoping thus to save her from some, which if but one, had been too much for such delicacy to endure.

But he, whose malice was such as the nearer he saw her succour, the more was his fury increased, looking up and seeing a brave knight accompany that voice, casting his hateful look again on her and throwing away the whips, drew his sword, saying 'Nor yet shall this new champion rescue thee', then ready to have parted that sweet breath from that most sweet body. Parselius came and struck down the blow with his sword, though not so directly but that it a little razed her on the left side, which she perceiving, looking on it, and seeing how the blood did trickle in some (though few) drops, 'Many more than these,' said she, 'have I inwardly shed for thee, my dear Perissus.' But that last word she spoke softlier than the rest, either that the strange knight should not hear her or that she could not afford that dear name to any but her own ears.

She being thus rescued, the knight strake fiercely at Parselius, who met him with as much furious strength, giving him his due in the cursedest and fullest measure, making such proof of his valour (justice being on his side, which best guides a good sword in a noble hand) as in short time he laid him at his feet, pulling off his helm to cut off his head. But then the lady cried unto him, beseeching him to stay that blow; the like did another knight newly arrived, who untied the lady—whereat Parselius was offended, thinking himself highly injured that any, except himself, should do her that service, telling him he much wondered at his boldness, which had made him offer that wrong unto him.

'I did it,' said the new knight, 'but to give her ease, and so to bring her that we both might acknowledge humble thankfulness for this brave and happy relief, which hath brought her blessed safety.' Parselius, hearing this courteous answer, was satisfied. Then, looking on the vanquished knight, he demanded why he had used that cruelty to so perfect a lady. As he was answering, the stranger knight knew him, casting his eye upon him, and without any word would as soon have deprived him of his life. But Parselius stayed him, blaming him for seeking the death of a man already dying. He, confessing his fault, asked pardon, and pulling off his helm, told him there he stood, ready to receive punishment for twice so offending him.

Parselius, though not knowing him, yet seeing his excellent personage and princely countenance, embraced him, telling him that honour might gain, nay challenge pardon for a greater fault than was possible to be committed by such a brave knight, he likewise taking off his helm. When Limena (who was this sad, tormented lady) saw her Perissus (for Perissus it was) the joy she conceived was just such as her love could make her feel, seeing him her soul had only loved after so many cruel changes and bitter passions in their crossed affection. This being past, the wounded knight began thus.

'First,' said he, 'let me know by whose hand I have received this worthy end, and indeed too worthy for so worthless a creature who now, and but now, could discern my rash and wicked error, which now I most heartily repent. Now are mine eyes open to the injuries done to virtuous Limena. Her chastity appears before my dying sight, whereto before my eyes were dim and ears deaf, seeing and hearing nothing but base falsehoods, being governed by so strong and undeserved jealousy. Next, I must ask pardon of you, my lord Perissus. Deny not these petitions I humbly beseech you both, unto a dying man, who in his life did offer you too foul and too unpardonable an injury.'

Perissus, seeing his speedy end approaching, having the noblest and freest heart, forgave him that offence, which proceeded from the same ground that his crosses came from, both taking root from love, and yet love in that kind changed nature with madness when attended on with so much jealousy. Then, with a mild voice, he spoke.

'Philargus,' said he, 'I am glad your punishment is accompanied with so happy and true repentance. I do freely forgive you and think no more of that past than if never done. But this I desire: you will demand the like of your excellently virtuous wife, who hath been the patient* of all your fury.'

'That I do,' said Philargus, 'and let my soul enjoy no happiness if I wish not her as well as it. Then, dear Limena, have you pardoned me? If not, O do, and forgive unfortunate and ill-deserving Philargus.' 'My lord,' said she, 'I most sincerely and heartily forgive you, and so I pray do you the like for me.' 'My dearest,' then said he, 'I happily and thrice happily now shall welcome death.'

'For your other demand,' said the brave prince, 'my name is Parselius Prince of Morea.' Philargus, kissing his hand, gave him thanks and weeping for joy said 'Most fortunate end, how do I embrace thee, coming so luckily, and brought thee by such royal hands.' Then, taking Perissus by one hand and Limena by the other, he said 'I have yet one request more to make, which granted I shall die with all content, and this is only in you two to consent to.' They promised that then he should not be refused.

'These misfortunes,' said he, 'which now are past, and I hope shall have burial in me, have nevertheless (it is most likely) left some false conceit remaining in the hearts of some people, which to remedy and utterly take away, desiring Limena's honour (which without question remains spotted) might flourish as deservedly as the clearness of itself is, without so much as the shadow of a thought to the contrary. I beseech you, for your own best fortunes, and my quiet departing, to promise me that after my death you will marry each other. One more worthy (my lord) more loyal, more chaste, the world holds not, and this you are bound to do for her, who for you hath been wronged. And Limena, deny not this to your dying husband, being the last he can ever ask you.'

He needed not urge them much to what they most coveted and purposed in their hearts before, yet to give him full satisfaction (though on her side with bashful and fearful consenting) they yielded to him. 'Then, my lord,' said he, 'take her and my heart's prayers with best wishes to you, and my best beloved Limena, in witness of my love to you I bestow on you this most worthy lord, far better befitting you, and my whole estate.' With that, embracing them, kissing her, and lastly lifting up his eyes to heaven, he departed, they, like true friends, closing his eyes.

Being now grown late, for that night they went into the cave which but lately had been the prison of sweet Limena. With them they carried the body, laying it in the further part of the hollowness. Then did Parselius tell them how infinitely happy he esteemed himself in having come so luckily to serve them, of whom and whose unfortunate affection he had heard, having had it from the rare shepherdess. Name her he could not, his breath being stopped with sighs and his tears falling down in all abundance, sent from his heart, which dropped like the weeping of a vine when men without pity wound it.

Perissus, seeing his sorrow, made haste to ask the cause, fearing some great harm had befallen that divine creature of whom he gave such praises as Limena thought they were too much, which he perceiving, left, with demanding of her safety and why his grieving was, which Parselius having passionately and truly related, he desired most earnestly to hear the rest of Limena's story, which she thus began.

'My lords, after I sent the letter and the time expired, Philargus came for my answer, or to perform his vow, which with desire I attended, although he, contrary to my wishes, prolonged it. When he had what I resolved to give him for satisfaction, which was a direct denial, being in these words: "I know, as I am your wife, I am in your power to dispose of; then use your authority, for so foul a stain will I never lay upon my blood as to betray the prince." Name you in truth I durst not, lest at the last that might move my affections. Then did he command me to go with him (to my death, I hoped) when he brought me into a great wood, in the midst whereof he made a fire, the place being fit and I think sure had been used in former time to offer sacrifice unto* the sylvan gods. Then he made me undress myself, which willingly and readily I did, preparing myself to be the poor offering, but the richest that richness of faith in love could offer.

'When I had put off all my apparel but one little petticoat, he opened my breast and gave me many wounds, the marks you may here yet discern'—(letting the mantle fall again a little lower, to show the cruel remembrance of his cruelty) which although they were whole, yet made they new hurts in the loving heart of Perissus, suffering more pain for them than he had done for all those himself had received in his former adventures. Therefore softly putting the mantle up again, and gently covering them, lest they might chance to smart, besought her to go on, longing to have an end of that tragical history and to come again to their meeting, which was the only balm could be applied unto his bleeding heart.

She, joyful to see this passion, because it was for her, and sorry it was Perissus did sorrow, proceeded. 'And after these, threatening many more, and death itself if yet I consented not. But seeing nothing could prevail, he took my clothes, and with them wiped the blood off from me, I expecting nothing but the last act, which I thought should have been concluded with my burning. His mind changed from the first resolution, so as taking me by the hair and dragging me into the wood among the bushes (whose cursedness seconded their master's fury) tearing my skin and scratching my bare legs, to a tree he there tied me, but not long continued there, for he going a little from me returned with a pastor's coat which he took from a poor man that was in that wood, seeking a lost beast. With this he disguised me, and also having taken the man's horse, took me behind him, putting a gag in my mouth for fear I should speak for help, posting unused ways through the desert to the seaside, where he got a boat and so passed over to this place, where ever since we have remained, for my part, with daily whippings and such other tortures, as pinching with irons and many more so terrible as for your sake (seeing your grief, my dearest lord) I will omit, declaring only this I must speak of, belonging to my story.

'Once every day he brought me to this pillar where you found me and in the like manner bound me, then whipped me, after washing the stripes and blisters with salt water. But this had been the last had not you thus happily arrived, for he determined, as he said, after my tormenting had been past, instead of washing me in the sea water, to cast me into her and so make a final end of his tormenting and of my torments. To this end he likewise went yesterday to the town and bought this armour, arming himself to the intent that after his purpose was accomplished he might take his journey which way best he pleased. Thus, my lords, have you heard the afflicted life of poor Limena, in whom these tortures wrought no otherwise than to strengthen her love and faith to withstand them. For could any other thought have entered into

my heart, that would have been a greater affliction to my soul
than the cursed strokes were to my body, subject only to his
unnaturalness, but now by your royal hand redeemed from
misery to enjoy the only blessing my heart can or ever could
aspire to wish. And here have you now your faithful love
Limena.'

Perissus embraced her with that love his best love could
express, and then speaking to the Morean prince, he said 'The
thanks, most brave prince, for this happiness belongs unto you,
which is so much as my life shall ever be engaged to pay that due
unto you, and my sword employed to the best of my power to
serve you, vowing that when I (and the same I profess for my
dearest here) prove ungrateful, we will no more see light. Nay, let
us be as wretched as ever we were if that sin know us.'

Parselius, with much affection, requited their protestations,
making the like for himself in his love to them. So, for that night,
they went to rest, the next day taking their journey to Naples, to
provide such things as were necessary for them. Thence went
they into Sicily, having a brave ship, which the governor of that
town, knowing Parselius, provided for them, going himself, and
many more brave gentlemen, to conduct them over. Whither
being come, they found the country in great trouble, the King
being dead and an usurper in his stead. But quickly were those
stirs appeased by the presence of Perissus, well helped by the
company which came out of Naples with him, but most, and
indeed chiefly, compassed by the valour of Parselius, who with
his own hands (in a battle which was fought between the usurper
and an army that came to aid Perissus, as soon as his arrival was
published), killed the false King and his two sons, being counted
the valiantest men of all Sicily, and in stature were little less than
giants.

This being finished, Perissus was crowned King, and soon
after was the last promise performed in the marriage, which was
solemnly and with great state accomplished. Then did Parselius
take his leave of the King and Queen, returning to Naples, and so
to the court of that King, where with all joy and welcome he was
received, the triumphs and feasts making testimony of it. Yet was
his sorrow such for Urania as all those sports were rather
troublesome than pleasing unto him.

Some few days after the triumphs began, the squire of Amphilanthus found him there, to whom he delivered his message. With much joy did the old King receive the squire, bringing him such joyful news of his son's being well, though much more welcome had he been if he could have told anything of his return thither. Parselius demanded of the squire how he found him out. 'Why Sir,' said he, 'my master, going away from Morea with Antissius and that company, sent me by sea to seek you in this country. By chance our ship sprung a leak, so as we were forced to put in again to mend her. After we had been a day at sea, before she was thoroughly mended, came a brave gentleman called Ollorandus, younger son to the King of Bohemia, who seeking my lord, to whom he hath vowed his love and service, knowing me to be his servant, enquired of me for him. I told him where at that time he might find him. Having done this, I took the boldness to ask him if he heard any news of you, and withal the cause why I asked. He answered me that, having passed Italy in search of Amphilanthus, and hearing he was cast upon Morea by shipwreck, he followed after him till he came to the court, which at that time was in Arcadia. There he heard that he had been there but was again gone into Italy to seek you, and that he would with you soon return again into that country to go into Albania, wherefore he, desiring to see something in those parts, passed up and down, sometime to Morea where in Elis he met with you having (as he merrily told me) passed a pretty adventure with a lady and her knights.

'From thence, he came to that part of the kingdom where I was put in by that chance, meaning there to ship once more for Italy. But I, telling him of my master's journey to Rumania, he with all speed followed him, there to deserve his friendship by his service, and thus came I to be so fortunate to meet you.'

Then did Parselius acquaint the King with his intent, which was to follow Amphilanthus. So, taking his leave, he went with as much fortunate speed as might be to overtake his friend, promising the old King to hasten his son's coming, withal letting him know the hope he had of Urania's being his daughter, which hope was as comfortable to him almost as if he had already enjoyed her.

Parselius in his journey travelled with great pain of mind. The like suffered Pamphilia, who all this while continued her love and life in Morea, who by love's force was, it seemed, transformed into the same passion, her lovesick companion still accompanying her till, one morning, her dear (though unquiet) affections calling her to attend them, made her see day sooner than otherwise she had by many hours, and seeing it, to make use of her light, for though the sight which she desired was hid from her, she might yet by the light of her imaginations (as in a picture) behold and make those lights serve in his absence. Even as the morning seems for clearness, fairness and sweetness, so did she rising, that daintiness waiting on her that the greatest light could say he excelled her only in heat, but not in brightness, and in some kind he gained at that time advantage on her, whom absence held in cold despair.

Quickly was she ready and as soon left her chamber, going into the gardens, passing out of one into another, finding that all places are alike to love: tedious. Then opened she a door into a fine wood, delicately contrived into strange and delightful walks, for although they were framed by art, nevertheless they were so curiously counterfeited as they appeared natural. These pleased her only to pass through into a little grove, or rather a pretty tuft of ashes, being environed with such unusual variety of excellent pleasures as, had she a heart to receive delight from anything but love, she might have taken pleasure in that place, for there was a purling, murmuring, sad brook weeping away her sorrows, desiring the banks to ease her even with tears but, cruel, they would not so much as stay them to comfort, but let them slip away with as little care as great ones do the humble petitions of poor suitors.

Here was a fine grove of bushes, their roots made rich with the sweetest flowers for smell and colour. There a plain, here a wood, fine hills to behold, as placed that her sight need not, for natural content, stray further than due bounds. At their bottoms, delicate valleys adorned with several delightful objects. But what were all these to a loving heart? Alas, merely occasions to increase sorrow, love being so cruel as to turn pleasures in this nature to the contrary course, making the knowledge of their delights but serve to set forth the perfecter mourning, triumphing in such glory where his power rules, not only over minds but on the best of minds, and this felt the perplexed Pamphilia, who, with a book in her hand, not that she troubled it with reading, but for a colour of her solitariness, she walked beholding these pleasures till grief brought this issue.

Seeing this place delicate without, as she was fair, and dark within as her sorrows, she went into the thickest part of it, being such as if Phoebus durst not there show his face for fear of offending the sad princess, but a little glimmeringly, as desirous to see and fearing to be seen, stole here and there a little sight of that all-deserving lady, whose beams sometimes ambitiously touching her did seem as if he shined on purest gold, whose brightness did strive with him, and so did her excellency encounter his rays. The tops of the trees joining so close as if, in love with each other, could not but affectionately embrace. The ground in this place where she stayed was plain covered with green grass, which being low and thick looked as if of purpose it had been covered with a green velvet carpet to entertain this melancholy lady, for her the softer to tread, loath to hurt her feet lest that might make her leave it.

This care proved so happy as here she took what delight it was possible for her to take in such kind of pleasures; walking up and down a pretty space, blaming her fortune, but more accusing her love, who had the heart to grieve her while she might more justly have chid herself, whose fear had forced her to too curious a secrecy, Cupid in her only seeking to conquer, but not respecting his victory so far as to allow so much favour as to help the vanquished, or rather his power being only able to extend to her yielding, but not to master her spirit.

Oft would she blame his cruelty, but that again she would salve with his being ignorant of her pain; then justly accuse herself, who in so long time and many years could not make him discern her affections (though not by words plainly spoken), but soon was that thought recalled, and blamed with the greatest condemnation, acknowledging her loss in this kind to proceed from virtue. Then she considered he loved another. This put her beyond all patience, wishing her sudden end, cursing her days, fortune and affection, which cast her upon this rock of mischief. Oft would she wish her dead, or her beauty marred—but that she recalled again, loving so much as yet in pity she would not wish what might trouble him, but rather continued according to her own wish, complaining, fearing, and loving: the most distressed, secret and constant lover that ever Venus or her blind son bestowed a wound or dart upon.

In this estate she stayed awhile in the wood, gathering sometimes flowers which there grew, the names of which began with the letters of his name, and so placing them about her. 'Well Pamphilia,' said she, 'for all these disorderly passions, keep still thy soul from thought of change, and if thou blame anything, let it be absence, since his presence will give thee again thy fill of delight. And yet what torment will that prove, when I shall with him see his hopes, his joys and content come from another? O love, O froward fortune, which of you two should I most curse? You are both cruel to me, but both alas are blind, and therefore let me rather hate myself for this unquietness, and yet unjustly shall I do too in that, since how can I condemn my heart for having virtuously and worthily chosen? Which very choice shall satisfy me with as much comfort as I felt despair. And now, poor grass,' said she, 'thou shalt suffer for my pain, my love-smarting body thus pressing thee.'

Then laid she her excelling self upon that then most blessed ground. 'And in compassion, give me some rest,' said she, 'on you, which well you may do, being honoured with the weight of the loyallest but most afflicted princess that ever this kingdom knew. Joy in this, and flourish still in hope to bear this virtuous affliction. O Morea, a place accounted full of love, why is love in thee thus terribly oppressed and cruelly rewarded? Am I the first unfortunate woman that bashfulness hath undone? If so, I suffer for a virtue, yet gentle pity were a sweeter lot. Sweet land, and thou more sweet love, pardon me, hear me, and commiserate my woe.'

Then, hastily rising from her low green bed, 'Nay,' said she, 'since I find no redress, I will make others in part taste my pain, and make them dumb partakers of my grief.' Then taking a knife, she finished a sonnet which at other times she had begun to engrave in the bark of one of those fair and straight ashes, causing that sap to accompany her tears for love, that for unkindness.*

> Bear part with me, most straight and pleasant tree,
>   And imitate the torments of my smart
>   Which cruel love doth send into my heart,

Keep in thy skin this testament of me
Which love engraven hath with misery,
Cutting with grief the unresisting part
Which would with pleasure soon have learned love's art,
But wounds still cureless must my rulers be.

Thy sap doth weepingly bewray thy pain,
My heart-blood drops with storms it doth sustain
    Love senseless, neither good nor mercy knows
Pitiless I do wound thee, while that I
Unpitied and unthought on, wounded cry:
    Then outlive me, and testify my woes.

And on the roots whereon she had laid her head, serving
(though hard) for a pillow at that time to uphold the richest world
of wisdom in her sex, she writ this.

My thoughts thou hast supported without rest,
My tired body here hath lain oppressed
With love and fear, yet be thou ever blessed;
Spring, prosper, last, I am alone unblest.

Having ended it, again laying her sad perfections on the grass,
to see if then some rest would have favoured her, and have
thought travel* had enough disturbed her, she presently found
passion had not yet allowed time for her quiet, wherefore rising,
and giving as kind a farewell look to the tree as one would do to a
trusty friend, she went to the brook, upon the bank whereof were
some fine, shady trees and choice thorn bushes, which might,
as they were mixed, obtain the name of a pretty grove, whereinto
she went and sitting down under a willow, there anew began her
complaints, pulling off those branches, sometimes putting them
on her head. But remembering herself, she quickly threw them
off, vowing however her chance was, not to carry the tokens of
her loss openly on her brows, but rather wear them privately in
her heart.

Further would she have proceeded but that she heard behind
her a rushing* in the bushes. Looking back, she perceived
Antissia close by her, who having noted the sadness in the
princess and her solitary retiredness, imagined (by her own
passions) the cause must needs be love. But that imagination
growing to belief, belief brought fear, fear doubt, and doubt the

restless affliction: suspicion, her excellencies making the assuredness of her no less excellent choice, so as the more perfect she confessed them both to be, the more did those perfections make her perfectly jealous.

This was the reason that she came thus forth, and in as private sort as she could, that so she might by chance overhear her secret complaints and so (though for a certain vexation) be sure of her most troubled knowledge. But herein she was deceived, for although she heard much of her sorrow, yet got she no assurance for whom the sorrow was, never in all her extremest sufferings once naming the mover of her pain, which kept her love in as much secrecy as that secretly after brought tormenting pain, proceeding from unhappy ignorance. But Pamphilia, perceiving her smiling yet blushing, doubting her passions were discovered and her love betrayed to her companion, she nevertheless to make the best of it, 'How came you hither fair Antissia?' said she. 'I did not think this sad place could have invited so much happiness to it as your presence, who being happy, must make all places partake with you.'

'This place,' said she, 'hath her blessing already in you, the saddest being forced to deserved joy, enjoying so good fortune as to have Pamphilia in it. But I pray, if I may be so bold to ask such a question of you (which the confidence of friend makes me venture upon) why are all these grievous complaints? For never heard I greater, neither was sorrow ever richlier apparelled than lately you have dressed her; if it be for love, tell me who that blessed creature is that doth possess such a world of treasure as your heart. And deny not this to your friend and servant, who will faithfully serve you in that or any other you will impose upon her, though sure in this little pain will serve to win your ease, if you will suffer yourself to have ease. No man breathing that will be so void of judgement or can have power to resist what you in love might demand, but must be so far from denying as he will without question venture his life to gain so precious a prize.'

'Your own worth,' said Pamphilia, 'makes you thus confident, and your happy fortune in meeting an answerable affection thus fearless. But alas for me, I that know worth (greatness, nor the truest love can bring one's desire, if destiny have otherwise appointed) can never let so much flattering hope blind me with conceit of mine own deserts (which it may be are seen but by my own eyes) as to imagine their merits may gain my ends. No, sweet Antissia, love is only to be gained by love equally bestowed, the giver and receiver reciprocally liberal, else it is no love; nor can this be but where affections meet, and that we must not all expect, nor can it reasonably be demanded, since how should the power of love be known but by his several usage of his subjects. If all were used alike, his justice must be examined. But be it as it will, some must and do suffer. Yet speak I not this of myself, or in confession that I am pinched with these tortures, for Lord knows how far am I from these like vanities. Then how can I satisfy your loving demand and friendly promise?'

'You cannot thus dissemble,' replied Antissia, 'your own hand in yonder fair ash will witness against you.' 'Not so,' said Pamphilia, 'for many poets write as well by imitation as by sense of passion, therefore this is no proof against me.' 'It is well,' said Antissia, 'in your own defence. But I pray, why did you but even now with sighs and tears (as I judged by your voice) blame both love and absence?' 'Many reasons there are to accuse both,' said Pamphilia, 'but let me be so much bound to you as to know the reason of your inquisitiveness. If it were only for my good, methinks you grow too near me, bare friendship not being able so cunningly to sift one. Therefore it makes me think some other cause moves this care in you. If so, freely speak it, and I will as freely satisfy you.'

'Well,' said Antissia, 'then confess you love, and I will soon follow with the other.' 'It were to small purpose,' replied Pamphilia, 'to deny it, since you have discovered me. I confess it, and am no whit ashamed of it, though grieved by it.' 'My curiosity,' said the other, 'was and is lest it should be he whom I affect.'

'Alas!' cried Pamphilia, 'can so base an humour as suspicion creep into so brave a heart as Antissia's, and to gain such power there as to make her mistrust her friend? Truly I am sorry for it, and would advise you for honour's sake quickly to banish that devil from you, which otherwise will daily increase new mischiefs.' 'I know,' said Antissia, 'it is the worst of monsters. Yet this is no answer to my question.'

''Tis true,' said Pamphilia, 'but I being innocent of it, forgot first to clear it. But I pray you Antissia, what do you see in me that

I should love Amphilanthus more than respectively?' 'This,' said she, 'that all perfections having joined and united their strengths to make you wholly excellent, it cannot be but you in all things must manifest it, and in judgement are you not called to express it? And if in judgement, wherein can there be more discerned than in the choice of friend or love? If so, can you choose other than the most deserving? And then, must it not be the most excellent of men? And is not Amphilanthus that most excelling prince?'

'In truth,' answered Pamphilia, 'I confess this latter part to be true, for assuredly there lives not his equal for all virtues, which well might make me (if I were such a one as you say) to have that ambition in me to affect the worthiest, but so much perfection I want as that part hath failed also in me. Yet this I will say: I love him as he merits, long conversation as from our youths, besides our blood, claiming an extraordinary respect.'

'You will not deny you are in love with him then?' 'Why should I not?' said she. 'I'm sure I know my own heart best, and truly so far is it from suffering in this passion as it grieves me you mistake me so much. But Lord, what strange and dangerous thoughts doth this bring into our breasts? Could any but a lover have so troublesome a conceit? Why, sweet Antissia, when did this opinion first possess you? Or what gave you occasion to conceive it. Hath my speech at any time betrayed me? Hath my fashion given you cause to suspect it? Did I ever enviously like a lover seek to hinder your enjoying him? Did I unmannerly press into your companies? Some of this surely I must have done, or you unjustly accuse me.'

'None of these could you fail in,' cried she, 'so great a wit and matchless a spirit would govern themselves better than to offend in such fond parts. But the reason I have already given, being equal excellencies, and the belief proceeds from this: that methought you did with as feeling an affection accompany my sorrow when he went away, and more nearly I imagined by your fashion it touched you than pity of my grief could have procured. Then I considered my eyes had been so fortunate as to look upon the best; why then should not the best of our sex also look on the rarest object, and looking so, must not the same conclusion be, that beholding as I did, love must come in and conquer? As on me, so then looking with my eyes, of force you must love him.'

'What a progress,' said Pamphilia, 'hath your troubled

imagination made to find a poor cause to forge a poorer
vexation. If all these things were true, and that I loved
Amphilanthus, what then? Were it any more than my extremest
torment, when I should see his affections otherwise placed? The
impossibility of winning him from a worthy love, the unblessed
destiny of my poor unblessed life, to fall into such a misery, the
continual afflictions of burning love, the fire of just rage against
my own eyes, the hatred of my breast for letting in so destroying a
guest that ruins where he comes—these were all, and these alone
touching me in all disquiets. What need should they have to
molest you, since so perfectly you are assured of his love as you
need fear no occasion, nor anybody to wrong you in that wherein
he will not wrong his worthy choice and constancy. What harm
then could it be to you if you [sic] should love him?'

'The loss of my content, since that you love,' said Antissia,
'must not be refused, but sought, and if obtained, woe be to any
other that aspires to that place. Better never to be born than know
the birth of so much folly as to adventure to be a rival with the
rarest princess Pamphilia. Therefore, knowing this harm, I had
rather you did not love him.' 'Well then, be satisfied,' said the
sweet but sad Pamphilia, 'my love to him proceeds from his never
enough praised merits, but not for love otherwise than I have
already expressed.'

Antissia was with this answer thoroughly satisfied, taking the
princess in her arms, protesting her life too little to pay for
requital for this royal freedom she had found in her, and the
favour received from her, expressing then her love in the best
manner she could, plainly making confession of all to her,
concluding that, had not her incomparable virtue bound her best
respects to her, yet the resemblance which she had in her face of
that famous prince and her only beloved would have forced her
to love her.

The delicate lady told her she could not better please her than
in telling her she did resemble him, since then she was sure she
was like to true virtue, for he was of that the only body. 'But this
love and his dependences do so vex us as they take away all other
society. To amend which, let us return to the court,' said she. 'I
am contented,' said Antissia. So rising, and holding each other by
the arm, with as much love as love in them could join, they took

their way back towards the palace. But in the great garden they met the King and Queen, so they attended back on them into the hall, whither they were no sooner come and settled in their places but they were entertained with this adventure.

Ten knights coming in russet armours, their beavers up, their swords in their hands, who, coming more than halfway to the state, making low reverence, stood still, parting themselves to either side of the chamber to let the followers better be discerned. Then came ten more, but in black armours, chained together, without helmets or swords. After them came six armed like the first, three carrying spears of infinite bigness; one, the shield and the other two the sword and helmet of a knight who for countenance seemed no lover. His colour like a moor, his fashion rude and proud, following after these six who, as the first, divided themselves.

Then came this man to the state, leading by the hand as sweet a lady as he was ugly; she as mild in countenance as he insolent; she as fearful as he bold. On the other hand of her, another knight, sad but, it seemed, amorous—the King and all the court beholding, and expecting the issue of this business, when the stout man in a hollow and hoarse voice delivered these words.

'King of Morea, I am Lansaritano, whose fame I doubt not hath spread itself to your ears. Lord I am of the islands of Cerigo, Dragonero and other lesser circling my chief island as subjects to my greatness. This lady you see here is my vassal by birth but by my choice honoured with my love, which she foolishly refuseth, judgement so far failing her as not to be able to discern the happiness and unspeakable good blind fortune hath given her in letting my high and noble thoughts abase themselves so low as to look on her, my creature, and favour her with my liking. She whom I might command I have been contented to woo; she, who should obey, ignorantly refuseth. Yet I, master of worth, will not force her but have compelled myself to consent to satisfy a fond request she hath made to me, which is to come into this court with her and this knight my cousin, whom she loves, and is the bar from my enjoying her, and here, if she can find a knight who for her sake will enter into this quarrel (which she calls the defence of true love) he must observe this: to give her to one of us and fight with the other.

'If it happen he choose him (as well it may be he will defend ladies, he will dispose of her to her beloved) he must combat me. If he overcome, she shall be free, else yielded to me, which I make no question of, since I never yet knew any had the fortune, how stout, valiant or hardy, could hold out with me. These bound men are knights, and her brothers two of them, the rest her friends and kindred, who upon her vain complaint, fearing violence would have been by me justly used upon her, made an insurrection, which soon I appeased and for the love of her would not yet put them to death, but have brought them with me likewise on this condition: that when I have fought and vanquished that bold and fond man whosoever that will adventure to combat with me, I shall strike off all their heads. This, Sir, is the cause of my coming, wherefore I desire leave of you that she may have one, if any knight will undertake it, or dare maintain her cause, which she accounts so fair and good.'

The King was sorry for the lady's sake his court was so unprovided of those brave knights which were wont to honour it, especially that his famous nephew and brave sons were all absent, who he knew would defend a lady's cause, especially a loving lady, as she seemed, wherefore he made this answer.

'Lansaritano, I am troubled so brave a man should fight in so ill a matter, since if I were as you, she that would not by my worth be won should not be thought worthy to be gained by the hazard of myself, into which you must run if you encounter knights of my court. For surely no brave man will give her from her own affection. But now indeed is your fortune good in coming when the worthies of our parts are absent. Yet doubt I not but I have still some here who honour ladies so much as they will venture to deliver them from force in love; therefore I give you free liberty to pronounce your challenge.'

'I am sorry,' said he, 'that all your worthies be not here, that I might for my glory overcome them one after another. But since they are absent, anyone here take her part that will, or give her to me if none will adventure combat. Otherwise I am ready to meet him with the lance three courses and then end the combat with the sword. If no-one dare undertake it, you must, sweet lady, be mine for want of a knight for your champion.'

She looked sadly and wept so love-likely as all pitied her, but none offered their service, the valour being known and the strength much feared of Lansaritano. Till Selarinus, disdaining such a man should have, though so little, a cause to add more fuel to the fire of his pride, stepped forth and said: 'Most mighty King, may it please you to honour me so much as to permit me the liberty of this adventure, wherein I doubt not but to do justly and to lay Lansaritano's pride as low as the earth will suffer his body to lie upon it.'

The King, glad to see the fine young prince so forward, but loath to venture him in so dangerous a business, told him that the true nobleness and bounty of the kings of Albania his predecessors did again live in him, to maintain which he was very willing to grant his request, but his tender years made him loath to adventure him alone. 'Then Sir,' said he, 'should I both shame myself and the brave princes before by you mentioned. But as I am alone left here of my blood, I will alone adventure.'

Then he asked the lady if she would accept him and stand to his censure. She answered, most willingly she would. He then gave her to her beloved, saying 'Prepare yourself and know, Lansaritano, that you shall find enough to do when you encounter justice and resolution, which are the two I take with me in this combat against you.'

The fury of the vain man was such, to see so young a man answer him, as he could scarce give one word again, but at last his breath smoked out these words. 'Alas, poor boy, I pity thee; wherefore pray thee be advised, and hereafter when thou hast a beard come, and it may be I will grace thee with fighting with thee. Unless thou dost hope I should have some pity on thy fair face and so forbear to hurt thee in the fight. But since you have no braver knights, great King of Morea, farewell. I will return. And now, fair lady, what think you of your servant, myself? Will you love me, or let this smug youth be your champion?'

The King was infinitely offended with the proud speech of Lansaritano; the like was all the company, yet none adventured to answer but brave Selarinus himself, who again courageously yet mildly told him that he need not learn to know words were not the weapons to be used in fight, therefore he would answer him no further in that kind, but he should give him satisfaction with his sword and spear for the lady's sake, before his parting thence, whether he would or no, and then have occasion to speak better of him if he left him to speak at all.

The King embraced the young prince and straight sending for an armour, which was the first that ever Amphilanthus had worn, having left it there, taking another which was brought him from Italy, after his first victory of fame which was there performed against two knights in the defence of an injured lady. This he put on, which was all white save just against the heart he had the figure of a heart wounded curiously made, and so artificially as one would have thought his heart had been seen to bleed through the armour. With these arms Selarinus was armed. The King, girting the sword to him and kissing him, wished as good fortune to him as the first lord of those arms had, and to prove as worthy to wear them.

He on his knee humbly gave him thanks, then turning to the lady, willed her to take her loved servant if she accepted him for her knight. She joyfully beholding him, and smiling on her love who equally expressed his joy, followed him, who now appeared a young Mars. Yet was her joy mixed with fear of falling again into his hands, till which time she (and this she told him) esteemed herself the happiest woman breathing, in such a defendant.

Then went they into the lists, the King and all the court taking places fit to behold the fight, Lansaritano cursing his destiny that brought him the dishonour to meet a child (as he termed him, though after he proved otherwise unto him) in the field. Lansaritano was conducted into the field by his own knights in the same manner as they entered the hall. The lady, who was called Nallinia, and her late distressed but now revived associates, were placed in a seat by themselves to see and to be seen as the prizes of the combat.

Then came Selarinus into the field, attended on by the marshall, master of the horse, and the chief officers of the kingdom of Morea. The marshall being a grave old man, but in his youth one of the best knights of that country, gave him his first spear. The King of Pamphilia (brother to the King, who was newly come thither to visit him, but principally his niece, who by his gift was to enjoy that kingdom after his decease, and therefore bore that name likewise given by him) was one of the judges, the prince of Elis the other for Selarinus, and these two did

Lansaritano accept also for him, doubting no wrong in so just a King's court.

They bravely encountered, running the two first courses without any advantage. The third, Selarinus received so strong a counter-buff on his breast as beat him back upon his saddle, being a pretty while before he recovered again. But Lansaritano having more strength, but as great a blow, showed no moving in himself, though the blow was so forcible as the girts broke, and he came over his horse by the slipping of his saddle. Selarinus, looking back, saw him on foot, which comforted him much, fearing that he had till then received the worst. But being satisfied, with new courage he leaped from his horse, scorning any advantage and drawing his sword, went towards his enemy, who met him puffed up with as much fury as a ship runs upon a rock withal, and alike did he prosper.

A long time did this combat endure, Lansaritano so bravely and valiantly behaving himself (as how could he do other, fighting before his lady to win his lady), as it won unexpected fame to the brave Albanian, who still continued with the better. For though Lansaritano* as valiant as most and as strong as any, yet had his enemy this advantage over him: that in valour he equalled him, and what in strength he failed of, in nimbleness and cunning he excelled him, which brought him the victory with the other's death, being given by a thrust in the face, his beaver* by chance flying up, the pin being cut in the last blow before.

Then were the knights and the lady set at liberty by the brother of Lansaritano, who was one of those, and the same that carried his helmet. He, now being to succeed his brother in his commands, took his leave of the King and the court. The lady had ever affected this knight, and was married before her parting to him, given in marriage by the brother, who was called Sarimatto. They returned, and she lived after with much content with her husband, who was no way like his cousin, though big and strong and as valiant, but mild, courteous and honest, proving a true friend and servant to the court of Morea.

With infinite joy the prince was conducted to the palace, there entertained by the King and ladies, who all joined in honouring him, who had so much honoured the sex, letting his first adventure be in the defence of a woman; then carried him to his chamber where his wounds were dressed, which were many but none dangerous—yet had the loss of much blood made him fainter than he was. This was his first adventurous trial of arms, and accordingly did he proceed bravely and happily.

But now to Leandrus, who was left in his way to Achaea to get forces to assist the princes. Long he rid not without an adventure, those places affording many, and pleasant ones, yet was his scarce one of that number. For after he had left court, he took his directest way to that part which was nearest for him to pass thence into Achaea, as he went thinking of his friends, but most of his love, his heart having received a cureless wound by the never-failing commanding eyes of Pamphilia, sometimes purposing to ask her in marriage, another time hoping first by his desert to win her love, then promising himself the furtherance of Parselius, the labour of Rosindy, the favour of Amphilanthus, the earnestness of his own affection, and lover-like importunity: these he resolved should woo for him, and thus he meant to have her.

Yet wanted he her consent, the better part of the gaining, and the harder to be gained. Yet these conceits pleased him, as mad folks delight in their own odd thoughts, and so was this little less than madness, had he had sense to have considered her worthy self not to be given but to her own worthy choice, and by it. But thus he satisfied himself till, wanting this happiness of self-framed delight also, he fell into such despair as proved far worse than many hells unto him.

As he passed (yet in his pleasure) along a way which divided itself (near a delicate fountain) into three parts, he sat down on the side of that fountain, drinking first of the spring, and then taking out a paper wherein he had written some sad verses, he read them to himself. They were these:

> Drown me not you cruel tears
> Which in sorrow witness bears
>   Of my wailing
>   And love's failing
> Floods but cover, and retire
> Washing faces of desire
>   Whose fresh growing
>   Springs by flowing.

Meadows ever yet did love
Pleasant streams which by them move.
    But your falling
    Claims the calling
Of a torrent curstly fierce
Past wit's power to rehearse,
    Only crying
    Or my dying
May, instead of verse or prose
My disastrous end disclose.

When he had read them, and was putting them up again,
having first kissed them because they should go to his mistress,
he heard the wailing of a man and, looking up, saw a knight (as he
seemed to be) lie by the side of the fountain on the other part
from him, and besides heard him use these speeches:

'I wonder when time will permit me ease and sorrow give
conclusion to my days or to itself; if not wearied, yet for pity's
sake tormenting me, the most afflicted soul breathing. Miserable
Clarimatto, accursed above all men and abused beyond all men,
and more dishonoured than any creature—and by whom, but by
the most esteemed creature, a woman, and a fair woman, but the
cage of a foul mind and the keeper of a corrupt soul and a false
heart, else would she not nor could she have given herself (once
mine) to any other. She was mine by vow, by solemn profession
but now another's. Fickle sex, unsteady creatures! Worse I will
not call you, because indeed I love her, though abused by her and
shamed in her.'

Leandrus went to him and kindly offered his service if he
needed it. He, casting up his weeping eyes, in tears thanked him,
but said one man was enough to suffer in so slight a cause and so
undeserving a creature. He desired to know the matter. He
answered, he had loved a lady, she had done the like to him, or
made him think so. But having what she would, she had changed,
and not only so, but given herself to his enemy, being first
betrothed unto him, and in that time he was providing for the
marriage, married the other.

'And this is the cause of my torment. Hither am I come to
revenge myself of him, and in him of her, if she love him still.
They are in a strong castle of his where they merrily live, while I

am miserably vexed with tortures and dishonour, the worst of torments.' 'What was the original cause of his malice?'

'Truly Sir, this cruelty he useth but to me as belonging to my destiny. Neglected I have been of my friends for bearing this disgrace from mine enemy and the hater of all my country. The reason of his hatred to us proceeding from this. The King of Morea in his youth was a brave man at arms, and followed and finished many adventures. By chance at a great joust held in Achaea for joy of the birth of the King's son, called Leandrus, as after I heard he was, and proved a prince worthily deserving the joy then showed for receiving of him. This lord's father was likewise there and, encountering the King, was by him thrown to the ground, which disgrace he took so heavily as he would have revenged it with his sword, but that being forbidden (the end of those triumphs reaching no further than sport) discontented, and burning in rage, he went thence, watching when the King returned in his journey.

'In this very place he set upon him troops of his, coming all these several ways, and at once charging him, who only for his pleasure had sent his greatest company before him, following with two knights and their squires. But in this conflict the King got so much of the victory as he slew his enemy with his own hands, but could not keep himself from being taken prisoner and carried almost to the castle, whither if he had gone without doubt he had thence never returned.

'But the squires seeing his distress, and the death of the other two, their masters, ran everyone a several way till they got a good number of the train together, who with all speed and fury pursued them, overtaking them hard by the castle and taking their lord from them. Most being killed, some few got into the hold where, relating their unlucky adventure, the wife of the slain lord, and mother to this lord (having as great a spirit as any woman breathing) made a vow to be revenged of all the court of Morea, of the King and his posterity especially. And this she hath hitherto performed with great cruelty. Her son having been nursed in this hatred doth likewise continue it with more violence, as his spirit is so much greater, as commonly a man's is in respect of a woman's. And this is the cause why he hateth all the Moreans, of which country I am, born in Corinth. My heart truly scorning him for his other injury done me, am invited hither for these two reasons to be revenged on him.'

Leandrus thanked him for his discourse, but told him he had by it made him long to try if he could be made a prisoner also for so just a cause, or deliver those so unjustly enclosed. 'And the rather,' said he, 'to serve one so much injured as yourself, whose quarrel lay on me, and do you defend the honour of your King and country, she not being worth fighting for.' He answered that was true, yet his honour he esteemed worth clearing, and that called upon him.

While they were thus discoursing, the lord and the false lady came lovingly hand in hand together down one of the paths, she smiling in his eyes and wantonly courting him, seeking to give him occasion of mirth, but he went on like a man to whom ill was succeeding. He had some servants with him armed, and his own armour was likewise carried by him, if he should have any occasion suddenly to use it. He was of a clear and pleasing complexion, a person amiable and lovely, curled hair, fair eyes, and so judicial a countenance as might have made the worthiest woman like him, and so well he deserved as it was pity he fell into her hands, who undid both his mind and body, making him as wicked as herself, which was the worst of her sex.

He looked upon her with love, but his speech was sparing, either that naturally he had not store of words, or his inward heaviness at that time made him silent. When he came near the fountain, Clarimatto approached to him. 'My lord,' said he, 'I am sure you know the cause of my coming into these parts. If not, examine your heart, and that will tell you the injuries you have done me. Or if that be so impure, or partial, as it will not, for offending, be true to so false a master, behold this creature by you, your shame and mine, and in her forehead, the fair field of our disgrace, you shall see it written in spots of infamy and wrong.'

The lord knew his face, and with it the offence, therefore answered him thus: 'Sir,' said he, 'if on these conditions I acknowledge the understanding of your rage I should make myself guilty of what I am free from. To my knowledge, I never wronged any. If unwillingly, I made amends, and am ready so to do.' 'Can you give me my honour again, thrown to the ground by

you and your insatiable love?' cried he. 'You wrong us both,' said
he, 'and this shall be the ground of my revenge and answer to
you.' With that he armed himself, she crying to him not to
adventure his dear self against that stranger whom she knew full
well. She kneeled to him, held him by the legs, kissed them,
gazed on him, in terms called him dearest. All would not serve.
He encountered his enemy and truly was he justly made so by his
own ill deserving.

They fought like two, one having got and earnest to keep a
mistress, the other having lost and revengeful to gain his honour
and kill his rival and undoer in his love. At last, the true cause got
the upper hand, and the lord came to the lower side of victory,
which the servants perceiving, rushed all upon Clarimatto.
Leandrus, finding the wrong they offered and the other was like
to suffer, stepped in to his rescue. A fight was among these
performed fit, and only the prize of love fit to be the end of it.
Clarimatto nimble, valiant and having justice on his side, fought
accordingly, and so as the lord, having lost much blood out of two
wounds given him by his foe, nor had he escaped free but was
hurt in some places, the lord then gave back a little, his men
circling Clarimatto about like busy bees when angered, using
their best (or better to say, more malicious) means to hurt him,
who protected by a brave spirit, and undaunted courage, laid
about him without fear, but not without such hurt to them,
assisted bravely by Leandrus, as they began to flee.

Their master, seeing that, reviled them, vowing to hang
whoever saved himself by base flight, and kill those that fought
not better, though he by that means let the hateful enemy pass.
This urged them again to perplex them, but could not now
compass him, he having to prevent that danger, got the fountain
at his back, there defending himself, but alas much like a stag at
bay, that must for all his courage yield to the multitude and force
of many dogs. And so was he like to do (Leandrus having a new
supply set on him) for having received a wound in the thigh, he
bled so fast as almost his powers failed him, his eyes beginning
with faintness to dazzle, and his strength so fast to decrease as he
leaned himself against the fountain, holding his sword straight
out, meaning he that first seized him should also meet his own
end, and with this resolution stood the brave, revengeful lover,

his soul bidding his friends and all farewell, Leandrus being but in a little better case, whenas an unexpected good hap befell them by the coming of a knight in black armour who, seeing this cruel fight and unmanly combating of many against two, came happily and speedily to their succour, even when one had done his last for that time to defend himself, which the lord perceiving pressed in upon Clarimatto, although almost as weak as he with loss of blood (spite procuring that, lest he might else want his will in having his end some way) so as both valiant, both strong, were now without ability to show valour if not in dying with their swords in their hands and without strength, having no more than hatred at that time allowed to both in those weak limbs, which was no more than, instead of running one at the other, they reeled and fell one upon the other, in the fall the sword of Clarimatto finding a way into an unarmed part of his rival's body, which a blow at the first encounter had left open, but till then well guarded by the skill and courage of his master, whose sword missed him, who else with that had with him taken a grave, both agreeing (by disagreeing) to death.

The new come knight made a quick dispatch of the rest, some by death, some by yielding. Leandrus, though weak, going with much care to Clarimatto and who had in all the fight behaved himself so worthily, not fearing anything but continuance of disgrace, and freeing all in true worth and love to truth.

The business ended, the stranger and Leandrus took up the wounded Clarimatto and having, with untying his helm, given him some air, he came a little to himself, but so besmeared with blood as at first he was not known to the knight, whose helm was likewise off. But when discovered, 'O Clarimatto' said he, 'happy I am to help thee, but unhappy to find thee thus, my dearest friend. What destiny brought thee hither? What happiness in unhappiness met, to make me meet thee thus? Accursed yet now blessed occasion, if thou outlive this victory.'

'If I had conquered,' said he, 'death yet might have honoured me, but to live vanquished, rather wish I to die.' 'Thou hast, brave Clarimatto,' said he, 'overcome and slain thine enemy with thine own hands.' 'Then am I contented,' said he, 'though straight I die, and most that I shall yet end in your arms, whom of all men I most love. None but yourself could have had the destiny to help me who only was and is best beloved of me, and herein hath destiny blessed me.'

Then came the lady, who with as much contempt of them as sorrow for her lover looked upon them both, the one dead, the other dying. She said nothing, but kneeled down by her latter-loved friend and kissed him, rose again, and looked with infinite hate upon Clarimatto, and then taking a knife she held under her gown, stabbed herself, falling between them both.

The black knight went to the castle whither Clarimatto was carried and soon after died. The bodies of the others were buried in the place where the fight was. The keys were delivered to the black knight, who delivered many brave and valiant knights caught by treason and unfortunate spite, and all Greeks. Then was Leandrus brought into a rich chamber, and the black knight, who had taken possession of that castle for the King of Morea, bestowed the keeping of it on Clorimundus his esquire. With many tears and sighs Clarimatto was buried, who was extremely beloved of this black knight, which was Rosindy, with whom he had been bred and nursed.

This being done, and Leandrus past danger, though not for weakness able to remove, Rosindy left him in the custody of the new governor and other knights, who loved him so well as there was a question which they more affected: their delivering joy and happy enjoying, or his safety who had been the first cause to bring them the other. Herein their worths appeared, and in better hands Leandrus cannot be left till his ability call him again to service in other parts.

But now Rosindy must be a little accompanied who, taking on his journey, still resolved to perform the command of his mistress, which was to pass all Greece and accomplish such adventures as might make him worthy of her love, and yet not to discover the end of his travel or himself to any without extraordinary occasion. To observe this he put on those black arms, bearing no device in his shield, because his desire was only to be called the unknown knight. The cause why she had thus commanded him was that the more his honour was known, the more he might be feared when time might serve for him to deliver her from her prison and bondage wherein she lived, from whence as yet she could not be released.

Thus unknown he passed among his best friends, and meaning so to continue, he passed from this place to his father's court, there to see what adventure would happen to add to his fame, besides to know the certain time of the pretended* journey for Albania, but especially when they appointed to free Meriana, the chief end indeed of his journey.

So he came to the court and, sending one squire of his, who well knew all the parts of it, came to Pamphilia's chamber, who hearing who it was that desired to speak with her, she straight sent for him, from whom she learned that her dearly beloved brother was hard by but, resolving not to be known, had entreated her to come into the pleasant grove, there to confer with him, which she with much willingness and desire performed.

Now this squire was not known of many besides Pamphilia, nor any whit of Antissia, whose jealousy infinitely upon this increased, and the more means were sought to alter it, the greater did the heat grow, like a smith that puts water into his forge to make the fire more violently hot. The sweet (but sad) princess, not mistrusting this, went as appointed into the grove. The suspicious lady, whose heart now lay in her eyes to discover her, soon and secretly followed her, where she discerned (being in the evening) a knight so like in proportion to hers, or so had the power of doubt made him, as she even believed it to be himself. But when she saw their affectionate embracements then was her heart like to break, not being able to sustain but for fear of discovering as softly but less quietly, being confident her confidence in his love, which had before but flattered her to his own ends, and not for love, had been a bait to draw on her destruction. With this dolorous opinion she retired into her chamber, where she fell into the most grievous complaints that ever poor, afflicted, suspicious lady had endured.

The princess continuing in the wood, with all love and kindness the black knight beginning his discourse: 'My best and only dear sister, know that after my departure hence I passed through most part of Greece to seek adventures till I came into Macedon, where I found the King dead and an usurper strongly placed and settled in his room. The fame of Meriana's beauty I likewise encountered, but (alas) she was shut up in prison by that traitor and so close kept as none could gain a sight of her but with much danger. The villain (though her near kinsman) keeping her thus with intent to marry her if he can gain her consent; if not, so to hold her enclosed during her life.

'But by a blessed chance, as it may happen, I got the sight of her: truly so rare a creature as my commendations which cannot with all worldly eloquence, if with best art employed to set forth the nearest of her praise, come near to the lowest degree of her perfections—what then should I venture to commend her, whose delicacy may receive wrong by my unperfect tongue, not sufficient to extoll her. Let it suffice, my eyes saw that which made my heart her slave, and thus I compassed my joy.

'I lay in a house, the master whereof had served her father and mother, waiting in the Queen's chamber, and now hath liberty to see her when he will, or hath any business with her, as to bring her new apparel or such necessary things, he being master of the wardrobe. This man, with whom I often conferred concerning the princess, finding my longing to behold her and heartily wishing her liberty, brake with me about it. I hearkened to him and so we grew so far as we were fast enough to each other for betraying our purpose. Then he caused me to put on a suit of one of his servants, who was just of my stature, and taking new apparel to carry her, sent it by me, withal his excuse that he was not then able himself to come.

'I went with it, imagining myself more than a prince in being so happy to be his servant to such an end. When I came, the maids that attended her told her of my coming and of myself, being a stranger and never there before. She sent for me, demanding many things of me, which (as well as so much amazedness as I was in, beholding her, could permit me) I answered. She took delight to see me so moved, imagining it had been out of bashfulness, which she made sport with.

'Thus for some time it continued, till one day my master went himself, with whom the princess had much discourse concerning me, and among the rest she very much pressed to know what countryman I was and at last directly who I was, "For," said she, "either he is a very foolish fellow, or some other than he seems to be, which I rather do imagine. Therefore fail not, but tell me, by the respect and love you bear me, what you know of him."

'He, who loved me as his son, was loath to discover me directly, for fear of danger. Yet, considering that if at all, he were

much better tell who I was and the cause of my disguise, which
would purchase me more good than dissembling. Upon promise
of her being no way offended nor discovering it, which if
known would cost me my life, he told her all, and withal added
my extreme affection to her.

'When she at first heard it, she seemed offended, yet after said
she was contented to keep counsel, upon condition that I
presently went thence and never more attempted to come where
she was, in so disguised a habit to wrong her.

'When I received this message of death, I knew not whether I
should thank or blame my friend. In an agony I was afflicted to
the highest, perplexed in soul. In brief, I was but torment,* and
with it tormented myself. Words I had none, nor other action, but
going straight to my chamber, throwing myself on the bed, and
there I lay senseless, speechless and motionless for some hours,
as they told me, in which time he went to her again, telling her
how he had left me, and that she had killed a brave prince and
her hopeful kinsman, adding "How do you think, madam, ever to
be freed, when you use such as would venture for your freedom
with this scorn. Long enough will you remain here and be a
prisoner for any hope you can have of delivery by these fashions.
But it may be you affect this life, or mean to marry Clotorindus.
If so, I have done amiss, for which I beseech you pardon me and
him with whom I will likewise leave Macedon; for what shall I do
here, where worth is condemned and slavery esteemed?"

'When she heard the honest speech of my master, and saw the
likelihood of losing him, in whom only she could have assurance
of truth and trust, she told him his love and truth had gained his
pardon, for she would not have him goe by any means. For me,
she would have me sent to her, with whom she would speak
(since she could not believe such a prince would take such a
course for her love) and direct me what I should do if she found I
was the man he spake of.

'He, returning, told me of it and the time being come, I
resolved (though for it I did die) since she did mistrust me, to go
like myself; so as, putting on my own clothes and my sword by my
side, but my master's cloak upon them, I passed into the garden
and so into a gallery, the honest man directing me there to tarry
till she came unto me. When she appeared, it was like a blazing
star foretelling my lost life and liberty if she did still persevere in

her cruelty. But when she spake my heart was so possessed as I had not one word to answer her, only throwing off my disguise, kneeling down and gazing on her, was the manner of my suing to her.

'She came then nearer and, taking me up, she said "My lord (for so my servant tells me I may call you) much do I wonder why disguised till this time you have continued. If for love, your judgement much erred to think I could affect so low as a servant; if for other ends, myself would never do myself the wrong to think of any unnoble course, and if the first, why did you not seek to discover it?"

' "Divine lady," said I, "far be it from me to have a thought to injure that virtue which I admiringly love and, loving, honour. The reason why I remained disguised and unknown was the happiness I conceived in seeing you, and the fear I had to lose that happiness, no way so much flattering myself as to have a hope to attain to that whereto my best thoughts ambitiously did flee. Fear kept me silent; love made me fear. Now you have it, dispose of me mercifully, else soon after this discovery be pleased to hear of my sad end."

'She, it seemed, had pity, but not so much as to express it, wherefore she only answered thus. "To assure me of your love, and you of pity, this is the course you must take: instantly leave this place, nor return unto it until such time as your fame by your noble deeds may prove such as shall make you worthy of my love. Then return, release me with your own hands, make me perfectly know you are prince Rosindy, and I will give myself unto you."

'I, with all joy, promised those conditions should be performed. She smiled and said a lover would promise anything. "I will die," said I, "but accomplish these." "Then will I be yours," said she. That gave me a full heaven of joy. So, kneeling down again and taking her hand, I kissed it and on it sealed my vow. "But one thing more," said she, "I would have you do. Let all these deeds be done while you still keep your name of The Unknown, and so be called till you return, unless some great occasion happen to reveal yourself."

'I promised likewise, and so by that name of Unknown I have passed these ten months, never discovering myself to any, but lately to Leandrus and a brave gentleman'—then told he her the whole adventure—'and now unto yourself. With promise of her love, my vow anew solemnly made, I took my leave, my heart filled with sorrow to part, and my soul ready to leave this earthly cage, grieving so much to leave my better self. She in like sort was sorry and prettily expressed it, yet would not let too much be seen, lest it might stay me. So we parted, I happy and sorry, she sorry and most happy in her own noble virtues. But now methinks the time is so long as desire makes me haste homewards, accounting that my home where my soul remains. But to this place I came first of purpose to hear what resolution was taken for the conquest of Albania, but most for the relief of Macedon. To obey my lady's command I came secretly, and so will remain unknown but to you, my dearest sister. Now tell me what you hear, and keep my knowledge to yourself.'

Pamphilia with infinite joy hearing this story, and the brave fortune like to befall her dear brother, took him affectionately by the hand, using these words: 'Most worthy to be held dearest brother, the happiness is much greater which I conceive than able to express, seeing the likelihood of your worthily-merited fortune. What I know, I were a poor, weak woman if I would conceal from you, or reveal of you. Therefore, know the intent was to conquer Albania first, but whether the absence of Steriamus will hinder it or no, I yet know not, but this I believe: that such means may be wrought as to prefer Macedon before the other, and since your content and fortunes lie that way, if you will trust me, I will order it so as that shall be first.'

'Bind me more if you can, sweet sister, and to make me happy, enjoy the authority over me and mine,' said he. Then did she entreat him that he would for a while tarry there, which he granted, till such time as they could order their affairs according to their own minds. While this content lasted to Pamphilia, as much grief increased to Antissia, which grief at last grew to rage, and leaving sorrow, fell to spite, vowing to revenge and no more complain. This thought did so far possess her as her count-enance bewrayed her heart, shunning the sight of Pamphilia, who with love and respect did covet hers.

This change made the sweet princess infinitely admire what the reason should be that now moved her, she seeming to have remained satisfied. But those who know that languishing pain, also know that no perfect satisfaction can be unless the humour itself with satisfaction do quite leave the possessed. For as long as one spark lives, though never so little, it is able with the least occasion or sign of occasion to make a great fire, and so did it now prove.

Pamphilia, desirous to have no unkindness between them, sought all ways to please her. This was as ill a course as if of scorn she had done it, or in pity (having deceived her) would show the most despised and contemptible friendship, which is pity. Madness grew so upon this as she burst out into strange passions, especially one day whenas ambassadors came from the young King of Rumania to give thanks to the King of Morea for his royal courtesy to his aunt, who by the Knight of Love he understood to be in his court, giving withal such infinite praises of him, to the unspeakable joy of the old King and all the court, knowing him to be Amphilanthus, as mirth liberally showed herself in all faces but Antissia's, the ambassador having delivered letters to her, both from Amphilanthus and the King, wherein she was entreated to come into Rumania to him, and by her servant advised not to refuse the King's demand, but to go with the ambassador, which was the new Duke Lysandrinus, whither in short time himself would also come.

But the more sweet and kind language he used in his letter, the greater was her conceit it was used to flatter her, compliment never being used in the time of her happiness, especially when she came to the point of going, she directly concluded that he had laid that trick upon her to be rid of her sight and the freelier to enjoy his new mistress, and this she angerly told Pamphilia, whispering in her ear, withal adding that he might as well have told her thus much himself, considering she saw him. 'And you, brave lady,' said she, 'last night in the garden wood . . . '

Pamphilia, between fear to have her brother discovered by her malice and disdain so unjustly to be accused, her blood, scorning to lie still when it was wronged, boldly showed itself in her face with threatening anger. But this moved a contrary effect than fear, increasing base jealousy instead of noble thoughts, and assurance of that she falsely conceived, proving this to be true: that mistrust, which is most times built upon falsehood, gains greatest assurance from the falsest grounds.

She, seeing her blush (as she called it), by that judging
guiltiness and that working spite, went away laden with scorn and
her own suspicion, which now wrought to fury. Into her chamber
she went where, throwing herself upon her bed, careless of ease
or handsomeness, she brake into these speeches. 'Accursed day
that first knew Antissia breathing, why was not the air pestilent,
the milk poison, the arms that held me serpents, and the breasts
that gave me suck venom, and all these changed from their
proper goodness to have wrought my destruction? Miserable fate
that brought me to be lost and found by him who now ruins me.
Treacherous love, but more treacherous lover, I might (wretch
that I was) have taken heed by others, and not have run into the
same danger myself. Now I am well requited and paid in the
same kind for glorying at them, and in my gain, while they wailed
under the weight of his forsaking them. Now must I tread with
them in the path of that misery. Fond creatures that joy in this,
beware! This must at last be your own; your turn 'twill be
(though last) to lead the dance.

'False creature, was it not enough to deceive me of my liberty
and honour, but to overthrow me utterly, to destroy my quiet
content, which in the smart of your love I enjoyed? Cursed be the
time I admired your sweetness and familiar kindness, your loving
care and tender respect, which made my heart too soft, yielding
to the power of your allurings. Is it come to this? Was all your
fondness for this purpose? Did you only strive to win, to cast away
at pleasure? Were all your desired meetings for this, to make me
the more miserably end with neglective forsakenness? If any man
could be true, I assured myself it must be you. O that I had
enough considered there was doubt justly made of man's truth in
love, then had I more safely defended myself from this disaster.

'Amphilanthus, thou wert noble, just, free; how is this change?
Can nobleness be where deceit rules? Can justice be where
cosinage governs? Can freedom be where falsehood lives? Those
were, but these are now in thee. Was thy sadness for this new
wound? Alas, I assured myself it was for parting from me that so
much change did grow. Could not I (blind fool that I was) have
marked his often frequenting Pamphilia's chamber; his private
discourse with her; his seeking opportunity to be in her presence;
his stolen looks; his fearful but amorous touching her hand; his

kissing his own hand, rather coming from hers than going to hers, loving it more for having touched that beloved hand than for being his? Oft would he do this, and look on me. Then did I believe all was meant to me which he did to her, and wished it had been I; his eyes betrayed me, my belief bewitched me, and his falsehood must kill me.

'Churlish affection, why torture you me alone? Make him likewise smart, make her likewise vex. But I need not curse her, since (poor lady) she is but entering into her following perplexity. Alas Pamphilia, I pity thee, and indeed love thee no whit less than before. I cannot nor may not blame thee for loving him, since none can resist his conquering force in love, nor for seeking him. For whose soul would not covet him? But I blame him for spoiling poor hearts to his glorious triumph. Unnatural man, that preys on his own kind, nourishing his life with the ruin of simple, innocent lovers: a cruel food, but crueller devourer of them—which hath wrought this hardness in me: as from hence to love thee but till I can be revenged of thee, and such a revenge will I have as thy hard heart shall melt for it, if any goodness be left in it, for over the world will I seek thee (my journey to Rumania once ended) to be thus quit with thee, that thy false eyes and flattering tongue shall be no longer able to deceive or betray thyself or others, but behold the true end of me, who gain my death by thy falsehood, and in thy presence will I conclude my life with my love to thee.

'I wondered, yet never had wit to doubt, why so much ceremony lately came from you. Ceremony indeed, being a shadow, not substance, of true love. Change wrought it, and change put on the habit of that which once was love, for once I know you loved me and was fond of me. Fond; aye, fondness it may most properly be called, for love is eternal, but this changeable. Many we see fond of sports, of horses, of dogs, and so was it my dogged fortune to have you fond of me. But the immortal part, the soul, is not fond but loving, which love for ever lives; and this love wanted I, only enjoying his fond, and fondly proved, desires, which are removed and have left nothing behind but the sad remembrance of my once great and highest-esteemed blessing. Now remain I, thrown down into the darkness of despair and loss by loss of his affection.'

Thus discoursing, tossing upon her bed, she remained; fed not nor slept all that night. The next morning early going to the garden woods whither she sooner came than Pamphilia where, being a while and sitting under the same ash wherein the other affectionate afflicted princess had written the sonnet, she was invited, either by her own passion or the imitation of that excellent lady, to put some of her thoughts in some kind of measure, so as she, perplexed with love, jealousy and loss as she believed, made this sonnet, looking upon the sun, which was then of a good height.

> The sun hath no long journey now to go
> While I a progress have in my desires
> Disasters dead-low-water-like do show
> The sand that overlooked my hoped-for hires.
>
> Thus I remain like one that's laid in briars,
> Where turning brings new pain and certain woe,
> Like one once-burned bids me avoid the fires,
> But love (true fire) will not let me be slow.
>
> Obedience, fear and love do all conspire
> A worthless conquest gained to ruin me,
> Who did but feel the height of blessed desire,
> When danger, doubt and loss I straight did see.
> > Restless I live, consulting what to do,
> > And more I study, more I still undo.

'Undo,' cried she, 'alas I am undone, ruined, destroyed, all spoiled, by being forsaken—restless affliction which proceeds from forsaking. Yet would I be beholding to this enemy of mine if forsaking in my torments would possess me, so I might remain forsaken by them. But that must not be, I must only know pleasure, happiness and the chief of happinesses, love, from my beloved forsake me,* but pain, torture and shame will still abide and dwell with me.'

Then went she a little further towards the river, where by the bank under the willow lay the supposed Amphilanthus, the cause of all this business. His helm was off, by reason of the heat, and secureness from being discovered, not indeed being possible for any except Antissia, who had by Pamphilia's leave a key to those walks to come within them of that side of the river. She had gone

to him rashly had not his voice stayed her, whereat she started at
first, and then trembled with fear and joy, thinking by that
likewise it had been her love. Jealousy had so transformed her as
it was impossible for her to hear or see or know anything but
Amphilanthus and her sorrow for him, when at another time she
would have laughed at herself for making such unlikeliness vex
her. He spake but low, as it were whispering to himself these
words.

'O my dear, when shall I (wretch) again enjoy thy sight, more
dear, more bright to me than brightest day or my own life? Most
sweet commandress of my only bliss, when, oh when shall I again
be blessed? Canst thou leave me, thy loyal servant, here or
anywhere but with thy best-deserving self? Shall I lie here in
secret complaining, when thyself mayest succour me? Quickly, alas,
relieve me, never more need, never more love sought it.'

These words gave her full assurance 'twas he, and jealousy
told her they were spoken to Pamphilia. Rage now outgoing
judgement, she flew to him. 'Ungrateful man, or rather monster
of thy sex,' said she, 'behold before thee thy shame in my
dishonour, wrought by my love and thy change.' Rosindy was
amazed and feared betraying, wondering his sister was so
careless of him; she, seeing her rash and unpardonable fault in
having thus wronged her love, stood in such a depth of
amazedness and torment (all affections working at once their own
ways in her) as she was a mere chaos, where unframed and
unordered troubles had tumbled themselves together without
light of judgement to come out of them.

The black knight beheld her, wondering more at her manner
and former speech than now heeding his being known, admiring
at her passion and not understanding her words, to his thinking
never having seen her, and therefore not guilty of her blaming
him. But now was she a little come to herself, but so as fear and
modesty caused so much bashfulness as scarce she could bring
forth what she desired. But with eyes cast down and a blushing
face, she with much ado said thus.

'Sir, I beseech you as a lover (for so I perceive you are) hide
the imperfections of one of that number, myself unfortunately
having fallen into the worst extremity, which is jealousy, and

worse, if may be worse, without cause as now I perceive, but falsehood, which hath caused it. I mistook you and more have mistaken myself, or indeed my better self. Conceal, I beseech, in this and if I may serve you in anything for requital, command and I will obey you.'

'Fair lady,' said he, 'I cannot but exceedingly pity your estate, and wish the happiest amendment to it. My humblest suit unto you shall be only this: that you will conceal my being here, not esteeming me so worthy as once (after your going hence) to remember you saw me, till such time as it may fortune I may do you service, or that I come to acknowledge this favour from you, and I shall in the like obey you.'

As she was answering and promising that, Pamphilia came, but with infinite discontent against Antissia for being there, whenas she, without dissembling, but with all unfeigned love and shame, fell at her feet, beseeching her pardon, crying out that never lived there a more unblessed creature than herself, who had now lived to wrong the two perfect mirrors of their sexes with the base (and most worthy of contempt) humour of suspicion.

Pamphilia took her up and quickly was the peace made, the one seeking to give all satisfaction, the other willing to receive any rather than for that business to make more stirring. Then, with promise of her secret holding the knight's being there, not so much as desiring to know his name, lest that might make suspicion she desired to know, to discover. Again she departed contented, and as happy as before she had been disquieted, only now grieved that she had wronged Amphilanthus.

She gone, the dear brother and sister sat down together, Pamphilia speaking thus: 'My long stay,' said she, 'might have marred your promise and my desired care of keeping you secret, had not this good chance of acknowledgement wrought the contrary. But howsoever, it had brought little harm to you, since long, I fear, you will not here abide after you understand the news I bring, which is this. My father was this morning in council, where it was set down that Macedon is fittest to be first relieved, and the rather because it is more easy to gain the kingdom out of one usurper's hand than out of many. My mother hath been infinite earnest, and as earnest as if she knew your mind, her reason being that the young Queen is her niece, as you know, and Macedon once quieted, Albania will be the sooner won.

'Selarinus, the younger brother, likewise hath desired the business of Albania may be laid aside till Steriamus be heard of, not willing to be thought hasty in winning honour and love in his own country in the absence of his brother—and in truth I must say he doth like himself in it, and that is like one of the finest princes I know, for so he is and the like will you say when you once know him, and know him you must, his ambition (as he terms it) being to gain the honour of your friendship and to be your companion in your travels. I have promised him to be the means for him, and believe me brother, you will thank me for it, since a sweeter disposition matched with as noble a mind and brave a courage you never (I believe) encountered.'

Rosindy was so joyed with this discourse as he knew not almost what this last part of her speech was. Wringing her hand, 'O,' said he, 'the blessed messenger of eternal happiness! But what forces shall go to redeem her?' 'The number from hence,' said she, 'are fifty thousand; from Achaea twenty; from Rumania twenty. The Achaeans are to be demanded by ambassadors now appointed, that army to be led by Leandrus; the Rumanians by Lysandrinus, the same duke who is here now with us and who certainly assures my father that number will not be refused by his master, but rather more forces added to them.

'Now doth my father wish for you to lead his men, desiring you should have the honour of this brave attempt; by strong working of divine knowledge, I think, understanding your mind. Choose now whether you will break promise or no to your mistress; yet do I not see but the liberty she gave you will permit you to do this.'

'No,' said he, 'dear Pamphilia, counsel me not to be unjust and in the greatest to mine own vow and that vow to my love. But thus you may help me: assure my father that you know where to find me, and let him reserve the honour of the charge for me, and you bring me to receive it, in which time I will post to Macedon and get leave to return and take the charge.'

This they agreed upon, so being somewhat late, she left her brother there, promising to come again to him after dinner, and then to let him know the King's answer, and so take leave of each other. She returned, whenas she found the King and the whole court assembled to see and hear a strange adventure.

An aged man of grave and majestic countenance, hair white as snow and beard down to his girdle, bound in strong chains of iron; a young man likewise enchained with him, four squires leading them, the old man with tears and pitiful groans telling his story thus. 'Most famous King, behold before you the distressed King of Negroponte, brought into this misery by mine own folly, so much doting on a daughter of mine as I suffered myself to fall into the sin of forgetfulness to this my son, too worthy, I confess, for me, deserving a far better title than my son, unless I had been a more natural father. For such was my affection to that ungrateful child of mine as I disinherited my son, called Dolorindus, whose virtues appear by the black sins of his sister, who I even now grieve to name. But why should my sorrow be increased with the sight of your noble compassions; or, better to say, why should so worthless a creature move sorrow in such royal minds? To avoid which, I will as briefly as my miserable relation will give me leave, discourse my tragic story to you.

'After I had unnaturally disinherited Dolorindus here present, I gave the kingdom (which came by my wife, and she dead) to Ramilletta, my ungracious daughter, who requited me as vipers do their dam, for no sooner had she the possession but she fell into such ill-government and indeed beastly living, as the report wounded my honour and stained my blood. I, ashamed, grieved at it, told her of it, persuaded her to leave it, telling her how cruel a blow it was to my soul to see her shame. She made me no answer, but with her eyes cast down, left the room where I was. I thought confession and repentance had caused this countenance, but alas I was deceived, for it was rage, and scorn procured it, as soon I found. For instantly came in a number of her servants, who took me and cast me into a dark, terrible prison, where they kept me one whole year. Then came Dolorindus, and strove with all his wit and power to release me, but finding it could not be wrought by other means than good nature, desiring that as he had life from me, he might have death also with me.

'She, taking some pity of him, or rather not willing to shed his blood herself (though she cared not who did), told him that if he

could overcome two knights which she would appoint to
encounter him, he should have his own and my liberty, else to be
at her dispose. This he agreed unto, glad that he had a shadow of
hope (for no more it proved) for my release, undertaken by him.

'The day was appointed, whenas I was brought into a little
place made of purpose for seeing the combat, she and her
servants hoping this would be the last day of my trouble to them,
when I should see Dolorindus slain and her cruelty increase,
both which must (as they did trust) end my life with breaking of
my heart. And so indeed it nearly had, and would assuredly had
my son been killed, whose love to me did make my fault so foul
before me, as affection proved curster* than affliction.

'But to the matter. So bravely did my Dolorindus behave
himself for our deliveries as although the other were such as still,
if a challenge were made, they were chosen; if any valiant man
had been named they had been instantly commended with him.
Nay, such confidence all had of their strength as if the kingdom
had been in danger to be lost, and only to be saved by combat,
these would have been set for the defenders, yet were these two
overcome by Dolorindus, and in our presence had their lives
ended by his brave arm, who yet had suffered his blood to
accompany their deaths, trickling down as fast as the tears from a
mother's eyes for the loss of her dearest son. So much indeed he
lost as he was for faintness forced to be carried away to
chirurgeons* (I thought) and so to safety.

'In some kind this was true, but not to liberty, for she seeing
the honour he had got, and fearing the love of the people would
fall upon him, seeing his worth, she kindly in show brought him
into a rich chamber and had his wounds dressed, taking infinite
care of him. But as soon as he recovered, he was for safety shut
into a strong tower, where he remained till within these few
months, myself carried back again into my prison, where I was
vexed with the continual discourse of her bravery, of Dolorindus'
death, and of her marriage with an undeserving man, who in my
life of government I ever hated, no worth being at all in him that
he should deserve mention, but that he had no worth in him
meriting mention: never so detestable a villain breathing.

'This creature she fell in love withal and lived withal, but now I
think is partly weary of, because she doth expose him to fight for

her honour, being before so fond of him as she was afraid the
wind should almost blow upon him. But him she hath brought,
and three more, his brothers, and if these four can be overcome
by any knights in this court, we shall be set at liberty, else remain
prisoners, which we have consented unto. Now Sir, if you please
to give us such knights, they shall enter.'

The King answered that such unnaturalness deserved a far
sharper punishment, and that there was no sense a combat
should end so foul a business. He replied that he was contented,
and therefore desired but the knights, and for the matter, it was
already determined. Then stepped Selarinus forth, desiring to be
one. Pamphilia likewise entreated she might have the favour to
bring another, who she would undertake for, meaning the prince
of Corinth. The prince of Elis would not be denied to be the
third, and Lysandrinus humbly besought in such a business he
might be the fourth.

This was agreed upon, so Pamphilia went to the wood and
there discoursing the business to her brother, he instantly
resolved to be one, and whether she would or no came with her,
his beaver close for fear of discovery, doubting nothing else but
his face to betray him, for so much was he grown in height and
bigness as he could not be taken for Rosindy.

The four defendants being there met, the rest entered,
Ramilletta going in the midst of the four challengers, two before
her, two behind her, but so far asunder as they made from corner
to corner the fashion of a Saltier cross.* So terrible were these to
behold as few could endure to look upon them; only her servant
was a little milder in his countenance and somewhat less than the
others. Their hair was of a brown red colour, and bristled; their
eyes of answerable bigness to their bodies, but furiously sparkling
fire.

When Pamphilia saw these monsters, she would as willingly
have had her brother thence as he ambitiously wished to have the
combat begin. Then followed fifty knights without swords, but
their beavers close, being such as, the old King told the court,
were taken seeking to deliver them from bondage, and who were
brought along with them for witness of their valour and power.

These huge men, who were called the terrible and unconquered brethren, nor the lady, made any reverence, but gazed

upon the company and ladies who there stood to behold them.
Then were they carried to the lists, the old man again speaking.
'Sir, these are the challengers. May it please you that the
defendants likewise go.' The King was sorry for the knights, and
in his mind more troubled than long time before he had been,
once being of the mind to have hindered it. But considering his
honour was engaged in that, he went on, commanding his Great
Marshall nevertheless to have some other number of knights
ready armed upon any occasion.

This was done, and so being all in the lists, the judges placed
and the trumpets sounding, Ramilletta was brought in her chariot
of pale green velvet made of an unusual fashion, and those fifty
knights standing round about her, the old man and his son being
in a seat behind her in the same chariot.

The jousts beginning, the Unknown Knight encountered the
greatest of the four; Selarinus the next in bigness and fierceness,
almost his equal; Lisandrinus the third; and the prince of Elis the
fourth. The first encounter was strong and terrible, for the
mourning knight was struck flat upon his back and his
adversary's horse was, with the blow, struck dead, his master by
that means falling to the ground, Selarinus and his enemy both
unwillingly saluting the earth with their heads. The rest had
likewise that fortune. Then bravely began the fight with the
swords which continued one whole hour, no advantage being
seen, till the prince of Elis, with extreme loss of blood and a
wound in his leg, fell to the earth. At that instant had the
Unknown Knight given his enemy a wound in the thigh, which
was so great, and besides given cross, as he could not stand, but
like a huge mast of a ship with the storm of his blow laid his
greatness along. The other, going to strike off the prince of Elis's
head, was by the Black Knight hindered, striking off that arm
which was depriving the prince of his life.

At this he cried out, giving the watchword which was among
them, so as the other, who had now even wearied their foes, left
them, running to the place where the princess sat, catching
Pamphilia in their arms and straight carrying her into the chariot.
The other fifty at the instant got swords for the accomplishing of
their wills, privately hid in the chariot, a place being made under
the seat for them, the hilts only out, which were taken to be but

artificially made to seem swords and placed for ornaments round about the body of the chariot, being all painted about and carved with trophies and such like devices.

Then did the old man, as soon as they had their prey, turn chariotman, driving the horses with great swiftness. The King cried for help, but alas in vain, as it seemed, tearing his hair for this oversight. But soon was this business ended, for Selarinus, marking their treason, leaped up upon his horse again, pursuing them and, overtaking them, killed the former horse. The rest, running, fell over him, so as the chariot was stayed. Then came two strange knights who by chance were going to the court, to whom the traitor cried for help, saying that that knight by force would take his lady from him, beseeching even with tears to have their help. 'For,' said he, 'here is the famous princess Pamphilia, whom this villain would take from me and abuse.'

With that, the strange knights began to prepare, but Selarinus told them they were best take heed. 'For,' said he, 'this is all false that he reports, and he hath stolen by treason this lady from the court where there is yet a cruel fight, I having left them to rescue this princess.'

One of them straight knew his voice, so as drawing their swords on his side, as before they were ready to do it against him, they drew to the chariot, demanding of the princess if this were true. She answered 'Yes, and therefore,' said she, 'assist this worthy prince.' Then they took the old man and youth, and as before they were in counterfeit chains, they made them sure in true ones, tying them with the false Ramilletta to the hind end of the chariot, so putting their squires to lead the horses.

With this brave princess they returned, and most fortunately for the other distressed knights at the court, who were so tired with the terrible brothers and fifty other as they were almost at their last, the poor unarmed courtiers lying as thick slain if they had strewed the place with their bravery instead of flowers. The Marshall came with his troop, but so little could he avail as only taking the King and carrying him away to safety with the Queen and such as did run with them, left the two brave combatants to defend themselves, who did so bravely as they had slain two of the brothers outright, Rosindy having killed one, wounded the other in the thigh, and now was fighting with him whom

Selarinus had first encountered, but very weak with weariness and loss of blood.

The fierce man pressed sorely on him when Selarinus again came and finished his begun work, giving him a blow on the head which made him stagger and, seconding it, laid him on the earth. Then leapt he from his horse, lifting the black knight up in his stead, and so strake he off the head of that traitor. Now was there but one left, and he wounded, yet the number of knights were little decreased, so as if the two new knights had not come, they would have been in a far worse case—who so bravely behaved themselves as soon the victory was clearly theirs, Rosindy bestirring himself in such manner as whoever had seen him and told the Queen his mistress of it, that alone, without any other conquest, had been enough to win her.

By this all was quiet. Then took they some of those knights who had yielded and demanded mercy, the wounded brother and the traitorous old man, Ramilletta and the youth, going with this troop into the palace. The body likewise of the prince of Elis they carried with them, which yet seemed but his body, no breath stirring nor any show of life appearing, till being laid in his bed and carefully looked unto, his old father being there grieved in heart, yet the better contented, since if he died it would be to his honour for ever to end his days in so noble an adventure.

Life again possessed him, but weakly expressing itself for many days, yet did he recover. When this company came into the hall, straight came the King unto them, running to Pamphilia and weeping with joy to see her free again, so as in a pretty space he could not speak unto her; but when: 'O my dear heart,' said he, 'what treason was there here against me, to deprive me of thy sight.' She comforting him, and letting some tears fall, as dutifully shed to wait on him, besought him, since she found that blessedness as his so great affection to her, that he would thank those who restored her to him. Then taking them all one after another in his arms, he desired to know the black knight.

Pamphilia then answered. 'Sir,' said she, 'this knight is so engaged by a vow as he can hardly let his name be known, yet since this liberty was given, that upon extraordinary occasion he might reveal himself, I will undertake the discovering, and fault (if fault there be in this) upon me.' And then turning to him, 'Brave brother,' said she, 'comfort our father's age with the happiness of the sight of such an incomparable son.' With that, Rosindy, pulling off his helm, kneeled down. But when the King beheld him, he fell upon his neck, with such affection kissing him as if all his love were at that instant in him, and joined together to express it to him.

Then was command given for a rich chamber for him, whither he was led, Selarinus accompanying him, being less hurt than he, yet had he not scaped free from remembrance of that devilish creature. All now at peace, no discourse was but of the valour of the defendants, but especially the honour of Rosindy was blazed abroad, having with his own hand killed one of the brothers, wounded another, and wearied the third to death, slain many of the knights, and by his example done so much as encouraged the weak bodies of the rest, whose hearts never failed.

Then Selarinus was commended exceedingly, and indeed with great cause, for his valour was equal with most, his care that day exceeding others, Pamphilia being saved from imprisonment by him. Lysandrinus with all honour respected, who made manifest proof of his valour and affection to the court. The prince of Elis did so well as made all assured of his being a brave knight, this the first of his adventures having so manfully performed, for had not an unlucky blow in the leg hindered him from standing, he had also slain his foe. The two last knights were of the court, one son to the Marshall, called Lizarino and the other Tolymandro, prince of Corinth. The traitors were all carried to a strong tower, where they remained till the knights were well again recovered, which in short time was, to the great joy and comfort of everyone.

Now did Pamphilia think it fit to acquaint the King with her brother's business, wherefore first asking leave of Rosindy, she did. The King, being infinite glad of this news, went straight unto his lodging, whom he found alone but for Selarinus, who never left him, as strict and firm an affection growing between them as ever lived in two men's hearts one unto another. Then did the King impart unto him what Pamphilia had told him, which was confirmed by Rosindy, the match liked and commended by the King. The resolution was as Pamphilia before had told him, and he chosen General of the Morean forces, Selarinus his lieutenant, and thus with preparing for these wars and everyone contented (except the loving ladies) love must again be a little discoursed of.

Parselius who, making haste after Amphilanthus, took his way through Morea, but after not as he was directed by the squires, but along Achaea, crossing the gulf of Lepanto, which course might make him miss the King, if he came short of the combat, they resolving to take their course back again by sea to Morea, as well to try adventures in the islands as to hasten the forces, that being a shorter way. But here did Parselius, as destined for him (for till now he still obeyed the other) meet a greater force than he imagined, being in a forest benighted and having none with him except his cousin's squire and his own.

In that solitary place they laid them down for that night, the next day going on in that desert till they came to a strong and brave castle, situated in a little plain, a great moat about it and over it a drawbridge, which at that time was down, and some servants upon it looking upon the water, which was broad and finely running. When the prince came near the place, they turned their eyes to him, who courteously saluted them and demanded whose castle that was. They replied it was the King's, and that there lived within it his fair daughter Dalinea.

'Is she,' said the prince, 'to be seen? If so, I pray let her know that here is a knight desires to kiss her hand, well known to her brother and who had the honour to be his companion.' One of the servants instantly ran in, others went to take their horses, while Parselius lighted and put off his helm, wiping his face with his delicate white and slender hand, rubbing his hair which, delicately and naturally curling, made rings every one of which were able to wed a heart to itself.

By that time the messenger returned, leading him first into a stately hall, then up a fair pair of stone stairs carved curiously in images of the gods and other rare workmanship. At the top they came into a brave room richly hanged with hangings of needlework, all in silk and gold, the story being of Paris his love and rape of Helen. Out of that they passed into another room, not so big but far richer, the furniture being every way as sumptuous, if not bettering it. But what made it indeed excel was that here was Dalinea sitting under a cloth of estate of carnation* velvet, curiously and richly set with stones, all over being embroidered with pearl of silver and gold, the gold made in suns, the silver in stars; diamonds, rubies and other stones plentifully and cunningly compassing them about and placed as if for the sky where they shined. But she, standing, appeared so much brighter, as if all that had been but to set forth her light, so far excelling them as the day, wherein the sun doth show most glorious, doth the drowsiest day.

Her ladies who attended her were a little distant from her in a fair compass window, where also stood a chair wherein it seemed she had been sitting till the news came of his arrival. In that chair lay a book. The ladies were all at work, so as it showed, she read while they wrought. All this Parselius beheld, but most the princess, who he so much admired as admiration wrought so far as to permit him to think that she equalled Urania. This was a sudden step from so entire a love as but now he vowed to his shepherdess, being an heresy, as he protested, for any man to think there lived a creature like his love. But into this he is now fallen, and will lead the faction against her. Uncertain tyrant love, that never brings thy favourites to the top of affection but turns again to a new choice! Who would have thought any but Urania's beauty could have invited Parselius to love? Or who could have thought any might have withdrawn it till this sight, which so much moved as he loves Urania but for being somewhat like to Dalinea, but her, for her own sake.

He was not so struck with wonder when he first saw Urania (though with it he lost his liberty) as he was now wounded to death, losing life if no compassion succeeded. This first sight won him and lost his former bondage; yet was he freed but to take a new bond upon him. He went towards her, who with a majestic yet gracious fashion met him, who saluted her thus.

'My fate leading me (I hope for my greatest happiness, I'm sure yet for my best content, bringing me thus to behold your excellencies) from far places unlooking for pleasures, am brought to the height of them, most incomparable lady, in coming thus into your presence whereto I was emboldened by the love I bare your brother, by the courtesies of your servants, the honour yourself granted me in licensing my approach, but most by my own soul, which told me I must not pass without paying the tribute of my best service to the princess of all women, for how would my conscience accuse me in such a neglect. How would

my heart blame me for such an omission. But how might brave
Leandrus chide Parselius if he yielded not himself at the feet of
his worthily admired sister.'

Dalinea, hearing him call himself Parselius, with a sweet and
pleasing blush desired pardon that she had so far forgot herself
as not to do him sufficient reverence. 'But yet a little blame
yourself, great prince,' said she, 'who unknown and undiscover-
ing yourself to any, you come among us. Pardon this rudeness
and be pleased to accept my submission for it, to deserve which
favour I will strive in giving you the best welcome to deserve it.'

He took her hand and kissed it, which although she could in
respect have hindered, yet so delicate was his hand as she was
content to let him hold and kiss hers. Then she brought him
under the State,* where two chairs being set, they passed away
some time discoursing of adventures and of the sweet content the
companion princes enjoyed in their youths, she infinitely
delighting in those stories, especially when they touched on her
brother, whom entirely she loved.

Parselius, finding which way her affection led her, made his
attend her and all his stories either beginning or ending with the
praise of Leandrus. Thus one pleased and the other contented
that it was in him to content her, they passed some days, love
creeping into the heart of Dalinea as subtly as if he meant to
surprise and not by open force take her. Discourse procured
conversation; sweet conversation, liking of itself; that liking,
desire to continue it; that desire, loving it; and that, the man that
afforded it. And thus far come, I should wrong her if I should not
say she yielded in her heart to love his person, whose discourse
had made his way by taking first her ears prisoners. Now her eyes
likewise execute their office, bring his excellent shape, his
beauty, his absolute brave fashion. Then her understanding
besets her, tells her how excellent his wit is, how great his valour,
how matchless his worth, how great his descent and royal
possessions.

All these, alas, joined and made a curious and crafty work to
compass that which love himself without half, or any in
comparison of these assistants, could have made his subject. But
as the rarest jewel is not to be had but at the highest rate, so her

peerless perfections must have all this business to gain her. But now she is won and he almost lost, not daring to think so, or venturing to win it. He would with his eyes tell her his heart, with kissing her delicate hand with a more than usual affection let her feel his soul was hers. She found it, and understood what he would have her understand. Nay, she would answer his looks with as amorous ones of her part, as straightly and lovingly would she hold his hand, but knowing modesty forbid, she would sigh and in her soul wish that he would once speak.

But bashfulness withheld him, and woman-modesty kept her silent, till one afternoon, walking into a most curious and dainty garden, where all manner of sweets were ready in their kind to entertain them—flowers of all sorts for smell and colour, trees of all kinds of fruits, and walks divided for most delight, many birds singing and with their notes welcoming them to that place. At last, a pair of innocent white turtles* came before them, in their fashion wooing each other, and so won, enjoying their gain in billing and suchlike pretty joy.

Parselius taking advantage on this, 'How blessed,' said he, 'are these poor birds in their own imaginations, thus having one another's love!' ' 'Tis true', said Dalinea, 'but more blessed are they if the story be true that they never change.' 'Having once,' said he, 'made a perfect choice, none sure can after change.' 'I never heard man accuse himself,' said she, 'but rather when he had run into that fault, find something amiss in his former love.'

'I am sorry,' replied the prince, 'you have so ill an opinion of men, since that, I fear, will hinder you from honouring any with your love.' 'Why should you fear that?' answered she. 'Because,' sighed he, 'I would not have such admirable beauties unaccompanied, but joined to a worthy associate.' 'These must,' said she, 'for anything I see remain as they do (if such as you say) long enough before they will be sought.' 'Fear,' cried he, 'makes men speechless, and admiration hinders the declaring their affections.' 'A poor lover,' said she, 'such a one must be who wants the heart of one such little bird as this.' 'I see, most perfect lady,' said he, 'then, that this bashfulness is neither profitable nor commendable, wherefore I will now, encouraged by your words, rather commit an error in honest plainness than in fine courtship, and if it be an error, take this with it, it is not meant amiss, though it may be rudely performed, as what but rudeness can come from wandering knight?

'Not then to colour that which is most clear and perfect in itself with fine and delicate phrases, or to go too far about from the right way of discovering, give me leave, most excellent princess, to say that so excelling was your power over me when I first saw you, and so strongly hath continued the honour in keeping the conquest, as I am, and ever must be, your devoted servant, my love being wholly dedicated to you. And this I would fain long since have said, but I feared your displeasure, nor had I now ventured but that methought you bid me be bold, taking your discourse wholly to myself.'

'Then did you take it right,' said she, 'for I confess . . .' With that she blushed so prettily, and looked so modestly amorous, as she need have said no more to make him know she loved him. Yet he, covetous to have the word spoken, taking her in his arms, 'Be not so cruel, my only life,' said he, 'to bar me from the hearing of my bliss.' 'Why then,' said she, 'I must confess I love you.' 'Blessedness to my soul,' cried he, 'these words are now. My dearer self, canst thou affect poor me?' 'I honour your worth, and love yourself,' said she, 'but let your love be manifested to me in your virtuous carriage towards me.' 'Virtue,' said he, 'made choice for me, then can she not abuse herself, and virtue in you made me most to love you, then assure yourself that only virtue shall govern me.'

Thus they lovingly and chastely lived awhile, only pleased with discourse; but that grew to leave place to more enjoying itself, being loath that any time should be spent without it, envying the night that kept them so long absent, to avoid which, he so earnestly sued and she so much loved as she could not refuse what he desired for their equal contents. So as making two of her maids and his squire only acquainted, one morning they stole out of the castle by a back door, which opened just upon the moat and, having a boat there, wherein they used to row for pleasure, they crossed the water and so walked unto an hermitage hard by where, after they had heard prayers, the hermit played the priest and married them.

With infinite joy they returned to come to the height of their desires, where we will leave them a little and speak of Berlandis, squire to Amphilanthus who, longing to see his lord, and seeing little hope of getting Parselius thence, resolved to try how he might get him from that lazy life and win him again to follow arms. But alas, this was as impossible as it was for Urania to believe that Parselius would forsake her. Many times he urged him, many times he told him of adventures which himself and his cousin had passed to their eternal fames. Oft he remembered him of the promises he had made and vows which ought to be performed, but these wrought nothing. Vows he remembered not but this last, holy one, which was most religiously to be observed. Promises he had made, but those might stay till some other time, or till he had longer solaced himself in these new delights.

To conclude, Berlandis concluded to leave him, and so telling and taking his leave of him, departed with this message to Amphilanthus: that he would in short time come unto him, in the meantime entreated to be pardoned, since in his time he had a little absented himself from him upon a like, though not so just, an occasion. Then he charged Berlandis not to let any know where he had left him except his own lord, and to entreat likewise his secrecy to all others to deny his finding of him.

Thus Parselius obscured himself for some time, while the fame of his brother bravely filled the world, and had shined alone like the greatest light had not one eclipsed it with his greater power, which was and is incomparable Amphilanthus who, with his two companions, left Rumania, intending to go to Morea, as I before said, hasting thither as in pretence of the Albanian business.

After they had taken ship, they came down the archipelago, and amongst those islands staying at Sio for fresh water, and to take in some passengers, left by that ship there, at her going to Constantinople, into the which island the Knight of the Forest would needs persuade the rest to enter, seeing it delightful, and loving naturally to see novelties, and venture as far and oft-times as happily as any. This motion was agreeable to Steriamus, whose heart yet failed him, for all Amphilanthus did warrant him to go where his soul was prisoner, for fear of offending her,

though so much he loved as if he had been sure to see her, and
with that sight to die instantly, rather than live and not see her, he
would so have suffered death.

But Amphilanthus was loath to lose time, yet he was contented
to content his friend, so as they passed up a good way into the
island themselves alone, without any other, not so much as their
squires with them. Long they had not gone before they met three
fine young maids, apparelled after the Greek manner, carrying
each of them a basket wherein were several delicate fruits. The
Knight of the Forest went to them, desiring to be resolved of the
manner of that place, and whether they could let them
understand any adventure.

The maids, with much sweetness and modest fashion, replied
they were but of mean parentage, and not accustomed to such
business. 'But,' said they, 'this last night a brave gentleman lay at
our father's house, much complaining of the loss of a young
prince called Dolorindus, prince of Negrepont, who landed here
and since was never heard of. Much he seemed to doubt his
danger, and especially to fear treason, the lord of this island
being indeed the most cruel and treacherous man breathing, old
and yet so ill as his white hairs have gained that colour from black
since he practised villainy, for these forty years plotting nothing
but the destruction of brave knights and delicate ladies, of which
he hath store in his castle, where in dark and ugly prisons he
continues them, only letting them have light when he sends for
them and sports himself in their torments, and this proceeds
from no other cause but out of a general hate to all where virtue
lives and beauty dwells.

'His wife of as sweet a condition, who is worn away to bare
bones with mere hateful fretting to hear that any should live
enriched with goodness. From this pair are brought forth a
couple of as hopeful branches as can proceed from so good
stocks, their parents' ill, which they have been many years
practised in, to come to perfection, being fully flowing in them, so
as they in this kind excel, having so many years fewer and yet as
much sin in them, falsehood and all treason abounding with ill
nature in them, one of them being a daughter, and the elder,
called Ramilletta, the most cunning, dissembling, flattering, false
creature that ever sweet air suffered to breathe in without

corrupting it with her poisonous treasons; the other a son, vile, crafty and beyond measure luxurious.*

'These three are now gone a journey, whither I cannot tell you, but surely to some villainous purpose. Bravely they are attended on and richly set forth, the old woman only left behind with her practices to help if occasion serve, or by as much ill to rescue, if harm befall them. It was a glorious sight to see the brave furniture they had, delicate horses and gallant troops of knights to the number of fifty, besides four who were the fiercest and strongest of this country, ugly and fearful to behold, being brothers, and called the terrible, being of stature little less than giants, and indeed such as surely for being so much above ordinary stature were anciently termed so. A joyful sight this also was, for everyone rejoiced so much at their going as in great troops the people followed them to the sea, heartily wishing never to see them return any more.'

'Hath there been no news of them since?' said the Knight of Love. 'None,' answered the maids, 'nor will be, we hope.' 'But are there any prisoners remaining in his castle?' said he. 'So the knight told my father,' said one of them, 'and we are all certain of it, if he put them not to death before his going, which I the less think because his wicked mate so much affects the like pleasure in torturing as she holds them surely living of purpose to delight herself.' 'Will you favour us with the guiding us to the castle?' said Amphilanthus. 'With all our hearts,' said they, 'if we were sure to bring you safe back again, but fearing that, we rather desire pardon than to be the means of bringing hurt to such gentlemen.' 'Let the hazard of that lie on us,' said the knights, 'and the content to this country, especially to yourselves, when you shall see it freed from such tyranny.'

Much ado they had to persuade the maids to conduct them, yet at last they prevailed, and all together went to the house of the traitor, by the way eating of those fruits they had in their baskets. Within few hours they arrived within sight of the castle and drawing nearer, they saw two gentlemen fighting on the bridge, but presently they lost the sight of one, being fallen. Then another advanced himself, who by that time that they came near enough to descry anything done on the bridge, they saw likewise betrayed by a false place in the bridge, which they but coming on it straight opened and, as soon as they were fallen, shut again; they of the house so well acquainted with it as they easily avoided it.

They, seeing this treason, hating deceit of anything, stood conferring what they might do to avoid this trick, whenas the man that combated the other two came unto them, courteously entreating them into the house, if it pleased them to enter without blows, or if they would try their forces, as all yet had done, he was the man that first would wait upon them in that exercise.

They, assuring themselves no good could be in that creature who had betrayed any, as curstly replied as he had mildly (but craftily) spoken, telling him that courtesy in traitors must be as dangerous as his kindness would prove if they were so ignorant as to trust him, who they saw before their faces had betrayed two who fought with him. Wherefore they were resolved to be so far from receiving his compliment as they would make him bring them to the surest entering into the castle, which if he refused, they would cut off his head, with which words they laid hands on him, and that but done when with a loud and terrible voice he gave notice to them within of his danger, which brought out many to his succour, that place never being without some always armed.

They rushed all on the knights, who bravely behaved themselves, making quick work amongst them. But then came more, and such numbers as, with their freshness and companies, they put the knights more to their skill than in long time they had been. Yet they, whose hearts were filled with true worth and valour, would not think themselves in hazard, but still confident of victory, pursued their enemies to the bridge who, seeing their want of strength to master the three, gave back of purpose to win them to their snare. But soon did they find their deceit, so as avoiding the bridge, they scaped the plot and got the knowledge of it, for they, fearful, and some unskilled, run upon the false place, which opened, they falling in, and the three knights, seeing the place opened, discovered the breadth to be no more than one might stride over, so as they bravely ventured, leaping over it, and entered the gate.

Presently was a great cry and noise in the castle, all now that could bear arms running upon the knights, and so did they perplex them as they forced them to take the benefit of putting their backs to a brave fountain, which was in the midst of a square court wherein they were. This gave them ease and safety, being sure to have no hurt but what they saw; thus they fought till none were left that durst fight with them.

Then stood they a while to breathe and rest them, when showers of arrows came upon them out of the windows and from the battlements. These vexed them more than anything, not knowing what to do against them, but only covering themselves with their shields, made them their defences while they rested a little. But no sooner had they gained breath but they ran up the stairs and, finding most of them women, yet cruel in that kind and skilful in shooting, they would not contend with them with their swords, but running forcibly (in spite of their skill and continual shots) within them, knowing no means to be secure, the number being so great, were forced for all their charitable mind to begin at home with that virtue and for their own good to hurt them, which in this manner they did: throwing such as they could lay hands on out of the windows, pursuing the rest who, running from them, yet still galled them with their arrows, such was their nimbleness and cunning as they would shoot when they ran fastest. But at last they got the end of their travail with the end of them, most killed or bruised with the fall, the rest throwing down their bows and craving mercy.

But now came they to the place where the spring of all mischief sat, the mistress of wickedness and that castle, in such distress because they were not distressed as malice and all vices mixed together could hardly be the figure of this woman. But what could she do? All cunning now failed her, though she began with humility, fawning and flatteringly begging life, succeeding with cursings, revilings and threatenings, but all prospered alike for they, taking her, commanded her to bring them where the prisoners were. When she saw no craft would prevail, she cast her hateful looks upon them and, by an unlucky chance espying a dagger at Ollorandus' back, stepped to him hastily, and as suddenly, being unmarked drawing it out struck Amphilanthus (who was then looking from herward, careless of her) under his armour, giving him such a wound as the blood fell in great abundance from him. But soon was that well revenged, if her life were answerable for such a mischance. Yet did they keep her alive till the castle was settled, one drop of his blood being more worth than millions of lives of better people. Then she was terribly tortured, and yet kept long in pain for her more lasting punishment, and lastly burned.

By this were most dead or yielded. All being safe, Amphilanthus was carried into a rich chamber where his wound was searched and dressed by the three sisters, who were now come into the castle, brought in by Steriamus of purpose to dress the prince; Ollorandus being so perplexed that it was his unlucky fate to have the weapon that hurt his friend as he was truly sorrow itself, even being ready with it to have parted his own life from him had not Amphilanthus conjured him by all loves and friendships and protestations to forbear.

Quickly did the sisters assure them of his safety, which as a blessing came unto them. After he was dressed, he sent his friend to fetch the prisoners all before him, which was done, where were of knights and ladies such store as (if in health and strength) there had been a fit number for the furnishing a brave court, but as they were, it was a sight of commiseration, so pale and weak they were with want of food and their bodies so abused with tortures, as they appeared like people of purpose made to show misery in extremity.

Among them was Dolorindus, whose own mind and this usage had brought him into a fit estate to answer his name. Amphilanthus, knowing him, first took care of him, calling for his own apparel, which was brought, and causing delicate food to be brought him, cherished him so, as by that time that he was able to travel for his wound, Dolorindus was likewise fit to accompany him, which in few days came to pass by the diligence and care of the three sisters, who were next in true succession by the mother's side to the ancient lords of Sio. Their father came unto them with the squires to the princes and those of the ship.

Then prepared they for their departure, Amphilanthus bestowing the castle and the island upon the sisters, his kind chyrurgeons, promising to send his faithful and best esteemed servant Berlandis to marry the eldest as soon as he could find him, and on the other two Steriamus and Ollorandus bestowed their squires, giving them the order of knighthood, who well deserved it, proving worthy of such masters, making the world

see that such examples as daily their master showed them must
needs make brave men, leaving that place in quiet, having taken
the oaths of all the inhabitants in Berlandis' name and his wife's.

Then took they ship again for Morea, but passing along the
Aegean sea, they entered many islands, seeking and finding
adventures, but in one being (though little) yet plentiful as a
greater, delicately compassed with snow-white rocks, yet mixed
with small fine trees whose greenness gave them hope to see, but
pleasure gave them heart to go into it, when they found within it
such a place as a lover would have chosen to have passed his time
in, and this did urge the four knights, all amorous, and yet in
several kinds, to express their passions several ways.

Amphilanthus left the other three, taking the direct way to the
heart of the land, as ever aiming at that place, having the best and
most power continually over that part. Steriamus took on the
right hand; Ollorandus to the left; but Dolorindus, who never
knew difference of fortune (still having lived in a constant state of
her displeasure) went away between them all, his thoughts (as
ever in action) better being able to utter forth his passions, being
alone, which in this kind he did. When he came into a dainty fine
wood of straight high oaks and young beeches mingled with a few
ashes and chestnut trees, in the midst of the wood was a mount
cast up by nature and more delicate than art could have framed it,
though the cunningest had undertaken it, in the midst of it was a
round table of stone, and round about it seats made of the same
stone, which was black marble.

Some letters, or rather characters, he found engraven in the
upper part of those seats, and on many of the trees which
curiously encompassed it, and many ciphers, although but one
for meaning, though in number many. Lovers had done these, as
he thought; lovers made him remember he was one, and that oft
he had carved his mistress's name upon bay trees to show her
conquest, which she had requited, cutting his name in willows to
demonstrate his fate. This afflicted him and moved so much in
him as he could not but frame some verses in his imagination,
which after were given to Amphilanthus and his other companions. The lines were these, place and fortune procuring them:

> Sweet solitariness, joy to those hearts
> That feel the pleasure of love's sporting darts,

Grudge me not, though a vassal to his might
And a poor subject to cursed changing's spite,
To rest in you, or rather, restless move
In your contents to sorrow for my love.
A love which, living, lives as dead to me
As holy relics which in boxes be
Placed in a chest that overthrows my joy,
Shut up in change which more than plagues destroy.
These, O you solitariness, may both endure,
And be a chirurgeon to find me a cure.
For this curst corsive* eating my best rest
Memory, sad memory in you once blessed,
But now most miserable with the weight
Of that which only shows love's strange deceit;
You are that cruel wound that inly wears
My soul, my body wasting into tears.
You keep mine eyes unclosed, my heart untied,
From letting thought of my best days to slide.
Froward remembrance, what delight have you
Over my miseries to take a view?
Why do you tell me in this same-like place
Of earth's best blessing I have seen the face?
But masked from me, I only see the shade
Of that which once my brightest sunshine made.
You tell me that I then was blessed in love
When equal passions did together move.
O why is this alone to bring distress
Without a salve but torments in excess.
A cruel steward you are to enroll
My once good days of purpose to control
With eyes of sorrow, yet leave me undone
By too much confidence my thread so spun,
In conscience move not such a spleen of scorn
Under whose swellings my despairs are born.
Are you offended (choicest memory)
That of your perfect gift I did glory?
If I did so offend, yet pardon me
Since 'twas to set forth your true excellency.
Sufficiently I thus do punished stand
While all that cursed is you bring to my hand.
Or, is it that I no way worthy was
In so rich treasure my few days to pass?
Alas, if so and such a treasure given

Must I for this to Hell-like pain be driven?
Fully torment me now, and what is best
Together take, and memory with the rest,
Leave not that to me, since but for my ill,
Which punish may, and millions of hearts kill.
Then may I lonely sit down with my loss
Without vexation for my losses cross
Forgetting pleasures late embraced with love
Linked to a faith the world could never move,
Chained with affection I hoped could not change
Not thinking earth could yield a place to range.
But staying, cruelly you set my bliss
With deepest mourning in my sight, for miss
And thus must I imagine my curse more
When you I loved add to my mischiefs' store.
If not, then memory continue still
And vex me with your perfectest known skill
While you dear solitariness accept
Me to your charge whose many passions kept
In your sweet dwellings have this profit gained
That in more delicacy none was pained.
Your rareness now receive my rarer woe
With change, and love appoints my soul to know.

When he had made this, and committed them to that keeper
who yet would not be persuaded to set him at liberty, but
continued the more to molest him, like a sore that one beats to
cure, yet smarts the more for beating, so did memory abide with
him. Then walked he on to meet his friends, who were all in their
kinds as much perplexed as himself.

Amphilanthus alone, and so the abler to be bold in speech,
began thus, walking (with his arms folded lovingly for love, one
within the other) along a sweet river. 'Unhappy man,' sighed he,
'that lives to be vexed with the same that once most delighted
thee, who could have thought inconstancy a weight, if not to
press me on to more delight? Left I till now any wherein change
brought not unspeakable content? When I took Antissia, thought
I not I was happy in the change? When I before had altered from
and to that love, did it not bring a full content of bliss? But now that
I have changed and for and to the best, alas how am I troubled,
how afflicted, how perplexed! Constancy, I see, is the only

perfect virtue, and the contrary, the truest fault, which like sins entices one still on of purpose to leave one in the height, as the height of enjoying makes one leave the love to it.

'I have offended, all you powers of love pardon me, and if there be any one among you that hath the rule of truth, govern me, direct me, and henceforth assure yourself of my faith and true subjection, error makes me perfect and shows me the light of understanding. But what talk I of truth? Why commend I faith when I am uncertain whether these will win? She, alas, she doth love and, woe is me, my hopes in this quite lost, she loves and so I see my end. Yet never shall that come without a noble conclusion and that her eyes and ears shall witness with my loss.

'Dearest, once pity, my sad looks shall tell thee I do love, my sighs shall make thee hear my pains, my eyes shall let thee see (if thou wilt but see me) that only thy sight is their comfort, for when from thee they stir, they must find a new seat to turn in and a head to dwell in, and so now they have, for nothing see they but thy delicacy, nothing view but thy perfections, turn from all to thee and only turn unto thee. My soul hath also eyes to see thy worth. Love hath now framed me wholly to thy laws. Command then, here I breathe but to thy love, from which, when I do swerve let me love unrequited, but dearest be thou kind and then have I all bliss. Why shouldst not thou leave one, since for thee I'll leave all? Be once unconstant to save me as 'twere from death, who for it will be true, I vow, and this vow still will keep, that only thou art worthy and alone will I love thee.'

Then casting up his eyes, he saw before him a rare meadow, and in the midst of it a little arbour, as he so far off took it to be, but drawing nearer he found a delicate fountain circled about with orange and pomegranate trees, the ground under them all hard sand. About the fountain (as next adjoining) was a hedge of jesamnis* mingled with roses and woodbines, and within that, paved with pavements of diverse colours, placed for show and pleasure. On the steps he sat down, beholding the work of the fountain, which was most curious, being a fair maid, as it were, thinking to ladle it dry, but still the water came as fast as it passed over the dish she seemed to ladle withal.

'And just thus,' said he, 'are my labours fruitless, my woes increasing faster than my pains find ease.' Then, having enough, as he thought, given liberty to his speech, he put the rest of his thought into excellent verse, making such excelling ones as none could any more imitate or match them than equal his valour, so exquisite was he in all true virtues and skill in poetry, a quality among the best much prized and esteemed, princes brought up in that next to the use of arms.

When he had finished them, he sat a while still; then, looking on the fountain, he said: 'Dear hopes spring as this water, flow to enjoying like this stream, but waste not till my life doth waste in me. Nay, die, run to my love and tell her what I feel. Say, and say boldly, till I knew herself I was but ignorant, and now do know that only she and she alone can save or ruin me.'

Many more and far more excellent discourses had he with himself, and such as I am altogether unable to set down, therefore leave them to be guessed at by those who are able to comprehend his worth and understanding. Such may express his passions, all else admire and admiringly esteem so incomparable a prince, who for a little while continued thus. But then, leaving the fountain, he went straight on and followed on his way till he came unto a hill, the sides appearing rocky, the top he might discern green and some trees upon it. He by little and little climbed to the top, where in the middle of it he saw a hole, and looking in at that hole perceived fire a pretty way below it, and that fire as if it were stirred by some hands, whereupon he concluded that this was some poor abode of some miserable people, either made so by want or misfortune, which likewise might be want, that being the greatest misery.

Round about the top he sought, but at last thought with himself that there was no way to see the inhabitants but by some way in the side of this rock, wherefore he went down again and half about the hill, when he found a little door of stone, the even proportion of the opening making him know it to be so, else nothing could have disordered* it, so close it was, appearing but like chinks or clefts. He pulled at it, but it would not stir. Then he knocked, when straight a little window was opened, and out of it an ugly old dwarf looked, whose face was as wrinkled as the rock, his complexion sand colour without so much red as to make a difference 'twixt his lips and face. His hair had been black, but now was grown grizzled, yet still kept the natural stubbornness of it, being but thin, and those few hairs, desirous to be seen, stood staring, neither were they of any equal length, but like a horse's mane new taken from grass, which by the wantonness of some of his companions had been bit and natched* in diverse places. Beard he had none to distinguish his sex, his habits* being forced to speak for him to that purpose. Only a wart he had on his right cheek, which liberally bestowed some hair according to the substance for the sight of such as saw him. He was not only a dwarf, but the least of those creatures, and in some sort the ill-favouredest. This youth, seeing Amphilanthus, straight cried 'Alas, we are betrayed, for here is an armed man that will assuredly destroy us!'

The prince promised on his word he, nor any there, should have the least harm if he would let him but come in unto him. The old dwarf scarce knew how to trust, having before been in his trust deceived, wherefore he desired first to know who he was that gave his word. The King answered, 'I am called and known by the name of the Knight of Love, but mine own name,' said he, 'is Amphilanthus.' 'Praised be heaven,' said he, 'that you are landed here, for alas my lord, I am your subject, miserably perplexed by a cruel and tyrannical man, lord of the island of Stromboli, and who hath undone me and my children.'

Then leaped he from the window and opened the door, which was made fast with many bolts of iron. The door open, the King went in, though with some difficulty at the entering, by reason the place was low and fitter for such a man as the host than the Rumanian King*. In the room he found a woman in height and loveliness answerable to the man, and three younger men than himself, but all of his proportion, who seemed to be his sons. Then did Amphilanthus desire to know the cause of his complaining against the lord of Stromboli, which the old dwarf began to relate in this manner:

'May it please you, great prince, to understand I am called Nainio, born in Stromboli to pretty possessions, the which I enjoyed some years after my father's decease. But the lord of the island (or better to say, the governor) passing that way, and seeing my living pleasant and delightful, groves of orange and lemon trees, all other fruits plentifully yielding themselves for our uses, grew in love with the place and in hate with me.

'First he peremptorily commanded me to bring my wife and these tall men, my sons, to attend him, his wife and children. I that was born free would not be made a slave, wherefore (I must confess, unadvisedly) I gave too rough an answer that bred dislike and gave just occasion against me. Then sent he for me, made me a scorn in the eyes of all men, and when he had gloried enough in my misery, scoffing at my shape and stature, saying I would make a fit commander against the infidels, he put me and my family into a little boat, and when shipping went for Greece, sent me along with them. But such kindness I found among them as they indeed carried me, but brought me back again. This was discovered, whereupon I was to die. But my pardon was got by the lady, wife to the lord, a virtuous and sweet lady, on condition if ever I were found in Stromboli or any part of Italy I should die for it.

'Then went I away, and with the first mentioned sailors got into this sea, and so unto this island, where I have remained; but in continual fear, for considering the danger I was in for my life, it so with the memory frights me as I had rather have starved here than gone hence for fear of harm, everyone that I hear or see in this place being as a sprite unto me, and so did you appear till you told me who you were, so much do I yet stand in awe of the cruel island lord.'

The King smiled to hear his discourse, but most to see his action, which was so timorous and affrighted as never any man beheld the like, and as he did so did his sons, like monkeys who, imitating one another, answer in gestures as aptly and readily as one echo to another and as like, and so the sport was doubled. Great delight did he take in these little men, wherefore gently and mildly he gained so much of them as they would with him leave that place, conditionally that he would not carry them into Italy, where they more feared their first enemy than trusted to the power of the King, such a lord is coward fear over base minds as understanding gains small place in their hearts, as by this appeared, else might they have been assured in his company in Stromboli itself.

But consents agreeing on both sides, they went out of the rock to meet the other princes, the dwarves quaking at every leaf that shook and fainted when they heard the armour a little clash in his

going, but directly they lost life for a while when they met the
other knights, not being able to believe they were their lord's
friends. But after they grew more valiant, like a coward who,
against his mind being brought into the middle of a battle, can
neither run nor his cries be heard, and therefore of force must
abide that Hell torment. So were these brought to it by sight of
fights when death could only have relieved them from fear.

Amphilanthus, following on, came to a great cave, into which
he went, putting the dwarves before him. A great way they passed
into it, till he came to a river, which either was black, or the
darkness of that shadowed place made appear so. The vault was
of height sufficient for him without trouble to walk in, and of
breadth for three to go afront, paved and covered round with free
stone; when he came to the river he desired to pass it, but at first
saw no means.

At last he discovered (or fear in his dwarfs discovered for him,
they being able to discern, having been long in the dark, which
though at first it blinds like love, yet it gives at last sight to get out
of it) so they found a board which was fastened with chains to the
top of the vault, and two pins of iron that held the chains being
stuck into the wall. Those being pulled out, the chains let the
plank fall gently down, just cross over the water, which was not
above six yards over, but being on it, they might see a great way
up and down the stream.

Then passed they on to a door which they opened a pretty way
along the same vault from the brook, and the end of it, through
which they entered into a dainty garden and so into a fair palace
of alabaster encompassed with hills, or rather mountains, of such
height as no way was possible to be found to come at it but
through the same vault the King came.

Diverse gardens and orchards did surround this palace; in
every one was a fountain and every fountain rich in art and
plentifully furnished with the virtue of liberality, freely bestowing
water in abundance. These places he passed, staying in a large
stone gallery set upon pillars of the same stone. There he sat
down, complaining still of his mistress, whose heart was stored
with pain and love equally oppressing her.

'O,' cried he, 'my dearest love, the sweetest cruel that ever
nature framed, how have I, miserable man, offended thee, that

not so much as a look or show of pity will proceed from thee to
comfort me? Are all thy favours locked up and only sad
countenances allotted me? Alas, consider women were made to
love and not to kill, yet you will destroy with cruel force while I,
changed to a tender creature, sit weeping and mourning for thy
cruelty, which yet I can hardly term so, since thou knowest not
my pain.'

Further he would have proceeded, when a door opened into
that room, and out of it came a grave lady apparelled in a black
habit and many more young women attending her. She straight
went to him, saluting him thus: 'Brave King, welcome to this
place, being the abiding of your friend and servant.' He, looking
upon her, perceived wisdom, modesty and goodness figured in
her face, wherefore with a kind acceptance he received this
salutation, desiring to be informed of the place, but most to know
how he came known to her.

'Sir,' said she, 'my name is Mellissea, and having skill in the
art of astrology I have found much concerning you, and as much
desire to do you service.' 'Can you find, good Madam,' said he,
'whether I shall be happy in my love or not?' 'In love, my lord,'
said she, 'you shall be most happy, for all shall love you that you
wish. But yet you must be crossed in this you now affect, though
contrary to her heart.'

'But shall I not enjoy her then? Miserable fortune, take all
loves from me so I may have hers.' 'She loves you,' said
Mellissea, 'and it will prove your fault if you lose her, which I
think you will and must, to prevent which, if possible, beware of a
treacherous servant. For this place, it is that anciently reverenced
and honoured island of Delos, famous for the birth of those two
great lights Apollo and Diana, the ruins of Apollo's and Latona's
temples remaining to this day on the other side of that mountain,
called Cynthus, once rich and populous, now poor and peopleless, none or very few inhabiting here besides this my family, the
sharp and cruel rocks which girdle this island guarding itself and
us from dangerous robbings.'

'But must I lose my love?' said Amphilanthus. 'Accursed fate
that so should happen. I yet do hope, if I may be assured she
loves me, this will never be.' 'Well my lord,' said she, 'to let you
see that hope is too poor a thing in comparison of truth to trust

to, I will give you these tokens to make you truly see my words are true. You have lately had a wound by a woman, but this a greater and more dangerous you must suffer, which will endanger your life far more than that last did, yet shall the cause proceed from your own rashness, which you shall repent when 'tis too late, and when time is past know the means might have prevented it. But to do what I may for your good, I advise you to this: alter your determination for your journey to Morea, and instead of it go straight to Cyprus, where you must finish an enchantment, and at your return come hither, and with you bring that company that you release there. Then shall I be more able to advise you, for this doth yet darken some part of my knowledge of you.'

He remained much perplexed with those words, yet as well as such affliction would permit him, he made show of patience. Then did Mellissea send one of her maids to bring his companions to him, hoping their sights and the discourse of their fortunes would a little remove his melancholy from him. In the meantime he, with crossed arms, walked up and down the gallery, musing in himself how he should so far and deadlily fall out with himself as to be the cause of his own misery, not being able, though he had the best understanding, to reach into this mystery. Sometimes the lady discoursed to him, and he for civility did answer her, yet oft-times she was content to attend his own leisure for his reply, so much power had his passions over him.

Thus he remained molested, while Steriamus, following his right-hand way, was brought into a fine plain, and thence to the foot of a mountain, where he found rich pillars of marble and many more signs of some magnificent building, which sight wrought pity in him, remembering how glorious they seemed to have been, now thrown down to ruin. 'And so,' said he, 'was my fortune fair and brave in show, but now cast low to despair and loss. O Pamphilia, goddess of my soul, accept me yet at last, if not for thy servant, yet for thy priest, and on the altar of thy scorn will I daily offer up the sacrifice of true and spotless love. My heart shall be the offering; my tears the water; my miserable body the temple; and thy hate and cruellest disdain, the enemy that lays it waste. Once yet consider, greatest beauty, mightiest riches, sumptuousest buildings, all have some end; brightest glory cannot ever dure, and as of goodness, must not ill have so? Grant this, and then thy rage must needs conclude.'

Yet thus did not his pain find conclusion, but a little further he went among those ruins, where he laid himself not down, but threw himself among those poor and destroyed relics of the rarest temples, where hard by he heard Ollorandus likewise complaining. 'My Melasinda,' said he, 'how justly mayest thou blame thy Ollorandus, who still travels further from thee, who strove to bring thy love still nearest to him. Canst thou imagine thy immaculate affection well bestowed when so great neglect requiteth it? Wilt thou or mayest thou think the treasure of thy love and richest gift of it well bestowed, when absence is the payment to it? If against me and these thou dost but justly except, yet what doth hold thee from killing that slave and setting thy dear soul at liberty? No, thy virtues will not like a murderer; it must be as it is, destiny must only work and despairing sorrow tire itself in me.'

Steriamus, wanting pity, knew the miss, and therefore would be as charitable as he could, to show which goodness he rose and went to Ollorandus to put him from his mourning, who was then again entering into his wailings, telling him they were too long from Amphilanthus. As he start up, behold Dolorindus, who came sadly towards them, whom they called to them and so together went from that place, meaning to ascend the mountain. But then came the servant of Mellissea to them, entreating their companies from her mistress to the palace, where they should meet their companion. They soon consented to that invitation, whither being come, they told all their adventures one to another. Then were they brought into a fair room where, after they had eaten, Mellissea again thus spoke:

'My lords, the time calls upon you, occasions being such as your presences are required in several places, wherefore first to you, my lord Steriamus, I must say you must haste hence, and as you desire your own happy ends in love, observe what I advise you. Go from hence into Arcadia; fear not, for nothing shall encounter you of harm. Dolorindus, do you the like, for much is your being there requisite. From thence, go to St Maura, and in a rock which lies just against it towards Cephalonia, privately remain till fortune call you thence by help, which shall appear death. This may seem hard and terrible, but fear it not, since it shall bring your happiness. Then go into Greece again, and help your friends and yourself in the conquest of Albania.'

They took her hand and kissed it, on it swearing to obey her counsel. Amphilanthus was sorry for his vow, especially that his journey was stayed to Morea, but he made the cause of his grief for parting with his friends.

Then to Ollorandus she thus spake: 'The good that shall come to you must proceed from this brave King, who shall give unto you both security of life and your only love. Life he shall venture for you, and save yours by the hazard of himself. Keep then together and still be your loves firm and constant, assisting one another, for a time will be when you shall merit this from Amphilanthus, giving him as great a gift. And credit what I say, for it is as true as by my means you received the armour in the forest when you were fast sleeping, it being laid by you, from which you have taken the name of Knight of the Forest.

'For you, my lord, think not but I am as careful or more of you than any, though I have left you last, for as yet I can say little. But fear nothing, except what I have already warned you of. My art shall attend you and I never fail to serve you. Make haste then to Cyprus and be careful.' Then all promising to perform her will, with tears in their eyes they took leave of each other. Steriamus and Dolorindus demanding what service Amphilanthus would command them, he answered they should honour him much in remembering him to the King and Queen, to whom by Steriamus he sent the old dwarves, and the youngest son, called after his father's name, he desired Dolorindus to present to Pamphilia from him.

Thus they parted, and Amphilanthus, Ollorandus and the other two dwarves, who served them for squires, took their way for Cyprus. Quick was the journey of the other two, arriving in Laconia, and so hasting to Mantinea where then the King was. But being near, Steriamus began to faint, fearing the sight of her he most desired to see. Yet encouraged by Dolorindus to perform what he had engaged his word to do, they went on, coming to the court when the King and all the princes were assembled to judge the traitors.

But Steriamus, whose fame was now far spread for his noble

acts at Constantinople and diverse others, was soon known in the hall, and as soon with great joy brought before the King, to whom he delivered the present and service of Amphilanthus. The King infinitely rejoiced to hear of his brave friend, and taking the dwarf (the Queen with as much love accepting the other), desired, before they passed to the judgement, to hear of their adventures. Then did Steriamus openly relate all that had happened him after his depart* until their coming thither, in so good words and princely a manner as all admired and loved him, especially for doing it with such affection and truth, to the eternal renown of incomparable Amphilanthus.

Then presented he Dolorindus to the King, whose name and presence was welcome too at that time, especially assuring himself now to have an end and true knowledge of the traitors, who were led (at their coming in) aside, so as they neither saw them nor heard the relation of the adventure at Sio, which was extreme strange and wondered at by all—the more the cause of admiration was, the more still increased their honours that achieved it.

Then went the princes to Pamphilia, who much commended Steriamus for his discourse, kindly of Dolorindus accepting the dwarf, promising to love him for his lord's sake. Then were all placed again, Rosindy taking Steriamus and setting him between him and his friend Selarinus, who was true joy itself to see Steriamus again. The traitors then entered, to whom the King thus spoke:

'Without any more falsehood, truly declare unto me who you are and your true names, for those you took upon you I know are false. Then discover the cause of taking my daughter. Deal truly, if any pity be expected by you to be showed unto you.' The old man curstly replied he wondered a King should have so ill a conceit of another of his own rank as to think falsehood could be in a royal breast, and more did he admire that the King of Morea, who before had been counted just, would offer that injustice to the King of Negrepont, who having been ill-used by an ungrateful child, and coming thither for succour, should be made a prisoner like a traitor and used like thieves.

Then answered the King: 'Behold my lords before you the vilest of men and falsest of traitors, to prove which, Dolorindus stand forth and witness against him.' Dolorindus indeed came forth, the traitor, seeing him straight, too well knew him, wherefore, roaring out, he cried 'I am undone for now all is betrayed!'

Then did Dolorindus again tell the manner of his treacherous taking and imprisoning him, and withal the winning and destroying of the castle and his servants, the burning of his wicked wife and the bestowing of the island upon Berlandis and the other two their squires, whom they had matched to the three sisters. These creatures, being past help to be saved, fell down on their faces, confessing the truth, which was this:

'The son to this wicked man, seeing the picture of Pamphilia, which was sent some two years before by Pamphilia to her uncle but was taken away by pirates, who after landed at Sio, and among other things sold that. He fell in love with it and so longed to enjoy her as nothing but death appeared in him, which the devil his father perceiving, plotted all ways he could, to which end he invented that false bridge, hoping to get some of her brothers or friends; if not, some that might bring them means to find a trick to gain her.

'Ten months this continued, then came the poor Dolorindus, who by treason they got, and having heard his story, which almost was the same he told for himself, only this differing: that the kingdom was not given by affection to the daughter but by right, as being a gift given by the grandfather to his daughter and her first born, which happened to be a daughter, and so she, elder, put Dolorindus by. The rest was true of her ill-deserving, but the father righted by his son, by a combat against two mighty men, was delivered from prison, she put down from government and committed to his prison where shortly after she died.

'This story the wicked man made his own, and his son took the name of brave Dolorindus, forging the rest and making that deceitful chariot of purpose to betray the princess, whom they purposed to have carried with them to Sio and to keep her by that treason against all, at least [until] the amorous lover should have his desire.'

This being confessed, and he no prince but an usurping lord of other men's rights, and a king's and prince's honour, they were all condemned and executed according to the Arcadian law.

Now is the time of Steriamus' departing come, and also for Dolorindus who, taking their leaves of the King and court, promised Rosindy and Selarinus to meet them soon after in Macedon. Kissing Pamphilia's hand once more to bless his lips with the last affectionate kiss he can ever have from her or give to her, he departed with his friend towards St Maura, perplexed in soul, love working more terribly now than ever, like that killing disease which parts not but with life, and so was this sickness come now to the height in him.

A little less ease felt Antissia, who now must soon leave Morea, the ambassador recovered of his hurts and others chosen to go in commission with him concerning the forces, being the two brave princes of Corinth and Elis, brother to the proud lover of Parselius, who he met as you have heard. More honourably Antissia could not be accompanied, and since she must go, 'twas thought fit she went with them.

The day before she was to go, not having all night taken any rest, she rose earlier than she was accustomed and sooner than any was stirring, she came into Pamphilia's chamber, who she found sweetly sleeping, but drawing the curtain she awaked and, seeing her, wondered what occasion had called her up so soon and at that hour to be dressed, wherefore she said 'Why, what disturbance, sweet Antissia, hath thus raised you? What disquiets molested you? Can your thoughts afford you no more rest, or is it joy for your departure makes you thus early, and takes away that dull humour of sleep from your spirits?'

'Joy to part! O me,' replied she, weeping. 'No Pamphilia, my heart doth break to think of it; my soul is tortured so as it enjoys no peace for grief's additions.' 'The loss of your company is much more to me,' said the princess, 'for you gone, who shall I have the blessing to converse withal? With whom or to whom may I freely say my mind? To whom speak my pain? To whom wail my misfortunes? Thus is the loss most in me, for you go to your nephew, where you soon will see your love, while I, lamenting, spend my time. I am to tarry here, which since you go will seem ages to me.'

'Why will you be thus cruel, most sweet Pamphilia,' said she, 'to add unto my torments by the expression of your favour to me? I shall go, 'tis true, to my nephew, rather to content him than myself, since what will his court be to me when I shall be in the dungeon of despair? For seeing my love, much hope I have, when he favours me not so much as by these princes to send one poor remembrance to let me know he thinks on such a soul, a soul indeed won and lost by him, who now despises the memory of her who disdained not to love and serve him and who, I know, suffers in honour for him. But let her suffer and be he as ungrateful as he will, I yet must love so much as to lament his loss. But methought you touched even now of parting; whither, rare lady, will you go? Or what quarrel have you to poor Morea to leave it desolate, as so it must be when you forsake it?'

'I shall leave it but for a while,' said she, 'and then it will be freer and safer from afflictions when the most afflicted shall be absent from it. Go I must with my uncle, to be seen to the Pamphilians, and acknowledged their princess, which country my uncle in his youth (being as brave and valiant a man as ever breathed) won from the subjection of tyrants, in requital whereof the people chose him their King, their love being then so great and still continuing as they have given him leave to choose his successor, which, by reason he never married, had else fallen to them again for choice. He long since chose me, and to that end gave me that name, but he growing old, or rather weak, and they desirous to know me, gained of him to make this voyage for me, with whom I do return speedily, and now rejoice in the soon coming of it, since you and I must part.'

'O name not that word great princess,' sighed she, 'but rather spend this little time in such content as our hearts can permit us, disposing these hours to a more pleasing purpose. Pray therefore rise, and go into the solitary wood, where we may unheard and unperceived better discourse our woes, sadly and freely complaining.' 'I will ever yield unto your desires,' said Pamphilia, 'then go you before, and I shall soon follow you.'

Antissia left her, taking the way to the walks. Pamphilia got up, and as she was making her ready, her passionate breast, scarce allowing her any respite from her passions, brought these verses to her mind, wherein she then imprinted them.

> Dear love, alas how have I wronged thee,
> That ceaselessly thou still dost follow me?
> My heart of diamond clear and hard I find

May yet be pierced with one of the same kind
Which hath in it engraven a love more pure
   Than spotless white, and deep still to endure,
Wrought in with tears of never-resting pain
   Carved with the sharpest point of cursed disdain.
Rain oft doth wash away a slender mark,
   Tears make mine firmer, and as one small spark
In straw may make a fire, so sparks of love
   Kindles incessantly in me to move,
While cruellest you do only pleasure take
   To make me faster tied to scorn's sharp stake,
'Tis harder and more strength must used be
   To shake a tree than boughs we bending see:
So to move me it was alone your power
   None else could ere have found a yielding hour.
Cursed be subjection, yet blessed in this sort,
   That 'gainst all but one choice my heart a fort
Hath ever lasted, though besieged, not moved,
   But by their miss my strength the stronger proved
Resisting with that constant might, that win
   They scarce could parley, much less foes get in.
Yet worse than foes your slightings prove to be
   When careless you no pity take on me.
Make good my dreams, wherein you kind appear,
   Be to mine eyes, as to my soul, most dear.
From your accustomed strangeness at last turn,
   An ancient house once fired will quickly burn
And waste unhelped, my long love claims a time
   To have aid granted to this height I climb.
A diamond pure and hard, an unshaked tree
   A burning house, find help and prize in me.

Being ready, she went into the garden woods, where she saw Antissia sadly walking, her eyes on the earth, her sighs breathing like a sweet gale claiming pity from above, for the earth, she said, would yield her none, yet she besought that too, and at last passion procured alteration from mourning. She began to sing a song, or rather part of one, which was thus:

    Stay mine eyes, these floods of tears
      Seems but follies weakly growing,
    Babes at nurse such wailing bears
      Frowardness such drops bestowing.

But Niobe must show my fate
She wept and grieved herself a state.

My sorrows like her babes appear
    Daily added by increasing,
She lost them, I lose my dear
    Not one spared from woes ne'er ceasing.
She made a rock, heaven drops down tears,
Which pity shows, and on her wears.

Assuredly more there was of this song, or else she had with her
unframed and unfashioned thoughts as unfashionably framed
these lines. But then Pamphilia came to her, saying 'Sweet
Antissia, leave these dolorous complaints. When we are parted
let our hearts bleed tears, but let us not deprive ourselves of this
little comfort: at least let us flatter ourselves and think we now
feel some, and when absence makes us know the contrary, then
mourn.'

'Alas,' said Antissia, 'I foresee my harm; my spirit tells me,
once being gone, gone will my joys be altogether.' 'Sadness will
presage anything,' said Pamphilia, 'especially where that may
procure more sadness, melancholy, the nurse of such passions,
being glad when her authority is esteemed and yielded to, and so
much hath it wrought in me as I have many hours sat looking on
the fire, in it making as many sad bodies as children do varieties
of faces, being pleased or displeased or as my own fancies have
felt pains, and all this was but melancholy, and truly that is
enough to spoil any, so strangely it grows upon one, and so
pleasing is the snare as, till it hath ruined one, no fault is found
with it, but like death, embraced by the ancient brave men like
honour and delight. This I have found and smarted with it.
Leave it then, and nip it in the bud, lest it blow to overthrow your
life and happiness; for my sake be a little more cheerful, and I
will promise you, when you are gone, I will as much bewail
absence.' Antissia took her hand and, though against her will,
kissed it, saying 'Admired princess, let your poor, unfortunate
friend and servant be in absence but sometimes remembered
with a wish to see her with you, and that will bring an
unspeakable content to that distressed creature on whom fortune
tries her curstest power in despiteful rage and cruelty.' 'Doubt
not me more, dear Antissia,' said she, 'for those wishes shall be,

and attended with others for your happiness. Then distrust not me, for Pamphilia must be just.'

Thus in kind discourse they continued, promising to each other what was in love demanded to demonstrate their affections, till it was time to retire. Little meat that dinner served them, whose hearts had filled their stomachs with love and sorrow. After dinner, going again to that sad place, that night being the last, lying together and with sad but loving discourse passing those dark hours, day being loath to see Antissia's tears, but grieved and afraid to see Pamphilia weep, did hide her face till the sun, greedy of so precious and sweet a dew, looking red, with haste came into the room, where they blushingly ashamed so to be surprised, put on their clothes, not to be in danger of his heat.

No sooner were they ready but Antissia was called for, who the sweetest lady accompanied to her coach with main* tears and sad, because parting, kiss, taking leave of each other, Antissia by her sorrow foretelling her coming, or indeed but showing her already befallen, loss. Pamphilia was sorry for her going, because she was now assured of her love. The court did in general lament, such love and respect she had gained by her courteous and sweet behaviour, many wishing her married to Parselius that so they might still keep her with them. So many well wishes she had as surely made her journey more prosperous for safety, and speedily (considering the way) she arrived at Constantinople, being lovingly and kindly entertained by the King and affectionately by her uncle, whose joy was greatest knowing what hazard she had suffered, aiming now at nothing more than how to get the brave Leandrus to perform what before was determined between their parents.

She gone, preparation was made for the journey of Pamphilia; rich chariots, coaches, furniture for horses and all other necessary things that could be demanded for service or state, the liveries for her servants being of the same colours the chariots and other furnitures were, and them all of her own chosen colours, which were watchet and crimson, as the chariots were watchet embroidered with crimson and pearl of silver, one with pearl, all the rest alike. The King and Queen did accompany her to the seaside, all the other princes bringing her aboard and there kissing her hands.

Thus away she went, sailing with gentle and pleasant wind, till the pilot told the King that a great fleet followed them, by their colours and the shape of the ships showing they were Italians. Wherefore they, not knowing the business, prepared for the worst, when they perceived, out of the greatest and fairest of these ships, knights unarmed and ladies armed with beauty able to conquer worlds of hearts, to issue and enter a delicate galley, which straight made way by oars towards them.

The King seeing it, and Pamphilia being above any princess courteous, commanded their ship to strike sail, lest harm might befall them in their coming aboard. Straight came they into the ship, the first and chief of those knights with a grave and manly fashion delivering these words, holding a lady (most exact in all perfections) by the hand:

'Most incomparable princess, the fame of whose worth the world is filled withal, and yet wants another to be able to comprehend the fullness of it. Be pleased to know that this lady and myself are your devoted servants Perissus and Limena of Sicilia, rescued and saved from ruin and death by your magnanimous brother Parselius, to whom we were now going to manifest our gratefulness to him, but hearing by a ship which came from Morea, just as we were putting ashore, that the prince is neither there nor hath been of sometimes* heard of, withal of your journey, we resolved to attend you and to you do the service we owe him, which by him I know will be alike taken. As to himself, such is his affection to you, such admirable perfections living in him, as love and affection to his friends are plentifully flourishing in him.

'Wherefore we beseech you to accept of our affectionate services, which shall ever (next to Parselius) be most devoutly observing to your commands. Him we love for his virtues, and the benefits we have received from him; you we love for him and your own merits, whose name doth duly claim all eyes and hearts to love and admire.'

Pamphilia, whose modesty never heard her own commendations without blushing, prettily did now express a bashfulness, but her speech delivered with confidence showed those words, nor the speaker of them, need for them blush. They were these:

'Brave and renowned King, of whose virtues mine ears have

long since been witness, be pleased to hear your servant say she
doth bless her eyes that presents such worth unto them, and
esteem this as my chiefest happiness: that for the first encounter
in my journey, fortune favours me with the meeting of such
excellent princes, in whom are all the powers of true worthiness
that can be in either or both sexes, and in you, most happy
Queen, the rare virtue of matchless and loyal constancy, and
much do I bless my destiny thus to enjoy your companies, which
Parselius shall thank you for, and I him for you.'

Then she presented them both to her uncle, who kindly
welcomed them, being glad such royal company would attend his
niece to honour her coronation, which he meant should be with
all speed after their arrival, he determining to retire to a religious
house he had built to that purpose. Thus with happy and pleasant
content she sailed towards Pamphilia, while Parselius all this
while continuing in sweet delight, it is now fit time to let him see
his fault committed in the greatest kind of ill, being breach of
faith in love.

One night in his sleep Urania appeared unto him, seeming
infinitely perplexed, but as if rather filled with scorn than sorrow,
telling him he was a traitor to love and the subtlest betrayer of
truth. 'Now may you joy,' said she, 'in your shame and change,
your cruel falsehood having undone my trust, but think not this
troubles me further than for your virtue's sake, so far are you now
from my thoughts as I study how I never more may hear of you, and
to assure you of this, you shall see me give myself before your
face to another more worthy, because more just.'

This in soul so grieved him as he cried, sobbed, groaned and
so lamentably took on as the kind Dalinea, lying by him, awaked,
having much ado to bring him out of his woeful dream. But when
he recovered his senses, they were but to make him more truly
feel pain, continuing in such extremity of weeping as she feared
his heart would break withal, which made her heart even rend
with compassion. Much she entreated, and even besought him to
tell her the cause, but this of any secret must be kept from her.
She begged, he continued in laments, till at last he saw he must
not leave her thus in fear. Wherefore, after he had a little studied
how to be more deceitful, or as equally as he had been before,
weeping still, and she accompanying him in tears, seeing his fall

so fast, which he finding made him weep the more, both now kindly lamenting each other, they remained the most perfect souls of affliction that ever had earthly bodies about them.

Compassion he had in great fullness to Dalinea, torment for Urania's scorn, affliction for her loss, hateful loathing his fault, condemning himself more cruelly than she would have done, all joining as it were for his utter destruction, yet remained he in his bed, framing this excuse to satisfy his wife: telling her that he imagined he saw all Arcadia on fire, the earth flaming, and in the midst his father burning, who with lamentable cries demanded help of him. 'Wherefore,' said he, 'certainly some ill is befallen, or befalling him, which makes me resolve instantly to go unto him.' 'O take me with you,' said she. 'My dear,' said he, 'pardon at this time my leaving you, for should I carry you where troubles are? No sweet, remain you here and be assured you soon shall hear of your Parselius, and if all be well, in short time I'll return for you. Besides, our marriage not yet known may wrong you if not carefully carried. Then, dear love, be patient and stay here.'

She could not deny, for words failed her. Only she sobbed and washed his face with her tears, who was as much afflicted. Then, rising he sent her maids unto her and so departed to his chamber, where he armed himself. Then being ready to go to her, he thought the word or show of farewell would but give new wounds, wherefore writing some few lines, he delivered them to the steward, and so with charge to give the letter to her own hands he took his horse, hasting he knew not whither, regarding neither way nor anything else.

Then came he to the seaside his squire not daring to speak one word to him all that journey. When he sent Clorinus (so was he called) to provide a boat for him, he thought it not fit to deny, nor durst he venture to counsel. In the meantime came a little bark into which he went, turning his horse loose, not considering what grief and trouble might come for his miss. But he, who sought for death, thought of no earthly content.

He being in, they put again from the land, and at Clorinus' return were quite out of sight. He, finding his master's horse without his lord, fell into pitiful complaining, not being able to guess other than the worst mishap. Long he was resolving what to do, but in conclusion he vowed to spend his life in solitary search of him and so to die, but by no means to go to Dalinea, nor to be an ill-news bringer to his parents. Heavily and afflictedly he passed on by the seaside, till he met the squire of Leandrus, who joyfully asked him for his lord. He as sadly replied he had lost him, then followed Leandrus who, knowing the youth, asked for his friend, but to him he could make no answer but in tears. Straight fear possessed him; the youth still wept, Leandrus sighed and, taking him aside, conjured him to tell what he knew of his lord.

Then did he relate all unto him, hiding only what might touch Dalinea. This much moved the prince, yet he sought to comfort Clorinus, telling him he did not see by this any other harm likely to follow but some private grief had made him take this course, and therefore willed him by any means to make no business of it, but go and seek him as carefully as he could, advising him by reason of his love, which he knew he bore to Urania, to go to Cyprus, lest thither he were gone to try the enchantment.

Thus they parted, Leandrus much grieved for Parselius, not indeed being able to judge of the matter, yet took he a good courage to him as a happy foretelling of his friend's safety, and so took his way to Dalinea's castle, whom he found in as much molestation as ever loving and faithful wife felt for the absence of her husband; but when she saw her brother, the joy of that, and her judgement contending with her passion, made her hide it so well as he only believed she had been ill of a fever, which was true, but 'twas the hectic fever of love. Some days he tarried there, all which time she held in good order, but he once gone, she fell into the most dolorous and unsufferable passions that violence in violent love could produce.

Parselius, with a heartless body and a wounded soul, never asking whither they carried him nor speaking one word, held on till they landed him in an island which they knew. So going away from them, he sought the most obscure place he could, but finding now none sad enough, desiring to outgo Perissus in his desolate living, which made him again remember the happiness he had in the finding Urania, for whom he now suffers, was assaulted with a new kind of sorrow, yet all but running to the end of torturing him, embracing memory for telling him all her perfections, as if the fault, the misery of her rage, the misfortune of her loss, were not enough to perplex him, but he must needs add memory as a plague of his own bringing and cherishing.

Then did he wish he were in that island and that he might spend his days in the same rock and that it might likewise include his miseries, cursing his indiscretion that suffered the ship to go away before she had conveyed him thither. Then, seeking for some other bark that might do it, he ran to the sea again, where he found a little boat and in her an old hermit. With him he would go, nor could the old father dissuade him. To a rock they came, being a pretty way within the sea, where being landed, the old man led the way up to the top, where it seemed there had been anciently a temple of great state and bigness, as yet by the ruins did appear. Among those sad places the cell of this good man was made. With this religious man and in this solitary place he resolved to end his days, thinking he could not do better than hide his face, which even himself was ashamed of for having committed so execrable an offence.

Then sat they down together, the old hermit consenting to his stay at last, but something against his will. At first he took him, and he happy (if that word may be used in that misery where happiness nor content or anything but afflictions are) but use what term you will to this, here he stayed, and being set, they told their own stories to each other, Parselius beginning.

'Aged and grave father, give me leave by way of confession to tell you my woeful life, which being so delivered claims secrecy of itself, did not your goodness otherwise warrant me that from you. My name is Parselius, born (in an unhappy hour and under a cursed planet) in Morea, prince thereof and of all miseries, my possessions so largely extending in that continent as none hath a more mighty inheritance. I was bred much at Athens, yet could I learn no way to avoid misfortune, but how to be subject to it I was most apt, humility to subjection reigning more in me than rule.

'My travels I began (as likewise all my good) with a cousin of mine, also bred there, and for the only happiness I ever tasted. We went sometime together in the search of one who I assure myself I have found, and with the finding lost myself, having before that parted from my friends, to the most excellent (and in that my sin the more excelling), I came into an island where I found her whose beauty excelled all things but her mind, which yet beautified that else matchless body. With her I fell in love, and loved her earnestly. Villain that I say, I loved, and so prove by the change my fault, much more that I must say I ever loved her who (sweetest creature) believing me, that then was just, went with, leaving that island where she was bred, trusting me who have deceived her.

'Many dangers we passed, she in all of them fearing nothing but my harm, who since have brought the greatest to her. At last a storm took us when we were, as we thought, safe and in sight of Italy, and wherein we might have landed, but destiny otherwise appointed for us. This tempest brought us from joy and comfort to despair and loss, for we were carried (in the many days that it endured) to Cyprus, where landing, by wicked charms our ship burned and we were forced to go up into the island for succour.

'Then arrived we at an enchanted palace made of purpose for my destruction, wherein Urania is enclosed—she whom once I did best love, who ought still to have been best loved, and she for whose loss in my falsehood thus tormenteth me. Thence parted I, deprived of all sense, but by leaving that land came again into them to be more vexed with them, a while (and wretch, too small a while) lamenting her imprisonment and my want, which wilfully I caused to be no longer want but direct loss.

'O fault unpardonable, why do I live to confess it, and shame in me, not quite devouring me, but I who was born to ill, led by the servants of Hell, or Hell itself conspiring my ruin, brought me into Achaea and so into the power of vile change. There I saw Dalinea, daughter to the King of Achaea; she blinded not alone mine eyes with admiration, but my judgement, blotting out and forcing my memory to be treacherous to me, made me forget all thoughts of my more deserving love and truth itself, letting me see nothing but desire of her love, she virtuous (and too perfect for such a worthless creature as myself) could but allow of virtuous yielding. I, to enjoy, granted anything, and so I married her, with whom I remained some while as happy as any blessing in a wife could make me, and yet in that am most unblessed, not being able to continue in that happy state of still enjoying her, too great a proportion of good for me (wretched man) to have.

'For one night I saw Urania in my sleep appear unto me, or

better to say, my conscience, taking the advantage of my body's rest, the hateful enemy to the soul's bliss, and in that quiet showed unto me my dearest shepherdess justly accusing me and condemning me. I had no way to escape, if not by this means: I rose, I left Dalinea for Urania's fury, whose sweet substance I lost for Dalinea's love. I have now left both, both injured, both afflicted by me. Why should I then continue such an affliction to the rarest of women and a vexation to the worst, as I am unto my unblessed self. Assist me, good father, in my misery. This is truth I have told you, and more than ought to live on earth or I hope can be found again, wherefore that as all ill is in me, I desire, nay covet to end, that the world may be no longer infected with that plague, but as knit in me, that knot may never be untied but end and conclude with me.'

Then wept he as if it had been to satisfy a drought with rain, shedding tears in such abundance as they left that name to be more properly termed little streams. Well it was that the sea was the place of receiving those springs which from the rock ran into her, which in madness of despair he would once have followed, offering to tumble into her. The old man, striving with him, stayed him, who had lost all power to resist, grief having taken away his strength and in place of it given him only might in weakening passions working for their glory to destroy.

Then did the aged hermit comfort him, chiding him for his wilful sin in seeking to murder himself. Religiously he wrought upon his fury, so as he brought him to a more peaceable bearing his afflictions, but not to any more easy.

This storm a little quieted (as after a tempest of thunder a shower of rain is thought little) the good man, to pass the time, began his story, the relation whereof gave some liking to Parselius. But because the drums beat and trumpets sound in Morea for the relief of Macedon, and the brave conquest of Rosindy, the hermit's discourse must a little stay, while wars, the noblest because professed by the noblest, take a little time for them.

The time come for the army's marching; brave Rosindy took his journey with his most noble companions, he general, Selarinus general of the horse, the princes of Corinth and Elis had their places reserved for them as sergeant major and commander of the archers. Many brave knights and bold men went along, some out of love, some for ambition, some for honour, many for preferment. The rendezvous was at Cariapa-iary in the confines of Macedon, not far distant from the river Devoda, where they met the Rumanian army led by Lisandrinus as desired, but with it came Antissius to see the brave wars and to receive knighthood of Amphilanthus, who not being there, he soon left the army to find him out, promising when he had from him received that honour (and only from him would he have it), he would return to them wherever they were.

Thus marched they on with all the bravery that might be, everyone striving who should be most sumptuous, to express their loves and respects to their general, who was more generally beloved than any prince except his cousin and brother, everyone wearing his colours in honour to him, which was orange-tawny and white.

Thither came to the place of meeting also the Achaeans, led by Leandrus, who after he had visited his sister, and once again seen his aged father, followed the army gone before and overtook them before their coming to the town. With them (and much true affection in himself to the general) he came to Rosindy, of whom he received most loving welcome. Whoever could imagine glory might here have seen it at the height of perfection: magnanimous spirits, brave and unconquered men, undaunted soldiers, riches of all gallantry in every respect and, what was most and best, all excellent soldiers and true soldiers, the excellentest men.

Thus then was all that could be wished in this army together joined. None refused passage, but willingly yielded it to be rid of their force, so as love or fear made free and open way for them till they came within the skirts of Macedon. There they met some, but poor, resistance, till they came to a great plain near the river of Devoda. There they saw a great army and by intelligence knew the usurper was there. They went as near him as discretion would permit them, considering night grew on, and as judicially provided for the army, the general himself going to settle every quarter in his right place, being so expert in the learning of the art of a soldier, as he could justly tell what compass of ground would serve from one hundred to thousands.

When he had settled them, he returned to his tent, where he

with the princes and commanders supped, after consulting what
would be fittest to be done the next day. Many opinions were
given: some to set upon the King and his army, but that Selarinus
liked not, 'For,' said he, 'we are but strangers, and all our hope
and power in the army. If we be overthrown, all is lost for us, if he
lose the day, he is in his own country, and may have aid instantly
brought to him. Therefore, I think fitter to let him urge us than
for us to press him to fight; besides, no question but he will do
that; why then should we be so forward? Let us patiently go on
with temper, and the greater will be our benefit.' Rosindy much
commended his advice and resolved to be persuaded by it.

While thus they sat, came a trumpet from Clotorindus with a
defy and a challenge to fight the next morning. This was
accepted, the hour appointed eight of the clock. Thus everyone
betook themselves to rest, hoping for the next day's victory. As
soon as day appeared, Rosindy took his horse and rid through all
the army, advising, entreating, commanding and using fair
words, entreaties, peremptory authority, and all in their kinds as
he found the subjects on whom they must be used, with such
judgement as bred not only love and fear, but admiration in all
hearts to see so great understanding and unusual excellency in so
few years.

But now all are ready; his army he ordered thus: the foot he
divided in three bodies, the vanguard led by himself, accompanied with Leandrus; the main battle by Selarinus accompanied
with Lysandrinus; the rear by the grave marshall, who went with
him out of love to his person, with him was his son Lizarino;
some of the horse (by reason of advantage was found in that
place) were put on either side as wings, the right-hand wing
given to Tolymandro, the left to the prince of Elis; some foot
placed to flank the horse and some horse put in each division.

Clotorindus had put his men much in this kind. So they
charged the vanguard of the Macedonians, led by a brave and
valiant gentleman called Thesarinus, prince of Sparta, who did
so bravely as, had there been but few more of his spirit, the day
had hardly been lost, at least not so soon won. Rosindy with the
vanguard charged the Macedonians, where there was a cruel
fight: the Morean horse first defeated, then the vanguard broken
and disordered, which Selarinus perceiving, came in with the

main-battle to the succour, where so bravely he found Rosindy
fighting as he had made walls of dead men of his own killing
round about him, as if they had been cast up of purpose for his
safety, or as a list roped in for the combat which he was in with
the young Phalerinus, prince of Thessalonica, who more delicately
and bravely held out than any he had yet encountered, but what
with weariness and besides seeing the new succour come was
forced to yield—Rosindy taking him in his arms instead of
disarming him, taking his word instead of his sword, which noble
act bred so much love in the young prince towards him, as he
after proved a true and faithful subject unto him.

Then did Rosindy and Sclarinus haste to the battle, which was
now, by the overthrow of the vanguard, required to come up, and
the rear with the strangers to advance against the Macedonian
horse. A great while the Moreans had the worst, but at last by the
valour of Selarinus, Leandrus (who had changed his white
armour's innocent colour to revengeful blood), Lisandrinus, the
princes of Corinth and Elis and the marshall with his son, but
especially by the judgement mixed with true valour and the care
matched with excellent skill of Rosindy, the victory came on their
side with the shameful flight of Clotorindus.

The execution was great and endured long; the conquest
greater, the booty very rich, and thus with the loss of ten
thousand on the one side and thirty on the other, the retreat was
sounded. The next day the dead of both sides buried, and
Rosindy with his brave troop marched on towards Thessalonica
where the Queen was, and into which town the usurper was got
of purpose, if not by strength, yet by tricks to save himself and
keep the crown—but neither he must do.

Then did the brave General set down before Thessalonica
and, encompassing it round, cutting off all victual by land and
blocking the sea and ships, hindered all good from their aid, so
making it a rare and cruel siege. Now did Rosindy endure the
length of this with much pain, longing in his very soul to see his
lady, which within some time after he did, but so as the great
longing he had satisfied by her sight was turned to sorrow for it,
his desire and joy to see her changed to grief, and wishing he had
not seen her, the cause and his affliction, as he termed it, proving
terrible. Thrice were there sallies made forth by the besieged,

but to as little purpose as if they meant only to come forth to be honoured with wounds and being vanquished by their mighty enemies.

One day they saw a white flag upon the wall, which gave them to understand a parly was demanded, by the beating likewise of a drum, which Rosindy did in the same manner answer. They came upon the wall, the prince and his companions to the wall, then did Clotorindus speak thus.

'Great prince Rosindy, and you brave princes his companions, what injustice do you go about in seeking to deprive me of mine own, who never wronged you, nor would have denied to have served any of you with my own person and means if you had required it. Now for you to seek to take a kingdom from me, lawfully my right both by being next heir male and besides mine now by marriage with Meriana, daughter and heir, as you term her, to the crown, what exceptions can you now take? Let me then, as a friend and kinsman (as by marriage I now am to you) gain peace. I, that have been by your own will made your enemy, desire an end of these cruel wars. Let me be accepted as a cousin and my friendship taken as proffered by a friend, rather than thus continue shedding of blood. Let the conclusion be welcome and the trumpets and drums turned to music of joy. This I demand for myself as your friend if you please, and for my wife, your cousin, who infinitely is grieved to have her own blood seek to shed the blood of her dear husband.'

'Husband, false traitor,' replied Rosindy, 'she whose matchless worth so well knows itself cannot abuse that knowledge of truth, to yield the treasure of it to so base a place, and which never had stain but by this thy wronging her, who cannot live to undo that with bestowing it on one so vile and treacherous as thyself. For thy friendship, I refuse it, and so I answer for my friends here present, condemning thy baseness so as we should hate ourselves if a thought of thy submission (if not to punish thee) could come into our hearts. Thy false tale of marriage we loathe to hear of, since as falsehood we hate that, and thee for it. Thou sayest we have no just quarrel. O monster, what justice more can be required than taking arms to the putting down a rebel and a traitor to his rightful princess? Alliance thou claimest; I acknowledge none, and had there been no other cause, this had

been enough to have made us ruin thee, for framing so false a
report and wronging (with thy filthy tongue) thy Queen and the
Queen of true virtue and of Macedon. Therefore, recant and
deliver her, or here I vow to fire the town and break open the
gates to let in our just revenge to thee and on thee.'

'Is this the requital of my kindness?' said Clotorindus.
'Farewell, do thy worst, proud prince, and all thy fond company.
But take this with thee: before the town be won, thy heart shall
ache more than ever any wound could come near thee to bring it,
or the wound of thy fond love.'

With that, he went from the wall, and instead of the white flag,
presently a bloody one was hung forth, which continued till the
next day, whenas to the same place Meriana was brought, with an
infinite number of armed men, dressed as to her wedding, a
crown on her head and her hair all down. To this sight was most
of the army drawn, but Rosindy with most haste, greedily
beholding her beauty and hearkening to her speech, which was
this:

'Clotorindus, thou hast now (I confess) some pity in thee, since
thou wilt free me from my miserable living. I thank thee for it,
and Rosindy, I hope, shall requite it, to whom I commend my
best and last love. Farewell brave prince, but be thus confident
that I am just.' With that, they enclosed her round in a circle,
often before seeking to hinder her last speech.

Presently was she out of Rosindy's sight, and presently again
brought into it, to his extremest misery, for only that peerless
head was seen of him, being set upon a pillar and that pillar being
upon the top of the palace, the hair hanging in such length and
delicacy as, although it somewhat covered with the thickness of it
part of the face, yet was that too sure a knowledge to Rosindy of
her loss, making it appear unto him that none but that excellent
Queen was mistress of that excellent hair. His soul and heart rent
with this sight, and the seeing it afar off, rising with such speed as
it seemed a comet to show before their ruin, or like the moon,
having borrowed the sun's beams to glorify her pale face with his
golden rays.

All the army made a most pitiful and mournful cry, as if every
one had lost a love, and the princes cried upon revenge. That
word wrought most upon Rosindy, the rest being before but a

time to lull his passions in their rest, which were restless
afflictions. Long it was before he spake; at last he cried: 'Arm,
and assault this wicked town!' Then went he in the head of the
army to the gates, which with engines that they had, and guided
with fury, by the next morning they broke open, not before when
judgement governed, being able to persuade themselves they
could have compassed it.

The gate open, they with furious rage and merciless cruelty
proceeded, sparing not one creature they met, hasting to take
down the head of his dearest love and hopes. But when he came
thither, he saw that taken away also. 'O cruelty unjust,' said he,
'wilt thou not suffer me to see her once more? Wretched fate,
that I must now be barred from taking yet the last kiss from thy
dear, though pale, dead lips, on them to seal the last part of my
life.'

He complained thus, yet his grief increased his rage, so as he
came into the palace, where he found Clotorindus in the hall with
a dagger in his hand who, as soon as he saw him, with a hellish
countenance, he looked on him and in a curst voice said: 'Thy
victory shall yet never be honoured by my death, which but with
mine own hand shall be brought me.' Then stabbed he himself in
many places of his body, and so fell. The prince, scorning to
touch him, commanded the soldiers to take him and throw him
into the ditch, esteeming that too good a burial for him.

Then went he on further, hoping in despair to know how his
soul was parted from him, and where the body did remain,
meaning on that place to make his tomb and in it to consume,
pine, and die. With this he went into many rooms but found no
body. Then went he to the gallery where he first spoke with her,
throwing himself upon the ground, kissing the place, and
weeping out his woe.

Selarinus stayed with him to hinder any rash or sudden
attempt he might make upon himself. Leandrus and the rest
made safe the town, and took all the people that were left (which
were but few) to mercy in Rosindy's name, who lying thus, at last
start up, crying he heard his lady call for help. Selarinus,
doubting it had been but some unruly passion, mistrusting more
his friend seeing the vehemency of his passion than hoping the
truth of this, followed him till he came into a tower at the end of

the gallery, where he also heard a voice pitifully complaining, at last hearing it bring forth these words: 'O Rosindy, how justly hast thou dealt with me, and royally performed thy word. But, wretch that I am, I shall not do so with thee, for here must I consume my days unknown to thee and, walled up with misery and famine, die.'

This was enough for the two brave men to make new comfort in new strength to relieve her, wherefore Rosindy cried out 'Dost thou live my Meriana? Here is thy faithful love and servant come to rescue thee.' 'O my lord,' said she, 'never in a happier time. Quickly then, give me life with your sight.'

Then ran Selarinus down with joy to call for help, Rosindy examining every place where he might find the fittest to come to throw down the wall, but then a new fear took him, how they might do that and not hurt her. But the greater danger must be avoided and the less taken, so the soldiers came and threw down the wall, Rosindy still crying to her to take heed, and when they came to the last blow that there was, a place appeared (though small) into the room, none then must work there but himself, lest dust or any the least thing might offend her.

But when the wall was so much down as she was able to come out, with what joy did he hold her and she embrace her love! Imagine excellent lovers, what two such could do when, after the sight of one dead, the other walled to certain death, seeing both taken away and met with comfort, what could they say? What joy possessed them, heavenly comfort and all joys on earth knit in this to content them!

Then did Rosindy as much weep with joy as he did before with mourning, and she weeped to see his tears, so as joy, not being to express itself, was forced to borrow part with sorrow to satisfy it. Selarinus chid them for that passion, and so brought them out of it, bringing them into the hall, whither by that time the other princes were come, and the chief of the army. In that brave and most warlike presence did Meriana give herself to Rosindy, being there betrothed. Then were the others of the people taken to Meriana, the Macedonians from all parts coming with exprestest* joy unto her, yielding themselves as her loyal subjects and taking others to her and Rosindy of allegiance.

Then sent he new governors and commanders to all the

frontier towns, and into the chief strength within the land, requiting the Moreans with the estates of those that were lost in the battle and the town, the strangers with the booty, which was infinite, and other such rewards as bound their loves to him forever, not being able to hope to thrive so well in the next business, which now must be for Albania.

The Queen Meriana and Rosindy in this content, the counterfeiting was found and the device discovered, which was told by a servant of Clotorindus used in the business, which was that pillar had been made and set there by her father, a man excellently graced in all arts, and especially in perspectives. To try his skill he made this which, though so big as one might stand in it, yet so far it seemed but as a small pillar, of purpose made to hold a head upon, and so had they raised her within it, as no more appeared above it than her chin coming over it; it was as if stuck into her throat, the just distance and art in the making being such and so excellent as none could but have thought it had been her head cut off, besides the grief and her own complexion, naturally a little pale, made her seem more than usually, and so nearer death, the intent being to make Rosindy believe she was dead, which conceit, he hoped, would lead him thence, she being gone for whose sake he came thither, which if it had taken effect, then she should have lived as she had done before, but seeing neither his false tale nor this took the way he wished, he walled her up, purposing that since he could not win nor keep her, none should else enjoy her. But now all is ended with the blessing of enjoying. In a better estate, who can be left?

Amphilanthus, following his way to Cyprus with his friend Ollorandus, quickly landed there, taking their way as they were directed by passengers (the country now full of people that came to see the end of this business) to the throne of love, the plain before it being all set with tents and covered with knights and ladies.

The first tent Amphilanthus knew to be some Italian's, wherefore he went into that and, finding it belonged to the Duke of Milan, whose opinion of his own worth and the beauty of his mistress had made him adventure the enchantment, was therein enclosed, he discovered himself unto his servants, who presently made offer of it to his service, which he accepted, yet did he charge the men not to let him be known by any but themselves. There they rested for that night, the next morning going among the tents, finding many brave princes and excellent ladies, some come to adventure, others only to behold the adventures of others. Many of these the two excellent companions knew, but they, keeping their beavers down, were not known of any.

One lady among the rest, or rather above the rest, for exquisite wit and rare spirit, so perfect in them as she excelled her sex so much as her perfections were styled masculine. This lady (as her judgement was greater than the rest, so her observation was likewise more particular) cast her eyes upon these strangers, but most on the Italian. She sighed at first sight, after grew sad, wondering why she was so troubled, not knowing the face of her trouble, never then resting till she had got the truth of whence he was, and so the means to see him. He, having enquired of everyone's name and title, came also to know her to be called Luceania, daughter to a nobleman who was brother to the famously virtuous but unfortunate lady Luceania, wife and mother to the first and this last Antissius, King of Rumania.

Wife she was to a great lord in the same country who, though unable to flatter himself with conceit of worth sufficient to end so rare an adventure, yet partly for novelties and most to please his spiritfull wife he came thither, loving the best company for these reasons.

The prince was glad to hear this because he was now sure of acquaintance quickly there. As soon as his name was known, she studying to have her ends by his knowledge, watched the next fit opportunity, which was offered the next day by a general meeting of all the knights and ladies. He, seldom bashful, put himself among them. Luceania must needs know him, wherefore she asked those that accompanied her who that stranger was. They all answered they knew him not, nor could they learn of any who he was.

'Is it possible,' said she, 'so brave a prince should be unknown?' Many, desiring to do her service, she being for noble behaviour, courtesy, wit and greatness of understanding loved and admired of all such as could be honoured with her conversation, to please her, everyone endeavoured, and one forwarder than the rest (as more bound in affection) went to him, telling him that a fair lady much desired to know his name.

'Can it be,' answered the King, 'that any fair lady should so much honour me as to desire so worthless a thing as my name?' 'There is one, Sir,' said he, 'who curiously desireth the knowledge of it, which must be more worthy than you do account it, otherwise could she not covet it, and such a one is she,' said he, 'as if you can deserve beauty you will acknowledge only deserves honour and service.'

'They belong,' said the King, 'to all such excellent creatures. Yet Sir,' said he, 'it is my ill fortune at this time that I am not able to satisfy her demand, although this grace shall ever make me her servant.' The knight, acquainted with such vows, went back to Luceania, truly telling her all that he had said, which although delivered by a far worse orator, yet gained they more favour for him, she esteeming wit beyond outward beauty, but both there joined, it is necessary for to yield as she did, for before she desired his name only, now finding judgement and brave courtship, she longs for his society, and these accompanied with seeing his excellently sweet and ever conquering loveliness, did join as to the conquest of her, for she who before had known love rather by name than subjection, now she finds herself love's prisoner, affection before but companion-like, now mastering, and now she finds it expedient to know that delightful cruel who had with so pleasing a dart wounded and seized her (till then commanding) heart.

The next evening was resolved of for her gain of knowledge and, rather than miss, there she would employ the same lovesick knight again, who to be graced with her commands would do anything. The evening come, Amphilanthus and his companion, assuring themselves they were unknown, freely came into the company. She who now was by the art of love taught to watch all opportunities and never to lose any, was walking with her husband forth to pass away the time in the cool air. Amphilanthus and his friend, discoursing of their own passions, finding the greatest miss ever in most company, their ladies being absent, were so transported with their passions as they were close to this amorous lady and her lord before they discovered it, which when they found, asked pardon for their rudeness.

They would have returned, but she, who was now not to put off her hopes till the next meeting, resolved to make use of this. So with as enticing a countenance as Caesar understood Cleopatra's to be, she told them she saw no error they had committed, that place being free to all, but turning herself towards her husband and smiling, said: 'Would you think, my lord, this knight were ashamed of his name?' 'I see small reason that he should,' said he, 'why think you that he is?' 'Because he refuseth to tell it,' said she.

'Although, excellent lady,' answered Amphilanthus, 'it may be my name is not so fortunate as to have come to your ears with any renown, yet am I not ashamed of it, a vow only having made me conceal it.' 'May not that vow be broken?' said she. 'This may, and shall,' said he, 'to satisfy your desire, though some vows are so dear as nothing nor any force may prevail against them.'

With that she saw Ollorandus had undertaken her husband, which gave her more liberty in her desires, again urging with fine and amorous countenances the breach of his vow. 'The commanding power,' said he, 'which your perfections carry with them must prevail. Then be pleased to know I am Amphilanthus, King of the Romans.'

'Pardon me, my lord,' said she, 'that I have been thus bold with you which was caused by . . . ' With that she, blushing, held her peace, desiring to be thought bashful, but more longing to be entreated for the rest. 'Nay, speak on excellent lady,' said he, 'and bar not mine ears from hearing what you surely once thought me worthy to know.' 'Well then, my lord,' said she, 'you shall have it. My desire to know you was caused by an unresisting power your excellencies have over my yielding affections to you. The first time I saw you I received the wound I now perish in, if you favour not.'

Amphilanthus was rather sorry than glad to hear this speech, being to him like as where the law is that a man condemned to die may be saved if a maid beg him for her husband. So he may be saved from death, but wedded against his heart to another; affection before having wounded him, he can scarce entertain this. But considering gratefulness is required as a chief virtue in every worthy man, he courteously replied that, till that time, fortune had never so honoured him as to bring him to the height of so much happiness as to be graced with such an affection.

She, who loved and desired, took the least word he spoke for a blessed consent, was about to answer again, when they saw Ollorandus come with her husband to them, who with much ado (as he counterfeited) had told who they were. The good man, hearing that these were two of them relieved and won Rumania to quiet by their own valour, but especially rejoicing that Amphilanthus (of whom the world was filled with fame) was there, came to welcome him, nor would be denied, but they must lodge with him in his tent.

Luceania was not grieved at this motion, though Amphilanthus would willingly have gone back to his Milan tent, where he might have comforted himself with discoursing to his own thoughts. But the lady now keeps him prettily well from those passions with continual discourse of other things.

Much he enquired after the manner of ending the enchantment, which he longed for, that then he might again see what he only coveted, love still increasing in her as longing grew in him to see his dearest love. He kindly entertained her favours and courteously requited them, and one day, the more to express his respect to her, he took this course, which in his own mind was plotted rather to get more freedom and to make proof of his valour, his friend and he only acquainting Luceania and her lord with it: changing their armours and colours the better to be unknown, came in the morning with trumpets before them, challenging everyone that desired to try his strength to the joust, to break six staves apiece, and this to continue six days in defence of their mistress's beauty.

Amphilanthus was in watchet and white, Ollorandus in orange colour, he having no favour, and therefore in spite wore that colour. The other had a scarf which Luceania sent him the night before, which he wore on his right arm. This challenge brought forth all the knights, and they the ladies. The first was an Italian, and encountered Ollorandus (who was to hold the first three days, if so long he could without fail, by Amphilanthus' appointment; if not, then he to come in).

This Italian was strong, and the stronger for that he was in love, and more because his mistress at that time made him the bolder, being favoured with her sight and blessed with her loving wishes. But these could not prevail against the Bohemian, who had the stronger spirit waiting on him of perfect love, which overthrew the Italian, lying on the ground, flatly confessing his overthrow.

Two days he thus kept the field, without show of losing the honour to any. But then came one who encountered him with such clean strength and valour as he was forced to confess he matched him, nor did it turn to any dishonour to him when it was known who it was, being Polarchus, bastard son to the King of that island. But soon did Amphilanthus revenge his friend, and so by conquest kept the field, though he confessed he had seldom felt such an encounter as the last of the six courses, the other five having lasted without any advantage, this with the loss of his stirrups, but the falling back of the other upon his horse's back and tumbling down, striving to recover his saddle. Thus he redeemed his friend's mischance, maintaining the field against all comers in the defence of his mistress's beauty

Two days he held it, in which time he won the fame of the bravest knight. The last day they were a little hindered from that sport by the coming of a great and brave troop of knights, having with them two of the beauties the world could hold excellent. They rode in a chariot of watchet velvet embroidered with crimson silk and pearl the inside, the outside with pearl of silver, and yet that riches poor in comparison of the incomparable brightness and clearness of their own beauties. Soon were they known, for who could be ignorant of the perfections of Pamphilia and Limena, for he that never saw Pamphilia but by report, seeing this unspeakable beauty, said it could be no other than that peerless Queen, none else could so excel in true perfection.

Two knights rid on each side of the chariot, one in armour of gold enamelled with leaves of laurel, the other all black. Thus they came with great magnificence and state, when Amphilanthus was ready to encounter a new knight, that would needs have the favour to be thrown down by the conquering prince, who soon received the honour his vanquishing power gave all other, kissing his mother* without desire or pleasure.

Then did the prince look about him, casting his eyes by chance towards the troop, at which sight he straight knowing the never enough exalted princess, he went towards her, his eyes meeting the unresisting power of her eyes, who was sovereign of all hearts, telling the new Queen that certainly now the charms must have conclusion, she being come to adventure for them. 'I hope my lord,' said she, 'there will be an end of them, since I know I am able to bring one part to the conclusion's demand, being that, I think you have not been much troubled withal, and in truth I cannot blame you much, since liberty is an excellent profit. But what colour shall we have next? The last I saw was crimson, now watchet and white. Do you add to your inconstancy as fast as to your colours?'

'None can be accused, dear lady,' said he, 'for their change, if it be but till they know the best, therefore little fault hath yet been in me. But now I know the best change shall no more know me.' 'Every change brings this thought,' said she, 'but here is the Queen Limena, whose noble virtues were rescued by your friend and my brother from cruelty and death, though not of them, but her person dying, they must (if not for him) have remained the outward tombs of her honour.' Then kissed he her hands, and so conducted the two Queens to the fittest place to see those begun sports and to be beheld of the knights.

Amphilanthus continuing his still enjoyed victories, none parting from him without flat falls or apparent loss of honour. Then the knight of victory and the black knight came unto him with these words: 'Victorious Sir, we see how bravely and happily you have carried yourself in this challenge, and so as we should be too bold flatterers of ourselves if we would hope to get the better of you, yet being knights and servants to fair ladies, we are engaged in honour to try our fortunes with you, defending that these two ladies are fairer and more truly worthy than your mistress.'

'I,' said the knight of victory, 'defend the Queen Limena.' 'And I,' said the other, 'the incomparable Pamphilia.' 'Your demand,' said Amphilanthus, 'shall be answered, although I must confess it rather should be yielded unto without blows. Yet will I proceed in the begun challenge, though against beauties matchless, and first answer you who defend the Queen Limena.'

All eyes were fixed upon these two, one known powerful and
not to be vanquished, the, other outwardly appearing excellent,
and so did he prove himself, for never were six courses run more
finely than these were, so as everyone said that none but another
Amphilanthus could have performed them so delicately. Yet a
little difference there was between them, which made a question
to whom the whole honour did belong. Amphilanthus lost his
stirrups, and the other was struck flat upon his horse. But the
prince himself ordered the business thus: that he would make an
end of that morning's triumph and the other should have the
afternoon's trial.

This was agreed on by all and he much commended for his
royal courtesy. When none came, Amphilanthus, lighting from
his horse, came to the stranger, who stood ready to receive him
with his right gauntlet off but his beaver down, to whom the
prince with a grave and sweet countenance delivered the spear
and liberty for the free accomplishing the rest of that exercise.
The stranger with all respect, and indeed affection, received that
favour, wishing the happiness to conclude the time with as much
bravery and good fortune as Amphilanthus had done the days
past.

Then did the prince boldly show himself to all, many there
knowing him and coming humbly to acknowledge their loves and
gratefulness unto him for infinite favours received by them from
him, for indeed, no man was ever enriched with a more noble,
free and excellent disposition than this exquisite prince had
flowing in him. After dinner this most honoured and beloved
prince, with the admired Queens, Ollorandus and the rest, came
again to see the conclusion of that brave sport, in which time the
knight of victory so stoutly behaved himself as thereby he gained
exceeding great fame. But now was evening beginning to
threaten him with her power to overcome his victories, which yet
remained whole unto him, few being left that were not by
Amphilanthus, Ollorandus or himself taught how to adventure in
such like businesses.

He now having a little time left him to breathe in, none coming
against him, he looked about and cast his eyes on her whose
beauty he so bravely defended, with such affection as he stirred
not them nor his mind from that beloved object, till a boy in

shepherd's apparel delivered these words to him, almost pulling him before he gave him hearing.

'My lord,' said he, 'for so my master bid me call you, I come from yon man, one who not skill in arms but truth of his lady's beauty brings forth and by me sends you word that your mistress Limena is not one half so fair as his Queen Pamphilia. It is, he says, no boldness to defend her, whose beauty is without compare, wherefore he desires you to prepare yourself. But take heed Sir, he is mighty strong.'

'Good boy,' said the knight, 'tell your master I will attend him, and I pray thee advise him as well for the love I bear thee.' Then came the shepherd knight, for so they called him, all in ash colour, no plume nor favour, only favoured with his lady's best wishes (the best of favours). The encounter was strong and delightful, shivers of their spears ascending into the air like sparks of a triumph fire. Four courses they ran, without any difference for advantage. The fifth, the knight of victory lost both stirrups and a little yielded with his body, the other passing with the loss of one stirrup. The sixth and last being, if it were possible, a more strong and excellent course, their ambitions equal to honour, glorious to love, and covetous of gain before their ladies, scorning any place lower than the face.

Both hit so luckily and equally as their beavers flew up, the knight of victory being known to be Perissus, the other Amphilanthus who, confident that now he had truth on his side, and desirous once more to try the strength of the other, while most eyes were on the champion, he stole away and armed himself. Amphilanthus at first knew not Perissus, many years having passed since their last meeting. But when he heard Perissus named, with what joy did he embrace him, being the man who from his youth he had like himself loved, admiring his virtues and loving his person.

This done, they went to Pamphilia's tent, where she gave Amphilanthus infinite thanks for the honour he had done her. 'But yet my lord,' said she, 'I must blame my poor beauty for the delay you had in your victory, which I confessed when I saw so long deferring of your overcoming, grieving then for that want which brought your stay in winning.'

'Detract not from your beauty, which all judgements know

without equal,' said he, ' nor from the bounty of the renowned and famous Perissus, but give the reason where it is, which is want in my fortune to obtain anything that most I desire or seek, such crosses hitherunto accompanied my life.' Then did Pamphilia entreat him to take knowledge of the other knight, whose name was Millisander, Duke of Pergamus and her subject, whose father, though newly dead and therefore wore that mourning armour, yet would not stay, but attend her thither. Then Amphilanthus desired to know how it came about that she honoured that place with her presence. The Queen, willing to satisfy his demand, began her discourse in this manner:

'Mine uncle, King of Pamphilia, coming for me to carry me into his country and there to settle me (as long since he resolved) by the consent and leave of my father, I went with him, by the way winning the happiness of the companies of these excellent princes, Perissus and Limena. After our arrival I was crowned, and being peaceably settled, mine uncle retired into a religious house, where he will end his days. I heard still the fame of this enchantment, of which I had understood by my brother Parselius, who had himself got some unfortunate knowledge of it. I desired to adventure it, being assured that I was able for one part to conclude it, since it is to be finished by that virtue I may most justly boast of. Thus resolved, honoured with the presence likewise of this excellent King and virtuous Queen, with the consent of my people leaving the government for this time with the council, we came to adventure for the Throne of Love.'

'Which,' said Amphilanthus, 'I am also to try, wherefore let me be so much favoured as I may be the knight to adventure with you, and you shall see I want not so much constancy as not to bring it to end, though it pleased you lately to tax me with it.' 'My lord,' said she, 'I taxed you only for Antissia's sake, who (poor lady) would die if she thought that you had changed, she so entirely loveth you.' 'Hath she spoken to you to speak for her?' said he. 'In truth she did well, since love much better suits with your lips than her own. But shall I have the honour that I seek?' 'You shall command, my lord,' said she, 'and we will surely bring an end to it, your valour and my loyalty being met together.'

He made no other answer than with his eyes, so for that night they all parted, everyone expecting the next morning's fortune,

when the Throne should be so bravely adventured for. All that
would try their fortunes had free liberty, so six couples ventured
before the peerless pair, but all were imprisoned, to be honoured
the more with having their delivery by the power of the most
excellent, who being ready to adventure, they were hindered a
little by the coming of a gentleman in white armour richly set
forth and bravely accompanied, who coming directly to Amphilanthus desired the honour of knighthood, telling him he had
sought many places and passed many countries to receive that
favour from him, which but from him he would not accept,
withal pulling off his helm, which presently made him to be
known to be Antissius, King of Rumania.

Amphilanthus, with due respect to him, welcomed him,
protesting he could never merit so high an honour as this was
unto him, wherefore without delay, in the sight of all that princely
company, he girt the sword to him, and he with Perissus put on
his spurs. Then came Allimarlus to kiss his hands, who most
kindly he received. 'And now my lord,' said he, 'you are very fitly
come to see the Throne of Love won (I hope) by this surpassing
Queen and your servant myself.'

Antissius went to salute the Queen; so together they passed
towards the bridge, Antissius and Ollorandus going together,
twined in each other's arms, Pamphilia being thus apparelled: in
a gown of light tawny or murray*, embroidered with the richest
and perfectest pearl for roundness and whiteness, the work
contrived into knots and garlands. On her head she wore a crown
of diamonds without foils, to show her clearness, such as needed
no foil to set forth the true brightness of it. Her hair (alas that
plainly I must call that hair, which no earthly riches could value
nor heavenly resemblance counterfeit) was prettily intertwined
between the diamonds in many places, making them (though of
the greatest value) appear but like a glass set in gold.

Her neck was modestly bare, yet made all discern it was not to
be beheld with eyes of freedom. Her left glove was off, holding
the King by the hand, who held most hearts. He was in ash
colour, witnessing his repentance, yet was his cloak and the rest
of his suit so sumptuously embroidered with gold as spoke for
him that his repentance was most glorious.

Thus they passed into the first tower, where in letters of gold

they saw written 'Desire'. Amphilanthus knew he had as much
strength in desire as any, wherefore he knocked with assured
confidence at the gate, which opened, and they with their royal
companions passed to the next tower, where in letters of rubies
they read 'Love'. 'What say you to this, brave Queen?' said he.
'Have you so much love as can warrant you to adventure for this?'
'I have,' answered she, 'as much as will bring me to the next
tower, where I must (I believe) first adventure for that.'

Both then at once extremely loving, and love in extremity in
them, made the gate fly open to them, who passed to the last
tower, where Constancy stood holding the keys, which Pamphilia
took, at which instant Constancy vanished, as metamorphosing
herself into her breast. Then did the excellent Queen deliver
them to Amphilanthus, who joyfully receiving them, opened the
gate. Then passed they into the gardens, where round about a
curious fountain were fine seats of white marble, which after, or
rather with the sound of rare and heavenly music, were filled with
those poor lovers who were there imprisoned, all chained one
unto another with links of gold enamelled with roses and other
flowers dedicated to love.

Then was a voice heard which delivered these words:
'Loyallest and therefore most incomparable Pamphilia, release
the ladies, who much* to your worth, with all other of your sex,
yield right pre-eminence, and thou Amphilanthus, the valiantest
and worthiest of thy sex, give freedom to the knights who, with all
other, must confess thee matchless. And thus is love by love and
worth released.'

Then did the music play again, and in that time the palace and
all vanished, the knights and ladies with admiration beholding
each other. Then Pamphilia took Urania and, with affection
kissing her, told her the worth which she knew to be in her had
long since bound her love to her, and had caused that journey of
purpose to do her service. Then came Perissus bringing Limena
to thank her, who heartily did it, as she deserved, since from her
counsel her fortunes did arise. Amphilanthus likewise saluted
her, having the same conceit of resemblance between her and
Leonius as Parselius had, and so told her with exceeding joy, all
after one another coming to her, and the rest.

Antissius, casting his eye upon Selarina, fixed it so as it was but as the setting of a branch to make a tree spring of it, so did his love increase to full perfection. Then all, desired by Pamphilia, took their way to her tent, everyone conducting his lady: Amphilanthus, Pamphilia; Perissus his Limena; Ollorandus, Urania; Antissius, Selarina; the King of Cyprus his Queen; his brave son, Polarchus, the lady he only loved, who was princess of Rhodes. Many other great princes and princesses there were, both Greeks and Italians, Allimarlus for old acquaintance leading Urania's maid.

Thus to Pamphilia's tent they came, where most sumptuously she entertained them. Then did all the great princes feast each other, the last being made by the King of Cyprus who, out of love to the Christian faith, which before he condemned, seeing such excellent and happy princes possessors of it, desired to receive it, which Amphilanthus infinitely rejoicing at, and all the rest, christened him with his wife, excellently fair daughter, and Polarchus his valiant son, and so became the whole island Christians. Then came he unto Amphilanthus, humbly telling him that the disgrace he had from him received he esteemed as a favour and honour sufficient to be overcome by the valiantest King, who none must resist, to manifest which he besought him to accept him unto his servant and friend, with whom he resolved to end his days.

Amphilanthus replied the honour was his to gain so brave a gentleman to his friendship, who should ever find him ambitious to express his love to him. 'But,' said he, 'assuredly you never adventured the throne but that you were in love.' He, blushing, told him it was true. 'But alas, my lord,' said he, 'I have no hope now to win her.' Then told he the King the whole story of his love, beseeching him to assist him, which he promised to do, and for that purpose to take their way by Rhodes, and so at the delivering of her to her father, to solicit his suit for him, she extremely loving him. He kissed the King's hands for it.

And thus everyone remained contented, Urania longing to see Parselius and yet not daring to demand anything of him, till one day (and the first of their journey) she prettily began with Pamphilia, taking occasion upon her own discourse, as you shall hear. But now that everyone resolves of going homeward, what can be imagined of loving Luceania, whose heart is now almost burst with spite and rage, which she showed to the King himself when he came to take leave of her, telling her that it must be his ill fortune to part with her, that being finished which brought him thither.

She answered it was true, it was finished now to her knowledge, which she doubted not had had many ends with such foolish creatures as herself. 'Else,' said she, 'had I never been deluded with your flatteries.' 'I never,' said he, 'protested more than I performed.' 'It was my folly then,' said she, 'to deceive myself and wrong mine own worth with letting my love too much express itself, to give advantage for my loss, whenas if you had first sued, your now leaving me might have been falsehood, whereas it is only turned to my shame and loss.' 'I am sorry,' said he, 'I shall part thus much in your displeasure, since I know I once was more favoured of you.' 'You cannot right me more,' said she, 'than to go and gone, never more to think of me, unless your own conscience call upon you.' 'It will not, I hope,' replied Amphilanthus, 'be overburdened with this weight, since I will (now as ever I did) obey you, and so, brave lady, farewell.'

She would not wish him so much good, who now she hated, so as only making him a small reverence, they parted, the prince going to the kings and queens who attended for him, the King of Cyprus bringing them to the sea the morning before their taking ship, presenting them with the shepherds and shepherdesses of those plains, who after their manner sang and sported before them to the great delight of all, especially Pamphilia who, much loving poetry, liked their pretty expressions in their loves, some of which she caused to be twice sung, and those that were at the banquet (which was made upon the sands, they being served by those harmless people) to be written out, which were two songs and one dialogue delivered between a neat and fine shepherd and a dainty loving lass. It was thus:

> SH. Dear, how do thy winning eyes
>   my senses wholly tie?
> SHE. Sense of sight wherein most lies
>   change and variety.
> SH. Change in me?
> SHE. Choice in thee some new delights to try.

SH. When I change or choose but thee
    then changed be mine eyes.
SHE. When you absent, see not me,
    will you not break these ties?
SH. How can I
    ever fly where such perfection lies?
SHE. I must yet more try thy love,
    how if that I should change?
SH. In thy heart can never move
    a thought so ill, so strange.
SHE. Say I die?
SH. Never I could from thy love estrange.
SHE. Dead, what canst thou love in me,
    when hope, with life, is fled?
SH. Virtue, beauty, faith in thee,
    which live will, though thou dead.
SHE. Beauty dies.
SH. Not where lies a mind so richly sped.
SHE. Thou dost speak so fair, so kind,
    I cannot choose but trust.
SH. None unto so chaste a mind
    should ever be unjust.
SHE. Then thus rest,
    true possessed of love without mistrust.

Another delicate maid, with as sweet a voice as her own lovely sweetness, which was in her in more than usual plentifulness, sang this song, being as it seemed fallen out of love, or having some great quarrel to him.

Love what art thou? A vain thought
    In our minds by fancy wrought,
    Idle smiles did thee beget
    While fond wishes made the net
    Which so many fools have caught.

Love what art thou? Light and fair,
    Fresh as morning, clear as th'air:
    But too soon thy evening change
    Makes thy worth with coldness range,
    Still thy joy is mixed with care.

Love what art thou? A sweet flower
    Once full blown, dead in an hour
    Dust in wind as stayed remains

As thy pleasure or our gains,
If thy humour change to lour.

Love what art thou? Childish, vain,
Firm as bubbles made by rain,
Wantonness thy greatest pride,
These foul faults thy virtues hide,
But babes can no stayedness gain.

Love what art thou? Causeless cursed,
Yet alas these not the worst,
Much more of thee may be said,
But thy law I once obeyed,
Therefore say no more, at first.

This was much commended and by the ladies well liked of; only Amphilanthus seemed to take love's part and blame the maid for accusing him unjustly, especially for describing him with so much lightness. Then, to satisfy him, a spruce shepherd began a song, all the others keeping the burden of it, with which they did begin.

Who can blame me if I love?
  Since love before the world did move.
When I loved not I despaired,
Scarce for handsomeness I cared,
Since so much I am refined,
  As new-framed of state and mind,
Who can blame me if I love,
Since love before the world did move.

Some in truth of love beguiled
  Have him blind and childish styled
But let none in these persist
Since so judging judgement missed,
  Who can blame me?

Love in chaos did appear
  When nothing was, yet he seemed clear,
Nor when light could be descried
To his crown a light was tied.
  Who can blame me?

Love is truth and doth delight
  Whereas honour shines most bright,
Reason's self doth love approve

Which makes us ourselves to love.
Who can blame me?

Could I my past time begin,
    I would not commit such sin
To live an hour and not to love,
Since love makes us perfect prove,
    Who can blame me?

This did infinitely please the brave King, so cunningly and
with so many sweet voices it was sung. Then, the banquet ended,
they took leave of the kind King of Cyprus and his company, all
the rest taking ship with Pamphilia, sailing directly to Rhodes,
where they received unspeakable welcome, being feasted there
eight days together, and for show of their true welcome, the
Duke of that island bestowed his consent for marriage of his
daughter with her long-beloved friend Polarchus, whose joy and
content was such as the other amorous knights wished to know.
Then took they their leaves of the Duke and all the Rhodean
knights and ladies, taking their way to Delos, Polarchus
promising within short time to attend them in Morea.

THE END OF THE FIRST BOOK

PERCY HERBERT

The Princess Cloria

(1653/1661)

The Princess Cloria: Or, The Royal Romance. In Five Parts. Embellished with diverse political notions and singular remarks of modern transactions. Containing the story of most part of Europe for many years last past. Written by a person of honour.

You have now the whole work of *The Princess Cloria*, otherwise called *The Royal Romance*, some of it being printed formerly in the worst of times, that is to say, under the tyrannical government of Cromwell, when but to name or mention any of the King's concernments was held the greatest crime almost could be committed against that usurpation, and so consequently to be punished by the high court of justice with more than ordinary severity, wherein perhaps it might be thought the author showed more fidelity than policy, especially by those that esteemed it best to comply with a man that never relented in his revenge, or was less cruel for his dissimulation.

However, do not look for an exact history in every particular circumstance, though perchance upon due consideration you will find a certain methodical coherency between the main story and the numerous transactions that passed, both at home and abroad, as may render people competently satisfied, for that the tediousness of repartees and impertinent discourses commonly used in inventions of this kind are for the most part omitted, that oftentimes not only weary readers with expectation, but make them cast away books before they are half read.

Of the other side, you may not think, however scarce any former precedent hath matched the wickedness of some in these latter days, that all other persons intended for patterns of virtue and gallantry did correspond fully with the relations made of their actions, neither in truth doth the present age in the general pretend to the exercise of such noble principles wherein gratitude, fidelity and constancy appear countenanced, much less practised in any high measure, so that I may conclude the author's meaning was rather to put persons in mind what they ought to do, than that he was altogether ignorant what passed in reality, wherefore, now and then, in regard of that deficiency was content to make use of his own invention to supply that defect, which serves well enough, notwithstanding to the history itself, and is more agreeing with the nature of any Romance.

It is to be considered also that not seldom one name stands for one or diverse parties, according as their faculties and employments were made use of, the better to avoid confusion, by reason of several repetitions of names which otherwise must have followed, whereby the reader might have been subject to have his memory put upon the rack to find out the meaning of the story, since in all writings clearness and facility is necessary for delight and satisfaction, but more especially where so many ends were to be brought together in some convenient periods.

For the style and manner of contrivance, being mixed between modern and antique,* although I shall leave them to the consideration and fancy of the reader, without giving my opinion, yet I must boldly profess the subject in my thoughts is not to be paralleled, which no doubt gave the writer greater appetite to proceed, for what faults soever may appear to rigid criticism, nevertheless it cannot be denied but the groundwork for a Romance was excellent, and the rather since by no other way almost could the multiplicity of strange actions of the times be expressed, that exceeded all belief and went beyond every example in the doing.

Notwithstanding, a key of plainer and more particular intelligence in many things hath been most earnestly solicited, however not thought altogether convenient to be printed with the rest, as well for that it might seem publicly too much to determine state particulars and eminent persons, as in regard also the story is no way difficult to be understood by any who have been but indifferently versed in the affairs of Europe, and for others of the more vulgar sort, a bare Romance of love and chivalry, such as this may be esteemed to be at the worst, will prove entertainment enough for their leisure, if the author have met with their appetites in his contrivance and expressions. Besides, too much explanation of mysterious conceptions of this nature would have taken off something from the quaintness of the design, and left many affected wits less matter for ampler discourse occasioned often by conjectural disputes.

But for that all capacities meet not in the same centre of knowledge and apprehension, I must inform the reader (in regard essentially it belongs to the body of the story intended) that the Princess Cloria is not only to be taken for the King's daughter, but also sometimes for his national honour, and so consequently appearing more or less in prosperity as accidents increased and diminished, by reason of the unnatural differences and rebellions were raised for so many years in this most glorious kingdom and monarchy; who for that purpose bears the chief title of the book, and so personally (if it be minded) with some decorum ends every part by itself, which hath not been observed by other modern writers, that scarce mention the parties most concerned in the whole story, as if rather accident set down their names than conveniency required their actions, which is an absurdity in my mind not to be pardoned by any indifferent judgement and understanding

Another advertisement I must give, that notwithstanding many and diverse stories are in the book of several natures, yet there is not one of them related but in some sort or other appertains to the main design, not brought in (as I may say) by the head and shoulders, as is frequently used nowadays; and as they are all digested into determinable periods within themselves, so are they of no more length than is convenient for any moderate communication either of recreation or discourse, whenas in other Romances they are oftentimes continued for five or six hours together without intermission,* which to my apprehension appears ridiculous, in that people would be altogether tired, either with hearing or making such relations, and indeed almost impossible to be performed by any, of what profession soever.

If there be exceptions against the many descriptions of countries, places and triumphs, I must say that as it hath neither perturbated or destroyed the matter, so do I not see why that should be any defect at all, but of the contrary, a pleasant divertisement to the reader, since nothing seems more to satisfy human nature than varieties, either to be continually seen or considered. Notwithstanding, I may make some doubt whether the hairbrainedness of the present world will give leisure enough to most to dwell upon anything at all, much less to practise heroical virtues with such a constant settledness as is necessary, being the chief intention of the author (as I conceive) in writing of this Romance, besides his affectionate duty to the royal family.

But here perhaps some may wonder why the perfect history might not have been as well undertaken for their honour, as to be thus mixed with several sorts of invention and fancies, that rather leads people's thoughts into a dark labyrinth of uncertainties than instructs their knowledges how matters passed indeed. Unto which this answer must be returned: that as the intricate transactions of other places, happening not seldom at the same instant, being otherwhiles only conjectural (wherefore point of time is not always observed) though conducing for the most part to the main design, could hardly have been explained by a bare historical relation that gives no liberty for inward disputations or supposed passions to be discovered, so on the other side counsels, for the most part being given in private, much of the lustre of the whole book would have been taken away, tending to the reader's satisfaction, and more especially seeing the common occurrences of the world do not arrive always at a pitch high enough for example, or to stir up the appetite of the reader, which things feigned may do* under the notion of a Romance, being it hath liberty to tell as well what might have been as what was performed in reality. And this certainly made most of the ancient and brave poets clothe their writings in figures and suppositions, whereby to set forth the virtues usually of famous persons, not confining themselves altogether to exact relations brought to their knowledge from authentical records, because they intended only the exalting of magnanimity and depressing of vice, which I conceive should be the principal object of every person's thoughts and desires.

Nevertheless, concerning the truth in the general, I must say that as there are no remarkable passages that have been agitated in Christendom for some years past, but may be found sufficiently set down in this writing, how they happened, and with what decorum they were performed, conducing to the ends and purposes intended, so in my opinion doth not the conjectural part, made up oftentimes by invention, any way alter the nature of the actions, no more than apparel may change the person of a man, who is not thereby transformed in essence but in circumstance only, and not seldom perhaps to the much more becoming and convenienter fashion. Wherefore, discourses probable, and not altogether so indeed, may put people in mind of what they may say and do another time, with more advantage to themselves or employment, especially seeing it is impossible otherwise to express inward passions and hidden thoughts that of necessity accompany all transactions of consequence, whenas statesmen now and then in treaties judge of effects by the very looks and countenances of such they have occasion to deal withal in businesses of any importance. Besides, bare and simple narratives speak little more, for the most part, than ordinary proceedings, for that others of a more transcendent nature do not often happen, serving to any great edification, and these, being now and then mixed with communications of arts and policy, cannot choose but prove as well delightful as beneficial, whenas the mere repetition of things we have already industriously learned is necessary sometimes, not only to put us in mind of virtues and their effects, but to continue them constantly in our thoughts and desires whereby to render them habitual to our natures.

For stories of former ages are no other than certain kind of Romances to succeeding posterity, since they have no testimony for them but men's probable opinions, seeing the historical part almost of all countries is subject to be questioned, neither is it any great matter as to our profit whether they were exactly so or no, provided bravery be cherished and baseness discountenanced to our instruction, in that all things are but to teach people how to do well and avoid the contrary, wherefore to be considered that the author had a greater desire to discourse the causes of accidents than the truth of actions. Nevertheless, I am confident in this Romance all passages are related with as little partiality as could well stand with books of this kind, since as it was something necessary matters should be mentioned a little above the ordinary way of proceedings to stir up the appetite of the reader to a continuance, so cannot it be said knowingly anything reacheth beyond the extremity of a wonder whereby to be questioned, either for impossible or improbable, for though twice or thrice mentions are made of dreams and visions, yet is it no otherwise to be understood than what hath often happened to particular persons formerly, who were famous or notorious for sanctity or wickedness, as preadmonitions from Heaven for people's better instruction.

So that now I have thus largely delivered my opinion, there rests no more behind but an admonition that this book, if read at all, may be considered with some leisure and circumspection, that neither the reader may be mistaken or the author too much prejudiced, since I am assured as the writer expects no vainglorious approbation from any (and less praise), so of the other side, he will not be much troubled to be put in mind of his faults, provided reasons be given for them, which the freer may be done in regard his name is not declared in these writings, however well enough known perhaps by other circumstances.

Nevertheless, it is confessed the poetry is but plain, though significant to the matter, being so only intended for the more convenient reading and apprehending the story without unnecessary trouble or interruption, which expressions in another strain might have procured, occasioning several interpretations and perhaps false conjectures, which in a Romance is not proper, the verses being commonly the main theme to be dilated upon, or at least the conclusive part that should sum up the business, so that they ought to be clear and expressive, whereas other strong lines of that kind (only belonging to themselves or to show poetical fancies in metre) may sometimes be of a nature more difficult to be understood, though often it falls out they are not to be unriddled by any.

As for the words that have miscarried in the printing (which I believe are not many, though some there be in all writings), I doubt not but they may be rectified easily in the reading by any reasonable capacity that will but cast over again their eyes, where they apprehend the defect to be, applying it to the sense of the rest, which in my opinion is a better way for direction than to set down the errors in the latter end of the book, since few people will take the pains to compare both places together, being rather willing to let the faults die to their memory than to busy themselves with trouble in another's concernment, especially having enough already in the story for their leisure or recreation. This being all I have to say, I bid you farewell.

The First Part of *The Princess Cloria*

BEAUTIFUL Aurora had newly dressed the pearled morning with a ruby coronet to entertain her lover, who began already to mount his golden chariot for the day's triumph, when unfortunate Cassianus,* in the great forest between the mountain Timolius and the city of Sardis, rose from his grassy bed under the large canopy of a well-spread oak, where the night past he underwent an inconvenient lodging for want of better shelter, and being seated upon the root of that tree that, however, had favourably contributed its best assistance towards his accommodation, with intention (according to his custom) to pay an early offering to his sorrow, whilst his page saddled his horse that procured more bountiful entertainment than his master, since the time of the year had provided plentiful provision for his appetite, of a sudden his ear was saluted by a well-tuned cry of deep mouthed hounds that seemed to charm the air with a delightful harmony, which consequently gave the prince some interruption to his resolutions.

But long he had not contemplated the pleasingness of the music, with a certain strife inwardly notwithstanding, whether his complaints or attentiveness should receive more friendly welcome in his discontented bosom, before he might see a young gentleman in a hasty hand-gallop to approach the place where he rested, which obliged him, as he thought, to quit the seat, whereby he might receive information concerning his travels towards Euarchus'* court, his absolute ignorance in the country having made him lose his way, that should have conducted him to some town that might have instructed his knowledge in the journey.

But the youth, beholding a stranger of a seeming quality in that posture, not only stopped the speedy course of his appearing well-breathed horse, but when he came at a nearer distance, in a gentle trot advanced towards him with intention to offer all courteous civilities, since he perceived the open heavens had only given him welcome, and to that purpose saluted him with this language.

'Sir,' said he, 'it hath been still the custom of Lydia* to comply with the necessity of strangers, of what quality soever, wherefore

I should commit a sin against the rules of hospitality in passing by your person with a regardless neglect to what you might stand in need of, finding you here at this time of the day, and the rather for that in outward appearance your condition may merit the highest respect, to which purpose I have resolved to leave my sport, whereby the more conveniently to conduct you to the King's presence, if your pleasure shall condescend to the intention, being now present in this exercise of hunting, who would no doubt correct my ill natured rudeness if I should commit so great a fault as not to let his Majesty know that the woods had entertained such a guest without his welcome and privity. And although I am but a gentleman that waits upon the King in his chamber, I may have yet the honour to attend you to him, where I dare presume your reception will in some sort be answerable to your worth, though my quality merit not your esteem.'

Cassianus, glad that he had happened upon a conductor that could so easily present him to the King, and that his Majesty's recreation gave him so speedy and convenient an occasion, after he had given him thanks for the offer, told him that as his ignorance in the passage had made him stand in need of the least assistance to wind him out of the intricate labyrinth of these woods that had employed his thoughts for the night past, since he could neither be safe from wild beasts or robbers according to his doubtful apprehension, but was more fortunate to have such a worthy guide to accompany him to the uttermost end of his journey, for that probably his arrival at the court would be the period of his business, and therefore he should, as he said, extremely oblige a wandering pilgrim in the office.

But because the King was so passionately employed (as he was informed) for the present with his fortunate sport, Cassianus supposed it scarce manners to give it interruption by his addresses, so that he walked up and down a green walk, demanding such questions as were necessary for his information, until the youth also modestly desired some satisfaction concerning his adventures, which was the easier granted since the relation not only suited well enough with the prince's intention of courtesy and affability, but with the conveniency of the time. When they were both seated upon the same root that had been Cassianus' uneasy pillow, he gave him this instruction of his fortunes, with few or no circumstances but what many deep sighs contrived.

'My father,' said he, 'Prince of Iberia was in his youthful years inflamed with the report of the excellent beauty of Elizana,* your King's sister, whose fame could not be circumscribed within the limits of Lydia, which made him after a long solicitation by letters take a journey in person to the court to tender the affection and respects due to a lady of so eminent birth and virtues, notwithstanding he seemed not to bring with him dignity, titles and riches sufficient to deserve so glorious a match. This, I must tell you, rendered the Queen her mother, then living, an absolute enemy to his courtships, supposing her daughter to be under-valued by the choice.

'Nevertheless, the state of Lydia finding not only a certain concurrency in their loves, but an agreement of their religions, for that both countries had left the obedience of Delphos,* persuaded the King her father to the alliance, supposing all other defects would be buried by those unities, so that in a short time the marriage was solemnized with most magnificent ceremonies, though in the interim the triumphs were somewhat obscured by the sudden death of the prince, her elder brother,* whose disposition in his life gave such opinions of his future greatness that the world began already to tremble with the very apprehension of his fate. Yet the accident advanced my mother a step nearer to the crown, since there was none left of the race to inherit but my uncle Euarchus and herself, and this by consequence made my father, in the apprehension of Asia,* a far greater prince than his own fortunes could pretend unto, insomuch as returning into his native country with his illustrious bride, what honour could be imagined was cast upon him by the admiring people, which honours raised excessively his aspiring thoughts, notwithstanding many of his own rank began to envy his prosperity, especially one Tygranes, Duke of Colchis, who ever esteemed himself in possession the more powerful prince.

'In fine, the kingdom of Mesopotamia revolting at the same time from the jurisdiction of Artaxis, King of Armenia, my father was earnestly solicited to take upon him the crown,* since he was only able by his power and alliance, as the people pretended, to defend their proceedings against their tyrannical lord, who had usurped too great a prerogative both over their laws and consciences.

'The offer in a manner was no sooner proposed to the ambition of his youth, being tickled with the desire of bearing the name of a king, though many had refused the same tender, but he accepted of the government, promising his protection, as the subjects did their fidelity, and in this hopeful agreement he was with all ceremony and state dignified with the diadem in the regal city of the kingdom. But the possession, however it brought with it honour and dignity, it lessened not his care or trouble since the glory was to be maintained now it was purchased. This enterprise gave as earnest warning to Artaxis to be diligent in providing forces to suppress the example and punish the esteemed rebellion, that else might prove a leading card, as he thought, to the quiet state of the rest of his dominions that began already to waver in their obedience, as it did desire in my father to maintain what he had got, though it were with never so great a violence and hazard.

'In the first place, Artaxis dispatches ambassadors not only to all his friends in other countries, laying before them the dangerous consequences of such a revolt, but also sent messengers to his own subjects, possessing them with the fear of the rebels' insolency. However, his endeavours so little prospered for the present to his advantage, the first sort being too far off to give him speedy assistance, as the other too disobedient to lend him much aid, that his General was constrained to take the field with a very small number, only the army within some few weeks became increased by an addition of Tygranes' forces, whose envy to my father, notwithstanding the near kindred between them, had rendered him a most mortal enemy.

'But Artaxis' General, finding it was full time to dispute the right by the sword, though upon any disadvantage, since all protraction did but increase the people's suspicion of the King's disability, that was not able to chastise one subject who seemed to rebel against his majesty and power with as much courage as could proceed from desperate hopes, marched against the city where my father continued his court, guarded with soldiers sufficient to have besieged Artaxis' whole army if their hearts and affections had been answerable to their number and accommodation. And in this posture, the General not only sets upon the wall (the garrison not expecting the boldness of the attempt) but in a short time became master both of the gates and streets, to the confused amazement of all the inhabitants, who seemed neither to have will nor power to resist, so that the strange news scarce giving conveniency and time to my father with his whole family to fly from the danger. He had not opportunity to draw his sword in the defence of himself and crown, but through private and obscure woods was constrained to convey his wife and children, until he arrived under the protection of a commonweal that at the beginning of the design had lent a willing and considerable aid to the action.

'Artaxis, hearing of this extraordinary success, not only beyond his expectation, but in a manner above all belief, caused public sacrifices to be made to the gods through the chief temples, that he might not seem in the people's apprehensions to be ungrateful for such large benefits, and to increase the more his subjects' opinions, that the very heavens intended to fight for his right; since he made religion the chief cause of the war, he gave it out the victory was no less than miraculous, since his General, as 'twas said, had been instructed in the assault by a divine revelation, which had made him venture upon so desperate an enterprise.

'But however, the King was thought by many over-superstitious, yet the General and Tygranes omitted no industry to render our house miserable, the first continuing in those parts after the battle with half the army to suppress the last sparkles of common rebellion, as the other led the rest into Iberia, my father's country, to make himself master of that territory, bestowed upon him by Artaxis in recompense of his service done against our family, in which employment they both thought and strived to exceed each other in cruelty, not only in undoing our present prosperity but also in rooting out our future remembrance, the one possessing himself of all the subsistence that should have nourished my father, his wife and children, as the other bereaved him of his honour, that would have made him and his posterity capable of better fortunes.

'And in this manner were we all turned abegging, as I may say, into the wide world, to converse with nothing but want, disgrace and trouble, whilst our enemies enjoyed our towns, castles, titles and country, which continued my poor father so discontent for some years, having nothing to live upon but what he received from the bounty of his father-in-law, until at last, not being able longer to endure the sharp frowns of his spiteful fates, accompanied with the cruel usage of his malicious enemies, he willingly paid nature her due and changed his inconstant habitation here for a perpetual one hereafter, leaving his wife and all his children not only to bewail his death, though they esteemed him much more happy than themselves, but to provide anew against the storms of other miseries, since we wanted a director to steer our courses.

'However, my mother being endued with admirable virtues and courage, endeavoured by the small though loving subsistence she received from her friends, not only to bring up her many children with all the exquisite breeding she could devise, but by the affability of her natural behaviour and conversation, strived to gain the love and compassion of all Asia, insomuch as for the first, she set us in the world at convenient years not to be a shame to our well-descended family, and for the latter, she so compassed her design that no heart in a manner but wished her prosperity.

'In this posture we remained until she sent me to be a suitor to a rich heir, with hopes again to raise our house to some eminency by obtaining the possession of another principality that rightly belonged to the young lady. But Tygranes, as if he had absolutely sworn himself an enemy to all that could do good to our family, not only became also a pretender to the same match, but prevailed so far with Artaxis, before the marriage could be obtained, that he sent a powerful army to besiege the lady in her castle, and so by force possessed themselves both of her person and patrimony, leaving me again to my desperate fortunes, not having any force to defend her rights or maintain my own pretensions. That ever since hath continued me a wanderer through most of the princes' courts of Asia to seek relief, which at last hath brought me into the quiet haven of Euarchus' country with the same intention to demand his willing assistance, my hopes being more increased by reason of the general fame of the peaceable state of his rich and powerful dominions.'

But scarce was he come to the end of this discourse when the King himself alighting to take a fresh horse near the place where they were, whereby the better to pursue his begun sport, Cassianus had opportunity to present himself to his view and consideration, the company in the meantime with a certain amazed haste making way for his approach, since the adventure of a stranger in such a posture seemed to invite all their expectations. Wherefore, when he came at so convenient a distance that his words might easily be heard, supporting his body by a small ebony lance he carried in his hand, with a confident modesty delivered these words.

'Mighty King,' said he, 'although your imperial diadems [*sic*] seems to flourish with olive branches, whilst the ambition of other princes make but the prerogative of their crowns nourish the lusts of their own tyranny, and by that means, instead of being protectors of their people, deliver them up to slaughter and oppression, yet certainly the gods have not only placed you upon a throne to be happy yourself by a lasting peace, but to render others satisfied by your power and justice, especially when the heavens are dishonoured by their injuries.' And with that wept, which for the present stopped the progress of his discourse. But being encouraged to further expressions by the King's pity, however his language seemed strange to his ears, as his person did to his eyes, when he had dried his fair face with a handkercher, he uttered this language.

'Great Sir,' said he, 'as I shall not need to trouble you with many particulars concerning the unhappy passages of my father's fortunes, since the story, I suppose, hath been sufficiently presented to your ears by common fame, if not by more exact relations, so must I at this time not only give you an account of my own actions, being encouraged thereunto by your Majesty's appearing favours, but also do presume upon redresses according to your power and goodness.

'To this purpose, be pleased to know that my name is Cassianus, your most unfortunate nephew, being driven from my rights and possessions in the fruitful country of Iberia by the tyrannical oppressions of Artaxis, King of Armenia, which hath caused me since my years gave me ability both to understand and prosecute my own affairs to travel through most part of Asia to seek assistance amongst other princes of my own rank, but finding them for the most part so much encumbered by reason of their troublesome occasions, or I may say not willing to expose themselves to any danger or hazard concerning another's benefit, though my injuries lie before them as warning examples for their own conditions, I could obtain from their courtesies no hopes of any assistance, though many compliments were used of good will and affection, unless I could procure other greater monarchs to join with them in the quarrel.

'These answers quickly carried my endeavours to the court of Syria,* where at present reigns Orsames,* that mighty King, who after I had also presented unto him my desires, he seemed to wonder why I should make my addresses to himself or any other prince in Asia, when you, notwithstanding your power, peace and tranquility, appeared to be so far from giving me any aid in my necessities that you appeared not at all sensible of my sufferings. However, he told me that if I could yet procure the breach of that amity between you and Artaxis, whereby some considerable supplies might come from Lydia, abounding, as he said, rather in luxuries than in activity, he would presently declare war against the Armenian King, by which means I might come again into the possession of my lost rights.

'These intimations I bring from one powerful monarch to another, and such supplications my own necessities require me to make, the rather for that not only your royal blood hath honoured my birth from my most illustrious mother, but the same worship of the gods are exercised both in Lydia and Iberia.' Which being said, he again rested silent, with tears in his eyes.

Euarchus, after he had fully understood with a pensive attentiveness his nephew's request, and entertained him with those compliments and that welcome his condition and alliance merited, he only for the present told him that as a matter of this consequence required a judicious consideration, so he might be confident of his love and affection, and withal invited him for diversion to be a partaker of the Lydian pastime, agreeing, as he said, with his youth and courage—which gave their thoughts for some hours sufficient employment.

However, the King being in his own nature extremely solicitous, though personally he followed the sport according to his custom with the foremost, yet having received, contrary to his expectation, a subject of such consideration, all the day did labour in his mind a resolution, one while reflecting upon the quiet and prosperity of his own kingdoms, and then again weighed the pretended injuries of his near kinsman, professing the same worship of the gods, besides the glorious offer of Orsames, which, as he thought, did in a manner compel him to be active.

But the night coming on so fast, the King was not only forced to put off his unprofitable meditation until a more convenient season, but to command the retreat from that delightful exercise to be sounded. Wherefore, taking the youth by the hand, with whose person and behaviour he seemed to be already in love, he placed him by him in his coach, and so entertained the time with discourses of his fortunes until they arrived at the palace, which for its singular beauty deserves a particular description.

The house was seated upon the banks of the river Pactoleus, by whose refreshing streams the delightful gardens, placed of all sides, seemed to flourish with an exact greenness. The portal was formed of white marble, with columns, architrave, frieze and cornish. On the top it was crowned with a cornucopia encompassing an azure globe supported by little cupids with gilded wings, under which they passed through a square court set round about with excellent statues of brass in niches. The structure itself was of oriental granite stone, so interlaced with Ionic and Corinthian pillars of diverse colours that as it gave the eye a most delectable object, so it rendered the edifice much more sumptuous. At the upper end was a large terrace elevated six steps. Upon the stairs stood Hiacinthia,* the Queen, to give her husband meeting accompanied by the new stranger.

As soon as Cassianus beheld that beauty mixed with a kind of sweet majesty, that both awed and pleased at the same time, he addressed himself to her presence like one that intended only to be Euarchus' suppliant. However, the Queen, that was ignorant in nothing but pride, with a gentle smile, which notwithstanding for the more grace, put a vermilion blush in her fair cheeks, gave him a gracious welcome into Lydia.

But turning his eye on one side, he was suddenly struck with such an amazement to behold the Princess Cloria,* the King's daughter, that he had strife enough with his own passions to perform the rest of those reverences due to her mother's dignity, since his thoughts imagined to look upon an earthly deity. She was clothed in light taffety for the commodity of the season, through which her dainty limbs seemed to appear in admirable proportion, leaving nothing to be hid that hindered the true knowledge of her excellent shape, but yet covered those beauties which are increased only by opinion and desire. She was crowned with a chaplet of white and red roses not yet fully blown; her hair was combed to the full length and braided with ribbons of the same colour, as if art were ambitious of nature's liberty. Her sleeves were open and lined with needlework of the story of Diana and Actaeon, wherein the nymphs, with a confused bashfulness, seemed to hide themselves amongst the rushes; and all the rest of her, scarce any apparel, was so becoming that either she made it so by her perfections, or her perfections could not be fitted by better inventions.

But the Queen quickly removed Cassianus from that object that began already so strongly to charm all his senses, for, taking him by the hand, she walked with him many turns about the terrace, whilst in the meantime he discoursed to her his adventures. However, now and then he could not choose but disturb his story by casting his looks where the princess stood, though at last she suddenly shot from his sight like a bright star in the firmament, which made him seek her with his eyes to as little purpose. After some time that the Queen seemed sufficiently to have recreated herself in the air, she was informed by an officer of the court that the King expected her company in the parlour.

The room was only divided from the gardens by a partition of bright glass, interwoven with certain silver terms, that afforded a most delectable prospect upon the orange trees and beautiful fountains. Not long after their entrance (in which space the King instructed Cassianus in the masters of his principal pictures) supper was served upon a marble table without covering, for the more coolness, near which was a lake of clear water where Neptune sat in majesty with his Tritons, that by the artificial turning of a cock sounded their trumpets, composed of shells, at the entrance of every course.

Cassianus was placed by fortune right over against Cloria, which not only gave him sufficient opportunity to contemplate her beauty, but the contemplation itself afforded him such abundant matter to work upon that he fed more his soul by that delight than his appetite with the delicious dishes of the King's table, and certainly had been absolutely lost in that ravishing lethargy if Euarchus had not often wakened him by diverse questions concerning his journey and the rest of his adventures in Armenia, to make a civil though scarce a satisfactory answer. But however, as if he esteemed his eyes bound to the duty, he cast his look again that way, which occasioned still more distractedness in his reply, so that the King, believing his nephew's travels required a necessary rest, not only presently rose from the table, but commanded the chief nobility of the court to conduct the prince to his lodging, where he had privacy enough fulfill the desires of his curious fancies, which entertained him all the night with little or no sleep, until the King's music the next morning saluted him with this ditty.

> Fair prince, your youthful presence here
> Is like the summer of the year,
> Welcomed by hearts of every sort
> To great Euarchus' royal court.
> May blessed visions sent by Jove
> Wait on your slumbers from above,
> Until bright Phoebus with his beams
> In season wake you from your dreams,
> And then may objects of delight
> In every place content your sight.
> Let fortune so observe your way
> That you command whilst others pray,
> And aged time prolong your life
> Beyond the sisters' fatal knife,
> Until you willingly resign
> Your soul to be installed divine.
> Then let old Sardis for its glory
> Raise up a Homer to your story,
> So as you are a summer here,
> A harvest may attend you there.

But however, after some weeks, Cassianus seemed to kindle in his youthful bosom new flames, with those small sparkles he had received from Cloria's beauty, which often separated him from the rest of the company, that made some believe he was too much discontented with the King's protraction. Yet Euarchus, mindful both of his affection to his nephew and the prosperity of his own countries, finding rumours began too frequently to fly about the court by reason of the violent desires of many to be employed in the wars, one day called unto him an ancient officer of his kingdom, on whose wisdom and fidelity he most relied in all his weighty affairs and leading him into the garden, where he might both enjoy privacy and recreation, after some necessary circumstances which seemed to usher in his discourse, he used these words:

'Polinex,' said he, for so was he called, 'as I have ever most trusted your knowledge and experience, so have I never been less confident of your loyalty and affection, since neither as yet hath deceived my expectation when I had most occasion to use your service, which deservedly renders you a worthy counsellor, as I desire to be a good prince that cannot I hope but produce consequents towards the happy government of my kingdoms. However, at the present your faithful advice is more requisite than ever, since expedition and danger cannot be separated from those undertakings I am violently pressed unto.

'You know that lately there is come to my court my nephew Cassianus, a prince whose person and merits deserve at least a kinsman's consideration, much more his injuries a King's justice. The one bids me cherish him with my affection; the other invites me to assist him with my power. However, the strict eye of sworn amity between princes persuades me to be circumspect in the breech, notwithstanding the headlong precipitation of many of my chief counsellors, who solicit me to a war, wherefore that I may avoid the hazard of a general disquiet, since I find my people begin to be sick of their own tranquillity, or make war upon such grounds that may conserve inviolably my faith with the King of Armenia, which the gods cannot else prosper, I require your opinion.'

Polinex, after he had with an humble gravity heard out the King's discourse, and taken some time to consider the weightiness of the counsel, in a distinct manner returned this answer, wherein he used no more eloquence than was necessary for the importance of so great a business, though nature and art had furnished him with parts excellent in that kind.

'Sir,' said he, 'as benefits had from princes are past requital in a subject, even like graces received from the gods, by which we are enabled to do something, so I, the unusefullest of your servants, though most honoured by your goodness, may by the reflection of your lustre merit the office of a counsellor because you have been pleased to make me one, but if I should in the least thought prove a traitor to your glory (as a heinous offence that ought to bury the remembrance of any good past) I did not only deserve to be divested of all your former benefits, but to be condemned to the worst of punishments, since your transcendent favours have rendered my defects considerable. However, if my weakness chance to err, and not my will, that mercy which makes you resemble the gods I must challenge, and thus, according to your royal command, I freely deliver my opinion.

'A war wisely undertaken ought chiefly to be accompanied with two considerations: the right of the quarrel and the power of the quarreller. The first makes a man a just enemy, the second a prevailing conqueror, without either of which certainly a prince cannot be fortunate, since he must be an oppressor or a loser, and why your Majesty should not give yourself the liberty of such a resolution, notwithstanding the pressing necessity of your kinsman, I know no reason, since your kingdoms are more to be valued than his country, and your honour than his benefit, though I will not at all dispute the worth of his person. Besides, you are to consider with what prince you are to have the difference, not only a neighbour that never yet injured your right in anything, but of the contrary, one with whom you have sworn a perfect friendship, which is an alliance the heavens have made to be preferred far before human kindred, since the one is sealed but with flesh and blood, as the other hath imprinted its character in the skies.

'Again, for you to proclaim a war of blood before you have demanded peace by a friendly disputation were to style you cruel, since no violence proceeding from the greatest ambition ever practised such an injustice to put in execution a force to obtain that which perhaps the enemy you intend to make will easily grant; and as it will be esteemed more charity and goodness to persuade than compel, although the cause be absolutely just, so if the contrary, you are a double injurer, one way in beginning an unlawful contention without provocation, the other in breaking those ties that ought to oblige all princes to an inviolable observation.

'Also, you may be pleased to consider your hazard, since your own safety is first to be valued, whether in honour or prosperity, for although your kingdoms do in some sort equal Armenia in multitude of men and warlike provision, yet in respect of the long neglect of martial discipline, they are rendered, as it is to be feared, wholly incapable of a present expedition, and your treasure, notwithstanding it be sufficient to maintain the expense of your peaceable government, yet it will be found no way able to undergo the charge of a powerful army. So that whether your people, so unaccustomed to oppression, and impatient of subjection, from whose purses must come the supply (inconstant by nature to their own desires, witness their promises lately upon the same occasion) will be brought blindfold to contribute, without being privy to every secret intention, in my judgement is scarce a question, and how dangerously destructive that would prove to any enterprise when the multitude must be made acquainted with each stratagem of state, I leave your Majesty to judge.

'Therefore, my opinion is that until you can provide a store out of your own revenue, without depending altogether upon the uncertainty of your subjects' bounty, no warlike undertaking can prove glorious or beneficial, but of the contrary dangerous and unprofitable. So that all you can do for the present is to send an ambassador with reasons to persuade, and not a herald with threatenings to denounce, which in all probability will not only give satisfaction to your distressed kinsman, but win time till you be better provided.'

This advice extremely pleased the King, who aimed rather at present content than future glory, although his courage might pretend to the greatest honour, not only for that it took away the occasion of exhausting his treasure, but was also, as he thought, a principal means still to maintain his state in tranquility and his government without perturbation. Wherefore, parting from Polinex with such a smile as sufficiently persuaded him he was well satisfied with his counsel, sent presently for prince Cassianus, to whom he communicated his determination, which was forthwith to employ an ambassador to demand reason of the King of Armenia.

But however, this determination did not much discontent

Cassianus, because it gave him opportunity to remain in Lydia, whereby he might the better prosecute his secret affections to the fair Princess Cloria. Yet those that violently desired employment in the wars, though it were bought with never so much prejudice to the King's affairs, extremely mutinied against Polinex his counsel, amongst which number there was a nobleman called Dimogoras, one whose birth exceeded his wit, as his ambition did his courage, and his fortune not answering either made him much more violent than the rest, since he supposed if he lost this opportunity for action, Euarchus' resolutions for peace would become more established. Besides, he hated the King's person because he had formerly received many court affronts procured by his own factious spirit, wherefore he took occasion by this means not only to inform the state of Syria that Euarchus could not be drawn to make war against any of the kindred of Soroasters, King of Egypt,* upon what pretence soever, but secretly possessed all manner of people either with the King's want of courage or good nature, since coldly he was content, as he said, to let sleep the oppressions of his injured nephew without revenge.

But principally he blamed the pernicious counsels, as he termed them, of Polinex, who strived to rock Euarchus' mind into a lethargy of repose, that he alone might rule the state with more conveniency towards the particular enriching of his own family, and the rather were these factious speeches dangerous because the King was resolved, out of the rules of hospitality, not to question anything that was said in Cassianus' behalf, which within short space began insensibly to penetrate the hearts of the vulgar, Dimogoras having a principal interest in their affections, not only because they knew he was not esteemed at court, but for that commonly men of least eminent worth have the fortune to gain the opinion of the multitude, since they hate virtue because they are resolved not to follow it.

However, Euarchus, to remedy (the sweetest way he could) these growing inconveniences which yet appeared not in full prospect, to divert his nephew's thoughts from entertaining discontented counsels, proclaimed a general hunting of the wild boar, at which time Cassianus, being summoned by the early morning to the delightful sport, he found the King ready

prepared for the forest upon the plain before the palace gate,
where Hyacinthia the Queen, not so much pleased with the chase
as to accompany her husband, soon repaired with the choicest
ladies, whose dress resembled the chaste goddess Diana in the
like exercise. Only upon her head she wore a hat, the more
commodiously to cover the fair tresses of her hair that were
embraced with rows of rich pearl, since no meaner ties were fit to
adorn so bountiful a treasure, and in this posture they issued out,
animated by the importunate solicitations of the huntsmen, who
seemed over-ambitious to be in their elements—at leastwise so
interpreted by love-sick Cassianus, who thought all the preparation nothing , since Cloria, the only star of his desires, was not to
be of the society, her mother judging her by much too young for
the pastime.

No sooner was the unhandsome beast dislodged from his
darksome habitation, when every person well-horsed endeavoured to show his own skill and his courser's vigour, whilst the
solitary woods resounded with the cheerful noise of diverse horns
that seemed to encourage the hunters. Only the women
complained that nature had not ordained them proper for the
sport, since their attire would not permit them to pass through
the thickest copses.

But Cassianus, who was willing otherwise to be employed,
thinking that confusion spoke not to his imagination the soft
language of a lover, retired presently from the crowd, though he
suffered his horse in a manner to be his own director, until the
permittance within a short space brought them both into an
ample plain, notwithstanding so environed with low wood that
the eye could scarce discern any other passage than what
Cassianus had found, where also a gentle though plentiful-
seeming spring had made a pretty brook, if the hot season had
not tyrannically suppressed part of its current, yet it appeared
beautiful in that littleness, because it contributed to the
flourishing greenness of the place, and that beauty invited
Cassianus to enjoy the delight thereof.

Wherefore, alighting from his horse and turning his bridle over
his head to give him the more liberty to please himself on that
luxurious pasturage, whilst he meant only to feed upon the
sadness of his own thoughts, sat down upon the bank of the river

into which he let fall many of his tears, as if he intended to supply the accidental defect thereof. But when the fountain of his eyes had paid a sufficient tribute to his grief, and that his sighs had awakened him to some expression, he discoursed to himself in this manner, since the ignorant woods seemed no way capable of his complaints, but in returning a doleful echo to augment his sufferings.

'Unfortunate Cassianus,' said he, 'whose youth hath scarce numbered years to make thee a perfect subject of misery, and yet thy crosses render thee the only unhappy spectacle of all Asia, for that almost at one instant thou didst not alone lose thy dear father and fruitful country, but art forced to become a wandering pilgrim through the whole world without compassion, since thy sufferings do not afford thee a competent pity amongst other princes of thy own rank, much less a necessary assistance from those which are above thee in dignity. And last of all, when thou hadst thought to have attained some harbour of consolation under the protection of thy powerful uncle, abounding in all plenty and tranquillity, thou art again cast upon a new rock that threatens thy ruin, in that thou neither darest own that love which destroys thy rest, nor hast hope to quench the flames of thy desire to give thyself ease, the one being too violent to be suppressed, as the other too impossible to be obtained.

'For canst thou think, fond Cassianus,' said he, 'that her innocency may be attempted without the consent of her parents, or that her parents can be won to so unprofitable a match. And yet, sweet Cloria, consider rather the virtue of an entire affection, that is the only tie required by the just heavens, than the sole commodity of empires, to make thee happy in a choice. But alas, alas, I foolishly bestow my vain breath upon the abundant air, and my sorrowful tears to increase the plentiful springs, since neither have power to contribute to my redress, when it must be action, if anything, that will afford satisfaction, and yet with what face thou canst present thy widow-love to so excellent a purity, the gods must only instruct, if they intend at all to be propitious in thy affairs.'

But as he was again taking a new career of passion, he might see of a sudden the hunted boar, foaming with his own choler, rush out of the thickest woods, and not long after a youth of manly proportion, who followed the chase with a bold eagerness. However, by his different attire he was easily to be discerned to be none of the morning company. This prospect invited Cassianus, with some curiosity, to attend the success of the encounter, since the valiant beast, finding himself to be pursued by so exact a courage, quickly turned with fury upon the young man, which represented to his expectation a spectacle not more dangerous than pleasant, for honour and cruelty seemed to contend for victory.

The conflict endured a long time, the one striving by a rude violence to avoid destruction, as the other with a handsome activity sought to become victorious, till at last both being heated with the fight began to approach at a nearer distance, since the youth's spear, broken in the encounter, afforded him no other convenience to offend his enemy, which however he managed with so much advantage that the boar, having received many wounds, was forced with open mouth to attempt his persecutor as his last refuge, though to his ruin. For, the stranger taking advantage of his unskilful rage, thrust his short weapon with his whole hand into the boar's throat, with so fortunate an issue that the point appeared in his neck behind, though the stroke deprived him not presently of life, but seemed rather to give him new courage, however less power, for turning afresh with a new fury upon the disarmed youth, he had no defence to prevent the danger but to traverse his ground until the beast's much loss of blood, by reason of his enraged agitation, made him become the trophy of his honour, who quickly separated his head from his body with a short sword he wore by his side as the testimony of a perfect conquest, and then placed it upon a little hill supported with the broken lance, whilst he himself approached the river to wash his hands that were bespotted in the fight with the boar's blood.

Cassianus, having beheld this combat with a most earnest delight, if anything could be termed delight that his sad imagination looked upon, thought he could do no less than congratulate so pleasing a tragedy, and to that purpose rose from his seat with the intention, which the stranger beholding, though until then he was not advertised of anybody's presence in that solitary habitation, as quickly prepared himself to give him the meeting, and the rather for that he appeared a person of some quality, until both their designs at last brought them to so near a distance that the youth was soon known to Cassianus to be his only friend Eumenes, a gentleman bred up in his mother's court, whose father had accompanied her out of Lydia into Iberia when she was first married.

As the gods can tell with what inward content these two companions performed their first embracement, wherein they seemed to be eternally united in fortune, not to be separated again by any disaster, so was it not very long before their desires of knowing each other's adventures separated their persons again, wherefore seating themselves by that riverside that had entertained them both, Eumenes was persuaded to begin the first story in order to the time it was acted, which he performed after this manner, though he kept still his eye as a watchful sentinel over his friend's person.

'Cassianus,' said he, 'you know that your virtuous mother, for my more absolute breeding, sent me into Cyprus* to be trained in the wars under the command of that excellent Duke, finding my disposition and years suited well enough with the profession, which for the time separated you and me to both our griefs, though the intention was honourable, and being so, I had reason to dispose my thoughts towards the accomplishment of some perfection in that noble exercise. Where, remaining two years, as you may have heard, fortune so favoured my actions that in many attempts upon the enemy I gained a convenient reputation. However, my ambition raised my imagination to higher fancies, insomuch as I not only thought upon a mistress unto whom I might consecrate all my military endeavours, as an essential part (as I thought) of a soldier, but was resolved to fly in no lower a place than in that region where the Duke's only daughter moved, the fair Eretheria, whose perfections (I conceived) were alone fit to captivate my intentions, and to that purpose upon all occasions I strived to let the world see my aims, which soon procured me a multitude of rivals of no mean quality, who thought it scarce justice to let a stranger carry away the glory of Cyprus.

'But not long after, by the violent solicitation of the youthful courtiers, a tournament was proclaimed upon the birthday of the princess, where everyone hoped to show that valour that might render him worthy of the high prize ordained for the conqueror. The time being come for the trial, the bright star, Eretheria, was placed upon a throne, like a deity sent by the heavens to captivate all mortal hearts, which sight certainly inflamed every courage with a new spirit, though we all beheld her as a comet threatening destruction to many, since but one pretender could hope to live by her favour.

'But the sounding of the trumpets quickly wakened us out of this admiring slumber, to be more gloriously active, which (in truth) performed such deeds of all sides that Eretheria seemed not to be dishonoured in the encounters. However, a young nobleman of Cyprus, passionately also taken with her beauty, seemed all the day to carry away the chief victory, which procured him, as you may imagine, a competent number of emulators, if not enviers, amongst which company, I must confess, I wished him not better than the rest, since I supposed myself as deeply interested in the quarrel. Wherefore, choosing one of the biggest spears I could find, though my heart was a great deal bigger with the desire of his disgrace, I sought him out in the crowd with so happy a success to my thoughts that I quickly unhorsed him in the midst of his prevailing glory, to the no small amazement of the people, who esteemed him almost immortal, and therefore crowned the action with so loud a shout that the heavens seemed to ring for a long time with the noise, which to my infinite content possessed me entirely with the rich prize from the fair hands of Eretheria, besides a multitude of other honours belonging to the ceremony.

'But however I seemed to be carried triumphantly in a chariot, beyond the reach of any envy, yet my rival forgot not the effects of revenge, since he esteemed himself not only to suffer in honour but in love, and the rather for that he imagined from that instant Eretheria turned, in some sort, her looks more graciously towards me than formerly she had done, by reason of the fortunate success I had in the tilting.

'Wherefore, one day meeting me half armed in the park belonging to the court, he set upon me with all violence, both with his language and weapon, insomuch as I had enough to do to avoid the one, as I did not at all dispute with him in the other, since my best faculties had employment sufficient to defend my person against so spiteful a valour, though the gods, favouring my innocency more than his injustice, at last gave me an unfortunate victory, since not only his life was the price of my conquest, but the fear of a dishonourable death compelled me quickly to quit Cyprus to avoid the prosecution of his powerful friends; where, however, I have left my heart a prisoner to be condemned or saved by the mercy of beauteous Eretheria, which occasioned also the slaughter of this beast before your eyes, for conceiving my own country my best place of refuge until this storm might be blown over, I retired hither with two servants only, who are not yet arrived, and travelling the woods, having lost my way, I accidentally met with this hunted boar that set upon me with some fury, which forced me at first to the encounter, else I should have scarce been so uncharitable as to have destroyed the sport. These accidents, dear Cassianus,' said he, 'have been the reasons that brought me into Lydia, only happy now in our meeting.'

Cassianus, having both kept silence, and observed attentiveness in his friend's discourse, as it were congratulating his story and welcome by four or five sad sighs, being compelled by his importunity to make relation of his own fortunes also, without many circumstances began in this manner: 'After my unfortunate father, as you well know,' said he, 'had paid the debt of his rash attempt (in taking upon him the crown of Mesopotamia, contrary to the good liking of Artaxis, great King of Armenia) with his death and loss of his fruitful country of Iberia, my infancy, as you were a witness, was carefully cherished by my mother's natural goodness, insomuch as she thought not my years capable of your employments in Cyprus, although both my desires and wishes accompanied you in your journey. However, after your departure she designed me to another war, though by much more gentle, yet not so honourable, which was to court the love of a rich heir, not far off the place where we lived. By whose power she conceived (if I could compass the marriage) I might be again rendered capable to contend with Tygranes, Duke of Colchis, who enjoyed the possession of my native country by the donation of Artaxis, in retribution of that service he did him in the prosecution of my father.

'But no sooner had a fitting preparation elevated my thoughts to the enterprise, but the King became advertised of the intention, so that arriving at her castle I was encountered by my double rival the Duke, contrary to my expectation, who came there also with the same design, though fortified, as he thought, with far greater pretensions, since he brought with him the strong recommendation of his mighty friend the King of Armenia. But the gods know with what labour I suppressed the passion of my soul that it might not burst out into a rude and inhospitable contention, to destroy absolutely my intended proceedings, so that both of us addressing ourselves to the lady's presence with a quiet civility, we were received in outward show with equal courtesy, which continued us for some weeks in her palace, only seeking occasions how we might best present our affections with most conveniency to deceive each other.

'But the Duke, whether impatient of his long attendance or suspecting I received private favours to his prejudice, of a sudden one morning before anyone was up in the house, took his leave both of his chamber and the castle, by which means he left me in full possession of my desires, since I thought no obstacle now was able to hinder my proceedings of a prosperous issue, in which paradise of felicity I continued for many days, solacing myself with delightful fancies, whilst in the meantime the Duke was preparing a snare not only to captivate the lady but to entrap me. For, not long after he marched in person with a powerful army to besiege the castle where we both remained, which news made me dispose of myself by flight into certain obscure woods not far off, whereby I might not only be secure from the danger of my mortal enemy, but have conveniency by my escape to procure some relief to succour the distressed lady, which accident hath brought me into Lydia to renew my father's old suit to Euarchus for the recovery of our ancient inheritance, the principality of Iberia, since the lady, as I hear, hath not only lost her castle but I my hopes, for she is constrained to become a captive wife to the cruel tyrant Tygranes, Duke of Colchis. And this, dear Eumenes, is the sad story of my fortunes, and the more to be lamented since I am not certain to what resolution my uncle's thoughts will be brought, he yet being determined but to send an ambassador to treat for a peaceable and friendly restitution, whilst in the meantime I languish between hope and despair.'

But scarce was he come to this issue, when they might hear the hounds in full cry pursue the footsteps of the dead boar towards the place where they were, which gave Eumenes no conveniency for reply, hardly time sufficient to protect the testimony of his victory from the violent cruelty of the dogs, who seemed not to be pacified in his death. Wherefore, rising from the seat where he sat, and snatching up the head, he held it upon the point of the spear in the air, whilst the hounds with open mouths seemed to besiege his person until the huntsmen themselves, coming in to the quarrel, were forced to defend him from their rude violence, and in that employment he continued while the other, almost lost company had leisure to assemble to perfect the triumph for the slaughter of that cruel beast that had done so much mischief in the country, terrifying the common people with the frightful apprehension of his aspect, who durst not travel by the places of his habitation to follow their necessary occasion.

But not long had the ladies satisfied their curiosities in beholding the dead boar, though yet at some distance, scarce believing him so in effect, as also infinitely commending Eumenes' valour, that had in single combat brought him to his destruction, as they understood by Cassianus that had been the eye-witness of the encounter. But the King and Queen, in a gentle hand-gallop made towards them through the same passage that Cassianus had found out in his solitary contemplation, which gave Eumenes occasion, accompanied with his friend Prince Cassianus, to present himself before their persons, not only offering to the Queen the boar's head as a sacrifice to her beauty, but desired humbly to be excused that he had unwillingly interrupted their sport.

When Cassianus had certified Euarchus fully of all the proceedings in that combat, wherein he let nothing pass that concerned his friend's honour, and also made the King acquainted with his breeding, condition and country, he soon obtained absolution for his valiant act. However, the envious evening coming on, which denied the undertaking of a new chase, a cessation from that sport was quickly proclaimed by the King's command, and the rather for that they returned with victory and spoil. Wherefore Euarchus and Hyacinthia taking the two friends into their own coach, whilst the skilful coachman made what haste he could through the rugged way, they required of Eumenes not only the relation of his own travels, but the satisfaction of the manner of the government of the island of Cyprus since their revolt from the King of Egypt.

Eumenes receiving this injunction from the King, however he supposed he rather desired to have his curiosity satisfied in his ability than that his knowledge could any way be instructed by his relation, excusing himself concerning his own particular adventures as not worthy his Majesty's attention, he prosecuted this discourse:

'Truly Sir,' said he, 'it is no small difficulty for a person of any mean capacity to particularize the true causes or motives of the first revolts in any kingdom, though you are pleased to give me the employment, since as the complaints for the most part are confused and uncertain, more governed perhaps by the passions and fancies of the common people than grounded upon right and knowledge, so, of the other side, it cannot be denied but that oftentimes prerogative and power will find out ways and shifts to cast off the aspersions either against themselves or favourites, though I must confess, both may have reason enough to defend their allegations before an indifferent auditory if such a tribunal could be instituted. But that not being possible to be had upon earth, most commonly such contentions are only ended by the sword, which fate hath befell the fruitful island of Cyprus, though now it be established in a perfect prosperity.

'To this purpose, the King of Egypt, natural lord of those countries, having placed a lady of eminent virtues as supreme governess for him, both in Cyprus and Pamphilia, whether the people presuming upon the supposed weakness of her sex, joined with the inconstancy of their own humours and dispositions, or rather being put on to demand something (though they knew not very well what) that seemed to appertain to their ancient privileges by the ambition of some of the nobility (that belike seemed not very well satisfied) of a sudden began most violently to complain of the obstruction of their customs, as also of the cruelty of the laws made (as they pretended) both against their freedom and consciences. And being transported with these furious fancies, when the court least thought of their disorders, they run violently to all the chief temples of the city where I may say they committed many outrages of nearest affinity with sacrilege and rebellion.

'But the governess's extraordinary mildness and temper not only quickly assuaged all these begun misdemeanors, but readily pardoned their offences, though she very well knew many principal persons were interested in the occasion of those tumults. Notwithstanding, she wisely and discreetly seemed not to take notice of them, in regard such intimations might create those jealousies that probably would again kindle a new fire of discontent and apprehension.

'However, the court and council of Egypt having understood these proceedings, whose greatness of empire and power in command could brook neither resistance nor dispute, thought it not agreeing with the honour and dignity of their King (whose authority before these accidents seemed rather to be adored than contraverted) to suffer these insolencies to escape without some remarkable severity, as well in regard of the nobility as the people, presently designed a huge army for these countries, composed of the best and oldest soldiers Egypt could produce, and these troops were put under the command of a person of the same nation that better knew how to punish facts committed by a kind of harsh cruelty than to compose differences newly begun with mildness and temper, rather imitating those physicians which use desperate remedies to perfect the body the sooner than by prolonging application to save part for fear the whole should perish. In short, whose experience in the wars was more ancient and glorious than his nature any way relenting, insomuch as like a storm coming afar off, demonstrated by lightning and thunder, he gave the people cause of fear and terror before the tempest arrived, which caused many of them, by the report only, to quit their dwellings, as of the other side not a few of the noblemen that were the least confident of their own loyalty presently engaged one another in private counsels.

'As soon as this great General arrived, he not only dispossessed the governess herself of her chief authority by producing a larger commission, but seized upon the persons of many of the nobility, whose lives were publicly sacrificed to his fury, whilst terror and amazement seized the hearts of the common people. Notwithstanding this rough demeanour, he proclaimed everywhere should be maintained by the sword until his own thoughts could become satisfied of the subjects' entire obedience to his commands.

'This rigorous and new proceedings quickly involved the whole island of Cyprus in a trembling confusion, as well as in a future rebellion, insomuch as almost all people entertained these strange beginnings as sad omens, if not prevented by some timely resistance, that threatened a general destruction as well to their lives as estates, whenas formerly they held themselves the freest subjects of the world by reason of those privileges they had gained by the indulgent natures of their many good and merciful princes.

'And thus, Sir, I must say, was the first fatal fire kindled in Cyprus, which since hath been augmented by the powerful interest of most of the potentates in Asia. For as upon these pretences the people presently flew out into open hostility, so did they call in as many foreign princes as they could to their assistance, who, glad of any occasion to give bounds to the Egyptian monarchy, that then began to swell to a vast largeness in command, readily contributed their best endeavours, especially the father of Orsames, King of Syria, insomuch as the effects since have produced so much blood and slaughter, with other varieties of success and fortune, that many books might be amplified with the story, until the succession of command fell to this gallant Duke that now bears sway in that region, who hath been so principal an instrument of the happiness and present flourishing condition of the island (being not more valiant in war than wise in peace) that the King of Egypt himself is not only reduced at present to that state by reason of his powerful contentions against him, both by sea and land, that he seeks peace upon any terms, with a resignation of all his pretended rights. Besides, the people, in regard of the Duke's prudent government, with their own industry (who at the beginning of these stirs were rather poor and contemptible fishermen than approved and credible merchants) are become now so terrible upon the sea that by their numerous vessels for trading they fetch home to their own quarters all the riches of the world.'

The Queen hereupon put a stop to Eumenes' discourse with this language: 'And yet I have heard,' said she, 'all the recompense he can procure from their gratitudes is only a bare pension for his support and subsistance, neither will they willingly allow him any other title than their servant, however his valour and conduct in the wars upon all occasions brings to their assistance the best spirits of Asia, as conceiving him most worthy to be their master in martial affairs.'

''Tis true madam,' answered Eumenes, 'I must needs confess the people themselves, although naturally they are no soldiers, being altogether addicted to the industry of the spade, by which faculty they have performed admirable things to the wonder of other nations, yet are they crafty enough to maintain their own liberties, and suffer the Duke to enjoy no other jurisdiction over them than what they are content from time to time to afford him for their best commodity and advantage. Nevertheless, it is thought, if his ambition were equal to his power, he might make himself absolute prince of the country without contradiction, having the army so entirely at his command as well in regard of many factions amongst their governors as by reason of the necessity of one head and governor, especially if they should purchase to themselves peace from the King of Egypt, who (as I said before) now seems with earnestness to desire it of them.'

After the King had a little smiled upon the Queen at Eumenes' discourse, so much pretending to the Duke's interest and commendation, being himself extremely perfect in the knowledge of those parts, he began to argue with him in this manner. 'Although I cannot,' said the King, 'but approve of your observations, and much more commend your affectionate rhetoric in the Duke's behalf, who no doubt in the general deserves as much as you have said, yet I must not conclude altogether with you in belief concerning this easy accession to sovereignty, though his intentions were directed to those ambitions. For, notwithstanding you may see him always attended with glorious and gallant troops in the field, a prospect, I must confess, that cannot but dazzle youthful or common eyes, yet when it shall be considered withal that the common soldiers (who for the most part are rather carried on to their employments by their own private gain than by the advancement of their general) are only paid by certain treasures* appointed by the people, entirely faithful to their designs, that upon the least disorders may obstruct or detain their wages, either in part or in the whole, it will be a very difficult matter to unite them absolutely in the Duke's designs against the commonwealth, especially when it shall be also remembered that most of all the towns in the island are not only strong both by nature and art, but are continually guarded by the burghers themselves, without having any relation at all to the General, and so by consequence are furnished with provisions of every sort, insomuch as the least fort of the country is neither to be surprised by any manner of stratagem or to be taken without a very long siege, which would give the Duke's army, without pay, occasion enough to change their resolutions in the interim, and rather seek to betray his person than advance his ambition.

'Wherefore, I hold him to be much a wiser man in desisting from those attempts than in entering upon designs that at the worst may ruin his posterity, and at the best cannot much mend his condition, since at the present the people afford him so large a pension for his entertainment, that doth more than equal the revenues of many absolute princes of the inferior rank, which is enjoyed, as I may say, without either hazard or trouble.

'And however the factions of the people, as you have intimated, may seem something to contribute to this probability, yet considering in their natures how much they are addicted to freedom and equality, though such a necessity should compel a change, I am most confident they would rather call in again their old prince than make election of any new, much less the Duke whom, however his birth and titles are more illustrious, yet in their hearts they rank him as once a fellow subject with themselves to the King of Egypt. And if peace, as you say, should be entirely restored to that island, the contrary now being a means the more strongly to unite them against the common enemy, yet such is their hate to a jurisdiction of that nature I am persuaded they would never be brought to that subjection without an absolute conquest and desolation, witness their not being able, as you have already related, to brook it in their lawful King, under whom they seemed to enjoy all manner of felicity and content.

' 'Tis true, it is otherwise with the subjects of Syria, who are so wedded to the honour and prosperity of their prince that it is unpossible to withdraw their fidelities by any taxations or almost oppressions whatsoever, though sometimes their nobility perhaps fly out against the power and greatness of favourites who seem something to obscure their interest with their sovereign, all dispositions not being alike. As, for example, I find my own subjects begin already to be weary of those happinesses under a peaceful monarch that other kingdoms can but only hope for after long and bloody experience.'

The King at these very words, as if he felt something inwardly at the soul, rested silent for a pretty space, and then again, as if he had anew recollected his spirits, kissing the Queen twice or thrice, he altered the subject of his serious discourse into another of more variety and delight, which continued them employed until they arrived at the palace gate, where many lighted torches attended to conduct him and the Queen up the stairs.

*   *   *   *   *   *   *   *   *   *

EUARCHUS' MEDITATION DURING HIS CAPTURE

Why should my unkind subjects, thought he, put me upon these straights that either I must confess myself guilty of those crimes I never intended to commit, or quit my interest to those crowns that have for so many lasting ages been worn by my predecessors, who perhaps were far more rigorous in their actions than myself.

'O you gods,' said he, 'where are those faults for which I am so deeply punished by your indignation, as well as my people's disobedience? If they be visible to be known to the world, why are they not in some measure made apparent to my understanding, that either knowingly I might suffer, or Asia be satisfied in my obstinacy, since the contrary doth but dishonour other princes without affording me the comfort to ask pardon, in that I know not who or wherein I have offended. If I follow not the tract of my ancestors, conserving those privileges belonging to my crowns, without demanding more of my subjects, or that I intended not to rule according to those principles, I confess they might have cause to quarrel with my proceedings, but when my reign hath been gentler than former kings and princes of the same line, that could challenge by right no greater prerogative than myself, why should they continue so cruel to my purposes?

'Is it not sufficient for the quieting of the hearts of my people that I willingly transfer part of my power to the Senate, whereby they may be able to make what laws they please, both against them and me, but I must also accuse my own innocency to give both honour and belief to their actions, whereby posterity might curse my very name and being to all eternity.'

*   *   *   *   *   *   *   *   *   *

EUARCHUS' SPEECH AT HIS TRIAL

When the noise was somewhat appeased, and the women by force sent out of the court, as esteemed too impertinent disturbers of the proceedings, Euarchus with a certain gentle admonition of his hand to be heard (which being at last granted him) with a constant grave countenance, though the sweetness of his favour was much decayed by his many miseries and continued afflictions, made this manner of speech* to the assembly.

'I hope there are some here,' said he, 'that are rather sorry for my misfortunes than condemners of my dignity, wherefore less persuaded of these my crimes than others, to whom I shall only address those few words I have to say, since I neither can or ever will acknowledge this jurisdiction, that seems to claim an unheard of authority over my person. You see your King not only brought before I know not what tribunal as a malefactor, but condemned to die by a law never yet put in practice by any power, however grounded, upon no other cause but that he desires satisfaction in the true constitution of the Lydian government, which ought to be the rules of comportment both for the prince and the subject.

'You may behold also a liberty extraordinary given to these men, rather by violence to execute what they please than justly to proceed in what they should, since the Senate is now no more what it was than myself when I was head thereof. If precedents were to be produced for these actions, certainly they would add much to the advantage of the cause in the opinion of the people; if none have been in former times, yet at leastwise let them derive their power from some visible authority, which may appear to have been supreme in past ages. If they challenge their jurisdiction from the ancient and hereditary privileges of the nobility, where are they themselves to make good the claim? If by the natural right of the people, why are not their consents demanded to justify the proceedings.

'But O you gods, it is the sword only (that never was ordained for government, but execution) by which Euarchus must fall. Alas, alas, my friends,' said he, 'to what a pass are your rights come, when the father of them all must perish because he desires still to make them good to your posterity?'

The judges being unwilling to hear any more of this language, for that the King's discourses seemed to draw from the assembly not only tears, but consideration even from the soldiers themselves, who began to be a little softened in their hearts, commanded them instantly to lead away the prisoner from the bar, since they perceived his obstinacy was not at all to be reformed.

MARGARET CAVENDISH
(DUCHESS OF NEWCASTLE)

The Blazing World

(1666)

The Description of a New World Called the Blazing World.
Written by the thrice noble, illustrious and excellent Princess the
Duchess of Newcastle.

To The Duchess of Newcastle on her New Blazing World.

Our elder world, with all their skill and arts
Could but divide the world into three parts.
Colombus then for navigation famed
Found a new world, America 'tis named.
Now this new world was found, it was not made,
Only discovered lying in time's shade.
Then what are you, having no chaos found
To make a world, or any such least ground?
But your creating fancy thought it fit
To make your world of nothing but pure wit.
Your blazing world beyond the stars mounts higher,
Enlightens all with a celestial fire.

William Newcastle*

TO THE READER

IF you wonder that I join a work of fancy to my serious
philosophical contemplations,* think not that it is out of a
disparagement to philosophy, or out of an opinion as if this noble
study were but a fiction of the mind, for though philosophers may
err in searching and enquiring after the causes of natural effects
and many times embrace falsehoods for truths, yet this doth not
prove that the ground of philosophy is merely fiction, but the
error proceeds from the different motions of reason, which cause
different opinions in different parts, and in some are more
irregular than in others, for reason being dividable, because
material, cannot move in all parts alike and since there is but one
truth in nature, all those that hit not this truth do err, some more,
some less, for though some may come nearer the mark than
others, which makes their opinions seem more probable and
rational than others, yet as long as they swerve from this only
truth they are in the wrong.

Nevertheless, all do ground their opinions upon reason; that is,
upon rational probabilities. At least, they think they do. But

fictions are an issue of man's fancy, framed in his own mind according as he pleases, without regard whether the thing he fancies be really existent without his mind or not, so that reason searches the depth of nature and enquires after the true causes of natural effects, but fancy creates of its own accord whatsoever it pleases and delights in its own work.

The end of reason is truth, the end of fancy is fiction. But mistake me not when I distinguish fancy from reason; I mean not as if fancy were not made by the rational parts of matter, but by reason I understand a rational search and enquiry into the causes of natural effects, and by fancy a voluntary creation or production of the mind, both being effects, or rather actions of the rational part of matter, of which, as that is a more profitable and useful study than this, so it is also more laborious and difficult, and requires sometimes the help of fancy to recreate the mind and withdraw it from its more serious contemplations.

And this is the reason why I added this piece of fancy to my philosophical observations, and joined them as two worlds at the ends of their poles, both for my own sake, to divert my studious thoughts which I employed in the contemplation thereof, and to delight the reader with variety, which is always pleasing. But lest my fancy should stray too much, I chose such a fiction as would be agreeable to the subject I treated of in the former parts.

It is a description of a new world, not such as Lucian's, or the Frenchman's world in the moon,* but a world of my own creating, which I call the blazing world, the first part whereof is romancical the second philosophical and the third is merely fancy or (as I may call it) fantastical, which if it add any satisfaction to you I shall account myself a happy creatoress; if not, I must be content to live a melancholy life in my own world. I cannot call it a poor world, if poverty be only want of gold, silver and jewels, for there is more gold in it than all the chemists ever did and (as I verily believe) will ever be able to make.

As for the rocks of diamonds, I wish with all my soul they might be shared amongst my noble female friends, and upon that condition I would willingly quit my part, and of the gold I should only desire so much as might suffice to repair my noble lord and husband's losses,* for I am not covetous, but as ambitious as ever any of my sex was, is or can be, which makes that though I cannot be Henry the Fifth or Charles the Second, yet I endeavour to be Margaret the First, and although I have neither power, time nor occasion to conquer the world as Alexander and Caesar did, yet rather than not to be mistress of one, since fortune and the fates would give me none, I have made a world of my own, for which nobody, I hope, will blame me, since it is in everyone's power to do the like.

The Description of a New World, Called the Blazing World

A MERCHANT, travelling into a foreign country, fell extremely in love with a young lady, but being a stranger in that nation and beneath her both in birth and wealth, he could have but little hopes of obtaining his desire. However, his love growing more and more vehement upon him, even to the slighting of all difficulties, he resolved at last to steal her away, which he had the better opportunity to do because her father's house was not far from the sea, and she often using to gather shells upon the shore accompanied not with above two or three of her servants, it encouraged him the more to execute his design.

Thus, coming one time—with a little light vessel, not unlike a packet-boat, manned with some few seamen, and well victualled for fear of some accidents which might perhaps retard their journey—to the place where she used to repair, he forced her away. But when he fancied himself the happiest man of the world, he proved to be the most unfortunate, for Heaven, frowning at his theft, raised such a tempest as they knew not what to do or whither to steer their course so that the vessel, both by its own lightness and the violent motion of the wind, was carried as swift as an arrow out of a bow towards the North Pole, and in a short time reached the icy sea, where the wind forced it amongst huge pieces of ice.

But being little and light, it did, by assistance and favour of the Gods to this virtuous lady, so turn and wind through those precipices as if it had been guided by some experienced pilot and skilful mariner. But alas, those few men which were it, not knowing whither they went nor what was to be done in so strange an adventure, and not being provided for so cold a voyage, were all frozen to death, the young lady only, by the light of her beauty the heat of her youth and protection of the Gods, remaining alive.

Neither was it a wonder that the men did freeze to death, for they were not only driven to the very end or point of the Pole of that world, but even to another Pole of another world which joined close to it, so that the cold, having a double strength at the conjunction of those two Poles, was insupportable.

At last the boat, still passing on, was forced into another world, for it is impossible to round this world's globe from Pole to Pole, so as we do from East to West, because the Poles of the other world, joining to the Poles of this, do not allow any further passage to surround the world that way, but if anyone arrives to either of these Poles he is either forced to return or to enter into another world; and lest you should scruple at it, and think if it were thus those that live at the Poles would either see two suns at one time, or else they would never want the sun's light for six months together, as it is commonly believed, you must know that each of these worlds having its own sun to enlighten it, they move each one in their peculiar circles, which motion is so just and exact that neither can hinder or obstruct the other. For they do not exceed their tropics, and although they should meet, yet we in this world cannot so well perceive them by reason of the brightness of our sun, which, being nearer to us, obstructs the splendour of the suns of the other worlds, they being too far off to be discerned by our optic perception except we use very good telescopes, by which skilful astronomers have often observed two or three suns at once.

But to return to the wandering boat, and the distressed lady: she, seeing all the men dead, found small comfort in life. Their bodies, which were preserved all that while from putrefaction and stench by the extremity of cold, began now to thaw and corrupt, whereupon she having not strength enough to fling them overboard, was forced to remove out of her small cabin upon the deck, to avoid that nauseous smell, and finding the boat swim between two plains of ice, as a stream that runs betwixt two shores, at last perceived land, but covered all with snow, from which came walking upon the ice strange creatures, in shape like bears, only they went upright as men.

Those creatures, coming near the boat, catched hold of it with their paws, which served them instead of hands. Some two or three of them entered first, and when they came out, the rest went in one after another. At last, having viewed and observed all that was in the boat, they spoke to each other in a language which the lady did not understand, and having carried her out of the boat, sunk it together with the dead men.

The lady now finding herself in so strange a place and amongst such a wonderful kind of creatures, was extremely strucken with fear, and could entertain no other thoughts but that every moment her life was to be a sacrifice to their cruelty. But those bear-like creatures, how terrible soever they appeared to her sight, yet were they so far from exercising any cruelty upon her that rather they showed her all civility and kindness imaginable. For, she being not able to go upon the ice by reason of its slipperiness, they took her up in their rough arms and carried her into their city, where instead of houses they had caves underground. And as soon as they entered the city, both males and females, young and old, flocked together to see this lady, holding up their paws in admiration.

At last, having brought her into a certain large and spacious cave, which they intended for her reception, they left her to the custody of the females, who entertained her with all kindness and respect and gave her such victuals as they were used to eat. But seeing her constitution neither agreed with the temper of that climate nor their diet, they were resolved to carry her into another island of a warmer temper, in which were men like foxes, only walking in an upright shape, who received their neighbours the bear-men with great civility and courtship, very much admiring this beauteous lady, and having discoursed some while together, agreed at last to make her a present to the emperor of their world.

To which end, after she had made some short stay in the same place, they brought her cross that island to a large river, whose stream run smooth and clear like crystal, in which were numerous boats much like our fox-traps, in one whereof she was carried, some of the bear and fox-men waiting on her, and as soon as they had crossed the river they came into an island where there were men which had heads, beaks and feathers like wild geese, only they went in an upright shape like the bear-men and fox-men; their rumps they carried between their legs, their wings were of the same length with their bodies, and their tails of an indifferent size, trailing after them like a lady's garment.

And after the bear and fox-men had declared their intention and design to their neighbours the geese or bird-men, some of them joined to the rest and attended the lady through that island, till they came to another great and large river, where there was a preparation made of many boats, much like birds' nests only of a bigger size, and having crossed that river they arrived into another island, which was of a pleasant and mild temper, full of woods, and the inhabitants thereof were satyrs, who received both the bear, fox and bird-men with all respect and civility. And after some conferences (for they all understood each other's language), some chief of the satyrs joining to them, accompanied the lady out of that island to another river, wherein were very handsome and commodious barges. And having crossed that river, they entered into a large and spacious kingdom, the men whereof were of a grass-green complexion, who entertained them very kindly and provided all conveniences for their further voyage.

Hitherto they had only crossed rivers, but now they could not avoid the open seas any longer, wherefore they made their ships and tacklings ready to sail over into the island where the emperor of their Blazing World (for so was it called) kept his residence. Very good navigators they were, and though they had no knowledge of the lodestone or needle or pendulous watches yet (which was as serviceable to them) they had subtle observations and great practice, insomuch that they could not only tell the depth of the sea in every place, but where there were shelves of sand, rocks and other obstructions to be avoided by skilful and experienced seamen.

Besides, they were excellent augurers, which skill they counted more necessary and beneficial than the use of compasses, cards, watches and the like. But above the rest, they had an extraordinary art, much to be taken notice of by experimental philosophers, and that was a certain engine which would draw in a great quantity of air and shoot forth wind with a great force. This engine, in a calm, they placed behind their ships, and in a storm, before; for it served against the raging waves like canons against an hostile army or besieged town: it would batter and beat the waves in pieces were they as high as steeples, and as soon as a breach was made, they forced their passage through, in spite even of the most furious wind, using two of those engines at every ship, one before, to beat off the waves, and another behind to drive it on, so that the artificial wind had the better of the natural, for it had a greater advantage of the waves than the natural of the ships; the natural, being above the face of the water, could not without a downright motion enter or press into the ships, whereas the artificial, with a sideward motion, did pierce into the bowels of the waves.

Moreover, it is to be observed that in a great tempest they would join their ships in battle array and when they feared wind and waves would be too strong for them if they divided their ships, they joined as many together as the compass or advantage of the places of the liquid element would give them leave, for their ships were so ingeniously contrived that they could fasten them together as close as a honeycomb without waste of place, and being thus united, no wind nor waves were able to separate them.

The Emperor's ships were all of gold, but the merchants' and skippers' of leather; the golden ships were not much heavier than ours of wood, by reason they were neatly made and required not such thickness, neither were they troubled with pitch, tar, pumps, guns and the like, which make our wooden ships very heavy; for though they were not all of a piece, yet they were so well soddered* that there was no fear of leaks, chinks or clefts, and as for guns, there was no use of them, because they had no other enemies but the winds. But the leather ships were not altogether so sure, although much lighter. Besides, they were pitched to keep out water.

Having thus prepared and ordered their navy, they went on in despite of calm or storm, and though the lady at first fancied herself in a very sad condition, and her mind was much tormented with doubts and fears, not knowing whether this strange adventure would tend to her safety or destruction, yet she being withal of a generous spirit and ready wit, considering what dangers she had passed, and finding those sorts of men civil and diligent attendants to her, took courage and endeavoured to learn their language, which after she had obtained so far that partly by some words and signs she was able to apprehend their meaning, she was so far from being afraid of them that she thought herself not only safe but very happy in their company. By which we may see that novelty discomposes the mind, but acquaintance settles it in peace and tranquility.

At last, having passed by several rich islands and kingdoms, they went towards Paradise, which was the seat of the Emperor, and coming in sight of it, rejoiced very much. The lady at first could perceive nothing but high rocks which seemed to touch the skies, and although they appeared not of an equal height, yet they seemed to be all one piece without partitions. But at last, drawing nearer, she perceived a cleft which was a part of those rocks, out of which she spied coming forth a great number of boats, which afar off showed like a company of ants marching one after another. The boats appeared like the holes or partitions in a honeycomb, and when joined together stood as close. The men were of several complexions, but none like any of our world; and when both the boats and ships met, they saluted and spoke to each other very courteously, for there was but one language in all that world, nor no more but one Emperor, to whom they all submitted with the greatest duty and obedience, which made them live in a continued peace and happiness, not acquainted with foreign wars or home-bred insurrections.

The lady, now being arrived at this place, was carried out of her ship into one of those boats, and conveyed through the same passage (for there was no other) into that part of the world where the Emperor did reside, which part was very pleasant and of a mild temper. Within itself it was divided by a great number of vast and large rivers, all ebbing and flowing into several islands of unequal distance from each other, which in most parts were as pleasant, healthful, rich and fruitful as nature could make them—and, as I mentioned before, secure from all foreign invasions, by reason there was but one way to enter and that like a labyrinth so winding and turning among the rocks that no other vessels but small boats could pass, carrying not above three passengers at a time.

On each side all along this narrow and winding river there were several cities, some of marble, some of alabaster, some of agate, some of amber, some of coral, and some of other precious materials not known in our world, all which after the lady had passed, she came to the imperial city, named Paradise, which appeared in form like several islands, for rivers did run betwixt every street, which together with the bridges, whereof there was a great number, were all paved. The city itself was built of gold, and their architectures were noble, stately and magnificent, not like our modern but like those in the Romans' time; for our modern buildings are like those houses which children use to make of cards, one storey above another, fitter for birds than men, but theirs were more large and broad than high. The highest of them did not exceed two stories, besides those rooms that were underground, as cellars and other offices.

The Emperor's palace stood upon an indifferent ascent from the imperial city, at the top of which ascent was a broad arch supported by several pillars, which went round the palace and contained four of our English miles in compass. Within the arch stood the Emperor's Guard, which consisted of several sorts of men. At every half-mile was a different gate to enter and every gate was of a different fashion. The first, which allowed a passage from the imperial city into the palace, had on either hand a cloister, the outward part whereof stood upon arches sustained by pillars, but the inner part was close.*

Being entered through the gate, the palace itself appeared in its middle like the aisle of a church, a mile and a half long and half a mile broad; the roof of it was all arched and rested upon pillars so artificially placed that a stranger would lose himself therein without a guide. At the extreme sides, that is, between the outward and inward part of the cloister, were lodgings for attendants, and in the midst of the palace, the Emperor's own rooms, whose lights were placed at the top of everyone because of the heat of the sun.

The Emperor's apartment for state was no more enclosed than the rest, only an imperial throne was in every apartment, of which the several adornments could not be perceived until one entered, because the pillars were so just opposite to one another that all the adornments could not be seen at once. The first part of the palace was, as the imperial city, all of gold, and when it came to the Emperor's apartment, it was so rich with diamonds, pearls, rubies and the like precious stones that it surpasses my skill to enumerate them all. Amongst the rest, the imperial room of state appeared most magnificent. It was paved with green diamonds (for in that world are diamonds of all colours) so artificially as it seemed but of one piece. The pillars were set with diamonds so close and in such a manner that they appeared most glorious to the sight. Between every pillar was a bow or arch of a certain sort of diamonds, the like whereof our world does not afford, which being placed in every one of the arches in several rows, seemed just like so many rainbows of several different colours.

The roof of the arches was of blue diamonds, and in the midst thereof was a carbuncle* which represented the sun. The rising and setting sun at the East and West side of the room were made of rubies. Out of this room there was a passage into the Emperor's bedchamber, the walls whereof were of jet, and the floor of black marble. The roof was of mother of pearl, where the moon and blazing stars were represented by white diamonds, and his bed was made of diamonds and carbuncles.

No sooner was the lady brought before the Emperor but he conceived her to be some goddess, and offered to worship her, which she refused, telling him (for by that time she had pretty well learned their language) that although she came out of another world, yet was she but a mortal, at which the Emperor, rejoicing, made her his wife and gave her an absolute power to rule and govern all that world as she pleased. But her subjects, who could hardly be persuaded to believe her mortal, tendered her all the veneration and worship due to a deity.

Her accoutrement after she was made Empress was as followeth: on her head she wore a cap of pearl and a half-moon of diamonds just before it; on the top of her crown came spreading over a broad carbuncle cut in the form of a sun; her coat was of pearl mixed with blue diamonds and fringed with red ones; her buskins* and sandals were of green diamonds. In her left hand she held a buckler* to signify the defence of her dominions, which buckler was made of that sort of diamond as has several different colours, and being cut and made in the form of an arch, showed like a rainbow. In her right hand she carried a spear made of a white diamond, cut like the tail of a blazing star, which signified that she was ready to assault those that proved her enemies.

None was allowed to use or wear gold but those of the imperial race, which were the only nobles of the state, nor durst anyone wear jewels but the Emperor, the Empress and their eldest son. Notwithstanding that, they had an infinite quantity both of gold and precious stones in that world, for they had larger extents of gold than our Arabian sands. Their precious stones were rocks and their diamonds of several colours. They used no coin, but all their traffic was by exchange of several commodities.

Their priests and governors were princes of the imperial blood and made eunuchs for that purpose, and as for the ordinary sort of men in that part of the world where the Emperor resided, they were of several complexions: not white, black, tawny, olive or ash-coloured, but some appeared of an azure, some of a deep purple, some of a grass green, some of a scarlet, some of an orange colour, etc. Which colours and complexions, whether they were made by the bare reflection of light, without the assistance of small particles, or by the help of well-ranged and ordered atoms, or by a continual agitation of little globules, or by some pressing and reacting motion, I am not able to determine.

The rest of the inhabitants of that world were men of several different sorts, shapes, figures, dispositions and humours, as I have already made mention heretofore Some were bear-men, some worm-men, some fish or mer-men, otherwise called syrens, some bird-men, some fly-men, some ant-men, some geese-men, some spider-men, some lice-men, some fox-men, some ape-men, some jackdaw-men, some magpie-men, some parrot-men, some satyrs, some giants, and many more, which I cannot all remember. And of these several sorts of men, each followed such a profession as was most proper for the nature of their species, which the Empress encouraged them in, especially those that had applied themselves to the study of several arts and sciences, for they were as ingenious and witty in the invention of profitable and useful arts as we are in our world—nay, more. And to that end she erected schools and founded several societies.

The bear-men were to be her experimental philosophers, the bird-men her astronomers, the fly, worm and fish-men her natural philosophers, the ape-men her chemists, the satyrs her Galenic physicians, the fox-men her politicians, the spider and lice-men her mathematicians, the jackdaw, magpie and parrot-men her orators and logicians, the giants her architects etc. But before all things, she, having got a sovereign power from the Emperor over all the world, desired to be informed both of the manner of their religion and government, and to that end she called the priests and statesmen to give her an account of either.

Of the statesmen she enquired first why they had so few laws, to which they answered that many laws made many divisions, which most commonly did breed factions and at last broke out into open wars. Next she asked why they preferred the monarchical form of government before any other. They answered that, as it was natural for one body to have but one head, so it was also natural for a politic body to have but one governor, and that a commonwealth which had many governors was like a monster of many heads. 'Besides,' said they, 'a monarchy is a divine form of government and agrees most with our religion, for as there is but one God, whom we all unanimously worship and adore with one faith, so we are resolved to have but one Emperor, to whom we all submit with one obedience.'

Then the Empress, seeing that the several sorts of her subjects had each their churches apart, asked the priests whether they were of several religions. They answered her Majesty that there was no more but one religion in that world, nor no diversity of opinions in that same religion; for though there were several sorts of men, yet had they all but one opinion concerning the worship and adoration of God. The Empress asked them whether they were Jews, Turks or Christians. 'We do not know,' said they, 'what religions those are, but we do all unanimously acknowledge, worship and adore the only, omnipotent and eternal God with all reverence, submission and duty.'

Again the Empress enquired whether they had several forms of worship. They answered, 'No, for our devotion and worship consists only in prayers, which we frame according to our several necessities in petitions, humiliations, thanksgiving, etc.' 'Truly,' replied the Empress, 'I thought you had been either Jews or Turks, because I never perceived any women in your congregations. But what is the reason you bar them from your religious assemblies?' 'It is not fit,' said they, 'that men and women should be promiscuously together in time of religious worship, for their company hinders devotion and makes many, instead of praying to

God, direct their devotion to their mistresses.' 'But,' asked the Empress, 'have they no congregation of their own to perform the duties of divine worship as well as men?' 'No,' answered they, 'but they stay at home and say their prayers by themselves in their closets.'*

Then the Empress desired to know the reason why the priests and governors of their world were made eunuchs. They answered, 'To keep them from marriage, for women and children most commonly make disturbance both in church and state.' 'But', said she, 'women and children have no employment in church or state.' ' 'Tis true,' answered they, 'but although they are not admitted to public employments, yet are they so prevalent with their husbands and parents that many times by their importunate persuasions they cause as much, nay more mischief secretly, than if they had the management of public affairs.'

The Empress, having received an information of what concerned both church and state, passed some time in viewing the imperial palace, where she admired much the skill and ingenuity of the architects and enquired of them first, why they built their houses no higher than two stories from the ground. They answered her Majesty that the lower their buildings were, the less were they subject either to the heat of the sun, to wind, tempest, decay, etc. Then she desired to know the reason why they made them so thick. They answered that the thicker the walls were, the warmer were they in winter and cooler in summer, for their thickness kept out both cold and heat. Lastly, she asked why they arched their roofs and made so many pillars. They replied that arches and pillars did not only grace a building very much and caused it to appear magnificent, but made it also firm and lasting.

The Empress was very well satisfied with their answers, and after some time, when she thought that her new-found societies of the virtuosos had made a good progress in their several employments which she had put them upon, she caused a convocation first of the bird-men and commanded them to give her a true relation of the two celestial bodies, viz. the sun and moon, which they did with all the obedience and faithfulness befitting their duty.

The sun, as much as they could observe, they related to be a firm or solid stone of a vast bigness, of colour yellowish and of an extraordinary splendour. But the moon, they said, was of a whitish colour, and although she looked dim in the presence of the sun, yet had she her own light and was a shining body of herself, as might be perceived by her vigorous appearance on moonshiney nights. The difference only betwixt her own and the sun's light was that the sun did strike his beams in a direct line, but the moon never respected the centre of their world in a right line, but her centre was always excentrical.

The spots both in the sun and moon, as far as they were able to perceive, they affirmed to be nothing else but flaws and stains of their stony bodies. Concerning the heat of the sun, they were not of one opinion. Some would have the sun hot in itself, alleging an old tradition that it should at some time break asunder and burn the heavens and consume this world into hot embers which, said they, could not be done if the sun were not fiery of itself. Others again said this opinion could not stand with reason, for fire being a destroyer of all things, the sun-stone after this manner would burn up all the near-adjoining bodies. 'Besides,' said they, 'fire cannot subsist without fuel, and the sun-stone, having nothing to feed on, would in a short time consume itself.' Wherefore they thought it more probable that the sun was not actually hot, but only by the reflection of its light, so that its heat was an effect of its light, both being immaterial.

But this opinion again was laughed at by others and rejected as ridiculous, who thought it impossible that one immaterial should produce another, and believed that both the light and heat of the sun proceeded from a swift circular motion of the ethereal globules, which by their striking upon the optic nerve caused light, and their motion produced heat. But neither would this opinion hold, for, said some, then it would follow that the sight of animals is the cause of light, and that, were there no eyes, there would be no light, which was against all sense and reason.

Thus they argued concerning the heat and light of the sun, but which is remarkable, none did say that the sun was a globous, fluid body and had a swift circular motion, but all agreed it was fixed and firm like a centre, and therefore they generally called it the sun-stone.

Then the Empress asked them the reason why the sun and moon did often appear in different postures or shapes, as

sometimes magnified, sometimes diminished, sometimes elevated, otherwhiles depressed, now thrown to the right, then to the left.
To which some of the bird-men answered that it proceeded from
the various degrees of heat and cold, which are found in the air,
from whence did follow a differing density and rarity, and
likewise from the vapours that are interposed, whereof those that
ascend are higher and less dense than the ambient air, but those
which descend are heavier and more dense.

But others did with more probability affirm that it was nothing
else but the various patterns of the air, for like as painters do not
copy out one and the same original just alike at all times, so, said
they, do several parts of the air make different patterns of the
luminous bodies of the sun and moon, which patterns, as several
copies, the sensitive motions do figure out in the substance of our
eyes.

This answer the Empress liked much better than the former,
and enquired further what opinion they had of those creatures
that are called the motes of the sun. To which they answered that
they were nothing else but streams of very small, rare and
transparent particles through which the sun was represented as
through a glass, for if they were not transparent, said they, they
would eclipse the light of the sun, and if not rare and of an airy
substance, they would hinder flies from flying in the air, at least
retard their flying motion. Nevertheless, although they were
thinner than the thinnest vapour, yet were they not so thin as the
body of air, or else they would not be perceptible by animal sight.
Then the Empress asked whether they were living creatures.
They answered, 'Yes, because they did increase and decrease,
and were nourished by the presence and starved by the absence
of the sun.'

Having thus finished their discourse of the sun and moon, the
Empress desired to know what stars there were besides. But they
answered that they could perceive in that world none other but
blazing stars, and from thence it had the name that it was called:
the Blazing World, and these blazing stars, said they, were such
solid, firm and shining bodies as the sun and moon, not of a
globular but of several sorts of figures; some had tails and some
other kinds of shapes.

After this, the Empress asked them what kind of substance or creature the air was. The bird-men answered that they could have no other perception of the air but by their own respiration. 'For,' said they, 'some bodies are only subject to touch, others only to sight and others only to smell, but some are subject to none of our exterior senses, for nature is so full of variety that our weak senses cannot perceive all the various sorts of her creatures, neither is there any one object perceptible by all our senses, no more than several objects are by one sense.' 'I believe you,' replied the Empress, 'but if you can give no account of the air,' said she, 'you will hardly be able to inform me how wind is made, for they say that wind is nothing but motion of the air.'

The bird-men answered that they observed wind to be more dense than air, and therefore subject to the sense of touch; but what properly wind was and the manner how it was made they could not exactly tell. Some said it was caused by the clouds falling on each other, and others that it was produced of a hot and dry exhalation which, ascending, was driven down again by the coldness of the air that is in the middle region and by reason of its lightness could not go directly to the bottom, but was carried by the air up and down. Some would have it a flowing water of the air, and others again a flowing air moved by the blades of the stars.

But the Empress, seeing they could not agree concerning the cause of wind, asked whether they could tell how snow was made, to which they answered that, according to their observation, snow was made by a commixture of water and some certain extract of the element of fire that is under the moon, a small portion of which extract being mixed with water, and beaten by air or wind, made a white froth called snow which being after some while dissolved by the heat of the same spirit, turned to water again.

This observation amazed the Empress very much, for she had hitherto believed that snow was made by cold motions, and not by such an agitation or beating of a fiery extract upon water. Nor could she be persuaded to believe it until the fish or mer-men had delivered their observation upon the making of ice, which, they said, was not produced, as some had hitherto conceived, by the motion of the air raking the superfices of the earth, but by some strong saline vapour arising out of the seas, which condensed water into ice, and the more quantity there was of that vapour, the greater were the mountains or precipices of ice. But the reason that it did not so much freeze in the torrid zone, or under the ecliptic, as near or under the poles, was that this vapour in those places, being drawn up by the sunbeams into the middle region of the air, was only condensed into water and fell down in showers of rain, whenas under the Poles, the heat of the sun being not so vehement, the same vapour had no force or power to rise so high, and therefore caused so much ice by ascending and acting only upon the surface of water.

This relation confirmed partly the observation of the bird-men concerning the cause of snow, but since they had made mention that that same extract, which by its commixture with water made snow, proceeded from the element of fire that is under the moon, the Empress asked them of what nature that elementary fire was; whether it was like ordinary fire here upon earth, or such a fire as is within the bowels of the earth and as the famous mountains Vesuvius and Etna do burn withal, or whether it was such a sort of fire as is found in flints etc.

They answered that the elementary fire which is underneath the sun was not so solid as any of those mentioned fires, because it had no solid fuel to feed on, but yet it was much like the flame of ordinary fire, only somewhat more thin and fluid. 'For flame,' said they, 'is nothing else but the airy part of a fired body.'

Lastly, the Empress asked the bird-men of the nature of thunder and lightning, and whether it was not caused by roves* of ice falling upon each other. To which they answered that it was not made that way but by an encounter of cold and heat, so that an exhalation being kindled in the clouds did dash forth lightning, and that there were so many rentings of clouds as there were sounds and cracking noises. But this opinion was contradicted by others, who affirmed that thunder was a sudden and monstrous blas stirred up in the air and did not always require a cloud.

But the Empress, not knowing what they meant by blas (for even they themselves were not able to explain the sense of this word) liked the former better, and to avoid hereafter tedious disputes, and have the truth of the phenomenas of celestial bodies more exactly known, commanded the bear-men, which were her experimental philosophers, to observe them through such instruments as are called telescopes, which they did according to her Majesty's command. But these telescopes caused more differences and divisions amongst them than ever they had before, for some said they perceived that the sun stood still and the earth did move about it; others were of opinion that they both did move; and others said again that the earth stood still and the sun did move. Some counted more stars than others; some discovered new stars never seen before. Some fell into a great dispute with others concerning the bigness of the stars, some said the moon was another world like their terrestrial globe, and the spots therein were hills and valleys; but others would have the spots to be the terrestrial parts and the smooth and glossy parts the sea.

At last, the Empress commanded them to go with their telescopes to the very end of the Pole that was joined to the world she came from, and try whether they could perceive any stars in it, which they did, and being returned to her Majesty, reported that they had seen three blazing stars appear there one after another in a short time, whereof two were bright and one dim. But they could not agree neither in this observation, for some said it was but one star which appeared at three several times and several places, and others would have them to be three several stars, for they thought it impossible that those three several appearances should have been but one star, because every star did rise at a certain time and appeared in a certain place and did disappear in the same place.

'Next, it is altogether improbable,' said they, 'that one star should fly from place to place, especially at such a vast distance, without a visible motion, in so short a time, and appear in such different places, whereof two were quite opposite, and the third sideways. Lastly, if it had been but one star,' said they, 'it would always have kept the same splendour, which it did not, for, as above mentioned, two were bright and one was dim.'

After they had thus argued, the Empress began to grow angry at their telescopes, that they could give no better intelligence 'For, 'said she, 'now I do plainly perceive that your glasses are false informers and instead of discovering the truth, delude your senses.* Wherefore I command you to break them, and let the bird-men trust only to their natural eyes and examine celestial objects by the motions of their own sense and reason.'

The bear-men replied that it was not the fault of their glasses which caused such differences in their opinions, but the sensitive motions in their optic organs did not move alike, nor were their rational judgements always regular. To which the Empress answered that if their glasses were true informers, they would rectify their irregular sense and reason. 'But,' said she, 'nature has made your sense and reason more regular than art has your glasses, for they are mere deluders and will never lead you to the knowledge of truth. Wherefore I command you again to break them, for you may observe the progressive motions of celestial bodies with your natural eyes better than through artificial glasses.'

The bear-men, being exceedingly troubled at her Majesty's displeasure concerning their telescopes, kneeled down and in the humblest manner petitioned that they might not be broken. 'For,' said they, 'we take more delight in artificial delusions than in natural truths. Besides, we shall want employments for our senses and subjects for arguments, for were there nothing but truth and no falsehood, there would be no occasion for to dispute, and by this means we should want the aim and pleasure of our endeavours in confuting and contradicting each other. Neither would one man be thought wiser than another, but all would either be alike knowing and wise, or all would be fools, wherefore we most humbly beseech your imperial Majesty to spare our glasses, which are our only delight, and as dear to us as our lives.'

The Empress at last consented to their request, but upon condition that their disputes and quarrels should remain within their schools and cause no factions or disturbances in state or government. The bear-men, full of joy, returned their most humble thanks to the Empress, and to make her amends for the displeasure which their telescopes had occasioned, told her Majesty that they had several other artificial optic glasses which they were sure would give her Majesty a great deal more satisfaction. Amongst the rest they brought forth several microscopes, by the means of which they could enlarge the shapes of little bodies, and make a louse appear as big as an elephant and a mite as big as a whale.

First of all they showed the Empress a grey drone-fly, wherein they observed that the greatest part of her face, nay of her head, consisted of two large bunches all covered over with a multitude of small pearls or hemispheres in a trigonal order, which pearls were of two degrees, smaller and bigger. The smaller degree was lowermost and looked towards the ground; the other was upward and looked sideward, forward and backward. They were all so smooth and polished that they were able to represent the image of any object. The number of them was in all 14,000.

After the view of this strange and miraculous creature, and their several observations upon it, the Empress asked them what they judged those little hemispheres might be. They answered that each of them was a perfect eye, by reason they perceived that each was covered with a transparent cornea containing a liquor within them which resembled the watery or glassy humour of the eye. To which the Empress replied that they might be glassy pearls and yet not eyes, and that perhaps their microscopes did not truly inform them. But they smilingly answered her Majesty that she did not know the virtue of those microscopes, for they did never delude, but rectify and inform their senses. 'Nay, the world,' said they, 'would be but blind without them as it has been in former ages before those microscopes were invented.'

After this they took a charcoal, and viewing it with one of their best microscopes, discovered in it an infinite multitude of pores, some bigger, some less, so close and thick that they left but very little space betwixt them to be filled with a solid body. And to give her imperial Majesty a better assurance thereof, they counted in a line of them an inch long no less than 2,700 pores, from which observation they drew this following conclusion: to wit, that this multitude of pores was the cause of the blackness of the coal. 'For', said they, 'a body that has so many pores from each of which no light is reflected must necessarily look black, since black is nothing else but a privation of light or a want of reflection.'

But the Empress replied that if all colours were made by reflection of light, and that black was as much a colour as any other colour, then certainly they contradicted themselves in saying that black was made by want of reflection. 'However, not to interrupt your microscopical inspections,' said she, 'let us see how vegetables appear through your glasses.' Whereupon they took a nettle and, by the virtue of the microscope, discovered that underneath the points of the nettle there were certain little bags or bladders containing a poisonous liquor, and when the points had made their way into the interior parts of the skin they, like syringe-pipes, served to convey that same liquor into them.

To which observation the Empress replied that if there were such poison in nettles, then certainly in eating of them they would hurt us inwardly as much as they do outwardly. But they answered that it belonged to physicians more than to experimental philosophers to give reasons hereof, for they only made microscopical inspections and related the figures of the natural parts of creatures according to the presentation of their glasses.

Lastly, they showed the Empress a flea and a louse, which creatures through the microscope appeared so terrible to her sight that they had almost put her into a swoon. The description of all their parts would be very tedious to relate, and therefore I'll forbear it at this present. The Empress, after the view of those strangely-shaped creatures, pitied much those that are molested with them, especially poor beggars which, although they have nothing to live on themselves, are yet necessitated to maintain and feed of their own flesh and blood a company of such terrible creatures called lice, who instead of thanks do reward them with pains and torment them for giving them nourishment and food.

But after the Empress had seen the shapes of these monstrous creatures, she desired to know whether their microscopes could hinder their biting, or at least show some means how to avoid them, to which they answered that such arts were mechanical and below that noble study of microscopical observations. Then the Empress asked them whether they had not such sorts of glasses that could enlarge and magnify the shapes of great bodies as well as they had done of little ones. Whereupon they took one of their best and largest microscopes and endeavoured to view a whale through it, but alas the shape of the whale was so big that its circumference went beyond the magnifying quality of the glass, whether the error proceeded from the glass or from a wrong position of the whale against the reflection of light, I cannot certainly tell.

The Empress, seeing the insufficiency of those magnifying glasses, that they were not able to enlarge all sorts of objects, asked the bear-men whether they could not make glasses of a contrary nature to those they had showed her, to wit, such as instead of enlarging or magnifying the shape or figure of an object could contract it beneath its natural proportion. Which, in obedience to her Majesty's commands, they did, and viewing through one of the best of them, a huge and mighty whale appeared no bigger than a sprat, nay through some no bigger than a vinegar-eel, and through their ordinary ones an elephant seemed no bigger than a flea, a camel no bigger than a louse, and an ostrich no bigger than a mite.

To relate all their optic observations through the several sorts of their glasses would be a tedious work, and tire even the most patient reader, wherefore I'll pass them by. Only this was very remarkable and worthy to be taken notice of: that notwithstanding their great skill, industry and ingenuity in experimental philosophy, they could yet by no means contrive such glasses by the help of which they could spy out a vacuum, with all its dimensions, nor immaterial substances, non-beings, and mixed-beings, or such as are between something and nothing, which they were very much troubled at, hoping that yet in time, by long study and practice, they might perhaps attain to it.

The bird and bear-men being dismissed, the Empress called both the Syrens or fish-men and the worm-men to deliver their observations which they had made, both within the seas and the earth. First she enquired of the fish-men whence the saltness of the sea did proceed, to which they answered that there was a volatile salt in those parts of the earth which as a bosom contain the waters of the sea, which salt being imbibed by the sea became fixed, and this imbibing motion was what they called the ebbing and flowing of the sea. 'For,' said they, 'the rising and swelling of the water is caused by those parts of the volatile salt as are not so easily imbibed, which, striving to ascend above the water, bear it up with such a motion as man, or some other animal creature, in a violent exercise uses to take breath.' This they affirmed to be the true cause both of the saltness and the ebbing and flowing motion of the sea, and not the jogging of the earth or the secret influence of the moon, as some others had made the world believe.

After this, the Empress enquired whether they had observed

that all animal creatures within the seas and other waters had blood. They answered that some had blood, more or less, but some had none. 'In crayfishes and lobsters,' said they, 'we perceive but little blood, but in crabs, oysters, cockles etc., none at all.' Then the Empress asked them in what part of their bodies that little blood did reside. They answered: in a small vein which in lobsters went through the middle of their tails, but in crayfishes was found in their backs. As for other sorts of fishes, some, said they, had only blood about their gills, and others in some other places of their bodies, but they had not as yet observed any whose veins did spread all over their bodies.

The Empress, wondering that there could be living animals without blood, to be better satisfied desired the worm-men to inform her whether they had observed blood in all sorts of worms. They answered that, as much as they could perceive, some had blood and some not. A moth, said they, had no blood at all, and a louse had but like a lobster, a little vein along her back. Also nits, snails and maggots, as well as those that are generated out of cheese and fruits as those that are produced out of flesh, had no blood. 'But,' replied the Empress, 'if those mentioned creatures have no blood, how is it possible they can live, for it is commonly said that the life of an animal consists in the blood, which is the seat of the animal spirits.' They answered that blood was not a necessary propriety to the life of an animal, and that that which was commonly called animal spirits was nothing else but corporeal motions proper to the nature and figure of an animal.

Then she asked both the fish and worm-men whether all those creatures that have blood had a circulation of blood in their veins and arteries. But they answered that it was impossible to give her Majesty an exact account thereof, by reason the circulation of blood was an interior motion, which their senses neither of themselves not by the help of any optic instrument could perceive, but as soon as they had dissected an animal creature to find out the truth thereof, the interior corporeal motions proper to that particular figure or creature were altered. 'Then,' said the Empress, 'if all animal creatures have not blood, it is certain they all have neither muscles, tendons, nerves, etc. But,' said she, 'have you ever observed animal creatures that are neither flesh nor fish, but of an intermediate degree between both?' 'Truly,' answered both the fish and worm-men, 'we have observed several animal creatures that live both in water and on the earth indifferently, and if any certainly those may be said to be of such a mixed nature, that is, partly flesh and partly fish.'

'But how is it possible,' replied the Empress, 'that they should live both in water and on the earth, since those animals that live by the respiration of air cannot live within water, and those that live in water cannot live by the respiration of air, as experience doth sufficiently witness.' They answered her Majesty that, as there were different sorts of creatures, so they had also different ways of respirations. 'For respiration,' said they, 'is nothing else but a composition and division of parts, and the motions of nature being infinitely various, it is impossible that all creatures should have the like motions, wherefore it was not necessary that all animal creatures should be bound to live either by the air or by water only, but according as nature had ordered it convenient to their species.'

The Empress seemed very well satisfied with their answer, and desired to be further informed whether all animal creatures did continue their species by a successive propagation of particulars, and whether in every species the offsprings did always resemble their generator or producer, both in their interior and exterior figures. They answered her Majesty that some species or sorts of creatures were kept up by a successive propagation of an offspring that was like the producer, but some were not. 'Of the first rank,' said they, 'are all those animals that are of different sexes, besides several others; but of the second rank are for the most part those we call insects, whose production proceeds from such causes as have no conformity or likeness with their produced effects as, for example, maggots bred out of cheese, and several others generated out of earth, water and the like.'

'But,' said the Empress, 'there is some likeness between maggots and cheese, for cheese has no blood, nor maggots neither; besides, they have almost the same taste which cheese has.' 'This proves nothing,' answered they, 'for maggots have a visible, local, progressive motion which cheese hath not.' The Empress replied that when all the cheese was turned into maggots it might be said to have local, progressive motion. They answered that when the cheese by its own figurative motions was changed into maggots it was no more cheese.

The Empress confessed that she observed nature was infinitely various in her works, and that though the species of creatures did continue, yet their particulars were subject to infinite changes. 'But since you have informed me,' said she, 'of the various sorts and productions of animal creatures, I desire you to tell me what you have observed of their sensitive perceptions.' 'Truly,' answered they, 'your Majesty puts a very hard question to us, and we shall hardly be able to give a satisfactory answer to it, for there are many different sorts of creatures which, as they have all different perceptions, so they have also different organs which our senses are not able to discover. Only in an oyster shell we have with admiration observed that the common sensorium of the oyster lies just at the closing of the shells, where the pressure and reaction may be perceived by the opening and shutting of the shells every tide.'

After all this, the Empress desired the worm-men to give her a true relation how frost was made upon the earth, to which they answered that it was made much after the manner and description of the fish and bird-men concerning the congelation of water into ice and snow, by a commixture of saline and acid particles, which relation added a great light to the ape-men, who were the chemists, concerning their chemical principles salt, sulphur and mercury. 'But,' said the Empress, 'if it be so, it will require an infinite multitude of saline particles to produce such a great quantity of ice, frost and snow. Besides,' said she, 'when snow, ice and frost turn again into their former principle, I would fain know what becomes of those saline particles.' But neither the worm-men nor the fish and bird-men could give her an answer to it.

Then the Empress enquired of them the reason why springs were not as salt as the sea is; also, why some did ebb and flow. To which it was answered that the ebbing and flowing of some springs was caused by hollow caverns within the earth where the sea water, crowding through, did thrust forward and drew backward the spring water according to its own way of ebbing and flowing. But others said that it proceeded from a small proportion of saline and acid particles which the spring water imbibed from the earth, and although it was not so much as to be perceived by the sense of taste, yet was it enough to cause an ebbing and flowing motion. And as for the spring water being fresh, they gave, according to their observation, this following reason: 'There is,' said they, 'a certain heat within the bowels of the earth proceeding from its swift circular motion upon its own axis, which heat distils the rarest parts of the earth into a fresh and insipid water, which water being through the pores of the earth conveyed into a place where it may break forth without resistance or obstruction, causes springs and fountains. And these distilled waters within the earth do nourish and refresh the grosser and drier parts thereof.'

This relation confirmed the Empress in the opinion concerning the motion of the earth and the fixedness of the sun, as the bird-men had informed her, and then she asked the worm-men whether minerals and vegetables were generated by the same heat that is within the bowels of the earth, to which they could give her no positive answer. Only this they affirmed: that heat and cold were not the primary producing causes of either vegetables or minerals or other sorts of creatures, but only effects. 'And to prove this our assertion,' said they, 'we have observed that by change of some sorts of corporeal motions, that which is now hot will become cold, and what is now cold will grow hot. But the hottest place of all we find to be the centre of the earth. Neither do we observe that the torrid zone does contain so much gold and silver as the temperate, nor is there great store of iron and lead wheresoever there is gold, for these metals are most found in colder climates towards either of the Poles.'

This observation the Empress commanded them to confer with her chemists the ape-men, to let them know that gold was not produced by a violent, but a temperate degree of heat. She asked further whether gold could not be made by art. They answered that they could not certainly tell her Majesty, but if it was possible to be done, they thought tin, lead, brass, iron and silver to be the fittest metals for such an artificial transmutation. Then she asked them whether art could produce iron, tin, lead or silver. They answered, not in their opinion. 'Then I perceive,' replied the Empress, 'that your judgements are very irregular, since you believe that gold, which is so fixed a metal that nothing has been found as yet which could occasion a dissolution of its interior figure, may be made by art, and not tin, lead, iron, copper or silver, which yet are so far weaker and meaner metals than gold is.' But the worm-men excused themselves that they were ignorant in that art, and that such questions belonged more properly to the ape-men, which were her Majesty's chemists.

Then the Empress asked them whether by their sensitive perceptions they could observe the interior, corporeal, figurative motions both of vegetables and minerals. They answered that their senses could perceive them after they were produced, but not before. 'Nevertheless,' said they, 'although the interior, figurative motions of natural creatures are not subject to the exterior, animal, sensitive perceptions, yet by their rational perception they may judge of them and of their productions if they be regular.'

Whereupon the Empress commanded the bear-men to lend them some of their best microscopes, at which the bear-men smilingly answered her Majesty that their glasses would do them but little service in the bowels of the earth because there was no light. 'For,' said they, 'our glasses do only represent exterior objects according to the various reflections and positions of light, and wheresoever light is wanting, the glasses will do no good.' To which the worm-men replied that although they could not say much of refractions, reflections, inflections and the like, yet were they not blind even in the bowels of the earth, for they could see the several sorts of minerals, as also minute animals that lived there, which minute animal creatures were not blind neither, but had some kind of sensitive perception that was as serviceable to them as sight, taste, smell, touch, hearing etc. was to other animal creatures, by which it is evident that nature has been as bountiful to those creatures that live underground or in the bowels of the earth as to those that live upon the surface of the earth or in the air or in water.

'But howsoever,' proceeded the worm-men, 'although there is light in the bowels of the earth, yet your microscopes will do but little good there, by reason those creatures that live underground have not such an optic sense as those that live on the surface of the earth, wherefore unless you had such glasses as are proper for their perception, your microscopes will not be anyways advantageous to them.' The Empress seemed well pleased with this answer of the worm-men, and asked them further whether minerals and all other creatures within the earth were colourless, at which question they could not forbear laughing and when the Empress asked the reason why they laughed: 'We most humbly beg your Majesty's pardon,' replied they, 'for we could not choose but laugh when we heard of a colourless body.'

'Why,' said the Empress, 'colour is only an accident, which is an immaterial thing, and has no being of itself but in another body.' 'Those,' replied they, 'that informed your Majesty thus, surely their rational motions were very irregular. For how is it possible that a natural nothing can have a being in nature? If it be no substance, it cannot have a being, and if no being, it is nothing. Wherefore the distinction between subsisting of itself and subsisting in another body is a mere nicety and nonsense, for there is nothing in nature that can subsist of or by itself (I mean singly) by reason all parts of nature are composed in one body, and though they may be infinitely divided, commixed and changed in their particulars, yet in general, parts cannot be separated from parts as long as nature lasts. Nay, we might as probably affirm that infinite nature would be as soon destroyed as that one atom could perish, and therefore your Majesty may firmly believe that there is no body without colour, nor no colour without body; for colour, figure, place, magnitude and body are all but one thing, without any separation or abstraction from each other.'

The Empress was so wonderfully taken with this discourse of the worm-men that she not only pardoned the rudeness they committed in laughing at first at her question, but yielded a full assent to their opinion, which she thought the most rational that ever she had heard yet. And then proceeding in her questions, enquired further whether they had observed only seminal principles within the earth free from all dimensions and qualities which produced vegetables, minerals and the like. To which they answered that, concerning the seeds of minerals, their sensitive perceptions had never observed any, but vegetables had certain seeds out of which they were produced.

Then she asked whether those seeds of vegetables lost their

species, that is, were annihilated in the production of their offspring. To which they answered that by an annihilation nothing could be produced, and that the seeds of vegetables were so far from being annihilated in their productions that they did rather numerously increase and multiply. 'For the division of one seed,' said they, 'does produce numbers of seeds out of itself.' 'But,' replied the Empress, 'a particular part cannot increase of itself.' ' 'Tis true,' answered they, 'but they increase not barely of themselves but by joining and commixing with other parts, which do assist them in their productions, and by way of imitation form or figure their own parts into such or such particulars.' 'Then I pray inform me,' said the Empress, 'what disguise those seeds put on, and how they do conceal themselves in their transmutations.' They answered that seeds did no ways disguise or conceal, but rather divulge themselves in the multiplication of their offspring, only they did hide and conceal themselves from their sensitive perceptions so that their figurative and productive motions were not perceptible by animal creatures.

Again the Empress asked them whether there were any non-beings within the earth, to which they answered that they never heard of any such thing, and that if her Majesty would know the truth thereof, she must ask those creatures that are called immaterial spirits, which had a great affinity with non-beings, and perhaps could give her a satisfactory answer to this question.

Then she desired to be informed what opinion they had of the beginning of forms. They told her Majesty that they did not understand what she meant by this expression. 'For,' said they, 'there is no beginning in nature, no not of particulars, by reason nature is eternal and infinite, and her particulars are subject to infinite changes and transmutations by virtue of their own corporeal, figurative self-motions so that there's nothing new in nature, nor properly a beginning of anything.'

The Empress seemed well satisfied with all those answers, and enquired further whether there was no art used by those creatures that live within the earth. 'Yes,' answered they, 'for the several parts of the earth do join and assist each other in composition or framing of such or such particulars, and many times there are factions and divisions which cause productions of mixed species, as, for example, weeds instead of sweet flowers and useful fruits. But gardeners and husbandmen used often to decide their quarrels and cause them to agree, which though it shows a kindness to the differing parties, yet 'tis a great prejudice to the worms and other animal creatures that live underground, for it most commonly causes their dissolution and ruin; at best they are driven out of their habitations.'

'What,' said the Empress, 'are not worms produced out of the earth?' 'Their production in general,' answered they, 'is like the production of all other natural creatures, proceeding from the corporeal figurative motions of nature. But as for their particular productions, they are according to the nature of their species. Some are produced out of flowers, some out of roots, some out of fruits, some out of ordinary earth.'

'Then they are very ungrateful children,' replied the Empress, 'that they feed on their own parents which gave them life.' 'Their life,' answered they, 'is their own and not their parents, for no part or creature of nature can either give or take away life, but parts do only assist and join with other parts, either in the dissolution or production of other parts and creatures.'

After this and several other conferences which the Empress held with the worm-men, she dismissed them, and having taken much satisfaction in several of their answers, encouraged them in their studies and observations. Then she made a convocation of her chemists, the ape-men, and commanded them to give her an account of the several transmutations which their art was able to produce. They began first with a long and tedious discourse concerning the primitive ingredients of natural bodies, and how by their art they had found out the principles out of which they consist. But they did not all agree in their opinions, for some said that the principles of all natural bodies were four elements, fire, air, water, earth, out of which they were composed. Others rejected this elementary commixture, and said there were many bodies out of which none of the four elements could be extracted by any degree of fire whatsoever and that, on the other side, there were diverse bodies whose resolution by fire reduced them into more than four different ingredients, and these affirmed that the only principles of natural bodies were salt, sulphur and mercury. Others again declared that none of the forementioned could be called the true principles of natural bodies, but that by their industry and pains, which they had taken in the art of chemistry, they had discovered that all natural bodies were produced but from one principle, which was water. 'For all vegetables, minerals and animals,' said they, 'are nothing else but simple water, distinguished into various figures by virtue of their seeds.'

But after a great many debates and contentions about this subject, the Empress, being so much tired that she was not able to hear them any longer, imposed a general silence upon them, and then declared herself in this following discourse.

'I am too sensible of the pains you have taken in the art of chemistry to discover the principles of natural bodies, and wish they had been more profitably bestowed upon some other than such experiments, for both by my own contemplation and the observations which I have made by my rational and sensitive perception upon nature and her works, I find that nature is but one infinite, self-moving body, which by the virtue of its self-motion is divided into infinite parts, which parts, being restless, undergo perpetual changes and transmutations by their infinite compositions and divisions. Now, if this be so, as surely according to regular sense and reason it appears no otherwise, it is in vain to look for primary ingredients or constitutive principles of natural bodies, since there is no more but one universal principle of nature, to wit, self-moving matter, which is the only cause of all natural effects.

'Next, I desire you to consider that fire is but a particular creature, or effect of nature, and occasions not only different effects in several bodies, but on some bodies has no power at all; witness gold, which never could be brought yet to change its interior figure by the art of fire. And if this be so, why should you be so simple as to believe that fire can show you the principles of nature, and that either the four elements, or water only, or salt, sulphur and mercury all which are no more but particular effects and creatures of nature, should be the primitive ingredients or principles of all natural bodies? Wherefore, I will not have you to take more pains and waste your time in such fruitless attempts, but be wiser hereafter and busy yourselves with such experiments as may be beneficial to the public.'

The Empress having thus declared her mind to the ape-men, and given them better instructions than perhaps they expected, not knowing that her Majesty had such great and able judgement in natural philosophy, had several conferences with them concerning chemical preparations, which for brevity's sake I'll forbear to rehearse. Amongst the rest, she asked how it came that the imperial race appeared so young, and yet was reported to have lived so long, some of them two, some three, and some four hundred years, and whether it was by nature or a special divine blessing.

To which they answered that there was a certain rock in the parts of that world which contained the golden sands, which rock was hollow within and did produce a gum that was a hundred years before it came to its full strength and perfection. 'This gum,' said they, 'if it be held in a warm hand will dissolve into an oil, the effects whereof are [as] following: it being given every day for some certain time to an old decayed man, in the bigness of a little pea, will first make him spit for a week or more. After this, it will cause vomits of phlegm, and after that it will bring forth by vomits humours of several colours, first of a pale yellow, then of a deep yellow, then of a green, and lastly of a black colour, and each of these humours have a several taste: some are fresh, some salt, some sour, some bitter, and so forth. Neither do all these vomits make them sick, but they come out on a sudden and unawares, without any pain or trouble to the patient.

'And after it hath done all these mentioned effects and cleared both the stomach and several other parts of the body, then it works upon the brain and brings forth of the nose such kinds of humours as it did out of the mouth, and much after the same manner. Then it will purge by stool, then by urine, then by sweat and lastly by bleeding at the nose and the emeroids,* all which effects it will perform within the space of six weeks or a little more, for it does not work very strongly, but gently and by degrees.

'Lastly, when it has done all this, it will make the body break out into a thick scab, and cause both hair, teeth and nails to come off, which scab being arrived to its full maturity, opens first along the back and comes off all in a piece liken armour, and all this is done within the space of four months. After this, the patient is wrapped into a cerecloth prepared of certain gums and juices, wherein he continues until the time of nine months be expired from the first beginning of the cure, which is the time of a child's formation in the womb.

'In the meanwhile, his diet is nothing else but eagles' eggs and hind's milk and after the cerecloth is taken away, he will appear of the age of twenty, both in shape and strength. The weaker sort of this gum is sovereign in healing of wounds and curing of slight distempers. But this is also to be observed: that none of the imperial race does use any other drink but lime-water or water in which limestone is immersed. Their meat is nothing else but fowl of several sorts; their recreations are many, but chiefly hunting.'

This relation amazed the Empress very much, for though in the world she came from she had heard great reports of the philosopher's stone, yet had she not heard of any that had ever found it out, which made her believe that it was but a chimera. She called also to mind that there had been in the same world a man who had a little stone which cured all kinds of diseases, outward and inward, according as it was applied, and that a famous chemist had found out a certain liquor called Alkahest, which by the virtue of its own fire consumed all diseases. But she had never heard of a medicine that could renew old age and render it beautiful, vigorous and strong. Nor would she so easily have believed it had it been a medicine prepared by art, for she knew that art, being nature's changeling, was not able to produce such a powerful effect, but being that the gum did grow naturally, she did not so much scruple at it, for she knew that nature's works are so various and wonderful that no particular creature is able to trace her ways.

The conferences of the chemists being finished, the Empress made an assembly of her Galenical physicians, her herbalists and anatomists, and first she enquired of her herbalists the particular effects of several herbs and drugs, and whence they proceeded. To which they answered that they could, for the most part, tell her Majesty the virtues and operations of them, but the particular causes of their effects were unknown. Only thus much they could say: that their operations and virtues were generally caused by their proper, inherent, corporeal, figurative motions, which being infinitely various in infinite nature, did produce infinite several effects.

'And it is observed,' said they, 'that herbs and drugs are as wise in their operations as men in their words and actions—nay wiser, and their effects are more certain than men in their opinions, for though they cannot discourse like men, yet have they sense and reason as well as men, for the discursive faculty is but a particular effect of sense and reason in some particular creatures, to wit, men, and not a principle of nature and argues often more folly than wisdom.'

The Empress asked whether they could not by a composition and commixture of other drugs make them work other effects than they did, used by themselves. They answered that they could make them produce artificial effects but not alter their inherent, proper and particular natures.

Then the Empress commanded her anatomists to dissect such kinds of creatures as are called monsters. But they answered her Majesty that it would be but an unprofitable and useless work, and hinder their better employments. 'For when we dissect dead animals,' said they, 'it is for no other end but to observe what defects or distempers they had, that we may cure the like in living ones, so that all our care and industry concerns only the preservation of mankind. But we hope your Majesty will not preserve monsters, which are most commonly destroyed, except it be for novelty. Neither will the dissection of monsters prevent the errors of nature's irregular actions, for by dissecting some, we cannot prevent the production of others, so that our pains and labour will be to no purpose unless to satisfy the vain curiosities of inquisitive men.'

The Empress replied that such dissections would be very beneficial to experimental philosophers. 'If experimental philosophers,' answered they, 'do spend their time in such useless inspections, they waste it in vain, and have nothing but their labour for their pains.'

Lastly her Majesty had some conferences with the Galenic physicians about several diseases and, amongst the rest, desired to know the cause and nature of apoplexies and the spotted plague. They answered that a deadly apoplexy was a dead palsy of the brain, and the spotted plague was a gangrene of the vital parts, and as the gangrene of outward parts did strike inwardly, so the gangrene of inward parts did break forth outwardly. 'Which is the cause,' said they, 'that as soon as the spots appear, death follows, for then it is an infallible sign that the body is throughout infected with a gangrene, which is a spreading evil, but some gangrenes do spread more suddenly than others, and of all sorts of gangrenes the plaguey gangrene is the most infectious, for other gangrenes infect but the next adjoining parts of one particular body and, having killed that same creature, go no further but cease, whenas the gangrene of the plague infects not only the adjoining parts of one particular creature, but also those that are distant; that is, one particular body infects another and so breeds a universal contagion.'

But the Empress, being very desirous to know in what manner the plague was propagated and became so contagious, asked whether it went actually out of one body into another, to which they answered that it was a great dispute amongst the learned of their profession whether it came by a division and composition of parts—that is, by expiration and inspiration—or whether it was caused by imitation. 'Some experimental philosophers,' said they, 'will make us believe that by the help of their microscopes they have observed the plague to be a body of little flies like atoms, which go out of one body into another through the sensitive passages, but the most experienced and wisest of our society have rejected this opinion as a ridiculous fancy and do for the most part believe that it is caused by an imitation of parts, so that the motions of some parts which are sound do imitate the motions of those that are infected, and that by this means the plague becomes contagious and spreading.'

The Empress, having hitherto spent her time in the examination of the bird, fish, worm and ape-men etc., and received several intelligences from their several employments, at last had a mind to divert herself after her serious discourses, and therefore she sent for the spider-men, which were her mathematicians, the lice-men, which were her geometricians, and the magpie, parrot and jackdaw-men, which were her orators and logicians.

The spider-men came first and presented her Majesty with a table full of mathematical points, lines and figures of all sorts, of squares, circles, triangles and the like, which the Empress notwithstanding that she had a very ready wit and quick apprehension, could not understand, but the more she endeavoured to learn, the more was she confounded. Whether they did ever square the circle I cannot exactly tell, nor whether they could make imaginary points and lines. But this I dare say: that their points and lines were so slender, small and thin that they seemed next to imaginary.

The mathematicians were in great esteem with the Empress as being not only the chief tutors and instructors in many arts, but some of them excellent magicians and informers of spirits, which was the reason their characters were so abstruse and intricate that the Empress knew not what to make of them. 'There is so much to learn in your art,' said she, 'that I can neither spare time from other affairs to busy myself in your profession, nor, if I could, do I think I should ever be able to understand your imaginary points, lines and figures, because they are non-beings.'

Then came the lice-men, and endeavoured to measure all things to a hair's breadth and weigh them to an atom, but their weights would seldom agree, especially in the weighing of air, which they found a task impossible to be done, at which the Empress began to be displeased, and told them that there was neither truth nor justice in their profession, and so dissolved their society.

After this, the Empress was resolved to hear the magpie, parrot and jackdaw-men which were her professed orators and logicians, whereupon one of the parrot-men rose with great formality and endeavoured to make an eloquent speech before her Majesty, but before he had half ended, his arguments and divisions being so many that they caused a great confusion in his brain, he could not go forward but was forced to retire backward with great disgrace both to himself and the whole society, and although one of his brethren endeavoured to second him by another speech, yet was he as far to seek as the former. At which the Empress appeared not a little troubled and told them that they followed too much the rules of art and confounded themselves with too nice formalities and distinctions. 'But since I know,' said she, 'that you are a people who have naturally voluble tongues and good memories, I desire you to consider more the subject you speak of than your artificial periods, connections and parts of speech, and leave the rest to your natural eloquence.' Which they did, and so became very eminent orators.

Lastly, her imperial Majesty being desirous to know what progress her logicians had made in the art of disputing, commanded them to argue upon several themes or subjects, which they did and, having made a very nice discourse of logistical terms and propositions, entered into a dispute by way of syllogistical arguments through all the figures and modes. One began with an argument of the first mode of the first figure thus:

> Every politician is wise:
> Every knave is a politician,
> Therefore every knave is wise.

Another contradicted him with a syllogism of the second mode of the same figure thus:

> No politician is wise:
> Every knave is a politician,
> Therefore no knave is wise.

The third made an argument in the third mode of the same figure after this manner:

> Every politician is wise:
> Some knaves are politicians,
> Therefore some knaves are wise.

The fourth concluded with a syllogism in the fourth mode of the same figure thus:

> No politician is wise:
> Some knaves are politicians,
> Therefore some knaves are not wise.

After this they took another subject, and one propounded this syllogism:

> Every philosopher is wise:
> Every beast is wise,
> Therefore every beast is a philosopher.

But another said that this argument was false, therefore he contradicted him with a syllogism of the second figure of the fourth mode thus:

> Every philosopher is wise:
> Some beasts are not wise,
> Therefore some beasts are not philosophers.

Thus they argued and intended to go on, but the Empress interrupted them. 'I have enough,' said she, 'of your chopped logic, and will hear no more of your syllogisms, for it disorders my reason and puts my brain on the rack. Your formal argumentations are able to spoil all natural wit, and I'll have you to consider that art does not make reason but reason makes art, and therefore as much as reason is above art, so much is a natural, rational discourse to be preferred before an artificial; for art is for the most part irregular and disorders men's understandings more than it rectifies them, and leads them into a labyrinth whence they'll never get out, and makes them dull and unfit for useful employments—especially your art of logic, which consists only in contradicting each other, in making sophisms and obscuring truth instead of clearing it.'

But they replied to her Majesty that the knowledge of nature— that is, natural philosophy—would be imperfect without the art of logic, and that there was an improbable truth which could no otherwise be found out than by the art of disputing. 'Truly,' said the Empress, 'I do believe that it is with natural philosophy as it is with all other effects of nature, for no particular knowledge can be perfect, by reason knowledge is dividable as well as composable. Nay, to speak properly, nature herself cannot boast of any perfection but God himself, because there are so many irregular motions in nature, and 'tis but a folly to think that art should be able to regulate them, since art itself is for the most part irregular. But as for improbable truth, I know not what your meaning is, for truth is more than improbability. Nay, there is so much difference between truth and improbability that I cannot conceive it possible how they can be joined together. In short,' said she, 'I do no ways approve of your profession, and though I will not dissolve your society, yet I shall never take delight in hearing you any more, wherefore confine your disputations to your schools, lest besides the commonwealth of learning they disturb also divinity and policy, religion and laws and by that means draw an utter ruin and destruction both upon church and state.'

After the Empress had thus finished the discourses and conferences with the mentioned societies of her virtuosos, she considered by herself the manner of their religion, and finding it very defective, was troubled that so wise and knowing a people should have no more knowledge of the divine truth. Wherefore she consulted with her own thoughts whether it was possible to convert them all to her own religion, and to that end she resolved to build churches and make also up a congregation of women, whereof she intended to be the head herself, and to instruct them in the several points of her religion.

This she had no sooner begun but the women, which generally had quick wits, subtle conceptions, clear understandings and solid judgements, became in a short time very devout and zealous sisters, for the Empress had an excellent gift of preaching and instructing them in the articles of faith, and by that means she converted them not only soon, but gained an extraordinary love of all her subjects throughout that world.

But at last, pondering with herself the inconstant nature of mankind and fearing that in time they would grow weary and desert the divine truth, following their own fancies and living according to their own desires, she began to be troubled that her labours and pains should prove of so little effect, and therefore studied all manner of ways to prevent it. Amongst the rest, she called to mind a relation which the bird-men made her once of a mountain that did burn in flames of fire, and thereupon did immediately send for the wisest and subtlest of her worm-men, commanding them to discover the cause of the eruption of that same fire, which they did and, having dived to the very bottom of the mountain, informed her Majesty that there was a certain sort of stone whose nature was such that, being wetted, it would grow excessively hot and break forth into a flaming fire until it became dry, and then it ceased from burning.

The Empress was glad to hear this news, and forthwith desired the worm-men to bring her some of that stone, but be sure to keep it secret. She sent also for the bird-men, and asked them whether they could not get her a piece of the sun stone. They answered that it was impossible unless they did spoil or lessen the light of the world. 'But,' said they, 'if it please your Majesty, we can demolish one of the numerous stars of the sky, which the world will never miss.'

The Empress was very well satisfied with this proposal, and having thus employed these two sorts of men, in the meanwhile builded two chapels, one above another. The one she lined throughout with diamonds, both roof, walls and pillars, but the other she resolved to line with the star stone. The fire stone she placed upon the diamond lining, by reason fire has no power on diamonds, and when she would have that chapel where the fire stone was appear all in a flame, she had by the means of artificial pipes, water conveyed into it, which by turning the cock did, as out of a fountain, spring all over the room, and as long as the fire stone was wet, the chapel seemed to be all in a flaming fire.

The other chapel, which was lined with the star stone, did only cast a splendorous and comfortable light. Both the chapels stood upon pillars just in the middle of a round cloister, which was dark as night, neither was there any light within them but what came from the fire and star stone[s], and being everywhere open, allowed to all that were within the compass of the cloister a free prospect into them. Besides, they were so artificially contrived that they did both move in a circle about their own centres, without intermission, contrary ways.

In the chapel which was lined with the fire stone, the Empress preached sermons of terror to the wicked and told them of the punishments for their sins, to wit, that after this life they should be tormented in an everlasting fire. But in the other chapel, lined with the star stone, she preached sermons of comfort to those that repented of their sins and were troubled at their own wickedness. Neither did the heat of the flame in the least hinder her, for the fire stone did not cast so great a heat but the Empress was able to endure it by reason the water which was poured on the stone, by its own self-motion turned into a flaming fire, occasioned by the natural motions of the stone, which made the flame weaker than if it had been fed by some other kind of fuel. The other chapel, where the star stone was, although it did cast a great light, yet was it without all heat, and the Empress appeared like an angel in it, and as that chapel was an emblem of hell, so this was an emblem of heaven.

And thus the Empress, by art and her own ingenuity, did not only convert the Blazing World to her own religion, but kept them in a constant belief without enforcement or bloodshed, for she knew well that belief was a thing not to be forced or pressed upon the people, but to be instilled into their minds by gentle persuasions, and after this manner she encouraged them also in all other duties and employments. For fear, though it makes people obey, yet does it not last so long nor is it so sure a means to keep them to their duties as love.

Last of all, when she saw that both church and state was now in a well ordered and settled condition, her thoughts reflected upon the world she came from and though she had a great desire to know the condition of the same, yet could she advise no manner of way how to gain knowledge thereof. At last, after many serious considerations, she conceived that it was impossible to be done by any other means by the help of immaterial spirits, wherefore she made a convocation of the most learned, witty and ingenious of all the forementioned sorts of men and desired to know of them whether there were any immaterial spirits in their world.

First she enquired of the worm-men whether they had perceived some within the earth. They answered her Majesty that they never knew of any such creatures, for whatsoever did dwell within the earth, said they, was embodied and material. Then she asked the fly-men whether they had observed any in the air. 'For you, having numerous eyes,' said she, 'will be more able to perceive them than any other creatures.' To which they answered her Majesty that although spirits, being immaterial, could not be perceived by the worm-men in the earth, yet they perceived that such creatures did lodge in vehicles of the air.

Then the Empress asked whether they could speak to them, and whether they did understand each other. The fly-men answered that those spirits were always clothed in some sort or other of material garments, which garments were their bodies, made, for the most part, of air, and when occasion served they could put on any other sort of substances, but yet they could not put these substances into any form or shape as they pleased.

The Empress asked the fly-men whether it was possible that she could be acquainted and have some conferences with them. They answered, they did verily believe she might. Hereupon the Empress commanded the fly-men to ask some of the spirits whether they would be pleased to give her a visit. This they did, and after the spirits had presented themselves to the Empress (in what shapes or forms I cannot exactly tell) after some few compliments that passed between them, the Empress told the spirits that she questioned not but they did know how she was a

stranger in that world, and by what miraculous means she was
arrived there, and since she had a great desire to know the
condition of the world she came from, her request to the spirits
was to give her some information thereof, especially of those
parts of the world where she was born, bred and educated, as also
of her particular friends and acquaintance—all which the spirits
did according to her desire.

At last, after a great many conferences and particular
intelligences which the spirits gave the Empress to her great
satisfaction and content, she enquired after the most famous
students, writers and experimental philosophers in that world,
which they gave her a full relation of. Amongst the rest, she
enquired whether there were none that had found out yet the
Jews' Cabala. 'Several have endeavoured it,' answered the spirits,
'but those that come nearest (although themselves denied it)
were one Dr Dee and one Edward Kelly, the one representing
Moses and the other Aaron, for Kelly was to Dr Dee as Aaron to
Moses, but yet they proved at last but mere cheats, and were
described by one of their own countrymen, a famous poet named
Ben Jonson, in a play called *The Alchemist*, where he expressed
Kelly by Capt. Face and Dee by Dr Subtle, and their two wives
by Doll Common and the widow. By the Spaniard in the play he
meant the Spanish ambassador, and by Sir Epicure Mammon, a
Polish lord.'

The Empress remembered that she had seen the play and
asked the spirits whom he meant by the name of Ananias. 'Some
zealous brethren,' answered they, 'in Holland, Germany and
several other places.' Then she asked them who was meant by the
druggist. 'Truly,' answered the spirits, 'we have forgot, it being
so long since it was made and acted.' 'What,' replied the
Empress, 'can spirits forget?' 'Yes,' said the spirits, 'for what is
past is only kept in memory if it be not recorded.' 'I did believe,'
said the Empress, 'that spirits had no need of memory or
remembrance, and could not be subject to forgetfulness.' 'How
can we,' answered they, 'give an account of things present if we
had no memory, but especially of things past unrecorded if we
had no remembrance?' Said the Empress: 'By present knowledge
and understanding.' The spirits answered that present knowledge and understanding was of actions or things present, not of

past. 'But,' said the Empress, 'you know what is to come without memory or remembrance, and therefore you may know what is past without memory and remembrance.' They answered that their foreknowledge was only a prudent and subtle observation made by comparing of things or actions past with those that are present, and that remembrance was nothing else but a repetition of things or actions past.

Then the Empress asked the spirits whether there was a threefold Cabala.* They answered Dee and Kelly made but a twofold Cabala, to wit, of the Old and New Testament, but others might not only make two or three, but threescore Cabalas if they pleased. The Empress asked whether it was a traditional or merely a scriptural, or whether it was a literal, philosophical or moral Cabala. 'Some,' answered they, 'did believe it merely traditional, others scriptural, some literal, and some metaphorical. But the truth is,' said they, ' 'twas partly one and partly the other, as partly a traditional, partly a scriptural, partly literal, partly metaphorical.'

The Empress asked further whether the Cabala was a work only of natural reason or divine inspiration. 'Many,' said the spirits, 'that write Cabalas pretend to divine inspirations, but whether it be so or not it does not belong to us to judge; only this we must needs confess, that it is a work which requires a good wit and a strong faith, but not natural reason; for though natural reason is most persuasive, yet faith is the chief that is required in Cabalists.'

'But,' said the Empress, 'is there not divine reason as well as there is natural?' 'No,' answered they, 'for there is but a divine faith, and as for reason, it is only natural. But you mortals are so puzzled about this divine faith and natural reason that you do not know well how to distinguish them, but confound them both, which is the cause you have so many divine philosophers who make a gallimaufry both of reason and faith.'

Then she asked whether pure natural philosophers were Cabalists. They answered 'No, but only your mystical or divine philosophers such as study beyond sense and reason.' She enquired further whether there was any Cabala in God, or whether God was full of Ideas. They answered there could be nothing in God, nor could God be full of anything, either forms or figures, but of himself, for God is the perfection of all things and an unexpressible being beyond the conception of any creature, either natural or supernatural.

'Then I pray inform me,' said the Empress, 'whether the Jews' Cabala or any other consist in numbers.' The spirits answered, 'No, for numbers are odd and different, and would make a disagreement in the Cabala.' 'But,' said she again, 'is it a sin then, not to know or understand the Cabala?' 'God is so merciful,' answered they, 'and so just that he will never damn the ignorant and save only those that pretend to know him and his secret counsels by their Cabalas, but he loves those that adore and worship him with fear and reverence and with a pure heart.'

She asked further which of these two Cabalas was most approved: the natural or theological. 'The theological,' answered they, 'is mystical and belongs only to faith, but the natural belongs to reason.' Then she asked them whether divine faith was made out of reason. 'No,' answered they, 'for faith proceeds only from a divine saving grace, which is a peculiar gift of God.' 'How comes it then,' replied she, 'that men, even those that are of several opinions, have faith more or less?' 'A natural belief,' answered they, 'is not a divine faith.' 'But,' proceeded the Empress, 'how are you sure that God cannot be known?' 'The several opinions you mortals have of God,' answered they, 'are sufficient witnesses thereof.'

'Well then,' replied the Empress, 'leaving this inquisitive knowledge of God, I pray inform me whether you spirits give motion to natural bodies.' 'No,' answered they, 'but on the contrary, natural material bodies give spirits motion, for we spirits, being incorporeal, have no motion but from our corporeal vehicles, so that we move by the help of our bodies and not the bodies by our help, for pure spirits are immovable.' 'If this be so,' replied the Empress, 'how comes it then that you can move so suddenly at a vast distance?' They answered that some sorts of matter were more pure, rare, and consequently more light and agile than others, and this was the reason of their quick and sudden motions.

Then the Empress asked them whether they could speak without a body or bodily organs. 'No,' said they, 'nor could we have any bodily sense, but only knowledge.' She asked whether they could have knowledge without body. 'Not a natural,' answered they, 'but a supernatural knowledge, which is a far better knowledge than a natural.' Then she asked them whether they had a general or universal knowledge. They answered, 'Single or particular created spirits have not, for not any creature but God himself can have an absolute and perfect knowledge of all things.' The Empress asked them further whether spirits had inward and outward parts. 'No,' answered they, 'for parts only belong to bodies, not to spirits.'

Again she asked them whether their vehicles were living bodies. 'They are self-moving bodies,' answered they, 'and therefore they must needs be living, for nothing can move itself without it hath life.' 'Then,' said she, 'it must necessarily follow that this living, self-moving body gives motion to the spirit, and not the spirit motion to the body as its vehicle.' 'You say very true,' answered they, 'and we told you this before.'

Then the Empress asked them of what forms of matter those vehicles were. They said they were of several different forms: some gross and dense, and others more pure, rare and subtle. 'If you be not material,' said the Empress, 'how can you be generators of all creatures?' 'We are no more,' answered they, 'the generators of material creatures than they are the generators of us spirits.' Then she asked whether they did leave their vehicles. 'No,' answered they, 'for we, being incorporeal, cannot leave or quit them, but our vehicles do change into several forms and figures according as occasion requires.'

Then the Empress desired the spirits to tell her whether man was a little world. They answered that if a fly or a worm was a little world, then man was so too. She asked again whether our forefathers had been as wise as men were at present, and had understood sense and reason as well as they did now. They answered that in former ages they had been as wise as they are in this present, nay wiser. 'For,' said they, 'many in this age do think their forefathers have been fools, by which they prove themselves to be such.'

The Empress asked further whether there was any plastic power in nature. 'Truly,' said the spirits, 'plastic power is a hard word, and signifies no more than the power of the corporeal, figurative motions of nature.' After this the Empress desired the spirits to inform her where the Paradise was; whether it was in the midst of the world as a centre of pleasure, or whether it was the whole world or a peculiar world by itself, as a world of life and not of matter, or whether it was mixed, as a world of living animal creatures. They answered that Paradise was not in the world she came from, but in that world she lived in at present, and that it was the very same place where she kept her court and where her palace stood in the midst of the imperial city.

The Empress asked further whether in the beginning and creation of the world all beasts could speak. They answered that no beasts could speak, but only those sorts of creatures which were fish-men, bear-men, worm-men and the like, which could speak in the first age as well as they do now. She asked again whether they were none of those spirits that frighted Adam out of the Paradise, at least caused him not to return thither again. They answered they were not. Then she desired to be informed whither Adam fled when he was driven out of the Paradise. 'Out of this world', said they, 'you are now Empress of, into the world you came from.'

'If this be so,' replied the Empress, 'then surely those Cabalists are much out of their story who believe the Paradise to be a world of life only without matter, for this world, though it be most pleasant and fruitful, yet it is not a world of mere immaterial life, but a world of living, material creatures.' 'Without question they are,' answered the spirits, 'for not all Cabalas are true.'

Then the Empress asked that since it is mentioned in the story of the creation of the world that Eve was tempted by the serpent, whether the Devil was within the serpent or whether the serpent tempted her without the Devil. They answered that the Devil was within the serpent. 'But how came it then,' replied she, 'that the serpent was cursed?' They answered, 'Because the Devil was in him, for are not those men in danger of damnation which have the Devil within them, who persuades them to believe and act wickedly.'

The Empress asked further whether light and the heavens were all one. They answered that that region which contains the lucid, natural orbs was by mortals named heaven, but the beatifical heaven, which is the habitation of the blessed angels and souls, was so far beyond it that it could not be compared to any natural creature. Then the Empress asked them whether all matter was fluid at first. They answered that matter was always as it is, and that some parts of matter were rare, some dense, some solid, some fluid, etc. Neither was God bound to make all matter fluid at first.

She asked further whether matter was immovable in itself. 'We have answered you before,' said they, 'that there is no motion but in matter, and were it not for the motion of matter, we spirits could not move nor give you any answer to your several questions.'

After this the Empress asked the spirits whether the universe was made within the space of six days, or whether by those six days were meant so many decrees or commands of God. They answered her that the world was made by the all-powerful decree and command of God, but whether there were six decrees or commands or fewer or more, no creature was able to tell.

Then she enquired whether there was no mystery in numbers. 'No other mystery,' answered the spirits, 'but reckoning and counting, for numbers are only marks of remembrance.' 'But what do you think of the number of four,' said she, 'which Cabalists make such ado withal, and of the number of ten, when they say that ten is all and that all numbers are virtually comprehended in four?' 'We think,' answered they, 'that Cabalists have nothing else to do but to trouble their heads with such useless fancies, for naturally there is no such thing as prime or all in numbers, nor is there any other mystery in numbers but what man's fancy makes. But what men call prime or all we do not know, because they do not agree in the number of their opinion.'

Then the Empress asked whether the number of six was a symbol of matrimony, as being made up of male and female, for two into three is six. 'If any number can be a symbol of matrimony,' answered the spirits, 'it is not six, but two, if two may be allowed to be a number, for the act of matrimony is made up of two joined in one.' She asked again what they said to the number of seven; whether it was not an emblem of God, because Cabalists say that it is neither begotten nor begets any other number. 'There can be no emblem of God,' answered the spirits, 'for if we do not know what God is, how can we make an emblem of him? Nor is there any number in God, for God is the perfection Himself, but numbers are imperfect, and as for the begetting of numbers, it is done by multiplication and addition, but subtraction is a kind of death to numbers.'

'If there can be no mystery in numbers,' replied the Empress, 'then it is in vain to refer the creation of the world to certain numbers, as Cabalists do.' 'The only mystery of numbers,' answered they, 'concerning the creation of the world is that, as numbers do multiply, so does the world.' The Empress asked how numbers did multiply. The spirits answered, 'to infinity'. 'Why,' said she, 'infinity cannot be reckoned, nor numbered.' 'No more', answered they, 'can the parts of the universe, for God's creation being an infinite action, as proceeding from an infinite power, could not rest upon a finite number of creatures, were it never so great.'

'But leaving the mystery of numbers,' proceeded the Empress, 'let me now desire you to inform me whether the suns and planets were generated by the heavens or ethereal matter.' The spirits answered that the stars and planets were of the same matter which the heavens, the ether and all other natural creatures did consist of, but whether they were generated by the heavens or ether they could not tell. 'If they be,' said they, 'they are not like their parents, for the sun, stars and planets are more splendorous than the ether, as also more solid and constant in their motions. But put the case the stars and planets were generated by the heavens, and the ethereal matter; the question then would be: out of what these are generated or produced? If these be created out of nothing, and not generated out of something then it is probable the sun, stars and planets are so too. Nay, it is more probable of the stars and planets than of the heavens or the fluid ether, by reason the stars and planets seem to be further off from mortality than the particular parts of the ether, for no doubt but the parts of the ethereal matter alter into several forms, which we do not perceive of the stars and planets.'

The Empress asked further whether they could give her information of the three principles of man according to the doctrine of the Platonists, as first of the intellect, spirit or divine light; 2. of the soul of man herself and 3. of the image of the soul, that is, her vital operation on the body. The spirits answered that they did not understand these three distinctions, but that they seemed to corporeal sense and reason as if they were three several bodies, or three several corporeal actions. 'However,' said they, 'they are intricate conceptions of irregular fancies.' 'If you do not understand them,' replied the Empress, 'how shall human creatures do then?' 'Many, both of your modern and ancient philosophers,' answered the spirits, 'endeavour to go beyond sense and reason, which makes them commit absurdities, for no corporeal creature can go beyond sense and reason; no, not we spirits, as long as we are in our corporeal vehicles.'

Then the Empress asked them whether there were any atheists in the world. The spirits answered that there were no more atheists than what Cabalists make. She asked them further whether spirits were of a globous or round figure. They answered that figure belonged to body but they, being immaterial, had no figure. She asked again whether spirits were not like water or fire. They answered that water and fire was material, were it the purest and most refined that ever could be, nay were it above the heavens. 'But we are no more like water or fire,' said they, 'than we are like earth; but our vehicles are of several forms, figures and degrees of substances.'

Then she desired to know whether their vehicles were made of air. 'Yes,' answered the spirits, 'some of our vehicles are of thin air.' 'Then I suppose,' replied the Empress, 'that those airy vehicles are your corporeal summer suits.' She asked further whether the spirits had not ascending and descending motions as well as other creatures. They answered that properly there was no ascension or descension in infinite nature, but only in relation to particular parts. 'And as for us spirits,' said they, 'we can neither ascend nor descend without corporeal vehicles, nor can our vehicles ascend or descend but according to their several shapes and figures, for there can be no motion without body.'

The Empress asked them further whether there was not a world of spirits as well as there is of material creatures. 'No,' answered they, 'for the word "world" implies a quantity or multitude of corporeal creatures, but we, being immaterial, can make no world of spirits.' Then she desired to be informed when spirits were made. 'We do not know,' answered they, 'how and when we were made, nor are we much inquisitive after it. Nay, if we did, it would be no benefit, neither for us, nor for you mortals to know it.'

The Empress replied that Cabalists and divine philosophers

said men's rational souls were immaterial and stood as much in need of corporeal vehicles as spirits did. 'If this be so,' answered the spirits, 'then you are hermaphrodites of nature; but your Cabalists are mistaken, for they take the purest and subtlest parts of matter for immaterial spirits.' Then the Empress asked when the souls of mortals went out of their bodies, whether they went to heaven or hell, or whether they remained in airy vehicles. 'God's justice and mercy,' answered they, 'is perfect and not imperfect, but if you mortals will have vehicles for your souls, and a place that is between heaven and hell, it must be purgatory, which is a place of purification, for which action fire is more proper than air, and so the vehicles of those souls that are in purgatory cannot be airy but fiery, and after this rate there can be but four places for human souls to be in, viz. heaven, hell, purgatory and this world; but as for vehicles, they are but fancies, not real truths.'

Then the Empress asked them where heaven and hell was. 'Your saviour Christ,' answered the spirits, 'has informed you that there is heaven and hell, but he did not tell you what nor where they are, wherefore it is too great a presumption for you mortals to enquire after it. If you do but strive to get into heaven it is enough, though you do not know where or what it is, for it is beyond your knowledge and understanding.'

'I am satisfied,' replied the Empress, and asked further whether there were any figures or characters in the soul. They answered where was no body, there could be no figure. Then she asked them whether spirits could be naked, and whether they were of a dark or a light colour. 'As for our nakedness, it is a very odd question,' answered the spirits, 'and we do not know what you mean by a naked spirit, for you judge of us as of corporeal creatures. And as for colour,' said they, 'it is according to our vehicles, for colour belongs to body, and as there is no body that is colourless, so there is no colour that is bodiless.'

Then the Empress desired to be informed whether all souls were made at the first creation of the world. 'We know no more,' answered the spirits, 'of the origin of human souls than we know of ourselves.' She asked further whether human bodies were not burdensome to human souls. They answered that bodies made souls active, as giving them motion, and if action was troublesome to souls then bodies were so too. She asked again whether souls did choose bodies. They answered that Platonics believed the souls of lovers lived in the bodies of their beloved. 'But surely,' said they, 'if there be a multitude of souls in a world of matter, they cannot miss bodies, for as soon as a soul is parted from one body it enters into another, and souls, having no motion of themselves, must of necessity be clothed or embodied with the next parts of matter.'

'If this be so,' replied the Empress, 'then I pray inform me whether all matter be soulified.' The spirits answered they could not exactly tell that, but if it was true that matter had no other motion but what came from a spiritual power, and that all matter was moving, then no soul could quit a body but she must of necessity enter into another soulified body, and then there would be two immaterial substances in one body. The Empress asked whether it was not possible that there could be two souls in one body. 'As for immaterial souls,' answered the spirits, 'it is impossible, for there cannot be two immaterials in one inanimate body, by reason they want parts and place, being bodiless; but there may be numerous material souls in one composed body, by reason every material part has a material natural soul, for nature is but one infinite, self-moving, living and self-knowing body, consisting of the three degrees of inanimate, sensitive and rational matter so intermixed together, that no part of nature, were it an atom, can be without any of these three degrees. The sensitive is the life, the rational the soul, and the inanimate part, the body of infinite nature.'

The Empress was very well satisfied with this answer, and asked further whether souls did not give life to bodies. 'No,' answered they, 'but spirits and divine souls have a life of their own, which is not to be divided, being purer than a natural life, for spirits are incorporeal and consequently indivisible.' 'But when the soul is in its vehicle,' said the Empress, 'then methinks she is like the sun, and the vehicle like the moon.' 'No,' answered they, 'but the vehicle is like the sun, the soul like the moon, for the soul hath motion from the body as the moon has light from the sun.'

Then the Empress asked the spirits whether it was an evil spirit that tempted Eve and brought all the mischiefs upon mankind, or whether it was the serpent. They answered that spirits could not commit actual evils. The Empress said they might do it by persuasions. They answered that persuasions were actions. But the Empress, not being contented with this answer, asked whether there was not a supernatural evil. The spirits answered that there was a supernatural good, which was God, but they knew of no supernatural evil that was equal to God.

Then she desired to know whether evil spirits were reckoned amongst the beasts of the field. They answered that many beasts of the field were harmless creatures and very serviceable for man's use, and though some were accounted fierce and cruel, yet did they exercise their cruelty upon other creatures, for the most part, to no other end but to get themselves food and to satisfy their natural appetite. 'But certainly,' said they, 'you men are more cruel to one another than evil spirits are to you, and as for their habitations in desolate places, we, having no communion with them, can give you no certain account thereof.'

'But what do you think,' said the Empress, 'of good spirits? May not they be compared to the fowls of the air?' They answered there were many cruel and ravenous fowls as well in the air as there were fierce and cruel beasts on earth, so that the good are always mixed with the bad. She asked further whether the fiery vehicles were a heaven or a hell, or at least a purgatory to the souls. They answered that if the souls were immaterial, they could not burn and then fire would do them no harm, and though hell was believed to be an undecaying and unquenchable fire, yet heaven was no fire. The Empress replied that heaven was a light. 'Yes,' said they, 'but not a fiery light.'

Then she asked whether the different shapes and sorts of vehicles made the souls and other immaterial spirits miserable or blessed. 'The vehicles,' answered they, 'make them neither better nor worse, for though some vehicles sometimes may have power over others, yet these by turns may get some power again over them, according to the several advantages and disadvantages of particular natural parts.' The Empress asked further whether animal life came out of the spiritual world and did return thither again. The spirits answered they could not exactly tell, but if it were so, then certainly animal lives must leave their bodies behind them, otherwise the bodies would make the spiritual world a mixed world; that is, partly material and partly immaterial. 'But the truth is,' said they, 'spirits, being immaterial, cannot properly make a world, for a world belongs to material, not to immaterial creatures.'

'If this be so,' replied the Empress, 'then certainly there can be no world of lives and forms without matter.' 'No,' answered the spirits, 'nor a world of matter without lives and forms, for natural lives and forms cannot be immaterial, no more than matter can be immovable. And therefore natural lives, forms and matter are inseparable.' Then the Empress asked whether the first man did feed on the best sorts of the fruits of the earth, and the beasts on the worst. The spirits answered that, unless the beasts of the field were barred out of manured fields and gardens, they would pick and choose the best fruits as well as men. 'And you may plainly observe it,' said they, 'in squirrels and monkeys, how they are the best choosers of nuts and apples, and how birds do pick and feed on the most delicious fruits and worms on the best roots and most savoury herbs, by which you may see that those creatures live and feed better than men do, except you will say that artificial cookery is better and more wholesome than the natural.'

Again the Empress asked whether the first man gave names to all the several sorts of fishes in the sea and fresh waters. 'No,' answered the spirits, 'for he was an earthly and not a watery creature, and therefore could not know the several sorts of fishes.' 'Why,' replied the Empress, 'he was no more an airy creature than he was a watery one, and yet he gave names to the several sorts of fowls and birds of the air.' 'Fowls,' answered they, 'are partly airy, and partly earthy creatures, not only because they resemble beasts and men in their flesh, but because their rest and dwelling places are on earth, for they build their nests, lay their eggs and hatch their young, not in the air, but on the earth.'

Then she asked whether the first man did give names to all the various sorts of creatures that live on the earth. 'Yes,' answered they, 'to all those that were presented to him or he had knowledge of, that is, to all the prime sorts, but not to every particular. For of mankind,' said they, 'there were but two at first, and as they did increase, so did their names.' 'But,' said the Empress, 'who gave the names to the several sorts of fish?' The posterity of mankind,' answered they.

Then she enquired whether there were no more kinds of creatures now than at the first creation. They answered that there were no more nor fewer kinds of creatures than there are now, but there are, without question, more particular sorts of creatures now than there were then. She asked again whether all those creatures that were in Paradise were also in Noah's ark. They answered that the principal kinds had been there, but not all the particulars.

Then she would fain know how it came that both spirits and men did fall from a blessed into so miserable a state and condition as they are now in. The spirits answered: 'By disobedience.' The Empress asked whence this disobedient sin did proceed. But the spirits desired the Empress not to ask them any such questions, because they went beyond their knowledge. Then she begged the spirits to pardon her presumption. 'For,' said she, 'it is the nature of mankind to be inquisitive.' 'Natural desire of knowledge,' answered the spirits, 'is not blameable, so you do not go beyond what your natural reason can comprehend.'

'Then I'll ask no more,' said the Empress, 'for fear I should commit some error. But one thing I cannot but acquaint you withal.' 'What is that?' said the spirits. 'I have a great desire,' answered the Empress, 'to make a Cabala.' 'What kind of Cabala?' asked the spirits. The Empress answered 'The Jews' Cabala.' No sooner had the Empress declared her mind, but the spirits immediately disappeared out of her sight, which startled the Empress so much that she fell into a trance, wherein she lay for some while.

At last, being come to herself again, she grew very studious, and considering with herself what might be the cause of this strange disaster, conceived at first that perhaps the spirits were tired with hearing and giving answers to her questions. But thinking by herself that spirits could not be tired, she imagined that this was not the true cause of their disappearing, till after diverse debates with her own thoughts, she did verily believe that the spirits had committed some fault in their answers, and that for their punishment they were condemned to the lowest and darkest vehicles.

This belief was so fixed in her mind that it put her into a very melancholic humour, and then she sent both for her fly- and worm-men and declared to them the cause of her sadness. ' 'Tis not so much,' said she, 'the vanishing of those spirits that makes me melancholic, but that I should be the cause of their miserable condition, and that those harmless spirits should, for my sake, sink down into the black and dark abyss of the earth.'

The worm-men comforted the Empress, telling her that the earth was not so horrid a dwelling as she did imagine. 'For,' said they, 'not only all minerals and vegetables, but several sorts of animals can witness that the earth is a warm, fruitful, quiet, safe and happy habitation, and though they want the light of the sun, yet are they not in the dark, but there is light even within the earth by which those creatures do see that dwell therein.'

This relation settled her Majesty's mind a little, but yet she being desirous to know the truth, where and in what condition those spirits were, commanded both the fly- and worm-men to use all labour and industry to find them out, whereupon the worm-men straight descended into the earth, and the fly-men ascended into the air. After some short time, the worm-men returned, and told the Empress that when they went into the earth they enquired of all the creatures they met withal whether none of them had perceived such or such spirits, until at last coming to the very centre of the earth, they were truly informed that those spirits had stayed some time there, but at last were gone to the antipodes on the other side of the terrestrial globe, diametrically opposite to theirs.

The fly-men seconded the worm-men, assuring her Majesty that their relation was very true. 'For,' said they, 'we have rounded the earth, and just when we came to the antipodes, we met those spirits in a very good condition, and acquainted them that your Majesty was very much troubled at their sudden departure, and feared they should be buried in the darkness of the earth. Whereupon the spirits answered us that they were sorry for having occasioned such sadness and trouble in your Majesty, and desired us to tell your Majesty that they feared no darkness, for their vehicles were of such a sort of substance as cats' eyes, glow-worms' tails and rotten wood, carrying their light along with them, and that they were ready to do your Majesty what service they could in making your Cabala.' At which relation the Empress was exceedingly glad, and rewarded both her fly and worm-men bountifully.

After some time, when the spirits had refreshed themselves in their own vehicles, they sent one of their nimblest spirits to ask the Empress whether she would have a scribe, or whether she would write the Cabala herself. The Empress received the proffer which they made her with all civility, and told them that she desired a spiritual scribe. The spirits answered that they could dictate, but not write, except they put on a hand or arm or else the whole body of man.

The Empress replied, 'How can spirits arms themselves with gauntlets of flesh?' 'As well,' answered they, 'as man can arm himself with a gauntlet of steel.' 'If it be so,' said the Empress, 'then I will have a scribe.' Then the spirits asked her whether she would have the soul of a living or a dead man. 'Why,' said the Empress, 'can the soul quit a living body and wander or travel abroad?' 'Yes,' answered they, 'for according to Plato's doctrine, there is a conversation of souls, and the souls of lovers live in the bodies of their beloved.' 'Then I will have,' answered she, 'the soul of some ancient famous writer, either of Aristotle, Pythagoras, Plato, Epicurus, or the like.'

The spirits said that those famous men were very learned, subtle and ingenious writers, but they were so wedded to their own opinions that they would never have the patience to be scribes. 'Then,' said she, 'I'll have the soul of one of the most famous modern writers, as either of Galileo, Gassendus, Descartes, Helmont, Hobbes, H. More, etc.'* The spirits answered that they were fine, ingenious writers, but yet so self-conceited that they would scorn to be scribes to a woman. 'But,' said they, 'there's a lady, the Duchess of Newcastle, which although she is not one of the most learned, eloquent, witty and ingenious, yet she is a plain and rational writer, for the principle of her writings is sense and reason and she will, without question, be ready to do you all the service she can.'

'That lady then,' said the Empress, 'will I choose for my scribe, neither will the Emperor have reason to be jealous, she being one of my own sex.' 'In truth,' said the spirit, 'husbands have reason to be jealous of Platonic lovers, for they are very dangerous, as being not only very intimate and close, but subtle and insinuating.' 'You say well,' replied the Empress, 'wherefore, I pray, send me the Duchess of Newcastle's soul'—which the spirit did, and after she came to wait on the Empress, at her first arrival the Empress embraced her and saluted her with a spiritual kiss. Then she asked her whether she could write.

'Yes,' answered the Duchess's soul, 'but not so intelligibly that any reader whatsoever may understand it, unless he be taught to know my characters, for my letters are rather like characters than well-formed letters.' Said the Empress: 'You were recommended to me by an honest and ingenious spirit.' 'Surely,' answered the Duchess, 'the spirit is ignorant of my handwriting.' 'The truth is,' said the Empress, 'he did not mention your handwriting, but he informed me that you writ sense and reason, and if you can but write so that any of my secretaries may learn your hand, they shall write it out fair and intelligible.'

The Duchess answered that she questioned not but it might easily be learned in a short time. 'But,' said she to the Empress, 'what is it that your Majesty would have written?' She answered, 'The Jews' Cabala.' 'Then your only way for that is,' said the Duchess, 'to have the soul of some famous Jew; nay, if your Majesty please, I scruple not but you may as easily have the soul of Moses as of any other.' 'That cannot be,' replied the Empress, 'for no mortal knows where Moses is.' 'But,' said the Duchess, 'human souls are immortal. However, if this be too difficult to be obtained, you may have the soul of one of the chief rabbis or sages of the tribe of Levi, who will truly instruct you in that mystery, whenas otherwise your Majesty will be apt to mistake, and a thousand to one will commit gross errors.'

'No,' said the Empress, 'for I shall be instructed by spirits.' 'Alas,' said the Duchess, 'spirits are as ignorant as mortals in many cases, for no created spirits have a general or absolute knowledge, nor can they know the thoughts of men, much less the mysteries of the great creator, unless he be pleased to inspire into them the gift of divine knowledge.' 'Then I pray,' said the Empress, 'let me have your counsel in this case.'

The Duchess answered, 'If your Majesty will be pleased to hearken to my advice, I would desire you to let that work alone, for it will be of no advantage either to you or your people, unless you were of the Jews' religion. Nay, if you were, the vulgar interpretation of the holy scripture would be more instructive and more easily believed than your mystical way of interpreting it, for had it been better and more advantageous for the salvation of the

Jews, surely Moses would have saved after ages that labour by his own explanation, he being not only a wise but a very honest, zealous and religious man. Wherefore the best way,' said she, 'is to believe with the generality the literal sense of the scripture, and not to make interpretations everyone according to his own fancy, but to leave that work for the learned, or those that have nothing else to do. Neither do I think,' said she, 'that God will damn those that are ignorant therein, or suffer them to be lost for want of a mystical interpretation of the scripture.'

'Then,' said the Empress, 'I'll leave the scripture and make a philosophical Cabala.' The Duchess told her that sense and reason would instruct her of nature as much as could be known, and as for numbers, they were infinite; but to add nonsense to infinite would breed a confusion, especially in human understanding. 'Then,' replied the Empress, 'I'll make a moral Cabala.' 'The only thing,' answered the Duchess, 'in morality is but to fear God and to love his neighbour, and this needs no further interpretation.' 'But then I'll make a political Cabala,' said the Empress. The Duchess answered that the chief and only ground in government was but reward and punishment and required no further Cabala. 'But,' said she, 'if your Majesty were resolved to make a Cabala, I would advise you rather to make a poetical or Romancical Cabala, wherein you may use metaphors, allegories, similitudes etc. and interpret them as you please.'

With that, the Empress thanked the Duchess, and embracing her soul, told her she would take her counsel. She made her also her favourite, and kept her some time in that world, and by this means the Duchess came to know and give this relation of all that passed in that rich, populous and happy world. And after some time, the Empress gave her leave to return to her husband and kindred into her native world, but upon condition that her soul should visit her now and then, which she did, and truly their meeting did produce such an intimate friendship between them that they became Platonic lovers, although they were both females.

One time, when the Duchess her soul was with the Empress, she seemed to be very sad and melancholy, at which the Empress was very much troubled and asked her the reason of her melancholic humour. 'Truly,' said the Duchess to the Empress, for between dear friends there's no concealment, they being like

several parts of one united body, 'my melancholy proceeds from an
extreme ambition.' The Empress asked what the height of her
ambition was. The Duchess answered that neither she herself nor
no creature in the world was able to know either the height, depth
or breadth of her ambition. 'But,' said she, 'my present desire is that
I would be a great princess.' The Empress replied, 'But so you
are, for you are a princess of the fourth or fifth degree, for a duke
or duchess is the highest title or honour that a subject can arrive
to, as being the next to a king's title, and as for the name of a
prince or princess, it belongs to all that are adopted to the crown,
so that those that can add a crown to their arms are princes, and
therefore a duke is a title above a prince. For example, the Duke
of Savoy, the Duke of Florence, the Duke of Lorrain, as also the
king's brothers, are not called by the name of princes, but dukes,
this being the higher title.'

''Tis true,' answered the Duchess, 'unless it be kings' eldest
sons and they are created princes.' 'Yes,' replied the Empress,
'but no sovereign does make a subject equal to himself, such as
kings' eldest sons partly are, and although some dukes be
sovereigns, yet I never heard that a prince by his title is sovereign,
by reason the title of a prince is more a title of honour than of
sovereignty, for, as I said before, it belongs to all that are adopted
to the crown.'

'Well,' said the Duchess, 'setting aside this dispute, my
ambition is that I would fain be as you are, that is, an empress of a
world, and I shall never be at quiet until I be one.' 'I love you so
well,' replied the Empress, 'that I wish with all my soul you had
the fruition of your ambitious desire, and I shall not fail to give
you my best advice how to accomplish it. The best informers are
the immaterial spirits and they'll soon tell you whether it be
possible to obtain your wish.' 'But,' said the Duchess, 'I have
little acquaintance with them, for I never knew any before the
time you sent for me.' 'They know you,' replied the Empress, 'for
they told me of you, and were the means and instrument of your
coming hither, wherefore I'll confer with them and enquire
whether there be not another world whereof you may be empress
as well as I am of this.'

No sooner had the Empress said this, but some immaterial
spirits came to visit her, of whom she enquired whether there

were but three worlds in all, to wit, the Blazing World where she was in, the world which she came from, and the world where the Duchess lived. The spirits answered that there were more numerous worlds than the stars which appeared in these three mentioned worlds. Then the Empress asked whether it was not possible that her dearest friend the Duchess of Newcastle might be empress of one of them.

'Although there be numerous, nay infinite worlds,' answered the spirits, 'yet none is without government.' 'But is none of these worlds so weak,' said she, 'that it may be surprised or conquered?' The spirits answered that Lucian's world of lights had been for some time in a snuff, but of late years one Helmont had got it, who since he was emperor of it had so strengthened the immortal parts thereof with mortal outworks as it was, for the present, impregnable.

Said the Empress: 'If there be such an infinite number of worlds, I am sure not only my friend the Duchess, but any other might obtain one.' 'Yes,' answered the spirits, 'if those worlds were uninhabited, but they are as populous as this your Majesty governs.' 'Why,' said the Empress, 'it is not impossible* to conquer a world?' 'No,' answered the spirits, 'but for the most part conquerors seldom enjoy their conquest, for they being more feared than loved, most commonly come to an untimely end.'

'If you will but direct me,' said the Duchess to the spirits, 'which world is easiest to be conquered, her Majesty will assist me with means and I will trust to fate and fortune, for I had rather die in the adventure of noble achievements than live in obscure and sluggish security, since by the one I may live in a glorious fame and by the other I am buried in oblivion.' The spirits answered that the lives of fame were like other lives, for some lasted long and some died soon. ''Tis true,' said the Duchess, 'but yet the shortest lived fame lasts longer than the longest life of man.' 'But,' replied the spirits, 'if occasion does not serve you, you must content yourself to live without such achievements that may gain you a fame. But we wonder,' proceeded the spirits, 'that you desire to be Empress of a terrestrial world whenas you can create yourself a celestial world if you please.'

'What,' said the Duchess, 'can any mortal be a creator?' 'Yes,' answered the spirits, 'for every human creature can create an immaterial world fully inhabited by immaterial creatures and populous of immaterial subjects, such as we are, and all this within the compass of the head or skull; nay, not only so, but he may create a world of what fashion and government he will and give the creatures thereof such motions, figures, forms, colours, perceptions etc. as he pleases, and make whirlpools, lights, pressures and reactions etc. as he thinks best. Nay, he may make a world full of veins, muscles and nerves, and all these to move by one jolt or stroke. Also, he may alter that world as often as he pleases, or change it from a natural world to an artificial. He may make a world of ideas, a world of atoms, a world of lights or whatsoever his fancy leads him to. And since it is in your power to create such a world, what need you to venture life, reputation and tranquility to conquer a gross, material world, for you can enjoy no more of a material world than a particular creature is able to enjoy, which is but a small part, considering the compass of such a world, and you may plainly observe it by your friend the Empress here, which although she possesses a whole world, yet enjoys she but a part thereof. Neither is she so much acquainted with it that she knows all the places, countries and dominions she governs.

'The truth is, a sovereign monarch has the general trouble, but the subjects enjoy all the delights and pleasures in parts, for it is impossible that a kingdom, nay, a country, should be enjoyed by one person at once, except he take the pains to travel into every part, and endure the inconveniencies of going from one place to another. Wherefore, since glory, delight and pleasure lives but in other men's opinions, and can neither add tranquility to your mind nor give ease to your body, why should you desire to be Empress of a material world and be troubled with the cares that attend government, whenas by creating a world within yourself you may enjoy all, both in whole and in parts, without control or opposition, and may make what world you please and alter it when you please and enjoy as much pleasure and delight as a world can afford you.'

'You have converted me,' said the Duchess to the spirits, 'from my ambitious desire, wherefore I'll take your advice, reject and despise all the worlds without me, and create a world of my own.' The Empress said, 'If I do make such a world, then I shall be mistress of two worlds, one within and the other without me.' 'That your Majesty may,' said the spirits, and so left these two ladies to create two worlds within themselves, who did also part from each other until such time as they had brought their worlds to perfection.

The Duchess of Newcastle was most earnest and industrious to make her world, because she had none at present, and first she resolved to frame it according to the opinion of Thales, but she found herself so much troubled with Demons that they would not suffer her to take her own will, but forced her to obey their orders and commands, which she being unwilling to do, left off from making a world that way and began to frame one according to Pythagoras' doctrine. But in the creation thereof, she was so puzzled with numbers, how to order and compose the several parts, that she, having no skill in arithmetic, was forced also to desist from the making of that world. Then she intended to create a world according to the opinion of Plato, but she found more trouble and difficulty in that than in the two former, for the numerous Ideas, having no other motion but what was derived from her mind, whence they did flow and issue out, made it a far harder business to her to impart motion to them than puppet players have in giving motion to every several puppet, in so much that her patience was not able to endure the trouble which those Ideas caused her, wherefore she annihilated also that world and was resolved to make one according to the opinion of Epicurus, which she had no sooner begun but the infinite atoms made such a mist that it quite blinded the perception of her mind, neither was she able to make a vacuum as a receptacle for those atoms, or a place which they might retire into, so that partly for the want of it and of a good order and method, the confusion of those atoms produced such strange and monstrous figures as did more affright than delight her, and caused such a chaos in her mind as had almost dissolved it.

At last, having with much ado cleansed and cleared her mind of these dusty and misty particles, she endeavoured to create a world according to Aristotle's opinion, but remembering that her mind, as most of the learned hold it, was immaterial, and that according to Aristotle's principle, out of nothing, nothing could be made, she was forced also to desist from that work, and then she fully resolved not to take any more patterns from the ancient philosophers but to follow the opinions of the moderns, and to that end she endeavoured to make a world according to Descartes' opinion. But when she had made the ethereal globules and set them amoving by a strong and lively imagination, her mind became so dizzy with their extraordinary swift turning round that it almost put her into a swoon, for her thoughts, by their constant tottering, did so stagger as if they had all been drunk. Wherefore she dissolved that world and began to make another according to Hobbes' opinion. But when all the parts of this imaginary world came to press and drive each other, they seemed like a company of wolves that worry sheep, or like so many dogs that hunt after hares, and when she found a reaction equal to those pressures, her mind was so squeezed together that her thoughts could neither move forward nor backward, which caused such an horrible pain in her head that although she had dissolved that world, yet she could not without much difficulty settle her mind and free it from that pain which those pressures and reactions had caused in it.

At last, when the Duchess saw that no patterns would do her any good in the framing of her world, she was resolved to make a world of her own invention, and this world was composed of sensitive and rational self-moving matter. Indeed, it was composed only of the rational, which is the subtlest and purest degree of matter, for as the sensitive did move and act both to the perceptions and consistency of the body, so this degree of matter at the same point of time (for though the degrees are mixed, yet the several parts may move several ways at one time) did move to the creation of the imaginary world, which world, after it was made, appeared so curious and full of variety, so well ordered and wisely governed, that it cannot possibly be expressed by words, nor the delight and pleasure which the Duchess took in making this world of her own.

In the meantime, the Empress was also making and dissolving several worlds in her own mind, and was so puzzled that she could not settle in any of them, wherefore she sent for the Duchess who, being ready to wait on the Empress, carried her beloved world along with her and invited the Empress's soul to observe the frame, order and government of it. Her Majesty was so ravished with the perception of it that her soul desired to live in the Duchess's world. But the Duchess desired her to make such another world in her own mind. 'For,' said she, 'your Majesty's mind is full of rational, corporeal motions, and the rational motions of my mind shall assist you, by the help of sensitive expressions, with the best instructions they are able to give you.'

The Empress, being thus persuaded by the Duchess to make an imaginary world of her own, followed her advice and after she had quite finished it and framed all kinds of creatures proper and useful for it, strengthened it with good laws and beautified it with arts and sciences, having nothing else to do unless she did dissolve her imaginary world or make some alterations in the Blazing World she lived in, which yet she could hardly do, by reason it was so well ordered that it could not be mended, for it was governed without secret and deceiving policy, neither was there any ambitious, factious, malicious detractions, civil dissensions or home-bred quarrels, divisions in religion, foreign wars, etc., but all the people lived in a peaceful society, united tranquility and religious conformity.

She was desirous to see the world the Duchess came from and observe therein the several sovereign governments, laws and customs of several nations. The Duchess used all the means she could to divert her from that journey, telling her that the world she came from was very much disturbed with factions, divisions and wars, but the Empress would not be persuaded from her design, and lest the Emperor or any of her subjects should know of her travel and obstruct her design, she sent for some of the spirits she had formerly conversed withal and enquired whether none of them could supply the place of her soul in her body at such a time when she was gone to travel into another world.

They answered yes they could, 'For not only one,' said they, 'but many spirits may enter into your body if you please.' The Empress replied she desired but one spirit to be viceroy of her body in the absence of her soul, but it must be an honest and ingenious spirit and, if it was possible, a female spirit. The spirits told her that there was no difference of sexes amongst them.

'But,' said they, 'we will choose an honest and ingenious spirit, and such a one as shall so resemble your soul that neither the Emperor nor any of his subjects, although the most divine, shall know whether it be your own soul or not.' Which the Empress was very glad at, and after the spirits were gone asked the Duchess how her body was supplied in the absence of her soul, who answered her Majesty that her body in the absence of her soul was governed by her sensitive and rational corporeal motions.

Thus those two female souls travelled together as lightly as two thoughts into the Duchess her native world and, which is remarkable, in a moment viewed all the parts of it and all the actions of all the creatures therein, especially did the Empress's soul take much notice of the several actions of human creatures in all the several nations and parts of that world, and wondered that for all there were so many several nations, governments, laws, religions, opinions, etc. they should all yet so generally agree in being ambitious, proud, self-conceited, vain, prodigal, deceitful, envious, malicious, unjust, revengeful, irreligious, factious, etc.

She did also admire that not any particular state, kingdom or commonwealth was contented with their own shares, but endeavoured to encroach upon their neighbours, and that their greatest glory was in plunder and slaughter, and yet their victories less than their expenses, and their losses more than their gains, but their being overcome, in a manner their utter ruin.

But that she wondered most at was that they should prize or value dirt more than men's lives, and vanity more than tranquillity. 'For the Emperor of a world,' said she, 'enjoys but a part, not the whole, so that his pleasure consists in the opinions of others.' 'It is strange to me,' answered the Duchess, 'that you should say thus, being yourself an empress of a world, and not only of a world but of a peaceable, quiet and obedient world.' ''Tis true,' replied the Empress, 'but although it is a peaceable and obedient world, yet the government thereof is rather a trouble than a pleasure, for order cannot be without industry, contrivance and direction. Besides, the magnificent state that great princes keep, or ought to keep, is troublesome.'

'Then by your Majesty's discourse,' said the Duchess, 'I

perceive that the greatest happiness in all worlds consists in moderation.' 'No doubt of it,' replied the Empress. And after these two souls had visited all the several places, congregations and assemblies both in religion and state, the several courts of judicature and the like in several nations, the Empress said that of all the monarchs of the several parts of that world, she had observed the Grand-Seigneur* was the greatest, for his word was a law and his power absolute. But the Duchess prayed the Empress to pardon her that she was of another mind. 'For,' said she, 'he cannot alter Mahomet's laws and religion, so that the law and church do govern the emperor, and not the emperor them.'

'But,' replied the Empress, 'he has power in some particulars; as, for example, to place and displace subjects in their particular governments of church and state, and having that, he has the command both over church and state and none dares oppose him.' ''Tis true,' said the Duchess, 'but if it pleases your Majesty, we will go into that part of the world whence I came to wait on your Majesty, and there you shall see as powerful a monarch as the Grand-Seigneur, for though his dominions are not of so large extent, yet they are much stronger, his laws are easy and safe and he governs so justly and wisely that his subjects are the happiest people of all the nations or parts of that world.'

'This monarch,' said the Empress, 'I have a great mind to see.' Then they both went and in a short time arrived into his dominions, but coming into the metropolitan city, the Empress's soul observed many gallants go into a house, and enquiring of the Duchess's soul what house that was, she told her it was one of the theatres where comedies and tragedies were acted. The Empress asked whether they were real. 'No,' said the Duchess, 'they are feigned.' Then the Empress desired to enter into the theatre and when she had seen the play that was acted, the Duchess asked her how she liked that recreation. 'I like it very well,' said the Empress, 'but I observe that the actors make a better show than the spectators, and the scenes a better than the actors, and the music and dancing is more pleasant and acceptable than the play itself, for I see the scenes stand for wit, the dancing for humour, and the music is the chorus.'

'I am sorry,' replied the Duchess, 'to hear your Majesty say so, for if the wits of this part of the world should hear you, they would condemn you.' 'What,' said the Empress, 'would they condemn me for preferring a natural face before a sign post, or a natural humour before an artificial dance, or music before a true and profitable relation?' 'As for relation,' replied the Duchess, 'our poets defy and condemn it into a chimney corner, fitter for old women's tales than theatres.' 'Why,' said the Empress, 'do not your poets' actions comply with their judgements? For their plays are composed of old stories, either of Greek or Roman, or some new-found world.'

The Duchess answered her Majesty that it was true that all or most of their plays were taken out of old stories, but yet they had new actions which, being joined to old stories, together with the addition of new prologues, scenes, music and dancing, made new plays.

After this, both the souls went to the court, where all the royal family was together, attended by the chief of the nobles of their dominions, which made a very magnificent show, and when the soul of the Empress viewed the King and Queen, she seemed to be in a maze, which the Duchess's soul perceiving, asked the Empress how she liked the King, the Queen and all the royal race. She answered that in all the monarchs she had seen in that world, she had not found so much majesty and affability mixed so exactly together that none did overshadow or eclipse the other, and as for the Queen, she said that virtue sat triumphant in her face and piety was dwelling in her heart and that all the royal family seemed to be endued with a divine splendour.

But when she had heard the King discourse, she believed that Mercury and Apollo had been his celestial instructors. 'And my dear lord and husband,' added the Duchess, 'has been his earthly governor.'* But after some short stay in the court, the Duchess's soul grew very melancholy. The Empress asking the cause of her sadness, she told her that she had an extreme desire to converse with the soul of her noble lord and dear husband and that she was impatient of a longer stay. The Empress desired the Duchess but to have patience so long until the King, the Queen and the royal family were retired, and then would bear her company to her lord and husband's soul, who at that time lived in the country some 112 miles off—which she did. And thus these two souls went towards those parts of the kingdom where the Duke of Newcastle was.

But one thing I forgot all this while, which is that although thoughts are the natural language of souls, yet by reason souls cannot travel without vehicles, they use such language as the nature and propriety of their vehicles require, and the vehicles of those two souls being made of the purest and finest sort of air and of a human shape, this purity and fineness was the cause that they could neither be seen nor heard by any human creature, whenas had they been of some grosser sort of air, the sound of that air's language would have been as perceptible as the blowing of Zephyrus.

And now to return to my former story, when the Empress's and Duchess's souls were travelling into Nottinghamshire (for that was the place where the Duke did reside), passing through the forest of Sherwood, the Empress's soul was very much delighted with it, as being a dry, plain and woody place, very pleasant to travel in both in Winter and Summer, for it is neither much dirty nor dusty at no time. At last they arrived at Wellbeck, a house where the Duke dwelled, surrounded all with a wood so close and full that the Empress took great pleasure and delight therein, and told the Duchess she never had observed more wood in so little compass in any part of the kingdom she had passed through.

'The truth is,' said she, 'there seems to be more wood on the seas' (she meaning the ships) 'than on the land.' The Duchess told her the reason was that there had been a long civil war in that kingdom, in which most of the best timber-trees and principal palaces were ruined and destroyed. 'And my dear lord and husband,' said she, 'has lost by it half his woods, besides many houses, land and movable goods, so that all the loss out of his particular estate did amount to above half a million of pounds.' 'I wish,' said the Empress, 'he had some of the gold that is in the Blazing World to repair his losses.' The Duchess most humbly thanked her imperial Majesty for her kind wishes. 'But,' said she, 'wishes will not repair his ruins. However, God has given my noble lord and husband great patience, by which he bears all his losses and misfortunes.'

At last they entered into the Duke's house, an habitation not so magnificent as useful, and when the Empress saw it, 'Has the Duke,' said she, 'no other house but this?' 'Yes,' answered the Duchess, 'some five miles from this place he has a very fine castle called Bolsover.' 'That place then,' said the Empress, 'I desire to see.' 'Alas,' replied the Duchess, 'it is but a naked house and unclothed of all furniture.' 'However,' said the Empress, 'I may see the manner of its structure and building.' 'That you may,' replied the Duchess.

And as they were thus discoursing, the Duke came out of the house into the court to see his horses of manage,* whom when the Duchess's soul perceived, she was so overjoyed that her aerial vehicle became so splendorous as if it had been enlightened by the sun, by which we may perceive that the passions of souls or spirits can alter their bodily vehicles.

Then these two ladies' spirits went close to him, but he could not perceive them. And after the Empress had observed that art of manage, she was much pleased with it and commended it as a noble pastime and an exercise fit and proper for noble and heroic persons. But when the Duke was gone into the house again, those two souls followed him, where the Empress observing that he went to the exercise of the sword, and was such an excellent and unparalleled master thereof, she was as much pleased with that exercise as she was with the former.

But the Duchess's soul being troubled that her dear lord and husband used such a violent exercise before meat, for fear of overheating himself, without any consideration of the Empress's soul, left her aerial vehicle and entered into her lord. The Empress's soul, perceiving this, did the like. And then the Duke had three souls in one body, and had there been but some such souls more, the Duke would have been like the Grand-Seigneur in his seraglio, only it would have been a Platonic seraglio.

But the Duke's soul being wise, honest, witty, complaisant and noble, afforded such delight and pleasure to the Empress's soul by his conversation that these two souls became enamoured of each other, which the Duchess's soul perceiving, grew jealous at first, but then considering that no adultery could be committed amongst Platonic lovers, and that Platonism was divine, as being derived from divine Plato, cast forth of her mind that idea of jealousy.

Then the conversation of these three souls was so pleasant that it cannot be expressed, for the Duke's soul entertained the Empress's soul with scenes, songs, music, witty discourses, pleasant recreations, and all kinds of harmless sports, so that the time passed away faster than they expected. At last, a spirit came and told the Empress that although neither the Emperor nor any of his subjects knew that her soul was absent, yet the Emperor's soul was so sad and melancholy for want of his own beloved soul that all the imperial court took notice of it. Wherefore he advised the Empress's soul to return into the Blazing World into her own body she left there; which both the Duke's and Duchess's soul was very sorry for, and wished that, if it had been possible, the Empress's soul might have stayed a longer time with them. But seeing it could not be otherwise, they pacified themselves.

But before the Empress returned into the Blazing World, the Duchess desired a favour of her, to wit that she would be pleased to make an agreement between her noble lord and Fortune. 'Why,' said the Empress, 'are they enemies?' 'Yes,' answered the Duchess, 'and they have been so ever since I have been his wife. Nay, I have heard my lord say that she hath crossed him in all things ever since he could remember.' 'I am sorry for that,' replied the Empress, 'but I cannot discourse with Fortune without the help of an immaterial spirit, and that cannot be done in this world, for I have no fly nor bird-men here to send into the region of the air where, for the most part, their habitations are.'

The Duchess said she would entreat her lord to send an attorney or lawyer to plead his cause. 'Fortune will bribe them,' replied the Empress, 'but I cannot discourse with Fortune without wherefore the best way will be for the Duke to choose a friend on his side and let Fortune choose another, and try whether by this means it be possible to compose the difference.'

The Duchess said, 'They will never come to an agreement unless there be a judge or umpire to decide the case.' 'A judge,' replied the Empress, 'is easy to be had, but to get an impartial judge is a thing so difficult that I doubt we shall hardly find one, for there is none to be had, neither in nature nor in hell, but only from heaven, and how to get such a divine and celestial judge I cannot tell. Nevertheless, if you will go along with me into the Blazing World I'll try what may be done.' ''Tis my duty,' said the Duchess, 'to wait on your Majesty, and I shall most willingly do it, for I have no other interest to consider.'

Then the Duchess spoke to the Duke concerning the difference between him and Fortune, and how it was her desire that they might be friends. The Duke answered that for his part he had always with great industry sought her friendship, but as yet he could never obtain it, for she had always been his enemy. 'However,' said he, 'I'll try and send my two friends, Prudence and Honesty, to plead my cause.'

Then these two friends went with the Duchess and the Empress into the Blazing World (for it is to be observed that they are somewhat like spirits, because they are immaterial, although their actions are corporeal) and after their arrival there, when the Empress had refreshed herself and rejoiced with the Emperor, she sent her fly-men for some of the spirits and desired their assistance to compose the difference between Fortune and the Duke of Newcastle. But they told her Majesty that Fortune was so inconstant that, although she would perhaps promise to hear their cause pleaded, yet it was a thousand to one whether she would ever have the patience to do it.

Nevertheless, upon her Majesty's request, they tried their utmost and at last prevailed with Fortune so far that she chose Folly and Rashness for her friends, but they could not agree in choosing a judge, until at last, with much ado, they concluded that Truth should hear and decide the cause.

Thus all being prepared, and the time appointed, both the Empress's and Duchess's souls went to hear them plead, and when all the immaterial company was met, Fortune, standing upon a golden globe, made this following speech:

'Noble friends, we are met here to hear a cause pleaded concerning the difference between the Duke of Newcastle and myself, and though I am willing upon the persuasions of the ambassadors of the Empress, the immaterial spirits, to yield to it, yet it had been fit the Duke's soul should be present also, to speak for herself. But since she is not here, I shall declare myself to his wife and his friends, as also to my friends, especially the Empress, to whom I shall chiefly direct my speech.

'First, I desire your imperial Majesty may know that this Duke who complains or exclaims so much against me hath been always my enemy, for he has preferred Honesty and Prudence before me, and slighted all my favours. Nay, not only thus, but he did fight against me and preferred his innocence before my power. His friends Honesty and Prudence, said he most scornfully, are more to be regarded than inconstant Fortune, who is only a friend to fools and knaves; for which neglect and scorn, whether I have not just reason to be his enemy, your Majesty may judge yourself.'

After Fortune had thus ended her speech, the Duchess's soul rose from her seat and spoke to the immaterial assembly in this manner:

'Noble friends, I think it fit, by your leave, to answer Lady Fortune in the behalf of my noble lord and husband, since he is not here himself, and since you have heard her complaint concerning the choice my lord made of his friends and the neglect and disrespect he seemed to cast upon her, give me leave to answer that, first concerning the choice of his friends. He has proved himself a wise man in it, and as for the disrespect and rudeness her Ladyship accuses him of, I dare say he is so much a gentleman that I am confident he would never slight, scorn or disrespect any of the female sex* in all his lifetime, but was such a servant and champion for them that he ventured life and estate in their service.

'But being of an honest, as well as an honourable nature, he could not trust Fortune with that which he preferred above his life, which was his reputation, by reason Fortune did not side with those that were honest and honourable, but renounced them. And since he could not be of both sides, he chose to be of that which was agreeable both to his conscience, nature and education, for which choice Fortune did not only declare herself his open enemy, but fought with him in several battles, nay, many times hand to hand. At last, she being a powerful princess and, as some believe, a deity, overcame him and cast him into a banishment, where she kept him in great misery, ruined his estate, and took away from him most of his friends. Nay, even when she favoured many that were against her, she still frowned on him, all which he endured with the greatest patience and with that respect to Lady Fortune that he did never in the least endeavour to disoblige any of her favourites, but was only sorry that he, an honest man, could find no favour in her court. And since he did never injure any of those she favoured, he neither was an enemy to her Ladyship, but gave her always that respect and worship which belonged to her power and dignity and is still ready at any time honestly and prudently to serve her. He only begs her Ladyship would be his friend for the future, as she hath been his enemy in times past.'

As soon as the Duchess's speech was ended, Folly and Rashness started up and both spoke so thick and fast at once that not only the assembly but themselves were not able to understand each other. At which Fortune was somewhat out of countenance, and commanded them either to speak singly or be silent. But Prudence told her Ladyship she should command them to speak wisely as well as singly. 'Otherwise,' said she, 'it were best for them not to speak at all.' Which Fortune resented very ill and told Prudence she was too bold, and then commanded Folly to declare what she would have made known. But her speech was so foolish, mixed with such nonsense, that none knew what to make of it. Besides, it was so tedious that Fortune bid her to be silent and commanded Rashness to speak for her, who began after this manner:

'Great Fortune, the Duchess of Newcastle has proved herself, according to report, a very proud and ambitious lady in presuming to answer you her own self in this noble assembly, without your command, in a speech wherein she did not only contradict you, but preferred Honesty and Prudence before you, saying that her lord was ready to serve you honestly and prudently, which presumption is beyond all pardon. And if you will allow Honesty and Prudence to be above you, none will admire, worship or serve you, but you'll be forced to serve yourself and will be despised, neglected and scorned by all, and from a deity become a miserable, dirty, begging mortal in a churchyard porch or nobleman's gate.

'Wherefore, to prevent such disasters, fling as many misfortunes and neglects on the Duke and Duchess of Newcastle and their two friends as your power is able to do, otherwise Prudence and Honesty will be the chief and only moral deities of mortals.'

Rashness having thus ended her speech, Prudence rose and declared herself in this manner:

'Beautiful Truth, great Fortune, and you the rest of my noble friends, I am come a great and long journey in the behalf of my dear friend the Duke of Newcastle, not to make more wounds but, if it be possible, to heal those that are made already. Neither do I presume to be a deity, but my only request is that you would be pleased to accept of my offering, I being an humble and devout supplicant. And since no offering is more acceptable to the gods than the offering of peace, in order to that, I desire to make an agreement between Fortune and the Duke of Newcastle.'

Thus she spoke, and as she was going on, up started Honesty (for she has not always so much discretion as she ought to have) and interrupted Prudence:

'I came not here,' said she, 'to hear Fortune flattered, but to hear the cause decided between Fortune and the Duke; neither came I hither to speak rhetorically and eloquently, but to propound the case plainly and truly. And I'll have you know that the Duke, whose cause we argue, was and is my foster son, for I, Honesty, bred him from his childhood and made a perpetual friendship betwixt him and Gratitude, Charity and Generosity, and put him to school to Prudence, who taught him wisdom and informed him in the rules of Temperance, Patience, Justice and the like. Then I put him into the university of Honour, where he learned all honourable qualities, arts and sciences. Afterwards I sent him to travel through the world of actions, and made Observation his governor, and in those his travels he contracted a friendship with Experience, all which made him fit for heaven's blessings and Fortune's favours.

'But she, hating all those that have merit and desert, became his inveterate enemy, doing him all the mischief she could, until the god of Justice opposed Fortune's malice and pulled him out of those ruins she had cast upon him. For this god's favourites were the Duke's champions, wherefore to be an enemy to him were to be an enemy to the god of Justice. In short, the true cause of Fortune's malice to this Duke is that he would never flatter her, for I, Honesty, did command him not to do it, or else he would be forced to follow all her inconstant ways and obey all her unjust commands, which would cause a great reproach to him. But on the other side, Prudence advised him not to despise Fortune's favours, for that would be an obstruction and hindrance to his worth and merit. And he, to obey both our advice and counsels, did neither flatter nor despise her, but was always humble and respectful to her so far as honour, honesty and conscience would permit—all which I refer to Truth's judgement and expect her final sentence.'

Fortune, hearing thus Honesty's plain speech, thought it very rude, and would not hearken to Truth's judgement, but went away in a passion, at which both the Empress and Duchess were extremely troubled that their endeavours should have no better effect. But Honesty chid the Duchess, and said she was to be punished for desiring so much Fortune's favours. 'For it appears,' said she, 'that you mistrust the gods' blessings'. At which the Duchess wept, answering Honesty that she did neither mistrust the gods' blessings nor rely upon Fortune's favours, but desired only that her lord might have no potent enemies.

The Empress, being much troubled to see her weep, told Honesty in anger, she wanted the discretion of Prudence. 'For though you are commended,' said she, 'yet you are apt to commit many indiscreet actions unless Prudence be your guide.' At which reproof Prudence smiled, and Honesty was somewhat out of countenance, but they soon became very good friends. And after the Duchess's soul had stayed some time with the Empress in the Blazing World, she begged leave of her to return to her lord and husband, which the Empress granted her upon condition she should come and visit her as often as conveniently she could, promising that she would do the same to the Duchess.

Thus the Duchess's soul—after she had taken her leave of the Empress, as also of the spirits, who with great civility promised her that they would endeavour in time to make a peace and agreement between Fortune and the Duke—returned with Prudence and Honesty into her own world. But when she was just upon her departure, the Empress sent to her and desired that she might yet have some little conference with her before she went, which the Duchess most willingly granted her Majesty.

And when she came to wait on her, the Empress told the Duchess that she, being her dear, Platonic friend, of whose just and impartial judgement she had always a very great esteem, could not forebear before she went from her to ask her advice concerning the government of the Blazing World. 'For,' said she, 'although this world was very well and wisely ordered and governed at first when I came to be Empress thereof, yet the nature of women being much delighted with change and variety, after I had received an absolute power from the Emperor, did somewhat alter the form of government from what I found it. But now, perceiving that the world is not so quiet as it was at first, I am much troubled at it. Especially, there are such continual contentions and divisions between the worm-, bear- and fly-men, the ape-men, the satyrs, the spider-men, and all others of such sorts, that I fear they'll break out into an open rebellion and cause a great disorder and the ruin of the government, and therefore I desire your advice and assistance how I may order it to the best advantage that this world may be rendered peaceable, quiet and happy as it was before.'

Whereupon the Duchess answered that since she heard by her imperial Majesty how well and happily the world had been governed when she first came to be Empress thereof, she would advise her Majesty to introduce the same form of government again which had been before; that is, to have but one sovereign, one religion, one law, and one language, so that all the world might be but as one united family, without divisions, nay, like God and his blessed saints and angels. 'Otherwise,' said she, 'it may in time prove as unhappy, nay, as miserable a world as that is from which I came, wherein are more sovereigns than worlds and more pretended governors than government; more religions than gods and more opinions in those religions than truths; more laws than rights and more bribes than justices; more policies than necessities and more fears than dangers; more covetousness than riches; more ambitions than merits; more services than rewards; more languages than wit; more controversy than knowledge; more reports than noble actions and more gifts by partiality than according to merit.

'All which,' said she, 'is a great misery, nay, a curse, which your blessed Blazing World never knew nor, 'tis probable, will never know of unless your imperial Majesty alter the government thereof from what it was when you began to govern it. And since your Majesty complains much of the factions of the bear-, fish-, fly-, ape- and worm-men, the satyrs, spider-men and the like, and of their perpetual disputes and quarrels, I would advise your Majesty to dissolve all their societies, for 'tis better to be without their intelligences than to have an unquiet and disorderly government.'

'The truth is,' said she, 'wheresoever learning is, there is most commonly also controversy and quarrelling, for there be always some that will know more and be wiser than others. Some think their arguments come nearer to truth and are more rational than others; some are so wedded to their own opinions that they'll never yield to reason, and others, though they find their opinions not firmly grounded upon reason, yet for fear of receiving some disgrace by altering them, will nevertheless maintain them against all sense and reason, which must needs breed factions in their schools, which at last break out into open wars and draw sometimes an utter ruin upon a state or government.'

The Empress told the Duchess that she would willingly follow her advice, but she thought it would be an eternal disgrace to her to alter her own decrees, acts and laws. To which the Duchess answered that it was so far from a disgrace as it would rather be for her Majesty's eternal honour to return from a worse to a better, and would express and declare her to be more than ordinary wise and good: so wise as to perceive her own errors, and so good as not to persist in them, which few did. 'For which,' said she, 'you will get a glorious fame in this world and an eternal glory hereafter, and I shall pray for it so long as I live.'

Upon which advice, the Empress's soul embraced and kissed the Duchess's soul with an immaterial kiss and shed immaterial tears that she was forced to part from her, finding her not a flattering parasite, but a true friend. And in truth, such was their Platonic friendship as these two loving souls did often meet and rejoice in each other's conversation.

The Second Part of the Description of the New Blazing World

THE Empress, having now ordered and settled her government to the best advantage and quiet of her Blazing World, lived and reigned most happily and blessedly, and received oftentimes visits from the immaterial spirits, who gave her intelligence of all such things as she desired to know and they were able to inform her of. One time they told her how the world she came from was embroiled in a great war, and that most parts or nations thereof made war against that kingdom which was her native country, where all her friends and relations did live, at which the Empress was extremely troubled, insomuch that the Emperor perceived her grief by her tears and, examining the cause thereof, she told him that she had received intelligence from the spirits that that part of the world she came from, which was her native country, was like to be destroyed by numerous enemies that made war against it.

The Emperor, being very sensible of this ill news, especially of the trouble it caused to the Empress, endeavoured to comfort her as much as possibly he could, and told her that she might have all the assistance which the Blazing World was able to afford. She answered that if there were any possibility of transporting forces out of the Blazing World into the world she came from, she would not fear so much the ruin thereof. 'But,' said she, 'there being no probability of effecting any such thing, I know not how to show my readiness to serve my native country.'

The Emperor asked whether those spirits that gave her intelligence of this war could not, with all their power and forces, assist her against those enemies. She answered that spirits could not arm themselves, nor make any use of artificial arms or weapons, for their vehicles were natural bodies, not artificial. 'Besides,' said she, 'the violent and strong actions of war will never agree with immaterial spirits, for immaterial spirits cannot fight, nor make trenches, fortifications and the like.'

'But,' said the Emperor, 'their vehicles can, especially if those vehicles be men's bodies, they may be serviceable in all the actions of war.' 'Alas,' replied the Empress, 'that will never do. For first,' said she, 'it will be difficult to get so many dead bodies for their vehicles as to make up a whole army, much more to make many armies to fight with so many several nations. Nay, if this could be, yet it is not possible to get so many dead and undissolved bodies in one nation, and for transporting them out of other nations, it would be a thing of great difficulty and improbability.

'But put the case,' said she, 'all these difficulties could be overcome, yet there is one obstruction or hindrance which can no ways be avoided, for although those dead and undissolved bodies did all die in one minute of time, yet before they could rendezvous and be put into a posture of war to make a great and formidable army, they would stink and dissolve, and when they came to a fight they would moulder into dust and ashes, and so leave the purer, immaterial spirits naked. Nay, were it also possible that those dead bodies could be preserved from stinking and dissolving, yet the souls of such bodies would not suffer immaterial spirits to rule and order them, but they would enter and govern them themselves, as being the right owners thereof, which would produce a war between those immaterial souls and the immaterial spirits in material bodies, all which would hinder them from doing any service in the actions of war against the enemies of my native country.'

'You speak reason,' said the Emperor, 'and I wish with all my soul I could advise any manner or way that you might be able to assist it. But you having told me of your dear, Platonic friend the Duchess of Newcastle, and of her good and profitable counsels, I would desire you to send for her soul and confer with her about this business.'

The Empress was very glad of this motion of the Emperor and immediately sent for the soul of the said Duchess, which in a minute waited on her Majesty. Then the Empress declared to her the grievance and sadness of her mind, and how much she was troubled and afflicted at the news brought her by the immaterial spirits, desiring the Duchess, if possible, to assist her with the best counsels she could, that she might show the greatness of her love and affection which she bore to her native country.

Whereupon the Duchess promised her Majesty to do what lay in her power, and since it was a business of great importance, she desired some time to consider of it. 'For,' said she, 'great affairs require deep considerations'—which the Empress willingly allowed her. And after the Duchess had considered some little time, she desired the Empress to send some of her sirens or mermen to see what passages they could find out of the Blazing World into the world she came from. 'For,' said she, 'if there be a passage for a ship to come out of that world into this, then certainly there may also a ship pass through the same passage out of this world into that.'

Hereupon the mer- or fish-men were sent out, who being many in number, employed all their industry and did swim several

ways. At last, having found out the passage, they returned to the
Empress and told her that, as their Blazing World had but one
emperor, one government, one religion and one language, so
there was but one passage into that world, which was so little that
no vessel bigger than a packet-boat could go through, neither was
that passage always open, but sometimes quite frozen up. At
which relation both the Empress and Duchess seemed somewhat
troubled, fearing that this would perhaps be an hindrance or
obstruction to their design.

At last the Duchess desired the Empress to send for her
shipwrights and all her architects, which were giants, who being
called, the Duchess told them how some in her own world had
been so ingenious as to contrive ships that could swim under
water, and asked whether they could do the like. The giants
answered they had never heard of that invention; nevertheless,
they would try what might be done by art, and spare no labour or
industry to find it out.

In the meantime, while both the Empress and Duchess were in
a serious council, after many debates the Duchess desired but a
few ships to transport some of the bird, worm and bear-men.
'Alas,' said the Empress, 'what can such sorts of men do in the
other world, especially so few? They will soon be destroyed, for a
musket will destroy numbers of birds at one shot.' The Duchess
said, 'I desire your Majesty will have but a little patience and rely
upon my advice, and you shall not fail to save your own native
country and in a manner become mistress of all that world you
came from.'

The Empress, who loved the Duchess as her own soul, did so.
The giants returned soon after and told her Majesty that they
had found out the art which the Duchess had mentioned, to
make such ships as could swim under water, which the Empress
and Duchess were both very glad at, and when the ships were
made ready, the Duchess told the Empress that it was requisite
that her Majesty should go herself in body as well as in soul. 'But
I,' said she, 'can only wait on your Majesty after a spiritual
manner; that is, with my soul.' 'Your soul,' said the Empress,
'shall live with my soul in my body, for I shall only desire your
counsel and advice.'

'Then,' said the Duchess, 'your Majesty must command a

great number of your fish-men to wait on your ships, for you know that your ships are not made for cannons, and therefore are no ways serviceable in war, for though by the help of your engines they can drive on, and your fish-men may by the help of chains or ropes draw them which way they will to make them go on or fly back, yet not so as to fight. And though your ships be of gold, and cannot be shot through but only bruised and battered, yet the enemy will assault and enter them and take them as prizes, wherefore your fish-men must do you service instead of cannons.'

'But how,' said the Empress, 'can the fish-men do me service against an enemy without cannons and all sorts of arms?' 'That is the reason,' answered the Duchess, 'that I would have numbers of fish-men, for they shall destroy all your enemy's ships before they can come near you.' The Empress asked in what manner that could be. 'Thus,' answered the Duchess, 'your Majesty must send a number of worm-men to the burning mountains (for you have good store of them in the Blazing World), which must get a great quantity of the fire stone, whose property, you know, is that it burns so long as it is wet. And the ships in the other world being all made of wood, they may by that means set them all on fire, and if you can but destroy their ships and hinder their navigation, you will be mistress of all that world, by reason most parts thereof cannot live without navigation.

'Besides,' said she, 'the fire stone will serve you instead of light or torches, for you know that the world you are going into is dark at nights, especially if there be no moonshine, or if the moon be overshadowed by clouds, and not so full of blazing stars as this world is, which make as great a light in the absence of the sun as the sun doth when it is present, for that world hath but little, blinking stars which make more shadows than light, and are only able to draw up vapours from the earth, but not to rarefy or clarify them or convert them into serene air.'

This advice of the Duchess was very much approved and joyfully embraced by the Empress, who forthwith sent her worm-men to get a good quantity of the mentioned fire stone. She also commanded numbers of fish-men to wait on her under water, and bird-men to wait on her in the air, and bear and worm-men to wait on her in ships, according to the Duchess's advice. And indeed the bear-men were as serviceable to her as the North star, but the bird-men would often rest themselves upon the decks of the ships; neither would the Empress, being of a sweet and noble nature, suffer that they should tire or weary themselves by long flights, for though by land they did often fly out of one country into another, yet they did rest in some woods or on some grounds, especially at night when it was their sleeping time. And therefore the Empress was forced to take a great many ships along with her, both for transporting those several sorts of her loyal and serviceable subjects and to carry provisions for them. Besides, she was so wearied with the petitions of several others of her subjects, who desired to wait on her Majesty, that she could not possibly deny them all, for some would rather choose to be drowned than not tender their duty to her.

Thus after all things were made fit and ready, the Empress began her journey. I cannot properly say she set sail, by reason in some part, as in the passage between the two worlds (which yet was but short), the ships were drawn under water by the fish-men with golden chains, so that they had no need of sails there or of any other arts but only to keep out water from entering into the ships and to give or make so much air as would serve, for breath or respiration, those land animals that were in the ships, which the giants had so artificially contrived that they which were therein found no inconveniency at all.

And after they had passed the icy sea, the golden ships appeared above water and so went on until they came near the kingdom that was the Empress's native country, where the bear-men, through their telescopes, discovered a great number of ships which had beset all that kingdom, well rigged and manned.

The Empress, before she came in sight of the enemy, sent some of her fish- and bird-men to bring her intelligence of their fleet, and hearing of their number, their station and posture, she gave order that when it was night, her bird-men should carry in their beaks some of the mentioned fire stones with the tops thereof wetted, and the fish-men should carry them likewise and hold them out of the water, for they were cut in the form of torches or candles, and being many thousands, made a terrible show, for it appeared as if all the air and sea had been of a flaming fire, and all that were upon the sea or near it did verily believe the time of judgement or the last day was come, which made them all fall down and pray.

At the break of day, the Empress commanded those lights to be put out and then the naval forces of the enemy perceived nothing but a number of ships without sails, guns, arms, and other instruments of war, which ships seemed to swim of themselves without any help or assistance, which sight put them into a great amaze. Neither could they perceive that those ships were of gold, by reason the Empress had caused them all to be coloured black or with a dark colour, so that the natural colour of the gold could not be perceived through the artificial colour of the paint, no not by the best telescopes—all which put the enemy's fleet into such a fright at night and to such wonder in the morning or at day time that they knew not what to judge or make of them, for they knew neither what ships they were nor what party they belonged to, insomuch that they had no power to stir.

In the meanwhile, the Empress, knowing the colours of her own country, sent a letter to their General and the rest of the chief commanders to let them know that she was a great and powerful princess and came to assist them against their enemies, wherefore she desired that they should declare themselves, when they would have her help and assistance.

Hereupon a council was called, and the business debated. But there were so many crosses and different opinions that they could not suddenly resolve what answer to send the Empress, at which she grew angry, insomuch that she resolved to return into her Blazing World without giving any assistance to her countrymen. But the Duchess of Newcastle entreated her Majesty to abate her passion, 'For,' said she, 'great councils are most commonly slow because many men have many several opinions. Besides, every councillor, striving to be the wisest, makes long speeches and raises many doubts, which cause retardments.'

'If I had long-speeched councillors,' replied the Empress, 'I would hang them, by reason they give more words than advice.' The Duchess answered that her Majesty should not be angry, but consider the differences of that and her Blazing World. 'For,' said she, 'they are not both alike, but there are grosser and duller understandings in this than in the Blazing World.'

At last a messenger came out, who returned the Empress

thanks for her kind proffer, but desired withal to know from whence she came, and how and in what manner her assistance could be serviceable to them. The Empress answered that she was not bound to tell them whence she came, but as for the manner of her assistance: 'I will appear,' said she, 'to your navy in a splendorous light, surrounded with fire.' The messenger asked at what time they should expect her coming. 'I'll be with you,' answered the Empress, 'about one of the clock at night.' With this report the messenger returned, which made both the poor councillors and seamen much afraid, but yet they longed for the time to behold this strange sight.

The appointed hour being come, the Empress appeared with garments made of the star stone, and was borne or supported above the water upon the fish-men's heads and backs, so that she seemed to walk upon the face of the water, and the bird and fish-men carried the fire stone, lighted both in the air and above the waters. Which sight, when her countrymen perceived at a distance, their hearts began to tremble, but coming something nearer, she left her torches and appeared only in her garments of light, like an angel or some deity, and all kneeled down before her and worshipped her with all submission and reverence.

But the Empress would not come nearer than at such a distance where her voice might be generally heard, by reason she would not have that any of her accoutrements should be perceived, but the splendour thereof. And when she was come so near that her voice could be heard and understood by all, she made this following speech:

'Dear countrymen—for so you are, although you know me not—I, being a native of this kingdom, and hearing that most part of this world had resolved to make war against it and sought to destroy it, at least to weaken its naval force and power, have made a voyage out of another world to lend you my assistance against your enemies. I come not to make bargains with you, or to regard my own interest more than your safety, but I intend to make you the most powerful nation of this world, and therefore I have chosen rather to quit my own tranquillity, riches and pleasure than suffer you to be ruined and destroyed.

'All the return I desire is but your grateful acknowledgement, and to declare my power, love and loyalty to my native country;

for, although I am now a great and absolute princess and empress of a whole world, yet I acknowledge that once I was a subject of this kingdom, which is but a small part of this world, and therefore I will have you undoubtedly believe that I shall destroy all your enemies before this following night—I mean those which trouble you by sea. And if you have any by land, assure yourself I shall also give you my assistance against them, and make you triumph over all that seek your ruin and destruction.'

Upon this declaration of the Empress, when both the General and all the commanders in their several ships had returned their humble and hearty thanks to her Majesty for so great a favour to them, she took her leave and departed to her own ships. But good Lord, what several opinions and judgements did this produce in the minds of her countrymen! Some said she was an angel; others, she was a sorceress; some believed her a goddess; others said the devil deluded them in the shape of a fine lady.

The morning after, when the navies were to fight, the Empress appeared upon the face of the waters dressed in her imperial robes, which were all of diamonds and carbuncles. In one hand she held a buckler made of one entire carbuncle, and in the other hand a spear of one entire diamond. On her head she had a cap of diamonds, and just upon the top of the crown was a star made of the star stone mentioned heretofore, and a half-moon made of the same stone was placed on her forehead. All her other garments were of several sorts of precious jewels, and having given her fish-men directions how to destroy the enemies of her native country, she proceeded to effect her design.

The fish-men were to carry the fire stones in cases of diamonds (for the diamonds in the Blazing World are in splendour so far beyond the diamonds of this world, as pebblestones are to the best sort of this world's diamonds) and to uncase or uncover those fire stones no sooner but when they were just under the enemy's ships, or close at their sides, and then to wet them and set their ships on fire. Which was no sooner done but all the enemy's fleet was of a flaming fire, and coming to the place where the powder was, it straight blew them up, so that all the several navies of the enemies were destroyed in a short time; which when her countrymen did see, they all cried out with one voice that she was an angel sent from God to deliver them out of the hands of their enemies. Neither would she return into the Blazing World until she had forced all the rest of that world to submit to that same nation.

In the meantime, the General of all their naval forces sent to their sovereign to acquaint him with their miraculous delivery and conquest, and with the Empress's design of making him the most powerful monarch of all that world. After a short time, the Empress sent herself to the sovereign of that nation to know in what she could be serviceable to him, who returning her many thanks, both for her assistance against his enemies and her kind proffer to do him further service for the good and benefit of his nations (for he was King over several kingdoms) sent her word that although she did partly destroy his enemies by sea, yet they were so powerful that they did hinder the trade and traffic of his dominions.

To which the Empress returned this answer: that she would burn and sink all those ships that would not pay him tribute, and forthwith sent to all the neighbouring nations who had any traffic by sea, desiring them to pay tribute to the King and sovereign of that nation where she was born. But they denied it with great scorn, whereupon she immediately commanded her fish-men to destroy all strangers' ships that trafficked on the seas, which they did according to the Empress's command, and when the neighbouring nations and kingdoms perceived her power, they were so discomposed in their affairs and designs that they knew not what to do.

At last they sent to the Empress and desired to treat with her, but could get no other conditions than to submit and pay tribute to the said King and sovereign of her native country, otherwise she was resolved to ruin all their trade and traffic by burning their ships. Long was this treaty, but in fine they could obtain nothing, so that at last they were enforced to submit, by which the King of the mentioned nations became absolute master of the seas and consequently of that world, by reason, as I mentioned heretofore, the several nations of that world could not well live without traffic and commerce by sea, as well as by land.

But after a short time, those neighbouring nations, finding themselves so much enslaved that they were hardly able to peep out of their own dominions without a chargeable tribute, they all agreed to join again their forces against King and sovereign of the said dominions, which when the Empress received notice of, she sent out her fish-men to destroy, as they had done before, the remainder of all their naval power, by which they were soon forced again to submit, except some nations which could live without foreign traffic, and some whose trade and traffic was merely by land—these would no ways be tributary to the mentioned King.

The Empress sent them word that in case they did not submit to him, she intended to fire all their towns and cities and reduce them by force to what they would not yield with a good will. But they rejected and scorned her Majesty's message, which provoked her anger so much that she resolved to send her bird and worm-men thither, with order to begin first with their smaller towns and set them on fire (for she was loath to make more spoil than she was forced to), and if they remained still obstinate in their resolutions, to destroy also their greater cities. The only difficulty was how to convey the worm-men conveniently to those places, but they desired that her Majesty would but set them upon any part of the earth of those nations, and they could travel within the earth as easily and as nimbly as men upon the face of the earth; which the Empress did according to their desire.

But before both the bird and worm-men began their journey, the Empress commanded the bear-men to view through their telescopes what towns and cities those were that would not submit, and having a full information thereof, she instructed the bird and bear-men what towns they should begin withal. In the meanwhile, she sent to all the princes and sovereigns of those nations, to let them know that she would give them a proof of her power and check their obstinacies by burning some of their smaller towns, and if they continued still in their obstinate resolutions, that she would convert their smaller loss into a total ruin. She also commanded her bird-men to make their flight at night, lest they be perceived.

At last, when both the bird- and worm-men came to the designed places, the worm-men laid some fire stones under the foundation of every house, and the bird-men placed some at the tops of them, so that both by rain and by some other moisture within the earth, the stones could not fail of burning. The bird-men, in the meantime, having learned some few words of their language, told them that the next time it did rain their towns would be all on fire, at which they were amazed to hear men speak in the air, but withal they laughed when they heard them say that rain should fire their towns, knowing that the effect of water was to quench, not produce, fire.

At last a rain came, and upon a sudden all their houses appeared of a flaming fire, and the more water there was poured on them, the more they did flame and burn, which struck such a fright and terror into all the neighbouring cities, nations and kingdoms that, for fear the like should happen to them, they and all the rest of the parts of that world granted the Empress's desire, and submitted to the monarch and sovereign of her native country, the King of ESFI,* save one, which having seldom or never any rain, but only dews, which would soon be spent in a great fire, slighted her power. The Empress, being desirous to make it stoop as well as the rest, knew that every year it was watered by a flowing tide which lasted some weeks, and although their houses stood high from the ground, yet they were built upon supporters which were fixed into the ground. Wherefore she commanded both her bird and worm-men to lay some of the fire stones at the bottom of those supporters and when the tide came in, all their houses were of a fire, which did so rarefy the water that the tide was soon turned into vapour, and this vapour again into air, which caused not only a destruction of their houses but also a general barrenness over all their country that year, and forced them to submit as well as the rest of the world had done.

Thus the Empress did not only save her native country, but made it the absolute monarchy of all that world, and both the effects of her power and her beauty did kindle a great desire in all the greatest princes to see her, who hearing that she was resolved to return into her own Blazing World, they all entreated the favour that they might wait on her Majesty before she went. The Empress sent word that she should be glad to grant their requests, but having no other place of reception for them, she desired that they would be pleased to come into the open seas with their ships and make a circle of a pretty large compass, and then her own ships should meet them and close up the circle, and she would present herself to the view of all those that came to see her. Which answer was joyfully received by all the mentioned princes, who came, some sooner, and some later, each according to the distance of his country and the length of the voyage.

And all being met in the form and manner aforesaid, the Empress appeared upon the face of the water in her imperial robes. In some part of her hair, near her face, she had placed some of the star stone, which added such a lustre and glory to it that it caused a great admiration in all that were present, who believed her to be some celestial creature, or rather an uncreated goddess, and they all had a desire to worship her, for surely, said they, no mortal creature can have such a splendid and transcendent beauty, nor can any have so great a power as she has, to walk upon the waters and to destroy whatever she pleases, not only whole nations but a whole world.

The Empress expressed to her own countrymen, who were also her interpreters to the rest of the princes that were present, that she would give them an entertainment at the darkest time of night; which being come, the fire stones were lighted, which made both air and seas appear of a bright, shining flame, insomuch that they put all spectators into an extreme fright, who verily believed they should all be destroyed. Which the Empress perceiving, caused all the lights of the fire stones to be put out, and only showed herself in her garments of light. The bird-men carried her upon their backs into the air, and there she appeared as glorious as the sun.

Then she was set down upon the seas again, and presently there was heard the most melodious and sweetest consort of voices as ever was heard out of the seas, which was made by the fish-men. This consort was answered by another, made by the bird-men in the air, so that it seemed as if sea and air had spoke and answered each other by way of singing dialogues, or after the manner of those plays that are acted by singing voices.

But when it was upon break of day, the Empress ended her entertainment, and at full daylight all the princes perceived that she went into the ship wherein the prince and monarch of her native country was, the King of ESFI, with whom she had several conferences, and having assured him of the readiness of her assistance whensoever he required it, telling him withal that she wanted no intelligence, she went forth again upon the waters, and being in the midst of the circle made by those ships that were present, she desired them to draw somewhat nearer that they might hear her speak, which being done, she declared herself in this following manner:

'Great, heroic and famous monarchs, I come hither to assist the King of ESFI against his enemies, he being unjustly assaulted by many several nations which would fain take away his hereditary rights and prerogatives of the narrow seas, at which unjustice heaven was much displeased, and for the injuries he received from his enemies, rewarded him with an absolute power, so that now he is become the head-monarch of all this world, which power, though you may envy, yet you can no ways hinder him, for all those that endeavour to resist his power shall only get loss for their labour and no victory for their profit. Wherefore my advice to you all is to pay him tribute justly and truly, that you may live peaceably and happily, and be rewarded with the blessings of heaven, which I wish you from my soul.'

After the Empress had thus finished her speech to the princes of the several nations of that world, she desired that their ships might fall back, which being done, her own fleet came into the circle without any visible assistance of sails or tide, and herself being entered into her own ship, the whole fleet sunk immediately into the bottom of the seas and left all the spectators in a deep amazement. Neither would she suffer any of her ships to come above the waters until she arrived into the Blazing World.

In time of the voyage, both the Empress's and Duchess's souls were very gay and merry, and sometimes they would converse very seriously with each other. Amongst the rest of their discourses, the Duchess said she wondered much at one thing, which was that since her Majesty had found out a passage out of the Blazing World into the world she came from, she did not enrich that part of the world where she was born, at least her own family, though she had enough to enrich the whole world.

The Empress's soul answered that she loved her native country and her own family as well as any creature could do, and that this was the reason why she would not enrich them. 'For,' said she, 'not only particular families or nations but all the world, their natures are such that much gold and great store of riches makes them mad, insomuch as they endeavour to destroy each other for gold or riches' sake.' 'The reason thereof is,' said the Duchess, 'that they have too little gold and riches, which makes them so eager to have it.' 'No,' replied the Empress's soul, 'their particular covetousness is beyond all the wealth of the richest world, and the more riches they have, the more covetous they are, for their covetousness is infinite. But,' said she, 'I would there could a passage be found out of the Blazing World into the world whence you came, and I would willingly give you as much riches as you desired.'

The Duchess's soul gave her Majesty humble thanks for her great favour and told her that she was not covetous, nor desired any more wealth than what her lord and husband had before the civil wars. 'Neither,' said she, 'should I desire it for my own, but my lord's posterity's sake.' 'Well,' said the Empress, 'I'll command my fish-men to use all their skill and industry to find out a passage into that world which your lord and husband is in.' 'I do verily believe,' answered the Duchess, 'that there will be no passage found into that world, but if there were any, I should not petition your Majesty for gold and jewels, but only for the elixir that grows in the midst of the golden sands for to preserve life and health, but without a passage it is impossible to carry away any of it, for whatsoever is material cannot travel like immaterial beings, such as souls and spirits are. Neither do souls require any such thing that might revive them or prolong their lives, by reason they are unalterable, for were souls like bodies, then my soul might have had the benefit of that natural elixir that grows in your Blazing World.'

'I wish earnestly,' said the Empress, 'that a passage might be found, and then both your lord and yourself should neither want wealth nor long life; nay, I love you so well that I would make you as great and powerful a monarchess as I am of the Blazing World.' The Duchess's soul humbly thanked her Majesty, and told her that she acknowledged and esteemed her love beyond all things that are in nature.

After this discourse they had many other conferences, which for brevity's sake I'll forbear to rehearse. At last, after several questions which the Empress's soul asked the Duchess, she desired to know the reason why she did take such delight, when she was joined to her body, in being singular both in accoutrements, behaviour and discourse. The Duchess's soul answered, she confessed that it was extravagant and beyond what was usual and ordinary, but yet her ambition being such that she would not be like others in anything, if it were possible. 'I endeavour,' said she, 'to be as singular as I can, for it argues but a mean nature to imitate others, and though I do not love to be imitated, if I can possibly avoid it, yet rather than imitate others I should choose to be imitated by others, for my nature is such that I had rather appear worse in singularity than better in the mode.'

'If you were not a great lady,' replied the Empress, 'you would never pass in the world for a wise lady, for the world would say your singularities are vanities.' The Duchess's soul answered she did not at all regard the censure of this, or any other age, concerning vanities. 'But,' said she, 'neither this present nor any of the future ages can or will truly say that I am not virtuous and chaste, for I am confident all that were or are acquainted with me and all the servants which ever I had will, or can upon their oaths, declare my actions no otherwise than virtuous. And certainly, there's none, even of the meanest degree, which have not their spies and witnesses, much more those of the nobler sort, which seldom or never are without attendants, so that their faults (if they have any) will easily be known and as easily divulged. Wherefore, happy are those natures that are honest, virtuous and noble; not only happy to themselves, but happy to their families.' 'But,' said the Empress, 'if you glory so much in your honesty and virtue, how comes it that you plead for dishonest and wicked persons in your writings?' The Duchess answered, it was only to show her wit, not her nature.

At last the Empress arrived into the Blazing World, and coming to her imperial palace, you may sooner imagine than expect that I should express the joy which the Emperor had at her safe return, for he loved her beyond his soul, and there was no love lost, for the Empress equalled his affection with no less love to him. After the time of rejoicing with each other, the Duchess's soul begged leave to return to her noble lord. But the Emperor desired that, before she departed, she would see how he had employed his time in the Empress's absence, for he had built stables and riding houses, and desired to have horses of manage such as, according to the Empress's relation, the Duke of Newcastle had.

The Emperor enquired of the Duchess the form and structure of her lord and husband's stables and riding house. The Duchess answered his Majesty that they were but plain and ordinary.

'But,' said she, 'had my lord wealth, I am sure he would not spare it in rendering his buildings as noble as could be made.' Hereupon the Emperor showed the Duchess the stables he had built, which were most stately and magnificent. Among the rest, there was one double stable that held a hundred horses on a side. The main building was of gold, lined with several sorts of precious materials. The roof was arched with agates, the sides of the walls were lined with cornelian, the floor was paved with amber, the mangers were mother of pearl, the pillars, as also the middle aisle or walk of the stables, were of crystal, the front and gate was of turquoise most neatly cut and carved. The riding house was lined with sapphires, topazes and the like. The floor was all of golden sand, so finely sifted that it was extremely soft and not in the least hurtful to the horses' feet, and the door and frontispiece was of emeralds curiously carved.

After the view of these glorious and magnificent buildings, which the Duchess's soul was much delighted withal, she resolved to take her leave. But the Emperor desired her to stay yet some short time more, for they both loved her company so well that they were unwilling to have her depart so soon. Several conferences and discourses passed between them. Amongst the rest, the Emperor desired her advice how to set up a theatre for plays. The Duchess confessed her ignorance in this art, telling his Majesty that she knew nothing of erecting theatres or scenes but what she had by an immaterial observation when she was with the Empress's soul in the chief city of E, entering into one of their theatres, whereof the Empress could give as much account to his Majesty as herself.

But both the Emperor and Empress told the Duchess that she could give directions how to make plays. The Duchess answered that she had as little skill to form a play after the mode as she had to paint or make a scene for show. 'But you have made plays,'* replied the Empress. 'Yes,' answered the Duchess, 'I intended them for plays, but the wits of these present times condemned them as uncapable of being represented or acted, because they were not made up according to the rules of art—though I dare say that the descriptions are as good as any they have writ.'

The Emperor asked whether the property of plays were not to describe the several humours, actions and fortunes of mankind.

' 'Tis so,' answered the Duchess. 'Why then,' replied the Emperor, 'the natural humours, actions and fortunes of mankind are not done by the rules of art.' 'But,' said the Duchess, 'it is the art and method of our wits to despise all descriptions of wit, humour, actions and fortunes that are without such artificial rules.'

The Emperor asked, 'Are those good plays that are made so methodically and artificially?' The Duchess answered they were good according to the judgement of the age, or mode of the nation, but not according to her judgement. 'For truly,' said she, 'in my opinion their plays will prove a nursery of whining lovers and not an academy or school for wise, witty, noble and well-behaved men.' 'But I,' replied the Emperor, 'desire such a theatre as may make wise men, and will have such descriptions as are natural, not artificial.'

'If your Majesty be of that opinion,' said the Duchess's soul, 'then my plays may be acted in your Blazing World when they cannot be acted in the blinking world of wit, and the next time I come to visit your Majesty, I shall endeavour to order your Majesty's theatre to present such plays as my wit is capable to make.'

Then the Empress told the Duchess that she loved a foolish farce added to a wise play. The Duchess answered that no world in nature had fitter creatures for it than the Blazing World. 'For,' said she, 'the louse-men, the bird-men, the spider and fox-men, the ape-men and satyrs appear in a farce extraordinary pleasant.'

Hereupon both the Emperor and the Empress entreated the Duchess's soul to stay so long with them till she had ordered her theatre and made plays and farces fit for them, for they only wanted that sort of recreation. But the Duchess's soul begged their Majesties to give her leave to go into her native world, for she longed to be with her dear lord and husband, promising that after a short time she would return again. Which being granted, though with much difficulty, she took her leave with all civility and respect, and so departed from their Majesties.

After the Duchess's return into her own body, she entertained her lord (when he was pleased to hear such kind of discourses) with foreign relations, but he was never displeased to hear of the Empress's kind commendations and of the characters she was pleased to give of him to the Emperor. Amongst other relations, she told him all what had passed between the Empress and the several monarchs of that world whither she went with the Empress, and how she had subdued them to pay tribute and homage to the monarch of that nation or kingdom to which she owed both her birth and education. She also related to her lord what magnificent stables and riding houses the Emperor had built, and what fine horses were in the Blazing World of several shapes and sizes, and how exact their shapes were in each sort, and of many various colours and fine marks, as if they had been painted by art with such coats or skins that they had a far greater gloss and smoothness than satin.

'And were there but a passage out of the Blazing World into this,' said she, 'you should not only have some of those horses, but such materials as the Emperor has to build your stables and riding houses withal, and so much gold that I should never repine at your noble and generous gifts.' The Duke smilingly answered her that he was sorry there was no passage between those two worlds. 'But,' said he, 'I have always found an obstruction to my good fortunes.'

One time the Duchess chanced to discourse with some of her acquaintance of the Empress of the Blazing World, who asked her what pastimes and recreations her Majesty did most delight in. The Duchess answered that she spent most of her time in the study of natural causes and effects, which was her chief delight and pastime, and that she loved to discourse sometimes with the most learned persons of that world. And to please the Emperor and his nobles, who were all of the royal race, she went often abroad to take the air, but seldom in the daytime, always at night, if it might be called night, 'For,' said she, 'the nights there are as light as days, by reason of the numerous blazing stars which are very splendorous, only their light is whiter than the sun's light, and as the sun's light is hot, so their light is cool; not so cool as our twinkling starlight, nor is their sunlight so hot as ours, but more temperate.

'And that part of the Blazing World where the Empress resides is always clear and never subject to any storms, tempests, fogs or mists, but has only refreshing dews that nourish the earth. The air of it is sweet and temperate and, as I said before, as much

light in the sun's absence as in its presence, which makes that
time we call night more pleasant there than the day. And
sometimes the Empress goes abroad by water in barges,
sometimes by land in chariots, and sometimes on horseback.

'Her royal chariots are very glorious: the body is one entire
green diamond; the four small pillars that bear up the top cover
are four white diamonds cut in the form thereof; the top or roof
of the chariot is one entire blue diamond, and at the four corners
are great springs of rubies; the seat is made of cloth of gold
stuffed with ambergris beaten small. The chariot is drawn by
twelve unicorns, whose trappings are all chains of pearl, and as
for her barges, they are only of gold.

'Her guard of state (for she needs none for security, there
being no rebels or enemies) consists of giants, but they seldom
wait on their Majesties abroad, because their extraordinary
height and bigness does hinder their prospect. Her entertainment when she is upon the water is the music of the fish and
bird-men, and by land are horse and foot-matches, for the
Empress takes much delight in making race-matches with the
Emperor and the nobility. Some races are between the fox and
ape-men, which sometimes the satyrs strive to outrun, and some
are between the spider-men and lice-men. Also there are several
flight matches between the several sorts of bird-men and the
several sorts of fly-men, and swimming matches between the
several sorts of fish-men.

'The Emperor, Empress and their nobles take also great
delight to have collations, for in the Blazing World there are most
delicious fruits of all sorts, and some such as in this world were
never seen nor tasted, for there are most tempting sorts of fruit.
After their collations are ended, they dance, and if they be upon
the water, they dance upon the water, there lying so many fish-
men so close and thick together as they can dance very evenly
and easily upon their backs, and need not fear drowning.

'Their music, both vocal and instrumental, is according to
their several places. Upon the water it is of water instruments, as
shells filled with water and so moved by art, which is a very sweet
and delightful harmony. And those dances which they dance
upon the water are, for the most part, such as we in this world call
swimming dances, where they do not lift up their feet high. In

lawns or upon plains they have wind instruments, but much better than those in our world. And when they dance in the woods, they have horn instruments, which although they are of a sort of wind instrument, yet they are of another fashion than the former. In their houses they have such instruments as are somewhat like our viols, violins, theorboes, lutes, citterns, guitars, harpsichords and the like, but yet so far beyond them that the difference cannot well be expressed. And as their places of dancing and their music is different, so is their manner or way of dancing. In these and the like recreations the Emperor, Empress and the nobility pass their time.'

The Epilogue to the Reader

BY this poetical description you may perceive that my ambition is not only to be Empress but authoress of a whole world, and that the worlds I have made, both the Blazing and the other philosophical world mentioned in the first part of this description, are framed and composed of the most pure—that is, the rational—parts of matter, which are the parts of my mind, which creation was more easily and suddenly effected than the conquests of the two famous monarchs of the world, Alexander and Caesar.

Neither have I made such disturbances and caused so many dissolutions of particulars, otherwise named deaths, as they did, for I have destroyed but some few men in a little boat which died through the extremity of cold, and that by the hand of justice, which was necessitated to punish their crime of stealing away a young and beauteous lady.

And in the formation of those worlds I take more delight and glory than ever Alexander or Caesar did in conquering this terrestrial world, and though I have made my Blazing World a peaceable world, allowing it but one religion, one language and one government, yet could I make another world as full of factions, divisions and wars as this is of peace and tranquillity, and the rational figures of my mind might express as much courage to fight as Hector and Achilles had, and be as wise as Nestor, as eloquent as Ulysses and as beautiful as Helen. But I, esteeming peace before war, wit before policy, honesty before beauty, instead of the figures of Alexander, Caesar, Hector, Achilles, Nestor, Ulysses, Helen, etc., chose rather the figure of honest Margaret Newcastle, which now I would not change for all this terrestrial world.

And if any should like the world I have made, and be willing to be my subjects, they may imagine themselves such, and they are such—I mean in their minds, fancies or imaginations. But if they cannot endure to be subjects, they may create worlds of their own and govern themselves as they please. But yet let them have a care not to prove unjust usurpers and to rob me of mine, for concerning the philosophical world, I am Empress of it myself, and as for the Blazing World, it having an Empress already who rules it with great wisdom and conduct, which Empress is my dear Platonic friend, I shall never prove so unjust, treacherous and unworthy to her as to disturb her government, much less to depose her from her imperial throne for the sake of any other, but rather choose to create another world for another friend.

THOMAS DANGERFIELD

Don Tomazo

(1680)

Don Tomazo, Or the Juvenile Rambles of Thomas Dangerfield

YOUTH has generally its extravagancies, and they that are seduced by the temptations of pleasures and bad company in great cities will have their times to sow their wild oats. For Don Tomazo's part, he has sowed his already and finding it such ill-husbandry to deal in that sort of grain, has resolved to give over. And now I have thought it convenient to give the world an account of his transgressions, to the end that people, as many have done, may not think him worse than he was, whatever self-interest would have made him. Nor does he expect that any man will henceforth upbraid him for what is past, as being under the protection of his sovereign's pardon,* to which all true subjects ought to give an aweful respect and obedience.

Had it not been for the high misdemeanours of Clavel,* we had missed a neat and excellent poem and the discovery of a great mystery of iniquity. The cheats and cunning contrivances of Gusman and Lazarillo de Tormes have been made English out of the Spanish language,* as well to instruct as to delight. And the greatest historians have taken as much pains to recount the lives of bad men as of the most deserving subjects of their pens. Mirrors that do not show the deformities as well as beauties of a face are of little use. In short, all sorts of men may gather hence how vain a thing it is to contend with the law, and that they must inevitably incur the misfortune of the pitcher by going often to the well. But the way to amendment is never out of date. St Austin himself had occasion enough to repent the follies of his youth.

Not that he goes about to excuse his offences, but this he hopes he may presume to say: that it was not his custom to put any man in danger of his life but himself. He only imposed upon the belief and understandings of others, which being deluded, misguided their wills. And it is no small argument that his being so proper for the designs for which he was called out was half a proof that his discoveries were true,* which perhaps had they not been ill-managed, might in some measure have made satisfaction for his past transgressions; nor does he despair but that some of them may yet take effect.

In the meantime, while he lives to show that Horace's 'Quo semel . . .'* is not always true, let the virtuous hence observe how laborious a thing it is to be wicked, and the vicious learn by his example to amend.

DON TOMAZO*

THE first corrupters and seducers of youth, especially if active and sprightly, are the whispers and temptations of pleasure, and that which boys call freedom, men extravagant looseness, which inclination in forward striplings being once inflamed by the inconsiderate severity of parents, labours with more violence to cast off the yoke of bondage, so that, unwilling to be under the continual awe and terror of the lash, they rather choose to stand to the favour of fortune and the compassion of the wide world than the cruel mercy of them that begat 'em. A cynical way of education, which perhaps many may have learnt from the morose documents of Solomon's whipping proverbs, and still as eagerly prosecute, not observing the ill success it met with in his own son. Upon which instigations no sooner has incensed extravagancy resolved to take its flight, but immediately vice appears in all her harlotry attire and, exposing all the splendour of her gaudy allurements, so hampers unwary innocence in the nooses of necessity that, not knowing which way to disengage itself, the scene quite alters.

So that of a sudden, innocence becomes criminal before it knows what a crime is, and young offenders incur the displeasure of the law ere they hardly understand what the law forbids. Till at length, perceiving what they have done, and not believing themselves safe from the punishment of lesser facts but by committing greater, they abandon themselves to those unhappy stratagems which, because they relieve at present, are by them looked upon as the effect of fortune's favour and their own prudence, so that encouraged by success, they cannot forsake the delightful practice of those enormities which maintain the sweet and tickling pleasures of riot and debauchery. So easy a thing it is for parents to beget, so difficult a task to hit the true method of education, for want of which so many lofty geniuses, so many active courages, so many soaring and refined wits, all tender pieces, ready for all the fair impressions of virtue, have quite altered their bias; so many blooming expectations have perished in the deep abysses of mistaken conduct and irregular severity.

How near the subject of this story was to falling from this fatal precipice the ensuing relation will declare, which, as may be well believed, will prove neither unpleasing nor unprofitable to the reader, or rather an incitement to acts of virtue, when he shall observe the pains and labours which extravagance undergoes to support itself in profuse and guilty luxury.

Don Tomazo (for so he must be called, as having put his name into the Spanish garb to which he was most accustomed in his travels) was by birth of English parents, born in Essex, no less famous for pleasure than plenty. His tender years were under the eye and government of his father, a person of a severe and disobliging austerity. In him perhaps it might be thought paternal care, who observing which way the current of his son's inclinations ran, deemed it the safest course by violence to stop the stream of his unruly passions. And indeed there was sufficient cause of suspicion, and the father had a fair prospect of what the future would produce by the early exercises of his son's childish talents. For which reason poor Don Tomazo was not only daily rated and rebuked, but frequently and vigorously chastised and exposed to the rigid lash for every trivial misdemeanour. This surly usage so disengaged the frank and generous humour of Don Tomazo, which was to have been corrected rather by lenitives than corrosives, that he looked upon his father as a master rather than a parent, and himself to be a slave rather than a son.

So then, for redress of these grievances, there must be a speedy remedy provided, for finding out of which his tender wits were soon employed. They argued in his brain that there was no living at home, therefore he must venture abroad, and that if a servitude must be endured, it was more easy to be borne under the frowns and spurns of strangers than of near relations, where extravagance had nobody to thank but itself for the hardship it suffered.

In the midst of these serious consultations, the Devil and ill-luck soon found him out a meet-help* for his purpose: a pure,

Satanical privy-counsellor, even a servant of his own father's. He was called by the name of Jemmy, a Scot by nation, nature and conditions: indigent, cunning and perfidious, true only to the son to cheat the father, perhaps out of a desire to revisit his household gods at the expenses of a defrauded master. To this instrument of Beelzebub the young disgusted squire discloses all the secrets of his heart, tells him the occasion of his discontents and his design to thrown off the yoke of paternal severity which, since there was no way to do but by travelling, he was resolved to take that course, and therefore requested both his advice and assistance.

Jemmy listened to this discourse like a sow i'th' beans. He applauded his design, magnified his youthful courage, and by a large encomium upon the worst of countries, persuaded the credulous stripling to steer toward the North Pole to the land of his nativity, whither he might be sure of a faithful guide and, when there, of an assistant in the midst of wealthy and generous relations. This being concluded, they were both sensible that it would be very uneasy travelling without horses, but that care was soon over when Don Tomazo called to mind that his father was well stored with that sort of cattle, and being their own casuists, they easily overcame all scruples of conscience upon a supposition that an heir in a case of necessity might anticipate a small pittance of his inheritance, and that the so doing was positively no theft.

But then again, well knowing that neither horse nor man could travel upon the road without corporal food, and that it was in vain to swear at a hostler or to kick a chamberlain without money in breeches, it was farther agreed that the young squire should fly to London, there to take up what money he could among his father's correspondents, and that trusty Jemmy, upon notice given of his success, should precisely meet him at the rendezvous which was before appointed at St Albans.

These blessed beginnings were so fortunately favoured by the assistance of their friend Monsieur Satan, who was loath to lose two such fair gamesters, that all things being accomplished according to their hearts' desire, away hastens Don Tomazo to St Albans and there meets his punctual companion with his father's two horses. And so, well mounted, the young master and the young man, knight errant-like, set forward upon their Northern progress. By the way, to make the journey the more pleasant, Jemmy, who was endued with a nimble utterance and the true faculty of Scotch lying, entertained his master with several discourses, and among the rest, told him such extravagant stories of the sweet pleasures, the contentment and plenty which he should meet with at his father's stately mansion that he had raised Don Tomazo's expectations steeple-high.

But after some days' travel, there befell them a small occasion of delay, which somewhat abated the squire's jollity. For it so happened that Jemmy, already possessed with one Devil, was seized with another Devil of an ague, which entered him with that violence that, to exorcise the robustious spirit, they were forced to lie still for four or five whole days and nights, in which time Don Tomazo's father had been amply informed which way the two Edomites were marched with the spoils of his purse and stable. How fatal this discovery might have proved to these young practitioners in iniquity may be easily conjectured had the father been eager to follow them. But he, being more tender of his credit, as disdaining the world should know how his grave experience had been over-reached by two raw whipsters, than to make a noise of his losses, neglected the pursuit.

So that upon Jemmy's recovery the two knight errants set forward again without any disturbance. But Jemmy, as unsound in body as in mind, having ventured too soon into the sharp winter air (for such was the season of the year which they chose for their journey of pleasure), before they could accomplish four days travel more, fell into a new distemper to the great grief and sorrow of Don Tomazo, who had then no small reason to doubt the loss of his guide and pillar of his hopes, as finding himself for the love and friendship which he bore to Jemmy now more likely to be exposed than ever to the misfortunes of unhappy undertakers, easily foreseen but not so easy to be prevented, especially considering the great expense he then and still was like to be at.

These reflections and the thoughts of being a stranger without having any bills of exchange for future supply, among a rude sort of people that would no longer respect him than his money lasted, which was not likely to be long at the rate of nurses' and 'pothecaries' bills, were sufficient to have confounded all the cogitations that an unexperienced stripling could muster together. But fortune and good husbandry so well agreed to encourage Don Tomazo in his first essays of Gusmanry* that in three weeks time Jemmy, not yet mellow enough for the Devil's palate, was well recovered and able to undertake the remaining part of the journey.

And indeed he had then more reason than ever to promise a retaliation of that care and kindness which his master had shown him in his sickness. Nor, to say truth, could Don Tomazo accuse him in the least while he was yet in England, where he was as lavish of his acknowledgements as could be expected, and protested such works of supererogation at home as if his father's opulent seat had been the mansion of gratitude itself. But the reader shall soon find the vast difference between Scotch promises and Scotch performances.

Well, after a cold and tedious journey, all weather-beaten as we* were, at length we arrived at Jemmy's father's palace, lying in the county of Anderdale near a town called Moffat.* When Don Tomazo beheld it, he was so far from being over-ravished with joy at the sight that he took it for some enchanted castle, in regard he could not see so much as one stone of all that magnificent pile which Jemmy all the way upon the road had been building in his fancy. Rather, he was more than usually surprised at the humility of the structure and the lowliness of the owner. Had he not been a Scot, you would have sworn him a Turk, regardless of his habitation in this world, in expectation of fool's paradise in the next.

It was a hovel, or rather sty, in length about six and thirty foot, not covered cathedral-like with lead, nor yet with glittering copper after the Swedish manner, but according to the Scotch custom, very meanly thatched with oaten reeds, not such as the Arcadian shepherds piped withal, but plain, downright illiterate straw. The fire was made near the bedside at one end, which for want of a chimney wrapped the whole family, guests and all, like so many Ixions in a continual cloud of eye-tormenting smoke.

Near to the bedside lay the corn and hay, which you may be sure was not worth its weight in gold, and at the other end, without the distinction of partitions, stood two sheep, a cow and the squire's horses, so that it may be verily believed that Virtue herself in all her exiles and persecutions never lived in such a homely hermitage, and Marius, when he lay hid among the bullrushes in the fens of Minturnus, might be thought to have lodged in a palace to this ill-favoured resemblance of Noah's ark.

So soon as we came to this unfortunate apartment, the old man, overtaken with joy not only to see his son, who had been absent from him several years, but to behold him in an equipage so genteel after the English mode, could not forbear bedewing his cheeks. But when Jemmy fell on his knee to crave his father's blessing, the old man, who well knew he had none to give, stood amazed. 'What a muckle Dee'l', quoth he, 'is the carl wood?'* Whereupon Tomazo, observing his astonishment, acquainted the old bacon-faced loon that it was the only customary way for children in England to acknowledge their respect and duty to their parents, and that Jemmy had done it purely out of natural affection and to show his improvement in English behaviour and education.

Thereupon the old man, seeming to be better satisfied, condescended to the breeding of his son and embraced him. Which ceremony being soon over, he requested the squire to enter his Polyphemes' den. But Don Tomazo, being very hungry, and not finding the place proper for many compliments, came close to the point and demanded what provision they had in the house. To which they made answer that they had good store of oatmeal and water, but neither flesh nor fowl, milk nor butter, bread nor drink and, which was worse, that none of these creature comforts were to be had for money within six miles of the place. So that poor Don Tomazo, who had always fared well at a plentiful table, began to curse his man Jemmy, who after such mountain-ous promises of a splendid entertainment and princely viands, had betrayed his longing appetite to such miserable commons, hardly worth the acceptance of a country mouse.

But Jemmy's mother, discovering discontent in Don Tomazo's face and taking pity of his youth, or rather for joy of her dear darling's return, began to comfort up our desponding stomachs with the hopes of a notable banquet. This, after the expense of all her huswifery, proved to be that sumptuous Scotch dish called a stean bannock, which was a certain composition of bean, pease, barley and oatmeal mixed together with water and made into the form of a large cake, and being set to the fire against a stone, and so baked, was to be eaten with water, and this, without first or second course, was the cream of their entertainment: a strange sort of philosophical diet that no way answered Don Tomazo's pampered expectations.

Supper—if so it might be called—being thus soberly dispatched at the mere instance of craving hunger, the weary guests were no less desirous of repose than they were before of food, to which the old man replied that 'twas the fashion in that country for the family to go to bed all together and not one before another, and therefore in regard that Don Tomazo and his son had prevailed with him to be conformable to an English ceremony, he would constrain them to be conformable to one of his country customs. Don Tomazo, not a little disgusted at his diet, and like to be worse pleased with his lodging, began to enter into a serious consideration of his forlorn condition. He found on the one side how miserably he had been frustrated by his man Jemmy, whose false tongue he now began too late to curse. He saw himself in a wild desert among a sort of savages more prone to make him a prey to their cruelty than afford him relief, which on the other side filled his head full of jealousies and fears, as now misdoubting that his trusty man Jemmy had some further designs, rather of mischief than of kindness, as being privy to the small treasure he had about him. To repent was irksome; to fear, below him. There were no shady woods for nightingales to lull him into soft slumbers, no murmuring rills to which he might make his sorrowful complaints, no kind hermits to invite him to their cells. All his comfort was in hope and the compassion of his guardian angel.

In the midst of these distractions, Don Tomazo perceived, through the thick smoke which forced those tears from his eyes that he ought more willingly to have shed, the two aged parents and five children, of which Jemmy was one, preparing for bed, which made him desire leave that he might sit up by the fire all night. But that request would by no means be granted him, so that poor Don Tomazo was constrained to unclothe and go to bed with the rest.

But in that comfortless place he was so far from finding any

sheets that he scarce found woollen enough to cover him from
the nipping cold. However, all things considered, the old man
was very friendly, for he laid the distressed Don Tomazo by one
of his brawny sides that smelt like hung beef; a kindness more
than ordinary, though it fell out to the unspeakable detriment of
the sadly tormented squire, for the warmth of his body had soon
summoned together multitudes of that creeping vermin, lice, the
common curse of the country, which finding the easy penetrable-
ness of the young squire's tender skin, and the sweetness of his
well-nourished blood, fell to their fresh viands with such an
eager appetite that the unhappy Don Tomazo, incessantly
tormented with the continual nippings of those hungry animals,
would be often starting up in his litter to throw off his shirt to
prevent those villainous insects from taking possession of the
folds of his under-linen, for which the old man as often rebuked
him.

But alas, it was impossible for the suffering Don Tomazo to
obey the checks of his surly moroseness while the sharpset
vermin were so busily employed upon his carcass, which it was as
natural for the rest to endure as it was to sleep. This restlessness
of Don Tomazo at length made the peevish cinque and quatre*
angry, so that at last he began to cry Don Tomazo was a subtle
carl and intended to be immodest with his daughter. Whereupon, in a grumbling tone, he commanded him to surcease his
cunning excuses and lie still, insomuch that the afflicted squire
was compelled to comply with his austere governor and to spend
the rest of the night in wishes for the slow-paced morning, which
had no sooner displayed her comfortable light but up he rises,
leaving the whole family asleep, designing to be gone forthwith,
and rather to expose himself to the mercy of the cold winds, the
severe weather, and the unknown passages of the rugged
mountains, than to the barbarous kindness of such a savage
entertainment for another night.

Thereupon, in order to his farther progress, he puts on his
boots and leads forth his horse, but going behind the house with
his steed in his hand (for to avoid the trouble of leading, he had
left his other courser at Jemmy's disposal as the reward of his
father's obligations), here fortune showed him one of her cursed
slippery tricks, which had like to have cost him his sweet life and put

an end to all his disconsolations. For, stepping by chance upon certain rotten boards covered with snow that lay over a deep well, the treacherous boards giving way, in dropped Don Tomazo, who had like to have drawn his horse also after him had not the bridle broke.

Well, it happened for the unfortunate squire that the water in the well was frozen to a considerable thickness, else you might have bid Don Tomazo goodnight by the name of Nicholas. But the ice putting a stop to his farther descent, he received no more hurt than a slight bruise by the fall. So oddly sometimes bad and good luck conjobble together. However, there he was forced to stand in a kind of cold little-ease* or Lobb's-pound*, being fallen much lower than was within his reach to get out again.

Now by that time he had remained there for some time, meditating upon his misfortune in chill-blood. Jemmy gets up and, perceiving his master gone, runs into the back side, where he finds the horse in a cold trance wondering what was become of the grass that used to grow in England, but could not imagine where Tomazo should be. In that amaze, he flies about to seek him, but not succeeding in his search, away he posts to Moffat.

In the meanwhile, the old man rises, who finding both his son and Don Tomazo absent, yet seeing their horses, could not conjecture what the De'el should be become of 'em. He waited for some hours with patience, expecting their return, but neither appearing, away goes he also to draw dry-foot after both. The old man proved a cunninger huntsman than the son, for he, tracing the footsteps which he observed in the snow, came directly to the well, where he found the unfortunate Don Tomazo who, espying the countenance of his supposed deliverer, invokes his aid and begs his assistance to help him out of his winter sweating-tub.

But Don Tomazo was extremely deceived in the humour of the churlish chuff,* for he, perceiving his prey in the snare, told the shivering squire that there were more words went to a bargain. 'You,' quoth he, 'would have deflowered my dear Moggie, and therefore you shall stay there a while to cool your courage. Nay farther,' quoth he, 'I am apt to believe that because I spoiled your sport, you have taken your revenge upon my son and made him away, so that until he be found, you are not like to stir.'

This was a sad morning lecture to poor Don Tomazo, who would have given all the shoes in his shop for a warm chimney corner, but there was no help for no remedy, for the old villain, full of mischief, leaving him to his soliloquies, returns to the house and there consults the hag his wife and his daughters, as ready as himself to exercise their cruelty upon poor Tomazo, well understanding by Jemmy's information that he had what they had been but little acquainted with, both silver and gold, about him. And therefore, having framed their design, they came to the well, let down a rope, and bid Tomazo to fasten it about him. To these glad tidings, as to a voice from Heaven, Don Tomazo cheerfully condescended, so that obeying such welcome orders, they presently drew him up. But he was no sooner come forth but the old caitiff was as yare* for his cash, who with a grim aspect threatened to stab him with his dirk,* a doleful sight God wot, if he did not fairly deliver all he had.

Thereupon, Don Tomazo, finding himself under the paws of an unavoidable violence, put his hands into a pocket that contained about three pound in silver, which the false old miscreant took. But not so contented, he further told Tomazo of the concealment of his gold, which he must either part with or with his life, and with that pulled him down by main force i'th' snow, menacing nothing less than downright murder if he did not speedily give it him.

Don Tomazo did by no means like this bitter breakfast. Loath he was to part with the life of his enterprise, and it was as sad a thing to think that he should take so much pains to travel into Scotland to be buried in a well. While he was in this peck of troubles, the wife and children, more merciful, prevailed with the old tyrant to spare his life, but to examine his clothes for the gold, which he soon found, and then fetching forth the despoiled Tomazo's horse, bid him begone, hoping in regard the ground was thick covered with snow, and Don Tomazo an absolute stranger in the country, that either he might fall into some hole and be starved, or else never be able to give any account of the place where he had been so courteously entertained. But Don Tomazo's better fortune so guided the horse, and the barbarism of the old ragamuffin had so imprinted all imaginable observations in Tomazo's memory, that they were never to be forgotten.

In this forlorn condition Don Tomazo, having wandered till some time before the next night, and about ten miles from the den of his grisly robber, happened to espy a small village, to which he rode with great joy. There the scene altered, and he found something of generosity in an ancient gentleman who was called the Laird of Corheid and owner of the village, to whom Don Tomazo, after he had made an apology for himself, gave an account of the old man's entertainment. Which being delivered by the dismantled squire in English, the Laird could scarce understand the meaning of his story, till by frequent repetition he better apprehended the matter and then gave credit to the relation, promising Don Tomazo withal that he would use him more kindly.

Upon which he bid the empty young gentleman welcome and commanded him to be as free as if he were at his father's house. Moreover, he assured the poor, disconsolate traveller that the next day he would send his warrant (for he was in commission of the peace) for the whole family which had been so barbarous to a stranger, which he performed accordingly, so that both the parents and all the children, together with Jemmy himself, were brought before him. There they met, to their sorrow, their injured guest, who charged the old man so home that he could not deny the fact, especially when, being searched, the joyful Don Tomazo's gold was found about him. Thereupon the old rogue, his son Jemmy and the daughter were all packed away to gaol.

By this time the good Laird of Corheid, being truly sensible of the heinous abuses that had been put upon the succourless Don Tomazo by this same crew of Scotch monsters, and also possessing a natural tenderness of heart, took such an affection to Don Tomazo that he requested him to remain in his house till he could more opportunely dispose of himself. Which kind and seasonable offer Don Tomazo was unwilling to refuse, especially finding the temper of that whole family so truly generous, so that he took the boldness to continue there near upon forty days, during which time he had so won the Laird's favour that he called Don Tomazo his son, and was often wont to take him, when he went avisiting, to the houses of several persons of quality, by whom he was so nobly and familiarly treated that it would be a foul ingratitude not to acknowledge their most obliging generosity.

Now was Don Tomazo, as it were, in a serene calm after a violent storm, living at ease and in plenty. He had seen himself revenged upon those violators of the laws of hospitality; he found his money all restored and his company acceptable to the chiefest in the province, which had inspired so much greatness into Don Tomazo's breast that he, according to the proverb, taking that for his country where he fared best, did not much care to quit his post. However, considering with himself, in the midst of his delights, that it would be a rudeness beneath the breeding he had shown to trespass upon the Laird's good nature beyond reason, he bethought himself that it was high time to take his leave, yet with a promise to return, for such was the Laird's obligation laid upon him, provided he could find no better quarters.

Whereupon he set forwards, being furnished with a letter of recommendation to a person of quality that lived about fifteen Scotch miles from the Laird's house, the most part of which way lay over the mountains. But now behold another jade's trick of that fickle whore that men call fortune. She had for forty days together given the exalted Don Tomazo her sweet milk, but now she resolves to kick down the pail, as if by checkering the accidents of his travels she intended betimes to teach him what he was to trust to, if he relied upon the mutability of her humour. For by that time Don Tomazo had rode about six of the forementioned miles, from a little cave between two rocks out leaped a brace of St Nicholas clerks,* who violently seizing the person of the squire, took away not only his gold and silver that had already been in so much jeopardy, but also his horse and clothes, stripping him to his very shirt, in lieu of which they gave him a piece of an old plaid, adding withal that that sort of clothing would make him as perfect a Scotchman as either of them. And thus, penniless, dismounted and naked, they left him to pilgrim it over the snowy mountains, without so much as directing him one step of his way.

You may now easily conjecture that this unfortunate youth had reason sufficient to condole the calamity of his condition. And indeed there was no person of pity that did not highly blame these rigorous proceedings of that hair-brained beldame fortune, but she made answer for herself that they could be no true-taught sons of hers that were not bred up in the school of affliction. Experience was not to be learned by living at a certain rate of content and plenty: it was the mixture of good and bad luck that was the mistress of knowledge. Quoth she: 'This young Gusman will be the better for these two robberies and this damned walk over the cursed rocks—as long as he lives. This is the way to try whether he have courage, whether he have patience, whether he have ingenuity.'

And so indeed it happened, for though at first the stripped and ransacked cavalier could not forbear lamenting the rashness of a journey that had brought him into so many almost intolerable misfortunes, yet resuming his natural courage, rather than return in that miserable condition to the good Laird (who would most certainly have clothed and entertained him as before), he resolved to march forward and to try, since he had no more to lose, how he might revenge himself by getting something from a people that had taken all from him—a task very difficult to be performed among the sons of poverty itself in a country as barren of riches as the mountains that disfigure it.

Full of these thoughts, Don Tomazo steers his course by accident to another Laird's house, whose title was the Laird of Crayback Bourn, to whom the rifled squire related his last misfortune only, omitting all the former passages, nor owning that he knew any person in the country, but only that he was travelling to Edinburgh, where he was in expectation of meeting with some friends.

This Laird's compassion was not much inferior to that of his first acquaintance, for when Don Tomazo had told him his story, he clad him with a suit of his son's clothes, civilly entertained him all night, and the next morning, after he had directed him the best way to Edinburgh, gave him also three pounds Scotch, which is five shillings sterling, to bear his charges.

From hence Don Tomazo walked on, till he came to the old town of Peebles, about ten miles from the last Laird's house and still in the same county, where it fell out that he met with the very persons that had so lately discharged him of the burden of his clothes and money. But though he kept 'em company and drank with 'em till he had spent half his small stock, their disguises were such as preserved them altogether from his knowledge, till it was too late to prosecute his revenge.

His tutoress Fortune had a mind to keep him fasting on

purpose, to put him upon trials of skill. She knew necessity and the lowness of his pocket would soon constrain him to summon his wits to a consultation for replenishment. Every fool can put the sweat of his tenants in his pocket; he's the darling of Fortune that carries his estate in his brains. She never forsakes the bold and daring. O brave wits, for by their prompt assistance Don Tomazo, now at a desperate pinch, had called to his remembrance a way what to do: not to laze under hedges; not to go whining from door to door to court penurious charity, but to cheat the crafty, out-knave the knave in grain; to whitewash boatles,* one of which is the sixth part of a penny, so as to make them pass currently for a certain Scotch piece of silver called a forty-penny piece, which amounts to twenty boatles in copper. Of these pieces Don Tomazo, by the help of some ingredients which he bought at Peebles, had got good store, which being by him vended for good, in a week's time put about five pounds in his pocket. And thus you see the wide world is no dangerous sea for one that can swim.

With this jolly recruit, Don Tomazo, now a Don indeed, returns to his friend the Laird of Corheid, to whom he related the manner of his being robbed the second time, which the good gentleman could hardly believe till Don Tomazo had described one of the persons most exactly well, and the other so near as could be possible. The first happened to be one of the Laird's tenants, who had often seen Tomazo, and knew of the gold and silver's being restored to him at the Laird's house, the temptation of which booty prompted him to act a crime which he had never been guilty of before. But that lame confession served neither his nor his companion's turn, for being both apprehended, they were both sent to gaol, companions in their punishment as they had been associates in the crime.

Which put Don Tomazo into some apprehension of his own danger, fearing lest his condition might be the same, should he linger much longer near the places where he had so lately been sowing his counterfeit pieces. But Fortune, that desired his improvement only, not his ruin, found out a way to deliver him. For about two nights after, as the Laird was sitting by the fire with his family and Don Tomazo, there arose a discourse concerning the misfortunes of Don Tomazo, at which the Laird fell into a rapture of admiration how miraculously Heaven had delivered the unfortunate stranger, saying very devoutly withal that surely providence had reserved him to be an instrument of some great work or other. And therefore, lest the noise of Don Tomazo's gold and silver might prove a bait for others to destroy this precious instrument, he resolved the next morning to go for Edinburgh to look after the prosecution of the prisoners and to take Don Tomazo along with him, as indeed the proceedings of justice required.

Now the road to Edinburgh lay through a village called Perkessen, where Don Tomazo had been very busy in vending his forty-penny pieces. So that as he passed through the town, the person who had exchanged the greatest part espying him, ran to stop his horse, at which the Laird, being surprised, demanded of the fellow whether he intended to rob him. 'No,' said he, 'but I want some money which that person,' pointing to Tomazo, 'cheated me of about five days since.'

But the Laird had too good an opinion of his son Don Tomazo to give credit to his story, but rather believed that the noise of his gold, being spread over the country, had set the people agog to be hanged for it. So that the Laird, putting Don Tomazo before him, without taking any further notice of the villager's complaint, rode on, by which means Don Tomazo 'scaped a scouring and got clear to Edinburgh with his true friend the good Laird, who carried him to one of the judges to give in his testimony against the prisoners. But Don Tomazo, being under age, could not be admitted as evidence against them, and so they were all acquitted.

At Edinburgh, Don Tomazo accidentally met with certain English gentlemen whose curiosity had led them to travel into those parts. These gentlemen knew Don Tomazo, to whom he related the occasion of his coming thither, as also how he had been treated, as well by the Laird in particular as others. He also gave them an account of his misfortunes and deliverances, which as they were stories pleasing to the ear, induced them to take Don Tomazo for a companion and to make the same provision for him as for themselves. After which they went with Don Tomazo to wait upon the Laird to give him thanks for the great favours he had shown their countryman, which piece of

complaisance was so grateful to the Laird that, after he had
drunk a bottle or two in the company, with tears in his eyes (for
such was his affection to his new son) he took his leave of
Tomazo in particular and then of the rest of the gentlemen.
Where note that it is not for clowns and men of sullen tempers,
but for persons of acute compliance and airy behaviour to be
gusmans.

With these gentlemen, Tomazo travelled through diverse parts
of Scotland, which proved a very pleasant journey, in regard
those gentlemen had letters of credit to most persons of quality in
the country, by whom they were for the most part very nobly
entertained with good music and other rarities. Nay, in some
parts their splendid equipage produced such credit of itself,
without their letters, that some gentlemen of the country would
stand at the back of a chair waiting while they sat at dinner, using
no less than the title of lord to the meanest of them, though they
endeavoured as much as in them lay to persuade them to the
contrary.

Thus, having travelled almost through the whole country and
meeting nothing worthy observation, the gentlemen faced about
homewards, when coming to a town called Dunfrieze,* upon the
borders of England, they concluded there to rest for a week or so,
in which time they became acquainted with several of the
inhabitants of the place, with whom they used to drink smartly.
One day among the rest, as they were merry at a tavern, an old
woman came into the room to beg a glass of wine, and in
particular of Don Tomazo, who for that very reason refused to
give her any, unwilling to assume a pre-eminence in the company
of friends to whom he was so much beholding. At which the
woman went away, refusing to take wine from any other person,
but threatening Don Tomazo with most dreadful misfortunes
and an immediate curse that should attend him, which the
gentlemen little regarding, drank on to that excess that very few,
if one, went home sober.

That night, Don Tomazo was not in a condition, but the next
morning he went to look after his horse, which he found in such
a posture as amazed him, for his body was drawn up in such a
strange manner that his head and his four feet were all in a
huddle together. Besides this, the colour of his hair was altered,

and a thick white foam bedaubed his chaps from one side to the other. This, putting Don Tomazo in mind of the woman's threats the night before, made him suspect her for a witch. Which he found upon enquiry had been the hard opinion of her neighbours for many years, upon which information Don Tomazo, possessed with immediate revenge, or rather to draw blood of her, according as his nurse had taught him, went to the old woman's house where he found her cutting of wood.

So soon as she saw him, it seemed to Tomazo that the anticness* of her behaviour was such as showed her jealous of Tomazo's design in coming to visit her, who while she discoursed him smoothly and calmly enough, waited for nothing but an opportunity to surprise her. At length, perceiving she had got a great stick in her hand that she could not easily cleave, Don Tomazo very officiously desires her to give him the bill and to hold one end of the stick, to which she readily consenting, Don Tomazo, having by some discourse or other obliged her to look another way, with a home stroke cut off one of her thumbs, and so leaving her to curse and ban him to the Devil, went immediately to the stable, where he found his horse upon his legs in decent order and feeding as well as if nothing had ever ailed him.

This accident of the witch, if such she were, exalted Don Tomazo to a very high pitch, as believing he was or should be some great hero. 'For,' quoth he, 'Ulysses was beloved by a witch, and Aeneas was beloved by a witch, St George was charmed by a witch, and Don Tomazo was beloved by a witch.' So that had he given her wine, and not cut off her thumb, who knows what happiness had been prepared for him? But having cut off her thumb, she withdrew her affections from him and was so far from advancing his fortunes that she complained to the magistrates of the town of the loss of her joint, for which she accused the English lad, as she called him. Whereupon the English lad was sent for and, upon a full examination of the matter, committed to prison. For indeed he owned the fact and upon what occasion he did it, but could not make out by any sort of reason why he should assume the doing of justice to himself.

The rest of the gentlemen offered to be his bail, but nothing would serve but one of Tomazo's thumbs, which the magistrate protested should be cut off and given to the old woman to burn before his face. Which rigorous sentence you may be sure did not a little trouble Don Tomazo. But Fortune, who knew he had more occasion for his thumb than the old woman, was for none of those Mosaical executions, so that what by her assistance and the gentlemen's industry, a rope was conveyed to Don Tomazo, by means whereof he made his escape out of the gaol without paying his fees, and so being privately conveyed out of town to a place where his horse stood ready, he received directions to post with all speed to Carlisle and there to stay at an inn appointed till the company came to him. Which, by the good conduct of Fortune and with no small hazard, he accomplished, being pursued almost to the walls of the city. About a week after arrived his companions, who being suspected to have been privy to Tomazo's escape, were detained by the magistrate till they had paid their ten crowns apiece to the poor of the town, which amounted to a considerable sum, there being five in number. These gentlemen, being come to Carlisle, found there their beloved Tomazo, for which they were not a little joyful, their kindness to him being nothing inferior to the Laird of Corheid's.

From Carlisle they set forward for London with all speed, where in a little time being safely arrived, the company separated and Don Tomazo was left to himself, who though so near his parents, was almost in as bad a condition as at his first entrance into Scotland. But necessity prompting him to some serious resolution, the story of the prodigal son took possession of his pate, and he began to study how to be reconciled to his father—a kind office which was soon accomplished by the intercession of a particular favourite of his father's, who so far prevailed that Tomazo, after a hearty sorrow and deep contrition for his crime, was again admitted into his father's favour, both expecting various effects of the past ramble: the father believing that the son, now well read in the lectures of necessity, would be more careful how he plunged himself into the same exigencies again, and the son presuming that the father, now knowing what it was to want a living child, would be more tender of provoking him for the future—in both which conjectures both were mistaken.

As for Tomazo (for while he is under his father's roof we must un-Don him) for about half a year he continued very patiently within the bounds of modesty. But the continued austerity of his father, together with certain impressions that love had made in his heart, soon put his discontents into an uproar and quite altered that composure of mind which had given such life to their hopes of his becoming a new creature. The Don began to close again with Tomazo, and all his passions being in a ferment, so alarmed his father that he was forced to double his guards. However, notwithstanding all the father's diligence and correction, the son, having laid aside all thoughts of reformation and forgotten all his vows and protestations of penitence, betook himself so far to his former more natural, and consequently more pleasing, extravagancies. So that the old man, no longer able to endure the bad examples which he gave in his family, one day in the garden took an occasion to acquaint Tomazo that he must depart those walls.

This sentence sounded very harshly in Tomazo's ears, and therefore duly weighing the misery of an eloignment* from his beloved mistress, a near neighbour, the great dangers he had escaped in Scotland, his present ease, and the apparent extremities he should be exposed to by the casualty of new travels, he began to intercede with his father, whose good nature at that time was easily prevailed with to have some further patience, provided his son would keep up to his promises of mortification. But Tomazo, being engaged in an amour with a loving female that was the sole and first mistress of his affections, had not the power to perform his engagements, and therefore found out a ready way to unravel all his father's hopes.

This mistress of his was daughter to a neighbouring gentleman, in her thirteenth year, of no great fortune more than what nature and art in point of education had accomplished her withal, which for the most part are the chief allurements of youth, especially such as are not capable of taking a prospect of their future well-being. Between these two children, as I may safely say, for Tomazo was not then above fourteen years of age, there was an amorous intrigue so cunningly managed as could hardly be expected from such early lovers. To which purpose, the damsel, who had a father as severe in all particulars as Tomazo's, had ordered our meetings in the night, to the end she might steal her enjoyments when the old gentleman thought her most secure —that is, in English, fast asleep.

Tomazo's condition was the same, so that for several nights they entertained each other with all the amorous caresses that an innocent and harmless converse could afford. But it so fell out that Tomazo was unfortunately suspected by his father, whose Argus eyes kept a continual watch upon him, even to that degree of strictness that nothing would serve but that Tomazo's quarters must be removed to a chamber, the passage to which lay through his father's, so that it was almost impossible for Tomazo to meet his mistress that night, as by solemn promise, sacred among lovers, he had engaged himself to do.

But love, that has more ways to the wood than one, furnished him with an expedient, for Tomazo, considering the vast damage it might be to him to disappoint a lady that ventured all for his sake, resolved to make the attempt, though it were through his father's chamber. With this resolution of a deeply smitten gallant, up he rises, puts on his clothes, and laying in his place a periwig and a block, with the face of the block turned to the wall and carefully healed up for fear of catching cold, he takes a sheet along with him and adventures cross the old gentleman's chamber, who being more wakeful than Tomazo expected, overheard him, but yet let him alone, well knowing the door to be fast and the keys of all the house to be safe by his bedside.

Tomazo understood all that before, and therefore, not to put himself upon vain and fruitless delays, he takes his napkin and his short stick, utensils that he had ready fixed, goes to the window and, having with much art but no noise drawn the bar, he fastens his sheet, lets himself down into the garden and thence, with no less speed than joy, repairs to his mistress, whose patience was almost tired with waiting for his company, which she had scarce enjoyed above two hours but break of daylight forced them to retire.

But before that time, Tomazo's father, having heard something trip through his chamber, concluded that it was his gracious son, but because he was almost assured that he could find no way out of the house, he therefore expected his immediate return, which not being made, the old gentleman, mistrusting some treachery in his own sense of hearing, consulted his wife. She was of the same opinion: that it was impossible for Tomazo to get out of the house, and therefore undertook to persuade her husband that Tomazo was returned to his chamber.

However, the old gentleman, not being satisfied, gets up and, taking a candle, examines the bed where, finding a head with hair that lay very snug and quiet in a true sleeping posture, he could not imagine but that slipstring was fast in Morpheus' chains, who was then indeed in the fetters of his mistress's arms. But jealousy and age, being generally such inseparable companions, it would not out of the old gentleman's pericranium but that either some hobgoblin or some thief had been visiting the secrets of his house, and therefore resolving to be further satisfied, once more up he takes the candle, down stairs he rumbles and examines all the doors. But finding all fast, in a pelting chafe to be put thus to dance about i'th' cold in his shirt, up he comes again when lo, as he ascended, he spied a pittance of the sheet hanging within the window, whither he marched immediately and, observing the posture of the contrivance, concluded there was a robbery in the case.

Thereupon the old gentleman calls up his servants and bid 'em search the house, who, finding all things in due decorum, brought in an absolute ignoramus, to the great amazement of the master and themselves. In which astonishment he returns to his warm wife and relates the story to her. She presently called 'em all fools, and bid 'em call up Tomazo, who there was no question to be made would soon unfold the mystery. Thereupon one of the maids was sent to wake him, who, receiving no answer, began to jog the block, believing it to have been the drowsy body of her master's son; which she did so rudely that the block turning, the black physiognomy of the graven image stared her full i'th' countenance. Which so terrified the maid that she ran to her master, crying out that Tomazo was murdered, for he looked black i'th' face.

Upon which the master and mistress both rose and went into Tomazo's chamber, where upon a true examination of the whole matter, they discovered the plot, and so leaving the wooden idol in the same posture as it lay when the maid first found it, they went to bed in expectation of Tomazo's return, who soon after made his silent entry, and having rectified the disorders of the window, stole barefoot through his father's chamber, who heard him well enough, into his own, and with much inward satisfaction for the purloined pleasures he had had, went to supply his broken rest, not dreaming he was discovered, in regard he found all things as he left them.

But woe is me, before Tomazo was well settled in his repose, the father, no longer able to conceal his passion, came to correct the amorous night-walker. Tomazo, by the cloud upon his father's brows perceiving the storm coming, pleaded hard for mercy, beseeching his father to consider that the innocency of his years could not draw him forth to any more than only a merry-making with honest and civil persons, some of whom he well knew. But that would not qualify the incensed old gentleman, who at first laid on very smartly, but observing no returns of childish howling, but rather a manly suffering and passive submission to paternal authority, he forbore any further schoolboy's chastisement, which he saw was but thrown away upon one that so little regarded it, and upon Tomazo's further entreaty came to a capitulation, which produced these articles of agreement: that the next fault that Tomazo did commit, he should be thrust out of doors, never more to see his father's face again.

This was a doleful sentence, yet but a flea bite to the irresistible commands of love. An article with a father was not to stand in competition with a promise made to a mistress. And the Devil would have it that he had made one to meet her again the night following in the same place. So that, after the mode of princes, Tomazo soon found a flaw i'th' treaty and was resolved to venture a breach, though he lost the reversion of all his father's dominions.

Thereupon, being informed, his father, who looked upon him as a Carthaginian of no faith, was resolved to lock him into his chamber the next night. By way of prevention, love inspired Tomazo to go in the daytime and pluck up one of the boards under his own bed, which gave him free passage into a cellar and so through a window as before. That done, the hopes of enjoying his mistress made Don Tomazo very pleasant the rest of the day, having made so fair a progress already, which gave his father no less cause to suspect that he had some notable stratagem in his pate that made his heart so light, and therefore that night he resolved to watch Tomazo's motion himself.

Which being come, and the usual hour having summoned the family to bed, Tomazo was locked into his room where, after he had made a seeming preparation to go to bed, he fell to work, and first having removed the board, he let down his clothes with a line, the passage not being otherwise wide enough for his body. Then he descended himself like an angel from the roof of a playhouse, and thinking himself as secure as a thief in a mill. But no sooner was he in the cellar but at the same moment his father was in the room, who immediately seizing the line, drew back all Tomazo's clothes and left him to meditate i'th' cold cellar all night in his shirt, having nothing to keep him warm but the heat of his desire—a sort of practice of piety which no way agreed with Tomazo's temper.

These disappointments did but serve to heighten Tomazo's resolutions, whose fires, meeting with reciprocal and equal flames, burnt with that ardent heat that the least separation from the object of his love was a gash that wounded to the heart, not to be endured. Love, of itself crafty and subtle enough, is a mere Devil in a young gusman, lawless as an Irish Tory, as impatient as Ajax and as choleric as Hector. So that had not his modesty argued hard against it, he had ventured as he was in his shirt to show himself a punctual lover to a most faithful Hero, who had spent all the night in waiting and moaning and moaning and waiting for her dear Leander, till the telltale sun began to peep into her amorous sanctuary. At what time, despairing, sighing, and accusing the infidelity of her young gallant, she retired to her broken rest, while on the other side the old gentleman came, not only to release his languishing prisoner, but also to discharge him without fees out of his house according to the conditions of the treaty so lately concluded. Which, as soon as he was apparelled, was absolutely performed, and poor peel-garlick* turned adrift into the wide world in a worse condition than when he travelled for Scotland, for then he had the blessings of money, now not a boatle in his pocket.

It was now high time to consider what course to steer. The last disappointment of his mistress had so confounded him in his amours that he had not the face to appear in his mistress's sight. He thought it a crime so far beyond forgiveness that he durst not crave it. And therefore, giving her over for lost (for he was yet but in his love-primer and had not yet learned those lessons of cajoling tender damsels which afterwards he became a Doctor in) he abandoned all his amorous thoughts and rather chose the retirement of a haycock the remaining part of that day, there to condole his destiny.

So soon as it was night, with the beasts of prey, to avoid his discovery, he began his rambles, steering directly for London, once more to try his father's credit, which proved not so hidebound as the old gentleman intended, who, suspecting that Tomazo would make bold with it as he had formerly done, had by way of prevention fairly warned all his correspondents not to pay any money upon his account without a warrant under his own hand.

Now was Tomazo, with a slender stock of ninepence, arrived at England's metropolis, where he was hard put to it to find a lodging. However, he ventured courageously into a public house and, having refreshed himself with a moderate supper, he calls for pen, ink and paper, and then drawing a letter of his father's out of his pocket, he did most exactly counterfeit the old gentleman's hand to a person of his acquaintance for thirty pound, who not at all suspecting the note, but extremely jealous of the messenger, of whom he had had some former experience, was at a wicked nonplus what to do about the delivery of the money.

At length, rather than run the risk of disobliging Tomazo's father, the politic citizen found out an expedient, which was that he would send his servant and the money with Tomazo to his father, to which Tomazo cheerfully agreed. So the money was immediately delivered to the servant, with positive orders not to part with his treasure to any person living but Tomazo's father. With these cautions, the knight of the burning pestle* and Tomazo set forward toward his father's forbidden gates. Upon the way Tomazo, full of invention, often courted his companion with the temptation of drink, a bait that would not take with a zealous writer of shorthand,* so jealous pated that when he came to a house upon the road where he had a mind to rest himself, he delivered his charge to the master of the house to secure it while he took a nap.

Tomazo, wholly intent upon his prey, and watching all

opportunities with the vigilance of a tiger, was not a little troubled at this reserved wariness of the coy purse-bearer. But such was Tomazo's patience that he stifled all his discontents and still beheld his companion with the careless glances of a merry countenance.

After some hours of slumber and repose, Tomazo and his cautious fellow-traveller set forward again, but going over a heath, they met with several persons that informed them that if they went such a road they would be certainly robbed, as they themselves had been but just before. Which so alarmed the cuckoo-brained prentice, who was ordered to deliver his money to none but Tomazo's father, that to prevent a compulsion to breach of trust he examined Tomazo what private ways there were that led to his father's house.

Blessed Mercury soon inspired Tomazo, so that he presently called to mind a solitary byway through long grass and corn, which proved so tiresome that the careful Londoner, to ease himself in some measure of his burden, believing that he could deal well enough with Tomazo, most inauspiciously desired Tomazo to relieve his weary arms. Tomazo most affectionately embraced both the opportunity and the bag, so that from that time they carried it by turns, to the great but different comfort of each other.

About eleven a clock at night (for so eager was the faithful trustee to be at his journey's end) it came to young Iscariot's turn to bear the sacred load, who had no sooner lodged it next his heart but Judas' own Devil possessed him, and presently taught him a trick that Monsieur Blunderbuss should be no more troubled with his burden. For Tomazo, passing by a heap of stones, privately but with a dextrous sleight of hand, takes up a good big brickbat and lays the adored Mammon in its place. Soon after, Tomazo being to go over a bridge, makes a false step as if he had been near a fall, and drops the stone into the river, which the city dromedary hearing, demanded what it was.

' 'Tis the money,' replied Tomazo, 'pox take it,' quoth he, 'let it go and be hanged. Better let the money fall than suffer myself to be soused at this time a night.' The poor seagull* was in such a dismal consternation at the news, so that his senses were just packing up their awls to be gone from a place where they prophesied that they should be but very rudely entertained by the passion of the master upon his booby's return, insomuch that Tomazo, who all the while laughed in his sleeve, would have given something to have had his picture as he then looked.

In this amazement, trusty Tom Fool would have persuaded Tomazo to have put off his clothes and to have gone into the water to make search for the money, which Tomazo, to avoid all suspicion, willingly offered to do, but withal told Nickapoop that it would be but a vain attempt without the help of a candle. So that he easily persuaded the tame dottrell,* now as submissive as a pumped bailiff, to stay by the bridge while he went back to certain houses about half a mile off to get a light.

In his way, Tomazo had recovered and secured his money, and so making forward to the houses, called up the people, told them the misfortune of young Nicodemus, desired their assistance, and sent them all for a company of fools to the bridge, where while they were poking and groping and treading a mortar i'th' water with their bare feet, Tomazo having traversed his ground and taken another road, had made a fair step in his way back to London, leaving Tom Totty to con the short lesson of experience which he had set him.

So far Tomazo had reason to applaud his own ingenuity. But Fortune would have her turns and her changes, to show him he was yet but a young gusman, and that there were others superior to him, whose art was not to be learnt by rules of accidence or grammar, but by a suffering experience. For he had no sooner secured himself in the city but he fell into the company of certain town bullies, who carried Tomazo to Speiring's ordinary,* where having easily allured the young squire into play, they soon reduced the thirty pound, for which he had taken so much pains, and which he looked upon as one of the trophies of his mercurial stratagems, to twenty shillings, to the great grief of Tomazo who, to add to his afflictions, had received information that his father was also in pursuit of him.

For the dejected counter-scrubber, perceiving as well by the vain search that the people had made, as by the not returning of Tomazo, that the serpent had been too crafty for him, with a heavy heart jogged on to the old gentleman's house and there told the uncomfortable story, not daring to venture his master's displeasure, though there were not above two inches difference in the depth of their understanding, only the master trusted the man and the man trusted Tomazo.

Upon this alarm, Tomazo makes down for Gravesend with all speed, where he was informed that several ships lay bound for the Straits, whither Tomazo resolved to venture, rather than fall again under the jurisdiction of his father. There it was that Tomazo, to whom Fortune was never more kind than when she had emptied his pocket, while he was treating with one of the captains for his passage to Cadiz, met with two of the gentlemen with whom he had travelled in Scotland, bound in the same ship for the same place.

To those gentlemen, as to his confidants, he made known his condition and related all that had befallen him since the time that they parted at London. True it is that the stories of his extravagance were not so pleasing to their more serious humours; however, for old acquaintance sake, they promised to take such care of Tomazo, provided he would be governed, that while he continued with them he should want nothing that was convenient for him (a kindness easily within their power, as being the sons of persons of quality and heirs to fair estates), and thus far Tomazo had Greymolkin's luck,* still to fall upon his legs.

While the ship was under sail, the two gentlemen and Tomazo had several consultations how to shape their travels after they came ashore, in order whereunto it was agreed that they should travel all Spain first, and after that set sail for Egypt, from whence they would visit India, China, Tartary and so through Muscovy and Germany home into England again. Full of these designed rambles, they arrived at Cadiz, from whence they made haste to Madrid, where they had not been above four days but one of the gentlemen happened to kill a Spanish count, which occasioned an immediate and diligent enquiry after all persons that had been in his company.

Thereupon, the gentlemen, upon notice of the search given them by a blackamoor maid that served in the house where they lived, stole away afoot through all the byways of the country, shaping their course for Ligorn and leaving miserable Tomazo behind without either money or credit, who in two days after was apprehended and in that blessed condition committed to gaol.

There he found several other English people, whose crimes were only their acquaintance with the gentleman that had killed the count, which gentleman's name (the sequel of the story so requiring) is to be henceforward Don Pedro Perguelio. But such was the kindness of the Spanish justice that, when the search was over, all the prisoners were brought before the court, where nothing appearing against them, they were all discharged. Had not Tomazo had a wonderful love for the light of the sun, it had been all one for him to have confessed the fact and been hanged, as to starve for want of mouldy crusts: such were the violent persecutions of a hungry stomach, under which Tomazo pined and wasted at that time. But, if it had not been for these blessed butts, of which you shall meet with anow before the story concludes, poor Tomazo had been half worm-eaten by this.

But then, I say, it so fell out one day, as Tomazo was walking upon the parade among the soldiers, for his inclinations were always martial, a certain captain, whose name was Don Pedro del Viejo Castello, perceiving Tomazo, by his habit, to be a foreigner, asked him his country, to which Tomazo replied of England. For which, the captain liking him much the better, persuaded him to list himself in his company, which lay then at Puerto Ferrara, promising him due payment of his wages, which came to three halfpence a day, but withal by his deportment giving Tomazo to understand that there might be some hopes of advance and better usage for an Englishman than for the riffraff of the country.

The offer, considering the nick of time, was as welcome to Tomazo as rain to the parched earth, he having been a stranger to all sort of sustenance for some time. So that now, being advanced on a sudden from the grave to be a gentleman soldier, he again resumes his forsaken title of Don, and marches away in state to his new quarters at Puerto Ferrara. There he lived about three quarters of a year upon his forementioned allowance and the augmentation of a pound of bread a day, at the end of which term the garrison was in a most violent manner besieged by the Portugueses, with whom the besieged had many encounters, in one of which the colonel of Tomazo's regiment being killed, Don Pedro del Viejo Castello succeeded him in the employment, who, not forgetting Don Tomazo in his advancement, whose courage and behaviour had very much won his heart, took such a special care of him that he raised his pay from three halfpence to four pence, and after that, for some works of supererogation that Don Tomazo performed, from four pence to eight pence a day.

About which time the besiegers drew off, leaving all their trenches in good order, and retreated home for some time, which gave the town both leisure and opportunity to recruit. During this calm, the rest of the soldiers, who had recovered their spirits, envying Don Tomazo's prosperity and the great esteem which his colonel had for him, entered into cabals and consultations among themselves to contrive his ruin. But finding no success in their Spanish plots, a brace of the conspirators undertook to attack him by main force, and in pursuance of their design, one evening, at the turning of a corner, set upon him with that violence that Don Tomazo was very severely wounded. But having recovered himself, he drew forth a pistol and shot one of his assailors, who soon after died of his hurts. And while he was in pursuit of the other, a corporal came in to his assistance, who took the other and secured him upon the guard. Nevertheless, upon the death of the first aggressor, Don Tomazo was tried by a council of war, where, upon a full examination of the fact, Don Tomazo was acquitted with great applause and the other assailant that was taken both degraded and cashiered.

This exploit made Don Tomazo more famous than before, and more esteemed and redoubted in the garrison. So that when the enemies returned again and renewed their attacks upon the town with that fury that the inhabitants began to be apprehensive of the loss of the place, several of the better sort delivered their jewels to a very considerable value to the custody of Don Tomazo, the better to secure 'em upon the surrender of the town. Which [being] no longer, after several rude assaults, able to hold out, yielded upon honourable conditions, and so the Spanish garrison marched forth, and as one of the number, Don Tomazo, who now possessed of so fair a booty, and knowing the danger of delays, went to his colonel for a passport.

The colonel, unwilling to part with Tomazo, promised to advance him to a commission and to make his fortune, provided he would stay in his service. But Tomazo, who had an unknown fortune within the compass of his breeches, gave those pressing arguments for his departure to his colonel and pressed him so home that at length, vanquished by importunity, the colonel granted him his pass, by virtue of which Don Tomazo posted away for Ligorn as fast as his legs would carry him, and there embarked for Scanderoon, whither, he was informed, some English gentlemen had taken shipping about fourteen days before, with a resolution to visit Grand Cairo.

When he came to Scanderoon, upon enquiry, by all descriptions he guessed them to be the persons that had left him to his shifts at Madrid, which was the reason he was not very solicitous to follow them. At Scanderoon, therefore, he stayed till, upon the sale of some of his jewels to a Jew that was bound for Ligorn, he was informed by his landlady, an Englishwoman, that there was an express come with orders to apprehend him. For the Jew, coming to Ligorn, presently offers his new purchase to sale and, as the Devil and ill luck would have it, to a merchant nearly related to the very person from whom Don Tomazo had received them, who had also particular order from his relation to seize all such persons as should expose any such sort of jewels to sale, of which he had sent a particular description.

So that the Jew, being questioned about the jewels, informs against his chapman, and discovers where he was. Thereupon Don Tomazo thought it high time to shift his quarters, and posts away with all imaginable speed for Grand Cairo, where if a man do but alter his habit, 'tis impossible to find him out. To which purpose he puts on the disguise of a Turk, and in that dress one day met with his old fellow-traveller Don Pedro Perguelio, who admired to find Don Tomazo in such a Mahometan garb, but being acquainted in few words with the occasion, he received ample satisfaction, more especially when Don Tomazo farther told him that at that distance from his country he could, in that heathenish city, command a thousand pound—which was at that time no rodomontado,* in regard the jewels were worth above four times the value.

Certainly there can be no greater pleasure in this world than for one distressed gusman to meet another of the same order, flush in the trophies of successful project, gusmans being the only relic of the golden age that have all things in common, so that if one has it, the rest never want. So that it is but reason that the purses of fools should pay tribute for the maintenance of such a noble generosity.

Don Pedro was upon his last legs, when the happy accident to meet a member of the fraternity so richly laden made his heart dance in his breast without a violin. On the other side, Don Tomazo understood that it had not been so much the ill-husbandry of Don Pedro which had brought him so low, but a generous charity to two English gentlemen his comrades, who died there of the plague, the expenses of whose sickness, together with their funeral charges, had exhausted him to a very small remainder. So that as if the two deceased gentlemen had left Don Pedro the executor of their gratitude, from thence forward, Don Pedro and Don Tomazo entered into an inviolable league as well offensive as defensive, insomuch that though they were two bodies, there were the same thoughts and the same mind in both, and a united force now managed all their intrigues.

Grand Cairo is a city famous for its situation and the variety of pleasures it affords all persons so well able to purchase 'em as then Don Tomazo was, who resolving to know the difference between three halfpence a day and the splendour of unlimited plenty, concluded with his friend to debar themselves of no freedom or recreation which money could command in the greatest mart of the world. But as the sea itself would dry up without the continual supply of swelling rivers, so it was impossible for Tomazo's unreplenished bag, had it been as deep as Virgil's passage to Hell, to answer the expectations of a brace of scattergoods that thought it would never be evening. Till at length, their inconsiderate profuseness having reduced their lean bank to the low ebb of not above a hundred and fifty pounds, repentance stepped in and put them in mind of the calamities of poverty: a very unsuccessful remedy to cure the surfeits of excess among the pitiless adorers of Mahomet.

Thereupon they began to think of a new ramble and understanding that there was a caravan of 800 passengers ready to depart for India, both the Dons agreed to make a part of the company. But the season of the year for passing the sandy deserts proving more tempestuous than usually, gave them leisure enough to spend a hundred and twenty pound out of their low stock (for the curses of the credulous Portugueses had by this time taken their desired effect), so that they, perceiving no more than thirty pound remaining, altered both their resolutions and their habits and embarked from Scanderoon to Genoa, where they continued fourteen months, to the total consumption of all the Portugal booty.

Then it was that necessity put Don Tomazo to employ the talents of his youth, to which purpose he made love to a Genoese widow, over whose affections in a short time he had obtained a conquest that very fairly answered both his own and his friend's expectations. But having made that post too warm by debauching the woman, getting her with child, and wasting her fortunes, they departed incognito in an English man of war that brought them safe to Cadiz, where they behaved themselves so well that the merchants gave them daily invitations and were very free in all manner of accommodations

But one day among the rest, Don Tomazo, to retaliate the kindnesses they had both received (for true gusmans never mind morality), proposed to his friend Don Pedro a design which, had it taken effect, would have made them masters of a new fortune to the value of above five hundred pound. But it so happened that as they were walking upon the beach in a deep consultation about the most compendious and effectual way to proceed in their attempt, not minding their way, they were rambled about a league from the town, where they were overtaken by three English gentlemen, who were in pursuit of eight land pirates for a robbery and murder they had committed the night before upon the person of Thomas Lucie Esq.

These gentlemen requested their assistance, which they readily promised, and joined in the pursuit. After a chase of four hours they found one of the criminals sitting upon a sand-hill, who pretended himself half dead. This crafty devil sat there as a decoy, having planted his other seven confederates under the sand, whence they were all ready to rise with pistols and stilettos if occasion required, as indeed it most unfortunately fell out. For the gentlemen eagerly falling to search and examine the single pickaroon, he presently gave the watchword to the rest, who presently rising from their ambuscado, fell upon the gentlemen, not a little surprised at their number and their instruments of death, with that violent fury that one of them was killed outright, having received near twenty stabs with a stiletto, and the other two so wounded that they were left for dead.

Tomazo was shot in the back and shoulder and Don Pedro pricked in five or six places with a Spanish tuck* and both conveyed by the victors among the great sand-hills. The other two, who were left for dead, made such hideous outcries through the extremity of their pain that a Spaniard, fishing not far from the shore, came and took them into his boat.

Don Tomazo and Don Pedro had the good luck to taste of the freebooters' mercy, who very carefully dressed their wounds, as if natural instinct had prompted them to be kind to persons who lived upon the spoil as they did, and when they were in a hopeful way of recovery, persuaded them to enter in their society and to run the risks of their fortune, which there was a necessity for the two Dons seemingly to condescend to. Nor was it long after the completing of their cures before those sons of rapine had cut them out an employment. For those miscreants, hearing of a parcel of merchants that were to pass by their territories, set the two Dons to guard a pass upon the road to Madrid, which was convenient for an escape if need required, while the master rogues, having met with the unfortunate merchants, robbed them of their goods and money to the value of six thousand pounds sterling, of which they gave a reasonable proportion, according to the justice of thieves one among another, promising that the next time they should be both equally concerned.

From thence they made to their sanctuary among the sand-hills, a place which did not afford those delights to the English gallants that their hearts panted after when their pockets were full. Whereupon Don Tomazo and Don Pedro agreed to make their escape in the night, which an odd accident much facilitated to their advantage. For one night among the rest, which proved darker than ordinary, one of the pickaroons being upon the watch, certain flashes of combustible meteors appearing among the sand hills so terrified the guilty sentinel that he awakened his companions, who believing the country was risen upon 'em, and hearing Don Tomazo and Don Pedro affirm withal that they had heard the voices of strange people, put the villainous crew into such a consternation that, for their better security, they concluded to march off several ways by couples, having appointed a rendezvous when the danger was over.

The two Dons, keeping together, steered directly for Cadiz, being followed by two more of the gang aloof off. Upon the way they met with two of their old acquaintance in the town, with whom they presently agreed to pillage the two pickaroons that came behind, which they did, leaving them sorely maimed and beaten upon the place, and so with light hearts and heavy purses continued their journey to Cadiz, where being arrived, they were entertained with great joy by their former correspondents.

Being thus got together among their friends, the main discourse of the company was about two English gentlemen that had been most barbarously used by eight thieves, and of two other Englishmen that were gone away with the robbers. Thereupon Don Tomazo, having first made enquiry how the gentlemen did, and understanding they were safe and well, began to relate the whole story, confessing himself and Don Pedro to be the two lost sheep, and after that gave them an account of the last robbery. Which happened not a little to their disadvantage, for one of the merchants that had been robbed, being then in company, spared not to bellow forth his losses and his usage, insomuch that the two Dons, being conscious that they had about them some of the goods which the merchant had described, and unwilling to run the risk of a discovery, thought it very conducing to their future safety to refund what the merchant laid claim to and to put the rest into the hands of the magistrates, who promised them an ample recompense for their fidelity, but were never so good as their words. Which cost one of the Spanish merchants, by way of revenge, a cornuting,* Don Tomazo having entered into a league of familiarity with his wife to the production of a very comfortable subsistence for himself and his friend while they continued in the town.

At length, perceiving no more good to be done there, and finding several ships bound for England, they embarked for the land of their nativity in one which, by the master's ill conduct, had the ill fortune to be cast away, so that there had been an end of all the ship's company and the two young gusmans had been coffined in some sea monster's belly had not a Dutch vessel been so kind as to send out their boat and save all the men, whom they carried along with them to Amsterdam, a place to which Don Tomazo and Don Pedro were both absolute strangers. But finding several English there, they told their tale so smoothly that they found very compassionate entertainment among their countrymen.

During which leisure time Don Tomazo, having made his interest with a burgher's wife, had soon weedled the loving soul out of three hundred guilders, which amounted to near thirty pound English. With this money, the two Dons having picked up and joined themselves in confederacy with two more Spaniards of the same order, Philippo de Mexico and Gulielmo Porfeire, fell to the national cheat of coining, wherein, after they had cut their own stamps, they were so successful that in two months' time they had filled all Amsterdam so full of double stivers composed of three parts copper blanched with arsenic and one-third silver, that there was hardly any other money stirring among the butter boxes. By which piece of dangerous industry they advanced their stock to twelve hundred pound sterling. All which being considered by the four engineers, they forsook Amsterdam and retired with their bank into Zeeland.

Where they were no sooner arrived, but the twelve hundred pound had so inspired them with high thoughts that then little gains were looked upon as ridiculous, and nothing would serve less than ten thousand pound apiece, for the raising of which princely sum there was a general consultation of all four heads, wherein it was concluded that doubloon stamps, ducatoon stamps, and all sorts of stamps for Spanish gold should be forthwith prepared. But the metal could not be fixed till near four hundred pound of the main stock was embezzled in experiments and necessary expenses.

But then Fortune, loath such men of art and industry should lie any longer idle, found them out a composition to their hearts' desire, consisting of one-third copper artificially tinctured with yellow, one half third gold and half third emery, and one third super fine silver. Of which metal they made about £2,000, according to their modest computation, and the conscience they used in putting them off. Which that they might do with the more facility and speed, they dealt with all persons, bought the best commodities and gave the largest rates. And for the better management of the affair, every confederate had his particular employment assigned to him: Philip de Mexico and Guglielmo Porfeire were to reside at Middleborough and prepare the coin;

Don Pedro was the merchant that bought the goods; and Don Tomazo the factor who resided at Gaunt, whither all commodities were sent and immediately exposed to sale or transported to places more secure.

But this trade lasted not long, for Philip de Mexico, being a person inclined to all sorts of debauchery, one day gave a certain female that had caressed him with more than ordinary civilities, one of his counterfeit pieces, who having a sudden occasion for money, as women of that profession are seldom hoarders, carried the piece to exchange for silver with a goldsmith, who had forfeited his judgement by being bitten with about thirty pieces of the same nature before. Whose revenge exasperating him to a strict examination of the woman, she was constrained to discover where she had it, and then to go along with the officers of the city and show them Philip's lodging, who was immediately surprised and apprehended with all his materials and instruments about him and, without enquiry after further proof, committed to prison.

This apparent discovery and the great alarm it gave the whole city was notice sufficient for Don Pedro and Guglielmo to shift for themselves, who made all imaginable haste to Don Tomazo, to whom they related the doleful disaster and the sad tidings of their interrupted commerce. Thereupon Don Tomazo sold off all his merchandise and, having quartered his companions in a village near to Gaunt, he went himself to Middleborough with an intention to use all his endeavours to help Philip out of the briars.

But by that time he had been twice with Philip in the prison and had ordered all things ready for his escape, there came in the middle of the night several of the officers of the town to seize Tomazo upon information given to the Heers* against him by Philip himself who, not believing it was in Don Tomazo's power to bring him off, was in hopes, by an ingenious confession and the conviction of Don Tomazo, to save his own bacon. But his treachery did him no kindness, for he wanted money, without which there is nothing to be done in that, nor in any other part of the world. On the other side, Tomazo had plenty, and with his golden showers so mollified the gaoler's daughter that she not only brought him an iron instrument to dig his way through the wall, a rope to let himself down and a boat to receive him, but accompanied him her none* tender self, leaving mother and father for the sweet satisfaction of her fleshly appetite.

Being both safe in the boat, away sailed Feliciano and his Feliciana to Flushing and from thence, without any provision put to sea, where they drove, almost starved to death, upon the wide ocean, till Fortune threw them at length upon the coast of Flanders, at what time they quitted the boat and travelled the country by land like a tinker and his doxy* till they came to Don Pedro and Guglielmo, to whom Don Tomazo gave an account of the kindness Philip would have done him in requital of his pains and friendly intentions.

Nor was it long after that we heard of poor Philip's being transported to the other world in a cauldron of boiling oil, according to the sentence of his judges, which sort of terrible execution did not little startle the rest of the confederates—yet not so as altogether to daunt 'em in the progress of their profession. For Don Tomazo, Don Pedro, Guglielmo and the gaoler's kind daughter, whose name was Mariana, removing to Brussels, they fell again in that place to their Zeeland sport, resolving to hazard t'other cauldron; where, after they had made a considerable quantity of coin, they took their several stations and employments of merchandising till all their pieces were gone. Which good success encouraged them to go on afresh.

But it so fell out that Mariana, who had altered her habit and went for a Dutch minheir, and Guglielmo, going one day to court to buy horses of Count Monterey's servants, were spied by a person of quality of whom they had purchased other horses before and paid him two hundred pistols of coin out of their own mint. This same person was a certain count, who made such a noise that the whole court was alarmed; the parties accused were both apprehended and sent to eat the bread of affliction in Lobb's pound, where they endured no small torment both of body and mind, especially Mariana, whose misfortune was the greater for want of her dear Don Tomazo.

But neither were his love nor his jealousy so importunate nor so vehement at that time, but that he was content rather to trust the Spaniard with his mistress than venture his carcass for them as he had done for Philip: a piece of ingratitude which his conscience and self-preservation were forced to dispense with at that time, in regard he was too well known to be their solicitor, which was the reason that both the wary Dons stole privately away for Dunkirk, there to attend the issue of Guglielmo's and Mariana's imprisonment, who in a short time after were both convicted by their own confessions and forced to evaporate their souls in boiling oil as Philip had done, by an infernal torment in this, the better to prepare them for the bituminous tarpits of the other world.

The news of which hellish execution reaching the ears of the two Dons at Dunkirk, the very thoughts of Dutch and Flemish crucibles so cooled their courages that, for the future, they resolved utterly to abandon the melting trade. And believing that time would obliterate the memory of these extravagancies, they resolved to employ themselves in travel, as they did through most parts of France. But returning for Calice,* with an intention to embark for England, the boiling oil had so perfumed those parts that, not able to endure the scent, they retreated to Dieppe, from whence they arrived safe and sound at Rye in Sussex where, when they came to cast up their accounts, they found themselves reduced to £500 apiece: a sound foundation, could they have had the patience to build upon it like either Sutton's or old Audley's.*

But they had no skill in grazing or malting or setting up of brewhouses, by which they had known as many ruined as raised. They were for the quick dispatch; they were for drink and be rich; they looked upon themselves like two children of Israel and all the world beside as Egyptians, from whom they thought it no crime to borrow in their necessity. And gusmans call that necessity when they want fuel to feed the heat of their prodigality.

The inseparable Don Tomazo and Don Pedro being thus returned into their native country, like two sons of Priam, *Per varios casus, per tot discrimina rerum,** made haste to London, the grand receptacle of all the most refined virtuosos in gusmanry, where they made it their business to repair the loss they had sustained by the parboiling of their Spanish companions. Nor was it long before they had found out a parcel of projectors as fit for intrigue as themselves, to whom they communicated a certain conundrum which they had just coddled in their continually working brains, the sum and shape of which piece of midwifery was this. That six persons should lay down £300 apiece to fit out a privateer to sea, a gudgeon quickly swallowed among persons that took all for fish that came to net.

Thereupon there was a person employed to go to Dunkirk to buy a vessel and to fit and victual her out to sea. They that made the grand council at London were to pick up men and to have them ready to go aboard when the vessel should arrive upon the coast of England, wherein the concording gusmans were so punctual (for the sinews of their war began to waste) that the men being conveyed away in boats, the little dreadnought set forward in pursuit of her design, which was no less than the intended destruction of the whole Guinea trade. See here the difference between a Spanish and an English gusman: the one pursuing a poor, hungry plot upon his penurious master's bread and cheese, the other designing to grasp the riches of the fourth part of the world by the ruin of a national commerce.

Thus, with a firm belief that they should have ballasted their ship with dust-ore, they hoisted their sails, but being driven by most violent storms upon the coasts of Ireland, they lost both their vessel and all their hopes, no other good luck attending that voyage but only that of saving the men, which were in number above three hundred who, dividing into small companies for convenience of travel, took several ways to seek for new employment, by which means the coast of Guinea 'scaped a most desperate scouring and the African company had a very great deliverance.

Don Tomazo and Don Pedro, so lately men, though now but mice, kept still together companions in misery, and coming to Dublin, by the instigation of pure necessity (a thing which the morose law never considers), fell to their old trade, which was to counterfeit guineas and broad pieces of gold. Which after they had done and carried on about two months, some as good and as expert at the sport as themselves, not enduring interlopers to their own prejudice, traced 'em out and found their quarters, where they gave the Dons very courteously to understand that that small city was already too well stocked with gravers of the King's image, and therefore desired the right worshipful copper-smiths to depart, lest worst befell them.

Upon which kind advice, the two Dons took shipping for Bristol, a place much more fit for their purpose. There, being loath to draw bills and break the bulk of their London stock, with a poor inconsiderable bank of thirty shillings, of which fifteen were milled, they began again. Those fifteen milled shillings did the two Dons knight's service, for being double gilt and inlayed with sceptres, they marched off currently. Upon which foundation they wrought so long with ease and little expense, till they had well lined their pockets, were well mounted and in a good condition to ramble.

From thence, well knowing the danger of staying too long in a place, they rode to Gloucester, where after they had made up near three hundred and fifty of their own St Martin's ware,* they were disturbed by an officious rumour and forced to ride the country, during which journey of pleasure, in exchange either for good money or commodities, they put out all their illegitimate pieces to nurse. After which, like a little running pestilence, they went to infect the city of Worcester. There the two Dons met accidentally with four other persons of the same profession, who being pursued by the country, were apprehended in their company. At what time one of the strangers, to prevent the fatality of a search, conveyed under the table into Tomazo's hands a certain bag both large and weighty.

Don Tomazo was with child to know the contents, and therefore being got to his lodging, his dear Pylades* and he made bold to open the bag, in which they found six letters to as many gentlemen in the neighbouring counties, a note of considerable sum of money left with an innkeeper at Bridgnorth, and 220 false guineas most artificially and elaborately ordered. The letters they opened, took copies, and sealed up again, having found by the contents how affairs stood with the gentlemen to whom they were directed.

Thus fortunately provided, Don Tomazo and Don Pedro departed forthwith, and galloping tantivy* to Bridgnorth, they received £337 from the innkeeper. From thence they took their rounds to visit the six gentlemen who, being all persons of valuable estates, and fearing to run the bloody hazard of having their spotless reputations brought upon so dangerous a stage, upon the delivery of the letters and a relation of the misfortune that attended the persons from whom they came, willingly bled their fifty pound apiece for an obligation of secrecy.

The two Dons, having thus made the best of their market, left the gentlemen for that time and took a ramble for Stourbridge, where being forced to continue, by reason of an accident that befell Don Tomazo's horse, they lived to the height of their estates. During which demorage,* Don Tomazo's behaviour (always taking among the tender sex) had infused such a passion into the heart of a gentlewoman in the town, who wanted neither wit nor caution to manage her amorous diversions, that partly out of gratitude, partly for profit (for he seldom loved but for his advantage), partly for pleasure, his friend and he were forced to encamp in that place much longer than they intended, Don Tomazo passing for a German and humouring that pretence with broken English.

All that while Don Tomazo lost no time in improving the advantage of his amours, nor spared for any sort of caresses which he thought were proper to entertain so kind and bountiful a lady. But that post growing too hot, through the jealousies and suspicions conceived of Don Tomazo and Don Pedro in regard of the high rate they lived at, the two sparks were forced to remove, though not without taking leave of the young lady, who was so concerned for the loss of her dear German's society that the magnetic virtue of his embraces had almost engaged her in a resolution to be the companion of his fortunes. But Don Tomazo, not desiring to travel with the expensive molestations and inconveniences of female luggage, diverted her affectionate humour with such powerful arguments that at length they parted, though not without some briny deluges that overflowed the sorrowful lady's rosy cheeks.

Don Tomazo having thus disengaged himself from the labyrinths of love after a prodigal waste of his venereal ammunition, set forward with his other self, Don Pedro, for London, where they ranted with a profuse pomp and vainglory for about half a year till, finding their exchequer grow low, they began to think it time to recruit. Neither was it for such extraordinary high-soaring gusmans as they to play at ordinary games, whose prodigality was not to be supplied by the dipping of country squires or the little cheats of high and low fullums.*

At that time, the French and Dutch were at daggers drawing, and they, understanding that there was a fleet of Holland merchantmen in the river of Thames very richly laden, to the value of eight hundred thousand pound, all outward bound under a convoy of two men of war of forty guns apiece and very well manned, concluded upon a design to surprise these ships and their convoy and to make them prize, by virtue of a French commission with which they were already furnished. First then, in order to this attempt, by their acquaintance with some of those seamen who had been fellow sufferers with them in their intended voyage to the coast of Guinea, they raised a very considerable number of men which, by the leave of the captains of the Dutch men of war, were to be put aboard their ships under pretence of being raised as recruits by certain officers employed from Holland for that purpose. And it so happened that Tomazo's great diligence had found out a parcel of such sons of necessity as had not only Dutch commissions, but as good a will to the design as himself.

These persons treated with the aforesaid captains for the carrying over so many men for the service of the States, which the captains were very willing to undertake for the good of their country. So that in two days' time, the whole fleet lying at Gravesend, the major part of the men were sent aboard in the habit of new-raised men, but all resolute sea-tories and privately well armed with poiniards and pistols. These were to have been the fatal instruments of the grand surprise. For, it being the custom at sea to divide the ship's company into three parts that make three watches, of which one is to be always upon the deck, it was so laid that the English, in the dead of the night, after they had secured the powder-rooms, should run upon the decks, shut down the hatches to keep down those that were below, and cut the throats of all that made resistance above. By which means, having got the command of the men of war, they might with ease have commanded the merchantmen and so have made for the French ports, where their commissions would have borne them out.

About two days after the men were thus disposed of, the pretended Dutch officers sent down about forty large trunks of a prodigious weight, with particular care to put them aboard in the night for fear of meeting with the searchers, all which trunks were filled only with hay and bricks, to possess the people with a belief of some considerable treasure or some great quantity of arms that might be in them, to avoid the suspicion of men whom they saw entrusted with such a ponderous charge.

By this time the wind stood fair and the English officers were ordered by the Dutch captains to repair aboard with the rest of their men, in order whereunto they went all down to Gravesend, where the officers, having sent their men aboard, went themselves ashore, and in their company Don Tomazo and Don Pedro, the master wheels of this confounded piece of mischief, under the notion of servants to one that passed for a Lieutenant-Colonel.

Thus far things went prosperously on, and the gale of Fortune blew as fair as the wind then favourable to the voyage. But the Devil's i'that thing called fond love, which has made me think that the poets did ill to couple Mars and Venus together, considering how many brave martial designs have proved abortive through the open-heartedness of amorous folly. For to the total destruction of this Babel-like structure of two unwearied brains, it happened that one of the men who went last aboard, and was to have been a private sentinel, was married forsooth to a Dutchwoman, who had so ravished or rather infatuated him upon the leavetaking night that, like the hair-brained Curius,* he could not conceal from his charming Fulvia the great design he was going upon.

Whereupon the plaguey Delilah, out of a pure affection for her countrymen, went and discovered the grand plot to the Dutch captains, who were at first struck with a strange kind of terror to see themselves so near the brink of danger; but soon recollecting themselves, they kept their discovery close, not making it known to any but the officers of the ships. After that, having prepared all things for a close fight, they ordered all the English which were above to go under deck upon pain of death, which they did, all but some resolute fellows who, being overpowered, were beaten, wounded and forced down. Which petty conquest being thus obtained, and the fatal Sinons secured in the bodies of the two Trojan seahorses, one of the captains was sent ashore to entreat the English officers to come aboard, in regard the fleet was ready to set sail.

But those sons of guilt and jealousy, reading something more than ordinary in the Dutch captain's face, one of them, with a loud oath, swore they were all undone and was making an offer to shift for himself, but the Dutch, having raised the town, had so beset the houses that they were apprehended every mother's son and delivered up to the magistrates with a general information against them of the crime and of the design they had in hand, but not a word in the least of the men which they had secured in the two vessels.

The Dutch captains, having thus escaped a danger ten times worse than that of Scylla or Charybdis, weigh anchor and, being safe arrived at their intended port, acquaint the great Mynheers what a whirlpool they had so narrowly missed and delivered up all their prisoners to the mercy of the Hogen Mogens,* who ordered them to be sent to the Indies for eight years, while they that were seized at Gravesend were discharged for want of further prosecution and so returned to London, in which wide place neither Don Tomazo nor Don Pedro durst show their heads, as having not only spent their own ill-got bank, but run in debt to defray the charges which you may be sure the expenses of such a design would require.

Such is the fate of gusmanry, sometimes to abound and sometimes to want bread. In which condition the two reduced projectors were forced for a while to sit and bite upon the bridle, till in some short time, having raised so much money as would pay for their passage to Harlem in the Low Countries, they embarked for that place, where the two Dons prevailed with a certain merchant to furnish them with thirty pound, for the repayment whereof they drew a bill upon another merchant of their own invention and nomination at London.

Thus set up again, they departed for Amsterdam, where they possessed the English with so firm a belief of their being young Irish merchants who had suffered shipwreck that they, compassionating their condition, assisted them with money and credit to the value of a hundred pound. Which good success in those two places made them resolve to try how high they could build upon this same oddly begun foundation of the world's opinion. Which is many times the beginning of a trade that advances several to vast and real fortunes.

In order to this design, away they go to Rotterdam, where they found an English merchant who, being newly crept into the world, struck in with Don Tomazo and Don Pedro, who pretended to be of the same profession, and that they would send for goods out of Ireland with the next opportunity. Upon which score the Dutch merchant furnished his two new partners with wines and other commodities to the value of £400, which were presently shipped off for Flanders by the general consent of all the three.

Into that country the inseparable couple followed their game, and at Bruges set up their staff. There, for a short apprenticeship served their turn, they fell to trade with the merchants of the city, and bartered their commodities very fairly for Irish goods, and with good advantage. And, which was more, very honestly from time to time sent the effects to their correspondent at Rotterdam, who by that hocus of just dealing was so satisfied with the reality and good intentions of his two Irish chapmen that they continued trading together for above a year, in which time he had furnished them with goods to the value of £3,457, for which the two Dons returned him still most punctually commodities of equal value, to the great content of the Rotterdamer and the great reputation of the two English gusmans, who in this time, by virtue of their commerce with the merchants of Bruges and the great entertainment which they gave them, were grown to be as high in the credit of the city merchants as with their correspondent at Rotterdam, everyone courting their custom and expressing how deeply they would trust 'em for their further encouragement.

One would have thought this genteel and gainful way of living, the kindness of strangers and their own gratitude, should have obliged these two Dons to have kept within the bounds of reason and common honesty. But there is that lechery in some men to triumph in their frauds, and to be profuse at the expenses of other people's purses, that they cannot be contented with other gains than those that will satisfy their prodigality, and the toil of keeping accounts was a labour too tedious to their mercurial brains, and therefore they were now for reaping the harvest which they saw ripe for their sickle; the sun shined and they must make their hay.

The merchants had fairly promised and they resolved to try how far they would be as good as their words. Volenti non fit

injuria* was a Machiavellian maxim that very much prevailed
upon their consciences, none of the tenderest at that time.
Thereupon they took up several parcels of goods to the value of
£2,000 or upwards, which being shipped off for England, away
marched they after their prey, and taking Ostend, Newport,
Dunkirk, Calice and indeed all the considerable ports between
that and St Malo's, at the same places, by virtue of several
counterfeit bills from several parts, but more particularly from
Rotterdam and Bruges, they raised, all expenses born, an
additional stock of ready money amounting to £1,507, with which
recruit they bore away to the port of Exeter, where the two Dons
thought to have found the ship which carried their goods.

But being arrived there, they understood by a merchant
concerned in the same ship that the master and some of the
company had carried the vessel and goods to Bayon, and had
there exposed them to sale. Nor was this all, for the same
merchant, keeping a correspondence at Bruges, and by the
intelligence he had received from thence concluding Don
Tomazo and Don Pedro to be the two persons complained of for
the exploit they had there so lately committed, caused them to be
both arrested in the names of his Flemish friends, to whom he
sent word of the embargo which he had laid upon their persons.

The Bruges merchants had no sooner received the information but they sent over a person to treat with the two young sparks
who, being unwilling to lose time by lying in prison, the worst
place in nature for men of their profession, came to a seasonable
composition, and having to their great grief refunded £1,360,
were presently discharged. Happily for them, for they were no
sooner gone but fresh orders came to the same merchant from
several persons out of France to detain them upon their
accounts. However, the birds being flown, there was an end of
that prosecution. The guilt of the two Dons made them wickedly
jealous of the diligence that would be used to entrap them, and
therefore they made all the haste they could to London, where
they lay still a while till they thought the danger over.

This terror being past, the two Dons fell to new consultations,
and finding the ill success of merchandising, they resolved to set
up the old trade of coining, wherein they were more expert, as
being more suitable to their geniuses. In order to the better

management of which affair, like men of gravity and prudence, they consulted the statutes of the kingdom, by which they found the counterfeiting of Spanish gold to be the least dangerous in point of penalty. And therefore, having got their materials and confederates, such as broken goldsmiths and gilders, all in a readiness, they fell so sedulously to their business that in fourteen days' time they had made as many doubloons and double doubloons as amounted to the value of £3,245, according to the price of their mint.

Part of these pieces Don Pedro and Tomazo undertook to put off in the West and Northwest parts of England. To which purpose they took their progress well-mounted, genteelly clad, well attended with servants, besides the travelling grandeur of led-horses. However, they did not always appear in this splendour, but at certain times, and for colour of some great designs, having for projects of lesser moment other disguises and pretences. Among the rest, they had an easy excuse for their stay at sea port towns, in expectation of ships from several parts, during which demorage it was no difficult thing to put off thirty or forty of their pieces and then remove to another place. Neither was Lyme in Dorsetshire the scene of one of their meanest exploits.

In that place lived a merchant nearly related to their correspondent at Rotterdam, upon whom they had a design of no less than three or four hundred pound thick. This man was a wary person and one that, having been often scalded, dreaded the fire, which made the enterprise much more difficult. However, the resolution of the two Dons was such that they resolved to attempt it, as they did in this manner.

Don Tomazo and Don Pedro, with their servants and horses, in great splendour went to Lyme, where they took up all the chiefest inns of the town, Don Tomazo (and Don Proteus himself could have done no more) having now metamorphosed himself into the shape of a Spanish Count, to whom he pretended the King of England and several of the nobility had given several horses and liberty to buy more and to transport them, at his pleasure, for the service of his own sovereign. In prosecution of which affair he had been in the adjacent counties and had made several purchases, which he daily expected in that town, and was therefore come to make provision of hay, corn and stabling for their accommodation till he could have the conveniency of shipping them off, insomuch that the country people that came thither to market were forced to set their unregarded beasts in the streets to make room for the Spanish Count's horses.

During the Spanish Count's continuance at Lyme, which was about four days, he sends for the merchant upon whom he had fixed his design, and after he had amused him with a noble entertainment, entered into a discourse with him about his horses and how he intended to have them transported; desiring him either to assist him with his advice, or else himself be pleased to hire him some vessels for that purpose. An employment which the merchant readily undertook and to that purpose brought four or five masters of ships to the Count, with whom his lordship soon agreed for the passage of his numerous cavalry.

The next day, the merchant being present, the Count received an account from one of his servants, who pretended he came from the horses that they were at such a place, but that his agents had bought more horses than they had money to pay for, and therefore desired the money might be sent them. Presently the Count, calling for his steward, bid him go and fetch as many pieces of Spanish gold as would make up the sum. Which being brought as soon, the Count desired the merchant to exchange them for silver. Which the merchant undertaking to do, went home, carries the gold along with him, and sending for three more of his friends, they all laid their heads together to make trial of the pieces, which they did by all the usual ways of touching, cutting, weighing and the like. But the metal was so superexcellently tempered that they could make no other discovery but that it was absolutely real, so that the merchant returned with the full change in silver, which the Count immediately delivered to one of his grooms, who carried it away.

The next day, the former messenger returns again to Lyme, and tells the Count that all his horses were seized, in regard the country people had consulted together and were of opinion that the horses were to be transported contrary to an Act of parliament, and without the King's leave. At which unexpected news the Count was seemingly strangely alarmed and surprised, and in a passion as well counterfeited as his Spanish gold, commanded his groom to make ready his horses, pretending to go in person to dispute a business so prejudicial to his grand affairs.

On the other side, for the prevention of all disturbance and delay, and to show that he came not into England upon a first of April day's errand, being as it were come to himself, he desired the favour of the merchant to ride post to London to give the King an account of the abuse and scandal he had suffered from the country and to pray his Majesty's warrant for the release of his horses, and in consideration of his trouble, allowed him one of his servants to wait upon him and ten pistols to bear his charges, with assurance that at his return he should find the Count at Lyme. The merchant, as well to oblige a person of so much honour as the Spanish Count as to serve his neighbours, who were not a little discomposed at the loss they should sustain by the Count's being so rudely disappointed, set forward with more than good speed to solicit for the Count.

For upon his arrival at London, the Count's gentleman, who had his private instructions to prevent the merchant's going to court, sent for a confederate that well understood his lord's affairs, who presently entered an action of £4,000 against the Spanish Count's ambassador and arrested him as he was going to Whitehall with a crew of pretended officers of his own garbling.* In this condition, they hurried the helpless merchant to prison, as they made him believe, but indeed to one of their own private haunts, a certain dark, diabolical cellar where they so roughly entertained the terrified stranger that, to free himself out of the clutches of such a surly sort of rake-shames, he was forced to draw bills upon his correspondents in several places, which being received and due intelligence given to the Count of all proceedings, the poor merchant of Lyme, who had by this means moulted a good part of his gayest feathers, was discharged out of captivity.

As for the Count himself and his retinue, they soon quitted that post and, having altered their habits and changed their horses, ranged further up into the country, not deeming the sea ports proper to be visited while such exploits as these were fresh in memory. So like are these sort of gusmans to the Tartars who, when they have devoured the products of one place, remove into fresh accommodation.

But though they had changed their horses, they did not alter their pretence of buying horses. To which purpose Don Tomazo, now acting the part of a jockey rather than a Spanish Count, made it his business to ride with a servant up and down to farmers' houses, having first enquired the names of such gentlemen as lived nearest thereabouts, and also taken a prospect as far as he could of their qualities, their honours and their conditions.

'Tis well known to be the custom in many parts of the West of England for many farmers to breed up horses of fifty or sixty pound a pair, and sometimes of greater value. Such horses as these Don Tomazo would often cheapen* and sometimes bargain for, but when the seller and the purchaser came to the point, Don Tomazo had no money which was passable, nor was it his intent it should be so, as knowing well the humour of those sort of people, which was to raise the country presently, to make a thousand hubbubs and put all the world into noise and uproar, whereas a gentleman, having been smitten under the fifth rib, will first consider his own reputation and hold a private emparlance with his own reason, of which some are so highly conceited that they would not have the world believe they could be out-noddled for the half of their estates. They observe themselves to be the great idols of wit and parts, to which the people offer in the high places of the country, but should it once appear that their divinity-ships had once been subject to the frailty of having been cullied and cunny-catched* by mortal gusmans, their oracles would be no more frequented among the vulgar and the smiles of the gentry would expose them to the satirical extension of the forefinger, which was a punishment of their unwary folly that so overawed their considerative prudences that hardly one in twenty ever divulged the tricks that Don Tomazo put upon them. And therefore, because they were best able to bear the loss, most ready to put it up and most easy to be played upon (as depending upon their own judgements), in point of morality, in point of policy and to save trouble, Don Tomazo seldom dealt with any other than those of his own rank: gentlemen.

Having made this digression for the better instruction of the reader, we shall clear the foregoing axiom by the following demonstration. For as has been already hinted, when Don

Tomazo had bargained with any farmers for one or more horses, he still told them he had not current money to pay for his markets, and therefore desired them to send one of their servants to such a gentleman's house, where he was certain to be furnished with English coin, delivering himself in such a manner as if he were most intimately acquainted there. Thereupon the farmer would presently order a servant to ride along with their genteel chapman who, by the way, never failed to intoxicate the credulous bumpkin with the promise of some gratuity for his pains, and then to make him perfect in his lesson, which was to give such a short account of Don Tomazo as he himself directed him.

The fellow, being thus prepared and inspired with expectation, so soon as they came somewhat near the house, was sent before to enquire whether the gentleman were within, a question which Don Tomazo could have resolved before, but done on purpose to give the gentleman opportunity to enquire of the servant who the person was that was coming behind. For then it was that the country fellow generally gave his worship this answer that either he was a person of quality and of his master's acquaintance, who had bought horses of one that lived in such a place, or else that he was a near relation to his master, who had bought horses of another of his acquaintance. Either of which pretences, so formal and so probable, were enough to prevail with a gentleman always ready to oblige his neighbours.

So that by these artifices Don Tomazo seldom failed of having his gold changed or silver lent upon it, with his promise of sending for it again in such a time. But the fish being caught, Don Tomazo had no more business either with that farmer or his servant, and therefore at parting he only gave the fellow a small reward and bid him tell his master that he was gone to such a place, quite contrary to that corner of the wind whither he was bound, and would be with him in three or four hours—in which time he was got out of reach to his next conveniency. For Don Tomazo and his brethren always so managed their business that they rode first about the country to inform themselves of everything material before they made any attempt, so that when they once began, two or three days put an end to all such designs as they had in those parts of the country.

During the time that these pranks were played, the Lyme merchant, being returned home full of choler and revenge, had made a strange hurly burly in the country, but could hear no tidings of his Count. So that all things being once more still and quiet, Don Tomazo and Don Pedro resolved to take the opportunity of the calm and to favour their beloved sea ports with a fresh visit. Among the rest, they arrived at length at a place called Kingsbridge in Devonshire. There coming in upon a market day, Don Tomazo found diverse gentlemen, and several of their number in whose faces he could read a chapter fit for his purpose better than some astrologers. And indeed the circumstantial accidents fell out so propitiously that they seemed, as it were, to assure him of success.

For upon a sudden, not only about the town but all the country round there fell so deep a snow that neither horse nor man could travel. By which confederacy of the season, Don Tomazo and Don Pedro came familiarly acquainted with several of the said gentlemen under the notion of persons that were newly arrived from Spain. This happy time of leisure afforded Don Tomazo a kind opportunity to enter his new acquaintance into play (which is one of the laudable exercises that waste our time in these parts of Europe), at which sport he gave them leave at first to win much of his Spanish gold, which some of the gamesters, having been travellers in that kingdom, pretended to understand as well as the losing stranger who, to give the better colour to his design, seemed not a little troubled at the loss of his summum bonum, the only true friend to a traveller.

But the fickle dice, y'faith, soon altered their career, and ran so much on Don Tomazo's side that in a short time he had taken captive good store of the gentlemen's coin, who were so fond of the gold that, rather than part with it, they borrowed money in the town to pay their losses. But this same sport was too hot to hold, so that the gentlemen, weary at length of ill luck and tired with the inconveniencies of losing, as having taken their leaves (besides the satisfaction for Don Tomazo's gold) of near a hundred pounds of their own money, thought it high time to knock off and return to their several habitations.

At their several departures, there was one of the company that prevailed with Don Tomazo and Don Pedro to ride with him home, where they were not only received with a most hospitable accommodation by the gentleman at his own, but by him also carried to a person of quality's house not far off, where they were likewise entertained with no less kindness than plenty. But such is the ill nature of gusmanry that it spares neither friend nor foe. For of this very person of quality, who had been so civil in his entertainment, did Don Tomazo very gratefully buy two horses, for which he paid 147 pistolets and sent them away by his servant. This scene being over, they were in haste to be gone, and therefore, to avoid the sour sauce that might happen to season the sweet viands of their entertainment, they took their leaves of the civility of those places and set forward for Plymouth, but giving out that they intended for London.

When the two Dons came to Plymouth, ere they had time to alight Don Tomazo was spied by a person that knew him, who informed him that his master was in the town. This news was to Don Tomazo like aloes and honey, a strange mixture of sweet and bitter. For the gentleman was his acquaintance, but one of the persons that had won some of his gold at Kingsbridge, so that Don Tomazo, suspecting that the gentleman was come thither to make trial of his gold, thought it not proper to stay there. Thereupon the two Dons turned their horses' heads, but as they rode by a goldsmith's shop, Don Tomazo's counterfeit pieces began to ferment in his pocket, so that at their instigation, Don Tomazo deeming it a foul shame that he should come into such a town as Plymouth and leave no monument of his fame behind him, alights at the goldsmith's shop and desires silver for as much gold as amounted to £14. 10s. 9d.

The goldsmith, satisfied with the trial he made, delivers the silver demanded, and so the two Dons, having given that great town a small taste of their ingenuity, steered directly for the county of Cornwall, where they found great opportunities of business, played several pranks, and among the rest, this in particular:

Don Tomazo, having taken up his quarters at a town called Penzance, and Don Pedro at another called St Ives, both sea ports, lay there without taking the least cognizance of each other. They had been such strangers one to another for some weeks that the one had not been in the other's company but once, and that, as it were, by an accidental meeting. So that it was impossible for the country to imagine or suspect any such thing as an intimacy between them, which was the foundation upon which many designs were laid and brought to perfection.

One time among the rest, it happened that Don Tomazo being at church upon a Sunday, paying his devotions to something or other, Cupid, finding him at a loss for an object of his zeal, fixed his eyes upon a very pretty lady whose beauty made no slight impression in Tomazo's heart. The inflamed lover, whose business it was always to use the swiftest expedition in his affairs, now more violently hastened by his amorous impatience, returns to his quarters and makes all those diligent enquiries after the lady that lovers are wont to do, which concluding with such a passionate joy that all their answers satisfied his expectations, the people easily from thence drew their wonted conjectures and presently reported that Don Tomazo, who passed for the son of a person of great quality in the North, was deeply in love with such a lady.

This report flew like lightning and was presently bandied from one tittle-tattle to another, till it came to the father's ear with all the embellishments of multiplication in reference to the behaviour and gallantry of the enamoured esquire. The father was tickled at the tidings and, as it is the fashion of the unwary to look upon distant prospects with a magnifying fancy, thought it but an act of paternal affection to advance his daughter's fortune, and the daughter herself, proud of the conquest of her victorious beauty, already imagined herself riding in her coach and six horses, the adored mistress of many tenants and the charming wife of a brisk, bonny and wealthy heir.

Thereupon the Justice comes thundering to Penzance to take view of his son-in-law, and having found him out, took an occasion to fall into a sifting discourse with Don Tomazo, who had all his story so geometrically framed, and delivered it with such a careless exactness without the least hesitation, that the Cornish chough was not only taken with his person and behaviour, but so intoxicated with his narrative that he invited him over to his house. Don Tomazo kindly accepted his invitation, and accordingly gave him the honour of his company home, where he had leisure enough to unbosom his affections to the young Isabella, the name by which henceforward she shall be known.

Some time after, the Justice, his wife and his daughter went to visit a gentleman of their acquaintance, that lived not far from St Ives, who after dinner informed the Justice of a gentleman that quartered at St Ives that was certainly the best company that ever he met with; withal, that he was a Spaniard whose curiosity had brought him thither to view the country. Upon which rare character of an intimate friend, the Justice desired he might be sent for, as he was, with all speed. But when he came, the country gentleman, who only thought to complete his pastime with the mirth of some comical droll, was strangely out of countenance and in a surprise, believing his old acquaintance had put some trick upon him. For such was Don Pedro's air and deportment that the Justice took him for no less than some person of high quality, which was no small trouble to the Justice, to be put out of the road of his rural addresses and country compliments, and forced on a sudden to recollect the exercises of his youth at the dancing school for new congees* and refined expressions.

For indeed, Don Pedro might well have passed for such a one as the Justice took him to be, in any part of the world. He was a person so comely that few Spaniards were like him: very fair, full-eyed, with a lovely head of long hair as black as a raven's wing, and a body most curiously proportioned, to which his graceful carriage, his affable, sweet and complaisant humour, his fluency of speech, and his noble equipage, were such charming additions that it was no wonder Cupid took his stand in such a face and bent his bow to kill two birds with one stone.

I say 'bent' because at that time, I believe, the God of love made use of a cross-bow in regard of the crossness of the shot. In short, the mother and the daughter were both shot plumb dead at the same time, insomuch that there was no peace or quiet in either of their bosoms till they had prevailed with the Justice (who could hardly think his mansion worthy such a guest) to invite Don Pedro to his house.

But at last, overcome by their importunity and his own ambition, he took the confidence to give him a solemn and Cardinal-like invitation, which Don Pedro readily accepted. You may be sure the entertainment could not choose but be splendid where the master consulted his honour, the mistress her deep affection, and no question but the daughter sat up late and had a finger in every pie and every tart. Nor was the female diligence of those two love-shot ladies less, to dress and trim and trick and adorn themselves with all the ornaments their trunks and cabinets could afford. What fairs and christenings saw but seldom and in parcels, that Don Pedro saw at once, and every day displayed, while the mother strove to renew the youth of her past beauty, the daughter to beautify her present youth.

All this Don Pedro contentedly observed, and as he was extremely acute in his observations, after dinner he gave Madam Isabella an occasion to convey a little billet into his hand, at what time the mother took an opportunity to slip another into his pocket, ignorant of what her rival daughter had done. Neither indeed was Don Pedro aware of the mother's contrivance. So ambitious they were, which of the two should make the first and deepest impression in Don Pedro's heart.

The two ladies having thus disburdened their affections, the one into his pocket, the other into his hand, Don Pedro, after a power of compliments and kindness, took his leave and, being returned to his quarters, drew forth the billet which he had received from Mrs* Isabella, wherein he read these following lines:

'Sir,
      the first time I saw you, the idea of your perfections caused a violent passion in my heart, which having ever since tormented me, pardon the flame that enforces me to let you know the wound you have given me. I doubt not but that a person of your quality will be careful to manage this secret with that prudence as shall be no way to the disadvantage of a person so young and tender, that languishes for your sake.'

Don Pedro was so startled at the reading these short ejaculations of a wounded heart that he wrote a letter to Don Tomazo and within enclosed the billet, desiring him to consider what design would be most likely to succeed among people that had laid themselves so fairly at the feet of their mercy and, as it were, put their lily white hands into the lion's mouth. Withal, he cautioned Don Tomazo for the future, to avoid suspicion, to write his mind and send his servant with it, to be left in a hole of a certain rock half way between Penzance and St Ives, which was afterwards observed.

But when Don Tomazo came to read the billet which Don Pedro had informed him came from the Justice's daughter, he was in a strange quandary, for he loved her himself even beyond the pleasures of his profession. He could not imagine the reason of his misfortune, not dreaming the young lady had been such an early May cherry so soon to allure the gatherer's hand, of whom he then himself had no other hopes but as the paternal heat of her father's care mellowed her for his embraces. Of his approbation, good will and favour he thought himself cocksure, as well for that they had been more intimate together, as in regard the deportment and natural parts of Don Tomazo were not much inferior to those acquired endowments of Don Pedro.

But while Don Tomazo's thoughts were thus tennis-balled between love and gusmanry, the lady herself sent him a cordial that soon composed this disorder of his senses. For within two days after, Mrs Isabella finding a convenient opportunity, and as young and innocent as Don Tomazo thought her, willing to have two strings to her bow, writ Don Tomazo the following letter in answer to one of his:

'Sir,

Your immediate passion surprises a person so great a stranger to things of this nature, and besides, you men (as I have been informed by my mother) are most kind things till your ends are accomplished, and then as full of flights. But if I could be satisfied of the reality of your affection, it would be more serviceable to your interest. But alas, how shall I credit anything from a man who burns and dies, swears vows and protests, and all in one single minute, quite contrary to the thoughts of his heart. This from a person so great a stranger, as well to yourself as to the thing called love, as I am, you may, if you please, value as a piece of liberty I allow you, to be what in yours you express.'

This letter, from so young and so unexpected a piece of female treason, did not a little damp the amorous Don Tomazo's flame.

He saw how the subtle traitoress was only coaxing poor Tomazo with the shadow, while she was disposing the substance to Don Pedro; cunningly providing that, if Don Pedro should slight her proffered fondness, then to accept of Don Tomazo's courtship.

This double-dealing of Mrs Isabella, though unlooked for, was upon better consideration the more welcome to Don Tomazo to support the morality of that injustice which he intended the family, which while he was meditating how to bring to pass, his servant brought him a letter from the rock with another billet in the belly of it. For by this time Don Pedro's servant, after his master had shifted his clothes, had found the Justice, Signior Cornuto Elect's wife's love letter in one of the pockets, which Don Tomazo reading, found these violent expressions of an amorous fury:

'Most fair and dear to me of all your sex, whose charms no creature is able to resist, I that have lived in the state of marriage this twenty-five years a just and dutiful wife and, as I thought, to the best of your sex, am now so altered in my respect to that thing called an husband that I hate him for your sake, for which I would quit all my immediate plenty to enjoy your dear company but one hour. Pity the weakness of a woman, and do not slight a passion so great that no breast can conceal, and consider how I break the impalement of a virtuous life forty-three years long to come to the embraces of yourself, whom I love above all the world. Let not my age render me insignificant, but meet me tomorrow at the mount.'

Don Tomazo, having read this letter, could not choose but laugh to see the infidelity of the daughter so prettily revenged by the wantonness of the mother, who was all this while in a fiery torment, like St Laurence upon the gridiron, believing that if Don Pedro had not slighted her, he either would have met her or else she should have heard from him.

It seems Don Pedro knew nothing of this letter before his man had found it, and therefore not to lose opportunities, having received some private instructions from Don Tomazo, he thought it high time to answer both his clients, beginning first with Madam Isabella in this language:

'Fair Isabella,

    when I had perused your little charm, I found myself under a thousand constructions. But by the contents thereof being truly sensible of your great affections for me, assure yourself nothing on earth shall labour more to retaliate those your favours, nor manage the whole matter with more safety to yourself than I will. So if you'll but meet me at the little rock, I shall there express what is now too much to expose in written lines.

                     Adieu.'

After he had wrote this and was assured of Isabella's coming to the place appointed, Don Pedro, apprehensive that the absence of the daughter might raise jealousies in the mother and put her upon the search, like Ceres after her daughter Proserpine, to prevent her sent her this julep to qualify the heat of her fever:

'Dear Madam,

    I cursed my ill fate a thousand times for concealing your billet so long from me, for I never knew of it till shifting my apparel, and then my valet du chambre found it by accident in the same pocket which I suppose you put it. But the contents thereof has given me such demonstrable satisfaction of your great and good inclination to me, that it puts me under no small surprise to qualify myself for the reception of so much honour, the least grain of which, as coming from you, I shall more esteem than my life, and finally make it my study how to embrace you with such a tenderness as may be most proper for a lady under the circumstances of so great a passion. And from henceforward, to prevent the jealousy of a husband, let us only meet and not write. For nothing is of more dangerous consequence than letters of such a nature as this when once discovered, especially by a man so apt as the Justice. I will meet you tomorrow at the same place you appointed and the same hour.

                      Adieu.'

At the receipt of this letter, the lady was so transported that for that day all the gaiety and pleasure she had ever shown or enjoyed in her whole life seemed to be recollected and rendezvoused in her countenance. She thought of nothing but of reinforcing her amorous heat, that she might be able to meet her dear Don Pedro's fires with equal flames. Her heart danced the Canaries in her bosom for joy that she should so soon be happy in the embraces of her beloved Spaniard, and the continual meditations of her brain upon these voluptuous felicities did so employ her thoughts that her daughter might have had the opportunity to have lost more maidenheads than Hercules got in one night, for any enquiry her mother made after her.

Thus was the mother's security the daughter's safety, who by this time had lost her troublesome virginity in those embraces, to which the other was the next day to resign the matrimonial loyalty of many years. So little does the continual sight of a gold thumb-ring control the temptations of a wanton appetite.

Isabella, having by this means obtained a full satisfaction from Don Pedro, and now become as wise in the natural philosophy of love as her mother, left her instructor a thousand sweet kisses in pawn for an assurance of her further society, and with the modesty of a nun, returned home to laugh in her sleeve at the cheat she had put upon the vigilance of her mother and all her female guardians. But before Don Pedro and she parted, there was an agreement made that whenever Don Pedro came to the Justice's house, it should be under pretence of making love to her who had already given him the surest pledge of her affection. For under that colour, Don Pedro being now to manage the intrigue between her mother and him, where lay the stress both of his and Don Tomazo's design and the prospect of their gain, it was necessary to uphold the amorous correspondence which he and Isabella had begun.

And now the happy hour was come. Don Pedro and the enamoured mother met, and he that had so deliciously fed the young kitlin* was now to purr it with the grey-maulkin the elder, whom he entertained with such variety of embraces that she protested all the Justice's Cornish hugs were but bavin-bands* to 'em. Which gave her such an intrinsic satisfaction that she enjoined Don Pedro to stay in those parts a month longer, and indeed till those quarters were grown almost too hot to hold either him or his company. In order whereunto she had contrived a way for his coming to the Justice's house. But Don Pedro, not deeming her way so commodious as his own, acquainted the mother with his affections to her daughter, who thereupon approved of his intentions and, having resolved to act conformably to the design, they parted for that time.

Don Pedro, being returned home, wrote a letter to be left at the rock for Don Tomazo, wherein he gave him an exact account of what had passed between him and the two ladies, and further desired Don Tomazo with all speed to get himself introduced into Isabella's company and to make his addresses to her, wherein he promised to be assisting so soon as there appeared any public acquaintance between them.

This letter Don Tomazo read with great regret, cursing Pedro's happiness and his own ill conduct, not so much for the love he bore the dissembling Isabella, as for that he had not made the same improvement of his opportunity that Don Pedro had done. But finding it was now Don Pedro's intention to carry on the common advantage, and that the design began to ripen, he easily rid his head of those impertinent imaginations, and two days after gave a visit to the Justice who, being at home, entertained him with great respect, and among the rest of the discourse, knowing Don Tomazo was well skilled in the Spanish tongue, informed him of a famous Spanish gentleman that was in those parts, well worth his acquaintance. Of which Don Tomazo seemingly made slight, telling the Justice that he was a young man and did not know what inconveniences the knowledge of that gentleman might produce. But the more Don Tomazo slighted it, the more earnest the Justice was to send for Don Pedro. So that Don Tomazo, unwilling to disoblige the Justice by his obstinacy, suffered himself to be overruled.

As soon as Don Pedro came, Don Tomazo entertained him with all ceremonies according to the gravity of Spain and afterwards discoursed him in the Spanish language, which fell out luckily for their business, in regard that none of the Justice's family understood what they said. This interview between the two pretended strangers, Don Tomazo and Don Pedro, first begat a familiarity, then frequent meetings, and at length, by the Justice's consent, his house became the general rendezvous. During which time Don Pedro, having had the frequent sight

and handling of his enamoured mistress's jewels, had got such a
perfect idea of the shape, form and bigness of the pearls and
stones and afterwards drawn them so exactly on paper, that there
was no question of the success of the design.

Thereupon Don Tomazo dispatched away his man to Exeter,
who there bought up several pendants of counterfeit pearl and
Bristol stones, so well matched that they were hardly to be
distinguished from the originals. Which being brought to Don
Tomazo, he delivered them to Don Pedro who, watching his
opportunity, which the fond dotage of Isabella's mother often
gave him, by opening her cabinet and displaying her wealth to
dazzle his eyes and oblige him to the satisfaction of her desires,
took an honest occasion to pay himself for his drudgery by taking
out the real substances and conveying the counterfeit shadows in
their places.

Which being done, for about three days after Don Tomazo
and Don Pedro drank the Justice very hard and indeed made it
their business to keep him elevated for the most part of their stay,
after the moral exchange which Don Pedro had made with his
wife. During which time, one evening, the Justice being bowsy,*
they took an occasion to make a repetition of the great favours he
had shown them, promising those returns which they neither
durst nor ever intended to perform. In the conclusion of which
most lofty compliments, some discourse arising about Mrs
Isabella, Don Pedro catched at it and spared not to say that he
loved her beyond measure and little less than his life. But he
came short of Don Tomazo, who swore, by way of reply, that she
was more dear to him than life itself and in pursuit of his zeal for
the lady, requested the Justice to declare if it were his intention to
dispose of his daughter in marriage and, if it were possible for
her to love Tomazo and Pedro both alike, on which of the two he
would soonest bestow her.

The Justice, being ravished to hear such a brisk contest about
his daughter between two such great persons of quality, was at
first in a dilemma, but at length, heightened by the t'other round
and the more generous protestation of Don Tomazo, frankly
declared in favour of him. At which Don Pedro seemed to take
snuff, but carried it off for the present, and so they drank on all
three till the ladies were gone to bed, but then Don Pedro and

Don Tomazo took an occasion to slip out of the room, leaving the Justice alone, who perceiving they did not immediately return, presently began to reflect upon the discourse that had passed between 'em. With that, he ran to the garden door at which they went out, where he had not stood long before he heard the clashing of swords, which so amazed his worship that in a trice the whole family was alarmed and the Justice, with some of his servants, came in great haste to part them.

In this counterfeit fray, Don Pedro had pricked Don Tomazo in the arm, more like a surgeon than an enemy, which with another green hurt that Tomazo had received but a little before, passed for two great wounds. The Justice caused his servants to take Don Tomazo into the house while he laboured to appease Don Pedro, who seemingly would fain have had the t'other touch with Don Tomazo. But his violent passion at length submitting to the Justice's mediation, he was prevailed with to go to bed.

The scuffle being thus over, and the great mischief prevented, the Justice visited Tomazo who, all in a boiling choler, lay swearing he would make Don Pedro smoke for the injury he had done him and what he would make him pay for damages. The old gentleman gave him all the sugar words he could think of, and sent for a surgeon, whose honesty Don Tomazo easily tempted to delay the cure to enhance the bill of costs.

After that time the two rivals never met, Don Tomazo returning to his quarters and the Justice, for his own reputation, so ordered it that there was no noise made of the dangerous duel. Nevertheless, Don Pedro, who all this while lay at rack and manger in the Justice's house, and took that care of his wife to find her other sport than visiting her cabinets, seemed to be not a little afraid of his rival, and therefore persuaded the Justice to give Don Tomazo a visit and withal to pump him in reference to his demands for satisfaction. To whom Don Tomazo protested that £500 should not reconcile 'em.

But the cure being over, Don Tomazo was persuaded by the Justice (whom they found very much pleased with his office of mediation) to treat with Don Pedro, who was willing to refer himself to Don Tomazo, as not thinking it convenient to encumber himself with the laws of the nation, to which he was a stranger. So that at length Don Tomazo was overruled by the

Justice to take £225. Accordingly, Don Pedro laid down the money in Spanish gold, which Don Tomazo refused as not being the coin of England. Thereupon Don Pedro, mainly desirous to be rid of trouble, requested the Justice to take the gold and furnish him with so much money, which he not having in the house, courteously sent to Penzance for and delivered it to Pedro who, upon the payment thereof to Don Tomazo, received a full and ample discharge, but refused to have any more to do with such a litigious gentleman.

By this time, having stocked all that country with their precious metal, by a letter from the rock they agreed to be gone, as they did in a most slovenly manner. For without taking leave of the Justice, who was so courteous, or his wife, who had been so kind, or the daughter, who had been so tenderly loving, they took horse of a sudden and vanished out of the country, leaving nothing behind 'em but the remarks of an old musty proverb: 'Happy are they that beware by other men's harms.' Neither were they very scrutinous to know what curses or lamentations followed 'em from the Justice's house, who they knew had no great reason to be over-zealous in their pursuit.

During this pleasant ramble, the two brethren in evil had returned several considerable sums to London, and disposed of all their counterfeit Peruvians.* And now, coming to a certain market town beyond Exeter, the little god with a muffler about his eyes found a way to shoot a new passion into Don Tomazo's heart. He that had so long defied the yoke of wedlock was now altogether for the bonds of matrimony. He had met with an object beautiful and rich that had enslaved him even to a sense of honour, as if the sickness of his love had caused a qualm of honesty in his mind. So that, having succeeded in his courtship, he resolved to be faithful to one he entirely loved. And now all things being concluded, and nothing wanting towards consummation but the ceremony of the church, Don Tomazo rides back to Exeter to provide the nuptial ornaments.

By the way, at another market town, he met with some gentlemen of the country who persuaded him to dine with 'em at an inn, where, after they had drank pretty hard, one of the company (who was master of the inn where Don Tomazo quartered at Lyme) began to relate the whole story of a certain exploit that was done at his town by a pretended Spanish Count, and at the conclusion of his story pointed to Tomazo, saying that the Count was as like him as ever he saw any man in his life, only that the Count wore a perruke* and Don Tomazo his own hair.

This narrative did not a little disorder Don Tomazo's cogitations, but he who had the confidence to out-brazen the stern looks of so many dangers, scorned to betray his fear of such a scarecrow as this, and so, putting a good face upon the matter with a story of the same nature with his own concern, which led to others quite different, he lulled the Lyme man's relation asleep, and for fear it should wake again, he kept the company so well sodered* together with pleasing healths that all manner of stories were forgot, there being not one in the company but what was carried to bed.

Only Don Tomazo, having been more careful of himself, rode to Exeter that night to meet a more unlucky misfortune. For early the next morning, after he came thither, the ostler of the inn where his horses stood taking one of them to the farriers upon some occasion or other, a certain person, casting his eye upon the beast, demanded of the ostler whose it was, who answered he knew not. Thereupon the person who asked the question waited till the horse was led back and, following him to the stable, there found the very horse on which Tomazo rode when he changed his Spanish pieces with him at Plymouth for £14 odd money, for so it fell out that this was the very individual goldsmith that had been nicked in that manner, who thereupon went to Don Tomazo's lodging and caused him to be apprehended—a sad catastrophe to a person that dreamt of nothing but epithalamiums and Hymeneal flambeaus.

Presently he was carried before a magistrate, by whom, upon the Justice's information, he was committed, but left bailable. Don Tomazo being thus in the climm,* and well knowing that the report of his being in prison would muster a wicked battalion of the same crimes to his destruction, to prevent the threats of his hard fate, writes away a letter to a gentleman who was a Justice of the Peace in the county of Devon, whose surname he then assumed to himself, wherein he gave him to understand his condition and that he was a person nearly related to him and therefore requested his worship (for nothing less than a Justice of the Peace of the same county would serve) to favour an innocent stranger so far as to stand for one of his bail; pretending, as well he might do, that his imprisonment would be his ruin, as being a person that came not into the country to utter false money, but to court a young lady that lived not far from him, of which he would give his worship a further account if his request were granted.

Don Tomazo's letter was well considered and scanned by the Justice before he sent an answer, and enquiry was also made by his order after this new-discovered kinsman, by which the Justice, finding many of the circumstances to be true as Don Tomazo had expressed, believed the rest and wrote him word that, though he knew him not personally, he was satisfied that he had such a kinsman in the world and believed him so to be, and therefore, rather than suffer a relation to lie under such a scandal, he promised to bail him off, which was immediately done by himself and another Justice of the Peace, whom he had engaged to stand with him.

With this new relation Don Tomazo went home, where he was civilly entertained till the time of his appearance at the sessions, during which interval, being brought acquainted by his cousin with the Justices of the Peace of the country, he had so insinuated himself into their favour that several of them had obliged themselves by promise to be his friends, which made him resolved to stand his trial.

When the time came, the goldsmith exhibited his indictment against Don Tomazo, wherein he charged him with having exchanged at his shop a certain weight of metal for so much real money, but that when he went to melt it down in his forge the whole matter, by putting a smart fire under it, evaporated with that violence that his servant, standing on the other side of the forge, having received some of the vapour into his nostrils, swooned away, to the great wonder of his master. Upon this indictment, Don Tomazo was found guilty of a high misdemeanour and fined £45, which was afterwards brought down to 40s. and presently paid with great joy. For upon payment of his fine, no other charge coming against him, he was acquitted by proclamation.

Don Tomazo having thus escaped the goldsmith's tongue,

almost as bad as St Dunstan's,* and made all the expedition he could to render his acknowledgements to the gentleman he was so much obliged to, made as much haste out of the country and with his other self, Don Pedro, set forward for London, no more regarding his intended marriage, which indeed had been to little purpose, for his mistress's relations, having heard of his misfortunes, and that he had been no sufferer for his religion, took that paternal care as to send their kinswoman far enough out of his reach.

When the two travellers arrived at London and had cast up their accounts, it appeared by their books that they and their confederates had uttered in this kingdom 4,050 pieces of their sorts of Spanish gold, amounting to near £5,000 sterling. Of which, being divided, £1,700 came to Don Tomazo's and Don Pedro's share, all which, together with the stock they had before and the jewels which they had borrowed of the Justice's lady (clear booty to them two), rose to a very considerable value—and yet no such vast sum neither for those that had been sowing and reaping all over England.

Now, you will say: 'What became of all this money?' O, never fear it, you shall have a faithful account of it by and by. You'll be impertinently questioning, too, why did not these two Dons put themselves in a way.* So they did, and that in as fair a way to be hanged as ever they did in all their progresses through all the ways of Great Britain. Now loosing and venturing life and limbs to impose upon princes and generals, as they did before to cozen goldsmiths and country gentlemen. But how you will approve of their ways is not for them to determine.

For, to tell you the truth, the two Dons, finding London the coolest place in England for men of their profession, now grown by continual persecutions rather like the stoves i'the new Bagnio than like a gentle Egyptian oven to hatch more mischief in, resolved to pass over into Holland with a resolution to serve the Prince of Orange,* and so they did more tricks than ever he thought they deserved thanks for. To which intent they took their leaves of their native soil like two philosophers, carrying all they had along with them—though it were a hard thing to judge whether their country were not as glad to be rid of them as they were to be rid of their country.

But let it be as it will, they were no sooner entered upon the stage of Holland but they were admitted to kiss the Prince's hands. Such an ascendant has the dazzle of garb and behaviour over all mankind, and all because the body of man is not as transparent as it is brittle. Soon after they had performed this ceremony, they had leave to enter themselves as volunteers, for there were no commissions to be had for money, it being then at the beginning of the campaign. During all which time of military duty and the Winter following, the two English sparks, not considering that their bank was to be fathomed, or rather, building upon the fair promises made them of employments that would soon replenish the vacuums of their empty bags, what with 'Item: for excessive expenses, Item: for gaming'—that bane of plethoric* pockets, were brought to sing lachrymae over the last penny.

So that, for want of foresight, seldom regarded by the great masters of art in gusmanry, having disposed of all their equipage and bravery, for it came to that at length, they were resolved, however, not to starve. And therefore, to prevent that miserable, pining death, Don Tomazo, who had some knowledge in the art of fortification, as being one that had often built sconces,* took the boldness to wait upon the Prince, to whom he expressed the great desire he had to serve his Highness to the utmost of what he was capable. Then—for Don Tomazo was always one that kept close to his text—he made known to the Prince the necessity he was in, not forgetting to mind him of the good services he and Don Pedro had done at several places, and more particularly the siege of Grave,* which were not unknown to the Prince, who thereupon bid Tomazo look about and find out something within his Highness's disposal and that then both he and his friend should not fail to see the effects of his Highness's favour answerable to their expectations.

But Don Tomazo, not to be baulked by those plausible evasions of courtship, came close to the point, for it was money he wanted, and thereupon he acquainted the Prince that if he would order him a hundred pound, he would undertake to serve him as a spy in the French army. This the Prince desired time to consider of, and in a short time communicated the secret to some of his council, who being as truly sensible as himself of the great want of intelligence among the Dutch, persuaded the Prince to employ Don Tomazo, since 'twas his own voluntary offer.

In pursuit of this advice, the Prince sent for Don Tomazo and told him, provided his friend Don Pedro would condescend to be left as a pledge, he should have a hundred pounds to put him into an equipage fit for the prosecution of his proposals. For the Prince had had several tricks put upon him by the English before, which made him the more cautious.

Upon this, Tomazo advises with his friend Don Pedro, and as they two were not wont to Spaniolize in their consultations, the matter was so ordered to the Prince's satisfaction likewise, that Don Tomazo, as much to his satisfaction likewise, received the hundred pound. Upon the receipt whereof, away went Don Tomazo for Brussels, altered all his habits and, in the disguise of a boor* of that country, trudged to the French army that then lay encamped near Sogny, under the command of the Prince of Condé. There Don Tomazo got a full view of all their standards, cannon, and the manner of their encamping, as also a very near account of the number of their men, both horse and foot.

With this discovery, Don Tomazo returned to Brussels, where he put all things into a formal draught, exactly representing the whole camp, which, being shown to the Prince of Orange, he compared it with one which he had received before from another person of the same occupation, by which comparison the Prince found Don Tomazo to be a very fit person for his employment, and therefore encouraged him and promised him that, so long as he could furnish them with good intelligence, he should want neither for money nor advance.

Thereupon, Don Tomazo returns to Brussels, where finding several of the country people, whose houses had been plundered and themselves stripped by the French, so miserably poor that they wanted bread, Don Tomazo picked up one of these forlorn creatures, which by conversation he found most acute, with whom he prevailed to undertake such enterprises as he should put him upon and to follow his directions, for which he promised him half a crown English a day. The boor, taking Don Tomazo for an angel sent from heaven to relieve his misery, embraced his offer with all the readiness imaginable. So that Don Tomazo, having given him full instructions, sent him about his business. Upon his return, the boor gave a very good account of things, which being put into form, together with such other discoveries which Don Tomazo had made (unknown to the boor), he presented them to the Prince, who still received more and more satisfaction from the labours of his new spy.

Some time after, Don Tomazo had, by the diligence of his new-acquired confederate, prevailed with ten or a dozen more of the same stamp and in the same condition to list themselves in his service for the same pay. By this increase of number his intelligence notably increased, insomuch that his double diligence had highly advanced him in the favour of the Prince, who believed that whatever Tomazo brought him was clearly gotten by his own hazard and industry, as indeed the best part of it was, for you must always allow the master to outdo the servants.

These smaller attempts so well succeeding, Don Tomazo was desired by the Prince of Orange to use all his art to insinuate himself into an acquaintance with some of the Prince of Condé's family or attendants, promising that if it could be accomplished and any service accrue from thence, no sum of money should be wanting for gratification, or reward, or remuneration, or whatever ye please to call it.

Don Tomazo, thirsting after fame and money, and believing that having so many irons in the fire it would not be long ere some of them proved hot enough to strike, readily undertakes the affair, to which purpose he provides a frock of sackcloth, a pair of wooden shoes (for such is the habit of boors in those parts), a rundlet* of brandy and a parcel of tobacco. This rundlet had two divisions, the one for the soldier's liquor of life and the other for black-lead pencils and parchment and such other necessary materials. In this garb, who the devil should know so great a person as Don Tomazo? So that under this disguise he walked about the French camp, grateful to the soldiers for the sake of his tobacco and brandy and, watching his opportunities, took several memorandums very considerable.

But loitering one day carelessly about the quarters of the Prince of Condé, one of the captains of the guard called to Don Tomazo who, believing him not worse than Cerberus, and in hopes that a sop would have stopped his mouth, proffered him a taste of his cordial liquor. But the captain, suspecting him to be what he was, ordered him to be searched and kept him upon the guard four whole hours. This was an accident that set all the pulses of Don Tomazo's brain at work, and all little enough to hammer out new spirits to supply the want of those which he had lost in the fright. But those little Vulcans soon recruited his arteries, and the Devil too, the father of lies, unwilling to lose a servant, gave him a list with a cast of his favour.

For, after something of a serious study upon such a ticklish point of life or death, Don Tomazo called for the captain, and desired he might be carried to the Prince of Condé, at which the captain laughed and saluted Don Tomazo's posteriors with a contemptible kick or two, asking in great derision what business such a beast as he could have with the Prince—so strangely may a captain be mistaken. But Don Tomazo urged his importunity so home that Mareschal D'Humières passing by, and hearing the brandy-man so boldly demand to speak with the Prince of Condé about business of importance, came up to him and asked him what it was. To whom Don Tomazo made a submissive answer that it was of that high consequence that, for his life, he durst not impart it to any but the Prince himself.

Away went the Mareschal, little thinking that Satan had sent him of an errand, and gave notice to the Prince of Don Tomazo's importunity, who thereupon sent for the brandy-merchant, not to buy any of his ware, but to understand his business. Then it was that Don Tomazo, with a respective bow not like that of a strong-water man, desired privacy with his Highness, as not daring to give any account of his business to any person living but himself. Thereupon, the Prince, considering there were such things as disguises in the world, and frequently made use of, and that it was in his power with one puff of a mort-bleu* as well to hang a varlet as to reward an instrument, ordered all people to withdraw, which being done, Don Tomazo opening his mouth without fear or trembling thus began:

'Sir, it is intended by the Prince of Orange that his whole army shall march to Oudenard about four days hence, in order to which all things are in preparation. Thirty battering cannon are to be sent from Gaunt to meet them, the Prince being resolved to besiege the town with all the vigour imaginable, and to render the enterprise more easy, four engineers are to be sent into the garrison tomorrow to dismount the cannon, which is to be done with the consent of some of the gunners already tampered with and made for their purpose. Further, when the Dutch are ready to open their trenches, the great water dam in the middle of the town is to be sprung by another engineer, by the consent of the persons there concerned, of whom they are already assured. Which being done, and the water fallen, the enemy intends to attack the town on that side. Now if your Highness think fit, I will return to the Dutch army and make further enquiry into the particulars of this design, which when I have done, I shall be ready to go to Oudenard and discover, to the persons your Highness shall appoint, the very engineers and their accomplices themselves.'

The Prince, hearing such a formal story from such an aniseed-water robin as he took Tomazo to be, was not a little surprised, which caused him, as any General of reason would have done, to ask Tomazo what he was, how he had lived, what had induced him to make this discovery, and how he came to be privy to such a considerable secret. Adding, withal, that he could not believe the Prince of Orange would ever communicate a design of such importance to a person of his low degree.

To this, Don Tomazo, not thinking it necessary to run through the whole course of his life, replied in short that he was a captain in the Prince of Orange's army, that he was intimately acquainted with all the chief officers, that he had been diverse times at their councils of war, and often had had the honour privately to discourse [with] the Prince of Orange, the Princes of Curland, Nassan and Friezeland, by which he made it out that there was probability enough that he might be acquainted with part, though not with all, their designs. And lastly, that as to his inducement to make the discovery, it proceeded merely from the great honour and esteem he had for His Majesty of France, whom he was most ambitious to serve.

The Prince, having thus duly weighed the circumstances of the story, and finding nothing but what was very likely to be true, surrendered his belief to Don Tomazo's smooth tale, and the more to oblige him, ordered his valet du chambre to present him with forty quadruples to the value of £160 sterling, which pleased

Don Tomazo much better than the kicks o'the breech which the surly captain gave him. Which being done, the Prince gave him further hopes of his favour, even to high advancement, if he made out the discovery as he had begun, and so, having enjoined him to return with all possible speed, in order to his going to Oudenard for the apprehension of Don Tomazo's traitors in the moon, he dismissed the well-satisfied mundungus* merchant from a most dreadful agony, with the sweet consolation of fiddler's fare.

Don Tomazo having thus by dint of wit delivered himself out of the lion's den, and finding that he was able to deal with two Princes at one time, resolved to play his game out. To this intent, away he goes directly to the Prince of Orange, and to him without any concealment, relates all that had passed between the Prince of Condé and himself, a story which very much pleased the Prince and caused him to laugh heartily. At the conclusion of his narrative, Don Tomazo was commanded by the Prince to return at the time appointed, which he did accordingly, and found immediate admittance to the Prince of Condé, to whom he told the same story as before, only with some alterations and additions, which so convinced the great General of the truth of the fable, not believing that though a man had counterfeited once, he would ever be such a fool to venture again with the same lie in his mouth, that he ordered Don Tomazo to go directly by such a token to the Marquis de Chamilly, then Governor of Oudenard, and give him an account of the whole matter as from the Prince.

All which Don Tomazo exactly performed, but then pretending to the Marquis that the persons were not yet come, and that it behoved him therefore to stay till they came, that liberty was soon allowed him. During which time he made it his business to walk and view all the fortifications, as well private as public, as also to take several memoirs of what he thought proper for his purpose. And though it was not to be expected that the Marquis should be so liberal as the Prince of Condé, yet did Don Tomazo so well order his Governorship that he Chamillyed him out of forty pistols,* and so having modelled all his draughts and observations, he watched his opportunity and stole out of the town, though with no small hazard, the French being the most careful in the world how they let any persons pass in or out at their garrisons without a strict examination.

By this time the Prince of Condé had received an account from some correspondent of his in the Dutch army that the Prince of Orange had sent an engineer to Oudenard and that he did intend to beleaguer it. Which piece of imperfect intelligence from a known friend, agreeing with Don Tomazo's story, so startled the Prince that he now believed every word Don Tomazo had said, and thereupon raises his camp from Charleroy and marches quite cross the country to cover Oudenard, into which he put three thousand fresh men with provisions, continuing his camp upon the downs in expectation of the Prince of Orange's coming. Of whom, in four days after, he heard another story, for the Dutch, taking the opportunity of the discamping and long march of the French, presently surrounded Charleroy, the place they had all along had their design upon, which forced the Prince, after a tedious march to Oudenard for the apprehension of Don Tomazo's invisible engineers, to hurry back again to the relief of Charleroy, where he had no small trouble to raise the besiegers, not daring to give them battle, though he had much the advantage. And it may be truly said that this invented chimera of Don Tomazo's, the product of a mere accident, had so disordered the measures of the French councils by sending their General from post to pillar that they could not recover their senses all that Summer. From such small beginnings oft times arise the most fatal revolutions in the world.

For, to say truth, the siege of Oudenard was never dreamt of till Don Tomazo's return from thence with the Marquis's pistols, and his presenting the Prince of Orange with the draughts and observations he had made. But then the Prince consulted all his engineers and diverse councils of war were held upon the occasion of Don Tomazo's discoveries, which were found to be of that consequence that the Dutch fell in good earnest to the siege of Oudenard, which put the Prince of Condé to another dance of attendance upon their masterships to rouse 'em from that haunt. Which happened very much to the loss of the besiegers and more for the Prince of Condé's honour, though Don Tomazo had put him to trot hard for it. However, there were some commanders of great experience among the Dutch, who were of opinion that had the directions which Don Tomazo gave them been rightly managed and kept private, the success of the enterprise could not have failed.

But that which occasioned the ill successes of the Dutch, I mean not only in this particular but at other times, was first their ill conduct in not concealing the good services, nor indeed the names of the persons, of those they put upon such employments as these, and then so often communicating their designs to such as gave immediate notice to the French, by whose advices the Dutch spies were so often discovered and hanged that, others being discovered, their intelligence was very insignificant till Don Tomazo undertook the business, who so ordered it that he had several emissaries up and down in the French army and some that waited even upon some of the principal officers themselves, which he had in daily pay, besides others that continually trotted between them in the army and himself, who with Don Pedro still kept his quarters in some Spanish garrison nearest his business, modelling collateral designs of another nature.

The next Summer, the face of affairs was somewhat altered, the Prince of Condé being removed into Alsatia and the Duke of Luxemburgh made general of the army in Flanders, which clearly disordered Tomazo's former settlement. So that he was forced to go himself to new model his affairs, which he effectually performed. For he got Don Pedro to be a valet du chambre to the Duke himself, by which means Don Pedro became very serviceable to him. His correspondence being thus settled and carried on for near four months, Don Tomazo found that some of the Spanish governors were not so kind to him as he expected, and therefore he made his complaint to the Prince of Orange, who soon after procured letters of recommendation from the Duke de Villa Hermosa, not only to those, but to all others which Don Tomazo had occasion to visit—a certain sort of utensils which he knew how to make use of.

Some time after, there happened certain disorders among the confederate spies which could not be well settled unless Don Tomazo appeared among them in person, and as it fell out, no other place would serve but the Duke of Luxemburgh's quarters themselves. In order to [undertake] this difficult journey, Don Tomazo puts on the habit of a merchant, gets as many passports as were requisite for a man under such circumstances to travel with, and so sets forward on foot towards the French camp. By the way he narrowly escaped the pursuit of several boors in the province of Artois, who would certainly have stripped, if not murdered him, had he not showed them a good pair of heels, the use of which he well understood, for it was common with him to travel fifty miles a day in that country.

He had no sooner got clear of this cursed crew but he met with another party, about half a mile off, as bad as themselves. Through these he had no other means to escape but by making his way by main force, which so provoked those bloody varlets that some of them let fly several shot at him from their fuzees,* while others set arunning after him, thinking to have overtaken him; and perhaps they might have won the race to the loss of his life had he not met with some of the horseguards of Lisle then scouting abroad who, observing what had passed between the boors and him, presently seized him and sent him away to the garrison, where he was detained by the captain of the guard, notwithstanding that he showed him his passports, who told Don Tomazo that he was a spy and only forced in by a party of their men who were gone out but a little before, and that therefore he should stay till the party returned.

Don Tomazo, vexed at this stop, acquainted the captain with the real occasion of his travelling that way, which was to wait upon the Duke of Luxemburgh, but nothing would serve, till at length the soldiers coming back and giving the captain an account how he had been pursued by the boors, and how they had seized him to secure him out of their clutches, he was presently discharged, but ordered to attend the Governor, who was desirous to see him, having heard of his deliverance out of the hands of the sons of Belial.

The Governor liked Don Tomazo so well that he would fain have entertained him in his house, as being unwilling to part with him, always acknowledging the great obligations the English had laid upon him in his extremity, in remembrance whereof he thought himself engaged to be kind to Don Tomazo. But he, knowing the urgency of his own affairs far better than the Governor, pretended that his errand was to the Duke of Luxemburgh and then told him so much of his business as concerned the French interest. Whereupon the Governor, sorry that he had detained Don Tomazo so long, to make him amends by expediting his journey, caused his groom to saddle two very good horses and to attend Don Tomazo till he saw him with the Duke.

This kindness of the Governor Don Tomazo could very well have borne with, had not the groom been ordered to see him with the Duke. For Don Tomazo, being resolved to make the Governor, who had given him nothing but a parcel of good words, pay for his loss of time, had already designed to take the horses in execution for his debt. All the matter was how to get rid of this impertinent groom. Which put Don Tomazo upon his invention that seldom failed, and at this time proved most faithful to him, for as he was riding before by a piece of enclosed ground, upon a pretence that he had seen a hare, he had flung his cane over the hedge and therefore prayed the groom to alight and fetch it him again, while he held his horse.

Don Tomazo, finding this the only time to prevent his being brought before the Duke of Luxemburgh, left his conductor to return home afoot, and rode clear away with the horses to Mons, a garrison of the Spaniards. Upon his arrival there he was presently carried by two files of musketeers to the Governor, then the Duke of Arescot, who had had letters of recommendation in the behalf of Don Tomazo from the Duke of Villa Hermosa before. To the Duke, Don Tomazo told the whole story of his travels and how he had served the Governor of Lisle for detaining him from his business. Thereupon the Duke caused the horses to be sold by beat of drum, upon the sale of which Don Tomazo received six and forty pound, which he put up in his pocket to drink the Governor of Lisle and his groom's health.

Two days after, the Duke sent a convoy of 800 dragoons to Brussels for provisions. Thither with them went Don Tomazo and there, considering the pressing want of his appearance among his confederates in the French army, he resolved to adventure once more. To which purpose he dressed himself up in a poor habit like a woman, and so setting forward, the next day made his private entry into the French camp, where, after he had settled all his affairs, scoured and oiled all his wheels and set 'em at work again, as he was coming away, it being in the evening, a certain lascivious horse officer, mad to be riding a fresh country wench, would needs have been forcing up Don Tomazo's coats, so that the young Amazon, not willing to be discovered, was forced to use her utmost strength to keep the boisterous officer honest.

Thereupon, as all repulses in love beget revenge, the disappointed cavalier, not believing so much strength in that sex, and disdaining to be so slighted by a bumpkinly trull, commanded some of his soldiers to search Tomazo, which when those rugged men midwives had done, and made the true discovery, th'enraged Hotspur caused Don Tomazo to be tied neck and heels and secured as a spy.

Now was Don Tomazo in a bushel of troubles and, one would think, past all redemption but give a man luck and quoit him into the sea.* In this condition therefore, Don Tomazo, arming himself with his wonted confidence, sends to speak in private with his amorous officer, which being condescended to, Don Tomazo gave him such a parcel of demonstrations so satisfactory to a fellow that had more treachery than wit, that he not only ordered no more noise to be made of the business, but at the request of Don Tomazo, went himself to tell the Duke of Luxemburgh that there was a person stolen out of the Prince of Orange his army in woman's apparel to make some discovery to his Excellency, whereupon the Duke sent for Don Tomazo.

But having heard how the Prince of Condé had been trout-tickled, and resolving that nobody should make a gudgeon of him, so soon as Don Tomazo was brought before him, sent for several officers, who had served in the army when the Prince of Condé commanded, to come and view Don Tomazo. But it so happened that now there was not one that could remember him, upon which assurance the Duke was willing to hear what Don Tomazo had to say, which was to this effect, as close as all the wit he had could prompt him to lay it: that an English colonel in the Dutch army had a great inclination to serve the King of France and to that purpose would so order his business that all his men and officers should privately convey themselves into the French camp, provided the Duke would assure them of the same employments in his service as they had under the Prince of Orange, and further, that the said colonel had employed him, who was one of his corporals, to treat with his Excellency about it.

This tale of a roasted horse seemed very probable to the Duke by reason of the frequent revolts of the English to the French, in regard of their better pay and usage. Thereupon the Duke obliged Don Tomazo to assure the officers that they should not only have the same employments, but also considerations of greater value, and to give Don Tomazo an occasion to applaud his bounty, with his own hand put into Don Tomazo's palm ten pistols for a taste, for which Don Tomazo, having made a scrape or a curtsy, he cannot well remember, with a most cheerful heart withdrew, and being now from a mouse in a trap advanced to be a man at full liberty, repairs to the Prince of Orange, to whom he related the good and bad fortune that had befallen him since the last time that he had waited upon his Highness, which so well pleased the Prince that he, remembering the proverb of the pitcher, kindly persuaded Don Tomazo not to venture any more—as indeed he did not intend, but seemingly refused to give over, keeping his private correspondence still with his agents in pay, though that knack of his were unknown to the Prince.

But by this time the Winter approached, and the rivulets of money not flowing so freely from the Prince's springs, as if there were no need of intelligence in the Winter, Don Tomazo, who thought he deserved as much in the Winter as in the Summer, and therefore apprehended himself to be slighted, sent for Don Pedro out of the French army and resolves to set some engine at work. To this purpose, Don Tomazo, taking Don Pedro along with him, went to the governor of Gaunt,* with whom he was sure there lay perdue* a letter of recommendation from the Duke of Villa Hermosa in his behalf, as there did with all the rest of the Spanish governors.

To this same great man of trust, Don Tomazo pretended that Don Pedro was going upon particular and immediate service into the French camp, but wanted money to defray the necessary expenses of the design. Upon which assertion of such a known minister among them as Don Tomazo, Don Pedro was presently furnished with £30. With which pretence they visited all the most considerable governors of the Spanish garrisons, which produced a notable heap, for they never got less than twenty pound at a place.

At length, having no more but one to visit, who was a great

grandee, they resolved to strike him home, to which intent they
took up their quarters in Antwerp, and as they never wanted tools
(for Don Tomazo had provided himself of a signet with the
Prince of Orange's arms), they counterfeited a letter from the
Prince to Count Salazar, then governor of Antwerp castle, in
these very words:

'Sir,
        let this person, the bearer hereof, be furnished with 400
pistols and four horses, at the request of

                                                        Prince Orange'

This letter was carried by Don Tomazo alone, and being
showed to the Count, who had not the least suspicion that it was
written at Don Tomazo's quarters in Antwerp, ordered the
money forthwith to be paid and the horses to be delivered, which
you may be sure were none of the worst. For the Count was so
civil to the Prince as to give Don Tomazo the liberty to go into his
stable and make choice of such as he should think most proper
for his purpose. And for prevention of the bad effects of second
thoughts, as well as for their own ease, Don Tomazo requested
the Count that he would permit one of his grooms to ride along
with him, a request soon granted to the spymaster-general of
Holland.

Having thus done all their business with success, Don Tomazo
and Don Pedro rode directly like Castor and Pollux to Dunkirk
where, being stopped by the out-guards, Don Tomazo, with a
kind of impatient countenance of business, desired to be carried
forthwith before the governor, to whom, so soon as he had the
liberty of a private audience, he related in part what he had done
to the advantage of the French, that his coming to that garrison
was to serve the King his master, and as such a one desired to be
entertained.

Upon this the governor received both Don Tomazo and Don
Pedro with great civility, giving them permission to dispose of
their booty. But Don Tomazo, being willing to lay some kind of
obligation upon the governor, for the proverb tells ye there is
daubing* in all trades, as an acknowledgement of his favour

presented him with two of the best. The other two they put i'their pockets and, having given the groom a small gratuity for his attendance and money to bear his expenses, they dismissed him with as ponderous a compliment to his master as they thought his memory was able to bear, which by that time was as welcome to the Count as the sound of his passing-bell.

For before the return of the groom with his vostre tres humbles,* the Prince of Orange, passing through Antwerp in his way to the Hague (the campaign being then broke up), the Spanish Count, believing he had laid a great obligation upon the Prince never to be forgotten, gave him to understand how ready he had been to observe his Highness's commands in furnishing Don Tomazo according to his request, expecting some mountainous compliment for his great care. But the Prince, not knowing what the Count meant, instead of applauding his sedulity fell alaughing, adding withal that it was a trick and that he must pay for his learning. 'No, not so,' replied the Count, 'for I have your Highness's hand to show for what I have done,' and presently drew the note out of his pocket.

The Prince read it and showed it to all the chief personages about him, who could not gainsay but that it was the Prince's subscription and his secretary's writing. However, in regard the Prince could not remember either the time or the occasion of such a bountiful piece of writing, it was by all condemned for a cheat and so the Count lost his cause. Nevertheless, the Prince, more sensible than the rest of the motives that had induced Don Tomazo to make such an ill use of his ingenuity, protested that, if Don Tomazo were with him again, he should not be so slighted as he had been, for that he had done him very great services, and therefore could not well be blamed for carving for himself what ought to have been with more freedom allowed him.

Weary now of the land service for a while, they resolved to commit themselves to the mercy of the ocean, and to venture the hazards of three unruly elements—fire, air and water—all at once. In order to which resolution the two bold sparks, flush with the spoils of the Flandrian governors, make a league with a privateer at Dunkirk, and so hoisting sail, they steer away for the North-East sea, where after they had taken several prizes, Don Tomazo was ordered by the captain to officiate in one of the best as his lieutenant.

Now would it not vex a man of sense to be in possession of a Peruvian mine and in a moment to lose it again through the folly, or rather madness, of a company of unruly beasts? For this same prize wherein Tomazo was, being well stored with wine as well as other rich commodities, had given the seamen such a fatal opportunity to steep themselves in the juice of the grape that, while their heads swam, the ship run aground upon the Isle of Amelandt,* in which condition Don Tomazo and the rest of the seamen, having pillaged her of the best of her lading, left her to the mercy of the next tide and got ashore, which being discovered by two Dutchmen that belonged to the vessel before she was made prize, the country rose upon the miserable sons of misfortune, took them every mother's son prisoners, and carried them to Harling in Friezeland, where after they had stripped and eased them of their rich plunder—which in gold, jewels, necklaces of pearl and other commodities of the highest value, found upon no more than thirteen men, amounted to no less than £15,000 sterling—they were so charitable as to deliver them some of their seamen's old clothes to cover their nakedness, and so with five shillings apiece to bear their expenses, turned 'em like a sort of Christian dogs out of the town to enquire their way home to Dunkirk, which is near a hundred leagues. So little compassion do malefactors find among the wicked themselves.

In their way, the chiefest place of note was Amsterdam, where Don Tomazo, having entered into a confederacy with two of the stoutest and acutest of the distressed gang, resolved to make a full stop, leaving the rest to take their own course. Here Don Tomazo, hourly instigated by his late sufferings and losses fresh in memory, thinking no injury he could do so merciless an enemy could equalise the miseries which they had caused him to endure, sought all opportunities to satisfy his importunate revenge.

Nor needed he long to wait, for those occasions are always at the elbow of those that dare adventure to attempt. And so it now happened, for at that time, several East India ships, being newly returned home, lay below a certain place called the Pampus, not being able to get over the sands till they had lightened themselves by unloading some part of their freight. To which purpose, several small vessels of thirty and forty ton apiece were employed to carry the goods so unladen up the river to Amsterdam, all which Don Tomazo and his comrades, with teeth watering and fingers itching, well observed. And therefore, knowing their condition to be desperate, and that if their courage did not put an end to their misery, their necessity would soon send them for another world, for which they were not yet ready, they resolved to play at hazard and venture neck or nothing.

With which resolution they made bold to borrow a small boat from Amsterdam and to set sail toward the Pampus, upon the trail of their fortune. By the way they met with a vessel of forty tons, laden with Indian goods, which in the height of their indigent fury they presently took, though guarded by nine men, whom they made prisoners. With this prize, the three daring adventurers sailed close by the ship from whence the goods were taken, whose company, well knowing that was not the way to Amsterdam, let fly several shot at Don Tomazo's prize; however, all to no purpose, they had as good ha' thrown their caps at it, for the vessel, running right before the wind, got presently out of their reach.

But coming up with the Texel at the mouth of the river, the gunner of that fort having observed the shot which the East India giant had made at Tomazo's pigmy, sent his iron round robins after him too, which made several loopholes in the sails and some few in the hull of the vessel, but all to little or no effect, so that now being quite out of their reach and, as they thought, out of danger, they put boldly to sea and steered their course directly for Dunkirk.

But when Fortune has a mind to play her Christmas gambols, the Devil's in her, she's as wanton as a kitten; nobody knows where to have her, sometimes she's as kind as an innkeeper's daughter, sometimes as froppish* as a Quaker's wife; sometimes as sweet as a whore in drink, sometimes as testy as a losing gamester. As, for example, you shall see how she dealt with poor Don Tomazo before she harboured him in his desired port. For no sooner were he and his two comrades, with their prize, upon the wide ocean making for Dunkirk, but they were kenned by a Rotterdam man of war, whose business it was to cruise about and clear the coast; who, judging by their course that they were no friends of his, gave them chase and about an hour after coming up with them, took the vessel.

Upon his first examination he found the Indian commodities, and upon a further search, the skipper, whom Don Tomazo had stowed in a little hole in the hold, who gave the captain a full account of the whole transaction. Whereupon the captain sent away the vessel for Rotterdam, but kept Don Tomazo and his associates in affliction on board his own ship, which was to continue at sea a month longer by order from the States General.

Thus much for Don Tomazo, whom Fortune had deprived of the profit of all his fair hazard and confined to an abstemious, poor-John diet. Now you shall see how she bobbed the captain of the man of war. For about a week after, certain privateers happening to pass the channel, being three in number, the captain made all his sail, and coming up with one of their prizes, retook her and after that another, which the three pickaroons observing, and well knowing their strength, for they had eight or ten guns and a hundred men apiece, two of them resolved to attack the man of war while the other was sent to retake their prizes, which being resolved, the Dutch man of war was boarded and, after a smart fight, compelled to yield.

The Dutch captain thus bejaded and his ship secured, Don Tomazo appeared in his likeness and gave the French an account of his exploits, which so well pleased the privateers that they highly applauded him. But Don Tomazo, full of revenge for the good booty he had lost, requested the captains to spare him a little money and six men besides his two comrades, for that he was resolved once more to try his fortune upon the same coast, which request of his was not only granted, but one of the French captains, mainly pleased both with Don Tomazo and his proposals, resolved to make one of the company, and for his security took his commission with him, which was for both land and sea.

By this time the other privateer had retaken the two lost prizes and so they all steered directly for Dunkirk, taking the valiant defender of his country along with them to feed upon the same bread of affliction which he had intended for Don Tomazo. So various are the chances of whimsical war. At the same time, Don Tomazo, the captain and his crew took a small boat and made for the land, and being got ashore, parted company and went by couples directly to Rotterdam, where, after they had continued four days, they found probability enough of good store of purchase, though not so rich as what Tomazo had already lost.

But the main booty they had fixed their eyes upon was a great fly-boat which lay in the road before Rotterdam, but that day returned from Cadiz very richly laden, having in her a month's provision, twenty-four guns mounted, all her sails furled to the yard, and above half her men gone ashore. This vessel Don Tomazo and his crew resolved to attack in the night. And for the better carrying on of their enterprise, Don Tomazo with the company went to a village called Lyrendam and set it afire, to the end that, while the people were busied for their own security, they might with more freedom do their own work.

Which fell out very luckily, for the fire had consumed six houses and four ships, during which time Don Tomazo and his company had taken the fly-boat from seventeen men that guarded it. Who being secured without any noise, they cut the cables and let the vessel drive with the tide before they loosed so much as one sail, till being almost out of sight, they spread their canvas wings and made all the way they could. So kindly does one mischief assist another.

Being now got below the Brill, they spied a very gay pleasure boat under sail and bound for Rotterdam, at the sight of which they brought their ship to an anchor, manned out their longboat and boarded the little yacht with the usual fury that the hope of purchase inspires, that they soon made themselves masters of her, four great mijnheers and their wives, together with nine men more and four seamen. These fine folks had been taking their pleasure all the day before at sea, but Don Tomazo and his company got the profit of their voyage at night, which consisted of several good watches, jewels, necklaces of pearl and chains of gold to a considerable value.

The pleasure boat they sunk and then carried all their prisoners aboard their great vessel, who being disposed of, they weighed anchor and set sail till they were clear out at sea. At what time they put the mijnheers and their company into two shallops, which they had made use of for the conquest of their prize, and sent them home to bewail their losses, having above a league to the shore. While the mijnheers and their wives were lamenting the sour sauce to their sweet jollity, Don Tomazo and his crew divided the spoil and, being assisted with a thumping gale at Nore Nore-East, in a short time arrived in Ostend road, where being spied by a privateer belonging to the town, who guessed her to be a prize taken by the French, he gave her chase and in two hours reached her.

Don Tomazo and the captain his comrade would not fire so much as one gun till the Ostender was come within half shot, but then bringing four guns double laden to bear upon him all at a time, they so raked his sides that, not liking his entertainment, he sprung his luff and lay by to repair his damages, while Don Tomazo kept on his course and in twelve or fourteen hours after arrived safe in the Splinter.

The arrival of Don Tomazo with this prize was more welcome to his owners than Summer to the swallow. Who, after they had highly caressed and entertained him, exposed the ship and goods to sail and upon receipt of their money gave Don Tomazo and his fellow captain £4,600 for their shares, the ship and cargo being worth eight times as much, considering that there was found at the bottom of the vessel a great chest crowded with pieces of eight not less worth than two-thirds of the purchase. Don Tomazo and the captain, thus contented and satisfied, generously rewarded the seamen with £300 a man and gave the prisoners which they had brought along with them twenty crowns apiece to bear their expenses home, wherein they showed nineteen times more full ounces of charity than the Dutch had shown them before at Harling.

Don Tomazo, being now at some leisure, began to enquire after his beloved friend Don Pedro, concerning whom he had this account: that Don Pedro had been also put into another prize, and that they feared he had undergone the same misfortune which Don Tomazo had suffered upon the coast of Amelandt. Soon after, Don Tomazo received a letter from Don Pedro that the ship with which he had been entrusted was cast away, which letter was writ not for any truth that it contained, but only for the cold comfort and satisfaction of the owners. For indeed the company had agreed with Don Pedro to run the ship to Leith and there expose her to sale. But the Scots, being too cunning for them, laid up the vessel and only gave Don Pedro and his mates enough to bear their charges to Dunkirk, so that upon their return they were forced to make good the truth of Don Pedro's letter by affirming the loss of the prize, which was too true, to their cost.

The two Dons being thus reunited, and having drowned in the pleasures of the land the memory of their salt-water afflictions, and purged themselves from the scorbutic humours of hung beef and Groynland fish, resolved to try their talents once more upon the terra firma. In pursuit of which resolution away they went to the Duke of Luxemburgh's army, then encamped not far from Mons. So soon as they came thither, upon their addresses to the Duke they were both admitted volunteers in his own regiment of foot and soon after advanced, Don Pedro to be youngest lieutenant and Don Tomazo to be youngest ensign in the same regiment, the Duke not suspecting in the least that one of these two was the person that had put so many furberies* upon himself and the Prince of Condé his predecessor.

About half a year had these two Dons enjoyed their commissions, at what time the French and Dutch armies met at Cenneff,* which occasioned a most terrible fight wherein, to the unspeakable grief of Don Tomazo, Don Pedro was slain, and Don Tomazo himself taken prisoner and, which was worst of all, by a party of horse that belonged to Salazar, Governor of Antwerp castle, of whom Don Tomazo had borrowed the money and horses in the Prince of Orange's name. These needy Spaniards, having uncased Don Tomazo, found in his pockets several rough draghts of Antwerp, Mechlen, Ipre, Louvain, Gant and several other Spanish garrisons, upon which they conjectured him to be a spy, and so publicly declared him to be.

The noise of a spy's being taken in time of fight, and by his own men, made the old Count eagerly desirous to see this same thief of intelligence. But no sooner did Don Tomazo appear in his sight but the cunning Governor, at first view without spectacles, knew him to be the person that he had furnished with the money and horses, as already has been related. So that without any further examination, Don Tomazo was committed close prisoner to Antwerp castle and, by the Count's order, guarded day and night by four sentinels to prevent any discourse or conveyance of letters.

This severe confinement lasted about four months, in which time the misfortunes of an English gentleman had entered the college of Jesuits at Antwerp, and was more particularly taken notice of by one Father Worseley, who was the only man among them that made it his business to gain proselytes. He therefore, at the instigation of his zeal, prevailed with the Count to discourse* Don Tomazo, a request easily obtained by one of his order and function.

When Father Worseley came to discourse Don Tomazo in English, Heavens, what a refreshing it was to him! For he had not spoken to any person whatever in ten weeks before. Presently, Don Tomazo besought the old father to take his confession (for Don Tomazo, shrewdly guessing at the occasion of his charitable visit, was resolved to prevent him of the trouble of a conversion), which he did accordingly, and therein, as Don Tomazo had ordered it, had some sort of information of Don Tomazo's case. From thenceforward the old Father looked upon him as his pupil, procured him a better provision of diet and lodging, and came often to visit him, as well to confirm him in his faith as to fathom the bottom of his crime. And at length the Father's good opinion of his penitent moved him to so much compassion that, having thoroughly sifted his case, and understanding that the draghts which the Spaniards found in his pockets were the effects of his employment under the Prince of Orange, and that the Prince had been presented with all the copies of them, he resolved to take a journey to the Prince to know the truth of the matter, which he soon found to be real, and that the Prince was sorry for Tomazo's misfortune.

During these negotiations of the old Father, Don Tomazo was brought before a court martial, convicted for a spy, and sentenced to be shot to death by two files of musketeers. But upon Don Tomazo's application, he was allowed five days' time for him to prepare himself for another world, neither he knowing of the Father's journey, nor the Father of his condition. But it luckily fell out that the old Father returned before two of the five days were expired, and brought along with him a letter from the Prince of Orange to the Duke de Villa Hermosa purporting the great desire he had that Don Tomazo should be discharged.

But the old Father, having all the Count's revenge and interest at court to deal with, found it hard to get the Prince's letter allowed, so that all he could obtain for the present was a reprieve for fourteen days longer. In that time, the Father made another journey to the Prince and then returned with two letters, one to the Duke and another to the Count, which gave them both such satisfaction that Don Tomazo was ordered to be discharged. But the old Father, desirous to try whether Don Tomazo were a true son of the church or no, kept him still in ignorance of his proceedings, and still admonished him to prepare for death, as Don Tomazo did according to all the ceremonies of the Romish church, as being indifferent to him, since he must die, of what religion he died.

So that now the time prefixed being quite expired, Tomazo was brought to the tree, bound fast, the soldiers in his sight ready presented, the old man on his right hand, the few ejaculations he had were spent and he ready to give the sign, when the old Father, seeing the constancy of his devout son, unbound him and with tears embraced him (an odd kind of ambition in those people to heighten the merits of their obligations), crying out, 'My son, thou shalt not die, for God has intended thee for some good and pious work.'

Don Tomazo, thus discharged, was taken by the old Father to the Jesuits' college, where the members of the order raised him a collection of thirty-seven pound, which put him into an equipage to return to the French army, where he was no sooner arrived but he was informed by an English soldier that Don Pedro was slain, that all their equipage and money was seized, for that the Duke of Luxemburgh had understood, as indeed their papers demonstrated no less, that his lieutenant and ensign had been both spies for the Prince of Orange. It was a hard case for a man to lose all the treasure and sweet booty for which he had so often ventured his life, but Don Tomazo rather chose to abandon all than stand to the mercy of the Duke of Luxemburgh, and so with a heavy and disconsolate heart he took his way for Calice. From thence he crossed over to Dover and so came directly to London.

Being come to London, his first endeavour was to find out an associate fit for his turn, of which he could not well miss among so much variety. So that, having leagued himself with one (as he thought) according to his heart's desire and raised a small sum of money, they two fell to the old trade of counterfeiting gold. So that in a short time, they had made and uttered a considerable quantity, presuming to visit several parts wherein Don Tomazo had been before, which bold attempt proved very unsuccessful. For, having dispersed several of their illegitimate guineas in Wiltshire, Dorset and Hampshire, they were pursued and taken in Dorsetshire and both upon information committed to Dorchester prison.

Some time after, Don Tomazo was removed to Sarum, there to be tried according to the law for his offences committed in those parts, a thing that could not be avoided. So that he was convicted and suffered the penalty of his sentence and, which added to his affliction, he had no fair prospect of his release, as not having wherewithal to satisfy the irresistible demands of the gaoler. But Fortune, sometimes his friend as well as sometimes his foe, soon found out a way to bring him out of this labyrinth. For in a short time after, one of the tender sex, among whom he had always a friend in a corner, came and made him a visit so full-handed that Don Tomazo soon purchased the liberty of his heels, which being obtained, away he comes for London, where he first sought out and soon found a companion, for iniquity seldom prospers without confederacy.

This companion of his lent him his helping hand to the old profession, for they knew that the readiest way to have money was to make it themselves. And therefore, after they had stored themselves with a sufficient parcel of their own manufacture, and were able to set up for themselves, away they gallop to Newmarket, where it was their course to bet high, but never both of the same side, so that if the one lost, the other was sure to win, and the gains of the one easily made good the other's losses. For the loss of near a hundred guineas of Don Tomazo's quaint sort of metal did not amount to above seven pound.

This trade continued for some time with good success, there being hardly a horse race or a cock match that escaped the two guinea merchants. But that trade failing at length, Don Tomazo and his companion turned graziers, and frequenting the fairs and markets up and down the country, bought several droves of cattle with their unlawful coin for which, when they had driven them off to another place, they soon found chapmen, as being persons that could easily afford good pennyworths.

But the cry of the country farmers began to be so loud, when they found what a bad exchange they had made, that Don Tomazo and his companion, not able to endure the noise, were forced, after a trade of four months' continuance, to quit a calling so prejudicial to all the landlords and tenants in the country. So true is the proverb 'That nothing violent is of long continuance.'

Thus, nowhere safe, and continually lying under the curse of wasting perpetually what was ill got, the two knights of the order of industry resolved to take their pleasure at sea. To which purpose they bought them a vessel of about forty tons, and having manned her with persons fit for their purpose, they lay perdue, sometimes in the river's mouth, sometimes in the channel, to meet with merchants' vessels that were homeward bound, out of which Don Tomazo and his friend bought several good pennyworths of the seamen with their counterfeit gold, till they had almost loaded their vessel. Which done, away they made for some convenient port and exposed their goods to sale for good money. This was a way less hazardous but very expensive, and therefore, not answering expectation, was soon laid aside.

The sea trade failing for this reason, and the two merchants near broke, Don Tomazo and his comrade parted, after which, Don Tomazo, taking a journey into Berkshire to sow his yellow grain in that soil, was apprehended and committed to prison for endeavouring to enrich that county with his precious wealth. There he was kept half a year in durance, and sorely threatened to be sent to Heaven in a string, but not liking that way of travelling to bliss, he so ordered his affairs that he was discharged without any trial, though cruelly gripped with the pangs of poverty. For when the prison doors were opened to him, all his revenue was but three shillings.

But industry soon increased it, for out of that small sum, one being a milled shilling, he presently made a counterfeit guinea and passed it off with a Certiorari* for good. Which fruitful return soon produced a new recruit, so that in a short time he saw himself the father of two goodly twins, or bags, of a hundred pound apiece, begot by his own labour. This round sum warmed his invention and put him in an equipage to go on with a new project, in order to which, away he returns for London, hires several servants fit for his purpose according to the method of trim-tram,* and takes at least fourteen or fifteen lodgings of good note in the city, which lodgings were generally near the shopkeeper or the merchant that was to suffer under his contrivance. These boroughs of his he would visit several times in a day, lying sometimes at one and sometimes at another, till he had lain a night apiece in each, which being, as he thought, long enough, he began his frolic as follows.

Don Tomazo stayed in his lodging and sent a servant, as it might be, cross the way to a goldsmith, to bring him such and such parcels of rings and jewels of such a sort to show them his master. Presently, either the goldsmith or his man came along with the servant, in hopes of some great customer. But when Don Tomazo had fixed upon such jewels and rings which he seemed to like best, and agreed upon the price, the goldsmith, having left the main purchase with Don Tomazo, was desired to walk up another pair of stairs with his servant—if the house admitted of such a conveniency—there to receive his money. But no sooner was the goldsmith in the trap but the servant, who you may be sure was a special trout, locked the door upon the poor mouse and presently both master and man slipped away together.

At another place, having bought another parcel of the same commodities at the same rate, he would send his servant with the owner of the goods to some cashier or banker of note, to be there paid for his costly ware, and while his trusty servant and the goldsmith were trotting to the receipt of custom, away tripped Don Tomazo to another lodging, leaving his servant to make his escape and shift for himself as well as he could. And of such an exploit as this, a certain goldsmith in Lombard Street had the misfortune to have the woeful experience to the loss of £275. 17s. 6d.

Now you are to understand that, when Don Tomazo had once begun his diabolical progress, he used all the expedition imaginable in his dispatches and removals from place to place, in regard it behoved him never to leave off till he had made an effectual visit at all his particular abodes, which was done to all intents and purposes in the space of nine hours, by which he got more than the best day labourer that works at Paul's, the reward of those few hours' pains amounting to no less than £1,625. For he looked upon it as a calling too mean for one of his quality to make children's shoes.

But this trick made too great a noise to be played over again, so that Don Tomazo was resolved to knock off and live for some time upon the spoil. In order whereunto, like an honest master, he first discharged all his servants, to whom he gave £35 apiece, which amounted to £525, there being fifteen in all, and then retired into the country. But neither could he there rest long, for though he went under the most absolute disguise imaginable, yet it would so happen that some or other still knew him. So that, in short, by removing from place to place and living at the rate of a lord, his massy sum in two years was reduced to a hundred and fifty pound, with which Don Tomazo set forward again for London, the only stage proper for a gusman to act his parts upon, in order to the projecting some new enterprise.

But no sooner was he come to town, but a gentleman of Worcestershire, with whom Don Tomazo had been trafficking by way of exchange to the value of £170, met him in the street and began to make a noise, which Don Tomazo finding no way convenient for his interest, whispered the gentleman in the ear, which gentle motion of Don Tomazo's lips, having conveyed to his irritated senses a short promise of satisfaction, stopped the violent motion of the gentleman's tongue. Thereupon, away they went to the tavern, where Don Tomazo would fain have been rid of his troublesome companion, but he stuck so close to him, and kept him so charily within the reach of his eye, that Don Tomazo, to his unspeakable grief, was forced to come to composition and to pay the gentleman £120.

This forced putt* of moral satisfaction brought Don Tomazo very low. Hating, therefore, that want should be his master, he resolved to have one stroke more with his hammer, and so fell to the old trade of coining. Which work, by the help of two more assistants, being completed, and a good stock of pieces being made, they had laid their design to take a ramble into Essex, to dispose of their gold that made others poor and themselves rich.

Being upon their journey, they took Hackney in their way, where one of the sparks, having his pockets full of gold, would needs have the world to take notice of it, and to that end, at a place where he and his companions had called to drink a bottle of wine, pulled out his gold by handfuls and exchanged one of his counterfeit guineas to pay the reckoning. The King's picture dazzled the vintner's eyes at first, but they were no sooner gone but, happily for Essex, the cheat was discovered, which put the whole town upon a swift pursuit, and such a one as proved indeed so very swift that the whole knot of money-changers was quite untied, all of them taken and carried over the fields to a Justice of the Peace. By which means Don Tomazo took the advantage to dispose of his guineas in the long grass. Nevertheless, that poor shift would not do; Don Tomazo was sent to Newgate for company, tried at the Old Bailey for company, and fined £50 for company, and so was remanded to Newgate for company, where he lay a whole year, not able to pay his fine, and at length obtained his Majesty's most gracious pardon, by which he was discharged.

Having this ill luck in company, he fell to the old trade alone, with the assistance only of one servant. But whether Fortune had taken a pique against coiners, or whether Mercury were turned honest and had disposed of his influences another way, so it happened that Don Tomazo, having sent his boy to the silver market one evening in the shape of a vintner's servant to exchange some few counterfeit guineas, the raw messenger was taken, carried before a magistrate, examined, and, upon his examination, discovered his master. Whereupon Don Tomazo was as soon apprehended and sent to wait upon his man to Newgate. 'Twas an ill job for one misfortune so soon to fall upon the neck of another, but there was no avoiding these home thrusts of fate.

And therefore, Don Tomazo, to make the best of a bad market, made all his applications to his servant, and so far prevailed upon his good nature to recant his charge against his master and take the whole business upon himself, which he did with that exactness and fidelity that Don Tomazo, being tried first, was acquitted. But being forced to lie a good while before he could purchase his liberty, as being charged with actions to a great value, then it was that Mrs Cellier, having heard of Don Tomazo's fame, and believing him brisk for her turn, gave him her first visits, which produced those transactions between them that have lately made so great a noise in the world; for an account whereof, the reader is referred to the narratives themselves.*

dazzled the farmer's eyes at first; but they were no sooner gone out happily for Lopez, the thief was discovered, which put the whole town upon a swift pursuit, and such a one as proved indeed so very swift, that the whole line of robber-chargers was confounded, all of them taken and carried over the fields to a justice of the Peace. By which means Don Tomato took the advantage to dispose of his entrees in the long peace. I say, that poor ability would not let Don Tomato was sent to Segovia for company, tried at the Old Bailey for company, and tried ... so for company, and so was remanded to Segovia for company, whereas by a whole year not able to pay his fine, and at length obtained his release a most generous pardon, by which he was disburthened.

Having laid all in company, he fell to the old trade alone, with the assistance only of one servant. But whether Fortune had taken a pique against others, or whether Mercury were turned sober, and had disposed of his influences another way, so it happened that Don Tobasco, having sent his boy to the silver market one evening, in the shape of a vanteck servant, to exchange some few counters purses, the raw messenger was taken out of his luck's company, exchanged also, upon his examination, discovered his master. Whereupon Don Tobasco was soon apprehended and sent to wait upon Lisander to Segovia. 'Twas a pitiful job for one that had runs so far upon the neck of another; but there was no avoiding these honours of his way.

And therefore, Don Tobasco, to make the best of a bad matter, made full his applications to his servant, and so far prevailed upon his good nature to recant his charge against his master, and take the whole business upon himself, which he did with that frankness and fidelity, that Don Tobasco, being tried, was thus acquitted. But being forced to lie a good while before he could purchase his liberty, as being charged with robbing to a great value, then it is that this Guzman swine-band of Don Tomato's Gang, and being now only brisk for the turn, gave him his freedom, which produced those transactions between them that have since made so great a noise in the world; to an account whereof the reader is referred to themselves.

JOHN BUNYAN

The Life and Death of Mr Badman

(1680)

The Life and Death of Mr Badman, Presented to the World in a Familiar Dialogue Between Mr Wiseman and Mr Attentive.

Mr Badman's Courtship

WISEMAN . . . he was for looking out for a rich wife, and now I am come to some more of his invented, devised, designed and abominable roguery, such that will yet declare him to be a most desperate sinner.

The thing was this. A wife he wanted; or rather, money, for as for a woman, he could have whores enough at his whistle. But, as I said, he wanted money, and that must be got by a wife or no way. Nor could he so easily get a wife, neither, except he became an artist at the way of dissembling; nor would dissembling do among that people that could dissemble as well as he. But there dwelt a maid not far from him that was both godly and one that had a good portion. But how to get her, there lay all the craft!

Well, he calls a council of some of his most trusty and cunning companions and breaks his mind to them, to wit, that he had a mind to marry, and he also told them to whom. 'But,' said he, 'how shall I accomplish my end? She is religious and I am not.' Then one of them made reply, saying: 'Since she is religious, you must pretend to be so likewise, and that for some time before you go to her. Mark, therefore, whither she goes daily to hear,* and do you go thither also, but there you must be sure to behave yourself soberly and make as if you liked the Word wonderful well. Stand also where she may see you, and when you come home, be sure that you walk the street very soberly and go within sight of her.

(margin) Badman is for a rich wife.

(margin) Badman has a godly maid in his eye. He seeks to get her, why, and how.

(margin) He calls his companions together, and they advise him how to get her.

'This done for a while, then go to her and first talk of how sorry you are for your sins, and show great love to the religion that she is of, still speaking well of her preachers and of her godly acquaintance, bewailing your hard hap: that it was not your lot to be acquainted with her and her fellow professors* sooner. And this is the way to get her. Also, you must write down sermons, talk of scriptures, and protest that you came awooing to her only because she is godly, and because you should count it your greatest happiness if you might but have such an one. As for her money, slight it; it will be never the further off. That's the way to come soonest at it, for she will be jealous at first that you come for her money. You know what she has, but make not a word about it. Do this, and you shall see if you do not entangle the lass.'

Thus was the snare laid for this poor, honest maid, and she was quickly catched in his pit.

Attentive. *Why, did he take this counsel?*

Wiseman. Did he? Yes, and after a while went as boldly to her and that under a vizard of religion, as if he had been for honesty and godliness one of the most sincere and upright-hearted in England. He observed all his points, and followed the advice of his counsellors, and quickly obtained her too, for natural parts he had: he was tall and fair and had plain but very good clothes on his back. And his religion was the more easily attained, for he had seen something in the house of his father and first master, and so could the more readily put himself into the form and show thereof.

So he appointed his day, and went to her, as that he might easily do, for she had neither father nor mother to oppose. Well, when he was come and had given her a civil compliment, to let her understand why he was come, then he began and told her that he had found in his heart a great deal of love to her person, and that, of all the damsels in the world, he had pitched upon her, if she thought fit, to make her

Badman goes to the damsel as his counsel advised him.

Badman's compliment, his lying compliment.

his beloved wife. The reasons, as he told her, why he had pitched upon her, were her religious and personal excellencies, and therefore entreated her to take his condition into her tender and loving consideration.

'As for the world,' quoth he, 'I have a very good trade, and can maintain myself and family well, while my wife sits still on her seat. I have got thus and thus much already, and feel money come in every day. But that is not the thing that I aim at; 'tis an honest and godly wife.' Then he would present her with a good book or two, pretending how much good he had got by them himself. He would also be often speaking well of godly Ministers, especially of those that he perceived she liked and loved most. Besides, he would be often telling her what a godly father he had, and what a new man he was also become himself. And thus did this treacherous dealer deal with this honest and good girl, to her great grief and sorrow, as afterward you shall hear.

Attentive. *But had the maid no friend to look after her?*

Wiseman. Her father and mother were dead, and that he knew well enough, and so she was the more easily overcome by his naughty, lying tongue. But if she had never so many friends, she might have been beguiled by him. It is too much the custom of young people now to think themselves wise enough to make their own choice, and that they need not ask counsel of those that are older and also wiser than they. But this is a great fault in them, and many of them have paid dear for it.

Well, to be short, in little time Mr Badman obtains his desire, gets this honest girl and her money, is married to her, brings her home, makes a feast, entertains her royally—but her portion must pay for all.

Attentive. *This was wonderful deceitful doings; a man shall seldom hear of the like.*

Wiseman. By this his doing he showed how little

Neglect of counsel about marriage dangerous.

Badman obtains his desire, is married, etc.

His carriage
judged
ungodly and
wicked.

he feared God, and what little dread he had of His judgements. For all this carriage and all these words were by him premeditated evil. He knew he lied, he knew he dissembled; yea, he knew that he made use of the name of God, of religion, good men and good books, but as a stalking horse, thereby the better to catch his game. In all this his glorious pretence of religion, he was but a glorious, painted hypocrite, and hypocrisy is the highest sin that a poor, carnal wretch can attain unto. It is also a sin that most dareth God, and that also bringeth the greater damnation. Now was he a whited wall; now was he a painted sepulchre; 'now was he a grave that appeared not', for this poor, honest, godly damsel little thought that both her peace and comfort and estate and liberty and person and all were going to her burial when she was going to be married to Mr Badman. And yet so it was. She enjoyed herself but little afterwards; she was as if she was dead and buried to what she enjoyed before.

Matt. 23.

The great alteration that quickly happened to Badman's wife.

Attentive. *Certainly some wonderful judgement of God must attend and overtake such wicked men as these.*

Wiseman. You may be sure that they shall have judgement to the full for all these things, when the day of judgement is come. But as for judgement upon them in this life, it doth not always come—no, not upon those that are worthy thereof. 'They that tempt God are delivered, and they that work wickedness are set up.' But they are reserved to the day of wrath, and then, for their wickedness, God will repay them to their faces. 'The wicked is reserved to the day of destruction; they shall be brought forth to the day of wrath; who shall declare his way to his face, and who shall repay him what he hath done? Yet shall he be brought to the grave and remain in the tomb.'

Mala. 3: 15.

Expectation of judgement is for such things.

Job. 21, 30, 31, 32.

That is, ordinarily they escape God's hand in this life, save only a few examples are made that others may be cautioned and take warning thereby. But at the day of judgement, they must be rebuked for their evil with the lashes of devouring fire.

Attentive. Can you give me no examples of God's wrath upon men that have acted this tragical, wicked deed of Mr Badman?

Wiseman. Yes: Hamor and Shechem and all the men of their city, for attempting to make God and religion the stalking horse to get Jacob's daughters to wife, were together slain with the edge of the sword. A judgement of God upon them, no doubt, for their dissembling in that matter. All manner of lying and dissembling is dreadful, but to make God and religion a disguise, therewith to blind thy dissimulation from others' eyes, is highly provoking to the Divine Majesty.

An example of God's anger on such as have heretofore committed this sin of Mr Badman. Gen. 24.

I knew one that dwelt not far off from our town, that got him a wife as Mr Badman got his. But he did not enjoy her long, for one night, as he was riding home from his companion's where he had been at a neighbouring town, his horse threw him to the ground, where he was found dead at break of day, frightfully and lamentably mangled with his fall and besmeared with his own blood.

Attentive. Well, but pray return again to Mr Badman. How did he carry it to his wife after he was married to her?

Wiseman. Nay, let us take things along as we go. He had not been married but a little while, but his creditors came upon him for their money. He deferred them a little while, but at last things were come to that point that pay he must, or must do worse. So he appointed them a time and they came for their money, and he paid them down with her money before her eyes for those goods that he had profusely spent among his whores long before (besides the portion that his father gave him), to the value of two hundred pounds.

After Badman is married his creditors come upon him, and his wife's portion pays for that which his whores were feasted with before he was married.

Attentive. This beginning was bad, but what shall I say? 'Twas like Mr Badman himself. Poor woman, this was but a bad beginning for her. I fear it filled her with

*trouble enough, as I think such a beginning would have
done one perhaps much stronger than she.*

Wiseman. Trouble! Aye, you may be sure of it, but
now 'twas too late to repent. She should have looked
better to herself when being wary would have done
her good. Her harms may be an advantage to others
that will learn to take heed thereby, but for herself, she
must take what follows: even such a life now as Mr
Badman her husband will lead her, and that will be
bad enough.

Attentive. *This beginning was bad, and yet I fear it
was but the beginning of bad.*

Wiseman. You may be sure that it was but the
beginning of badness, for other evils came on apace.
As, for instance, it was but a little while after he was
married but he hangs his religion upon the hedge, or
rather, dealt with it as men deal with their old
clothes, who cast them off or leave them to others to
wear. For his part, he would be religious no longer.
Now, therefore, he had pulled off his vizard and
began to show himself in his old shape: a base,
wicked, debauched fellow, and now the poor woman
saw that she was betrayed indeed. Now also his old
companions begin to flock about him and to haunt
his house and shop as formerly. And who with them
but Mr Badman, and who with him again but they?

Now those good people that used to company with
his wife began to be amazed and discouraged; also,
he would frown and gloat upon them as if he
abhorred the appearance of them, so that in little
time he drove all good company from her and made
her sit solitary by herself. He also began now to go
out a nights to those drabs who were his familiars
before, with whom he would stay sometimes till
midnight, and sometimes till almost morning, and
then would come home as drunk as a swine. And this
was the course of Mr Badman.

Now, when he came home in this case, if his wife
did but speak a word to him about where he had

Marginal notes:

Now she reaps the fruits of her unadvisedness

Now Badman has got him a wife by religion, he hangs it by as a thing out of use, and entertains his old companions.

He drives good company from his wife.

He goes to his whores.

been and why he had so abused himself, though her words were spoken in never so much meekness and love, then she was whore and bitch and jade, and 'twas well if she missed his fingers and heels. Sometimes also he would bring his punks* home to his house, and woe be to his wife when they were gone, if she did not entertain them with all varieties possible, and also carry it lovingly to them. *He rails at his wife.*

Thus this good woman was made by Badman her husband to possess nothing but disappointments as to all that he had promised her, or that she hoped to have at his hands. But that that added pressing weight to all her sorrow was that, as he had cast away all religion himself, so he attempted, if possible, to make her do so too. He would not suffer her to go out to the preaching of the word of Christ, nor to the rest of His appointments for the health and salvation of her soul. He would now taunt at, and reflectingly speak of her preachers, and would receive, yea raise scandals of them, to her very great grief and affliction. *He seeks to force his wife from her religion.* *He mocks at her preachers.*

Now she scarce durst go to an honest neighbour's house or have a good book in her hand, specially when he had his companions in his house, or had got a little drink in his head. He would also, when he perceived that she was dejected, speak tauntingly and mockingly to her in the presence of his companions, calling of her his religious wife, his demure dame, and the like. Also, he would make a sport of her among his wanton ones abroad. *He mocks his wife in her dejections.*

If she did ask him (as sometime she would) to let her go out to a sermon, he would in a currish manner reply: 'Keep at home, keep at home, and look to your business. We cannot live by hearing of sermons.' If she still urged that he would let her go, then he would say to her: 'Go if you dare!' He would also charge her with giving of what he had to her Ministers when, vile wretch, he had spent it on his vain companions before. *He refuses to let her go out to good company.*

This was the life that Mr Badman's good wife lived within few months after he had married her.

Attentive. *This was a disappointment indeed!*

Wiseman. A disappointment indeed, as ever, I think, poor woman had. One would think that the knave might a little let her have had her will, since it was nothing but to be honest, and since she brought him so sweet, so lumping a portion, for she brought hundreds into his house. I say, one would think he should have let her had her own will a little, since she desired it only in the service and worship of God. But could she win him to grant her that? No, not a bit, if it would have saved her life. True, sometimes she would steal out when he was from home on a journey, or among his drunken companions, but with all privacy imaginable. And, poor woman, this advantage she had, she carried it so to all her neighbours that, though many of them were but carnal, yet they would not betray her or tell of her going out to the Word if they saw it, but would rather endeavour to hide it from Mr Badman himself.

She gets out sometimes by stealth.

Attentive. *This carriage of his to her was enough to break her heart.*

Wiseman. It was enough to do it indeed; yea, it did effectually do it. It killed her in time; yea, it was all the time a killing of her. She would oftentimes, when she sat by herself, thus mournfully bewail her condition: 'Woe is me, that I sojourn in Meshech and that I dwell in the tents of Kedar. My soul hath long time dwelt with him that hateth peace. O what shall be given unto thee, thou deceitful tongue, or what shall be done unto thee, thou false tongue? I am a woman grieved in spirit; my husband has bought me and sold me for his lusts. 'Twas not me but my money that he wanted. O that he had had it, so I had had my liberty!'

Her repentance and complaint. Psal. 120.

This she said, not of contempt of his person, but of his conditions, and because she saw that, by his hypocritical tongue, he had brought her not only almost to beggary, but robbed her of the Word of God.

Attentive. *It is a deadly thing, I see, to be unequally yoked with unbelievers. If this woman had had a good husband, how happily might they have lived together. Such an one would have prayed for her, taught her, and also would have encouraged her in the faith and ways of God. But now, poor creature, instead of this there is nothing but the quite contrary.*

The evil of being unequally yoked together.

Wiseman. It is a deadly thing indeed, and therefore, by the word of God, his people are forbid to be joined in marriage with them. 'Be not', sayeth it, 'unequally yoked together with unbelievers, for what fellowship hath righteousness with unrighteousness; and what communion hath light with darkness; and what concord hath Christ with Belial; or what part hath he that believeth with an infidel; and what agreement hath the temple of God with idols?' There can be no agreement where such matches are made. Even God Himself hath declared the contrary from the beginning of the world. 'I', says he, 'will put enmity betwixt thee and the woman, betwixt thy seed and her seed.' Therefore, he sayeth in another place, they can mix no better than iron and clay. I say, they cannot agree, they cannot be one, and therefore they should be aware at first and not lightly receive such into their affections. God has often made such matches bitter, especially to his own. Such matches are, as God said of Eli's sons that were spared, 'to consume the eyes and to grieve the heart.' O the wailing and lamentation that they have made that have been thus yoked, especially if they were such as would be so yoked against their light and good counsel to the contrary.

2 Cor. 6. 13.

Gen. 3. 15.

Deut. 2. 43.

Attentive. *Alas, he deluded her with his tongue and feigned reformation.*

Wiseman. Well, well, she should have gone more warily to work. What if she had acquainted some of

Good
counsel to
those godly
maids that
are to marry.

her best, most knowing and godly friends therewith? What if she had engaged a godly Minister or two to have talked with Mr Badman? Also, what if she had laid wait round about him to espy if he was not otherwise behind her back than he was before her face? And besides, I verily think (since in the multitude of counsellors there is safety) that if she had acquainted the congregation with it, and desired them to spend some time in prayer to God about it, and if she must have had him, to have received him as to his godliness upon the judgement of others, rather than her own, she knowing them to be godly and judicious and unbiased men, she had had more peace all her life after than to trust to her own poor, raw, womanish judgement as she did. Love is blind, and will see nothing amiss, where others may see an hundred faults. Therefore, I say she should not have trusted to her own thoughts in the matter of his goodness.

As to his person, there she was fittest to judge, because she was to be the person pleased; but as to his godliness, there the Word was the fittest judge, and they that could best understand it, because God was therein to be pleased. I wish †that all young maidens will take heed of being beguiled with flattering words, with feigning and lying speeches, and take the best way to preserve themselves from being bought and sold by wicked men, as she was, lest they repent with her, when (as to this) repentance will do them no good, but for their unadvisedness go sorrowing to their graves.

†A caution
to young
maidens.

Attentive. *Well, things are past with this poor woman, and cannot be called back. Let others† beware by her misfortunes, lest they also fall into her distress.*

† Let Mr
Badman's
wife be your
example.

Wiseman. That is the thing that I say; let them take heed, lest for their unadvisedness they smart, as this poor woman has done. And ah, methinks that they that yet are single persons, and that are tempted to marry to such as Mr Badman, would, to inform and warn themselves in this manner before they entangle themselves, but go to some that already are in the snare and ask them how it is with them, as to the suitable or unsuitableness of their marriage, and desire their advice. Surely they would ring such a peal in their ears about the unequality, unsuitableness, disadvantages and disquietments and sins that attend such marriages, that would make them beware as long as they live.

But the bird in the air knows not the notes of the bird in the snare until she comes thither herself. Besides, to make up such marriages, Satan and carnal reason and lust, or at least inconsiderateness, has the chiefest hand, and where these things bear sway, designs, though never so destructive, will go headlong on, and therefore I fear that but little warning will be taken by young girls at Mr Badman's wife's affliction.

Attentive. But are there no dissuasive arguments to lay before such, to prevent their future misery?

Wiseman. Yes, there is the law of God, that forbiddeth marriage with unbelievers. These kind of marriages also are condemned even by irrational creatures. It is forbidden by the law of God both in the Old Testament and in the New. 1. In the Old: 'Thou shalt not make marriages with them; thy daughter thou shalt not give unto his son, nor his daughter shalt thou take unto thy son', Deut. 7.4,5. 2 In the New Testament it is forbidden: 'Be not unequally yoked together with unbelievers; Let them marry to whom they will, only in the Lord.'

Here now is a prohibition plainly forbidding the believer to marry with the unbeliever; therefore they should not do it. Again, these unwarrantable marriages are, as I may so say, condemned by irrational creatures, who will not couple but with their own sort. Will the sheep couple with a dog, or the partridge with a crow, or the pheasant with an owl? No, they will strictly tie up themselves to those of

Deut. 7. 4, 5.

1 Cor. 7. 39.
2 Cor. 6. 14,
15, 16.

Rules for
those that
are to marry.

their own sort only. Yea, it sets all the world a wondering when they see or hear the contrary. Man only is most subject to wink at and allow of these unlawful mixtures of men and women, because man only is a sinful beast, a sinful bird, therefore he, above all, will take upon him by rebellious actions to answer, or rather to oppose and violate, the law of his God and creator. Nor shall these or other interrogatories (what fellowship, what concord, what agreement, what communion can there be in such marriages?) be counted of weight, or thought worth the answering by him.

If you love your souls take heed.

But further, the dangers that such do commonly run themselves into should be to others a dissuasive argument to stop them from doing the like, for besides the distresses of Mr Badman's wife, many that have had very hopeful beginnings for Heaven have, by virtue of the mischiefs that have attended these unlawful marriages, miserably and fearfully miscarried. Soon after such marriages, conviction (the first step towards Heaven) hath ceased; prayer (the next step toward Heaven) hath ceased; hungerings and thirstings after salvation (another step towards the kingdom of Heaven) have ceased. In a word, such marriages have estranged them from the Word, from their godly and faithful friends, and have brought them again into carnal company, among carnal friends, and also into carnal delights, where and with whom they have in conclusion both sinfully abode and miserably perished.

Deut. 7.

And this is one reason why God hath forbidden this kind of unequal marriages. 'For they,' sayeth he, meaning the ungodly, 'will turn away thy son from following me, that they may serve other gods, so will the anger of the Lord be kindled against you and destroy you suddenly.' Now mark, there were some in Israel that would, notwithstanding this prohibition, venture to marry to the heathens and unbelievers, but what followed? They served their idols; they

sacrificed their sons and their daughters unto devils.
Thus were they defiled with their own works, and
went a whoring with their own inventions. Therefore
was the wrath of the Lord kindled against his people,
insomuch that he abhorred his own inheritance.

Psal. 106. 35,
36, 37, 38,
39, 40.

Wiseman Tells Attentive Stories of God's Judgements

IN our town there was one W.S., a man of a very
wicked life, and he, when there seemed to be
countenance given to it, would needs turn informer.
Well, so he did, and was as diligent in his business as
most of them could be. He would watch a nights,
climb trees, and range the woods a days, if possible,
to find out the meeters,* for then they were forced to
meet in the fields. Yea, he would curse them bitterly
and swear most fearfully what he would do to them
when he found them. Well, after he had gone on like
a Bedlam in his course a while, and had done some
mischiefs to the people, he was stricken by the hand
of God, and that in this manner.

Mark.

1. Although he had his tongue naturally at will,
now he was taken with a faltering in his speech and
could not, for weeks together, speak otherwise than
just like a man that was drunk.

2. Then he was taken with a drooling or slabber-
ing at his mouth, which slabber sometimes would
hang at his mouth well nigh half way down to the
ground.

3. Then he had such a weakness in the back
sinews of his neck that oft times he could not look up
before him, unless he clapped his hand hard upon
his forehead and held up his head that way, by
strength of hand.

4. After this, his speech went quite away and he
could speak no more than a swine or a bear.
Therefore, like one of them, he would gruntle and

make an ugly noise, according as he was offended, or pleased, or would have anything done, etc.

In this posture he continued for the space of half a year or thereabouts, all the while otherwise well, and could go about his business, save once that he had a fall from the bell as it hangs in our steeple, which 'twas a wonder it did not kill him. But after that he also walked about, till God had made him a sufficient spectacle of his judgement for his sin, and then on a sudden he was stricken and died miserably, and so there was an end of him and his doings.

☞ I will tell you of another. About four miles from St Neots, there was a gentleman had a man, and he would needs be an informer, and a lusty young man he was. Well, an informer he was, and did much distress some people, and had perfected his informations so effectually against some, that there was nothing further to do but for the constables to make distress on the people, that he might have the money or goods and, as I heard, he hastened them much to do it.

Now, while he was in the heat of his work, as he stood one day by the fireside, he had (it should seem) a mind to a sop in the pan (for the spit was then at the fire), so he went to make him one. But behold, a dog (some say his own dog) took distaste at something, and bit his master by the leg, the which bite, notwithstanding all the means that was used to cure him, turned, as was said, to a gangrene. However, that wound was his death, and that a dreadful one too, for my relator said that he lay in such a condition by this bite (as the beginning) till his flesh rotted from off him before he went out of the world. But what need I instance in particular persons, when the judgement of God against this kind of people was made manifest, I think I may say, if not in all, yet in most of the counties in England where such poor creatures were. But I would, if it had been the will of God, that neither I nor anybody else could tell you more of these stories: true stories, that are neither lie nor romance.

Mr Badman's False Remorse

ATTENTIVE. *But it is† a rare case, even this of Mr Badman, that he should never in all his life be touched with remorse for his ill-spent life.*

† a rare thing.

Wiseman. Remorse I cannot say he ever had, if by remorse you mean repentance for his evils. Yet twice I remember he was under some trouble of mind about his condition: once when he broke his leg as he came home drunk from the ale-house, and another time when he fell sick and thought he should die. Besides these two times, I do not remember any more.

Mr Badman under some trouble of mind.

Attentive. Did he break his leg then?

Wiseman. Yes. Once, as he came home drunk from the ale-house.

Attentive. Pray how did he break it?

Wiseman. Why, upon a time he was at an ale-house, that wicked house, about two or three miles from home, and having there drank hard the greatest part of the day, when night was come, he would stay no longer, but calls for his horse, gets up, and like a madman (as drunken persons usually ride) away he goes, as hard as horse could lay legs to the ground. Thus he rid till, coming to a dirty place where his horse, flouncing in, fell, threw his master and with his fall broke his leg, so there he lay. But you would not think how he† swore at first. But after a while, he coming to himself, and feeling by his pain and the uselessness of his leg what case he was in, and also fearing that this bout might be his death, he began to cry out after the manner of such:† 'Lord help me, Lord have mercy upon me, good God deliver me' and the like. So there he lay till some came by who took him up, carried him home, where he lay for some time before he could go abroad again.

Mr Badman broke his leg.

† He swears.

† He prays.

Attentive. And then, you say, he called upon God.

Wiseman. He cried out in his pain, and would say 'O God' and 'O Lord, help me!', but whether it was that his sin might be pardoned and his soul saved, or whether to be rid of his pain, I will not positively determine, though I fear it was but for the last, because when his pain was gone and he had got hopes of mending, even before he could go abroad he cast off prayer and began his old game, to wit, to be as bad as he was before. He then would send for his old companions; his sluts also would come to his house to see him, and with them he would be, as well as he could for his lame leg, as vicious as they could be for their hearts.

It has no good effect upon him.

Attentive. 'Twas a wonder he did not break his neck.

Wiseman. His neck had gone instead of his leg, but that God was long suffering towards him; he had deserved it ten thousand times over. There have been many, as I have heard and as I have hinted to you before, that have taken their horses when drunk, as he, but they have gone from the pot to the grave, for they have broken their necks twixt the ale-house and home. One hard by us also drank himself dead; he drank, and died in his drink.

☞

Attentive. 'Tis a sad thing to die drunk.

Wiseman. So it is. But yet I wonder that no more do so. For considering the heinousness of that sin, and with how many other sins it is accompanied, as with oaths, blasphemies, lies, revellings, whorings, brawlings, etc., it is a wonder to me that any that live in that sin should escape such a blow from Heaven that should tumble them into their graves. Besides, when I consider also how, when they are as drunk as beasts, they, without all fear of danger, will ride like Bedlams and madmen, even as if they did dare God to meddle with them, if He durst, for their being drunk. I say, I wonder that He doth not withdraw his protecting providences from them and leave them to those dangers and destructions that by their sin they

How many sins do accompany drunkenness.

Acts 17. 30, 31, 32.

had deserved, and that by their Bedlam madness they would rush themselves into. Only I consider again that He has appointed a day wherein he will reckon with them, and doth also commonly make examples of some to show that he takes notice of their sin, abhors their way, and will count with them for it at the set time.

Attentive. It is worthy of our remark to take notice how God, to show his dislike of the sins of men, strikes some of them down with a blow, as the breaking of Mr Badman's leg, for doubtless that was a stroke from Heaven.

Wiseman. It is worth our remark indeed. It was an open stroke; it fell upon him while he was in the height of his sin. And it looks much like that in Job: 'Therefore he knoweth their works and overturneth them in the night, so that they are destroyed. He striketh them as wicked men in the open sight of others', or, as the margent reads it, 'in the place of beholders'. He lays them with his stroke in the place of beholders. There was Mr Badman laid; his stroke was taken notice of by everyone; his broken leg was at this time the town-talk.† 'Mr Badman has broken his leg', says one. 'How did he break it?' says another. 'As he came home drunk from such an ale-house,' said a third. 'A judgement of God upon him,' said a fourth. This his sin, his shame and punishment, are all made conspicuous to all that are about him. I will here tell you another story or two.

I have read in Mr Clark's *Looking Glass for Sinners,** that upon a time, a certain drunken fellow boasted in his cups that there was neither Heaven nor Hell. Also, he said he believed that man had no soul, and that for his own part, he would sell his soul to any that would buy it. Then did one of his companions buy it of him for a cup of wine, and presently the Devil in man's shape bought it of that man again at the same price, and so in the presence of them all laid hold on this soul-seller and carried

Job 34. 24, 25, 26.

† An open stroke.

Pag. 41.

him away through the air, so that he was never more heard of.

In page 148 he tells us also that there was one at Salisbury in the midst of his health-drinking and carousing in a tavern, and he drank a health to the Devil, saying that if the Devil would not come and pledge him, he would not believe that there was either God or Devil. Whereupon his companions, stricken with fear, hastened out of the room, and presently after, hearing a hideous noise and smelling a stinking savour, the vintner ran up into the chamber and, coming in, he missed his guest and found the window broken, the iron bar in it bowed and all bloody, but the man was never heard of afterwards.

Again, in page 149 he tells us of a bailiff of Headley, who upon a Lord's day, being drunk at Melford, got upon his horse to ride through the streets, saying that his horse would carry him to the devil, and presently his horse threw him and broke his neck. These things are worse than the breaking of Mr Badman's leg, and should be a caution to all of his friends that are living, lest they should also fall by their sin into these sad judgements of God.

But, as I said, Mr Badman quickly forgot all; his conscience was choked before his leg was healed. And therefore, before he was well of the fruit of one sin, he tempts God to send another judgement to seize upon him, and so He did quickly after. For not many months after his leg was well, he had a very

Mr Badman fallen sick.

dangerous fit of sickness, insomuch that now he began to think he must die in very deed.

Attentive. *Well, and what did he think and do then?*

His conscience is wounded.

Wiseman. He thought he must go to Hell. This I know, for he could not forbear but say so. To my best remembrance, he lay crying out all one night for fear, and at times he would so tremble that he would

† *He cries out in his sickness.*

make the very bed shake under him.† But O, how the thoughts of death, of Hell-fire and of eternal judgement did then wrack his conscience. Fear might be seen in his face and in his tossings to and fro; it might also be heard in his words, and be understood by his heavy groans. He would often cry: 'I am undone, I am undone, my vile life has undone me.'

Attentive. *Then his former atheistical thoughts and principles were too weak now to support him from the fears of eternal damnation?*

Wiseman. Aye, they were too weak indeed. They may serve to stifle conscience when a man is in the midst of his prosperity, and to harden the heart against all good counsel when a man is left of God and given up to his reprobate mind. †But alas, atheistical thoughts, notions and opinions must shrink and melt away when God sends, yea comes with sickness to visit the soul of such a sinner for his sin.

† His atheism will not help him now.

There was a man dwelt about twelve miles off from us, that had so trained up himself in his atheistical notions that at last he attempted to write a book against Jesus Christ, and against the divine authority of the scriptures (but I think it was not printed). Well, after many days God struck him with sickness, whereof he died. So, being sick, and musing upon his former doings, the book that he had written came into his mind, and with it such a sense of his evil in writing of it, that it tore his conscience as a lion would tear a kid. He lay, therefore, upon his death-bed in sad case and much affliction of conscience. Some of my friends also went to see him, and as they were in his chamber one day, he hastily called for pen, ink and paper, which when it was given him, he took it and writ to this purpose: 'I, such an one, in such a town, must go to Hell-fire for writing a book against Jesus Christ and against the holy scriptures', and would also have leaped out of the window of his house to have killed himself, but was by them prevented of that, so he died in his bed, such a death

A dreadful example of God's anger.

as it was. 'Twill be well if others take warning by him.

Attentive. *This is a remarkable story.*

Wiseman. 'Tis as true as remarkable; I had it from them that I dare believe, who also themselves were eye and ear witnesses, and also that catched him in their arms and saved him when he would have leaped out of his chamber-window to have destroyed himself.

Attentive. *Well, you have told me what were Mr Badman's thoughts, now being sick, of his condition. Pray tell me also what he then did when he was sick.*

Wiseman. Did! He did many things which I am sure he never thought to have done, and which, to be sure, was not looked for of his wife and children. In this fit of sickness his thoughts were quite altered about his wife. I say his thoughts, so far as could be judged by his words and carriages to her. For now she was his 'good' wife, his 'godly' wife, his 'honest' wife, his 'duck' and 'dear' and all. Now he told her that she had the best of it, she having a good life to stand by her, while his debaucheries and ungodly life did always stare him in the face. Now he told her the counsel that she often gave him was good, though he was so bad as not to take it. Now he would have her talk to him, and he would lie sighing by her while she so did. Now he would bid her pray for him, that he might be delivered from Hell.

He would also now consent that some of her good Ministers might come to him to comfort him, and he would seem to show them kindness when they came, for he would treat them kindly with words and hearken diligently to what they said; only he did not care that they should talk much of his ill-spent life, because his conscience was clogged with that already. He cared not now to see his old companions, the thoughts of them was a torment to him; and now he would speak kindly to that child of his that took after its mother's steps, though he could not at all abide it before.

What Mr Badman did more when he was sick.

Great alteration made in Mr Badman.

He also desired the prayers of good people, that God of His mercy would spare him a little longer, promising that if God would but let him recover this once, what a new, what a penitent man he would be toward God and what a loving husband he would be to his wife. What liberty he would give her; yea, how he would go with her himself to hear her Ministers, and how they should go hand in hand in the way to Heaven together.

Attentive. Here was a fine show of things. I'll warrant you, his wife was glad for this.

Wiseman. His wife! Aye, and a good many people besides. It was noised all over the town what a great change there was wrought upon Mr Badman, how sorry he was for his sins, how he began to love his wife, how he desired good men should pray to God to spare him, and what promises he now made to God in his sickness, that if ever he should raise him from his sick-bed to health again, what a new, penitent man he would be towards God and what a loving husband to his good wife.

The town-talk of Mr Badman's change.

Well, Ministers prayed, and good people rejoiced, thinking verily that they now had gotten a man from the Devil; nay, some of the weaker sort did not stick to say that God had begun a work of grace in his heart. And his wife, poor woman, you cannot think how apt she was to believe it so; she rejoiced and she hoped as she would have it. But alas, alas, in little time things all proved otherwise.

His wife is comforted.

After he had kept his bed a while, his distemper began to abate and he to feel himself better, so he in little time was so finely mended that he could walk about the house and also obtained a very fine stomach to his food, and now did his wife and her good friends stand gaping to see Mr Badman fulfil his promise of becoming new towards God and loving to his wife. But the contrary only showed itself, for so soon as ever he had hopes of mending, and found that his strength began to renew, his trouble began to go off his heart and he grew as great

Mr Badman recovers and returns to his old course.

a stranger to his frights and fears as if he had never had them.

But verily, I am apt to think, that one reason of his no more regarding or remembering of his sick-bed fears, and of being no better for them, was some words that the doctor that supplied him with physic said to him when he was mending. For as soon as Mr Badman began to mend, the doctor comes and sits him down by him in his house, and there fell into discourse with him about the nature of his disease, and among other things, they talked of Badman's trouble, and how he would cry out, tremble and express his fears of going to Hell when his sickness lay pretty hard upon him. To which the doctor replied that those fears and outcries did arise from the height of his distemper, for that disease was often attended with lightness of the head, by reason the sick party could not sleep, and for that the vapours disturbed the brain. 'But you see Sir,' quoth he, 'that so soon as you got sleep and betook yourself to rest, you quickly mended, and your head settled, and so those frenzies left you.'

Ignorant physicians kill souls while they cure bodies.

'And was it so indeed,' thought Mr Badman, 'was my troubles only the effects of my distemper, and because ill vapours got up into my brain? Then surely, since my physician was my saviour, my lust again shall be my God.' So he never minded religion more, but betook him again to the world, his lusts, and wicked companions. And there was an end of Mr Badman's conversion.

WILLIAM CONGREVE

Incognita

(1692)

Incognita: Or, Love and Duty Reconciled. A Novel.

To The Honoured and Worthily esteemed Mrs Katherine Leveson.*

Madam,

a clear wit, sound judgement and a merciful disposition are things so rarely united, that it is almost inexcusable to entertain them with anything less excellent in its kind. My knowledge of you were a sufficient caution to me to avoid your censure of this trifle, had I not as entire a knowledge of your goodness. Since I have drawn my pen for a rencounter,* I think it better to engage where, though there be skill enough to disarm me, there is too much generosity to wound, for so shall I have the saving reputation of an unsuccessful courage if I cannot make it a drawn battle.

But methinks the comparison intimates something of a defiance, and savours of arrogance; wherefore, since I am conscious to myself of a fear which I cannot put off, let me use the policy of cowards and lay this novel, unarmed, naked and shivering at your feet, so that if it should want merit to challenge protection, yet as an object of charity it may move compassion. It has been some diversion to me to write it; I wish it may prove such to you when you have an hour to throw away in reading of it. But this satisfaction I have at least beforehand: that in its greatest failings it may fly for pardon to that indulgence which you owe to the weakness of your friend, a title which I am proud you have thought me worthy of, and which I think can alone be superior to that

Your most humble and obliged servant,

CLEOPHIL*

THE PREFACE TO THE READER

Reader,

some authors are so fond of a preface that they will write one, though there be nothing more in it than an apology for itself. But to show thee that I am not one of those, I will make no apology for this, but do tell thee that I think it necessary to be prefixed to a trifle to prevent thy overlooking some little pains which I have taken in the composition of the following story.

Romances are generally composed of the constant loves and invincible courages of heroes, heroines, kings and queens, mortals of the first rank, and so forth; where lofty language, miraculous contingencies and impossible performances elevate and surprise the reader into a giddy delight, which leaves him flat upon the ground whenever he gives off, and vexes him to think how he has suffered himself to be pleased and transported, concerned and afflicted, at the several passages which he has read, viz., these knights' success to their damsels' misfortunes and such like, when he is forced to be very well convinced that 'tis all a lie.

Novels are of a more familiar nature; come near us, and represent to us intrigues in practice; delight us with accidents and odd events, but not such as are wholly unusual or unprecedented—such which, not being so distant from our belief, bring also the pleasure nearer us. Romances give more of wonder, novels more delight. And with reverence be it spoken, and the parallel kept at due distance, there is something of equality in the proportion which they bear in reference to one another with that between comedy and tragedy; but the drama is the long extracted from romance and history: 'tis the midwife to industry and brings forth alive the conceptions of the brain. Minerva walks upon the stage before us and we are more assured of the real presence of wit when it is delivered viva voce:

> Segnius irritant animos demissa per aurem,
> Quam quae sunt oculis subjecta fidelibus et quae
> Ipse sibi tradit spectator—Horace.*

Since all traditions must indisputably give place to the drama, and since there is no possibility of giving that life to the writing or repetition of a story which it has in the action, I resolved in another beauty to imitate dramatic writing, namely in the design, contexture and result of the plot. I have not observed it before in a novel. Some I have seen begin with an unexpected accident, which has been the only surprising part of the story: cause enough to make the sequel look flat, tedious and insipid, for 'tis but reasonable the reader should expect it not to rise, at least to keep upon a level in the entertainment, for so he may be kept on in hopes that at some time or other it may mend. But the t'other is such a baulk to a man, 'tis carrying him upstairs to show him the dining room and after forcing him to make a meal in the kitchen.

This I have not only endeavoured to avoid, but also have used a method for the contrary purpose. The design of the novel is obvious after the first meeting of Aurelian and Hippolito with Incognita and Leonora, and the difficulty is in bringing it to pass, maugre* all apparent obstacles, within the compass of two days. How many probable casualties intervene in opposition to the main design, viz. of marrying two couple so oddly engaged in an intricate amour, I leave the reader at his leisure to consider, as also whether every obstacle does not, in the progress of the story, act as subservient to that purpose which at first it seems to oppose. In a comedy, this would be called the unity of action;* here it may pretend to no more than an unity of contrivance. The scene is continued in Florence from the commencement of the amour, and the time from first to last is but three days.

If there be anything more in particular resembling the copy which I imitate, as the curious reader will soon perceive, I leave it to show itself, being very well satisfied how much more proper it had been for him to have found out this himself, than for me to profess him with an opinion of something extraordinary in an essay began and finished in the idler hours of a fortnight's time, for I can only esteem it a laborious idleness which is parent to so inconsiderable a birth. I have gratified the bookseller in pretending an occasion for a preface. The other two persons concerned are the reader and myself, and if he be but pleased with what was produced for that end, my satisfaction follows of course, since it will be proportioned to his approbation or dislike.

Incognita: Or, Love and Duty Reconciled

AURELIAN was the only son to a principal gentleman of Florence. The indulgence of his father prompted, and his wealth enabled him, to bestow a generous education upon him, whom he now began to look upon as the type of himself: an impression he had made in the gaiety and vigour of his youth, before the rust of age had debilitated and obscured the splendour of the original. He was sensible that he ought not to be sparing in the adornment of him, if he had resolution to beautify his own memory. Indeed, Don Fabio (for so was the old gentleman called) has been observed to have fixed his eyes upon Aurelian, when much company has been at table, and have wept through earnestness of intention if nothing happened to divert the object; whether it were for regret at the recollection of his former self, or for the joy he conceived in being, as it were, revived in the person of his son, I never took upon me to enquire, but supposed it might be sometimes one and sometimes both together.

Aurelian, at the age of eighteen years, wanted nothing (but a beard) that the most accomplished cavalier in Florence could pretend to. He had been educated from twelve years old at Siena, where it seems his father kept a receiver,* having a large income from the rents of several houses in that town. Don Fabio gave his servant orders that Aurelian should not be stinted in his expenses when he came up to years of discretion, by which means he was enabled not only to keep company with, but also to confer many obligations upon, strangers of quality and gentlemen who travelled from other countries into Italy, of which Siena never wanted store, being a town most delightfully situate upon a noble hill and very well suiting with strangers at first, by reason of the agreeableness and purity of the air. There also is the quaintness and delicacy of the Italian tongue most likely to be learned, there being many public professors of it in that place. And indeed, the very vulgar of Siena do express themselves with an easiness and sweetness surprising and even grateful to their ears who understand not the language.

Here Aurelian contracted an acquaintance with persons of worth of several countries, but among the rest, an intimacy with a gentleman of quality of Spain, and nephew to the Archbishop of Toledo, who had so wrought himself into the affections of Aurelian through a conformity of temper, an equality in years, and something of resemblance in feature and proportion, that he looked upon him as his second self. Hippolito, on the other hand, was not ungrateful in return of friendship, but thought himself either alone or in ill company if Aurelian were absent. But his uncle having sent him to travel under the conduct of a governor, and the two years which limited his stay at Siena being expired, he was put in mind of his departure. His friend grew melancholy at the news, but considering that Hippolito had never seen Florence, he easily prevailed with him to make his first journey thither, whither he would accompany him and perhaps prevail with his father to do the like throughout his travels.

They accordingly set out, but not being able easily to reach Florence the same night, they rested a league or two short at a villa of the great Duke's called Poggio Imperiale, where they were informed by some of his Highness's servants that the nuptials of Donna Catharina (near kinswoman to the great Duke) and Don Ferdinand de Rivori were to be solemnised the next day, and that extraordinary preparations had been making for some time past to illustrate the solemnity with balls and masques and other divertisements; that a tilting had been proclaimed and to that purpose scaffolds erected around the spacious court before the church Di Santa Croce, where were usually seen all cavalcades and shows performed by assemblies of the young nobility; that all mechanics and tradesmen were forbidden to work or expose any goods to sale for the space of three days, during which time all persons should be entertained at the great Duke's cost, and public provision was to be made for the setting forth and furnishing a multitude of tables, with entertainment for all comers and goers and several houses appointed for that use in all streets.

This account alarmed* the spirits of our young travellers, and they were overjoyed at the prospect of pleasures they foresaw. Aurelian could not contain the satisfaction he conceived in the welcome fortune had prepared for his dear Hippolito. In short, they both remembered so much of the pleasing relation had been made them that they forgot to sleep, and were up as soon as it was light, pounding at poor Signior Claudio's door (so was Hippolito's governor called) to rouse him, that no time might be lost till they were arrived at Florence, where they would furnish themselves with disguises and other accoutrements necessary for the prosecution of their design of sharing in the public merriment. The rather were they for going so early because Aurelian did not think fit to publish his being in town for a time, lest his father, knowing of it, might give some restraint to that loose* they designed themselves.

Before sunrise they entered Florence at Porta Romana, attended only by two servants, the rest being left behind to avoid notice. But, alas, they needed not to have used half that caution, for early as it was, the streets were crowded with all sorts of people passing to and fro, and every man employed in something relating to the diversions to come, so that no notice was taken of anybody. A Marquis and his train might have passed by as unregarded as a single fachin* or cobbler. Not a window in the streets but echoed the tuning of a lute or thrumming of a guitar, for, by the way, the inhabitants of Florence are strangely addicted to the love of music, insomuch that scarce their children can go* before they can scratch some instrument or other.

It was no unpleasing spectacle to our cavaliers (who, seeing they were not observed, resolved to make observations) to behold the diversity of figures and postures of many of these musicians. Here you should have an affected valet who mimicked the behaviour of his master, leaning carelessly against the window with his head on one side in a languishing posture, whining in a low, mournful voice some dismal complaint, while from his sympathising theorbo* issued a bass no less doleful to the hearers. In opposition to him was set up, perhaps, a cobbler with the wretched skeleton of a guitar, battered and waxed together by his own industry, and who with three strings out of tune and his own tearing, hoarse voice would rack attention from the neighbourhood to the great affliction of many more moderate practitioners, who no doubt were full as desirous to be heard.

By this time, Aurelian's servant had taken a lodging and was returned to give his master an account of it. The cavaliers, grown weary of that ridiculous entertainment, which was diverting at first sight, retired whither the lackey conducted them, who, according to their directions, had sought out one of the most obscure streets in the city. All that day to the evening was spent in sending from one broker's shop to another to furnish them with habits, since they had not time to make any new.

There was, it happened, but one to be got rich enough to please our young gentlemen, so many were taken up upon this occasion. While they were in dispute and complimenting one another, Aurelian protesting that Hippolito should wear it, and he, on t'other hand, forswearing it as bitterly, a servant of Hippolito's came up and ended the controversy, telling them that he had met below with the valet de chambre of a gentleman who was one of the greatest gallants about the town, but was at this time in such a condition he could not possibly be at the entertainment. Whereupon the valet had designed to dress himself up in his master's apparel and try his talent at court, which he hearing, told him he would inform him how he might bestow the habit for some time much more to his profit, if not to his pleasure; so acquainted him with the occasion his master had for it.

Hippolito sent for the fellow up, who was not so fond of his design as not to be bought off it, but upon having his own demand granted for the use of it, brought it. It was very rich and, upon trial, as fit for Hippolito as if it had been made for him. The ceremony was performed in the morning, in the great dome,* with all magnificence correspondent to the wealth of the great Duke and the esteem he had for the noble pair. The next morning was to be a tilting, and the same night a masqueing ball at court. To omit the description of the universal joy that had diffused itself through all the conduits of wine, which conveyed it in large measure to the people, and only relate those effects of it which concern our present adventurers.

You must know that, about the fall of the evening, and at that time when the equilibrium of day and night for some time holds the air in a gloomy suspense between an unwillingness to leave the light and a natural impulse into the dominion of darkness, about this time our heroes, shall I say, sallied or slunk out of their lodgings and steered toward the great palace, whither before they were arrived, such a prodigious number of torches were on fire that the day, by help of these auxiliary forces, seemed to continue its dominion. The owls and bats, apprehending their mistake in counting the hours, retired again to a convenient darkness, for Madam Night was no more to be seen than she was to be heard, and the chemists were of opinion that her fuliginous* damps, rarefied by the abundance of flame, were evaporated.

Now, the reader I suppose to be upon thorns at this and the like impertinent digressions, but let him alone and he'll come to himself, at which time I think fit to acquaint him that when I digress, I am at that time writing to please myself; when I continue the thread of the story, I write to please him. Supposing him a reasonable man, I conclude him satisfied to allow me this liberty, and so I proceed.

If our cavaliers were dazzled at the splendour they beheld without doors, what surprise, think you, must they be in when, entering the palace, they found even the lights there to be but so many foils to the bright eyes that flashed upon 'em at every turn. A more glorious troop no occasion ever assembled. All the fair of Florence, with the most accomplished cavaliers, were present, and however nature had been partial in bestowing on some better faces than others, art was alike indulgent to all, and industriously supplied those defects she had left, giving some addition also to her greatest excellencies. Everybody appeared well-shaped, as it is to be supposed none who were conscious to themselves of any visible deformity would presume to come thither. Their apparel was equally glorious, though each differing in fancy.

In short, our strangers were so well bred as to conclude from these apparent perfections that there was not a mask which did not at least hide the face of a cherubim. Perhaps the ladies were not behind hand in return of a favourable opinion of them, for they were both well dressed and had something inexpressibly pleasing in their air and mien;* different from other people and, indeed, differing from one another. They fancied that, while they stood together, they were more particularly taken notice of than any in the room, and being unwilling to be taken for strangers, which they thought they were, by reason of some whispering they observed near them, they agreed upon an hour of meeting after the company should be broke up, and so separately mingled with the thickest of the assembly.

Aurelian had fixed his eye upon a lady whom he had observed to have been a considerable time in close whisper with another woman. He expected with great impatience the result of that private conference, that he might have an opportunity of engaging the lady whose person was so agreeable to him. At last, he perceived they were broke off, and the t'other lady seemed to have taken her leave. He had taken no small pains in the meantime to put himself in a posture to accost the lady, which no doubt he had happily performed had he not been interrupted. But scarce had he acquitted himself of a preliminary bow (and which, I have heard him say, was the lowest that ever he made), and had just opened his lips to deliver himself of a small compliment which nevertheless he was very big with, when he unluckily miscarried by the interposal of the same lady whose departure, not long before, he had so zealously prayed for. But, as providence would have it, there was only some very small matter forgot, which was recovered in a short whisper. The coast being again cleared, he took heart and bore up and, striking sail, repeated his ceremony to the lady who, having obligingly returned it, he accosted her in these or the like words:

'If I do not usurp a privilege reserved for someone more happy in your acquaintance, may I presume, Madam, to entreat for a while the favour of your conversation, at least till the arrival of whom you expect, provided you are not tired of me before; for then, upon the least intimation of uneasiness, I will not fail of doing myself the violence to withdraw for your release.'

The lady made him answer, she did not expect anybody, by which he might imagine her conversation not of value to be bespoke, and to afford it him were but further to convince him to her own cost. He replied, she had already said enough to convince him of something he heartily wished might not be to his cost in the end. She pretended not to understand him, but told him if he already found himself grieved with her conversation, he would have sufficient reason to repent the rashness of his first demand before they had ended, for that now she intended to hold discourse with him on purpose to punish his unadvisedness in presuming upon a person whose dress and mien might not, maybe, be disagreeable to have wit.

'I must confess,' replied Aurelian, 'myself guilty of a presumption and willingly submit to the punishment you intend, and though it be an aggravation of a crime to persevere in its justification, yet I cannot help defending an opinion, in which now I am more confirmed, that probable conjectures may be made of the ingenious disposition of the mind, from the fancy and choice of apparel.'

'The humour* I grant ye,' said the lady, 'or constitution of the person, whether melancholic or brisk; but I should hardly pass my censure upon so slight an indication of wit, for there is your brisk fool as well as your brisk man of sense, and so of the melancholic. I confess, 'tis possible a fool may reveal himself by his dress, in wearing something extravagantly singular and ridiculous, or in preposterous suiting of colours, but a decency of habit, which is all that men of best sense pretend to, may be acquired by custom and example, without putting the person to a superfluous expense of wit for the contrivance, and though there should be occasion for it, few are so unfortunate in their relations and acquaintance not to have some friend capable of giving them advice, if they are not too ignorantly conceited to ask it.'

Aurelian was so pleased with the easiness and smartness of her expostulation, that he forgot to make a reply when she seemed to expect it, but being a woman of a quick apprehension, and justly sensible of her own perfections, she soon perceived he did not grudge his attention. However, she had a mind to put it upon him to turn the discourse, so went on upon the same subject. 'Signior,' said she, 'I have been looking around me and by your maxim I cannot discover one fool in the company, for they are all well dressed.' This was spoken with an air of raillery that awakened the cavalier, who immediately made answer.

''Tis true, Madam, we see there may be as much variety of good fancies as of faces, yet there may be many of both kinds borrowed and adulterate if inquired into, and as you were pleased to observe, the invention may be foreign to the person who puts it in practice, and as good an opinion as I have of an agreeable dress, I should be loath to answer for the wit of all about us.'

'I believe you,' says the lady, 'and hope you are convinced of your error, since you must allow it impossible to tell who, of all this assembly, did or did not make choice of their own apparel.' 'Not all,' said Aurelian, 'there is an ungainliness in some which betrays them. Look ye there,' says he, pointing to a lady who stood playing with the tassels of her girdle, 'I dare answer for that lady, though she be very well dressed, 'tis more than she knows.' His fair unknown could nor forbear laughing at his particular distinction, and freely told him he had indeed light upon one who knew as little as anybody in the room, herself excepted. 'Ah Madam,' replied Aurelian, 'you know everything in the world but your own perfections, and you only know not those because 'tis the top of perfection not to know them.' 'How,' replied the lady, 'I thought it had been the extremity of knowledge to know oneself.'

Aurelian had a little overstrained himself in that compliment, and I am of opinion would have been puzzled to have brought himself off readily, but by good fortune the music came into the room and gave him an opportunity to seem to decline an answer, because the company prepared to dance. He only told her he was too mean a conquest for her wit, who was already a slave to the charms of her person. She thanked him for his compliment and briskly told him she ought to have made him a return in praise of his wit, but she hoped he was a man more happy than to be dissatisfied with any of his own endowments, and if it were so, that he had not a just opinion of himself, she knew herself incapable of saying anything to beget one.

Aurelian did not know well what to make of this last reply, for he always abhorred anything that was conceited, with which this seemed to reproach him. But however modest he had been heretofore in his own thoughts, yet never was he so distrustful of his good behaviour as now, being rallied so by a person whom he took to be of judgement. Yet he resolved to take no notice, but with an air unconcerned and full of good humour, entreated her to dance with him. She promised him to dance with nobody else, nor, I believe, had she inclination, for notwithstanding her tartness, she was upon equal terms with him as to the liking of each other's person and humour, and only gave those little hints to try his temper, there being certainly no greater sign of folly and ill breeding than to grow serious and concerned at anything spoken in raillery.

For his part, he was strangely and insensibly fallen in love with her shape, wit and air, which, together with a white hand he had seen (perhaps not accidentally), were enough to have subdued a more stubborn heart than ever he was master of. And for her face, which he had not seen, he bestowed upon her the best his imagination could furnish him with. I should, by right, now describe her dress, which was extremely agreeable and rich, but 'tis possible I might err in some material pin or other, in the sticking of which, maybe, the whole grace of the drapery depended.

Well, they danced several times together, and no less to the satisfaction of the whole company than of themselves, for at the end of each dance, some public note of applause or other was given to the graceful couple. Aurelian was amazed that, among all that danced or stood in view, he could not see Hippolito. But concluding that he had met with some pleasing conversation, and was withdrawn to some retired part of the room, he forbore his search till the mirth of that night should be over, and the company ready to break up, where we will leave him for a while, to see what became of his adventurous friend.

Hippolito, a little after he had parted with Aurelian, was got among a knot of ladies and cavaliers who were looking upon a large gold cup, set with jewels, in which his royal Highness had drunk to the prosperity of the new married couple at dinner, and which afterward he presented to his cousin, Donna Catherina. He among the rest was very intent, admiring the richness, workmanship and beauty of the cup, when a lady came behind him and, pulling him by the elbow, made a sign she would speak with him.

Hippolito, who knew himself an utter stranger to Florence and everybody in it, immediately guessed she had mistaken him for her acquaintance, as indeed it happened. However, he resolved not to discover himself till he should be assured of it. Having followed her into a set window, remote from company, she addressed herself to him in this manner.

'Signior Don Lorenzo,' said she, 'I am overjoyed to see you are so speedily recovered of your wounds, which by report were much more dangerous than to have suffered your coming abroad so soon, but I must accuse you of great indiscretion in appearing in a habit which so many must needs remember you to have worn upon the like occasion not long ago; I mean at the marriage of Don Cynthio with your sister Atalanta. I do assure you, you were known by it, both to Juliana and myself, who was so far concerned for you as to desire me to tell you that her brother, Don Fabritio, who saw you when you came in with another gentleman, had eyed you very narrowly and is since gone out of the room, she knows not upon what design. However, she would have you, for your own sake, be advised and circumspect when you depart this place, lest you should be set upon unawares. You know the hatred Don Fabritio has born you ever since you had the fortune to kill his kinsman in a duel.'

Here she paused, as if expecting his reply, but Hippolito was so confounded that he stood mute and, contemplating the hazard he had ignorantly brought himself into, forgot his design of informing the lady of her mistake. She, finding he made her no answer, went on. 'I perceive,' continued she, 'you are in some surprise at what I have related and, maybe, are doubtful of the truth. But I thought you had been better acquainted with your cousin Leonora's voice than to have forgot it so soon. Yet in complaisance to your ill memory, I will put you past doubt by showing you my face.'

With that, she pulled off her mask and discovered to Hippolito (now more amazed than ever) the most angelic face that he had ever beheld. He was just about to have made her some answer when, clapping on her mask again without giving him time, she, happily for him, pursued her discourse—for 'tis odds but he had made some discovery of himself in the surprise he was in. Having taken him familiarly by the hand, now she had made herself known to him, 'Cousin Lorenzo,' added she, 'you may, perhaps, have taken it unkindly that during the time of your indisposition, by reason of your wounds, I have not been to visit you. I do assure you, it was not for want of any inclination I had, both to see and serve you to my power, but you are well acquainted with the severity of my father, whom you know how lately you have disobliged. I am mighty glad that I have met with you here, where I have had an opportunity to tell you what so much concerns your safety, which I am afraid you will not find in Florence, considering the great power of Don Fabritio and his father, the Marquis of Viterbo, have in this city.

'I have another thing to inform you of: that whereas Don Fabio had interested himself in your cause, in opposition to the Marquis of Viterbo, by reason of the long animosity between them, all hopes of his countenance and assistance are defeated. For there has been a proposal of reconciliation made to both houses, and it is said it will be confirmed (as most such ancient quarrels are at last) by the marriage of Juliana, the Marquis's daughter, with Aurelian, son to Don Fabio, to which effect the old gentleman sent t'other day to Siena, where Aurelian has been educated, to hasten his coming to town. But the messenger, returning this morning, brought word that the same day he arrived at Siena, Aurelian had set out for Florence in company

with a young Spanish nobleman, his intimate friend, so it is
believed they are both in town and not unlikely in this room in
masquerade.'

Hippolito could not forbear smiling to himself at these last
words, for ever since the naming of Don Fabio he had been very
attentive. But before, his thoughts were wholly taken up with the
beauty of the face he had seen, and from the time she had taken
him by the hand, a successive warmth and chillness had played
about his heart and surprised him with an unusual transport. He
was in a hundred minds whether he should make her sensible of
her error or no, but considering he could expect no farther
conference with her after he should discover himself, and that as
yet he knew not of her place of abode, he resolved to humour the
mistake a little further.

Having her still by the hand, which he squeezed somewhat
more eagerly than is usual for cousins to do, in a low and
undistinguishable voice he let her know how much he held
himself obliged to her, and avoiding as many words as
handsomely he could, at the same time entreated her to give him
her advice toward the management of himself in this affair.
Leonora, who never from the beginning had entertained the least
scruple of distrust, imagined he spoke faintly as not being yet
perfectly recovered in his strength, and withal considering that
the heat of the room, by reason of the crowd, might be uneasy to
a person in his condition, she kindly told him that if he were as
inclinable to dispense with the remainder of that night's diversion,
as she was, and had no other engagement upon him, by her
consent they should both steal out of the assembly and go to her
house, where they might with more freedom discourse about a
business of that importance, and where he might take something
to refresh himself if he were (as she conceived him to be)
indisposed with his long standing.

Judge you whether the proposal were acceptable to Hippolito
or no. He had been ruminating with himself how to bring
something like this about, and had almost despaired of it, when
of a sudden he found the success of his design had prevented his
own endeavours. He told his cousin in the same key as before
that he was unwilling to be the occasion of her divorce from so
much good company, but for his own part, he was afraid he had

presumed too much upon his recovery in coming abroad so soon, and that he found himself so unwell he feared he should be quickly forced to retire. Leonora stayed not to make him any other reply, only tipped him upon the arm and bid him follow her at a convenient distance to avoid observation.

Whoever had seen the joy that was in Hippolito's countenance, and the sprightliness with which he followed his beautiful conductress, would scarce have taken him for a person grieved with uncured wounds. She led him down a back pair of stairs, into one of the palace gardens, which had a door opening into the piazza not far from where Don Mario, her father, lived. They had little discourse by the way, which gave Hippolito time to consider of the best way of discovering himself. A thousand things came into his head in a minute, yet nothing that pleased him, and after so many contrivances as he had formed for the discovery of himself, he found it more rational for him not to reveal himself at all that night, since he could not foresee what effect the surprise would have she must needs be in at the appearance of a stranger, whom she had never seen before, yet whom she had treated so familiarly.

He knew women were apt to shriek or swoon upon such occasions, and should she happen to do either, he might be at a loss how to bring himself off. He thought he might easily pretend to be indisposed somewhat more than ordinary, and so make an excuse to go to his own lodging. It came into his head too, that under pretence of giving her an account of his health, he might enquire of her the means how a letter might be conveyed to her the next morning, wherein he might inform her gently of her mistake and insinuate something of that passion he had conceived, which he was sure he could not have opportunity to speak of if he bluntly revealed himself.

He had just resolved upon this method as they were come to the great gates of the court, when Leonora, stopping to let him go in before her, he of a sudden fetched his breath violently as if some stitch or twinging smart had just then assaulted him. She enquired the matter of him, and advised him to make haste into the house, that he might sit down and rest him. He told her he found himself so ill that he judged it more convenient for him to go home while he was in a condition to move, for he feared if he should once settle himself to rest he might not be able to stir.

She was much troubled, and would have had a chair made ready and servants to carry him home, but he made answer he would not have any of her father's servants know of his being abroad, and that just now he had an interval of ease, which he hoped would continue till he made a shift to reach his own lodgings. Yet if she pleased to inform him how he might give an account of himself the next morning in a line or two, he would not fail to give her the thanks due to her great kindness, and withal would let her know something which would not a little surprise her, though now he had not time to acquaint her with it.

She showed him a little window at the corner of the house where one should wait to receive his letter, and was just taking her leave of him, when, seeing him search hastily in his pocket, she asked him if he missed anything. He told her he thought a wound, which was not thoroughly healed, bled a little, and that he had lost his handkerchief. His design took, for she immediately gave him hers, which indeed accordingly he applied to the only wound he was then grieved with, which though it went quite through his heart, yet thank God was not mortal.

He was not a little rejoiced at his good fortune in getting so early a favour from his mistress, and notwithstanding the violence he did himself to personate a sick man, he could not forbear giving some symptoms of an extraordinary content, and telling her that he did not doubt to receive a considerable proportion of ease from the application of what had so often kissed her fair hand. Leonora, who did not suspect the compliment, told him she should be heartily glad if that, or anything in her power, might contribute to his recovery, and wishing him well home, went into her house as much troubled for her cousin as he was joyful for his mistress.

Hippolito, as soon as she was gone in, began to make his remarks about the house, walking round the great court, viewing the gardens and all the passages leading to that side of the piazza. Having sufficiently informed himself, with a heart full of love and a head full of stratagem, he walked toward his lodging, impatient till the arrival of Aurelian, that he might give himself vent. In which interim let me take the liberty to digress a little, and tell the reader something which I do not doubt he has apprehended himself long ago, if he be not the dullest reader in the world. Yet only for order's sake, let me tell him. I say that a young gentleman (cousin to the aforesaid Don Fabritio) happened one night to have some words at a gaming house with one Lorenzo, which created a quarrel of fatal consequence to the former, who was killed upon the spot, and likely to be so to the latter, who was very desperately wounded.

Fabritio, being much concerned for his kinsman, vowed revenge (according to the ancient and laudable custom of Italy) upon Lorenzo if he survived, or in case of his death (if it should happen to anticipate that much more swinging* death which he had in store for him), upon his next of kin, and so to descend lineally, like an English estate, to all the heirs males of his family. This same Fabritio had indeed (as Leonora told Hippolito) taken particular notice of him from his first entrance into the room, and was so far doubtful as to go out immediately himself and make enquiry concerning Lorenzo, but was quickly informed of the greatness of his error in believing a man to be abroad who was so ill of his wounds that they now despaired of his recovery, and thereupon returned to the ball very well satisfied, but not before Leonora and Hippolito were departed.

So reader, having now discharged my conscience of a small discovery which I thought myself obliged to make to thee, I proceed to tell thee that our friend Aurelian had, by this time, danced himself into a net which he neither could nor, which is worse, desired to untangle. His soul was charmed to the movement of her body; an air so graceful, so sweet, so easy and so great he had never seen. She had something of majesty in her, which appeared to be born with her, and though it struck an awe into the beholders, yet was it sweetened with a familiarity of behaviour which rendered it agreeable to everybody. The grandeur of her mien was not stiff, but unstudied and unforced, mixed with a simplicity free, yet not loose nor affected. If the former seemed to condescend, the latter seemed to aspire, and both to unite in the centre of perfection. Every turn she gave in dancing snatched Aurelian into a rapture, and he had like to have been out two or three times with following his eyes, which she led about as slaves to her heels.

As soon as they had done dancing, he began to complain of his want of breath and lungs to speak sufficiently in her commenda-tion. She smilingly told him he did ill to dance so much then. Yet in consideration of the pains he had taken more than ordinary upon her account, she would bate him a great deal of compliment, but with this proviso: that he was to discover to her who he was. Aurelian was unwilling for the present to own himself to be really the man he was, when a sudden thought came into his head to take upon him the name and character of Hippolito, who he was sure was not known in Florence.

He thereupon, after a little pause, pretended to recall himself in this manner: 'Madam, it is no small demonstration of the entire resignation which I have made of my heart to your chains, since the secrets of it are no longer in my power. I confess I only took Florence in my way, not designing any longer residence than should be requisite to inform the curiosity of a traveller of the rarities of the place. Whether happiness or misery will be the consequence of that curiosity, I am yet in fear, and submit to your determination. But sure I am not to depart Florence till you have made me the most miserable man in it and refuse me the fatal kindness of dying at your feet.

'I am by birth a Spaniard, of the city of Toledo, my name Hippolito di Saviolina. I was yesterday a man free as nature made the first; today I am fallen into a captivity which must continue with my life and which it is in your power to make much dearer to me. Thus, in obedience to your commands, and contrary to my resolution of remaining unknown in this place, I have informed you, Madam, what I am. What I shall be, I desire to know from you. At least, I hope, the free discovery I have made of myself will encourage you to trust me with the knowledge of your person.'

Here a low bow and a deep sigh put an end to his discourse, and signified his expectation of her reply, which was to this purpose—but I have forgot to tell you that Aurelian kept off his mask, from the time that he told her he was of Spain, till the period of his relation—'Had I thought,' said she, 'that my curiosity would have brought me in debt, I should certainly have forborne it, or at least have agreed with you beforehand about the rate of your discovery; then I had not brought myself to the inconveniency of being censured, either of too much easiness or reservedness. But to avoid, as much as I can, the extremity of either, I am resolved but to discover myself in part, and will endeavour to give you as little occasion as I can either to boast of, or ridicule, the behaviour of the women of Florence in your travels.'

Aurelian interrupted her and swore very solemnly (and the more heartily, I believe, because he then indeed spoke truth) that he would make Florence the place of his abode, whatever concerns he had elsewhere. She advised him to be cautious how he swore to his expressions of gallantry, and further told him she now hoped she should make him a return to all the fine things he had said, since she gave him his choice whether he would know whom she was, or see her face.

Aurelian, who was really in love, and in whom consideration would have been a crime, greedily embraced the latter, since she assured him at that time he should not know both. Well, what followed? Why, she pulled off her mask and appeared to him at once in the glory of beauty. But who can tell the astonishment Aurelian felt? He was, for a time, senseless; admiration had suppressed his speech and his eyes were entangled in light. In short, to be made sensible of his condition we must conceive some idea of what he beheld, which is not to be imagined till seen, nor then to be expressed.

Now see the impertinence and conceitedness of an author who will have a fling at a description, which he has prefaced with an impossibility. One might have seen something in her composition resembling the formation of Epicurus his world, as if every atom of beauty had concurred to unite an excellency. Had that curious painter* lived in her days, he might have avoided his painful search when he collected from the choicest pieces the most choice features, and by a due disposition and judicious symmetry of those exquisite parts made one whole and perfect Venus. Nature seemed here to have played the plagiary, and to have moulded into substance the most refined thoughts of inspired poets.

Her eyes diffused rays comfortable as warmth and piercing as the light; they would have worked a passage through the straitest pores and with a delicious heat have played about the most obdurate, frozen heart until 'twere melted down to love. Such majesty and affability were in her looks; so alluring, yet commanding was her presence that it mingled awe with love, kindling a flame which trembled to aspire. She had danced much, which, together with her being close masked, gave her a tincture of carnation more than ordinary.

But Aurelian (from whom I had every tittle of her description) fancied he saw a little nest of cupids break from the tresses of her hair, and every one officiously betake himself to his task. Some fanned with their downy wings her glowing cheeks, while others brushed the balmy dew from off her face, leaving alone a heavenly moisture blubbing* on her lips, on which they drank and revelled for their pains. Nay, so particular were their allotments in her service that Aurelian was very positive a young cupid, who was but just pen-feathered,* employed his naked quills to pick her teeth. And a thousand other things his transport represented to him, which none but lovers, who have experience of such visions, will believe.

As soon as he awaked and found his speech come to him, he employed it to this effect. '' 'Tis enough that I have seen a divinity. Nothing but mercy can inhabit these perfections. Their utmost rigour brings a death preferable to any life but what they give. Use me, Madam, as you please, for by your fair self I cannot think a bliss beyond what now I feel. You wound with pleasure, and if you kill, it must be with transport. Ah, yet methinks to live—O Heaven, to have life pronounced by those blessed lips— did they not inspire where they command, it were an immediate death of joy.'

Aurelian was growing a little too loud with his admiration, had she not just then interrupted him by clapping on her mask and telling him they should be observed if he proceeded in his extravagance; and withal, that his passion was too sudden to be real, and too violent to be lasting. He replied indeed it might not be very lasting (with a submissive, mournful voice), but it would continue during his life. That it was sudden, he denied, for she had raised it by degrees from his first sight of her by a continued discovery of charms in her mien and conversation, till she thought fit to set fire to the train she had laid by the lightning of her face, and then he could not help it if he were blown up.

He begged her to believe the sincerity of his passion, at least to enjoin him something which might tend to the convincing of her incredulity. She said she should find a time to make some trials of him, but for the first, she charged him not to follow or observe her after the dissolution of the assembly. He promised to obey, and entreated her to tell him but her name, that he might have recourse to that in his affliction for her absence, if he were able to survive it. She desired him to live by all means, and if he must have a name to play with, to call her Incognita,* till he were better informed.

The company breaking up, she took her leave, and at his earnest entreaty, gave him a short vision of her face which, then dressed in an obliging smile, caused another fit of transport which lasted till she was gone out of sight. Aurelian gathered up his spirits and walked slowly towards his lodging, never remembering that he had lost Hippolito till, upon turning the corner of a street, he heard a noise of fighting and, coming near, saw a man make a vigorous defence against two who pressed violently upon him. He then thought of Hippolito, and fancying he saw the glimmering of diamond buttons such as Hippolito had upon the sleeves of his habit, immediately drew to his assistance and with that eagerness and resolution that the assailants, finding their unmanly odds defeated, took to their heels.

The person rescued by the generous help of Aurelian came toward him, but as he would have stooped to have saluted him, dropped fainting at his feet. Aurelian, now he was so near him, perceived plainly Hippolito's habit, and stepped hastily to take him up, just as some of the guards (who were going the rounds, apprehensive of such disorders in a universal merriment) came up to him with lights, and had taken prisoners the two men whom they met with their swords drawn, when looking in the face of the wounded man, he found it was not Hippolito but his governor Claudio in the habit he had worn at the ball. He was extremely surprised, as were the prisoners, who confessed their design to have been upon Lorenzo, grounding their mistake upon the habit, which was known to have been his. They were two men who formerly had been servants to him whom Lorenzo had unfortunately slain.

They made a shift to bring Claudio to himself, and part of the guard carrying off the prisoners, whom Aurelian desired they would secure, the rest accompanied him, bearing Claudio in their arms to his lodging. He had not patience to forbear asking for Hippolito by the way, whom Claudio assured him he had left safe in his chamber above two hours since; that his coming home so long before the divertisements were ended and undressing himself had given him the unhappy curiosity to put on his habit and go to the balance, in his return from whence, he was set upon in the manner he found him, which if he recovered, he must own his life indebted to his timely assistance.

Being come to the house, they carried him to his bed, and having sent for surgeons, Aurelian rewarded and dismissed the guard. He stayed the dressing of Claudio's wounds, which were many, though they hoped none mortal, and leaving him to his rest, went to give Hippolito an account of what had happened, whom he found with a table before him, leaning upon both his elbows, his face covered with his hands, and so motionless that Aurelian concluded he was asleep. Seeing several papers lie before him half written and blotted out again, he thought to steal softly to the table and discover what he had been employed about. Just as he reached forth his hand to take up one of the papers, Hippolito started up so on the sudden as surprised Aurelian and made him leap back. Hippolito, on the other hand, not supposing that anybody had been near him, was so disordered with the appearance of a man at his elbow (whom his amazement did not permit him to distinguish) that he leaped hastily to his sword, and in turning him about, overthrew the stand and candles.

Here were they both left in the dark, Hippolito groping about with his sword and thrusting at every chair that he felt oppose him. Aurelian was scarce come to himself when, thinking to step back toward the door, that he might inform his friend of his mistake without exposing himself to his blind fury, Hippolito heard him stir, and made a full thrust with such violence that the hilt of the sword, meeting with Aurelian's breast, beat him down and Hippolito atop of him, as a servant, alarmed with the noise, came into the chamber with a light. The fellow trembled and thought they were both dead, till Hippolito, raising himself to see whom he had got under him, swooned away upon the discovery of his friend.

But such was the extraordinary care of providence in directing

the sword, that it only passed under his arm, giving no wound to
Aurelian but a little bruise between his shoulder and breast with
the hilt. He got up, scarce recovered of his fright, and by the help
of the servant, laid Hippolito upon the bed, who, when he was
come to himself, could hardly be persuaded that his friend was
before him and alive till he showed him his breast, where was
nothing of a wound. Hippolito begged his pardon a thousand
times, and cursed himself as often, who was so near to
committing the most execrable act of amicide.*

They dismissed the fellow and, with many embraces, congratu-
lated their fortunate delivery from the mischief which came so
near them, each blaming himself as the occasion: Aurelian
accusing his own unadvisedness in stealing upon Hippolito,
Hippolito blaming his own temerity and weakness in being so
easily frighted to disorder, and last of all, his blindness in not
knowing his dearest friend. But there he gave a sigh and, taking
Aurelian by the hand, cried, 'Ah, my friend, love is indeed blind
when it would not suffer me to see you!' There arose another
sigh. A sympathy seized Aurelian immediately (for, by the way,
sighing is as catching among lovers as yawning among the
vulgar). Beside, hearing the name of love made him fetch such a
sigh that Hippolito's were but fly-blows in comparison. That was
answered with all the might Hippolito had. Aurelian plied him
close, till they were both out of breath. Thus not a word passed,
though each wondered why the t'other sighed; at last concluded
it to be only complaisance to one another.

Aurelian broke the silence by telling him the misfortune of his
governor. Hippolito rejoiced as at the luckiest accident which
could have befallen him. Aurelian wondered at his unseasonable
mirth, and demanded the cause of it. He answered, it would
necessitate his longer stay in Florence, and for ought he knew be
the means of bringing a happy period to his amour.

His friend thought him to be little better than a madman, when
he perceived him of a sudden snatch out of his bosom a
handkerchief, which having kissed with a great deal of ardour, he
took Aurelian by the hand and, smiling at the surprise he saw him
in, 'Your Florentine Cupid is certainly,' said he, 'the most expert
in the world. I have, since I saw you, beheld the most beautiful of
women. I am fallen desperately in love with her, and those papers

which you see so blotted and scattered are but so many essays which I have made to the declaration of my passion. And this handkerchief, which I so zealously caress, is the inestimable token which I have to make myself known to her. O Leonora,' continued he, 'how hast thou stamped thine image on my soul! How much dearer am I to myself, since I have had thy heavenly form in keeping. Now, my Aurelian, I am worthy thee; my exalted love has dignified me and raised me far above thy poor, former despicable Hippolito.'

Aurelian, seeing the rapture he was in, thought it in vain to expect a settled relation of the adventure, so was reaching to the table for some of the papers, but Hippolito told him if he would have a little patience he would acquaint him with the whole matter, and thereupon told him word for word how he was mistaken for Lorenzo and his management of himself. Aurelian commended his prudence in not discovering himself, and told him if he could spare so much time from the contemplation of his mistress, he would inform him of an adventure, though not so accidental, yet of as great concern to his own future happiness— so related all that had happened to him with his beautiful Incognita.

Having ended the story, they began to consider of the means they were to use toward a review of their mistresses. Aurelian was confounded at the difficulty he conceived on his part. He understood from Hippolito's adventure that his father knew of his being in town, whom he must unavoidably disoblige if he yet concealed himself, and disobey if he came into his sight, for he had already entertained an aversion for Juliana in apprehension of her being imposed on him. His Incognita was rooted in his heart, yet could he not comfort himself with any hopes when he should see her. He knew not where she lived, and she had made him no promise of a second conference. Then did he repent his inconsiderate choice in preferring the momentary vision of her face to a certain intelligence of her person. Every thought that succeeded distracted him, and all the hopes he could presume upon were within compass of the two days' merriment yet to come, for which space he hoped he might excuse his remaining concealed to his father.

Hippolito, on the other side (though Aurelian thought him in a much better way), was no less afflicted for himself. The difficulties which he saw in his friend's circumstances put him upon finding out a great many more in his own than really there were. But what terrified him most of all was his being an utter stranger to Leonora; she had not the least knowledge of him but through mistake, and consequently could form no idea of him to his advantage. He looked upon it as an unlucky thought in Aurelian to take upon him his name, since possibly the two ladies were acquainted, and should they communicate to each other their adventures, they might both reasonably suffer in their opinions and be thought guilty of falsehood, since it would appear to them as one person pretending to two.

Aurelian told him there was but one remedy for that, which was for Hippolito, in the same manner that he had done, to make use of his name, when he writ to Leonora, and use what arguments he could to persuade her to secrecy, lest his father should know of the reason which kept him concealed in town. And it was likely, though perhaps she might not immediately entertain his passion, yet she would, out of generosity, conceal what was hidden only for her sake.

Well, this was concluded on after a great many other reasons used on either side in favour of the contrivance. They at last argued themselves into a belief that fortune had befriended them with a better plot than their regular thinking could have contrived. So soon had they convinced themselves in what they were willing to believe.

Aurelian laid himself down to rest; that is, upon the bed, for he was a better lover than to pretend to sleep that night, while Hippolito set himself again to frame his letter designed for Leonora. He writ several, at last pitched upon one, and very probably the worst, as you may guess when you read it in its proper place. It was break of day when the servant, who had been employed all the foregoing day in procuring accoutrements for the two cavaliers to appear in at the tilting, came into the room and told them all the young gentlemen in the town were trying their equipage and preparing to be early in the lists. They made themselves ready with all expedition at the alarm, and Hippolito, having made a visit to his governor, dispatched a messenger with the letter and directions to Leonora.

At the signal agreed upon, the casement was opened and string let down, to which the bearer, having fastened the letter, saw it drawn up and returned. It were a vain attempt to describe Leonora's surprise when she read the superscription: 'The Unfortunate Aurelian to the Beautiful Leonora.' After she was a little recovered from her amaze, she recollected to herself all the passages between her and her supposed cousin, and immediately concluded him to be Aurelian. Then several little circumstances, which she thought might have been sufficient to have convinced her, represented themselves to her, and she was in a strange uneasiness to think of her free carriage to a stranger.

She was once in a mind to have burned the letter, or to have stayed for an opportunity to send it again. But she was a woman, and her curiosity opposed itself to all thoughts of that nature. At length, with a firm resolution, she opened it, and found word for word what is underwritten.

THE LETTER

'Madam,

if your fair eyes, upon the breaking up of this, meet with somewhat too quick a surprise, make thence, I beseech you, some reflection upon the condition I must needs have been in at the sudden appearance of that sun of beauty, which at once shone so full upon my soul. I could not immediately disengage myself from that maze of charms to let you know how unworthy a captive your eyes had made through mistake. Sure, Madam, you cannot but remember my disorder, of which your innocent (innocent, though perhaps to me fatal) error made a charitable but wide construction. Your tongue pursued the victory of your eyes, and you did not give me time to rally my poor, disordered senses so as to make a tolerable retreat.

Pardon, Madam, the continuation of the deceit, and call it not so, that I appeared to be other than myself, for Heaven knows I was not then myself, nor am I now my own. You told me something that concerned me nearly as to a marriage my father designed me, and much more nearly in being told by you. For Heaven's sake, disclose not to anybody your knowledge of me, that I may not be forced to an immediate act of disobedience, for if my future services and inviolate love cannot recommend me to your favour, I shall find more comfort in the cold embraces of a grave, than in the arms of the never so much admired (but by me dreaded) Juliana.

Think, Madam, of those severe circumstances I lie under, and withal I beg you, think it is in your power, and only in your power, to make them happy as my wishes, or much more miserable than I am able to imagine. That dear, inestimable (though un-designed) favour which I received from you shall this day distinguish me from the crowd of your admirers; that which I really applied to my inward bleeding wound, the welcome wound which you have made, and which, unless from you, does wish no cure. Then pardon and have pity on, O adored Leonora, him who is yours by creation as he is Heaven's, though never so unworthy. Have pity on

Your,
Aurelian.'

She read the letter over and over, then flung it by, then read it again. The novelty of the adventure made her repeat her curiosity and take more than ordinary pains to understand it. At last, her familiarity with the expressions grew to an intimacy, and what she at first permitted, she now began to like. She thought there was something in it a little more serious than to be barely gallantry. She wondered at her own blindness, and fancied she could remember something of a more becoming air in the stranger than was usual to Lorenzo. This thought was parent to another of the same kind, till a long chain successively had birth, and every one somewhat more than other in favour of the supposed Aurelian. She reflected upon his discretion in deferring the discovery of himself till a little time had, as it were, weaned her from her persuasion, and by removing her further from her mistake, had prepared her for a full and determinate convincement. She thought his behaviour, in personating a sick man so readily upon the first hint, was not amiss, and smiled to think of his excuse to procure her handkerchief, and last of all, his sifting out the means to write to her, which he had done with that modesty and respect she could not tell how to find fault with it.

She had proceeded thus far in a maze of thought, when she started to find herself so lost to her reason, and would have trod back again that path of deluding fancy, accusing herself of fondness and inconsiderate easiness, in giving credit to the letter of a person whose face she never saw and whose first acquaintance with her was a treachery; and he who could so readily deliver his tongue of a lie upon a surprise, was scarce to be trusted when he had sufficient time allowed him to beget a fiction and means to perfect the birth.

How did she know this to be Aurelian, if he were? Nay further, put it to the extremity: what if she should, upon further conversation with him, proceed to love him? What hopes were there for her, or how could she consent to marry a man already destined for another woman? Nay, a woman that was her friend, whose marrying with him was to complete the happy reconciliation of two noble families, and which might prevent the effusion of much blood likely to be shed in that quarrel. Besides, she should incur share of the guilt which he would draw upon him by disobedience to his father, whom she was sure would not be consenting to it.

'Tis strange now, but all accounts agree that just here Leonora, who had run like a violent stream against Aurelian hitherto, now retorted with as much precipitation in his favour. I could never get anybody to give me a satisfactory reason for her sudden and dextrous change of opinion just at that stop, which made me conclude she could not help it, and that nature boiled over in her at that time when it had so fair an opportunity to show itself. For Leonora, it seems, was a woman beautiful, and otherwise of an excellent disposition, but in the bottom a very woman. This last objection, this opportunity of persuading man to disobedience, determined the matter in favour of Aurelian more than all his excellencies and qualifications, take him as Aurelian, or Hippolito, or both together.

Well, the spirit of contradiction and of Eve was strong in her, and she was in a fair way to love Aurelian, for she liked him already. That it was Aurelian, she no longer doubted, for had it been a villain who had only taken his name upon him for any ill designs, he would never have slipped so favourable an opportunity as when they were alone and in the night, coming through the garden and broad space before the piazza. In short, thus much she resolved: at least to conceal the knowledge she had of him, as he had entreated her in his letter, and to make particular remarks of his behaviour that day in the lists, which, should it happen to charm her with an absolute liking of his person, she resolved to dress herself to the best advantage and, mustering up all her graces, out of pure revenge, to kill him downright.

I would not have the reader now be impertinent, and look upon this to be force, or a whim of the author's, that a woman should proceed so far in her approbation of a man whom she never saw; that it is impossible, therefore ridiculous to suppose it. Let me tell such a critic that he knows nothing of the sex if he does not know that a woman may be taken with the character and description of a man, when general and extraordinary. That she may be prepossessed with an agreeable idea of his person and conversation, and though she cannot imagine his real features or manner of wit, yet she has a general notion of what is called a fine gentleman, and is prepared to like such a one who does not disagree with that character.

Aurelian, as he bore a very fair character, so was he extremely deserving to make it good, which otherwise might have been to his prejudice; for oftentimes, through an imprudent indulgence to our friend's merit, we give so large a description of his excellencies that people make more room in their expectation than the intrinsic worth of the man will fill, which renders him so much the more despicable as there is emptiness to spare. 'Tis certain though, the women seldom find that out, for though they do not see so much in a man as was promised, yet they will be so kind to imagine he has some hidden excellencies which time may discover to them, so are content to allow him a considerable share of their esteem and take him into favour upon tick.*

Aurelian, as he had good credit, so he had a good stock to support it, and his person was a good promising security for the payment of any obligation he could lie under to the fair sex. Hippolito, who at this time was our Aurelian, did not at all lessen him in appearing for him. So that, although Leonora was indeed mistaken, she could not be said to be much in the wrong.

I could find in my heart to beg the reader's pardon for this digression if I thought he would be sensible of the civility, for I promise him I do not intend to do it again throughout the story, though I make never so many, and though he take them never so

ill. But because I began this upon a bare supposition of his
impertinence, which might be somewhat impertinent in me to
suppose, I do, and hope to make him amends by telling him that,
by the time Leonora was dressed, several ladies of her
acquaintance came to accompany her to the place designed for
the tilting, where we will leave them drinking chocolate till 'tis
time for them to go.

Our cavaliers had by good fortune provided themselves of two
curious suits of light armour, finely enamelled and gilt. Hippolito
had sent to Poggio Imperiale for a couple of fine led horses,
which he had left there with the rest of his train at his entrance
into Florence. Mounted on these, and every way well equipped,
they took their way, attended only by two lackeys, toward the
church De Santa Croce, before which they were to perform their
exercises of chivalry.

Hippolito wore upon his helm a large plume of crimson
feathers, in the midst of which was artificially placed Leonora's
handkerchief. His armour was gilt and enamelled with green and
crimson. Aurelian was not so happy as to wear any token to
recommend him to the notice of his mistress, so had only a plume
of sky colour and white feathers suitable to his armour, which
was silver enamelled with azure. I shall not describe the habits of
any other cavaliers or of the ladies; let it suffice to tell the reader
they were all very fine and very glorious, and let him dress them
in what is most agreeable to his own fancy.

Our gallants entered the lists, and having made their obeisance
to his Highness, turned round to salute and view the company.
The scaffold was circular, so that there was no end of the
delightful prospect. It seemed a glory of beauty which shone
around the admiring beholders. Our lovers soon perceived the
stars which were to rule their destiny, which sparkled a lustre
beyond all the inferior constellations, and seemed like two suns
to distribute light to all the planets in that heavenly sphere.

Leonora knew her slave by his badge, and blushed till the lilies
and roses in her cheeks had resemblance to the plume of crimson
and white handkerchief in Hippolito's crest. He made her a low
bow, and reined his horse back with an extraordinary grace into a
respectful retreat. Aurelian saw his angel, his beautiful Incognita,
and had no other way to make himself known to her but by

saluting and bowing to her after the Spanish mode. She guessed
him by it to be her new servant Hippolito, and signified her
apprehension by making him a more particular and obliging
return than to any of the cavaliers who had saluted her before.

The exercise that was to be performed was in general a
running at the ring, and afterwards two cavaliers undertook to
defend the beauty of Donna Catherina against all who would not
allow her pre-eminence of their mistresses. This thing was only
designed for show and form, none presuming that anybody
would put so great an affront upon the bride and Duke's
kinswoman as to dispute her pretensions to the first place in the
court of Venus. But here our cavaliers were under a mistake, for
seeing a large shield carried before two knights with a lady
painted upon it, not knowing who, but reading the inscription,
which was (in large gold letters) 'Above the Insolence of
Competition', they thought themselves obliged, especially in the
presence of their mistresses, to vindicate their beauty, and were
just spurring on to engage the champions when a gentleman,
stopping them, told them their mistake: that it was the picture of
Donna Catherina, and a particular honour done to her by his
Highness's commands, and not to be disputed.

Upon this they would have returned to their post, much
concerned for their mistake, but notice being taken by Don
Ferdinand of some show of opposition that was made, he would
have begged leave of the Duke to have maintained his lady's
honour against the insolence of those cavaliers, but the Duke
would by no means permit it. They were arguing about it when
one of them came up, before whom the shield was borne, and
demanded his Highness's permission to inform those gentlemen
better of their mistake by giving them the foil. By the intercession
of Don Ferdinand, leave was given them, whereupon a civil
challenge was sent to the two strangers, informing them of their
error, and withal telling them they must either maintain it by
force of arms, or make a public acknowledgement by riding bare-
headed before the picture once around the lists.

The stranger cavaliers remonstrated to the Duke how sensible
they were of their error, and though they would not justify it, yet
they could not decline the combat, being pressed to it beyond
an honourable refusal. To the bride they sent a compliment,

wherein having first begged her pardon for not knowing her picture, they gave her to understand that now they were not about to dispute her undoubted right to the crown of beauty, but the honour of being her champions was the prize they fought for, which they thought themselves as able to maintain as any other pretenders. Wherefore they prayed her that, if fortune so far befriended their endeavours as to make them victors, that they might receive no other reward but to be crowned with the titles of their adversaries, and be ever after esteemed as her most humble servants. The excuse was so handsomely designed, and much better expressed than it is here, that it took effect. The Duke, Don Ferdinand and his lady were so well satisfied with it as to grant their request.

While the running at the ring lasted, our cavaliers alternately bore away great share of the honour. That sport ended, marshals were appointed for the field and everything in great form settled for the combat. The cavaliers were all in good earnest, but orders were given to bring 'em blunted lances, and to forbid the drawing of a sword, upon pain of his Highness's displeasure. The trumpets sounded and they began their course. The ladies' hearts, particularly the Incognita and Leonora's, beat time to the horses' hoofs, and hope and fear made a mock fight within their tender breasts, each wishing and doubting success where she liked. But as the generality of their prayers were for the graceful strangers, they accordingly succeeded.

Aurelian's adversary was unhorsed in the first encounter, and Hippolito's lost both his stirrups and dropped his lance to save himself. The honour of the field was immediately granted to them, and Donna Catherina sent them both favours, which she prayed them to wear as her knights. The crowd breaking up, our cavaliers made a shift to steal off unmarked, save by the watchful Leonora and Incognita, whose eyes were never off from their respective servants. There was enquiry made for them, but to no purpose, for they, to prevent their being discovered, had prepared another house, distant from their lodging, where a servant attended to disarm them, and another carried back their horses to the villa, while they walked unsuspected to their lodging. But Incognita had given command to a page to dog 'em till the evening at a distance, and bring her word where they were latest housed.

While several conjectures passed among the company, who were all gone to dinner at the palace, who those cavaliers should be, Don Fabio thought himself the only man able to guess, for he knew for certain that his son and Hippolito were both in town, and was well enough pleased with his humour of remaining incognito till the diversions should be over, believing then that the surprise of his discovery would add much to the gallantry he had shown in masquerade. But hearing the extraordinary liking that everybody expressed—and in a particular manner the great Duke himself—to the persons and behaviour of the unknown cavaliers, the old gentleman could not forbear the vanity to tell his Highness that he believed he had an interest in one of the gentlemen whom he was pleased to honour with so favourable a character, and told him what reason he had to believe the one to be his son and the other a Spanish nobleman, his friend.

This discovery having thus got vent was diffused like air; everybody sucked it in and let it out again with their breath to the next they met withal, and in half an hour's time, it was talked of in the house where our adventurers were lodged. Aurelian was stark mad at the news, and knew what search would be immediately made for him. Hippolito, had he not been desperately in love, would certainly have taken horse and rid out of town just then, for he could make no longer doubt of being discovered, and he was afraid of the just exceptions Leonora might make to a person who had now deceived her twice. Well, we will leave them both fretting and contriving to no purpose, to look about and see what was done at the palace, where their doom was determined much quicker than they imagined.

Dinner ended, the Duke retired with some chosen friends to a glass of wine, among whom were the Marquis of Viterbo and Don Fabio. His Highness was no stranger to the long feud that had been between the two families, and also understood what overtures of reconciliation had been lately made, with the proposals of marriage between Aurelian and the Marquis's daughter. Having waited till the wine had taken the effect proposed, and the company were raised to an uncommon pitch of cheerfulness, which he also encouraged by an example of freedom and good humour, he took an opportunity of rallying the two grave signiors into-an accommodation. That was seconded with the praises of the young couple, and the whole company joined in a large encomium upon the graces of Aurelian and the beauties of Juliana.

The old fellows were tickled with delight to hear their darlings so admired, which the Duke perceiving, out of a principle of generosity and friendship, urged the present consummation of the marriage, telling them there was yet one day of public rejoicing to come, and how glad he should be to have it improved by so acceptable an alliance, and what an honour it would be to have his cousin's marriage attended by the conjunction of so extraordinary a pair, the performance of which ceremony would crown the joy that was then in agitation, and make the last day vie for equal glory and happiness with the first.

In short, by the complaisant and persuasive authority of the Duke, the Dons were wrought into a compliance, and accordingly embraced and shook hands upon the matter. This news was dispersed like the former, and Don Fabio gave orders for the enquiring out his son's lodging, that the Marquis and he might make him a visit as soon as he had acquainted Juliana with his purpose, that she might prepare herself.

He found her very cheerful with Donna Catherina and several other ladies, whereupon the old gentleman, pretty well warmed with the Duke's good fellowship, told her aloud he was come to crown their mirth with another wedding; that his Highness had been pleased to provide a husband for his daughter, and he would have her provide herself to receive him tomorrow.

All the company at first, as well as Juliana herself, thought he had rallied, till the Duke coming in confirmed the serious part of his discourse. Juliana was confounded at the haste that was imposed on her, and desired a little time to consider what she was about. But the Marquis told her she should have all the rest of her life to consider in; that Aurelian should come and consider with her in the morning, if she pleased, but in the meantime, he advised her to go home and call her maids to council.

Juliana took her leave of the company very gravely, as if not much delighted with her father's raillery. Leonora happened to be by and heard all that passed. She was ready to swoon and found herself seized with a more violent passion than ever for Aurelian. Now, upon her apprehensions of losing him, her active fancy had brought him before her with all the advantages imaginable, and though she had before found great tenderness in her inclination toward him, yet was she somewhat surprised to find she really loved him. She was so uneasy at what she had heard that she thought it convenient to steal out of the presence and retire to her closet, to bemoan her unhappy, helpless condition.

Our two cavalier lovers had racked their invention till it was quite disabled, and could not make discovery of one contrivance more for their relief. Both sat silent, each depending upon his friend, and still expecting when t'other should speak. Night came upon them while they sat thus thoughtless, or rather, drowned in thought. But a servant, bringing lights into the room, awakened them, and Hippolito's speech, ushered by a profound sigh, broke silence.

'Well,' said he, 'what must we do Aurelian?' 'We must suffer,' replied Aurelian faintly. When, immediately raising his voice, he cried out: 'O ye unequal powers, why do ye urge us to desire what ye doom us to forbear; give us a will to choose, then curb us with a duty to restrain that choice? Cruel father, will nothing else suffice? Am I to be the sacrifice to expiate your offences past— past ere I was born? Were I to lose my life I'd gladly seal your reconcilement with my blood. But, O, my soul is free; you have no title to my immortal being; that has existence independent of your power. And must I lose my love, the extract of that being, the joy, light, life and darling of my soul? No, I'll own my flame and plead my title too.

'But hold, wretched Aurelian, hold. Whither does thy passion hurry thee? Alas, the cruel fair Incognita loves thee not. She knows not of thy love. If she did, what merit hast thou to pretend? Only love, excess of love. And all the world has that. All that have seen her. Yet I had only seen her once, and in that once I loved above the world; nay, loved beyond myself, such vigorous flame, so strong, so quick, she darted at my breast. It must rebound and, by reflection, warm herself. Ah, welcome thought! Lovely, deluding fancy, hang still upon my soul; let me but think that once she loves, and perish my despair.'

Here a sudden stop gave a period also to Hippolito's expectation, and he hoped, now that his friend had given his passion so free a vent, he might recollect and bethink himself of what was convenient to be done. But Aurelian, as if he had mustered up all his spirits purely to acquit himself of that passionate harangue, stood mute and insensible, like an alarm clock that had spent all its force in one violent emotion. Hippolito shook him by the arm to rouse him from his lethargy, when his lackey, coming into the room out of breath, told him there was a coach just stopped at the door, but he did not take time to see who came in it.

Aurelian concluded immediately it was his father in quest of him, and without saying any more to Hippolito than that he was ruined if discovered, took his sword and slipped down a back pair of stairs into the garden, from whence he conveyed himself into the street. Hippolito had not bethought himself what to do, before he perceived a lady come into the chamber close veiled, and make toward him. At the first appearance of a woman, his imagination flattered him with a thought of Leonora, but that was quickly over upon nearer approach to the lady, who had much the advantage in stature of his mistress.

He very civilly accosted her and asked if he were the person to whom the honour of that visit was intended. She said her business was with Don Hippolito di Saviolina, to whom she had matter of concern to import,* and which required haste. He had like to have told her that he was the man, but by good chance reflecting upon his friend's adventure, who had taken his name, he made answer that he believed Don Hippolito not far off, and if she had a moment's patience, he would enquire for him.

He went out, leaving the lady in the room, and made search all round the house and garden for Aurelian, but to no purpose. The lady, impatient of his long stay, took a pen and ink and some paper which she found upon the table, and had just made an end of her letter when, hearing a noise of more than one coming upstairs, she concluded his friend had found him, and that her letter would be to no purpose, so tore it in pieces—which she repented when, turning about, she found her mistake and beheld Don Fabio and the Marquis of Viterbo just entering at the door.

She gave a shriek at the surprise of their appearance, which much troubled the old gentlemen and made them retire in confusion for putting a gentlewoman into such a fright. The

Marquis, thinking they had been misinformed, or had mistaken the lodgings, came forward again and made an apology to the lady for their error. But she, making no reply, walked directly by him downstairs, and went into her coach, which hurried her away as speedily as the horses were able to draw.

The Dons were at a loss what to think when Hippolito, coming into the room to give the lady an account of his errand, was no less astonished to find she was departed and had left two old signiors in her stead. He knew Don Fabio's face, for Aurelian had shown him his father at the tilting, but being confident he was not known to him, he ventured to ask him concerning a lady whom just now he had left in that chamber. Don Fabio told him she was just gone down, and doubted they had been guilty of a mistake in coming to enquire for a couple of gentlemen, whom they were informed were lodged in that house. He begged his pardon if he had any relation to that lady, and desired to know if he could give them any account of the persons they sought for. Hippolito made answer he was a stranger in the place, and only a servant to that lady whom they had disturbed, and whom he must go and seek out. And in this perplexity he left them, going again in search of Aurelian, to inform him of what had passed.

The old gentlemen at last meeting with a servant of the house, were directed to Signior Claudio's chamber, where they were no sooner entered but Aurelian came into the house. A servant, who had skulked for him by Hippolito's order, followed him up into the chamber and told him who was with Claudio then making enquiry for him. He thought that to be no place for him, since Claudio must needs discover all the truth to his father, wherefore he left directions with the servant where Hippolito should meet him in the morning. As he was going out of the room, he espied the torn paper which the lady had thrown upon the floor. The first piece he took up had 'Incognita' written upon it, the sight of which so alarmed him he scarce knew what he was about, but hearing a noise of a door opening overhead, with as much care as was consistent with the haste he was then in, he gathered up the scattered pieces of paper and betook himself to a ramble.

Coming by a light which hung at the corner of a street, he joined the torn papers and collected thus much: that his Incognita had written the note, and earnestly desired him (if there were any reality in what he pretended to her) to meet her at twelve a clock that night at a convent gate. But unluckily, the bit of paper which should have mentioned what convent was broken off and lost.

Here was a large subject for Aurelian's passion, which he did not spare to pour forth in abundance of curses on his stars. So earnest was he in the contemplation of his misfortunes, that he walked on unwittingly, till at length a silence (and such as was only to be found in that part of the town whither his unguided steps had carried him) surprised his attention. I say, a profound silence roused him from his thought, and a clap of thunder could have done no more.

Now because it is possible this, at some time or other, may happen to be read by some malicious or ignorant person (no reflection upon the present reader), who will not admit, or does not understand, that silence should make a man start, and have the same effect in provoking his attention with its opposite, noise, I will illustrate this matter to such a diminutive critic by a parallel instance of light, which though it does chiefly entertain the eyes, and is indeed the prime object of the sight, yet should it immediately cease, to have a man left in the dark by a sudden deficiency of it would make him stare with his eyes and, though he could not see, endeavour to look about him. Why, just thus did it fare with our adventurer, who seeming to have wandered both into the dominions of silence and of night, began to have some tender for his own safety, and would willingly have groped his way back again when he heard a voice, as from a person whose breath had been stopped by some forcible oppression and just then, by a violent effort, was broke through the restraint.

'Yet—yet,' again replied the voice, still struggling for air, 'forbear, and I'll forgive what's past.' 'I have done nothing yet that needs a pardon,' says another, 'and what is to come will admit of none.' Here the person who seemed to be the oppressed made several attempts to speak, but they were only inarticulate sounds, being all interrupted and choked in their passage.

Aurelian was sufficiently astonished, and would have crept nearer to the place whence he guessed the voice to come, but he was got among the ruins of an old monastery, and could not stir so silently but some loose stones he met with made a rumbling.

The noise alarmed both parties, and as it gave comfort to the
one, it so terrified the t'other that he could not hinder the
oppressed from calling for help. Aurelian fancied it was a
woman's voice, and immediately drawing his sword, demanded
what was the matter. He was answered with the appearance of a
man, who had opened a dark lantern which he had by him, and
came toward him with a pistol in his hand ready cocked.

Aurelian, seeing the irresistible advantage his adversary had
over him, would fain have retired, and, by the greatest providence
in the world, going backwards, fell down over some loose stones
that lay in his way just in that instant of time when the villain fired
his pistol, who, seeing him fall, concluded he had shot him. The
cries of the afflicted person were redoubled at the tragical sight,
which made the murderer, drawing a poniard, to threaten him
that the next murmur should be his last.

Aurelian, who was scarce assured that he was unhurt, got
softly up and, coming near enough to perceive the violence that
was used to stop the injured man's mouth (for now he saw plainly
it was a man), cried out: 'Turn, villain, and look upon thy death!'
The fellow, amazed at the voice, turned about to have snatched
up the lantern from the ground, either to have given light only to
himself, or to have put out the candle that he might have made
his escape. But which of the two he designed nobody could tell
but himself, and if the reader have a curiosity to know, he must
blame Aurelian, who, thinking there could be no foul play offered
to such a villain, ran him immediately through the heart, so that
he dropped down dead at his feet without speaking a word.

He would have seen who the person was he had thus happily
delivered, but the dead body had fallen upon the lantern, which
put out the candle. However, coming up toward him, he asked
him how he did, and bid him be of good heart. He was answered
with nothing but prayers, blessings and thanks, called a thousand
deliverers, good geniuses and guardian angels, and the rescued
would certainly have gone upon his knees to have worshipped
him had he not been bound hand and foot, which Aurelian
understanding, groped for the knots and either untied them or
cut them asunder; but 'tis more probable the latter, because more
expeditious.

They took little heed what became of the body, which they left behind them, and Aurelian was conducted from out the ruins by the hand of him he had delivered. By a faint light issuing from the just rising moon, he could discern that it was a youth, but coming into a more frequented part of the town, where several lights were hung out, he was amazed at the extreme beauty which appeared in his face, though a little pale and disordered with his late fright.

Aurelian longed to hear the story of so odd an adventure, and entreated his charge to tell it him by the way; but he desired him to forbear till they were come into some house or other, where he might rest and recover his tired spirits, for yet he was so faint he was unable to look up. Aurelian thought these last words were delivered in a voice whose accent was not new to him. That thought made him look earnestly in the youth's face, which he now was sure he had somewhere seen before, and thereupon asked him if he had never been at Siena. That question made the young gentleman look up, and something of a joy appeared in his countenance which yet he endeavoured to smother. So, praying Aurelian to conduct him to his lodging, he promised him that as soon as they should come thither, he would acquaint him with anything he desired to know. Aurelian would rather have gone anywhere else than to his own lodging, but being so very late, he was at a loss and so forced to be contented.

As soon as they were come into his chamber and that lights were brought them and the servant dismissed, the paleness, which so visibly before had usurped the sweet countenance of the afflicted youth, vanished and gave place to a more lively flood of crimson, which with a modest heat glowed freshly on his cheeks. Aurelian waited with a pleasing admiration the discovery promised him, when the youth, still struggling with his resolution, with a timorous haste pulled off a peruke which had concealed the most beautiful abundance of hair that ever graced one female head. Those dishevelled spreading tresses, as at first they made a discovery of, so at last they served for a veil to the modest, lovely blushes of the fair Incognita, for she it was and none other.

But O, the inexpressible, inconceivable joy and amazement of Aurelian! As soon as he durst venture to think, he concluded it to be all vision, and never doubted so much of anything in his life as of his being then awake. But she, taking him by the hand, and desiring him to sit down by her, partly convinced him of the reality of her presence. 'This is the second time, Don Hippolito,' said she to him, 'that I have been here this night. What the occasion was of my seeking you out, and how by miracle you preserved me, would add too much to the surprise I perceive you to be already in, should I tell you. Nor will I make any further discovery till I know what censure you pass upon the confidence which I have put in you, and the strange circumstances in which you find me at this time. I am sensible they are such that I shall not blame your severest conjectures, but I hope to convince you when you shall hear what I have to say in justification of my virtue.'

'Justification,' cried Aurelian, 'what infidel dares doubt it!' Then, kneeling down and taking her hand: 'Ah Madam,' says he, 'would Heaven would no other ways look upon than I behold your perfections. Wrong not your creature with a thought he can be guilty of that horrid impiety as once to doubt your virtue. Heavens,' cried he, starting up, 'am I so really blessed to see you once again? May I trust my sight, or does my fancy now only more strongly work? For still I did preserve your image in my heart, and you were ever present to my dearest thoughts.'

'Enough, Hippolito, enough of rapture,' said she, 'you cannot much accuse me of ingratitude, for you see I have not been unmindful of you; but moderate your joy till I have told you my condition, and if for my sake you are raised to this delight, it is not of a long continuance.'

At that (as Aurelian tells the story) a sigh diffused a mournful sweetness through the air, and liquid grief fell gently from her eyes; triumphant sadness sat upon her brow, and even sorrow seemed delighted with the conquest he had made. See what a change Aurelian felt! His heart bled tears and trembled in his breast. Sighs, struggling for a vent, had choked each other's passage up. His floods of joys were all suppressed; cold doubts and fears had chilled 'em with a sudden frost, and he was troubled to excess, yet knew not why. Well, the learned say it was sympathy, and I am always of the opinion with the learned, if they speak first.

After a world of condolence had passed between them, he

prevailed with her to tell him her story. So, having put all her sighs into one great sigh, she discharged herself of 'em all at once, and formed the relation you are just about to read.

'Having been in my infancy contracted to a man I could never endure, and now by my parents being likely to be forced to marry him, is, in short, the great occasion of my grief. I fancied,' continued she, 'something so generous in your countenance and uncommon in your behaviour, while you were diverting yourself and rallying me with expressions of gallantry at the ball, as induced me to hold conference with you—I now freely confess to you, out of design that if things should happen as I then feared, and as now they are come to pass, I might rely upon your assistance in a matter of concern, and in which I would sooner choose to depend upon a generous stranger than any acquaintance I have.

'What mirth and freedom I then put on were, I can assure you, far distant from my heart, but I did violence to myself out of complaisance to your temper. I knew you at the tilting, and wished you might come off as you did, though I do not doubt but you would have had as good success had it been opposite to my inclinations. Not to detain you by too tedious a relation, every day my friends urged me to the match they had agreed upon for me before I was capable of consenting. At last their importunities grew to that degree that I found I must either consent, which would make me miserable, or be miserable by perpetually enduring to be baited by my father, brother and other relations.

'I resolved yesterday on a sudden to give firm faith to the opinion I had conceived of you, and accordingly came in the evening to request your assistance in delivering me from my tormentors, by a safe and private conveyance of me to a monastery about four leagues hence, where I have an aunt who would receive me, and is the only relation I have averse to the match. I was surprised at the appearance of some company I did not expect at your lodgings, which made me in haste tear a paper which I had written to you with directions where to find me, and get speedily away in my coach to an old servant's house, whom I acquainted with my purpose.

'By my order, she provided me of this habit which I now wear. I ventured to trust myself with her brother, and resolved to go under his conduct to the monastery. He proved to be a villain, and pretending to take me a short and private way to the place where he was to take up a hackney coach (for that which I came in was broke somewhere or other with the haste it made to carry me from your lodging), led me into an old, ruined monastery, where it pleased Heaven, by what accident I know not, to direct you. I need not tell you how you saved my life and my honour by revenging me with the death of my perfidious guide. This is the sum of my present condition, bating the apprehensions I am in of being taken by some of my relations and forced to a thing so quite contrary to my inclinations.'

Aurelian was confounded at the relation she had made, and began to fear his own estate to be more desperate than ever he had imagined. He made her a very passionate and eloquent speech in behalf of himself (much better than I intend to insert here) and expressed a mighty concern that she should look upon his ardent affection to be only raillery or gallantry. He was very free of his oaths to confirm the truth of what he pretended, nor I believe did she doubt it, or at least was unwilling so to do. For I would caution the reader, by the by, not to believe every word which she told him, nor that admirable sorrow which she counterfeited to be accurately true. It was indeed truth so cunningly intermingled with fiction, that it required no less wit and presence of mind than she was endowed with so to acquit herself on the sudden. She had entrusted herself indeed with a fellow who proved a villain to conduct her to a monastery, but one which was in the town, and where she intended only to lie concealed for his sake, as the reader shall understand ere long. For we have another discovery to make to him, if he have not found it out of himself already.

After Aurelian had said what he was able upon the subject in hand, with a mournful tone and dejected look he demanded his doom. She asked him if he would endeavour to convey her to the monastery she had told him of. 'Your commands, Madam,' replied he, 'are sacred to me, and were they to lay down my life, I would obey them.' With that, he would have gone out of the room to have given order for his horses to be got ready immediately, but with a countenance so full of sorrow as moved compassion in the tender hearted Incognita.

'Stay a little, Don Hippolito,' said she, 'I fear I shall not be able to undergo the fatigue of a journey this night. Stay and give me your advice how I shall conceal myself, if I continue tomorrow in this town.' Aurelian could have satisfied her she was not then in a place to avoid discovery, but he must also have told her then the reason of it, viz. whom he was, and who were in quest of him, which he did not think convenient to declare till necessity should urge him, for he feared lest her knowledge of those designs which were in agitation between him and Juliana might deter her more from giving her consent.

At last he resolved to try his utmost persuasions to gain her, and told her accordingly he was afraid she would be disturbed there in the morning, and he knew no other way (if she had not as great an aversion for him as the man whom she now endeavoured to avoid) than by making him happy to make herself secure. He demonstrated to her that the disobligation to her parents would be greater by going to a monastery, since it was only to avoid a choice which they had made for her, and which she could not have so just a pretence to do till she had made one for herself.

A world of other arguments he used, which she contradicted as long as she was able, or at least willing. At last, she told him she would consult her pillow, and in the morning conclude what was fit to be done. He thought it convenient to leave her to her rest, and having locked her up in his room, went himself to repose upon a pallat* by Signior Claudio.

In the meantime, it may be convenient to enquire what became of Hippolito. He had wandered much in pursuit of Aurelian, though Leonora equally took up his thoughts. He was reflecting upon the oddness and extravagance of his circumstances, the continuation of which had doubtless created in him a great uneasiness, when it was interrupted with the noise of opening the gates of the Convent of St Lawrence, whither he was arrived sooner than he thought for, being the place Aurelian had appointed by the lackey to meet him in.

He wondered to see the gates opened at so unseasonable an hour, and went to enquire the reason of it from them who were employed, but they proved to be novices, and made him signs to go in where he might meet with somebody allowed to answer him. He found the religious men all up and tapers lighting everywhere. At last he followed a friar who was going into the garden, and asking him the cause of these preparations, he was answered that they were entreated to pray for the soul of a cavalier who was just departing or departed this life, and whom upon further talk with him he found to be the same Lorenzo so often mentioned. Don Mario, it seems, uncle to Lorenzo and father to Leonora, had a private door out of the garden belonging to his house into that of the Convent, which door this Father was now a going to open, that he and his family might come and offer up their orisons for the soul of their kinsman.

Hippolito, having informed himself of as much as he could ask without suspicion, took his leave of the friar, not a little joyful at the hopes he had, by such unexpected means, of seeing his beautiful Leonora. As soon as he was got at convenient distance from the friar (who, 'tis like, thought he had returned into the Convent to his devotion), he turned back through a close walk which led him, with a little compass, to the same private door where just before he had left the friar, who now he saw was gone and the door open.

He went into Don Mario's garden and walked round with much caution and circumspection, for the moon was then about to rise, and had already diffused a glimmering light sufficient to distinguish a man from a tree. By computation now (which is a very remarkable circumstance) Hippolito entered this garden near upon the same instant when Aurelian wandered into the old monastery and found his Incognita in distress. He was pretty well acquainted with the platform and sight of the garden, for he had formerly surveyed the outside and knew what part to make to if he should be surprised and driven to a precipitate escape.

He took his stand behind a well grown bush of myrtle, which, should the moon shine brighter than was required, had the advantage to be shaded by the indulgent boughs of an ancient bay tree. He was delighted with the choice he had made, for he found a hollow in the myrtle as if purposely contrived for the reception of one person, who might, undiscovered, perceive all about him. He looked upon it as a good omen that the tree consecrated to Venus* was so propitious to him in his amorous distress. The consideration of that, together with the obligation he lay under to the Muses for sheltering him also with so large a crown of bays, had like to have set him a rhyming.

He was, to tell the truth, naturally addicted to madrigal, and we should undoubtedly have had a small dessert of numbers* to have picked and criticised upon, had he not been interrupted just upon his delivery; nay, after the preliminary sigh had made way for his utterance. But so was his fortune, Don Mario was coming towards the door at that very nick of time, where he met with a priest just out of breath, who told him that Lorenzo was just breathing his last, and desired to know if he would come and take his final leave before they were to administer the extreme unction. Don Mario, who had been at some difference with his nephew, now thought it his duty to be reconciled to him, so calling to Leonora, who was coming after him, he bid her go to her devotions in the chapel, and told her where he was going.

He went on with the priest, while Hippolito saw Leonora come forward, only accompanied by her woman. She was in an undress, and by reason of a melancholy visible in her face, more careless than usual in her attire, which he thought added as much as was possible to the abundance of her charms. He had not much time to contemplate this beauteous vision, for she soon passed into the garden of the Convent, leaving him confounded with love, admiration, joy, hope, fear and all the train of passions which seize upon men in his condition, all at once.

He was so teased with this variety of torment that he never missed the two hours that had slipped away during his automachy* and intestine conflict. Leonora's return settled his spirits, at least united them, and he had now no other thought but how he should present himself before her, when she, calling her woman, bid her bolt the garden door on the inside that she might not be surprised by her father if he returned through the Convent, which done, she ordered her to bring down her lute, and leave her to herself in the garden.

All this Hippolito saw and heard to his inexpressible content, yet had he much to do to smother his joy and hinder it from taking a vent, which would have ruined the only opportunity of his life. Leonora withdrew into an arbour so near him that he could distinctly hear her if she played or sung. Having tuned her lute, with a voice soft as the breath of angels, she sung to it this following air.

I.

Ah, whither, whither shall I fly,
  A poor, unhappy maid,
To hopeless love and misery
  By my own heart betrayed?
Not by Alexis' eyes undone,
Nor by his charming, faithless tongue,
  Or any practised art,
Such real ills may hope a cure,
But the sad pains which I endure
  Proceed from fancied smart.

II.

'Twas fancy gave Alexis charms,
  Ere I beheld his face.
Kind fancy, then, could fold our arms
  And form a soft embrace.
But since I've seen the real swain
And tried to fancy him again
  I'm by my fancy taught,
Though 'tis a bliss no tongue can tell
To have Alexis, yet 'tis Hell
  To have him but in thought.

The song, ended, grieved Hippolito that it was so soon ended, and in the ecstasy he was then wrapped, I believe he would have been satisfied to have expired with it. He could not help flattering himself (though at the same time he checked his own vanity) that he was the person meant in the song. While he was indulging which thought, to his happy astonishment he heard it encouraged by these words:

'Unhappy Leonora,' said she, 'how is thy poor, unwary heart misled! Whither am I come? The false, deluding lights of an imaginary flame have led me, a poor, benighted victim, to a real fire. I burn and am consumed with hopeless love; those beams in whose soft, temperate warmth I wantoned heretofore, now flash destruction to my soul. My treacherous, greedy eyes have sucked the glaring light; they have united all its rays and, like a burning-glass, conveyed the pointed meteor to my heart. Ah, Aurelian, how quickly hast thou conquered, and how quickly must thou forsake. O happy (to me, unfortunately, happy) Juliana, I am to be the subject of thy triumph. To thee, Aurelian comes laden with the tribute of my heart and glories in the oblation of his broken vows.

'What then, is Aurelian false? False, alas, I know not what I say; how can he be false, or true, or anything to me? What promises did he ere make or I receive? Sure I dream, or I am mad, and fancy it to be love. Foolish girl, recall thy banished reason. Ah, would it were no more; would I could rave, sure, that would give me ease and rob me of the sense of pain. At least, among my wandering thoughts I should at sometime light upon Aurelian, and fancy him to be mine. Kind madness would flatter my poor, feeble wishes and sometimes tell me Aurelian is not lost—not irrecoverably, not for ever lost.'

Hippolito could hear no more; he had not room for half his transport. When Leonora perceived a man coming toward her, she fell a trembling and could not speak. Hippolito approached with reverence, as to a sacred shrine, when, coming near enough to see her consternation, he fell upon his knees. 'Behold, O adored Leonora,' said he, 'your ravished Aurelian; behold at your feet the happiest of men. Be not disturbed at my appearance, but think that Heaven conducted me to hear my bliss pronounced, by that dear mouth alone whose breath could fill me with new life.'

Here he would have come nearer, but Leonora (scarce come to herself) was getting up in haste to have gone away. He catched her hand, and with all the endearments of love and transport, pressed her stay. She was a long time in great confusion; at last, with many blushes, she entreated him to let her go where she might hide her guilty head and not expose her shame before his eyes, since his ears had been sufficient witnesses of her crime. He begged pardon for his treachery in overhearing, and confessed it to be a crime he had now repeated. With a thousand submissions, entreaties, prayers, praises, blessings and passionate expressions, he wrought upon her to stay and hear him.

Here Hippolito made use of his rhetoric, and it proved prevailing. 'Twere tedious to tell the many ingenious arguments he used, with all her nice distinctions and objections. In short, he convinced her of his passion, represented to her the necessity they were under of being speedy in their resolves. That his father (for still he was Aurelian) would undoubtedly find him in the morning, and then it would be too late to repent. She, on the other hand, knew it was in vain to deny a passion which he had heard her so frankly own (and no doubt was very glad it was past and done), besides apprehending the danger of delay and having some little jealousies and fears of what effect might be produced between the commands of his father and the beauties of Juliana, after some decent denials, she consented to be conducted by him through the garden into the convent, where she would prevail with her confessor to marry them.

He was a scrupulous old Father, whom they had to deal withal, insomuch that ere they had persuaded him, Don Mario was returned by the way of his own house where, missing his daughter, and her woman not being able to give any further account of her than that she left her in the garden, he concluded she was gone again to her devotions, and indeed he found her in the chapel upon her knees with Hippolito in her hand, receiving the Father's benediction upon conclusion of the ceremony.

It would have asked a very skilful hand to have depicted to the life the faces of those three persons at Don Mario's appearance. He that has seen some admirable piece of transmutation by a Gorgon's head* may form to himself the most probable idea of the prototype. The old gentleman was himself in a sort of a wood,* to find his daughter with a young fellow and a priest, but as yet he did not know the worst, till Hippolito and Leonora came, and kneeling at his feet, begged his forgiveness and blessing as his son and daughter.

Don Mario, instead of that, fell into a most violent passion, and would undoubtedly have committed some extravagant action, had he not been restrained, more by the sanctity of the place than the persuasions of all the religious who were now come about him. Leonora stirred not off her knees all this time, but continued begging of him that he would hear her.

'Ah, ungrateful and undutiful wretch,' cried he, 'how hast thou requited all my care and tenderness of thee? Now, when I might have expected some return of comfort, to throw thyself away upon an unknown person and, for ought I know, a villain; to me, I'm sure he is a villain, who has robbed me of my treasure, my darling joy, and all the future happiness of my life prevented. Go, go, thou now to be forgotten Leonora; go and enjoy thy unprosperous choice. You who wanted not a father's counsel cannot need, or else will slight, his blessing.'

These last words were spoken with so much passion and feeling concern that Leonora, moved with excess of grief, fainted at his feet just as she had caught hold to embrace his knees. The old man would have shook her off, but compassion and fatherly affection came upon him in the midst of his resolve, and melted him into tears. He embraces his daughter in his arms and wept over her, while they endeavoured to restore her senses.

Hippolito was in such concern he could not speak, but was busy employed in rubbing and chafing her temples, when she, opening her eyes, laid hold of his arm and cried out, 'O, my Aurelian, how unhappy have you made me!' With that, she had again like to have fainted away, but he shook her in his arms and begged Don Mario to have some pity on his daughter, since by his severity she was reduced to that condition. The old man, hearing his daughter name Aurelian, was a little revived and began to hope things were in a pretty good condition. He was persuaded to comfort her, and having brought her wholly to herself, was content to hear her excuse, and in a little time was so far wrought upon as to beg Hippolito's pardon for the ill opinion he had conceived of him, and not long after gave his consent.

The night was spent in this conflict, and it was now clear day, when Don Mario, conducting his new son and daughter through the garden, was met by some servants of the Marquis of Viterbo, who had been enquiring for Donna Leonora to know if Juliana had lately been with her, for that she was missing from her father's house, and no conjectures could be made of what might become of her. Don Mario and Leonora were surprised at the news, for he knew well enough of the match that was designed for Juliana, and having enquired where the Marquis was, it was told him that he was gone with Don Fabio and Fabritio toward Aurelian's lodgings.

Don Mario, having assured the servants that Juliana had not been there, dismissed them and advised with his son and daughter how they should undeceive the Marquis and Don Fabio in their expectations of Aurelian. Hippolito could oftentimes scarce forbear smiling at the old man's contrivances, who was most deceived himself. He at length advised them to go all down together to his lodging, where he would present himself before his father and ingenuously confess to him the truth, and he did not question his approving of his choice.

This was agreed to, and the coach made ready. While they were upon their way, Hippolito prayed heartily that his friend Aurelian might be at the lodging, to satisfy Don Mario and Leonora of his circumstances and quality, when he should be obliged to discover himself. His petitions were granted, for Don Fabio had beset the house long before his son was up or Incognita awake.

Upon the arrival of Don Mario and Hippolito, they heard a great noise and hubbub above stairs, which Don Mario concluded was occasioned by their not finding Aurelian, whom he thought he could give the best account of. So that it was not in Hippolito's power to dissuade him from going up before, to prepare his father to receive and forgive him. While Hippolito and Leonora were left in the coach at the door, he made himself known to her, and begged her pardon a thousand times for continuing the deceit. She was under some concern at first to find she was still mistaken, but his behaviour and the reasons he gave soon reconciled him to her. His person was altogether as agreeable, his estate and quality not at all inferior, to Aurelian's.

In the meantime, the true Aurelian, who had seen his father, begged leave of him to withdraw for a moment, in which time he went into the chamber, where his Incognita was dressing herself, by his design, in woman's apparel. While he was consulting with her how they should break the matter to his father, it happened that Don Mario came upstairs where the Marquis and Don Fabio were. They undoubtedly concluded him mad to hear him making apologies and excuses for Aurelian, whom he told them, if they would promise to forgive, he would present before them immediately.

The Marquis asked him if his daughter had lain with Leonora that night. He answered him with another question in behalf of Aurelian. In short, they could not understand one another, but each thought t'other beside himself. Don Mario was so concerned that they would not believe him that he ran downstairs and came to the door out of breath, desiring Hippolito that he would come into the house quickly, for that he could not persuade his father but that he had already seen and spoke to him. Hippolito by that understood that Aurelian was in the house, so taking Leonora by the hand, he followed Don Mario, who led him up into the dining room, where they found Aurelian upon his knees, begging his father to forgive him that he could not agree to the choice he had made for him, since he had already disposed of himself, and that before he understood the designs he had for him, which was the reason that he had hitherto concealed himself. Don Fabio knew not how to answer him, but looked upon the Marquis, and the Marquis upon him, as if the cement had been cooled which was to have united their families.

All was silent, and Don Mario, for his part, took it to be all conjuration. He was coming forward to present Hippolito to them when Aurelian, spying his friend, started from his knees and ran to embrace him. 'My dear Hippolito,' said he, 'what happy chance has brought you hither, just at my necessity?' Hippolito pointed to Don Mario and Leonora, and told him upon what terms he came. Don Mario was ready to run mad hearing him called Hippolito, and went again to examine his daughter. While she was informing him of the truth, the Marquis's servants returned with the melancholy news that his daughter was nowhere to be found.

While the Marquis and Don Fabritio were wondering at and lamenting the misfortune of her loss, Hippolito came towards Don Fabio and interceded for his son, since the lady perhaps had withdrawn herself out of an aversion to the match. Don Fabio, though very much incensed, yet forgot not the respect due to Hippolito's quality, and by his persuasion spoke to Aurelian, though with a stern look and angry voice, and asked him where he had disposed the cause of his disobedience, if he were worthy to see her or no. Aurelian made answer that he desired no more than for him to see her, and he did not doubt a consequence of his approbation and forgiveness. 'Well,' said Don Fabio, 'you are very conceited of your own discretion. Let us see this rarity.'

While Aurelian was gone in for Incognita, the Marquis of Viterbo and Don Fabritio were taking their leaves in great disorder for their loss and disappointment, but Don Fabio entreated their stay a moment longer, till the return of his son. Aurelian led Incognita into the room veiled, who, seeing some company there which he had not told her of, would have gone back again. But Don Fabio came bluntly forwards and, ere she was aware, lifted up her veil and beheld the fair Incognita, differing nothing from Juliana but in her name.

This discovery was so extremely surprising and welcome that either joy or amazement had tied up the tongues of the whole company. Aurelian here was most at a loss, for he knew not of his happiness, and that which all along prevented Juliana's confessing herself to him was her knowing Hippolito (for whom she took him) to be Aurelian's friend, and she feared, if he had known her, that he would never have consented to have deprived him of her.

Juliana was the first that spoke, falling upon her knees to her father, who was not enough himself to take her up. Don Fabio ran to her and awakened the Marquis, who then embraced her, but could not yet speak. Fabritio and Leonora strove who should first take her in their arms. For Aurelian, he was out of his wits with joy, and Juliana was not much behind him, to see how happily their loves and duties were reconciled. Don Fabio embraced his son and forgave him. The Marquis and Fabritio gave Juliana into his hands; he received the blessing upon his knees. All were overjoyed, and Don Mario not a little proud at the discovery of his son-in-law, whom Aurelian did not fail to set forth with all the ardent zeal and eloquence of friendship. Juliana and Leonora had pleasant discourse about their unknown and mistaken rivalship, and it was the subject of a great deal of mirth to hear Juliana relate the several contrivances which she had to avoid Aurelian for the sake of Hippolito.

Having diverted themselves with many remarks upon the pleasing surprise, they all thought it proper to attend upon the great Duke that morning at the palace, and to acquaint him with the novelty of what had passed, while, by the way, the two young couple entertained the company with the relation of several particulars of their three days' adventures.

APHRA BEHN
The Unfortunate Happy Lady
(1698)

The Unfortunate Happy Lady. A True History.

To Edward Cook of Norfolk, Esquire.
Honoured Sir,

if so considerable a name as Mrs Behn's did not
justify my choice of your patronage, Sir, for the following novel, I
might perhaps be thought too presumptuous in sheltering the
unhappy fortunate under your name. But being secured by her
established reputation from injuring yours, I gave way to that
desire I had to show myself in the number of your admirers. For,
there being a sort of merit in admiring merit, everyone that has
the least ambition would desire to show himself master of that
desert.

Your virtues as well as fortunes are too conspicuous not to be
observed by all; your affability, generosity, goodness, are what
give hope to your inferiors and comfort and satisfaction to your
equals and admiration to all. For 'tis seldom that fortune alone
can draw our hearts, though it draw our eyes, but when
embellished with such qualifications it makes the possessor truly
great and happy, as well as rich.

'Tis well, Sir, I am no panegyrist; I should else, on so engaging
a theme, be apt to forget the violence I did your modesty in the
satisfaction I found in the contemplation of your excellencies.
But I leave that task to happier pens, and content myself with the
generous ambition of what my stars deny me, and only beg leave
to subscribe myself, Sir,

Your most obedient and devoted servant,

Sam. Briscoe.*

The Unfortunate Happy Lady. A True History*

I CANNOT omit giving the world an account of the uncommon
villainy of a gentleman of a good family in England, practised
upon his sister, which was attested to me by one who lived in the
family and from whom I had the whole truth of the story. I shall
conceal the unhappy gentleman's own, under the borrowed
names of Sir William Wilding, who succeeded his father, Sir
Edward, in an estate of near £4,000 a year, inheriting all that

belonged to him except his virtues. 'Tis true, he was obliged to pay his only sister a portion of £6,000, which he might have very easily have done of his patrimony in a little time, the estate being not in the least encumbered. But the death of his good father gave a loose to the extravagance of his inclinations, which till then was hardly observable.

The first discovery he made of his humour was in the extraordinary rich equipage he prepared for his journey to London, which was much greater than his fair and plentiful fortune could maintain, nor were his expenses any way inferior to the figure he made here in town, insomuch that in less than a twelvemonth he was forced to return to his seat in the country, to mortgage a part of his estate of a thousand pounds a year to satisfy the debts he had already contracted in his profuse treats, gaming and women, which in a few weeks he effected, to the great affliction of his sister Philadelphia, a young lady of excellent beauty, education and virtue, who, foreseeing the utter ruin of the estate if not timely prevented, daily begged of him, with prayers and tears that might have moved a Scythian or wild Arab, or indeed anything but him, to pay her her portion.

To which, however, he seemingly consented, and promised to take her to town with him and there give her all the satisfaction she could expect. And having dipped some paltry acres of land deeper than ever Heaven dipped 'em in rain, he was as good as his word, and brought her to town with him, where he told her he would place her with an ancient lady with whom he had contracted a friendship at his first coming to London, adding that she was a lady of incomparable morals and of a matchless life and conversation.

Philadelphia took him in the best sense, and was very desirous to be planted in the same house with her, hoping she might grow to as great a perfection in such excellent qualifications as she imagined 'em. About four days, therefore, after they had been in town, she solicits her brother to wait on that lady with her. He replied that: 'It is absolutely necessary and convenient that I should first acquaint her with my design and beg that she will be pleased to take you into her care, and this shall be my chief business today.'

Accordingly, that very hour he went to the Lady Beldam's,* his reverend and honourable acquaintance, whom he prepared for the reception of his sister, who he told her was a cast mistress* of his and desired her assistance to prevent the trouble and charge, which she knew such cattle would bring upon young gentlemen of plentiful estates. 'Tomorrow morning about eleven I'll leave her with your ladyship who, I doubt not, will give her a wholesome lesson or two before night, and your reward is certain.'

'My son,' returned she, 'I know the greatness of your spirit; the heat of your temper has both warmed and inflamed me. I joy to see you in town again. Ah, that I could but recall one twenty-years for your sake. Well, no matter, I won't forget your instructions, nor my duty tomorrow. In the meantime, I'll drink your health in a bottle of sherry or two.' 'O, cry your mercy, good my Lady Beldam,' said the young debauchee, 'I had like to have forfeited my title to your care in not remembering to leave you an obligation. There are three guineas, which I hope will plead for me till tomorrow. So—your Ladyship's servant humbly kisses your hand.' 'Your Honour's most obedient servant most grate-fully acknowledges your favours. Your humble servant, good Sir William,' added she, seeing him leave her in haste.

Never were three persons better pleased for a time than this unnatural man, his sweet innocent sister, and the Lady Beldam, upon his return to Philadelphia, who could not rest that night for thinking on the happiness she was going to enjoy in the conversation of so virtuous a lady as her brother's acquaintance, to whom she was in hopes that she might discover her dearest thoughts and complain of Sir William's extravagance and un-kindness, without running the hazard of being betrayed, and at the same time reasonably expect, from so pious a lady, all the assist-ance within her capacity. On the other side, her brother hugged himself in the prospect he had of getting rid of his own sister and the payment of £6,000, for the sum of forty or fifty guineas, by the help and discretion of this sage matron who, for her part, by this time had reckoned up and promised to herself an advantage of at least three hundred pounds, one way or other, by this bargain.

About ten the next morning, Sir William took coach with his sister for the old lady's enchanted castle, taking only one trunk of hers with 'em for the present, promising her to send her other things to her the next day. The young lady was very joyfully and respectfully received by her brother's venerable acquaintance, who was mightily charmed with her youth and beauty. A bottle of the best was then straight brought in, and not long after a very splendid entertainment for breakfast. The furniture was all very modish and rich and the attendance was suitable. Nor was the Lady Beldam's conversation less obliging and modest than Sir William's discourse had given Philadelphia occasion to expect.

After they had eaten and drunk what they thought convenient, the reverend old lady led 'em out of the parlour to show 'em the house, every room of which they found answerably furnished to that whence they came. At last, she led 'em into a very pleasant chamber, richly hung and curiously adorned with the pictures of several beautiful young ladies, wherein there was a bed which might have been worthy the reception of a Duchess. 'This, Madam,' said she, 'is your apartment, with the antechamber and a little withdrawing room.' 'Alas Madam,' returned the dear, innocent, unthinking lady, 'you set too great a value on your servant, but I rather think your Ladyship designs me this honour for the sake of Sir William, who has had the happiness of your acquaintance for some months.'

'Something for Sir William,' returned the venerable Lady Beldam, 'but much more for your Ladyship's own, as you will have occasion to find hereafter.' 'I shall study to deserve your favours and friendship, Madam,' replied Philadelphia. 'I hope you will, Madam,' said the barbarous man, 'but my business now calls me hence. Tomorrow at dinner I will return to you and order the rest of your things to be brought with me. In the meanwhile,' pursued the traitor, kissing his sister, as he thought and hoped, the last time, 'be as cheerful as you can, my dear, and expect all you can wish from me.' 'A thousand thanks, my dearest brother,' returned she, with tears in her eyes. 'And Madam,' said he to his old mischievous confederate, giving her a very rich purse which held fifty guineas, 'be pleased to accept this trifle as an humble acknowledgement of the great favour you do this lady and the care of her which you promise, and I'm sure she cannot want. So once more,' added he, 'my dear, and Madam, I am your humble servant. Jusqu' a revoir,'* and went out bowing. 'Heavens bless my dear brother,' cried Philadelphia. 'Your Honour's most faithful and obedient servant,' said the venerable Beldam.

No sooner was the treacherous brother gone than the old lady, taking Philadelphia by the hand, led her into the parlour where she began to her to this effect. 'If I mistake not, Madam, you were pleased to call Sir William brother once or twice of late in conversation. Pray be pleased to satisfy my curiosity so far as to inform me in the truth of this matter. Is it really so, or not?' Philadelphia replied, blushing: 'Your Ladyship strangely surprises me with this question, for I thought it had been past your doubt that it is so. Did not he let you know so much himself?'

'I humbly beg your pardon, Madam,' returned the true offspring of old mother Eve, 'that I have so visibly disturbed you by my curiosity, but indeed Madam, Sir William did not say your Ladyship was his sister when he gave me charge of you, as of the nearest and dearest friend he had in the world.' 'Now our father and mother are dead,' said the sweet innocent, 'who never had more children than us two, who can be a nearer or dearer friend unto me than my brother Sir William, or than I, his sister, to him? None!'

'Certainly you'll excuse me, Madam,' answered t'other, 'a wife or mistress may.' 'A wife indeed,' returned the beautiful innocent, 'has the pre-eminence, and perhaps a mistress too, if honourably loved and sought for in marriage. But,' she continued, 'I can assure your Ladyship that he has not a wife, nor did I ever hear he had a mistress yet.' 'Love in youth,' said old venerable, 'is very fearful of discovery. I have known, Madam, a great many fine young gentlemen and ladies who have concealed their violent passions and greater affection under the notion and appellation of brother and sister.' 'And your Ladyship imagines Sir William and I do so?' replied Philadelphia, by way of question. ''Twere no imprudence if you did, Madam,' returned old Lady Beldam, with all the subtlety she had learned from the serpent. 'Alas Madam,' replied she, 'there is nothing like secrecy in love. 'Tis the very life and soul of it. I have been young myself, and have known it by experience.'

'But all this, Madam,' interrupted Philadelphia, something nettled at her discourse, 'all this can't convince me that I am not the true and only sister, both by father and mother, of Sir William Wilding, however he would impose upon your ladyship, for what ends, indeed, I know not, unless (unhappily which

Heaven forbid) he designs to gain your ladyship's assistance in defeating me of the portion left me by my father. But,' she continued with tears, 'I have too great an assurance of your virtue to fear that you will consent to so wicked a practice.'

'You may be confident, Madam,' said t'other, 'I never will. And supposing that he were capable of perpetrating so base an act of himself, yet if your Ladyship will be guided and directed by me, I will show you the means of living happy and great without your portion or your brother's help, so much I am charmed with your beauty and innocence. But pray Madam,' pursued she, 'what is your portion? And what makes you doubt your brother's kindness?'

Philadelphia then told her how much her brother was to pay her, and gave her an account of his extravagancies as far as she knew 'em, to which t'other was no stranger and doubtless could have put a period to her sorrows with her life, had she given her as perfect a relation of his riotous and vicious practices as she was capable of. But she had farther business with her life, and in short, bid her be of good comfort, and lay all her care on her, and then she could not miss of continual happiness. The sweet lady took all her promises for sterling, and kissing her impious hand, humbly returned her thanks.

Not long after, they went to dinner, and in the afternoon, three or four young ladies came to visit the right reverend the Lady Beldam, who told her new guest that these were all her relations, and no less than her own sister's children. The discourse among 'em was general and very modest, which lasted for some hours, for our sex seldom wants matter of tattle. But whether their tongues were then miraculously wearied, or that they were tired with one continued scene of place, I won't pretend to determine, but they left the parlour for the garden, where after about half an hour's walk, there was a very fine dessert of sweetmeats and fruits brought into one of the arbours. Sherbets, ros solis,* rich and small* wines, with tea, chocolate etc. completed the old lady's treat, the pleasure of which was much heightened by the voices of two of her Ladyship's sham-nieces, who sung very charmingly.

The dear, sweet creature thought she had happily got into the company of angels, but, alas, they were angels that had fallen more than once. She had heard talk of nunneries,* and having never been out of her own country till within four or five days, she had certainly concluded she had been in one of those religious houses now, had she but heard a bell ring and seen 'em kneel to prayers and make use of their beads, as she had been told those happy people do. However it was, she was extremely pleased with the place and company. So nearly does Hell counterfeit Heaven sometimes.

At last, said one of the white devils: 'Would my dear Tommy were here!' 'O sister,' cried another, 'you won't be long without your wish, for my husband and he went out together and both promised to be here after the play.' 'Is my brother, Sir Francis, with him there?' asked the first. 'Yes,' answered a third, 'Sir Thomas and Sir Francis took coach from St James' about two hours since.' 'We shall be excellent company when they come,' said a fourth. 'I hope they'll bring the fiddlers with 'em,' added the first.

'Don't you love music, Madam?' asked the old Lady Beldam. 'Sometimes, Madam,' replied Philadelphia, 'but now I am out o' tune myself.' 'A little, harmless mirth will cheer your drooping spirits, my dear,' returned t'other, taking her by the hand, 'Come! These are all my relations, as I told you Madam, and so, consequently, are their husbands.' 'Are these ladies all married, Madam?' Philadelphia asked. 'All, all, my dear soul,' replied the insinuating mother of iniquity, 'and thou shalt have a husband too, ere long.' 'Alas Madam,' returned the fair innocent, 'I have no merit nor money. Besides, I never yet could love so well as to make choice of one man before another.' 'How long have you lived then, Madam?' asked the Lady Beldam. 'Too long, by almost sixteen years,' replied Philadelphia, 'had Heaven seen good.'

This conversation lasted till word was brought that Sir Francis and Sir Thomas, with two other gentlemen, were just lighted at the gate, which so discomposed the fair innocent that, trembling, she begged leave to return to her chamber. To which, after some persuasion to the contrary, the venerable Beldam waited on her—for these were none of the sparks to whom Philadelphia was designed to be sacrificed.

In her retirement, the beautiful, dear creature had the

satisfaction of venting her grief in tears and addressing herself to Heaven, on which only she trusted, notwithstanding all the fair promises of her reverend hostess. She had not been retired above an hour ere a she-attendant waited on her to know if she wanted anything, and what she would please to have for her supper, if she would not give her Lady the honour of her company below. To which she returned that she would not sup, and that she wanted nothing but rest, which she would presently seek in bed.

This answer brought up the officious old lady herself, who by all means would needs see her undressed, for other reasons more than a bare compliment, which she performed with a great deal of ceremony and a diligence that seemed more than double. For she had then the opportunity of observing the delicacy of her skin, the fine turn of her limbs and the richness of her nightdress, part of the furniture of her trunk. As soon as she had covered herself, she kissed and wished her a good repose.

The dear soul, as innocent and white as her linen, returned her thanks and addressed herself to sleep, out of which she was wakened by a loud consort of music in less than two hours time, which continued till long after midnight. This occasioned strange and doubtful thoughts in her, though she was altogether so unskilled in these mysteries that she could not guess the right meaning. She apprehended that (possibly) her brother had a mistress, from the Lady Beldam's discourse, and that this was their place of assignation, suspecting too that either Sir Francis or Sir Thomas, of whom she had heard not long before, was Sir William, her brother.

The music and all the noise in the house ceased about four o' clock in the morning, when she again fell into a sleep that took away the sense of her sorrows and doubts till nine, when she was again visited from her Lady by the same she-attendant to know how she had rested and if she would please to command her any service. Philadelphia replied that she had rested very well most part of the morning, and that she wanted nothing but to know how her Lady had slept and whether she were in health, unless it were the sight of her brother.

The servant returned with this answer to her Lady, while Philadelphia made shift to rise and begin to dress without an assistant. But she had hardly put on anything more than her

nightgown ere the Lady Beldam herself came in her dishabille*
to assure her of her brother's company with 'em at dinner exactly
at one o' clock, and finding Philadelphia doing the office of a
waiting woman to herself, called up the same servant and in a
great heat (in which, however, she took care to make use of none
of her familiar devilish dialect) asked the reason that she durst
leave the Lady when she was rising. The wench, trembling,
replied that indeed the lady did not let her know that she had any
thoughts of rising. 'Well then,' said her seeming offended lady,
'stir not from her now, I charge you, till she shall think fit to
dismiss you and command your absence.'

'Dear Madam, good morrow to you,' said she to Philadelphia,
'I'll make haste and dress too.' 'Good morrow to your Ladyship,'
returned the designed victim. When she was habille, she desired
the servant to withdraw, after which she betook herself to her
devotion, at the end of which the Lady Beldam returned,
attended by a servant, who brought some bread and wine for her
breakfast, which might then be seasonable enough to Philadelphia who could not forbear discovering the apprehensions she
had of her brother's unkindness, still entertaining her Reverence
with the fear she had of his disappointment that day at dinner,
which t'other opposed with all the seeming reasons her art could
suggest, till the clock had struck twelve, when a servant came to
tell the Lady Beldam that one Sir William Wilding would
certainly wait on her precisely at one, and desired that he might
dine in the young lady's apartment to avoid being seen by any
visitants that might come, and besides, that he had invited a
gentleman, his particular friend, to dinner with him there.

This message, being delivered aloud by the servant, was no
little satisfaction to the poor, desponding young lady, who
discoursed very cheerfully of indifferent matters till the clock
gave 'em notice that the hour was come, within three minutes
after which, word was brought to the Lady Beldam that a
gentleman below enquired for Sir William Wilding, whom she
immediately went down to receive, and led up to Philadelphia.

'Madam,' cried the great mistress of her art, 'this is the
gentleman whom Sir William has invited to dinner with us, and I
am very happy to see him, for he is my worthy friend and of a
long acquaintance. Trust me Madam, he is a man of honour and

has a very large estate. I doubt not,' added she, 'that you will find
his merits in his conversation.' Here Gracelove (for that was the
gentleman's name) saluted Philadelphia, and acquitted himself
like a person of good sense and education in his first address to
her, which she returned with all the modesty and ingenuous
simplicity that was still proper to her.

At last, she asked him how long he thought it would be ere Sir
William came, to which he replied that Sir William told him
unless he were there exactly at half an hour after one, they should
not stay dinner for him, that he had not parted with him much
above a quarter of an hour, when he left him engaged with
particular company about some weighty business. But however,
that if he should be so unhappy as to lose their conversation at
dinner, he would not fail to wait on 'em by four at farthest.

The young lady seemed a little uneasy at this, but the
gentleman appearing so very modest, and speaking it with such
an assured gravity, took away all thoughts of suspicion. To say
truth, Gracelove was a very honest, modest, worthy and
handsome person, and had the command, at present, of many a
thousand pounds. He was, by profession, a Turkey merchant.*
He had travelled much for his age, not having then reached
thirty, and had seen most of the courts in Christendom. He was a
man of sweet temper, of just principles and of inviolable
friendship where he promised, which was nowhere but where
'twas merited.

The minute came then at length, but without any Sir William,
so dinner was served up in the room next to Philadelphia's
bedchamber. What they had was nice and seasonable, and they
were all three as pleasant as could be expected without Sir
William, to whose health the glass went round once or twice.
Dinner over, and the table cleared, the old Lady Beldam
entreated Mr Gracelove to entertain the young lady with a
discourse of his travels, and of the most remarkable passages and
encounters of 'em, which he performed with a modesty and
gravity peculiar to himself, and in some part of his discourse
moved the innocent passions of the beauteous and compassionate Philadelphia, who was as attentive as she used to be in church
at divine service.

When the old lady perceived that he had made an end, or at

least that he desired to proceed no farther, she took occasion to leave 'em together in haste, pretending that she had forgotten to give orders to one of her servants about a business of moment, and that she would return to 'em in a very little time. The gentleman, you may believe, was very well pleased with her retreat, since he had a discourse to make to Philadelphia of a quite contrary nature to the preceding, which required privacy. But how grateful her absence was to Philadelphia, we may judge by the sequel.

'Madam,' said Gracelove, 'how do you like the town? Have you yet seen any man here whom you could love?' 'Alas Sir,' she replied, 'I have not seen the town, only in a coach as I passed along, nor ever was in any house except this and another, where my brother lodged. And to your other question, I must answer that I love all men.' 'That's generous indeed, Madam,' cried he, 'there is then some hope that I am one of the number.' 'No doubt, Sir,' she returned, 'that I love you as well as any, except Sir William.' 'Is he the happy man then, Madam?' said Gracelove. 'If to be loved best by me may make any man happy, doubtless it must be he, for he is my own brother.'

'I fancy Madam,' returned he, 'that you may make me as dear a relation to you as Sir William.' 'How is that possible, Sir?' she asked. 'Thus Madam,' replied he, drawing closer to her, 'by our nearer approaches to one another.' 'O, Heaven defend me,' cried she aloud, 'what do you mean? Take away your hand, you uncivil man! Help! Madam! My Lady!' 'O,' said Gracelove, 'she's gone purposely out of hearing.' 'Am I betrayed then?' she cried. 'Betrayed! As if your pretty, innocent Ladyship did not know where you were lodged. Ah Lady,' said he, 'this faint will, will never do. Come child,' pursued he, 'here are an hundred guineas for you, and I promise you yearly as much, and two hundred with every child that I shall get on thy sweet body. Faith, I love thee, thou pretty creature. Come, let's be better acquainted—you know my meaning.'

'Hell does, no doubt of [that],' she returned, 'O monster a man! I hate the sight of you.' With that, she flung from him and ran into the bedchamber, where she thought to have locked herself in, but the key was conveyed into his pocket. Thither, therefore, he pursued her, crying: 'Ah Madam, this is the proper field for our dispute.' Perceiving her error, and animated by despair, she rushed between him and the door into the outward room again, he still following and dodging her from chair to chair, she still shrieking.

At last cried he: 'A parley, Madam, with you. Let me ask you one question and will you answer me directly and truly to it?' 'Indeed I will,' said she, 'if it be civil.' 'Don't you know, then, that you are in a naughty* house, and that old Beldam is a rank procuress, to whom I am to give two hundred guineas for your maidenhead?' 'O Heaven,' cried she, kneeling with tears gushing out from her dear eyes, 'thou asserter and guardian of innocence, protect me from the impious practices intended against me.' Then, looking steadfastly on him, 'Sir,' pursued she, 'I can but difficultly guess what you mean. But I find that unless you prove what at first you seemed to me, I would say an honest, worthy gentleman, I shall be in danger of eternal ruin. You, Sir, are the only person that may yet preserve me. Therefore, I beseech you Sir, hear my story, with the injuries and afflictions that so dreadfully torment me, of which, I am sure, none of those barbarians of which you had occasion to speak but now, would have been guilty. O hear, and help me, for Heaven's sake, hear and help me!'

'I will, poor creature,' returned he, 'methinks I now begin to see my crime and thy innocence in thy words and looks.' Here she recounted to him all the accidents of her life since her father's decease, to that very day ere Gracelove came to dinner. 'And now,' cried she, sobbing and weeping, 'how dare I trust this naughty brother again. Can I be safe with him, think you Sir?' 'O no, thou dear, sweet creature, by no means. O infernal monsters! Brother and bawd!'

'If you distrust that I am yet his sister, here Sir, take this key,' said she, 'and open that trunk within, where you will find letters from him to me in his own hand and from my own dear, dead father too, Sir Edward, that gracious, that good man. He showed us both the paths of virtue, which I have not yet forsaken. Pray satisfy me Sir, and see the truth.' 'For your satisfaction I will Madam,' said he, 'but I am now fully convinced that you have greater beauties within than those I admire without.' Saying this, he opened the trunk, where he read a line or two from her father and as many from her brother, which having again laid down, returned to her with this advice.

'I see Madam,' said he, 'that you have money there and several things of value, which I desire you to secure about you this moment, for I mean to deliver you out of this cursed place—if you dare put any confidence in a stranger, after your own brother has acted the part of so great a villain. If you dare trust a stranger, too, Madam, who had himself a design upon you, Heaven forgive me for it. But, by all things sacred, I find my error. I pity you and I fear I shall love you.'

'Do you fear that, Sir,' said she, 'why, I love you dearly now, because I see you are going to be good again; that is, you are going to be your self again.' 'I hope, nay, I resolve I will, though it cost me my life,' said he, 'can you submit, Madam, to attend on a young lady of my acquaintance here in town, till I can provide better for you?' 'O, I can be anything: a chambermaid, a cookmaid, a scullion, what you shall think fit, though never so mean, that is not naughty.' 'Well Madam,' said he, 'compose yourself then, and seem a little pleasant when I bring up that old factoress of Hell.' 'I will endeavour it, Sir,' she returned, and he went down to the Devil's chief agent, to whom he said that the poor thing was at first very uneasy, but that now she had consented to go along with him for an hour or two to some other place: 'Doubting your secrecy, for she would not have her brother know it, as she calls him, for a thousand worlds and more money.'

'Well, my son,' replied old Beldam, 'you may take her with you, but you remember your bargain.' 'O, fie mother,' cried he, 'did you ever know me false to you?' 'No, no, you smock-faced* wag,' said she, 'but be sure you bring her again tonight, for fear Sir William should come.' 'Never doubt it! Come up with me,' cried he, 'you'll see a strange alteration, I believe.' To Philadelphia they came then, whom they found walking about the room and looking something more pleasantly than she had ever done since she came thither.

After she had taken her money and other things of value: 'So, Madam,' said Beldam, 'how does your Ladyship now? I find the sight of a young, handsome gentleman has worked wonders with you in a little time. I understand you are going to take a walk with my worthy friend here, and 'tis well done. I dare trust you with him, but with no other man living except Sir William.' 'Madam,' returned the fair, afflicted lady, 'I am strangely obliged to you for your care of me, and am sure I shall never be able to return your obligations as I ought, and as I could wish.'

'You won't stay late, Mr Gracelove?' said the mother of mischief. 'No, no,' replied he, 'I will only show the lady a play, and return to supper.' 'What is played tonight?' asked the old one. '*The Cheats*,* mother, *The Cheats*,' answered Gracelove. 'Ha,' said Beldam, laughing, 'a very pretty comedy indeed.' 'Aye, if well played,' returned he.

At these words, they went down, where a coach was called, which carried 'em to Counsellor Fairlaw's house in Great Lincoln's Inn Fields, whom they found accidentally at home, but his lady and daughter were just gone to chapel, being then turned of five. Gracelove began his apology to the good old Councillor, who was his relation, for bringing a strange lady thither, with a design to place her in his family. 'But Sir,' continued he, 'if you knew her sorrowful story, you would be as ambitious of entertaining her as I am earnest to entreat it of you.'

'A very beautiful lady 'tis,' returned the Counsellor, 'and very modest, I believe.' 'That I can witness,' replied t'other. 'Alas, Sir,' said the fair unfortunate, 'I have nothing but my modesty and honest education to recommend me to your regard. I am wronged and forsaken by my nearest relation . . . ' Then she wept extravagantly. 'That gentleman can give you an account of my misfortunes, if he please, with greater ease and less trouble than myself.'

'Not with less trouble, believe me Madam,' returned Grace-love, and then began to inform Fairlaw in every point of her unhappy circumstances. The good old gentleman heard 'em with amazement and horror, but told her, however, that she need not despond, for he would take care to right her against her brother, and that in the meantime she should be as welcome to him as any of his nearest kindred, except his wife and daughter. Philadelphia would have knelt to thank him, but he told her that humble posture was due to none but Heaven, and the King sometimes.

In a little while after, the Lady Fairlaw and her daughter came home, who were surprised at the sight of a stranger, but more at her beauty, and most of all at her story, which the good old gentleman himself could not forbear relating to 'em; which ended, the mother and daughter both kindly and tenderly embraced her, promising her all the assistance within their power, and bid her a thousand welcomes. Gracelove stayed there till after supper, and left her extremely satisfied with her new station. 'Twas here she fixed, then, and her deportment was so obliging that they would not part with her for any consideration.

About three days after her coming from that lewd woman's house, Gracelove took a constable and some other assistants and went to Beldam's to demand the trunk and what was in it, which at first her reverence denied to return, till Mr Constable produced the emblem of his authority, upon which it was delivered without so much as reminding Gracelove of his bargain, who then pretended he would search the house for Sir William Wilding, but her graceless reverence swore most devoutly that he had never been there, and that she had neither seen nor heard from him since the day he left Philadelphia with her.

With these things and this account, he returned to Counsellor Fairlaw's, who desired Gracelove, if possible, to find out Sir William, and employed several others on the same account. In less than a month's time, Gracelove had the good fortune to find him at his lodgings in Soho Square, where he discoursed him about his sister's portion and desired Sir William to take some speedy care for the payment of it, otherwise she had friends that would oblige him to it, though never so contrary to his intentions.

Wilding asked where she was. T'other enquired where he left her. Sir William replied that he had placed her with an old, grave gentlewoman of his acquaintance, and that he thought she was there still. 'No Sir,' returned Gracelove, 'I have delivered her out of the jaws of perdition and Hell. Come, Sir William,' answered* he, ' 'twas impiously done to leave your beautiful, young and virtuous sister to the management of that pernicious woman. I found her at old Beldam's, who would have prostituted her to me for two hundred guineas, but her heavenly virtues might have secured and guarded her from more violent attempts than mine. Blush if you can, Sir, and repent of this. It will become you. If not, Sir, you will hear further from your servant,' added he, and left him staring after him.

This discourse was a great mortification to the knight, whose conscience, hardened as it was, felt yet some pain by it. He found he was not like to continue safe or at ease there, wherefore he immediately retreated into a place of sanctuary, called the Savoy,* whither his whole equipage was removed as soon as possible, he having left order with his servants to report that he went out of town that very afternoon for his own country.

Gracelove, in the meantime, returned to the Counsellor's with a great deal of joy for having discovered Sir William at his lodgings, which was likewise no little satisfaction to Fairlaw, his lady and daughter. Philadelphia only was disturbed when she heard the good old gentleman threaten to lay her brother fast enough. But alas, he was too cunning for 'em, for in a whole twelvemonth after, all which time they made enquiry and narrowly searched for him, they could not see him nor anyone that could give an account of him, for he had changed his true name and title for that of Squire Sportman. The further pursuit of him then seemed fruitless to 'em, and they were forced to be contented with their wishes to find him.

Gracelove by this time had entertained the sincerest affections and noblest passion that man can be capable of for Philadelphia, of which he had made her sensible, who had at that time complied with his honourable demands, had she not entreated him to expect a kind turn of providence which might happily, ere long, put her in possession of her right, without which, she told him, she could not consent to marry him, who had so plentiful a fortune, and she nothing but her person and innocence. 'How Madam,' cried he, 'have you no love in store for me?' 'Yes Sir,' returned she, 'as much as you can wish I have in store for you, and so I beg it may be kept till a better opportunity.'

'Well Madam,' said he, 'I must leave you for some months—perhaps for a whole year. I have received letters of advice that urge the necessity of my going to Turkey. I have not a week's time to endeavour so dreaded a separation as I must suffer. Therefore, thou beautiful, thou dear, thou virtuous creature, let me begin now. Here, thou tenderest part of my soul,' continued he, giving her a rich diamond ring, 'wear this till my return. I hope the sight of it may sometimes recall the dying memory of Gracelove to your better busied thoughts.' 'Ah Gracelove,' said she, 'nothing can so well, nothing I'm sure can better employ my thoughts than thy dear self, Heaven only excepted.'

They enlarged a great deal more on this subject at that time, but the night before his departure was entirely spent in sighs, vows and tears on both sides. In the morning, after he had again entreated his cousin's and the lady's and her daughter's care and kindness to Philadelphia, the remaining and best part of his soul, with one hearty kiss accompanied with tears, he took a long farewell of his dear mistress, who pursued him with her eyes till they could give her no further intelligence of him, and they helped her kindness to him, and eased her grief for his absence, in weeping for above a week together, when in private.

He never omitted writing to her and his cousin by every opportunity for near nine months as he touched at any port, but afterwards they could not hear from him for above half a year when, by accident, the Counsellor met a gentleman of Gracelove's acquaintance at a coffee house, who gave him an account that the ship and he were both cast away near five months since; that most, if not all, of the ship's company perished, of which 'twas feared that Gracelove was one, having never since been heard of; that his loss in that ship amounted to above twelve thousand pounds.

With this dreadful and amazing news, the good old gentleman returns home, afflicts his poor, sorrowful lady and daughter, and almost kills unhappy Philadelphia, who the next day, by mere chance, and from a stranger who came on business to the Counsellor, heard that one Sir William Wilding, an extravagant, mad young spark of such a county, who lately went by the borrowed name and title of Esquire Sportman, had mortgaged all his estate, which was near four thousand a year, and carried the money over with him into France on Saturday last.

This, added to the former news, put so great a check on her spirits that she immediately dropped down in a swoon, whence she only recovered to fall into what was of a much more dangerous consequence: a violent fever, which held her for near six weeks ere she could get strength enough to go down stairs, in all which time Madam Fairlaw and Eugenia her daughter attended her as carefully and constantly as if they had been her own mother and sister, the good old Counsellor still commending and encouraging their care.

The roses and lilies at last took their places again, but the clouds of her sorrow were still but too visible. Two years more passed without one word of advice from Gracelove or any account of him from anyone else, insomuch that they all concluded he was certainly dead. And 'twas true, indeed, that his ship and he were cast away much about that time that the gentleman gave Fairlaw a relation; that 'twas certain he had lost above £12,000 and had like to have lost his life, but being very expert in swimming, he got to shore upon the coast of Barbary,* the wreck happening not to be above three leagues thence.

He was in almost as bad a condition as if he had been drowned, for here he was made a prisoner to one of the natives, in which miserable circumstance he languished for above six years for want of a ransom, which he had often endeavoured to raise by letters that he sent hither to his friends in England, amongst which Counsellor Fairlaw was one of his most particular and assured. But however, providence, or accident if you please, ordered it, not a line came to the hands of any of his friends, so that had not Heaven had yet a future blessing in store for him, he had certainly have better perished in the sea than to have fallen into the power of a people less merciful than seas, winds or hungry wild beasts in pursuit of their prey. But this could not be learned, it seems, from any man but himself upon his return after his redemption.

Two years more passed on, towards the latter of which the old Lady Fairlaw took her bed, desperately sick, insomuch that she was given over by all her physicians. She continued in great misery for near two months, in all which time Philadelphia was constantly with her all the day or all the night. Much about that time she died, and dying, told her husband that she had observed he had a particular esteem or kindness [for] Philadelphia, which was now a great satisfaction to her, since she was assured that if he married her, she would prove an excellent nurse to him and prolong his life by some years. 'As for Eugenia,' added she, 'you need not be concerned, I'm sure. She will consent to anything that you shall propose, having already so plentifully provided for her.'

The good old gentleman answered that he would fulfil her will as far as lay in his power, and not long after, she departed this life. Her burial was very handsome and honourable. Half a year was now expired since her interment, when the old Counsellor began to plead his own cause to young Philadelphia, reminding her that now the death of Gracelove was out of question, and that therefore she was as much at her liberty to make her own choice of an husband as he was of a wife, not forgetting at the same time to let her know that his widow, whoever had the good fortune to be so, would be worth above thirty thousand pounds in ready money, besides a thousand a year. But above all, he urged his dying lady's last advice to him that he would marry her, and hoped she would see the will of the dead satisfied.

The young lady, being broken in sorrows, and having mortified all her appetites to the enjoyments of this world, and not knowing where to meet with so fair an overture, though at first in modesty she seemed to refuse it as too great an honour, yet yielded to less than a quarter of an hour's courtship. And the next Sunday, married they were, with the consent and to the perfect satisfaction of his daughter, Madam Eugenia, who loved Philadelphia sincerely. They kept their wedding very nobly for a month at their own house, in Great Lincoln's Inn Fields, but the memory of the old lady was still so fresh with the young Lady Fairlaw, that she prevailed with him to remove to another, more convenient, as she fancied, in Covent Garden.

They had dwelt there not much more than four months ere the good old gentleman fell sick and died—whether it were the change of an old house for a new, or an old wife for a young, is yet uncertain, though his physicians said, and are still of opinion, that doubtless it was the last. 'Tis past all doubt that she did really mourn for and lament his death, for she loved him perfectly, and paid him all the dutiful respect of a virtuous wife while she lived within that state with him, which he rewarded as I have said before.

His funeral was very sumptuous and honourable indeed, and as soon as it was over, Eugenia desired her young, beautiful mother-in-law to retreat a little with her into the country, to a pleasant house she had not twenty miles distant from town, urging that she could by no means enjoy herself under that roof where her dear father died. The obliging stepmother, who might more properly have been called her sister, being exactly of the same age with her, readily complied, and she passed away all that Summer with Eugenia at their country seat, and most part of the Winter too. For Eugenia could by no means be prevailed on to lie one night in her mother's house; 'twas with some reluctancy that she consented to dine there sometimes.

At length, the whole year of Philadelphia's widowhood was expired, during which you can't but imagine that she was solicited and addressed to by as many lovers, or pretended lovers, as our dear King Charles,* whom God grant long to reign, was lately by the Presbyterians, Independents, Anabaptists, and all those canting, Whiggish brethren. But she had never liked any man so well as to make him her husband by inclination, unless it was Gracelove, devoured by the greedy inhabitants of the sea.

Whilst her fortune began to mend thus, her brother's grew worse, but that was indeed the effect of his extravagancy. In less than two years' time, he had spent eight thousand pounds in France, whence he returned to England, and pursuing his old profuse manner of living, contracted above £100 debts here in less than four months' time, which not being able to satisfy, he was arrested and thrown into a gaol, whence he removed himself into the King's Bench on that very day that old Fairlaw died. There at first, for about a month, he was entertained like a gentleman, but finding no money coming, nor having a prospect of any, the Marshal and his instruments turned him to the common side, where he learnt the art of peg-making, a mystery to which he had been a stranger all his life long, till then.

'Twas then he wished he might see his sister, hoping that she was in a condition to relieve him, which he was apt to believe from the discourse he had with Gracelove some years past. Often he wished to see her, but in vain. However, the next Easter after the old Counsellor's death, Philadelphia, according to his custom, sent her steward to relieve all the poor prisoners about town. Among the rest, he visited those in the common side of the King's Bench, where he heard 'em call Sir William Wilding to partake of his lady's charity. The poor prodigal was then feeding on the relief of the basket, not being yet able to get his bread at his new trade.

To him the steward gave a crown, whereas the others had but half a crown apiece. Then he enquired of some of the unhappy gentlemen, Sir William's fellow collegians, of what country Sir

William was, how long he had been there and how much his debts were, all of which he received a satisfactory account. Upon his return to his lady, he repeated the dismal news of her brother's misfortunes to her, who immediately dispatched him back again to the prison, with orders to give him twenty shillings more at present, and to get him removed to the master's side into a convenient chamber, for the rent of which the steward engaged to pay, and promised him, as she had commanded, twenty shillings a week as long as he stayed there, on condition that he would give the names of all his creditors and of all those to whom he had engaged any part of his estate, which the poor gentleman did most readily and faithfully.

After which the steward enquired for a tailor, who came and took measure of Philadelphia's unkind brother and was ordered to provide him linen, a hat, shoes, stockings, and all such necessaries, not so much as omitting a sword, with all which he acquainted his lady at his return, who was very much grieved at her brother's unhappy circumstances, and at the same time extremely well pleased to find herself in a condition to relieve him.

The steward went constantly once a week to pay him his money, and Sir William was continually very curious to know to whom he was obliged for so many and great favours. But he was answered that they came from a lady who desired to have her name concealed. In less than a year, Philadelphia had paid £25,000 and taken off the mortgages on £2,500 per annum of her brother's estate, and coming to town from Eugenia's country house one day to make the last payment of two thousand pounds, looking out of her coach on the road near Dartford, she saw a traveller on foot who seemed to be tired with his journey, whose face she thought she had formerly known.

This thought invited her to look on him so long that she at last persuaded herself it was Gracelove, or his ghost, for to say truth, he was very pale and thin, his complexion swarthy and his clothes perhaps as rotten as if he had been buried in 'em. However, unpleasant as it was, she could not forbear gazing after this miserable spectacle, and the more she beheld it, the more she was confirmed it was Gracelove, or something that had usurped his figure. In short, she could not rest till she called to one of her servants who rode by the coach, whom she strictly charged to go to that poor traveller and mount him on his horse till they came to Dartford, where she ordered him to take him to the same inn where she baited,* and refresh him with anything that he would eat or drink, and after that to hire a horse for him to come to town with them. That then he should be brought home to her own house and be carefully looked after till further orders from her—all which was most duly and punctually performed.

The next morning early she sent for the steward, whom she ordered to take the stranger to a sale-shop and fit him with a suit of good clothes, to buy him shirts and other linen and all necessaries as he had provided for her brother, and gave him charge to use him as her particular friend during his stay there, bidding him withal learn his name and circumstances, if possible, and to supply him with money for his pocket expenses. All which he most faithfully and discreetly performed, and brought his lady an account of his sufferings by sea and slavery among the Turks, as I have before related, adding that his name was Gracelove.

This was the greatest happiness, certainly, that ever yet the dear, beautiful creature was sensible of. On t'other side, Gracelove could not but admire and praise his good fortune, that had so miraculously and bountifully relieved him, and one day, having some private discourse with the steward, he could not forbear expressing the sense he had of it, declaring that he could not have expected such kind treatment from anybody breathing, but from his cousin, Councillor Fairlaw, his lady, or another young lady whom he placed and left with his cousins.

'Councillor Fairlaw,' cried the steward, 'why Sir, my lady is the old Councillor's widow; she is very beautiful, and young too.' 'What was her name, Sir, before she married the Councillor?' asked Gracelove. 'That I know not,' replied t'other, 'for the old steward died presently after the old lady, which is not a year and a half since, in whose place I succeed, and I have never been so curious or inquisitive as to pry into former passages of the family.' 'Do you know, Sir,' said Gracelove, 'whereabouts in town they lived before?' 'Yes Sir,' returned the steward, who was taught how to answer, 'in Great Lincoln's Inn Fields, I think.' 'Alas,' cried Gracelove, ''twas the same gentleman to whom I designed to apply myself when I came to England.' 'You need not despair now Sir,' said t'other, 'I dare say my lady will supply your wants.' 'O wonderful goodness of a stranger,' cried Gracelove, 'uncommon and rare amongst relations and friends. How have I, or how can I, ever merit this?'

Upon the end of their conference, the steward went to Philadelphia and repeated it almost verbatim to her, who ordered Gracelove should be taken measure of by the best tailor in Covent Garden; that he should have three of the most modish, rich suits made that might become a private gentleman of a thousand pounds a year, and hats, perukes, linen, swords, and all things suitable to 'em, all to be got ready in less than a month, in which time she took all the opportunity she could either find or make to see him and not to be seen by him.

She obliged her steward to invite him to a play, whither she followed 'em and sat next to Gracelove and talked with him, but all the while masked. In this month's time she was daily pestered with the visits of her addressors. Several there were of 'em, but the chief were only a lord of a very small estate, though of a pretty great age; a young blustering knight who had a place of £500 a year at court; and a country gentleman of a very plentiful estate, a widower and of a middle age. These three only of her lovers, she invited to dinner on the first day of the next month.

In the meanwhile, she sent a rich suit, and equipage proportionable, to her brother, with an invitation to dine with her on the same day. Then she writ to Eugenia to come and stay in town, if not in the same house with her, for two or three days before, which her affectionate daughter obeyed, to whom Philadelphia related all her brother's past extravagancies and what she had done for him in redeeming most part of his estate, begging of her that if she could fancy his person, she would take him into her mercy and marry him, being assured that such a virtuous wife as she would prove must necessarily reclaim him, if yet he were not perfectly convinced of his follies, which she doubted not his late long sufferings had done. Eugenia returned that she would be wholly directed and advised by her in all things, and that certainly she could not but like the brother, since she loved the sister so perfectly and truly.

The day came, and just at twelve Gracelove, meeting the steward on the stairs coming from his lady, Gracelove then told him that he believed he might take the opportunity of that afternoon to go over to Putney and take a game or two at bowls. The steward returned: 'Very well Sir, I shall let my lady know it, if she enquires for you.' Philadelphia, who overheard what they said, called the steward in haste and bid him call Gracelove back and tell him she expected his company at her table today, and that she desired he would appear like himself.

The steward soon overtook him at the door, just going out as Eugenia came in, who looked back on Gracelove. The poor gentleman was strangely surprised at the sight of her, as she was at his, but the steward's message did more amaze and confound him. He went directly to his chamber to dress himself in one of those rich suits lately made for him, but the distraction he was in made him mistake his coat for his waistcoat, and put the coat on first. But recalling his straggling thoughts, he made shift to get ready time enough to make his appearance without a second summons.

Philadelphia was as pleasant at dinner as ever she had been all her life. She looked very obligingly on all the sparks and drank to every one of 'em particularly, beginning to the Lord—and ending to the stranger, who durst hardly lift up his eyes a second time to hers to confirm him that he knew her. Her brother was so confounded that he bowed and continued his head down till she had done drinking, not daring to encounter her eyes, that would then have reproached him with his villainy to her.

After dinner, the cloth was taken away. She began thus to her lovers: 'My Lord, Sir Thomas, and Mr Fat-Acres, I doubt not that it will be of some satisfaction to you to know whom I have made choice for my next husband, which now I am resolved no longer to defer. The person to whom I shall next drink must be the man who shall ever command me and my fortune, were it ten times greater than it is, which I wish only for his sake, since he deserves much more. Here,' said she to one that waited, 'put wine into two glasses.'

Then she took the diamond ring from her finger and put it into one of 'em. 'My dear Gracelove,' cried she, 'I drink to thee, and send thee back thy own ring with Philadelphia's heart.' He startled, blushed and looked wildly, whilst all the company stared on him. 'Nay, pledge me,' pursued she, 'and return me the ring, for it shall make us both one the next morning.' He bowed, kissed and returned it after he had taken off his wine. The defeated lovers knew not how to resent it. The lord and knight were for going, but the country gentleman opposed it, and told 'em 'twas the greatest argument of folly to be disturbed at the caprice of a woman's humour. They sat down again, therefore, and she invited 'em to her wedding on the morrow.

'And now brother,' said she, 'I have not quite forgotten you, though you have not been pleased to take notice of me. I have a dish in reserve for you, which will be more grateful to your fancy than all you have tasted today. Here,' cried she to the steward, 'Mr Rightman, do you serve up that dish yourself.' Rightman then set a covered dish on the table. 'What, more tricks yet,' cried my Lord and Sir Thomas. 'Come, Sir William,' said his sister, 'uncover it.' He did so, and cried out: 'O matchless goodness of a virtuous sister! Here are the mortgages of the best part of my estate. O, what a villain, what a monster have I been!'

'No more, dear brother,' said she, with tears in her eyes, 'I have yet a greater happiness in store for you. This lady, this beautiful, virtuous lady, with twenty thousand pounds, will make you happy in her love.' Saying this, she joined their hands. Sir William eagerly kissed Eugenia's, who blushed and said: 'Thus Madam, I hope to show how much I love and honour you.' 'My cousin Eugenia,' cried Gracelove. 'The same, my dear, lost, dead cousin Gracelove,' replied she. 'O,' said he in a transport, 'my present joys are greater than all my past miseries. My mistress and my friend are found and still are mine.'

'Nay, faith,' said my Lord, 'this is pleasant enough to me, though I have been defeated of the enjoyment of the lady.' The whole company in general went away very well that night, who returned the next morning and saw the two happy pair firmly united.

EXPLANATORY NOTES

URANIA

3 *When the Spring*: *Urania*'s opening sentence closely echoes the opening of Sir Philip Sidney's *New Arcadia* (1590).

4 *disease*: lack of ease.

19 *except the own fellow to a cockleshell can fit the other*: except for a perfect mirror-image, like two cockleshells?

20 *Urania*: possibly Urania loosely represents Susan, Countess of Montgomery.

24 *beasts will keep their own natures*: cf. a parallel scene in Sidney's *Arcadia* of Pamela and Philoclea pursued by a lion and a bear.

27 *watchet*: light or sky blue.

30 *she died*: i.e. his wife.

40 *two springs*: an example of one of Wroth's dangling sentences, rhetorically effective, but almost impossible to punctuate in an orderly fashion.

46 *steepy*: steep.

50 *These*: i.e. these aspersions.

52 *meaning*: intent.

tapist: lurking, hiding.

58 *palace*: the Throne of Love is depicted in *Urania*'s engraved title page, reproduced in Graham Parry, 'Lady Mary Wroth's *Urania*', *Proceedings of the Leeds Philosophical and Literary Society*, 16 (1975), 55–6.

67 *toil*: trap.

73 *bewailed absence*: bewailed Urania's absence.

77 *being excelling*: being particularly excellent.

88 *spriteless*: spiritless.

worth: emended from 'wroth'.

92 *murry*: mulberry coloured (reddish purple).

ties: bind; entice?

104 *patient*: patient [sufferer].

105 *unto*: emended from 'into'.

111 *that for unkindness*: a word seems to be missing here, though the sense is clear.

112 *travel*: travail.

rushing: rustling.

121 *Lansaritano*: 'was' needs to be understood.

beaver: the face-guard of a helmet.

129 *pretended*: portended; intended.

131 *I was but torment*: I contained nothing but torment.

137 *from my beloved forsake me*: exact sense unclear, perhaps 'from my beloved who has forsaken me'.

142 *curster*: more cursed.

chirurgeons: surgeons.

143 *Saltier cross*: a Saltire cross, similar to St Andrew's cross.

148 *carnation*: crimson or pink.

150 *State*: a raised canopy, usually above a throne.

151 *turtles*: turtledoves.

155 *luxurious*: lecherous.

160 *corsive*: corrosive.

162 *jesamnis*: jasmine.

163 *disordered*: perhaps a misprint for 'discovered'.

164 *natched*: nipped. *habits*: clothing.

Rumanian king: Amphilanthus is king of Rome, not Rumania.

171 *depart*: departure.

177 *main*: many.

178 *of sometimes*: for some time?

191 *exprestest*: most clearly manifested.

197 *his mother*: i.e. his mother earth.

202 *murray*: mulberry coloured (reddish purple).

203 *much*: perhaps should read 'must'.

PRINCESS CLORIA

212 *modern and antique*: the 'manner and contrivance' refers to what would now be called the plot, which uses both older romance structure and more modern narrative techniques.

213 *five or six hours together without intermission*: referring to the long *récits* (monologues) in the French heroic romances which were popular at the time.

214 *things feigned may do*: here and elsewhere the Preface echoes Philip Sidney's *Defence of Poetry* (1580).

217 *Cassianus*: Charles Louis, son of Frederick V.

Euarchus: King Charles I.

Lydia: England.

219 *Elizana*: Princess Elizabeth, Queen of Bohemia.

Delphos: Rome, i.e. Catholicism.

her elder brother: Prince Henry, d. 1612.

Asia: Europe.

the crown: Frederick was crowned King of Bohemia in 1619, after Emperor Ferdinand was deposed.

224 *Syria*: France.

Orsames: Louis XIII.

225 *Hiacinthia*: Henrietta Maria.

Princess Cloria: Mary, who married William II, Prince of Orange (Narcissus in the romance); though Cloria, as the preface indicates, stands also for other things, and in the narrative she does not always consistently play out the events of Mary's life.

231 *Soroasters, King of Egypt*: Philip IV of Spain.

235 *Cyprus*: United Dutch Provinces.

243 *treasures*: treasurers.

246 *speech*: in fact, Charles was prevented from delivering his final speech, see C. V. Wedgwood, *The Trial of Charles I* (London, 1967), 185–6.

THE BLAZING WORLD

251 *William Newcastle*: Margaret Cavendish's husband, the Duke of Newcastle.

my serious philosophical contemplations: *The Blazing World* was published together with Cavendish's *Observations Upon Experimental Philosophy*, in part a critique of Robert Hooke's *Micrographia* (1665).

252 *Lucian's, or the Frenchman's world in the moon*: Lucian's *True History* (2nd cent. AD), perhaps the earliest imaginary voyage, trans. into English in 1634; Cyrano de Bergerac, *Histoire comique contenant les états et empires de la lune* (1657).

husband's losses: Newcastle's loyalty to the royalist cause in the Civil War was not very amply rewarded at the restoration of Charles II.

257 *soddered*: sealed.

259 *close*: enclosed.

260 *carbuncle*: garnet.

buskins: low boots.

buckler: shield.

263 *closets*: small, private rooms.

267 *roves*: slivers.

268 *delude your senses*: the first of a number of attacks on such observations,

continued from the critique of Robert Hooke's advocacy of the micro-scope.

282 *emeroids*: haemorrhoids.

293 *a threefold Cabala*: it is worth stressing the connections in the seventeenth century between 'science', mysticism, and magic. Caven-dish's interest in these matters parallels that of the leading figures of seventeenth-century 'science'; see Christopher Hill, *Intellectual Origins of the English Revolution* (Oxford, 1965); Keith Thomas, *Religion and the Decline of Magic* (New York, 1971); Frances Yates, *The Occult Philosophy in the Elizabethan Age* (London, 1979). The Cabala, the Jewish mystical system, Christianized in the Renaissance, seems to be used loosely by Cavendish to describe seventeenth-century syntheses of religion, science, and mysticism.

306 *Gassendus . . . Helmont . . . H. More*: Pierre Gassendi (1592–1655), French philosopher; Jan Baptista Van Helmont (1577–1644), Flemish physician and chemist, interested in hermetic philosophy and a proponent of the theory that the world consisted of matter and an efficient cause; Henry More (1614–87), English philosopher and neo-Platonist.

310 *impossible*: emended from 2nd edn., 'possible' in 1st.

316 *Grand-Seigneur*: ruler of the Ottoman Empire.

317 *governor*: Newcastle was made Charles's governor in 1638.

319 *horses of manage*: Newcastle was a famous horseman, and published two books on the subject.

320 *cast*: convicted.

322 *female sex*: Newcastle, when acting as his governor, is reported to have told Charles 'above all be civil to women', Antonia Fraser, *King Charles II* (London, 1979), 19.

338 *ESFI*: imaginary country, significance of the name is uncertain.

343 *plays*: Cavendish wrote a number of unperformed plays, collected in two main volumes, *Plays* (1662) and *Plays Never Before Printed* (1668).

DON TOMAZO

(A number of notes have used information taken from Spiro Peterson's excellent edition of Don Tomazo in *The Counterfeit Lady Unveiled*, New York, 1961.)

351 *Sovereign's pardon*: Dangerfield's ignoble part in the events surrounding the aftermath of the Popish Plot included receiving a royal pardon to allow him to testify to the existence of the Meal Tub Plot (an alleged Catholic conspiracy to falsely concoct a Protestant plot against Charles II). Dangerfield's testimony was revealed to be entirely fallacious.

Clavel: John Clavel, *A Recantation of An Ill Led Life* (1628).

351 *Spanish language*: Mateo Aleman, *Guzman* (1599), trans. by James Mabbe as *The Rogue* (1622); *Lazarillo de Tormes*, trans. David Rowland (1576, repr. 1624, 1639) and trans. James Blakeston (1653). These are the 2 pioneering Spanish picaresque novels.

discoveries were true: Peterson points out that when Dangerfield produced his final set of charges against the Duke of York, 'no one believed a single word he said' (183).

352 *Horace's 'Quo semel . . .'*: Horace, *Epistles*, I. ii. 69–70, 'The jar will long keep the fragrance of what it was once steeped in when it was new'.

Don Tomazo: a long, descriptive table of contents has been omitted.

353 *meet-help*: helpmate.

356 *Gusmanry*: roguery, from Aleman's picaro.

we: it is hard to tell if the narrative's occasional lapses into the 1st person are inadvertent revelations of its autobiographical nature, or disingenuous contrivances intended to convey that impression.

Moffat: near the Lowther Hills in Scotland.

357 *is the carl wood*: what a great fuss, is the fellow mad?

359 *cinque and quatre*: cinquante = 50 year old.

360 *little-ease*: a dungeon or prison.

Lobb's pound: jail for foolish bumpkins.

churlish chuff: rough boor.

361 *yare*: ready.

dirk: a small dagger.

363 *St Nicholas clerks*: poor scholars.

365 *boatles*: a bodle was the smallest Scottish coin.

367 *Dunfrieze*: Dumfries.

368 *anticness*: grotesque nature, oddness.

370 *eloignment*: removal to a distant place.

374 *peel-garlick*: pilgarlic = poor creature (from baldheaded, like a peeled garlic).

375 *knight of the burning pestle*: credulous, like the citizens in Francis Beaumont's play *The Knight of the Burning Pestle* (1613).

zealous writer of shorthand: over-zealous clerk? Origin unknown, the first recorded use of the word 'shorthand' in OED is 1636.

376 *seagull*: gull = dupe.

377 *dottrell*: foolish person.

ordinary: a tavern.

378 *Greymolkin's luck*: the luck of a cat (grimalkin).

381 *rodomontado*: boast.

384 *tuck*: rapier.

385 *cornuting*: cuckolding (made horned, the sign of a cuckold).

387 *Heers*: mynheers (mijnheers) = Dutch title for a man, like Mr.

388 *none*: possibly a misprint for 'own'.

   a tinker and his doxy: a gipsy and his mistress.

389 *Calice*: Calais.

   Sutton's or old Audley's: Thomas Sutton and Hugh Audley, two famous self-made wealthy men in the seventeenth century.

   Per varios casus, per tot discrimina rerum: *Aeneid*, I, l. 204, 'through diverse mishaps, through so many perilous chances', not a reference to the sons of Priam.

391 *St Martin's ware*: counterfeit coins, from the St Martin's area of London, where imitation jewellery was made.

   Pylades: friend of Orestes = dearest friend.

   tantivy: at full speed.

392 *demorage*: demurrage = stay or delay.

   high and low fullums: types of loaded dice.

394 *Curius*: revealed Catiline's conspiracy to his wife Fulvia, who told Cicero.

395 *Hogen Mogens*: Dutch, from Hoogmogendheiden = High-Mightyness, title of the States-General.

396–7 *Volenti non fit injuria*: wrong cannot be done to a willing victim.

400 *garbling*: selection.

401 *cheapen*: appraise, bid for.

   cunny-catched: conned, duped (cony = rabbit).

406 *congees*: ceremonial bows (usually of farewell).

407 *Mrs*: i.e. Mistress.

411 *kitlin*: kitten.

   bavin-bands: thin ties for bundles of brushwood.

413 *bowsy*: boozy = drunk.

415 *Peruvians*: counterfeit coins, derivation unknown.

416 *perruke*: wig.

   sodered: soldered [Peterson]? foddered? sodden?

   climm: jail, probably derived from clem = confine, pinch.

418 *St Dunstan's*: St Dunstan was taught to sing by an angel after a fight with the Devil.

   in a way: on a set path.

   Prince of Orange: William III.

419 *plethoric*: full.

sconces: small forts, perhaps punning on 'head' or 'fine/tax'.

Grave: perhaps siege of Gravelines, 1659.

420 *boor*: peasant.

421 *rundlet*: runlet = small cask.

422 *mort-bleu*: morbleu = Mort Dieu (God's death), an oath.

424 *mundungus*: refuse, offal.

424 *pistols*: pistoles = Spanish gold coins.

427 *fuzees*: muskets.

429 *give a man luck and quoit him into the sea*: abandon him to his fate, M. P. Tilley, *A Dictionary of Proverbs in England in the Sixteenth and Seventeenth Centuries* (Ann Arbor, Mich., 1966), Proverb M146: Give a man luck and throw him into the sea.

430 *Gaunt*: Ghent.

perdue: hidden.

431 *daubing*: falsity.

432 *vostre tres humbles*: great humbleness to you.

433 *Amelandt*: island off the north coast of The Netherlands.

434 *froppish*: peevish, fretful.

438 *furberies*: fourberies = tricks, cheats.

Cenneff: probably battle of Seneff, 1674.

439 *discourse*: discourse with, often used in this way in *Don Tomazo*.

442 *Certiorari*: certificate of authenticity (a writ).

trim-tram: ornament of little value, absurdity.

444 *putt*: stroke.

445 *the narratives themselves*: Elizabeth Cellier enlisted Dangerfield in 1679 to play his part in the aftermath of the Popish Plot. Dangerfield purportedly wrote *A Particular Narrative of the Late Popish Design* (1679) and *A True Narrative of the Popish Plot* (1680).

MR BADMAN

449 *to hear*: i.e. to hear the Word of God preached.

450 *professors*: professing Christians.

455 *punks*: whores.

461 *meeters*: Puritan sects, like Bunyan's, persecuted during the Restoration.

465 *Looking Glass for Sinners*: Samuel Clarke's *Mirror or Looking Glass for Sinners* (1646), a compilation of sensational and moralistic examples of God's judgement.

INCOGNITA

473 *Mrs Katherine Leveson*: daughter of Robert Leveson of Staffordshire, home of the Congreve family.

rencounter: skirmish, battle.

CLEOPHIL: used as a pseudonym only for *Incognita*, which was published anonymously.

474 *Segnius irritant . . . Horace*: Horace, *Art of Poetry*, ll. 180–2, 'Less vividly is the mind stirred by what finds entrance through the ears, than by what is brought before the trusty eyes and what the spectator can see for himself'.

475 *maugre*: despite.

unity of action: the three unities, time, place, and action, were presented as rules for correct dramatic composition by the seventeenth-century neo-classical critics, following suggestions made by Aristotle and Horace.

476 *receiver*: rent collector.

477 *alarmed*: excited.

478 *loose*: freedom.

fachin: porter.

go: walk.

theorbo: base lute.

479 *great dome*: duomo = hall of state.

fuliginous: sooty.

480 *mien*: bearing, manner.

481 *humour*: nature, from the idea of four humours in the body, one of which would determine a person's character.

489 *swinging*: swingeing = powerful.

491 *painter*: Apelles of Macedon.

492 *blubbing*: swelling, pouting.

492 *pen-feathered*: pin-feathered, newly feathered.

493 *Incognita*: Unknown.

495 *amicide*: the murder of a friend.

501 *upon tick*: on credit.

508 *import*: impart, communicate.

516 *pallat*: small straw bed.

517 *the tree consecrated to Venus*: the myrtle.

518 *numbers*: verses of poetry/song.

518 *automachy*: self-conflict.

521 *Gorgon's head*: turned those who saw it to stone.

wood: violent, confused anger.

THE UNFORTUNATE HAPPY LADY

529 *Sam. Briscoe*: editor of posthumous editions of Behn's works.

A True History: most of Behn's fiction professes truth, and some of it was based on true incidents, but no source has been suggested for *The Unfortunate Happy Lady* .

530 *Lady Beldam's*: Beldame = old woman, used mostly pejoratively.

531 *cast mistress*: cast off/abandoned mistress.

532 *Jusqu' a revoir*: until we meet again.

534 *ros solis*: rosa solis = a kind of blended liqueur.

small: light, fine.

535 *nunneries*: in view of the true nature of Beldam's house, nunnery was often used as a euphemism for brothel in the seventeenth century.

537 *dishabille*: state of undress, casually dressed.

538 *a Turkey merchant*: dealing in trade with Turkey and the Middle East.

540 *naughty*: immoral.

541 *smock-faced*: effeminate, smooth faced.

542 *The Cheats*: probably John Wilson's popular play *The Cheats* (1663), or perhaps Behn's close friend Thomas Otway's *Titus and Berenice with the Cheats of Scapin* (1677).

543 *answered*: should probably read 'continued'.

544 *the Savoy*: perhaps refers to the area that became a hospital.

546 *Barbary*: north coast of Africa, kingdom of the Saracens.

548 *our dear King Charles*: an indication that Behn wrote *The Unfortunate Happy Lady* prior to 1685.

550 *baited*: stopped for rest and refreshment.

THE WORLD'S CLASSICS

A Select List

HANS ANDERSEN: Fairy Tales
Translated by L. W. Kingsland
Introduction by Naomi Lewis
Illustrated by Vilhelm Pedersen and Lorenz Frølich

JANE AUSTEN: Emma
Edited by James Kinsley and David Lodge

Mansfield Park
Edited by James Kinsley and John Lucas

J. M. BARRIE: Peter Pan in Kensington Gardens & Peter and Wendy
Edited by Peter Hollindale

WILLIAM BECKFORD: Vathek
Edited by Roger Lonsdale

CHARLOTTE BRONTË: Jane Eyre
Edited by Margaret Smith

THOMAS CARLYLE: The French Revolution
Edited by K. J. Fielding and David Sorensen

LEWIS CARROLL: Alice's Adventures in Wonderland
and Through the Looking Glass
Edited by Roger Lancelyn Green
Illustrated by John Tenniel

MIGUEL DE CERVANTES: Don Quixote
Translated by Charles Jarvis
Edited by E. C. Riley

GEOFFREY CHAUCER: The Canterbury Tales
Translated by David Wright

ANTON CHEKHOV: The Russian Master and Other Stories
Translated by Ronald Hingley

JOSEPH CONRAD: Victory
Edited by John Batchelor
Introduction by Tony Tanner

DANTE ALIGHIERI: The Divine Comedy
Translated by C. H. Sisson
Edited by David Higgins

VIRGIL: The Aeneid
Translated by C. Day Lewis
Edited by Jasper Griffin

HORACE WALPOLE: The Castle of Otranto
Edited by W. S. Lewis

IZAAK WALTON and CHARLES COTTON:
The Compleat Angler
Edited by John Buxton
Introduction by John Buchan

OSCAR WILDE: Complete Shorter Fiction
Edited by Isobel Murray

The Picture of Dorian Gray
Edited by Isobel Murray

VIRGINIA WOOLF: Orlando
Edited by Rachel Bowlby

ÉMILE ZOLA:
The Attack on the Mill and other stories
Translated by Douglas Parmée

A complete list of Oxford Paperbacks, including The World's Classics, OPUS, Past Masters, Oxford Authors, Oxford Shakespeare, and Oxford Paperback Reference, is available in the UK from the Arts and Reference Publicity Department (BH), Oxford University Press, Walton Street, Oxford OX2 6DP.

In the USA, complete lists are available from the Paperbacks Marketing Manager, Oxford University Press, 200 Madison Avenue, New York, NY 10016.

Oxford Paperbacks are available from all good bookshops. In case of difficulty, customers in the UK can order direct from Oxford University Press Bookshop, Freepost, 116 High Street, Oxford, OX1 4BR, enclosing full payment. Please add 10 per cent of published price for postage and packing.